Born in the village of Moore in the Borough of Halton, located midway between Runcorn and Warrington in Cheshire, England, where his father was a licensed victualler, Richard de Mora gave up a promising career with the Mersey Ferries to follow his dream of being a session musician at Abbey Road. He never actually played his guitar in any Beatles' sessions, though he often claimed that he had.

Tiring of the hand-to-mouth existence of a poorly-paid session musician in London, he returned to Liverpool and had a range of lucrative jobs in local attractions in the city's growing tourist industry. These included trainee crocodile-handler at a local adventure park; specialist scouse-chef at a Pier Head hostelry; and mushroom forager in Sefton and Prince's Parks, where he also worked as a tennis coach. During most of this time, he attended creative writing classes at local colleges and wrote several quite successful professional texts and guidebooks. Now, he's decided to write fiction and it's up to you to decide how well that's turned out.

Dedicated to the Clason family of Härnösand in Sweden, who did all this with ships made of wood; and the Moore family of Bankhall in Liverpool, Hawarden in Flintshire, and Stockport in Cheshire who helped me in so many ways.

Rik de Mora

STARSHIP-101

AUSTIN MACAULEY PUBLISHERS™

LONDON • CAMBRIDGE • NEW YORK • SHARJAH

A CIP catalogue record for this title is available from the British Library.

ISBN 9781035859313 (Paperback)
ISBN 9781035859320 (ePub e-book)

www.austinmacauley.com

First Published 2024
Austin Macauley Publishers Ltd®
1 Canada Square
Canary Wharf
London
E14 5AA

Sincere thanks to William Burton Fears, M.D., F.A.C.E. of DeSoto, Texas, for generous and kindly encouragement.

Synopsis

Suppose you have just received a radio message reporting safe arrival and successful landing on a habitable planet from the first sub-lightspeed human expedition that was sent to Earth's nearest neighbouring star system: the Centauri triple star system. You know this message has been in transit at the speed of light for four and a half years. You know that any reply you send by radio will also take four and a half years to get back to Proxima-Centauri-b, which is where they have landed and are now struggling to establish humanity's first interstellar colony.

You also know that in the one hundred years or so since their Starship was built and launched, humanity's quantum technology has advanced so much that the speed of light is no longer the barrier to long-distance travel it once was. What do you tell them? What do you do? There's no point sending them many radio messages that will take four and a half years to arrive when, these days, the best of the Superposition Navigators are able to translocate their vehicles, and even fleets, instantaneously across the quantum space-time continuum (that's assuming the concepts of 'space' and 'time' have any meaning in the quantum realm).

Providing only that they have a decent quantum map of their destination, which, surely, the Proxima-b settlers can help with. Seems to me, the best thing to do would be to send a radio reply as a matter of courtesy and support, but to issue a contract for the best of the best Superposition Navigators, the Clason brothers, Tarvin and Harden, to put together a *modern* interstellar expedition that will create a pathway to Proxima-b and resupply and upgrade the technology available to these brave and distant first extrasolar human settlers, to bring their colony into the Solar System's trading family.

Oh, and by the way, these Proxima-b settlers own a valuable antique—their Starship. It's the first *successful* sub-lightspeed Starship you know about, because its sister-ship, Starship-102, is still in flight to Tau Ceti, and it's a cryo-hibernation ship and no one knows what's happened to that. So, how about getting the Clason brothers to bring Starship-101 back home?

Day 1

The town mayor of the Proxima Alpha settlement, Mervyn Castlefield ("call me Merv, only the wife calls me Mervyn and it usually means doom for the rest of the week!"), had behaved like a child with a new toy ever since we had delivered the swamp boat that he'd particularly requested. We waited on the makeshift landing stage that had been jury rigged to the bottom of one of the ship's riverside airlocks as he raced the boat around in circles just offshore. He approached with such a flourish that I was glad we were wearing fully waterproof fatigues when the bow wave from the swamp boat swept across the landing stage.

'Hi Tarvin,' he called, 'are you two about ready to go?'

'Sure, just give us a moment to drip-dry,' was all that I could say as my co-pilot, Kat, and I tried to brush off the worst of the water before stepping aboard the swamp boat. We had barely settled into its passenger seats before the mayor gunned the motor and turned the boat towards the centre of the stream marking our departure by shouting 'Yee Haw' at the top of his voice, revealing the settlement's very limited, and very old, library of entertainment videos.

As the boat raced across the more turbulent waters at the centre of the river, it was not possible to converse over the amazing volume of sound produced by the boat's propeller. Its whine shattered the tranquillity of the permanent state of twilight that enveloped the settlement. Anticipating this, we had previously settled on the route of this initial trip to assess the lie of the land around the grounded Starship and Mayor Castlefield set the swamp boat skimming across the immensely wide river estuary towards a rocky outcrop that marked the tip of the ridge that was just visible on the other bank of the river from the settlement itself.

The boat sped down the shallower water near the opposite bank pretty much at full throttle. It was hair-raising to those of us who led a more sedentary life on a Navigator's couch, but certainly exhilarating.

I whispered quietly into my helmet microphone, issuing instructions to record this expedition from now on and add the video to my ship's log for return home.

At this speed, we reached the outcrop in only a few minutes and swept around it into a previously hidden little bay, skimming over the extensive mudflat that had collected there in the shelter of the ridge. The speed was reduced, and the propeller noise settled down to a gentle murmur, so I was able to ask, 'Is the river tidal?'

'Yes, it's tidal,' shouted Mayor Castlefield. 'But we've not been able to work out the tide tables yet. With three stars and three planets dancing around each other in the skies above us, it's a complex bit of mathematics to work out the tides just here. But it's no big deal as we don't use the river for much. And then there's the impossible difficulty of forecasting our weather patterns and the added problem that we've only recently realised that the planet precesses around the North Pole quite a bit, and even that seems to add even more variability, so it adds up to being too complex a problem for our resources. It takes the scale of the calculation way beyond the capabilities of the knowledge, much less the computers, we brought with us. I hope the present-day knowledge those flashy computers you've brought for us will be able to do the job.'

Merv Castlefield throttled back even more as he was talking and turned the boat in towards the bank. I started to recognise that the water at the river's edge was filled with a low-lying vegetation that, in this reddish twilight, was almost black in colour. The vegetation continued up the approaching riverbank and only the continued splashing of the boat's skis showed that we were still floating on water. Then, with a little more throttle, Merv drove the boat straight up the mossy riverbank towards the closest tree in what looked like an open stand of upright, but sparse and branch-less tree trunks.

Merv jumped down from the boat with a mooring rope in hand and proceeded to tie it to the nearest tree trunk. Kat and I followed and as I got up close to the tree that now served as our mooring post, I realised I had seen these things before.

'What happened to your forest?' asked Kat. 'There are no branches, it looks like all the treetops have been sheared off.'

'No idea,' Merv replied. 'Our biologists have been concentrating on the other bank of the river, around and to the west of the settlement,' he explained, 'so we've not been able to survey this bank in any detail.'

'Well, they ain't trees,' I volunteered, 'they're much more like giant club fungi.'

'Oh yeah?' responded Kat in a challenging tone. 'Hey Boss, when did you become an authority on Proxima-b's biology?'

'As you well know, 'Doubting Kat', we've only just arrived here. But I have seen these things before.'

'Oh yeah? Where? On Earth?' she asked, in a more than slightly mocking tone.

'Yes,' I replied, 'but not in the present day.'

'Oh! Come on! You must explain that.'

'OK, OK. When I was a Nav-cadet, my grandfather developed the first of the Timeships and he took Harden and me, and the rest of our class, on a little expedition back in time to Earth's Devonian period of about 400 million years ago. These things were all over the place then.'

'You and HARDEN?' Kat protested loudly, eyes wide.

'Hey, quieten down, children,' Merv cut in, 'this place was quiet and peaceful before you two started arguing like an old married couple.'

'Oh, I may be a Clason by marriage, but I'm not married to Tarvin,' said Kat, more quietly. 'I'm married to his twin brother, Harden. The slimeball who's never told me about this Timeship expedition. Even though he knows perfectly well that I've always wanted to go on one.'

'Be fair, Kat, this was one of the pioneer trips. The maiden flight of the first passenger ship. We served as cheap crew members and disposable passengers. And it was about 15 or 20 years ago. They're just tacky tourist jaunts now.' I was trying to calm her down because she had such a lively temper sometimes.

Merv cut in again: 'Could you stop the argument and start the climb to the top of this ridge? We have a town meeting and barbecue in a couple of hours.'

We all started to climb away from the riverbank as Merv continued: 'If you can talk *and* walk, Tarvin, I'd like to know more about the Timeships and this expedition of yours. I've been away from Earth for a long time and things have obviously changed a great deal.'

I didn't savour the climb to the top of this ridge that dominated this river valley. This much exercise was a new experience for me. I'd spent too long in the Navigator's couch in my ship's control room for it to be an easy walk, so I was even less happy about the prospect of giving a long lecture on current interstellar travel protocols, but I made a start as we scrambled up the ridge, weaving our way over and between what looked like moss-covered boulders, through the tree-like things.

'It all results from our improved understanding of quantum mechanics. My ship depends on quantum entanglement for instantaneous point-to-point travel in the present time thread and the Timeships use quantum time threads that have one end attached to their past and the other end in a fragment of one of today's fossils. The Timeship's quantum computer identifies a suitable thread in an original atom of the fossil and then MASER-pumps energy from some truly massive fusion reactors to expand the thread into a wormhole to the distant past through which the Timeship travels.'

I paused, to take a few gasping breaths, and was pleased when Kat chipped in: 'Over a ten-to-fifteen-year timeframe, the programme included purely scientific trips to just about every period in Earth's geological past. The United Planetary Authority decided to build a *Museum of the Solar System* in a stable orbit between Uranus and Neptune and then established an asteroid train that makes a grand tour around the most amazing sights in the Solar System.'

'A what? Asteroid train?' gasped Merv, who, I was pleased to note, was also breathing heavily. 'That's something else that's new to me. The old place has certainly moved on.'

'It's a set of asteroids moving along the same orbit' I contributed, 'it loops around Venus and then, providing the planetary orbits allow, goes past all the other major centres of population, Earth, the Moon and the Lagrange-2 StarCorp Starship graving docks, Mars, and the mining camps that harvest materials from the moons of Jupiter and Saturn. It's created a regular transport service between these sites. The asteroids are exhausted mines that have self-sustaining holiday resorts built into their hollowed-out interiors. They're big enough to have some artificial gravity on the inside of the walls when we spin them up. And we keep adding new asteroids to the train as their mines are exhausted.'

'Jeez,' wheezed Merv. 'It's almost worth going back home for that!'

'You don't have to go back home to enjoy the views,' said Kat. 'Each asteroid in the train has a camera array that broadcasts continuously to the Solar System's satellite internet constellation. Before we leave, we will be building you a ground station to connect to the internet nodes we've stationed along our route to here. Once that's up and running, you'll be able to tune in to all the broadcasts from home.'

'Yes, that's all true,' I interjected, 'but remember that, in this universe, the TV news travels at the speed of light. So, what you'll be able to tune into with your ground station will be four and a half years late!'

'But we'll be equipping the ground station with a massive library of vids that were current when we left Earth,' added Kat, 'and if Frankie and Lana's teams can really find a way to make that quantum megacomputer we're installing here use quantum entanglement for comms links, we'll be able to beat the lightspeed barrier with communications as we've done with physical travel.'

'Seems like you've thought of everything,' replied Merv. 'But, hey Tarvin, we're almost at the summit of this ridge. Are you going to tell me what these tree-things are?'

'Aye, OK,' I responded, 'if these things of yours really are similar to what we saw on Grandpa's Timeship trip to the Earth of 400 million years ago, then they are giant fungi.'

'Fungi? You mean, like mushrooms?' asked Merv incredulously. He stopped and started stroking the surface of the nearest tree-thing. Kat and I did the same. The surface was smooth to the touch, but quite soft and velvety.

'Well, it doesn't feel like a tree,' Kat remarked. 'But this one is, what, five metres tall? And half a metre in diameter? That's some mushroom!'

'The Earth-variety was more primitive than genuine mushrooms. We brought some samples back with us and the fungi-people went into rhapsodies about them. Finally concluding they were most like things called club fungi that still exist on Earth, though present-day ones are only a few centimetres tall.'

'Oh, I'd love to see that!' sighed Kat. 'I must get Harden to book us onto one of those trips for our next leave. Can we get a discount?'

'I reckon we have so many strings to pull that you could get a very hefty discount. But, from what I remember of their ads, the Devonian is probably not the most popular Timeship Tour. By far the most popular is the one that follows the Chicxulub meteor into its collision with Earth. You know, the one that killed off the dinosaurs. Harden and I have been there, too and if you want real excitement, that's the place to go!'

A few more steps climbing the hill and I went on: 'But Kat, I believe we are walking through something almost indistinguishable from Earth's Devonian period. Just look around! Here, look at it in white light.' I unhitched my torch from my belt and swung it from side to side. The change in the view was astonishing. As the beam of my torch splashed over the ground, the low growing carpet of moss-like plants all brightened up from a dull black to various shades of bright green! And the trunks of the huge club fungi were shades of orange and pale browns, covered with green speckles and blotches, mainly around their bases.

'Wow!' Kat exploded, reaching for her own torch. 'That's unexpected! How come the plants look green?'

'Yeah, it surprised us, or at least the non-biologists among us,' said Merv, 'the first time anyone ventured out to explore around the Starship. It's a headline in the pioneer's diary.

'Our biologists soon explained,' he went on. 'By analysing some of the 'black' plants we found and proving that they used chlorophyll pigments for their photosynthesis that match, atom-by-atom, the chlorophyll used by plants on Earth. The point is, that chlorophyll works best with red and blue light. And that's the part of the light spectrum 'green plants' absorb. Earth's sunlight includes yellow and green wavelengths that the plants can't absorb so they reflect it, and your eyes see green leaves. But Proxima-Centauri is a red dwarf, emitting mostly red and infrared but with some blue and ultraviolet, most of which the leaves of Proxima's plants absorb. They don't reflect any visible light, so to our eyes they just look black in Proxima-Centauri's ambient light.'

'Wow!' Kat said again, asking: 'So what does that mean for evolution here and on Earth? Is it convergent evolution or do I remember something called parallel evolution?'

'You'll have to ask the biologists about that,' Merv responded. 'They've mostly been muttering about both, but just a little louder about convergent evolution recently.

'But remember,' Merv continued, 'we only have two biologists and they've never even seen Earth's biology. It was their parents who left Earth on this trip; so, our present team's had an entirely ship-bound education. And now they have an entire planet to explore! They seem to spend most of their time on the western river delta marshlands. I'm not sure they've seen much of this bank of the river.'

'We brought a fair-sized science team with us,' I said. 'I must get them to send a few over to this bank. Analysis and specimens from this club fungus 'forest' would be an essential comparison with the marshes.'

During this conversation we had reached the top of the ridge that dominated the river valley. Even in this reddish twilight, the view was spectacular, and well worth all the physical effort.

The river valley swept from our right to our left. If we were effectively facing 'North' this sweep was from East to West in terms of Earth's geography. But similarities to Earth are difficult to find here because this planet, Proxima-b, is tidally locked by the gravitational pull of its star, Proxima-Centauri. With the result that one side of the planet is always facing the star. And this makes the one similarity with our own home Earth-Moon system being that our Moon is tidally locked to Earth and only ever shows one side to the inhabitants of Earth.

The Proxima Alpha settlement is in the far north of the side of Proxima-b that is facing its star. This is, of course, the 'hot' side of permanent day, though as Proxima-Centauri is a faint red dwarf, Proxima-b only receives, on average, about 60% of the radiant energy the Earth receives from the Sun. So, the 'hot' side experiences quite reasonable temperatures, well above freezing, and allowing liquid water to flow. The opposite side of the planet faces deep space and is permanently dark and frozen and covered in glaciers. Although the planet doesn't rotate, the temperature differentials between the two sides cause huge cloud masses to swirl and circulate above the 'dividing line' or terminator between day and night leading to enormous quantities of rain, hail and snow being dumped unexpectedly on Proxima Alpha as the clouds swirl into the warm side, while clouds swirling from the warm and into the cold night side take enormous quantities of warm water vapour into the night to fall as snow that replenishes the glaciers.

Proxima-Centauri was known to have one unpleasant habit that affects Proxima-b: intense solar flares occasionally erupt from the star that could sweep the planet with fluxes of hostile radiation. When Starship-101 was landed, the pilot chose to de-orbit on the cold side of the planet and fly the ship down towards the terminator in the mountains of the far north, aiming for the marshlands of this river delta and neatly bringing it to rest in the shadow cast by the rocky mountain ridge we had just climbed. The wide river, swollen with meltwater from the cold-side glaciers at the terminator, reached towards the coast behind us. I knew from our own orbital surveys that this river valley was the eastern boundary of a huge river delta which opened out on our left, and beyond the Proxima Alpha settlement. Straight ahead, I could just make out the mountains in the far north, the most distant ones being just beyond the terminator. They were high enough for their snow-capped, glacial tops to be glittering redly in the light from Proxima-Centauri that was melting their snows and ice; to make the runoff that fed the river below.

17

And right ahead of us, that river; full and turbulent, a broad swathe of white-water seeming to emerge over the rocks beneath Starship-101 that otherwise seemed to be neatly parked on the valley floor in front of us. It all looked perfectly natural, unless you knew, as I certainly did, that Starships as big as this were no longer built to land on a planet's surface. But then, this is not a present-day Starship. This is the very first of the sub-light speed generation Starships that left Earth orbit to journey to the stars before I was born.

'Well, what do you think?' It was Kat, breaking into my reverie, gasping out the question through some decidedly heavy breathing. Another one who spent too much of her life nestled in a Nav Couch. 'They did well to avoid those mountains and get it down here. It looks undamaged from here.'

'It's structurally intact,' she went on, 'certainly worth salvaging. There's been some collapse of internal structures that were not designed to support weight in a gravity well, so some parts look a mess internally; and they're the parts you see first when you go aboard in the rear-most sections. That's why I wanted you to see it from here, because the hull structure is basically OK, and the power units are all in working order despite their age.'

'Yeah, they told me all that when I took the contract,' I replied. 'On the basis of Merv's early reports. I didn't believe it entirely then; and now I don't entirely believe what I'm seeing!'

Ten kliks long; a flat ellipse in section which is one klik in maximum diameter but, though it's not easily seen from this vantage point, essentially triangular, like a medieval arrowhead in shape. In rocket man technospeak, it would be called a lifting body—sleek enough to create lift to glide in any decent atmosphere. Tough enough to withstand landing like a brick-on-a-sledge. But, and it's a big 'but', requiring superhuman flying skills to make such a landing.

'The guys on that flight deck were barnstorming pilots,' I whispered in appreciative reverence. 'The ship's log shows that the co-pilot brought the bird out of orbit and then Captain Billy Westwood took control, slowing the ship nicely in the atmosphere, and finally bringing the thing into a landing where you see it now. Totally, superbly, brilliant. How would you fancy doing that Kat?'

'Not without quantum jumps,' replied Kat, adding, 'No, wait, I don't think I'd even know how to quantum jump into a soft landing on that riverbank.'

'Did you know them, Merv?' I asked.

'Oh, yes. Billy Westwood died only about ten years ago. He was effectively Proxima Alpha's first mayor as he took control of the disembarkation and initial establishment of the settlement. In fact, we're talking about naming the new village that you guys will be building on the site left by old-101 when you remove her, Westwood, in his honour.'

'And the co-pilot?'

'Cleo Westwood. Yes, they were a husband-and-wife team. She was a superbly loyal second-in-command through all the inevitable early disputes in the colony. Died about a couple of years after Billy.'

Suddenly, the voice of my chief engineer, Frankie Burton, cut into this conversation through my helmet comms: 'Hey, Boss, we're about ready to launch the drone squads and it looks from your helmet cam that you've got a good view of the ship now. Can we go?'

'Hold on, Frankie,' I replied. 'I'll just get the mayor's OK on that. Will you be able to create the 3D model in real time?'

'Oh, yes,' Frankie came back to me, 'Lana has arranged for enough bandwidth on the uplink so we can use our own NeuroNet in orbit. The model will be streamed to your NeuroModem while it's being constructed. As usual.'

'Sorry, Merv,' I said to the mayor, 'my chief cyber engineer is ready to launch the clouds of video drones that will allow us to create the 3D model of 101 that I need to use for the quantum jump into orbit. Is that OK with you?'

'Sure,' Merv replied, 'is it likely to be intrusive for the local settlers?'

'Minimally, I hope.' I explained, 'there are two squads that Frankie will release from the cargo truck you can see just drawing up at the nose of your Starship down there. Macro drones will survey the ship and its surroundings from the outside. They have sensors for just about everything, from gamma rays to low frequency sound, gravity anomalies, magfields and anything else Frankie and her computers can think up. Then there's a squad of micro drones that will make a matching survey of the inside of the ship. The internal drones are really tiny. Smaller than a housefly.'

'Er, well hold on there, Tarvin,' Merv responded. 'We don't have insects here. And I was born on the ship during the flight, so I've never seen a housefly. But a winged insect the size of a house sounds pretty intrusive to me!'

'Behave yourself, Merv,' I responded. 'You know perfectly well I'm talking about drones less than a centimetre in size.'

Merv grinned at me broadly, then turned back to watch the show. 'Almost gotcha, there.' Adding, 'Hey, I can see smoke over the settlement.'

'That'll be Ilsa and Emma's team firing up their barbecue kitchens,' said Kat.

'OK Frankie, we have the mayor's permission to fly the drones,' I said. 'So we can blame him for anything that goes wrong now!'

'Copy that, Boss. On record, locked in. Drone launch … … now!'

Looking like two dense puffs of smoke at the nose of the Starship down there in the middle distance, two squads of drones were released from Frankie's parked cargo truck. The heavier, darker cloud spread over the nose of the ship, lighting it up with white light as they did so. The greyer, paler 'puff of smoke' hung over Frankie's truck, patiently waiting for the first drone squad to get to work and move away. Then it assembled itself into an orderly linear whisp and disappeared into the Starship through the main forward access hatch, which was located just under the nose. And then the external show was over.

But almost immediately my NeuroModem started building a visualisation in my mindscape. It looked exactly like the stairway into the main forward access hatch of Starship-101 that I had climbed earlier this morning on my way to Merv's makeshift landing stage. I thought of different properties; metal density, surface temperatures, static fields, radiation emissions were my favourites, and my visualisation changed, becoming a ghostly image for weak signals, or multicoloured for those properties with a range of levels. And all the time, the extent of the model in my visualisation was increasing as the drones swept from the nose and into and around the main body of the Starship. I tried thinking a few changes in magnification, and then pulled back on my point of view to examine the outside of the model. Turning the visualisation over in my mind to examine its underside and the damage caused to the ship's skin during the landing. It all seemed to be fine.

'Are you getting this, Kat?'

'Yes, you were right about the featherlight landing that pilot pulled off. I can see that the ship has nose skids. But there doesn't seem to be any damage to the hull itself. How did he manage that?'

I changed the point of view of my visualisation and thought the ship itself away, so I could examine the impression the nose section had made in the riverbank. There was a huge cushion of dried mud on the starboard side that could be seen as far towards the stern as the drones had reached.

'There's the answer to your question,' I thought towards Kat. 'This riverbank was just part of the marshes. That genius Billy Westwood brought the whole thing down into a mud bath!'

Satisfied with the progress of the modelling I switched back to conventional comms: 'Hi Frankie, those surveys are doing fine; so is the streaming. Carry on and stream into my NeuroModem's memory. I'll sign off and make my way back.'

'Copy that, Boss. We're losing a few of the internal micro drones for some reason, but I'll fix it. Out'

I turned to Merv Castlefield 'I think we've finished our business here, Merv, we could go back to 101 now.'

'Agreed,' said Kat, 'but I'd like to scoot all along this bank as we return and shoot a close-up video of the entire length of the Starship.'

And that's just what we did, but before we set off, I called Geoff Moore, the head of our BioScience Group. 'Hi Geoff, we are over on the east bank of the river, and there are some interesting things to see over here. I'll patch in a vid I've just made on the south side of the rocky promontory that overshadows the Starship. It's a small plantation of what I think are giant club fungi—they're three to five metres tall. I'm sure I've seen similar things growing on Earth during a Timeship visit to the Devonian era. I'd like you to check it out and collect enough specimens for me to take some back home.'

'O.K. Tarvin,' Geoff replied. 'I've been on that Devonian trip back home and agree your video looks astonishingly like the Devonian fungi. I think the Earth-fossils are called *Prototaxites*. But that's something else to read up about. We've got masses of stuff from these marshlands which parallels what we can find in similar ecosystems anywhere on Earth. It's astonishing how much the small team of biologists in 101's crew managed to achieve during the past twenty to thirty years. They've had field trips to all the major locations on the hot side, North, South, East and West. They've found photosynthetic plants all over the planet. And they look very similar to what we'd call bryophytes back on Earth, you know, things like liverworts and mosses.' Geoff's enthusiasm gushed on, 'And, of course, there are cyanobacteria-like cells and lichen-like organisms, and all the stretches of water are full of what we'd call algae back home, ranging from microscopic to massive. So, I'm not surprised the fungus-like things are expressing their dominance of the land! There's several lifetimes of taxonomy to do here!'

'Sounds like you'll need to expand your team,' I remarked, trying to cope with Geoff's excitement. 'So, if you draft a case, accompanied by a collection of suitable biosamples, I will take it back to Oort Station with me and make your case for you. After all, making these interstellar comparisons is one of the major reasons for chasing after these early sub-lightspeed Starships, so Proxima-b is literally our first opportunity to study the biology of a non-Solar planet. Anyway, I must go, we're about to start our return trip to Starship-101. I'll catch up with you after the barbie, or maybe tomorrow. Over and out.'

We ambled back to the ski-boat, making a few more video observations of the giant fungi, and then scooted north along the eastern riverbank, all of us making vids of Starship-101 on the west bank, from nose to tail, these to be combined with Frankie's drone models at some stage later.

The coffee bar, carefully placed in a long-emptied cargo hold just inside the Starship's main entrance, was our most urgently required venue as it was roasting and brewing some of the fresh beans we had brought with us from Earth. The smell of this activity enticed us immediately to claim one of the tables. We also took advantage of their range of cakes. And thus fortified I decided to broadcast to my senior officers about the barbecue planned for later in the afternoon.

'Attention all team leaders and deputies. I would like you all to attend this afternoon's barbecue so that you and the settlers can get to know each other. I will be saying a few words about our mission in two hours' time; make the effort to arrive before that. I want to get over what our visit means for the future of this colony and the fact that there will be ongoing support from the Solar planets into the foreseeable future. We're expecting a full turnout of the settlers, and I would like to introduce you all to the audience at the start of my little speech. So, this is a 'full dress uniform' occasion, complete with team IDs so you can circulate and answer questions. Oh, and David, I don't want a repetition of the pantomime you provided at our full dress uniform departure reception.'

'Aw, Boss, don't bring that up again!' David Wood, our deputy chief engineer, protested.

'David, I know your off-duty time is devoted to vintage vids and computer games, but none of your senior officers have enough service awards to match the chest full of glittering 'Star Wars Stormtrooper' and 'Death-Star Slayer' honours you can display. So, cool it. Understood?'

'Yeah, I guess so.'

'That's a relief,' I heard David's chief engineer, Jim Igwe, mutter in the background.

'One last thing,' I went on. 'Remember, when you are talking to the settlers, this is not a rescue mission; this is a support and resupply mission, and the intention is for us to be the first of an ongoing line of such missions to support the colony towards self-sufficiency and, in due course, active trading between the Centauri system and the Solar System. Starship-101 left Earth nearly a century ago. It was crewed by the parents, in some cases grandparents, of the people you will be talking to. Nobody asked these people if they wanted to be interstellar pioneers, travelling four and a half lightyears away from Earth. But they are here, the first of humanity's interstellar children. But the technology their parents used when they set out is a century old. Our first job is to bring them the knowledge and technology that's been developed in the Solar System while they were in flight.' I paused, to let that sink in, making the mental note to my NeuroModem that this little speech might be useful at the barbecue.

'Please remember when you are talking to these settlers, that we have the capacity to take all of them back to Earth in the next couple of months if they want that. But we don't want that. We want to support them in every way with all the present-day technology, training and services they need to stay here, and succeed in making this, humanity's first interstellar colonising experiment, a thriving success. Over and out.' I thought that was a fine, stirring, mission statement with which to end. We just have to achieve those fine aims, now. Anyway, as I didn't hear too much giggling after I finished, I took that as a good sign and assumed it had gone down OK with the crew, at least.

A couple of hours later came my opportunity to try my speech on the settlers. Ilsa Blaine, and Emma Halton's teams, with the assistance of the settler's own catering squad and various helpful bystanders, had brought dozens of tables and chairs from the Starship-101's canteens into the 'Town Square' and set up their barbecue kitchen across the north side of the square. The south side was left free of tables and featured a makeshift stage, to which Lana Mancot had added a couple of microphones and loudspeaker units, and a small lighting rig.

As the settlers started to assemble, claiming the tables set out in the square, I messaged the NeuroModems of my senior officers to ask them to congregate on the stage, and before too long Merv Castlefield drifted over to me, glad-handing the seated settlers as he came. He had Frankie in tow.

'Hi Tarvin, you do brush up well, I like the captain's insignia. Very smart!' Merv greeted me.

'Actually, Merv,' I replied 'this is a Commodore's insignia, one cut above Captain,' I smiled at Frankie as she seemed to be bubbling over with something to say, before I ended my sentence, 'In recognition of my exceptional navigational ability and because my ship is classed as a squadron as it's made up of several independent units, some of which we've stationed in deep space along the way to here, some of which we will leave here.'

'OK, Commodore,' Merv butted in again. 'We've got a small problem with your small survey drones in Starship-101.'

'What is it, Frankie?' I asked.

'Well,' started Frankie, uncomfortably, 'one of the settlers who lives in the ship has been swatting them claiming that they're hornets, coming to sting him to death!'

'Really? Who is this guy, Merv?'

'He's the last living member of the original crew,' said Merv. 'We call him The Priest, because he's become a real weirdo. He's claimed the Pilot's Stateroom and turned it into some sort of a shrine to something called 'Microsoft', claiming it's the 'Window onto The New Universe'. He's a nut, but usually quite a nice, gentle, and, for a lot of people, entertaining nut. He's great with children. Doing actual damage to electronic equipment is right out of character for him. In the original crew he was a very young, very junior, but very brilliant software engineer who came on board straight from Mars.'

'He must be ancient,' I suggested.

'He admits to being 80 years old, sometimes even 85, but he must be closer to 95. Some years ago, he simply deleted his date of birth and all dates related to his education and life before embarkation from our computer.'

'So, what damage has he done?' I asked Frankie.

'Half a dozen of our microdrones completely smashed, and another five swatted to the deck and unable to fly,' Frankie reported. 'We've got plenty of drones and the rest of the swarm worked out not to go near him, that's not the problem. But with him on the warpath like this we can't complete our internal surveys. That stateroom runs right across the spine of 101's fuselage and the hull plates around it are crucial to the structural integrity of the forward section of the ship when we try to lift it into orbit.'

An important argument suddenly crystallised in my NeuroModem: 'Frankie, what's the form factor of the drones you are using? I mean the size and shape specs.'

'Their basic form and structure are supposed to be derived from flying insects, mainly the ones called bumble bees,' Frankie replied. 'Though the drones fly silently, and they're programmed to avoid interacting with people.'

24

'Have you got any microdrones, that could carry out your survey, that look more friendly, like butterflies, or dragonflies?' I asked.

'Sure, we could get the computer to improvise a small mixed squadron like that; they could carry different sensors to suit their flying patterns. But why?' she asked.

'Because I reckon that 'The Priest' is the only person surviving on Starship-101 who's ever seen a real live hornet and might even have been stung by one.' I turned to Merv Castlefield: 'Have I got it right, Merv? There are no flying insects on Proxima-b?'

'Quite right,' said Merv, adding: 'As far as I know there's been no sign of insects of any sort. Indeed, our biology team have not found anything at all that might be classed as an animal, large or small. They just don't seem to have evolved here yet. Your team has started a much more in-depth analysis of the western marshland, so there's no knowing what they might find in the mud there.'

'Does 'The Priest' have a normal name?' I asked.

'Undoubtedly,' replied Merv, hesitantly. 'Though everyone who knew it probably died several years ago. He's very reclusive, you know. Doesn't emerge from his shrine very often.'

'Will he come here to the barbie?'

'Nah, he shuffles as far as the canteen, and as that's where Ilsa's put all those chocolate biscuit supplies, he'll watch the video of the event there.'

'Okay, here's what we do,' I announced. 'Frankie, you get a sample of a butterfly and/or dragonfly drone and towards the end of the barbie you and I will take a picnic and make a friendly visit to The Priest to get things sorted. Merv, when we've finished our introductory talks and the barbie gets underway, will you drift into the ship and warn The Priest that Frankie and I will come visiting, with a picnic, as this party finishes? It sounds to me as though this guy might be a candidate for repatriation Earthside; you might suggest that. If he really is in his nineties, he'll find life a lot easier in microgravity.'

I NeuroModemed a message to Ilsa to ask for a picnic for three to be set aside for Frankie to pick up later; and then I thought an instruction into my NeuroModem for my flight computer in my ship, which was in synchronous orbit above: 'Malik, can you penetrate the computer on Starship-101 and reinstate the personal data about the person known as 'The Priest'? And then stream it to my NeuroModem.' The thought-thread 'Affirmative' drifted across my mind.

With all that settled, I looked around to see that the Town Square had filled up nicely and there was a full gallery of senior officers at the back of the stage. 'I guess we should make a start, Merv?' I suggested. Merv nodded, and the two of us ambled towards the microphones, while Frankie aimed towards Lana and the other officers.

Merv grabbed one of the radio microphones, and after a bit of faffing around while Lana helped him find the on-switch, he finally spoke to his settlers.

'Friends, we are here to welcome Commodore Tarvin Clason and his crew, who arrived just a day or so ago on what promises to be the first of a regular sequence of visits to Proxima-b by Starships from Earth.' That announcement raised an appreciative round of applause.

'Settle down,' Merv continued, 'save your applause, because the news will be getting better and better. Now, we all know the history of Starship-101. Crewed by our parents, or even grandparents, she left the Solar System eighty years ago, heading for Proxima-Centauri, the nearest star to Earth's Sun. Theirs was, no, that's not the right word; theirs *IS* the first venture by humanity into interstellar space. A fifty-year flight time! But we made it. We found Proxima-b to our liking. And then that great Pilot of treasured memory, Billy Westwood, landed us here and we built our settlement.' Merv paused a moment, then went on: 'You know, friends, if you want to applaud something. I think that's the something that deserves applause!' He put the microphone down on his lectern and lead us all in a lengthy round of applause in memory and appreciation of Starship-101's original crew. As the applause faded, I noticed that more than a few tears were being wiped from the eyes of those around me: and not just by the settlers.

Merv held up his hands to quieten the audience and then resumed: 'Ironically, the only thing that was damaged in the landing here was the ship's main radio antenna. So, it was some while, nearly a year of effort, before we were able to rebuild a sufficiently powerful transmitter array. On the very first day that the transmitter came into operation, we sent our report of our safe landing on its four-and-a-half-year journey to the Solar planets. And nine years after that day, we received their reply!' Merv paused, for dramatic effect.

'Earth offered help and support; and asked what we most wanted. It took us almost a year to assemble our shopping list. But then, you don't worry too much about delay in preparing the grocery order when your recipient won't get it for over four and a half years!' Merv paused again, more dramatic effect to let the chuckling settle down. 'We received their reply after another four and a half years, of course, and that was only a year ago, but that message from Earth is the one that's changed our lives most amazingly.' Another pause, and then an aside: 'I hope you're keeping up with the mental arithmetic, here. That message received a year ago arrived at Proxima-b twenty years, yes *twenty years*, after our announcement of safe arrival here. Yet it promised delivery of our entire shopping list, and a whole lot more, in about a year. They 'explained' that while our back was turned and we flew to Proxima, long-distance travel in the Solar System had been revolutionised. Somehow or other, the lightspeed barrier is no longer a barrier.'

Merv turned to me, with a smile, 'But as I'm not going to pretend that I understand the explanation for this heresy, this is where I hand over to Tarvin.' To which he mischievously added the comment: 'I've heard the senior officers of his crew call him 'Boss', and I guess we might all get into that habit before long. For now, though, give a warm welcome to Commodore Tarvin Clason.'

The applause was loud and welcoming and several people around the tables shifted their positions as though this was their main event.

'Thank you, Merv. And thank you to all you settlers on behalf of all my crew for the welcomes you have given us, despite the disruption and extra work we've caused you so far.' I paused briefly, and then got down to business, 'I *will* take up Merv's challenge, and try to explain the revolutionary technological advances that took place while your expedition was in flight, and which enable us to be here now. But first, I have a few words about why we have been sent here.' Another pause, as I looked around the audience.

'I'm a contractor, not a 'government' employee. I'm part of a family business that's been built by my grandfather over the past 50 years, called Deep Space Haulage. To take this Proxima-Centauri contract my brother and I started an offshoot of this company which we have called Interstellar Haulage, and that's the name you will see on our badges. We don't represent the government of Earth, Mars or Venus, or the Jovian Moons or any of the smaller administrations in the asteroid or Oort belts. The contract we are here to fulfil is financed by all of the above acting as a consortium.' I paused again, as a little murmur of comments mixed with a little quiet applause, rolled around the audience.

'In our eyes, people of Proxima-b, this is not a rescue mission. True, we are aware that it was your parents, not you, their children, who chose to take their families on this great expedition to Proxima-Centauri. It's also true that my ship will be returning to the Solar System in a couple of weeks, and we do have the capacity to repatriate to Earth any of you who wish to reverse your parents decision. But we are here as a support and resupply mission, and the intention is that we are the first of an ongoing line of such missions, intended to support the colony towards self-sufficiency. In due course, Earth foresees active trading between the Centauri System and the Solar System. Earth is proud of you guys. You are the ones who are here. Four and a half lightyears from humanity's home. The first of humanity's interstellar children.' I was forced to a stop as another, this time more triumphal, round of applause broke out, first among the settlers, though it was quickly taken up by all my crew who had continued to crowd into the Town Square. I took a few sips of the drink that Ilsa had placed on the lectern for me as I had started my speech. Waiting, as the applause faded, and the audience made it clear from their attentive attitudes that they wanted to know more.

'So, I want to get over what our visit means for the future of this colony, which is that there will be ongoing support for you from the Solar planets into the foreseeable future. The technology your parents used when they set out for Proxima, is a century old. Our first job is to bring you the knowledge and technology that's been developed in the Solar System during that century. We want to support you in every way with all the present-day technology, training, and services you need to stay here, and make this, humanity's first interstellar colonising experiment, a thriving success.'

I paused, again, to let that sink in, making the mental note to my NeuroModem that the little speech I had made earlier to the crew, was indeed useful at the barbecue. Another box ticked!

'Let me just summarise the major technology advances that enable us to get to you so quickly. For the most part they derive from improved understanding of quantum mechanics, so before we get too smug about that, let me remind you of the wise old saying: 'if you think you understand quantum mechanics, then you don't'. But even if we don't fully understand quantum mechanics, we can use it. And we use it for long-distance travel, which is effectively faster than lightspeed, using the quantum entanglement drive, or QE drive, though informally, we call the process quantum jumping.' I took another sip of my drink.

'Quantum jumping depends on another advance which was in development when Starship-101 left the Solar System, which was quantum computing. When your expedition left home, this was the latest thing in large scale computation, and, as I understand it, the navigation computer in Starship-101 still operates an array of q-bit chips. But we all know Moore's Law about doubling the transistor count of computer chips every 2 years, so there's no surprise that the quantum computing capacity of our computer chips on Earth rapidly increased beyond anything imagined when Starship-101 was fitted out. AI-quantum megacomputers were soon coming out of the factories to contribute to every technological job we do; from deep space navigation, sickness diagnosis and medical treatments, to the crucial work of programming and selling video broadcasts around the Solar System.' There was an agreeable quiet round of laughter at that last comment. I waited for it to fade away.

'But the biggest surprise came when the first quantum NeuroModems were installed in volunteers. The q-bit NeuroModems all merrily reported successful interfacing with another, preexisting, quantum computer, which turned out to be the human brain.' That statement set off a wave of disbelief circulating around my audience. 'With the benefit of fifty years hindsight, no great revelation,' I continued, 'That's how we can multitask. That's how our distant ancestors could navigate through forests and simultaneously walk, talk, eat, drink, scratch their butts, and still be keenly aware of threats from their predators and opportunities offered by their prey. For us, at this time, a q-bit NeuroModem,' pausing slightly, I patted the interface installed just behind my right ear, 'Like this, enables us to interface with a quantum megacomputer and, through that computer, with other q-bit NeuroModems worn by other members of our work teams. And we can do things that were unimaginable when your parents left Earth. Our mission is to bring all these advances to Proxima-b. To enable Earth's first interstellar outpost to flourish. That's you, if you are willing.' I took another swig from my glass before resuming.

'I think this lecture has gone on long enough, and that barbecue smells ready to go; but I want to end by introducing my senior officers to you, so you know who can answer your questions about our mission. Though the way that barbecue is smelling at the moment I think I'd better start by introducing Captain Ilsa Blaine, and her deputy, Commander Emma Halton, who are responsible for bringing to Proxima Alpha the tons of catering supplies that will update the food and drink available here. Most urgently, it's Ilsa and Emma who are managing the catering teams providing the barbecue, and Emma's team has been busy throughout today, firing up the barbecues along the back of this Town Square! Judging by the delicious smells they are stirring up, it's about time we started eating, rather than talking.' I theatrically led the two ladies to the front of the little stage we were using and said, 'I think I detect a barbecue calling your names, Ilsa and Emma, you'd best go and tend to it.' Then, turning back to the audience: 'Oh, one last thing: Ilsa also brought a microbrewery down from our orbital transport; so, you might like to sample its products too!'

The two ladies jogged through the expectant diners, high-fiving the hopeful diners as they went, to fulfil their duties at the portable kitchens ranged along the far side of the Town Square. A few of the more desperately hungry of those expectant diners followed Ilsa and Emma to get to the head of the queues. I thought I should say something about that.

'Yes, don't stand on ceremony. If you're hungry, go get some food and drink. I'll just keep talking into the background, as usual!'

'I should add that Ilsa and Emma have a wide range of food technology responsibilities beyond this afternoon's catering. Ilsa will be installing some very large horticultural units on the outskirts of the settlement. These have their own fusion power plant and full spectrum lighting so you can immediately start high-intensity cultivation of food plants brought from Earth. Emma is also responsible for the meatier side of your diet. She's brought some live farm animals and frozen embryos with which you can establish smallholdings on the marshlands in the delta west of the settlement. Your biologists found, in their first surveys, plenty of nutritious algae and other primitive plants growing in these marshes, so our planners chose sheep, cattle and pigs that thrive in salt marshes and on rocky coastlines on Earth which can, we hope, make best use of Proxima-b's vegetation.'

Emma interrupted, shouting over from her place in the barbecue kitchen: 'I've brought more animals, Boss. I've got a small herd of goats, and incubators full of bantams, chickens and ducklings,' to which she added emphatically: 'but you're not having any of my ducklings for this barbie!' Then, as an afterthought: 'Oh, I got fish, too. Ready-to-go fishponds full of fry. We got carp, we got catfish, we got trout, we got tilapia.'

She was stopped as a tall young man held on to her high-fived hand and asked 'Fish? To eat? I've never had fish to eat. 101's supplies were all finished by the time I was born here.'

Unfazed, Emma held onto his hand and pulled him out of his seat. 'Well, come to my barbie, darlin'; I'm cooking fish sticks for the discriminating palate, which you'll love, and tuna steaks drizzled with fresh lime juice, a great way of getting more omega-3 fatty acids into your diet, which you'll like even more!' The two of them strode off towards the barbecue kitchens, followed by the rest of the occupants of the young settler's table, and quite a few more besides.

I was left trying to regain the attention of the audience, before too many of them noisily abandoned me in favour of the barbecues 'I hope all of this floorshow is good news to all you intrepid pioneers,' I continued, 'but the best news may be is that Ilsa and Emma also brought with them an entire Starship cargo segment crammed with foods for every palate and every diet. They'll be brought down from orbit as we build storage parks for their container units.'

My NeuroModem caught Kat's whispered: 'That girl could cause a riot in a nunnery.'

'Yes,' I thought back, 'it's the laughing eyes, one-glance can be devastating!'

Then, back to the microphone: 'As an aside, Ilsa's husband, Richard Blaine, was left in charge of establishing, completing the build, and commissioning Proxima Station 4, which is the Waystation we positioned at four lightyears out from Earth. It will eventually be responsible for collecting and controlling future incoming flights to the Centauri Tristar System. A job full of potential difficulties because of the complexity of the gravity wells that are dancing around each other in this stellar neighbourhood.'

'Let's introduce a few more members of my crew. I'm the Command Pilot and my job in quantum jumps is to build a quantum entanglement view of the ship and its cargo at the departure point.' I paused to beckon Kat over to the lectern. 'This is my co-pilot, Captain Katharina Hope Clason, known as Kat for short. In the jargon of our trade, we are both 'Superposition Navigators', or SN's for short. We translocate our vehicles instantaneously across the space-time continuum; and for this we need complete quantum maps of the origin and target positions. The co-pilot is really the ship's navigator because Kat is responsible for building the quantum entanglement view of the ship's destination when we are preparing for a jump. When we're ready, I merge the two quantum maps, departure and destination, together in my mindscape to create the entanglement and then the computer destabilises it and we are transferred from the departure point and emerge into the destination.'

'You make it sound like a cut-and-paste operation in a word processor,' commented someone in the audience.

'Yes, that's a fair analogy. But it's only as easy as that sounds if you have a couple of quantum megacomputers interfaced with a couple of human brains trained to make it happen,' I responded.

As Kat moved off towards the other side of the Town Square, I continued: 'Kat is also the expedition's Chief Astrophysics Officer and leads a team that will collect the astronomical and astrophysical data of the Proxima-Centauri local stellar region, to refine what we know about the complex Centauri system, which is so far mainly dependent on Earth-based observations.'

I moved on to the next ship's officer. 'This is Captain Igwe. He is the loadmaster for my flotilla, and therefore third in line of seniority, but he is also Chief Civil Engineer, so he is the member of our team responsible for bringing down materials from the cargo transport segments of our ship, and especially for deploying the big industrial machines that will support the development of Proxima Alpha's infrastructure. Most immediately, this means several large state-of-the-art fusion power plants and a fleet of mobile mini-fusion-reactors. The mobile reactors will power a fleet of 3D printers that will rebuild and re-equip the settlement, as well as many other basic industrial 3D printers to establish factories able to make and assemble everything from coffee cups to trucks, helicopters, and shuttle rockets. You'll see a lot of Captain Igwe around Proxima, but I'll leave it to him to pronounce his full name. 'Ah,' he said, showing some astonishingly white teeth in the biggest of grins, 'duckin' out again, eh, Commodore? You should keep tryin', man, you'll manage it someday! My full name, ladies, and gentlemen is Orahjimetochukwu Igwe. Igwe is a royal name, meaning 'heaven' that's rooted in the Igbo peoples of Nigeria. My given name, Orahjimetochukwu, means 'people praise The Great Spirit because of me'! But you all can call me Jim, like everyone else does!

As the audience's amused shouts of 'Welcome to Proxima, Jim' settled, I continued to introduce engineering, saying, 'And this is Jim's deputy, Lieutenant Commander David Wood, the two of them are currently assembling all the ready-made components of the new Proxima SpacePort, which is crucial to shuttling materials from orbit, and includes everything needed to make oxygen and hydrogen rocket fuels by electrolysis of water to refuel the shuttles. Jim also deploys the crews of AI-robots that build and operate these and other facilities. We brought a couple of hundred robots, all 'latest version' specification.' A slight pause, as I urged Jim and David to depart towards the barbecue kitchens.

As they left the lectern the thunder of rocket engines swept repeatedly overhead as a squadron of heavy lift shuttles settled out of orbit onto the SpacePort site over to the east of us. I continued as the thunder quieted down, 'David will also be responsible initially for installing and programming the giga-presses for the vehicle production lines in what will become your own Gigafactory. Of course, the priority for Giga-Alpha will be all the new building equipment, diggers, cranes, road graders and such, including self-drive cargo trucks, that will be needed to upgrade the settlement's buildings.'

Moving further down the line, 'Another of the ready-made facilities Jim will be bringing down from orbital storage are a full set of medical and hospital units, assembly of which will be done by our medics working with yours. Meet Captain Bill Roberts and Commander Mary Warwick, who will commission your new medical services, installing q-bit NeuroModem upgrades for you and your existing bots, adding a brigade of state-of-the-art AI medical bots all NeuroModemed to your new mainframe computer; and deploying training facilities for your existing medical staff. This initial 'medical school' will also form the nucleus for a graduate education and training resource that will upgrade the settlement's education facilities to be the equal of any of the universities on the home planets today.'

'This young lady, Captain Lydia Connah, will spend most of her time well above your heads because she will be responsible for converting the cargo transport segments of our ship, as they are emptied of cargo, into a residential waystation facility for Proxima-b. She will be down here at the settlement some of the time as this task includes integrating upload and download crewing movements with SpacePort shuttles and interacting with Lieutenant Commander David Wood on initial ground transport facilities for the SpacePort.'

'We're reaching the end of the line, now, so after these introductions we'll all be making a sprint for the barbecue! This is Captain Francesca Burton. Frankie is our chief cyber engineer; at the moment she is in charge of the macro and micro surveyor drones, and everything related to making Starship-101 structurally sound and fit for return to Earth neighbourhood. She is also responsible for the deployment of the settlement's new megacomputer. She works closely with this young lady: Captain Lana Mancot, who is our communications officer and responsible for establishing the main comms satellite in Proxima-stationary orbit immediately above the settlement and in communication with the satellite constellation that's been left along the route and the GroundLink station in the settlement itself. And as her most immediate task, over the next few days she will use these facilities to set up broadcast and streaming of TV explanatory documentaries and podcasts that explain everything that's going on now on Proxima-b and everything that's happened in the Solar System since Starship-101 set off for Proxima-Centauri.'

Frankie butted into this final part of my speech, 'Hey Boss, don't forget what Lana and me are staying to do.'

'Oh, yes,' I resumed. 'Frankie is reminding me that when I take my Starship back towards the Solar System, Frankie and her team will stay on here, with Lana and her team, to set up an experimental communications link between your new quantum megacomputer on Proxima-b and the Earth-local Satellite Network using the principles of quantum entanglement. This is really important for the future of communication in deep space. Initial experiments across the Solar System have been very promising, but this journey is our first opportunity to experiment across a four-lightyear distance. Now, food!'

I thought that was the end of my talking, but an elderly settler at one of the front tables stood up saying:

'Hold on, Commodore, before we do all sprint to the barbecue, did I just hear you say that your chief engineer is surveying our Starship-101 to make it fit for return to Earth?'

I was a bit taken aback by my slip of the tongue, but fortunately Merv Castlefield butted in:

'Relax, Clint, we will be the ones who decide what happens to Starship-101, and I tell you all now, I will reconvene this Town Meeting later this evening, in 101's theatre, where we can all chew it over in private. But though all of us on Proxima-b have as much devotion to the ship as we had to our biological parents, the simple fact is that the old girl is an antique. Hell, we are antiques; we only know how to live in the century during which Starship-101 was built, sealed up and launched towards Proxima-Centauri. And while 'old-101' is past it, we're being given the opportunity to move our entire expedition into the present century.'

'And the price?' asked Clint.

'Our unique but antique Starship,' Merv replied. 'But we can discuss all this later, and everyone can have their say, and we'll have a vote. One question Tarvin is best placed to answer is 'why'. Why does the Solar System want

Starship-101 back? Can you say a few words about that, Tarvin? But keep it brief, we're hungry!'

'Sure, Merv, I'm hungry, too. If, as you say, I'm talking to antique settlers, or colonists if you prefer, then let me start by saying this: imagine all your wildest dreams of interplanetary travel around the Solar System; well, in the past 100 years those dreams have been brought into reality. Next, on the basis of your experience of it, imagine your wildest dreams about interstellar travel in deep space. I suggest to you that our presence here now brings even those dreams into reality. Compared with Starship-101's fifty-year flight time, our flight time from the Solar System's Oort Station into stationary orbit over Proxima-b was a month. And it only took that long because we stopped at each lightyear mark, at which, by the way, Starship-101 had dropped off comms satellites to survey the localities. Thanks to their radioed observations we could follow your exact route. And at each marker we stopped for a week to detach and deploy independent ships from my flotilla, each of which will become permanent residential waystations on the route between the Solar System and the Centauri system.'

'And we hope, with your permission, to return Starship-101 to become the most important exhibit in an Interstellar Museum which will tell the epic story of 101's pioneering flight. The United Planetary Authority has already established a *Museum of the Solar System* in a stable orbit between Uranus and Neptune. The *Museum of Interstellar Humanity*, or whatever title it's given, could be located alongside the Museum of the Solar System or thereabouts. Along with updating and resupplying Proxima-b, I've been tasked with posing this question to you. If you say 'yes', then I will take Starship-101 back to Oort Station where it will be quarantined and cleaned down and turned into the first specimen for that Museum of Interstellar Humanity.'

I put the microphone down on the lectern and moved off the platform to make it clear that I hoped my part in the proceedings was over. The last few members of the audience who were still sitting around listening, took the cue and started to move off towards the food.

As I passed Clint he fell into step beside me, saying 'I'm Clint Stapleton, Commodore, I'm the town treasurer, though before you arrived, we had precious little treasure to be taken care of. My father was 101's astronavigator, and he was responsible for releasing 101's lightyear-marker comms satellites; he'd be pleased, as I am, to find they've served their purpose in such a decisive way. There's just one more thing I'd like to ask you about. I remember Dad talked often about Starship-102 while he was teaching me astronomy. Before our departure I think there was discussion about 102 going to Eridani, but it hadn't been decided. Do you know what happened, and were there any more sub-lightspeed expeditions?'

'No more expeditions left after 101 and 102,' I said. 'Earth decided to wait for the results of those two experiments and concentrate on developing travel infrastructure within the Solar System. But 102, which left 20-years after 101 left Earth, didn't go to Eridani. It became a much bigger expedition, and much bigger ship, that headed out to Tau Ceti, which is only 1 lightyear further away from Earth than Eridani.'

'Ah, yes,' said Clint. 'Now you mention that, I remember Dad's lectures. Tau Ceti is slightly smaller than the Sun, but otherwise very similar. And with, what, 8 planets?'

'Yeah, two in the habitable zone; though there's so much debris orbiting the star in an accretion disk that it might not be very comfortable inhabiting the habitable zone.'

'So, any news of the flight?'

'No direct information. Hopefully, 102 is still safely in flight, but she's a cryo-hibernation ship. At any one time, most of her crew will be in cryosleep. Her computer was programmed to deposit lightyear-marker satellites, like Starship-101, along her flightpath and we've detected four of them, which all report, essentially, 'so-far-so-good', and which we will replace with our big residential Waystations in due course. But that means that 102 is, at best, only halfway to destination. My company has been commissioned to chase after her. These contracts take ages to work out in detail. We have to be prepared for anything we might find when we catch her, and cryosleep chambers of that time are notoriously unreliable.'

'No other sub-lightspeed missions? Asked Clint, as we approached the end of the line for the barbecue serveries.

'None. Quantum jumping made sub-lightspeed very unpopular for long-distance direct travel. In the twenty years between Starships-101 and 102 there was a lot of talk about 'the next interstellar expedition', with TRAPPIST-1, about 40 lightyears from Earth, being one favourite target because it has at least seven Earth-like planets. But the star is another red dwarf and, apart from being a lot older than the Solar System, offers no obvious advantages for new knowledge over 101's trip to Proxima-Centauri. The most scientifically interesting destination that was considered at the time, I think, was Vega, about 25 lightyears from Earth, as it seems to be a very young star that may be in the process of planet formation. Though such an environment doesn't offer very relaxed colonising. But then quantum jumping put paid to all these ideas.'

By this time both Clint and I had amassed decent quantities of food, trimmings and condiments on a couple of plates, so we settled into occupation of the nearest table. Conversation became a matter of exchanges like 'Mmmmm!', 'Glorious!' and 'Whoa, so that's a real barbecue?' though most people were enjoying the food treats too much to interrupt their eating with unnecessary words.

My barbie behaviour was interrupted by a message to my NeuroModem from my ship's computer, Malik, 'This is The Priest's minibio: name is Thomas William Fraser, age 94, profession: senior computer engineer, designing and building software, and firmware; shipboard function: member of a team of five human computer engineers responsible, with their AI service-bots and micro-bots, for overseeing the maintenance of Starship-101's computer equipment. Fraser's responsibility was the medical centre's diagnostic/treatment machines and robots. Malik out.'

This communication woke me up to my next task: my interview with The Priest. If he's really 94, he's going to need a care-specialist robot, and if he's really a med lab computer tech, he might even accept one of ours!

I messaged Bill and Mary's NeuroModems: 'Bill, Mary, I'm in urgent need of a geriatric-care robot. Have you brought any down from orbit yet?'

'Hey, Boss, overdone the barbie, have you?' was Mary's immediate response, to which Bill chimed in 'Don't worry. You only feel close to death. It's just flatulence. At your age you should be more careful in your choice of sauces. You know what too much chilli does to you!'

I tried to growl my reply, but found you can't growl when you're smiling, 'OK, OK, you need to cut some slack for a man in my condition. But the robot's not for me. I'm about to visit the last surviving member of the original crew. The locals call him The Priest. He's 94 years old, reclusive, and he's set up what he calls a 'Microsoft Shrine' in Starship-101. So, he might be off his head. But if he's coherent his first-hand reminiscences of 101's mission would be gold dust for the planned museum. Either way I need specialist help to deal with him.'

'Yes, we have a full med-robot brigade in sleep mode in 101's own med centre. I'll wake one and tell it to meet you at the top of the gangway at 101's forward hatch. It'll be one of our latest multimode bots. Able to morph between looking like a robot, a male nurse, or a female nurse, to suit all patient-preferences.'

Almost instantly, Mary continued: 'Right that's done. This one is called Carlo or Carla, depending on the patient's gender preference. It's interfaced with Malik and will communicate with your NeuroModem. Mary, out.'

I thought a 'Thank You' through my NeuroModem and caught sight of Ilsa, Frankie and Merv approaching my table. Ilsa was carrying an elaborate wickerwork basket.

'What's with the fancy wicker basket, Ilsa?' I asked.

'Well,' she replied, 'we have a container loaded with picnic foods, so I thought I'd throw in a couple of dozen of these baskets to enhance the settlers' experience. Trouble is that half of them have gone missing already. Emma's the main culprit. Because they have lids and a food warmer inside, she carries her ducklings and other chicks around in them. Anyway, this one's got a fair-sized picnic in it. Frankie will lay it out for you when you get settled.'

'Thank you, Ilsa!' said Merv. 'I'm sure I'll find room for the odd morsel, or two, though I don't plan to stay long myself. Now, I can see that Frankie is ready to go, shall we try to find The Priest?' Frankie, who had a dragonfly drone perched on one shoulder and a butterfly drone on the other, just smiled, but I said 'Yes, I've got it all sorted from my end; we'll be meeting a geriatric-specialist care-robot at the top of the gangway. I just need you to make the introductions, Merv. After that you can make your excuses and skedaddle.'

Merv accompanied us inside the Starship, where we made contact with the care-robot. My NeuroModem offered a plan of the Starship's interior derived from the recently completed drone surveys, but I declined it for the moment. Like most of my ground crews, I was already well aware of the geography of this region of the ship. We had all become regular customers of the coffee bar and canteen even in the few hours we'd been down here. It was a vast hall where the initial crew's flight couches and escape pods had been located, which had been converted into a canteen and several snack bars and comfortable lounges. Merv guided us past the eateries, further towards the stern of the ship where the main corridor ended as a circular arcade of three regular hatchways, all closed, but clearly labelled: 'Command Deck', 'Astronavigation' though the original label on the third, still evident as 'Stateroom', had an additional neatly printed

'Microsoft Shrine' on it, with yet another addition immediately below: 'Your Window onto The New Universe'.

'Right, this is it,' said Merv.

'Hold on a moment, Merv,' I said, 'before you do anything drastic, like knocking on the door, let's be sure we all know what we're here for.' I turned to the care-robot, who had been keeping one step behind us so far. 'Come into the huddle, Carla, I'm hoping you will be able to help me with this.

'Ostensibly,' I went on, 'we are here to deal with, and bring to an end, the drone-swatting business. But, in addition, as a mark of goodwill, we've come with a picnic version of the barbecue specifically for him, and with it the opportunity for a personal explanation of anything he might have missed from the video of our discussion. While that's happening, Carla, I want you to carry out as much of an assessment of The Priest as you can from the back of the room and stream your conclusions to my NeuroModem. Before we go much further, I need to know if he's a nut, or just a cantankerous old man. And either way, I also need to know if he's healthy enough to survive shuttle transfer to orbit.'

'If I may interrupt, here,' said Carla, who had now morphed into a very convincing female nurse. 'I see that Frankie is accompanied by two survey drones, which I understand from the files of past conversations, you want to introduce to The Priest as acceptable drones to complete the structural survey of the area around his 'shrine'. If Frankie can persuade The Priest to allow one or both drones to alight on his skin, Malik can reprogramme them as medi-drones and I can use their sensors to give him a complete medical examination.'

'Brilliant,' was all I needed to say. 'That's what we'll do. OK, Merv, into the lion's den!'

Merv touched the 'open' symbol on the hatch, it swished to one side, and we shuffled in. It was the stateroom set aside for the original pilots and their guests of Starship-101, so the room was a generous size and well equipped; albeit in a 100-year-old fashion. The Priest was lying on a launch-couch far from the door, surrounded by active, but silenced, video screens. He was very noisily fast asleep.

Merv strode over to the couch and shook The Priest, gently. 'Hey fella, wake up there! I've brought some people to see you, and as you didn't come down to the barbecue, we've brought the barbecue to you!'

If Merv was expecting thanks for our thoughtful largesse, he was disappointed. As Frankie started to set out the barbecue picnic on one of the side tables in the lounge area of the stateroom, The Priest slowly swung his legs off the couch and punctuated with a variety of grunts and groans, went through an elaborate routine of muscle and joint massage, as though trying to get a recalcitrant mechanism up and running just one more time. But all the time during this performance he was watching Frankie's activities very carefully. And then, after a fit of coughing and the odd sneeze, he spoke, gruffly.

'What do you want, Castlefield? I've told you before, I don't welcome interruption while I'm meditating.' He finally ventured onto his feet and then tottered, though with improving steadiness as lazy joints got back to work, towards the table Frankie was just completing. 'Thank you, young lady,' he said much kindlier, as his eyes scanned the table 'What do you recommend?'

'Yes, well, sorry to wake you from your meditation,' Merv responded, trying to match the gruff tones. 'The young lady you're trying to flirt with is chief cyber engineer, Captain Frankie Burton, you've been destroying the microdrones she must use to make structural surveys of this ship. And you've got to stop.'

The Priest didn't respond beyond smiling at Frankie and shrugging his shoulders as he took the selection plate from her. Then he spoke directly to me.

'I was awake long enough during the video stream of the barbecue to recognise you, Commodore Clason. Are you here to whisk Starship-101 from under my feet?'

'Not immediately,' I acknowledged. 'But we do need to talk about it. Call me Tarvin.'

'OK, Tarvin, but who is that other young lady lurking there in the background?' and then, quickly adding, 'No, don't tell me, let me find out for myself.' Turning his attention to Carla, he said, much more briskly, 'Robot ID Tom's override routine immediate.'

To which Carla responded: 'Med-robot, geriatric care specialist, morph capable, this unit name Carlo, Carla or Default-C. Presently in morph-form Carla.'

'And very nice, too, Carla,' said The Priest. 'Robot Tom's override routine immediate, show me Carlo, then show me Default-C.'

We watched, spellbound, as the robot morphed its body into its three characters, its 'skin' moulding itself from the diminutive Latina Carla, into the considerably taller and Italian-looking Carlo and then to the almost skeletal, metallic, default robot body.

'Beautiful,' whispered The Priest, with tears in his eyes. 'You know, when I was writing that code, what, seventy years ago, was it? The best we could do was stick a bloody great video screen on their shoulders and do all that morphing with graphics on the screen. Robot Tom's override routine immediate revert to Carla.' Followed by the instruction 'Carla Robot Tom's override routine immediate state assignment.'

To which Carla returned 'Carla is a geriatric-care specialist, assigned to Thomas William Fraser, age 94, sole survivor of Starship-101's original crew. Senior computer engineer, responsible for service and maintenance of Starship-101's computer equipment. Carla is managed by Malik and reports covertly directly to Commodore Tarvin Clason's q-bit NeuroModem.'

'Beautiful, truly beautiful. I guess Malik is your Starship's quantum megacomputer, eh, Tarvin?' I nodded, as he continued, 'Commodore, as far as I am concerned, you can do anything you like with Starship-101, just keep this robot assigned to me. The three of us have got a hundred years of coding to talk about, and I'm including Malik in that trio!'

He turned his attention back to Carla and holding out his now empty plate to the robot, asked 'Carla, could you find me another one of those chicken legs? No, wait, I've not eaten chicken legs like that for 50 years, see if you can find three, and another of those little lamb chops, and I guess if I'm going to make a pig of myself, I could use a few more tissues, too.'

The years seemed to be falling away from him as he turned to the rest of us, saying 'Castlefield, you can go about your mayoral duties, me and my new friends, Tarvin and Frankie, need to talk things over in private.'

Merv looked at me, shrugged, raising his eyes to the ceiling. 'I'll go organise that Town Meeting, then.' He left.

'Don't be so hard on Merv,' I ventured out loud. 'He's doing his best.'

'Oh, Tarvin,' he spluttered through his next chicken leg. 'You're forgetting what Carla's just told you. I've been locked up in this tin can with Merv 'doing his best' for his entire life. He was a fool of a child and now he's an uptight, full-his-own-importance, fool of a Town Mayor, and his father was a full-his-own-importance fool as a ship's administrator, too, and probably came from a long line of the same. Though, thankfully, I didn't have to live with his ancestors.'

He pointed at me with the remains of a lamb chop. 'I was glad to hear you say that Starship-103 was cancelled because the problem with generation Starships like us is that the parents turn their children into miniature versions of themselves. They have to, because that's the deal; the shipboard responsibilities of the parents are inherited by their children. But the ship is the children's one and only world. They can't leave home to live in the next town, there isn't one. They can't take a gap year 'to see the world'; it only takes a week to walk down every corridor on the ship. Fortunately, we were in flight for only one lifetime. I hate to think what's in store for Starship-102 or what might have happened to 103 if it had been launched. Not having a family of my own, my complaints about the way the children were being educated was seen as me preaching about things about which I could know nothing. That's how I got the nickname 'Priest'. The older I got, the more I appreciated being isolated from the rest of the crew. So, I played-up to 'The Priest' monicker, because it suited me to be thought of as a reclusive nutcase. And when I broadened out my little story to this claptrap about a Microsoft 'shrine' the second-generation settlers left me alone.'

Finally, he said: 'Now, come on guys, let's all cheer up, settle around the Captain's Table and deal with our business rather than ancient history. Carla, can you get us some drinks? And are they pigs-in-blankets in that dish? Any bread rolls?'

'Certainly, Sir,' said Carla.

'None of the 'Sir', Carla. I hereby defrock and resign my priesthood; call me Tom. In fact, everybody: call me Tom!'

We settled around the table, and I happily tucked into my second barbecue of the day, promising my nagging NeuroModem health monitor that I'll get a bit more exercise 'tomorrow'. Frankie guided the conversation around to drone swatting and Tom Fraser apologised, explaining: 'The older I get, the more I hark back to my childhood, almost as a reflex action. When your drones flew in here, they triggered childhood memories of me and my brother disturbing a hornet's nest in the woods behind our holiday home somewhere in central Europe when I was about ten or eleven years old. I have this visual mindscape of both of us running back to the house, flailing our arms about, trying to drive them away, but still being stung painfully. It wasn't until I'd slapped down a few of your drones that I recognised them for what they are. They are impressive little things.'

'I've brought a couple of drones fabricated to mimic insects that might have more tranquil memories for you. We still need to complete the structural surveys in this part of the ship,' said Frankie, setting the dragonfly and butterfly into flight. While the butterfly flapped gracefully around the table, the dragonfly hovered in front of Tom's face. He leaned towards it to examine more closely and stuck out his finger. The dragonfly obligingly settled on his finger, and he watched closely as a proboscis emerged from the head of the thing and began sucking around his skin, apparently seeking out food.'

Tom smiled and held out his other hand in front of the fluttering butterfly. This drone also settled, then unrolled its proboscis and probed around his skin. Tom's smile broadened and, still holding his hands out so the drones could finish their work, he said: 'Brilliantly done, Carla! My arms are getting tired, though. Have you got all the information you need?'

'Yes, Tom,' Carla replied 'Your medical scan is complete. The drones can be released.'

With that the drones flew back towards Frankie, one settling onto each shoulder.

'Nice demonstration, Frankie!' Tom said 'I'm sorry I trashed so many drones this morning. I have no further objections to your completing your structural survey.'

'Thank you, can I get on with that now?' Frankie asked, looking at me. 'My truck is still parked at the entrance.'

'Sure,' I said. 'Call up the drones.'

Frankie went to the door and opened the hatchway. She stood there for a few moments using her NeuroModem to issue orders to her drone squads. Then, standing to one side of the entrance, she ushered in a squad of dragonflies and another of butterflies. They buzzed and fluttered about their business and Tom looked on benignly.

'OK, Boss,' said Frankie. 'I'll get back to my truck to manage the data from these guys. Keep the door open, if you will. The drones have a route to follow when they've finished here. Bye.'

'You know, when we left Earth, most people were still using mobile phone devices to communicate,' Tom remarked, biting into another chicken leg. 'Computer jockeys like me were the fortunate ones, fitted with NeuroModems. What's the chance of me having an upgrade to a q-bit NeuroModem?'

'That's up to your medical adviser. What's your opinion, Carla?'

'I see no reason to deny such an upgrade,' replied the robot. 'Tom is remarkably healthy for his age and sedentary lifestyle. But then, he has spent his life as maintenance engineer and first treatment volunteer in Starship-101's medical centre so his health has been well monitored over the years. I can oversee the upgrade and associated training if that's agreeable to you, Tarvin.'

'Yes, go ahead; that's fine. As you know, we will be offering q-bits to all the settlers after Frankie and Lana get the settlement's new quantum megacomputer up and running. So, Malik and you can continue to treat Tom as a guineapig and make him the first upgrade.'

'Nice one!' muttered Tom. 'Will that include a direct link to Malik?'

'We'll have to wait and see about that. I'm unwilling to agree to that until we establish how many of 'Tom's override routines' are embedded in the legacy coding of my principal ship's computer. I'll set Malik to checking that, PDQ,' I said aloud and mentally sent a duplicate of it through my NeuroModem to Malik. 'Copy that. Commodore,' the computer responded.

I thought it was about time to broach the subject of taking Tom back to the Solar System with the hulk of Starship-101: 'There's another idea I wanted to float with you,' I said. 'Are you determined to stay on Proxima-b, or would you be willing to come back to the Solar System with me?'

Tom smiled, saying 'Oh, Tarvin, my dear, this is so sudden. Is this a proposal?'

'Don't laugh it off before I've finished,' I resumed. 'As you know, our basic intention is to take Starship-101 back home to establish it as prime exhibit in a museum about interstellar travel, which, personally, I think will be located at the Oort Station, because that's the obvious place to develop as our gateway to other stars. And it seems to me that the last surviving member of Starship-101's original crew could make a really important contribution to establishing that museum.'

'Erm,' mused Tom, looking innocently vacant. 'Are you talking about me?'

'Sure, but again, I need medical advice. Carla, I can't risk to quantum jump 101 with passengers until we know that this century-old hulk will stay intact, so Tom would have to be lifted into orbit on one of our shuttles. What do you think about this idea?'

'Healthwise, the risks can be managed,' Carla reported. 'Malik recommends using the return launch of one of the heavy lift shuttles. They can make a long and slow lift into orbit, which would cause minimum stress to Tom's body. I would accompany him, so it's perfectly manageable. And, of course, once in orbit, microgravity minimises all the stresses for geriatric patients.'

'Fine, we've asked everybody else,' I said. 'So Tom, what do you think about going back to the Solar System?'

There was a long pause. So long that I was beginning to think he might say no, but finally he almost whispered, 'Given the chance, I'd leave tomorrow!' I believe I saw a tear trickling over his wrinkled cheek as he continued: 'Humanity's first visit to an extrasolar star system, and I return to tell the tale! What a tale to tell! Like one of the ancient Greek myths, isn't it? Oh, yes; I like the sound of that. When can Carla and I leave?'

'I'm happy to leave that to Carla and Malik,' I said. 'Carla can sort out your health and NeuroModem upgrade, and Malik can fit you into the shuttle timetable. It will be a couple of weeks before we make our jumps back to the Solar System. We have a lot of work to do here. You can be accommodated in a guest stateroom in my Starship until we jump out of orbit. Gives you plenty of time to acclimatise.' I was sorry about that last sentence as soon as I uttered it. Tom was sharp enough to pick me up about it.

'No worries there, Mate. I've spent 50 years acclimatising to Starship travel!'

'OK, OK, I admit, not the best thing to say in the circumstances!'

'It's a lot more than 50 years, anyway,' Tom continued. 'And I got used to the climb into orbit in my early days.'

'How did that come about?' I asked, rummaging about in the remains of the picnic for further morsels.

'Oh, my first job after qualifying on Earth was in writing basic operating code for what were then the latest AI-robots and that finished with me taking a small army of robots to Mars as part of the Mars atmosphere replacement programme.'

That made me sit up and take notice. 'Really?' I exclaimed 'My grandpa was involved in that, too. It was the first major interplanetary contract for our company. Grandpa was responsible for collecting ice-asteroids from the asteroid belt and soft-landing them on the surface of Mars. The idea was to replace the shallow oceans the planet used to have. What was your programme about?'

'Our programme was to cover Mars with moss!' said Tom, smiling. 'And I remember those big icebergs being brought into land and melting all over the deserts. That struck me as something worth doing. I was never too keen on our job. It involved hauling to Mars huge tanker loads of fermented milk, yoghurt, basically, mixed with chopped-up fragments of mosses, algae and similar stuff collected mainly from Iceland. My job was training autonomous trucks to deliver the muck to the latest iceberg landing site with squads of AI-robots to smear it over the ground.' He paused to drink the rest of his beer, before continuing.

'Apparently it was all good science, and I quite enjoyed it for a couple of years. But by then I had tuned the software so that the machines could work reliably without me and soon started to think that a lifetime's career in yoghurt smearing was not for me. I started to look for alternative employment and almost immediately the Proxima-Centauri mission started inviting applications for its crew. So, I jumped on the bandwagon. They needed coding engineers and as I'd written a lot of the code for the then most up-to-date medical robots, I sailed through the selection procedures and was offered a ride on the first interstellar emigration.'

'Great story, that, Tom,' I said 'And so like my grandpa's experiences. We'll have to get the two of you together. And Carla, while I'm thinking about it, archive Tom's story as the start of his reminiscences, and you build the files and pass them on to Malik for editing.'

'My grandpa's best story about that water replacement programme on Mars,' I went on, warming to the recollections. 'And the one he's most proud of, is that he was the one who sent the infamous radio message: 'Hello Earth, this is Mars. It's snowing here! Please advise.' It made the home page of every news blog in the Solar System!'

'It must be nice to be in at the conclusion of one of these planetary engineering projects. I'd love to see the Red Planet now,' remarked Tom, unsuccessfully stifling a yawn.

'You'll be able to do that in a few months,' I responded. 'And you will not be disappointed. It's a distinctly greenish-red planet now, thanks to the Icelandic programme you were involved with.' I found myself trying not to yawn and noticed the room's lighting had begun to dim. Realising that this might mean it was getting late, I asked Tom: 'What's the local time, Tom?'

'Nearly midnight,' was the response. 'As we're on the bright side of a planet that keeps one hemisphere facing its sun, we use the ship's computer to make all interior lighting maintain our circadian rhythms. We found in the first few weeks after landing that the constant red twilight of Proxima-b screwed up our body clocks, so we returned to the Universal Time standard we'd been flying with on the journey here.'

'Just as we do,' I said. 'My ship and all the others my company operates all run on the Greenwich Earth time zone of the Universal Time standard. So, I'd better clear off before it gets too late for you, but there is one other question with which I'd appreciate your help.'

'Well, go on then, ask the question. At my age I can sleep anywhere, anytime but I've not been asked for my help for many a long year!' Was the robust response.

'What's been bothering me since I first saw the settlement in our ground scans as we brought my Starship into orbit above it,' I continued, 'is how the people in that settlement would react to us turning up in the blink of an eye with loads of stuff that will change their lifestyles drastically. Will they object? We're here because the Solar System wants to draw the Centauri system into an interstellar trading union to establish humanity as an interstellar species. But the original crew chose to embark on Starship-101 to get away from the Solar System, maybe they still want to maintain their independence. You know these people, Tom, so tell me, will they object to us telling them how to live their lives?'

'Tarvin, my boy, you have no need to worry about objections. I can tell you they are all delighted with your arrival and everything you have to offer!' Tom chuckled, 'You're not thinking it through, lad! You need to add a hundred years of subsistence living, and a couple of generations to your guesses about the opinions and beliefs of the settlers who are out there now. Sure, the original crew had a wide variety of opinions and motives that drove us to accept all the risks and choose to escape the clutches of the Solar System's Authorities. I'm sure that many of them would object, some of them violently, to the Solar System reaching out to take us back into its clutches. But the strength of attitudes like that has been diminished by fifty years flying through deep space in a titanium box and another twenty years existing on a planet that's not exactly a welcoming holiday home!' Tom paused to drink some of the fresh coffee with which Carla had provided us. He held up his cup when he resumed. 'See?' he started. 'Fresh coffee! Real coffee! We ran out of stocks of that about twenty years into the flight. So, we've lived through fifty years of dependence on processed and synthetic food and drink. Of course, we have whole sections of the Starship, two or three kilometres long, devoted to industrial food production. Hydroponics produces cereals, peas and several types of beans, and from the plant wastes and straw, together with reclaimed human wastes we produce more mushrooms than you can shake a stick at. We also have a section full of fermenters that produce fungi and yeasts, and even animal cells, all of which we use to make simulated meat. Apart from me, none of the people at your barbecue will have ever eaten real meat, or real fish, or drunk real coffee or tea, or hot chocolate. For those we have the chemical synthesis machines which make everything else we need for a healthy existence, like synthetic coffee! And when you've tasted our synthetic coffee, you realise how the dregs of the reclaimed human wastes are used! The truth is, that without your intervention the settlers alive now have got nothing to look forward to but a slow decline into increasing adversity as the machines on which they depend wear out and fail on a planet that demands survival skills that the later generations simply don't have.'

Tom paused again, to drain his cup. 'That tastes good!' he said, and added, 'And that's why sub-lightspeed generation starships can never succeed in creating an interstellar civilisation. Unless you can build them the size of a planet with all the support infrastructure that size implies, the crew that embarked and the generations it produces during and after the flight will exhaust the capability of the original ship to support them, with no chance of help from back home at anything other than sub-lightspeed. What you are doing, Tarvin, is giving the Proxima-b settlers a future. And not just any old future, but a future updated to your present century. You'll not find anyone objecting to that! You know, I've not talked that much in decades, and now I feel as though I've had enough of today.'

'I advise you both to go to bed,' said Carla. 'Do you have accommodation on Starship-101, Commodore Tarvin?'

'Oh yes,' I replied. 'I was allocated the captain's cabin which, if I remember rightly, is just above this stateroom.'

Stretching, I stood up and fist-bumped Tom. 'I'm immensely grateful for your comments and advice, Tom. This little chat has helped me a lot. But now, Carla, I'm going to follow your advice and take to my bunk, and I'll leave you to follow up on what we've agreed. Arrange with Malik to fit Tom's q-bit NeuroModem and organise his orbital transfer.'

'Copy that, Commodore,' the robot replied.

Tom was standing in front of me as I turned towards the still-open doorway, but there were no more fist-bumps. This time he just hugged me. 'Thanks for everything, Tarvin,' he whispered into my ear. 'I'm really looking forward to going home!'

I called a final 'goodnight' through the open doorway, and as the microdrones were long gone onto their next venue, I closed the hatchway behind me as I walked into the circular arcade at the end of the entrance corridor. I remembered Merv conducting me early this morning into the elevator that was behind the door labelled Command Deck, so I just followed my nose and went up there. The lift opened into a small atrium with a door into the forward control room straight ahead, and a second door on my left labelled 'Captain's Cabin', which I knew was 'mine'.

The cabin was rather more generous than I was used to on my own ship, having a comfortable lounge area leading to two bedrooms with ensuites; but then I recalled that the original pilot and co-pilot were a married couple, and I was benefitting from that history. As I entered the lounge the robot steward came to life. This AI-robot was, of course, 100 years old, so interaction with my NeuroModem was out of the question, but it was controlled by the ship's computer, and I knew that Malik would have already updated that machine with all my personal preferences, so I was confident of relying on voice commands. Certainly, the steward had unpacked the contents of my overnight bag and laid out fresh clothes for tomorrow which included a newly ironed shirt, so the machine was on the ball. I gave it verbal instructions to wake me at 6.30 a.m. next morning and retired; sleeping contentedly until the steward did wake me at the allotted time.

Day 2

Declining the steward's offer of breakfast, I decided to shave myself rather than trust that activity to a century-old robot, though before leaving the cabin to follow the smell of freshly brewed coffee emanating from the coffee bar on the deck below, I did thank the thing for steaming and pressing my uniform overnight. Its care had made me look like a reasonably tidy flotilla commodore for the second day in a row.

I reached the coffee bar just behind Merv Castlefield and he introduced me to a display of freshly baked breakfast goodies. Every time I had visited the coffee bar in the short time I'd been here, the place had been full of settlers. But this morning it was almost empty, apart from a few of my gang chiefs, relaxing after a hard night supervising the overnight robot brigades.

Over breakfast I brought Merv up to date with the Tom Fraser story of the previous evening and asked if he had received any feedback comments from the settlers about yesterday's barbecue.

'They were all amazed at the quality and taste of the food; and most had eaten far too much of it!' He reported. 'That doesn't surprise me, of course, all of us have grown up eating ship's rations, and as we didn't bring any farm animals with us, all we've been able to do since landing with regards to fresh food has been to grow plants. Nice enough, but Ilsa and Emma's barbecued meat and fish were a revelation to all of us!'

'Glad to hear it,' I said. 'It was a bit of a gamble. For all we knew you might all have grown up as dedicated vegans. I'll ask Malik to report that to Ilsa and Emma and suggest they get your canteen chefs involved in making a cookout a weekly event. Was there any feedback about our purposes here?'

'Oh, yes, very appreciative comments, and not just for the food!' said Merv as we sauntered back to the counter for a coffee top-up. I don't think there'll be many takers for the trip back to Earth you mentioned. At least, not this time around. Everyone I talked to said they'd like to stay and make a go of the settlement IF they can rely on the regular support you mentioned in your talk.'

'Yes, definitely,' I said. 'That's a given. My brother is organising the next supply operation right now. We plan to meet at Oort Station when I return. Harden's part of the contract is to pioneer and test out the quantum jump route and its four waystations that we established on the way here. Once that route's been commissioned and certified it will be opened up to commercial quantum jump pilots working for the likes of the tourist, general travel and prospecting industries. All of which could be a major source of revenue for Proxima-b,' I concluded.

'Yeah, I understand that,' said Merv. 'And I guess that more and more of my settlers will come to appreciate the potential future they have here. I understand your robot teams have built and equipped a new studio complex in the settlement overnight, and Lana's already broadcasting the first of the podcasts and documentaries that explain it all. I guess that's where everyone is. This place is deserted; they're probably all brewing their own coffee in front of their video screens.'

'So, how did the town meeting go?' I inquired.

'Pretty brilliant, actually,' Merv responded, grinning over his coffee mug. 'It was the least argumentative Town Meeting I've ever experienced! I don't think anyone aired a negative comment. Very 'gung-ho' about the whole thing. I was expecting at least some reservations about you making off back towards the Solar System with old 101, but whenever there was any hint of nostalgia for the ship, somebody else piped up with stories about the century-younger items coming down from your cargo ships.' Merv gulped another mouthful of coffee and continued, 'I think most of the settlers must have spent most of their time before the barbecue yesterday picking through the newly delivered crates and drooling over the contents!'

'Does anyone object to me hauling Starship-101 off-planet and into orbit?' I asked.

'Nah,' was Merv's response. 'I suggested a vote, but then Clint asked if anyone was likely to vote 'no', to which there was complete silence, so I declared a unanimous vote in favour of transferring ownership of Starship-101 to you. The meeting broke up and lots of people galloped back to the Square to see if the barbecue had any leftovers.'

'All good news, then. Though I don't want to own Starship-101, I'm just its heavy haulage driver, you'll need to get your Town Council's approval of ownership transfer to the United Planetary Authority.' And then through my NeuroModem, I continued, 'Malik, I know you have the authority to effect this transfer, will you sort it out with the mayor's office?'

'Affirmative, Commodore,' was the thought Malik placed in my NeuroModem.

It was quickly followed by a message from Kat: 'Boss, can we discuss arrangements to haul my observatories around this planet and its near neighbours?'

'Sure, where are you?'

'Back onboard ship.'

Standing, I turned back to Merv and offered a fist-bump. 'I need to get back to my ship. Malik will send all the ownership transfer bumph to your office and the two of you can sort it out between you. I don't need to be further involved.'

I wandered off to the forward gangway and went from the bright white light of the Starship's interior to the red twilight of the outside world of Proxima-b. Near the bottom of the gangway I saw that Jim's team had already brought down some of the latest hydrogen powered all-terrain trikes for the settlers' use, and I commandeered one of them and set off towards the SpacePort to hitch a ride back to my ship on a returning cargo shuttle.

When the shuttle docked with my ship, I found the transition from gravity to microgravity just as entertaining as usual and I flew through the corridors towards the command deck, having as much fun as any first-year space cadet.

Kat was already in the control room, surrounded by active video screens. 'Hi Boss, do you want a quick sitrep on overnight progress before we get down to observatory business?' She went on without waiting for my reply. 'Everyone's got at least the first fix sorted for the various replacement facilities. The power station was first in and started sharing load with Starship-101's fusion reactors in the wee small hours of this morning. It all seems to be working well and Malik expects to have the new reactors fully commissioned in the next hour or so; at which point he will retire 101's reactors and leave them as power for the ship only, switching the settlement's power grid over to the new reactors.' Kat didn't seem to take a breath before she continued: 'Second machine to be put in place was Malik-2, the megacomputer we've brought for the settlement. Frankie experienced a few issues with the new machine's cooling plant, but that's been sorted now. The only ongoing issue is that Malik wants the new machine given a different name; he says he doesn't like the idea of training such a capable AI that has a name so like his own. He's getting a bit bolshie about it!'

'I suppose, I could ask Merv and the settlers to choose a name,' I ventured, but it could take a while for them to come to a decision.' Then I had a brainwave. 'Wait, here's an idea. Merv told me they plan to name the new village we'll be building down there after we lift the Starship into orbit, 'Westwood' in honour of the original pilots, Billy and Cleo Westwood, who brought Starship-101 into land on Proxima-b. So, why don't we pre-empt that plan and name their new computer Westwood?'

Malik placed the thought in my NeuroModem: 'I like that idea.'

'OK,' I thought back. 'That's what we'll do.'

'Any other reports, Kat? I understand that Lana's got her broadcasts up and running.'

'Yes,' Kat pointed to two neighbouring sections of the wraparound screen. 'That's the studio, though it looks deserted at the moment, and the next one is what she's broadcasting live right now.'

'Hey, Lana!' I thought into my NeuroModem. 'Congrats on getting your videos on air! Can you talk at the moment?'

'Morning, Boss,' she replied, walking into view of the studio camera and waving. 'Thanks. We've got Malik organising the broadcast and streaming programmes at the moment. We'll swap over to Frankie's computer, which I'm just being told will be called 'Westwood', when Frankie gives us the thumbs-up.'

'You approve of the name?' I asked.

'Oh yeah! I realise we couldn't call the place 'Hollywood', so Westwood is close enough. But maybe, as a homage to the original, we could put the word Westwood in 15-metre-high letters on that rocky outcrop downstream that the Boss was climbing around breathlessly yesterday morning. Are you listening, Malik?'

'I listen to everything, Lana, but I'll take a rain check on that suggestion!'

'Rain check? What do you know about rain to check? You're just a handful of sand that lives in a tin can!' was Lana's immediate rejoinder.

'Oh, hurtful! There's much more than a handful, and the can is mostly made of titanium.'

'OK, kids, bickering bores the adults around here!' Kat broke in. 'Get some work done.'

'I am working,' Lana protested to Kat. 'Me and my production team are just about to grab a few of Jim's all-terrain trikes and buzz around Starship-101 to find good vantage points for our cameras to record your historic removal of a Starship from its landing site on the ground and back into orbit. And Malik, stick with me kid and I'll take you outside and you can check for rain.'

'I am always with you, Lana, there's a thread of me that lives in your NeuroModem,' Malik remarked, adding, 'It's one of the aspects of my job I treasure least.'

'Oh, hurtful!' Lana giggled.

Ignoring the continued exchange of minor insults, I interrupted, 'You're planning to make a major production of the lift into orbit, are you, Lana?'

'I certainly am,' Lana replied, going on to explain, 'As far as I can discover, there are no vids of the preparation and conduct of a quantum jump other than the ones used for training cadets at space schools. So that alone is an original opportunity. And then, what makes it even more essential that we go to town on the project are all the other 'firsts' that we can add to the jump itself. For a start it would be the first ever documentary recorded in a non-Solar star system; the first ever interviews of *interstellar* travellers; the first ever in-your-face views of a non-Solar star system. I got some great views of our insertion into orbit as we first approached and by now Malik's got petabytes of orbital observations of the whole surface of Proxima-b, and the local space environment.'

'It's getting close to an exabyte, by now,' Malik interjected.

Lana continued, 'We could spend the rest of our lives editing all that into vids the streaming services all over the Solar System would be falling over themselves to buy into. And all copyright *Interstellar Haulage*! Loadsamoney!'

'Right,' I said. 'Did you say 'money'? Now I'm really interested. You'd better get going to make a start on this money-making opus.'

'Copy that, Boss. Lana out.'

I made a call for refreshment 'Catering, can we have coffee for two in the control room, please?'

'Certainly, Sir,' replied the Command Centre steward.

Then, pointing to the last screen image, I asked, 'What else is that you have on the screen, Kat?'

'That's the new medical centre. Lots of activity there. All the rooms were fitted out with basic services overnight and now the robot decorating teams are finishing off. Bill and Mary, with 101's own existing medical staff are beginning to commission the new diagnostic and treatment units. The brigade of new medical bots was trooped in just before you got here.' Kat paused as she wound up the magnification of the screen image. 'And that door label says 'Neurosurgery', so I guess they're planning to push forward with installing q-bit NeuroModem upgrades for both humans and the brigades of old bots.'

After all this talking, Kat looked gratefully towards the door as the steward interrupted proceedings, floating into the control room with a tray of bulb-like microgravity coffee 'mugs' and a 'coffee-pot' dispenser.

With coffee bulb in hand, Kat then continued, 'And that brings me to our next activity. I'd like to discuss the deployment of both our ground-based and satellite-based astrophysical observatories.

'OK, what do you have in mind.'

Kat waved a hand at the wraparound screen and a 3-D model of the planet's surface came into view 'This,' she said 'is the topography of the terminator of Proxima-b directly north of the settlement. Cold side at the top. I'd like to locate the ground observatories well into the cold side to shield the instruments from Proxima-Centauri's radiations. We're already using heavy lift shuttles to deliver an automatic stellar observatory to the equatorial desert on the hot side which will give us all the observations we need of the star, so it doesn't matter that our main ground-based observatory will be hidden from the star we're orbiting.' Kat paused and took a quick pull on the nozzle of her coffee.

'The compromise I want advice on,' she went on, 'is this: just how far should we go into the cold side. If we go close to the terminator, it makes travel relatively easy between the settlement and observatory, but I worry about snowfall from the eddies of moisture-laden atmosphere that swirl from the warm side of the terminator to the cold side. The places that are most convenient to reach are also subject to almost continuous blizzards. On the other hand, the further we look into the cold side, the better the seeing conditions because it's so cold that the atmosphere itself freezes down to the permanent glaciers, but travel to and from the facility becomes a major undertaking.'

'Have you identified potential locations?' I asked.

'Not close to the terminator, there's always too much snow,' Kat replied. 'But if you look up here, well into the cold side.' Kat adjusted the image magnification and started a fly-through towards an extremely high mountain range. 'Here,' she pointed. 'There's a flat-topped peak that stands clear of the surrounding glaciers. It's the second tallest mountain on Proxima-b and could have been made for the job. But how do you travel over that much of that terrain?'

'I think I can tell you that,' I said. 'But tell me how often human travel would be necessary. I thought these facilities, like the orbital observatories, were operated by AI-robots.'

'Oh, yes, that's true,' Kat replied. 'And, indeed,' she went on, 'the robot squads we'll use are the latest 'fax' robots, that have q-bit NeuroModems capable of interfacing so deeply with a remote human NeuroModem that they become a facsimile of that human. The human experiences directly everything the robot experiences. This is fully tested and fully functional, and there are enough spare fax-bots in the squads for whole teams of human astronomers to work together. The issue we have is that our main sponsor, the Interplanetary Astronomical Union, wants to maintain the tradition of regular site visits by human astronomers. And they've paid a fair wedge of cash up front for that service. We have to provide it.'

'OK, Kat, here's what we'll do. If that flat mountain top is the best place for your observatory, we'll put it there. You coordinate with Malik and Jim to get Jim's civil engineering teams to do the necessary surveys to build what needs to be built and install what needs to be installed. But, add to your plans a SpacePort apron and a hydrogen/oxygen refuelling facility, because what you need for travel to-and-fro is a good old-fashioned rocket sled.'

'Malik, do we carry stocks of hydrogen/oxygen-fuelled rocket sleds?'

'Not in our general supplies,' Malik reported. 'These so-called 'Skippers' are generally classed as 'vintage' vehicles. But my manifest shows two of them mothballed and stowed in the commodore's quarters as part of the commodore's personal belongings. According to my records, they've not been touched for some time.'

'Oh, so that's where they are. Malik, please arrange for both to be reconditioned, recommissioned, refuelled and delivered to a Commodore's Personal Lockup on Proxima-b's SpacePort. And include deep-space-rated personal space suits for Captain Katharina Clason and me.'

'Copy that, Commodore.'

I grinned at Kat. 'You're going to enjoy this, Kat. When we were teenagers, and training to be quantum jumpers, Harden and I rode Skippers all around near-Earth space. They're space-travelling motor trikes we could quantum jump into orbit and then rocket around the Earth in orbit. We even used them to quantum jump to local Waystations at Lagrange points around Earth and Moon where the museums, interplanetary travel hubs and shipyards were located, and where other space-bums hung out.'

'Yes,' said Kat, slowly and doubtfully. 'Harden's confessed a few little tales about your teenage tearaway years charging around the Solar System. Not all of them respectable.'

'But all forgivable!' I volunteered, quickly, not wanting to delve further into those reminiscences. 'When Malik's got my Skippers sorted out, I'll take you on a trip to 'Observatory Mountain' so we can experience the site conditions for ourselves. We could take Jim, as well, so that he can get a feel for the place too.'

'I'm getting confused now, Tarvin. How does your enthusiasm for reliving your childhood solve the issue of to-and-fro travel to the observatory? Are you planning to donate your Skippers to the IAU with which their visitors can risk life and limb reliving your teenage escapades?'

'Certainly not,' I protested. 'They are really very straightforward machines to build and I'm sure David will be able to recover the build specs from his transport factory's memory, update them to modern standards of safety and build a few new ones, long before the IAU sends anybody up here. Flying them is well within the capabilities of any of our standard AI-driving units. And by the time we've been to Observatory Mountain and back, we'll have flight plans on record to be used in AI training, just like any other transport jockey on a regular route.'

I drained the dregs from my coffee mug, saying, 'I'm getting close to needing some brunch, and I'd enjoy it more in the gravity field of the planet's surface. Do you need decisions about any other observatory issues?'

'Yes. I'm afraid so,' Kat replied. 'We carry two large astrophysical observatories that we are contracted to place in orbit around Proxima-c and Proxima-d. Their purposes are both to map their local space environments in sufficient detail for quantum jumping, and to map the planets they orbit in sufficient detail for prospecting. We dispatched comms satellites into the Proxima system during our own approach into Proxima-b orbit and they are already indicating that the gravity gyrations in this TriStar/TriPlanet system are much messier than we anticipated from Earth-based observations. There's a complex mix of short period orbital motions—planets around the stars, and the orbit of Proxima-c is not only eccentric, but crosses the orbit of Proxima-b. As well as long period stellar orbits—the binary star pair Alpha Centauri A and B are only about the same distance apart as the distance between the Sun and Uranus, but Proxima-Centauri has an extremely eccentric, half-million-year, orbit around the binary stars which varies from close, about 0.07 lightyears, to fairly distant, about 0.2 lightyears.'

A slight pause, then, 'And all that leaves us with the classic dilemma that we need to have the astrophys satellites in stable orbits to make observations for a long period of time, but we need to have all those observations in hand before we can calculate the stable orbits into which we have to drop the satellites!'

'But you have a solution, right?' I asked.

'Yes, but it means sacrificing two of our heavy lift shuttles as partners to the astrophys satellites because the satellites might need to have their orbits adjusted more frequently and more drastically than anticipated, and the satellites themselves don't have the fuel or the grunt force to make the unanticipated adjustments.'

'I don't see that as a problem, Kat. You need to use heavy lift shuttles as tugs to take big satellites to the other planets and then leave them shackled to the astrophys satellites. No problem. Do it.'

'But those heavy lift shuttles cost an arm and a leg!' Kat protested.

'True, but it's not a permanent loss. Leaving the shuttles as tugs in this way is OK because it will not be long before David's teams get the settler's factories capable of manufacturing space tugs of their own that could be sent out to replace our shuttles. And then our shuttles can be taken back into our ownership on a later visit by Interstellar Haulage. You do what you must do to fulfil our contracts. Details can be tidied up later.'

'Now,' I continued, 'is that everything? I'm wasting away into utter starvation here. Do you want to come planetside for brunch?'

'Yes, that's everything I wanted to ask about; but no to a brunch trip, I'll get a bite to eat here and get on with these observatory placements.'

'OK,' I said, pushing away from the control desk and floating towards the door. 'Malik, is there a cargo shuttle about to depart any time soon?'

'Cargo bay 19, Commodore. A load of Emma's animals is due to depart in 10 minutes for a gentle flight down to the settlement.'

'That sounds ideal for me. Please tell the loadmaster that I'd like to hitch a lift, I'm leaving the control room now, but it may take me more than ten to reach Bay 19.'

'Copy that. Malik out'

With a final wave to Kat, I thrust myself out of the control room towards the central supply corridor that ran the full length of the ship and had a travellator along its walls. Revelling again in the joys of flying in microgravity I swung myself from one handgrip to the other, into the fast lane and then settled into dealing with some of my accumulated NeuroModem messages and acknowledging the salutes and greetings from passing fellow travellers. The deck numbers clicked along, the passage of their ID-numbers slowing greatly as we travelled towards the stern of the ship where the enormous cargo bays were located. It wasn't too much more than ten minutes before the number 18 was emblazoned on the corridor walls I was flying past, and I swung myself into the slow lane to decelerate for the off lane into Bay 19.

The bay was almost empty. Just a few remaining cargo containers being gently assembled into a group near the bay's airlock doors to which the travellator was taking me. Emma was stationed at the entrance, alongside a couple of our AI-loadmasters, one of which was holding one of Ilsa's picnic baskets.

'Hi Emma, I hope I've not delayed you too much?'

'Hi Boss, no probs. Malik's kept us informed. He also knew that I'd revived one of the barbecue's before coming up here to collect my little fish. So, I've got a picnic,' she pointed towards the picnic basket, 'and there's enough grilled cheese and sausage sarnies for two, Boss!'

'Emma, you're a life saver,' I said gratefully, 'do you have much more to load?'

'Nah, we can leave it to the tin men now.'

She retrieved her picnic basket from her tin man, and I followed her into the shuttle. I went, automatically, to the control cabin and sat in the pilot's seat. The flight down to the Proxima-b SpacePort would be entirely automatic, of course; controlled by the built-in AI-pilot. Call me paranoiac, if you will, but I just felt better about AI-flying if I was in reach of the controls.

When the two of us were settled, Emma started to open her picnic basket and I contacted flight control.

'Commodore in the control cabin,' I reported. 'Permission to depart, flight control?'

'Bay 19 doors sealed. All umbilicals detached. Push-off in 5-4-3-2-1-Go. Have a good trip, Commodore.'

And that's where the shuttle's AI took over, firing the cold gas thrusters to move the shuttle a respectful distance away from my Starship before firing the oxy-hydrogen retrorockets to start slowing us down. My enormous Starship seemed to be streaking past us, serenely onto its next orbit of the planet it was servicing.

We were, as usual, de-orbiting over the cold side of Proxima-b, which was illuminated at the moment only by distant starlight. But the high-sensitivity cameras that were showing our progress on the control cabin screens were nevertheless providing a fine display of the rugged mountains and almost planet-wide glaciers and ice fields below.

Emma thrust a, very welcome, sausage sandwich into my hand, and that brought my attention firmly back from the outside world below and into the shuttle.

'Thanks, Emma. So, the cargo on this flight is all fishy, is it?'

'Sure is,' she replied, 'I've been working with some of the young guys I met at the barbecue to set up the initial fish farms in the marshes. Geoff Moore's team is doing field studies there, so we have some baseline environmental data.'

Why, I asked myself, am I not surprised that Emma has already recruited a team of 'young guys she met at the barbecue' to help her out alongside her squads of tin men?

But Emma continued with her account, 'In this load, we have all my fingerlings. Young fish ready to go into the rearing ponds. These guys are the last to be moved down from orbit because we had to create their ponds by netting off the marshlands of the river delta. The nets were made by a 3D-printer using cell wall polymers extracted from local aquatic plants and algae. And while we were waiting for that to be done, we offloaded the hatcheries and nursery incubator units into one of Starship-101's disused cargo bays.'

Emma paused while she chased a floating piece of cheese-encrusted sausage that had detached itself from the sarnie she'd been waving about while she talked. The shuttle was now low enough in the atmosphere for us to feel the effects of Proxima-b gravity, so the escaped sausage described a gentle arc from sandwich towards what was becoming 'the floor'. She caught it expertly and then continued her description.

'It's all a big experiment to test how best to transport fish to Proxima-b. The problem being how to keep their water oxygenated in microgravity during the trip. But the eggs and hatchlings we've already successfully transferred to the incubators set up in Starship-101 suggest that the little guys are tougher than they look.'

We were now definitely aware of the gravity field we were landing into, and Emma jumped down from her seat saying, 'You'll have to excuse me now. As we transition to planetside gravity, I have to switch my fingerlings' tanks from artificial lung oxygenation to standard fish tank bubbling; and see how they handle being back on planet gravity. You know, buoyancy depends on gravity and these little brutes have swim bladders.' With that she threw herself down the hatchway into the cargo hold below the control cabin.

The AI-pilot was now guiding the descending shuttle into sweeping but gentle side to side manoeuvres as it shed height and speed onto the northerly approach to the landing pattern of the settlement's new SpacePort. A calm automatic voice announced over the intercom: 'Shuttle 559, this is Proxima-b SpacePort. Your landing acquired and approved. All personnel prepare for landing. Prepare for landing.'

Emma scrambled up the access ladder from the hold and jumped into the co-pilot's seat beside me, and the seat restraints tightened on both of us. 'The fingerlings look great,' she grinned at me. 'Couldn't see any losses, though they were sloshing about a bit. But that's another half-dozen of Earth's animals that copes perfectly well with interstellar travel!'

The shuttle then cruised out of the cold dark side of the planet, and as it crossed the terminator the top of our display screens lit up, showing the twilight redness that was all that Proxima-Centauri bestowed on this planet. But Starship-101, the settlement itself with the SpacePort beyond were picked out by the numerous white lights that were lighting the enormous range of activities that were underway on this early afternoon.

'There's my fish farm,' said Emma, excitedly pointing towards the right-hand side of the wraparound display. And, sure enough, the vast western side of the river delta was in view to starboard with numerous squares outlined by pinpoints of white light were clearly visible along a bank of one of the delta's bigger tributaries.

'I didn't realise you were establishing so many farms, Emma,' I said.

'I've got several species, carp, catfish, trout, and tilapia, and three life cycle stages of each in the transport methods experiment. So, I need a dozen, minimum. And then the young lads and lasses I met at the barbie asked for a few extra for their own attempts at farming. That's what we're here for, ain't it?'

I could only agree; but I had to suppress too much of a grin to say 'Yeah, ain't that the truth.'

By this time the view screen was clearly showing that we were now in the statutory, final approach pattern with another shuttle, one of the big lift types, 300 metres ahead of us, and yet another big lift shuttle the same distance behind. Our shuttle shuddered and rocked as the landing jets ignited and the AI-pilot made micro-adjustments to cope with the turbulence generated by the big brute ahead of us. And then we were sweeping over the runway threshold and the landing jets were winding up to bring us to a hover, and finally we settled onto our wheeled undercarriage.

The intercom announced, 'All jets off. Airlocks unsealed. Doors to manual. Passengers prepare for disembarkation. Be aware that we are about to be towed to our arrival gate.'

The screens showed an AI-ground tug busily linking up to our shuttle's nosewheel and then dragging us off the runway towards the line of cargo sheds to the west.

As the control cabin's housekeeping bots buzzed around my feet, I cleared up the remains of our picnic. It always amazed me how much filth the house-bots found to remove. It settled out of the internal atmosphere as soon as we entered planetside gravity, of course. But that meant that while we were in microgravity the muck was floating around in the atmosphere we were breathing. Not good, though not many cargo shuttles carried human passengers. I then followed Emma, who had dropped through the hatchway into the cargo hold.

By the time I got into the hold, its doors were already open wide and forklift loaders were sliding in alongside the shuttle to offload what were now happily bubbling fish tanks directly onto waiting trucks. Trying to keep out of the way, I tried to get a closer look at the contents of the tank that was being lifted past me and saw dense shoals of fish that were indeed each about the size of my fingers.

I saw Emma standing beside the cabin of this truck, so I jumped down from the shuttle and went over to return her picnic basket.

'Thanks for the ride, and for lunch,' I said.

'You're welcome, Boss. Would you like to visit my fish farms to see for yourself what we're doing out there?'

'Yeah, I've not been out to the western side of the delta yet, so I would like to do that. But don't you have to meet up with your happy band of young settlers?'

'Oh, don't worry about them,' Emma replied. 'When last seen, they had found Jim's free-to-use all-terrain trikes and were tearing around making fools of themselves. They'll come to Momma when this convoy of trucks roll up. In fact, we'll have to keep an eye on the trucks, I don't want them being nicked; David's only just released them to me!'

We climbed up into the drive cabin of the truck and Emma keyed in the destination and sent the instructions to the rest of the trucks in the convoy; then she hit 'go'.

As we drove off towards the SpacePort's perimeter road, I was delighted to see one of the smaller new buildings proudly displaying 'Commodore's Personal Lockup'. I already had somewhere to house my old Skippers! Malik caught my thoughts about this and reported to my NeuroModem 'Both machines have been reconditioned in the Starship's workshops, and will be transported planetside, with personal space suits, on the next general cargo shuttle. The machines will be refuelled and recommissioned by the SpacePort's light engineering teams. Malik out.'

As we approached the fish farms, a half-dozen all-terrain trikes came out of the red twilight and formed up as an escort for our convoy. Emma flashed the truck's headlights in recognition and the overspill of white light again made that magical transformation in the local vegetation from unsavoury-looking black to bright spring green.

As the convoy came to a halt alongside the checkerboard pattern of fish farm boundaries and access walkways, Emma swung down to the roadway, saying 'I need to concentrate on getting the right fish into the right ponds now, Boss, but you will probably find some of Geoff Moore's crew in the farmhouse over there. They could give you a guided tour of the marshes.'

Emma was pointing towards a newly printed, and well-lit, building on the bank of the tributary just ahead, so, after saying my thanks to Emma for such a pleasant ride down from orbit, I made for that.

The farmhouse was deserted, but that didn't deter me from marching straight in and poking around on my own. There was a small domestic area at one end—

a small kitchen with basic kitchen appliances, a table, and a bunch of chairs. But the other end of this ground floor room was covered in view screens and control panels. Some of the vids were displaying images of fish tanks being offloaded from the truck convoy and placed into the netted-off sectors of the fish farm. The young settlers certainly seemed to be earning their keep, while Emma was marshalling their activities with vigorous arm waving.

I began to think that we might all merit a refreshing drink in the near future, so I drifted down to the kitchen to see what I could find there. I introduced the contents of a tap labelled 'drinking' to a kettle and switched on. The cupboards were woefully bare, but there was a large box of tea bags, and the fridge offered several containers of soymilk, so I elected myself chaiwallah and started a hunt for mugs.

I'd just found the crockery supplies when Geoff Moore and a boisterous trio of his assistants and students barged into the farmhouse, hurling bags and boxes to the floor.

I offered tea all round, and while I fulfilled those orders the new arrivals tidied up their mess and we all settled down around the kitchen table.

'I rode down from orbit with Emma and her fish tanks,' I explained. 'And she suggested I impose on you for a tour of the delta.'

'We'd be delighted to drink this very welcome and superbly made tea and tell you all about results so far,' Geoff said. 'But we can't show you very much more than you can see outside the farmhouse door because the rest of my team have taken all our marsh buggies for a joint expedition with 101's resident biologists to the far western side of the delta. They'll be away for a few days.'

'No matter,' I said. 'We'll have to get David to make you a few more buggies, and I'll come back some time in the future.'

'Oh, I put an order in with David Wood's team,' Callum Selby, Geoff's chief technician, interrupted. 'But they're working full time at the moment producing trucks and machines for all the building projects in the settlement that are getting under way now. So, we must wait.'

'And we've arranged to borrow the mayor's swamp boat tomorrow,' Geoff resumed. 'The media girl Lana is using it today, but we're planning to collect specimens for you from the east bank of the river tomorrow. And then we'll take it downriver as far as we can go to survey the eastern side of the delta, coming back westward around the coast of the Inland Sea.'

'Merv's boat is not very big,' I warned. 'A four-seater, if I remember rightly.'

'That's right,' Geoff replied. 'We'll be followed by a small AI-cargo drone, which is loaded with sensors and will be doing the bulk of the survey work from 50 metres altitude. It also has a useful space for cargo and can resupply us as needed, by making to-and-fro flights to our base here if necessary. We've got used to surveying the delta like this.'

Geoff paused to pay more attention to his mug of tea and then went on, 'The images of this area that are being made from orbit suggest that we should be able to navigate from the seacoast back to this location, using tributaries well to the west of the main river. We're keen to establish that route, if we can, because it might allow the settlement to establish some sort of 'river' port here on its western side to mirror the access that's planned on the riverbank to the east when you remove Starship-101.'

'I didn't realise that town planning was part of your remit, Geoff,' I commented.

'All of our survey data ends up in Malik and he combines it for the general good,' put in Callum Selby.

Nodding, I continued, 'You mentioned collecting specimens for me, so you should know that I've been allocated a shed at the SpacePort rather grandly called the 'Commodore's Personal Lockup'. When you've got the specimens in a state suitable for repatriation Earthside you can store them there. Tip off Malik, and he will sort out transport and warehousing.'

'Will do,' Geoff said. 'Callum sent a drone over to that promontory to have a look at your giant club fungi and I reckon you may be right about what they are. Is there any more tea?' He added.

'Relax, Boss,' said Callum, putting a hand on my shoulder as I started to rise from my seat. 'I'll do the honours.'

'Really?' I directed at Geoff.

'Aye, just from the drone footage, you understand; but they're a dead ringer for the *Prototaxites* Earth-fossils. The sooner we can get samples back Earthside the sooner we can stir up the whole evolution hornet's nest,' Geoff commented, with a grin, continuing, 'I'm going to put one of my students onto it back home. It's the sort of project that could make her name for life.'

'Excellent. So, those specimens you are collecting for me; if you put her name and address on them, I'll see that they're delivered.'

'Just picking up on your mention of a hornet's nest,' I continued. 'We found that the last surviving member of Starship-101's original crew, the guy the settlers called 'The Priest', had been swatting Frankie's microdrones because of a childhood memory trace of doing just that; disturbing a hornet's nest.'

'Honestly? He must be the only person on Proxima-b who can remember what a hornet looks like!' Geoff turned to the other members of his team as he said, 'I'm strictly a plant man myself. Have any of you guys encountered hornets back home?'

The question drew only headshaking accompanied by the word 'No' from everyone, including Callum who was now delivering refills to our tea mugs. 'I've never sought them out and, thankfully, never come across them.' Callum continued, 'If The Priest suffered from a hornet attack as a child, I'm not surprised he started to slaughter the microdrones flying around 101.'

'True,' I said. 'We got him sorted out and he'll be returning to the Solar System with me. He's an asset for the proposed museum! The only surviving old-school interstellar traveller!'

'That we know of,' Geoff corrected. 'We still don't know what's happened to Starship-102. It may be cruising nicely towards Tau Ceti as planned or it might be a frozen coffin-ship.'

'That's a cheerful thought!' I protested. 'Since this Proxima-Centauri contract has gone so well, Harden and I are planning to bid for the contract to chase after 102. It's only the coffin-ship thought that's a bit of a downer on those plans.'

I turned in my seat to look at the digital glass at the other end of the room; nodding towards them, I said, 'I see that the vid screens show only one of Emma's trucks still on site, and Emma's troop of bikers seem to be departing. So, before I have to start chasing after a lift back to the settlement, tell me, quickly, about Proxima's animal life.'

'Zilch!' all my companions chorused together.

Geoff expanded, 'Literally nothing convincing found so far but we've not had enough time to carry out the more sophisticated analyses. There's a richly diverse population of motile organisms we'd call chytrids at home.'

'Chytrids?' I queried.

'Yeah. Be aware we're talking in terms of Earth's biology because that's the only comparison we can make right now, and it will take a lifetime or two, or more, to complete the analysis we need to establish if that comparison is valid. But, on Earth, chytrids are one of the most ancient groups of fungi, and in their ancient habitats Earthside they swam around using flagella, but they had cell walls made of chitin, like the filamentous moulds.'

Geoff paused to finish off his mug of tea, before going on, 'Now, everywhere we've looked so far on Proxima-b, we've found a full inventory of things we'd call 'prokaryotes' at home, including ones we'd class as really ancient types and call 'archaea' and photosynthetic ones we'd call 'cyanobacteria'. All of which are the earliest forms of life known on Earth. And it looks likely they've evolved here on Proxima-b completely independently of what was happening on Earth four and a half lightyears away. Then you only have to look casually around this marshland, and you can see a fair range of organisms we'd classify as 'eukaryotes' on Earth, that have nuclei and mitochondria and lots of other membranes and stuff that make them the so-called 'higher' organisms on Earth. Here, we have 'algae', of all sorts from the microscopic to kelp like organisms down towards the coast, we've got 'lichens', we've got 'moss-like' plants all over the place and wherever we look we've got these 'chytrids', things you might call 'fungal moulds', and now your giant 'club fungi'. It's overwhelming.'

He paused again, before concluding, 'We need busloads of biologists to examine this planet's biology. And we can't wait four and a half years for our plea for help to get back to Earth. You've got to take it, Tarvin. I'll put together a broad collection of samples and interim reports for you to take back home. But you'll have to make the case for us. Galvanise the fat cats back home into realising how much we can learn about life on Earth by studying life on Proxima-b!'

'I'll do my honest best for you, Geoff,' I assured him. 'A few of the more adventurous fat cats may be travelling with my brother Harden, so be sure to give me a bunch of copies of your interim reports. I'll make sure the fattest cats have something to read while Harden's bringing them up here.'

'Thanks, Tarvin, that's all I can ask for. I appreciate it.' He paused a moment, and then resumed, 'Well, there is one other thing that's been developing in the back of my mind while we've been finding the enormous native biodiversity in our field surveys here. Before we, I mean humanity, even began to colonise Mars and the other near-Earth planets and satellites, there was an awful lot of debate about what was called ethical colonisation of those planets and satellites. I've always been interested in the history of science, and I wrote a dissertation on this ethics topic. The essence of it is the belief that before we impose Earth-biology on any other body that lies in the habitable zone we must take steps to safeguard any and all indigenous biology that might have arisen on the planets or satellites that we visit. What worries me, is that there's no record of any such debate taking place when the original Proxima-Centauri Expedition was being planned and launched, and certainly, none before we were sent out here. And now we're starting to build fish and poultry farms, and greenhouses for a healthy number of Earth's crop plants.'

I held up my hand to stop him going any further, saying, 'You urgently need to talk to Lana, our 'media girl'. She's working up grand plans for a series of TV and radio documentaries, podcasts and blogs of all sorts along the lines of 'the first interstellar this, that, or the other'. You must talk to her about what you've just described: 'the first interim report from an interstellar habitable zone'. Malik, will you summarise what we've just been talking about, you can leave out the bit about Starship-102, and then send it to Lana's NeuroModem with my suggestion that she adds it to her to-do list?'

'Copy that, Commodore. Malik out.'

Geoff's eyes had widened considerably, and he nodded slowly, but Callum said 'Wow, can we use that title? It's great!'

'Sure,' I said. 'Lana's planning to swamp the Solar System's video industry with these broadcasts, and we'll be taking back with us whatever programmes she can get finished for our departure.'

'Lana is much more than our 'media girl' though, guys,' I continued. 'She is head of our communications team, and will be staying here when I leave, to work with our other wunderkind, Frankie, to develop a quantum jump method of quantum computer-to-quantum computer instantaneous communication that bypasses the speed of light limitation. We've recently got it working for point-to-point messaging within the Solar System, but the Solar System is only one thousandth of a lightyear across, so it's nice to be able to do it, but it ain't crucial. This trip to Proxima-Centauri is our first opportunity to test quantum jump communication across a genuine interstellar distance.'

I finished off my mug of tea, then finished off my story, 'We're laying the foundation now; Frankie is installing a quantum megacomputer in the settlement, the AI of which Malik, my ship's computer, will train. Then we will have two quantum megacomputers, independent but perfectly in tune, one of which, Malik of course, we will jump towards home, one lightyear at a jump, down the route we established by coming here. From Proxima Waystation 4 to Waystation 3 and so on, all the way back to Oort Station and the Kuiper Belt Station. Hopefully,

Frankie and Lana will be able to exchange coordinated universal time signals with Malik at each Waystation and calculate time-of-flight for the message. If the whole thing works, by the time we get to Oort Waystation, we will meet with my brother Harden waiting to bring his flotilla along the Proxima Route to test out the whole thing. At Oort Station, again, if it's all worked OK, Malik will train Sasha, my brother's flight computer. If it's not worked OK, Sasha will try to establish what went wrong on his way up the Proxima Stations.'

'Amazing,' whispered Geoff. 'And the end result?'

'We're hoping for instantaneous transmission. We believe quantum jumping is instantaneous as soon as decoherence of the superposition of origin and destination is triggered. That certainly seemed to apply to our journey here, which is the furthest any Superposition Navigator like me has travelled. But,' I shrugged, 'it's quantum mechanics, so who knows how weird it might behave over several lightyears' distance?'

Behind me, the farmhouse door banged open and Emma swept into the room, 'Hi guys,' she smiled as we all twisted in our seats to look at her, 'I'm taking this truck back to the SpacePort Park, do you want a lift back there, Boss?'

'I sure do, Emma, thanks.'

'Hold on, Boss,' said Callum. 'Just one more little question: why do you give your flight computers such weird names?'

'Company policy, mate,' I replied. 'We choose the names from different Earth languages. I chose Malik, which is Urdu for 'supervisor'. Bruv Harden chose Sasha which is Russian for 'helper of mankind'. Which probably tells you more about us, than about our computers!'

'OK, I'll make no further comment,' said Callum, turning back to Emma, 'Now Emma, I've got the kettle boiling again, would you like to take a drink out there with you?'

'Yes please, one mug of tea to go,' Emma stressed the please, then offered, 'Anyone want a biscuit? I've still got some in my picnic basket.' Silly question really, we all dived into the basket and had cleared it of biscuits by the time Emma received her mug of tea.

'Well, they went down well!' Emma commented.

'Yes, they did,' I said. 'And that reminds me. Malik, will you arrange for this farmhouse to be properly provisioned? Get catering to supply a normal domestic range of provisions and kitchen gear and have a housekeeping bot assigned to the site. Oh, and I'd like you to arrange for two or three vehicle charging bays to be installed.'

'Copy that, Commodore. Malik out'

'Hey, thanks for that, Boss,' said Emma, delightedly. 'I thought I'd have to pay for that sort of stuff myself.'

'Don't be silly, Emma,' I replied. 'You're working for Interstellar Haulage now. The biccies are on us! Now let's get truckin.'

As the truck drove itself back towards its parking lot at the SpacePort, I asked Emma if she was partying tonight.

'Oh no,' she said. 'It's a big day tomorrow. Overnight, Jim's tin men will be building me a nice big barn alongside the farmhouse and tomorrow me and my team will be supervising its fitting out, while the tin men will be building a range of poultry houses, duck houses and chicken coops alongside; these are demonstration builds, mainly. To show the range of structures that the building-printers and their attendant tin men, the ones we'll be leaving here that is, can do.'

'And the big barn?' I queried. 'What's that for?'

'Oh, it's really big, and sectioned off for lots of different purposes. First thing to be transferred to it will be everything that I've got scattered in and around Starship-101. That means the various 3-D printers I need to make fish farm and poultry nets, farm vehicles, including boats and remotely operated submersibles for the fish farms. Then we have hatcheries and nursery incubator units for both fish and poultry that are currently stored in one of Starship-101's disused cargo bays, and then all the young animals we have housed temporarily in the adjoining cargo bay.'

'A Starship deck is not the best place to set up a small holding, but it's a great place to encourage the locals to start thinking 'I could do that.' People have been dropping by to cuddle a lamb or a piglet and play with the chicks and ducklings, and you can watch their Starship-isolation moods fading away. Give them a few freshly laid eggs as they leave, and they're hooked!'

'Is that how you hooked the young tearaways on the trikes?'

'Not really, they were hooked by the barbecued fresh fish! If they stay committed, they'll make decent fish-farmers. Their main problem is that, like all the settlers, their general education is a hundred years behind the times. I just hope that they'll really start to flourish when we give their NeuroModems their q-bit upgrades. The youngsters are keen to make a go of it here, but their thought processes are hampered by the lack of that quantum link.'

'I'll have to see Bill about progress with those upgrades,' I said. At which point the truck's AI cut into our conversation with the announcement 'Passengers prepare to disembark. Be sure to remove all your possessions. We have reached our destination.'

There was a trike park near the transport office where we each claimed a trike and went our separate ways back to Starship-101. I went directly to my quarters with the intention of having some downtime watching Lana's TV broadcasts, but the downtime soon became snooze time!

I was woken by Malik, wanting to report his findings about Tom Fraser's override routine that enabled him to extract information from his nurse Carla, one of our newest AI service robots.

'Sorry to disturb, Commodore. The effective phrase is '*Tom's override routine immediate*' and there's a voice recognition locked to Tom's own voice signature. It's not a virus or a Pegasus-like trojan but is neatly hidden encrypted in the machine code of all AI-robot units, including non-humanoid AIs. It is a legacy of Tom Fraser's contribution to the development of AI work units on Mars at the start of his career in software engineering. Fortunately, the override is not a legacy in AI-supercomputers. With your permission, I will remove it from all such robots except the care-robot Carla and will spread the repair around the Solar System as soon as we return.'

'Yes,' I replied. 'That sounds like the best option, so that's what we'll do. Leaving Carla unchanged means that Tom can continue to play, without the risks of leaving it scattered around everywhere.'

'Two final messages, Commodore. Your Skippers have been refurbished with current generation rocket drives, refuelled and are ready to use. They are parked in your Personal Lockup at the SpacePort. Secondly, Captain Katharina Clason would like to discuss getting her observatories launched and suggests meeting tomorrow for breakfast in Starship-101's canteen.'

'Please tell Kat 'yes' to breakfast around 8 a.m. tomorrow, and I'll catch up with the Skippers after that meeting because she'll want to see them. That's all.'

'Copy that, Commodore. Malik out.'

After a shower and change of clothes, and a little more TV, and alright, I confess it, a few more minutes snooze, I drifted down to the canteen to see what was available for dinner. The canteen was decorated like a Cantonese tearoom, so I had to check out what was on offer. Merv Castlefield was just wandering into the canteen as well, and we agreed to share a dim sum banquet for two. When we were comfortably settled and had been sufficiently revived by our tea and dim-sums, we resumed our discussion of the ownership of Starship-101, or 'the old heap' as Merv was now disparagingly describing his ancestral home.

'We got the legals all stitched up to Malik's satisfaction,' Merv reported. 'The old heap is all yours.'

'Did you have any trouble getting the Council's agreement?' I asked, trying manfully to cope with chopsticks again.

'Nah,' Merv responded. 'There are only three of us. Aside from me there's Clint, the Treasurer, you've met, and our chief medical officer, Sally Gates. You've probably not come across her as she's been in the new medical centre ever since it was brought down from orbit.'

Merv sloshed a baked bun around what was left of the dipping sauce and continued, 'Everybody in the settlement now is immensely happy with what you're doing for us. Obviously, we had a few doubts at first. Doubts that Earthside could be that generous without wanting something in return. But those doubts are gone, and the more you bring down from orbit for us, the further they go. Left to ourselves we could only see a future based on 100-year-old technology. Quaint, but true. On a daily basis, we can see that you're dragging us up a 100-year step. And we're very happy about it!'

'Have some more tea, Merv,' I offered. 'I think you've just written an outline for another documentary for our media queen, Lana, to produce. She's got great plans for taking the Solar System's video markets by storm, let me ask Malik to tell her about it.' I paused conversation with Merv to address Malik, 'Malik, here's another conversation for you to summarise and send to Lana's NeuroModem with my suggestion that she contacts Merv to talk about the history of the settlement and the impact of first contact from home on an interstellar colony. And, Malik, please download all of Starship-101's video streams to computer Westwood and tell Lana there's 50 years of historical broadcasts there.'

'Copy all that, Commodore. Malik out.'

'Merv,' I went on, 'you and your settlers need to get your business hats on. At the moment the Solar System is exchanging all the material goods we've brought here for the carcase of Starship-101. There's no further charge. But the Solar System is a profit-making enterprise and when we've finished here 'enterprise Solar System' will expect to trade with 'enterprise Proxima-Centauri'. You must get the settlement geared up for that because small though the settlement might be the settlers are now the rightful owners of the Proxima-Centauri system. So, it's you guys who have to establish the basic rules, governance and contract terms that can make fair profits, and I mean fair to you, from future trade between 'enterprise Proxima-Centauri' and the Solar System.'

Merv looked shocked at this. 'How? When?' he muttered.

'Don't worry, Merv, getting the basic essentials in place is not that difficult,' I replied. 'Malik's legal engine will tell you what to do and will map out the timetable of steps for you and the settlers to take. And when Malik's finished training your new settlement computer, which will be called Winwood, by the way, your computer will be fully clued up on Solar System legalities and when you have your q-bit NeuroModems installed, so will you. What you need to do first is call Town Meetings, and from what I've seen so far, you're pretty good at that!' I held up my teacup before draining it as a mock toast to him.

'What things do we discuss?' He asked.

'Well, the first thing that occurs to me is that you need to agree your attitude to copyright. Lana's video plans are all aimed at producing vids copyright Interstellar Haulage. Now, as one of the owners of Interstellar Haulage, That's fine by me. But you're in more need of money than I am. We're already making a mint out of this contract. I'd reckon 'enterprise Proxima-Centauri' should be due at least a 50% share of the copyright, maybe more if you can negotiate it. And then individuals who appear in these vids will be due fees. You need to make sure they are properly represented. And talking of money, you have to decide the currency you'll use for both local and interstellar transactions. You could invent one—the Proxima-dollar, maybe. But I think life would be easier if you just make use of the Solar System's trading currency—the Solar-dollar. But you'll need a bank into which you can put all those $solar you're all going to earn. And the bank will need to be connected to the Solar System's banking system to allow electronic financial transactions. Remembering, of course, that at the moment if you ask for a statement of account from an Earthside bank, it will take nine years to get back to you.'

'And that's just for copyright?' asked Merv, still a bit shocked.

'Sure, but it's only the start. Brother Harden will be bringing representatives of mining, manufacturing, commercial travel, and tourism industries with him. So, you will need to deal with the legalities of whatever they might want to do in a couple of months' time.' I paused but then resumed with another thought, 'I guess you should also get your citizenship, immigration and emigration policies sorted out pretty soon. I don't recall being asked to prove my identity since I arrived. I've told you who I want you to believe I am, but you could be talking to the Earth's number 1 Starship thief. There's a lot of very valuable metals in that hulk of yours! Oh, sorry, my mistake, it's mine now, isn't it?' I grinned. Merv frowned.

'I guess I'll put a call out for a town meeting lunchtime tomorrow,' he said, finally.

'Yeah, that sounds like a good plan. Get things started off. Now, thinking of meetings, I've got a breakfast meeting with Kat tomorrow. So, I need to turn in, goodnight, Merv.' He waved me off, distractedly.

I went back to my captain's cabin and asked the steward to fix me a whisky and water. At first, planning to relax, I settled down to watch whatever Lana was broadcasting on her video channel. It was a dramadoc about q-bit NeuroModem upgrades and rather than relax me, it reminded me I needed to talk to both Lana and Bill. As it was only just past 9 p.m., I asked Malik to set up personal calls to both, Lana first.

'Hi Lana, I hope you've received from Malik the video ideas I've had recently.'

'Yes, Boss. All received and noted in my team's production diary.'

'Have you got enough AI-bots to do all the work?'

'Yeah,' she said. 'Enough to make a start; and I've asked David to build me another squad. In the meantime, I can use spare med-bots because they have inbuilt interview skills and enough AI to modify those skills.'

'Excellent,' I replied. 'How are you fixed for camera crews? Let me explain why I'm asking. I'll be talking to Kat at breakfast tomorrow; we're planning to survey a mountain top on the cold side where she thinks she wants to place the Proxima-b observatory, and I thought you might like to add a camera bot to the expedition to make a travelogue about the cold side. Do you have one free?'

'You bet,' Lana answered with enthusiasm. 'But you'll need two. It's always better to have two cameras in operation. And one of them could be a fax-bot that I could dial into to direct the operation from here. When is this going down?'

'Well, we ain't discussed the 'when' yet, but I'd like to do it sooner rather than later, so, personally, I'd prefer tomorrow afternoon or the following morning. Either way we'll be leaving from the SpacePort and using Skippers.

74

I'm assuming your bots could travel as pillion passengers, so they'd have to be space-hardened.'

'Skippers, eh? How very old-fashioned! That's a blast and no problemo; I've got a few crews that are certified for filming on the outside of our Starship. I'll get them down from orbit overnight and station them at the SpacePort. Is that all, Boss?

'You have Captain Bill Roberts on the line, Commodore,' Malik whispered in my ear.

'Hi Bill, sorry to bother you at this hour, but I wondered how the med centre and the settlers' q-bit upgrades programme were progressing.'

'Progressing according to plan, Boss,' Bill said. 'The medical centre is finished, fitted out, commissioned and accepting patients. Thankfully, there's not much illness around here, but we have had two deliveries and parents and babies are doing well! The settlement's chief medical officer, Sally Gates, and your friend Tom Fraser have had their q-bit NeuroModem upgrades and are staying in the med centre overnight, under observation. Providing they have no adverse reactions, we'll start to rollout the upgrades to the rest of the settlers tomorrow. And overnight tonight our cyber-engineering teams will make a start on fitting q-bit upgrades to Starship-101's own brigade of AI-bots.'

'Great, Bill,' I responded. 'Congratulations to all concerned. Will you make Merv Castlefield and Clint Stapleton priority candidates for q-bit upgrades, they're going to need a lot of guidance directly from Malik and Westwood in the next few days.'

'Will do. Is that all, Boss?'

'Yes, that's all, Bill. Goodnight.'

I asked the steward for another whisky and tried to watch a little more TV, but when I could no longer keep my eyes open, I retired, thankfully, to my bed.

Day 3

After the previous evening's Cantonese tearoom extravaganza, breakfast next morning was a strictly traditional toast, marmalade and freshly brewed coffee. The middle-aged settler who managed the servery counter chided me for my meagre choice, trying to entice me with what was on offer on the fry-up counter. But I declined, saying 'If I dared to choose a 'heart-attack on a plate' breakfast my flight computer would never stop nagging me.'

'Too true,' Malik floated the thought into my NeuroModem.

Kat is a 'morning person' so she was already eating breakfast as I settled myself and my tray at her table. 'Is that all you're having for breakfast?' she asked, grinning.

'Now, don't you start, Mrs Clason,' I said defensively. 'That fry-up counter does smell good, but Malik has already made his opinion known to me!'

'Hm, well, your girlfriend over there, Commodore Clason, obviously thinks you need feeding-up.'

'I'll certainly not allow that to happen,' cut in Malik. 'And I might start my nagging by pointing out that the shipboard gymnasium has not seen much of Commodore Clason since we arrived here.'

Changing the topic while I spooned marmalade onto toast, I asked 'What's the position with your various observatories, Kat?'

'Nicely swerved! Malik out.'

'It's good news about the satellite observatories I'm sending to Proxima-d and Proxima-e,' Kat said. 'Jim found a couple of heavy lift tugs I can have. They're powerful enough to haul Starships around in orbital graving docks and he'd rather I used them than any of his orbital shuttles as he still needs all the shuttles, he has to bring cargo down from orbit. I spent yesterday afternoon positioning the satellites and their tugs in high orbit over Proxima-b.'

'Excellent,' I said. 'When do they launch?'

'This afternoon sometime. We want them to take a slingshot route around Proxima-Centauri. This is really important for Proxima-c because it has such an eccentric orbit. So, after we've finished here, I will cadge a lift on a returning shuttle to direct the launches from our control room.'

'OK, so when is the best time for our trip to Observatory Mountain?' I asked.

'Tomorrow morning would suit me best,' said Kat. 'But we should bring Jim in on planning this. I mentioned it to him yesterday, when we were talking about the tugs and he was quite willing to bring an entire survey and building team to the mountain. He said he'd check the orbital telemetry and hi-res imaging of the site.'

'Right, so Malik, will you ask Captain Igwe, if it's convenient to talk now, and if it is, setup a 4-way conference call.'

'Copy that, Commodore. Malik out'

'Shall we get more coffee?' I asked Kat and gesticulated towards the nice lady at the servery counter.

'Captain Igwe is now on the line. And do you really need more caffeine this early in the morning, Commodore?' asked Malik.

'Oh, give me a break, Malik. Go boil your CPU. Hello Jim.'

'Good morning, Commodore, morning Kat,' said Jim. 'If you can recall your 'computers for commodores-101' course, Boss, AI-central processing units do not do well in any kind of water, let alone the boiling variety.'

'Thank you for your advice, Jim,' I said. 'But Malik is in a peculiar mood this morning, and I'm the one who has him permanently in my head. Right now, a boiled CPU would greatly improve him.' At which a banner bearing the phrase 'Scz who?' drifted silently across my vision.

'Jim let's get down to business, Malik, pay attention,' I said out loud. 'Have you been able to make any assessment of the mountain top on the cold side where Kat wants to site her ground-observatory?'

'Yes, I must have caught Malik on one of his good days and we've done a thorough survey from orbit and, subject to a site visit to confirm this, it looks like an ideal spot for everything we want to locate on the cold side at high altitude. It's almost perfectly flat and high enough for most of the ices to ablate off in the high-altitude winds. An hour or two with our AI-graders and we'll have a perfect site for a cold side base-station.'

'Can you build up there?' I asked.

'Sure,' Jim assured us. 'It's cold and windy but all we need to do building-wise is consolidate the stone surface. Once that's done, we'll configure a small SpacePort, drop in a terminal building, and then add a mobile fusion power unit, which can begin producing hydrogen and oxygen from the local ice. We've got an ice mining unit ready to deploy in the foothills of Observatory Mountain. The observatory itself is also a ready-to-deploy unit we can deliver directly to site by hover-shuttle, leaving its own brigade of AI-bots to complete its fitting out. We add a range of space-rated habitation units, the kind developed for the Ice Moons of Jupiter and Saturn. They're essentially spaceships lying on platforms on the ice. Again, we just need to drop them into place and the bots that travel with them will anchor them down to set them up. And that's it.'

'And there's me thinking it might be difficult,' I commented. 'Done in an afternoon?'

'Not quite, Boss,' retorted Jim. 'We'll have enough bots for it to take about eight 12-hour shifts, so that's four days.'

'Can you do a site survey tomorrow?' asked Kat.

'I can,' said Jim. 'Could meet you onsite at 2 p.m. How's that?'

'We're going to travel on my vintage Skippers,' I said. 'Do you want a lift?'

'NO, thank you!' Jim said, emphatically. 'I've got my own transport in which I can travel in shirtsleeves and with zero chance of arriving as a crumpled bloody mess of flesh and metal!'

'Oh well, don't hold back, Jim. After all this time we've worked together, you don't trust my piloting skills?'

'It's not your piloting skills, Boss, well, not entirely,' Jim responded. 'It's the lethal whizz-bang exploding thing you choose to pilot!'

'And another thing,' Jim continued. 'Kat mentioned that you were planning to have Skippers as the main visitor transport to and from Observatory Mountain. But that's neither necessary nor advisable. We carry the specs for David's transport factories to produce various aircraft and Airspeeders as well as a couple of useful sub-orbital transports that are comfortable, reliable and don't require passengers to wear spacesuits! One is a six-passenger taxi, the other a 15-passenger minibus. Both are built using our standard truck panels so it's just a matter of switching the production line from one to the other. But because the aerial vehicles have wings, we'll have to expand the size of the factory before we can start producing them. At the moment, David is concentrating on wheeled transport units while we develop the infrastructure around the Proxima Alpha settlement, but when we want to go further afield with outstations around the bright side, David will switch to constructing flying machines.'

'Fine, nobody likes my Skippers. So, do you have a sub-orbital taxi to hand?' I asked.

'Sorry, but no,' said Jim. 'We have the specs but not the finished machines yet.'

'Then we either wait for a taxi, or we go tomorrow by Skipper. So, Kat, how do you feel about travelling on a 'lethal whizz-bang exploding thing' tomorrow,' I asked.

Kat's response was rather more positive than Jim's. 'Oh, Tarvin. You forget how like your brother you are! Harden has hauled me all over Earth and Mars on the pillion seat of his Skipper. And I've flown it back with Harden on the pillion. So, like you, I'm looking forward to reliving old times. We Skip tomorrow! See you at Observatory Mountain at two p.m., Jim?'

'Affirmative,' said Jim. 'I'll be the one in shirtsleeves. I'll bring a shuttle load of goodies to revive you after your hair-raising trip; like a fusion power unit, SpacePort terminal and habitation unit equipped with sick bay and a full team of medical bots! Enjoy your ride. Jim out.'

'Copy that, Jim. Malik out.'

'Our conference seems to have ended. Do you have anything else, Kat?'

'No, I'll get back to our ship and deal with those orbital insertions. I might come down for dinner later on, so could catch up with you then.'

'OK, I just have one more item of information, which is that when we do fly to Observatory Mountain, we will both have one of Lana's camera bots on the pillion to record the flight and film the location. It'll be the first chance for her production team to film the cold side. Now, I don't know what's going on, but they seem to be dismantling this canteen around us.'

'Have you not been outside before breakfast?' asked Kat. 'One of Jim's new buildings is right outside, sporting a brand-new banner title saying 'Proxima Alpha Canteen'. They're evacuating this canteen into the new facility around us. So, let's not continue to get in their way. I'm off.' She waved and scooted out while I was pushing my chair back into the hands of a patiently waiting general assistance AI-bot.

I followed the bot and my chair out of what was now rapidly becoming an ex-canteen, down 101's nose gangway and into the unearthly red morning twilight of Proxima-b. Sure enough, just across what was rapidly being turned into a paved roadway by a team of Jim's civil engineering AI-bots, was the new Proxima Alpha canteen, with brightly lit windows spilling white light over the trike park in front. Inside, a couple of settlers were working with an AI-bot, fitting a flashing green LED sign declaring 'OPEN' in the centre of the acrylic frontage windows. This place was really changing fast.

I pushed through the new entrance door and sat down at one of tables meaning to use it just to initiate a discussion with Malik about lifting Starship-101 into orbit. 'Malik, the locals seem to be vacating Starship-101 at an alarming rate, we should start planning its translocation into orbit.'

'Yes, Commodore,' returned Malik. 'Most of the legacy resources have now been transferred to newly built facilities in the settlement. The medical centre was the first to move and its new site is now fully operational. The new fusion power station has been online for a couple of days, but overnight the Electricity System Operator was brought online, and the settlement's power grid load was transferred to the new reactor and Starship-101's power plant output was limited to the Starship itself. The computer centre is fully operational and overnight I completed Westwood's AI training and he is now fully capable of managing the transfer of data from Starship-101's Flight computer, hopefully overnight tonight, so the activities of that machine can also be limited to the Starship itself.'

'That sounds good, Malik. Just hold on a moment, will you, while I deal with something here.'

Although I hadn't requested it, my 'breakfast girlfriend' who had tried to interest me in the old servery's fry-ups earlier in the morning had just quietly deposited a tray onto my table that carried a cafetière of fresh coffee, mug, jug of soycream and plate of biscuits. Well, I couldn't do anything other than gracefully accept, could I?

'OK, Malik, please continue.' (Crunch! Crunch!)

'Just a moment, Commodore. You have an incoming message from Merv Castlefield via Westwood. Go ahead caller. Malik out'

'Hey Tarvin, this is Merv. Good morning. Hey this is weird, like telepathy. No phone or tablet. Weird.'

'Good morning, Merv. I gather you've had your q-bit NeuroModem upgrade fitted. Yes, it can feel weird at first, just don't get too excited. Stay calm and rest. Your quantum megacomputer, called Westwood, by the way, will train your brain while you rest.'

'Yeah, it's just been fitted. I'm in the medical centre. Just been trolleyed into the general ward. They want me to stay overnight.'

'Well, don't try to rush things, Merv. You'll feel drowsy, so the best thing to do is sleep. While you sleep, Westwood, will be giving you all the memory traces you need to make full use of your new NeuroModem. When you wake tomorrow morning, you'll be able to use it as though it's been part of you all your life.'

'Yeah, I've heard that before. Oh, yeah, Sally Gates just told me that.' Merv yawned.

'Sounds like you need to sleep Merv. Just say, or think 'Merv out' to end this call.'

'Yeah, right. Merv out.'

'Malik, is Westwood happy with Merv's upgrade?'

'Yes, Commodore, all went well. The mayor insisted on calling you immediately the upgrade was fitted, but Westwood reports he now has control of the mayor's sleep induction pathways and will proceed with the training programme.'

'Fine,' I said, biting into another biscuit. 'You were telling me about how much of Starship-101 has been vacated.'

'Yes,' said Malik. 'I've just done a full inventory and, providing all the planned moves go well during the day, it appears that by this evening, you will be the sole occupant of Starship-101, Commodore.'

'I suppose that's quite fitting,' I muttered. 'We need to plan how we're going to lift Starship-101 into orbit. It's a big brute, so, I also need to build a thorough feeling for the whole ship. I'll finish here and then stroll over to 101's control deck to have a poke around there. I'll resume contact from there. Commodore out.'

I downed the last of my coffee and picked up the last biscuit (where had they all gone?). Before leaving, I returned my tray to the servery counter and thanked my 'girlfriend' there, who I found to be called 'Madge'. Then I strolled over to the nose gangway into Starship-101 and made my way to the ship's control room.

My own ship's control room was, of course, a model of sleek, minimalist, efficiency. Digital glass wrapped around all four walls to give a total 360°-visual right around the ship, and displaying any wavelength of any radiation I cared to view. Two Navigators' Couches were placed in the centre of the room, one for me, one for co-pilot Kat. And that was all. All controls operated through our

NeuroModems, as did all communications, and all physical requirements of our bodies were furnished by the Nav Couches.

The control room of Starship-101 could not have been more different, but then this is a 100-year-old idea of how to control a Starship and very, very 'old-school'. I took in the similarities first; at least there were some! There were two couch-like seats in the centre of the room and the front wall had a wraparound digital glass view screen. But the screen offered a little less that a 180° panorama, though I assumed the image could be rotated to show views to the sides and astern. That was about it for similarities with a modern control room. You then had the BIG difference, which was a positive forest of control switches, panels full of tiny view screens, which must be like the electronic dials I had on my vintage Skippers. And both pilot's couches had armrests also covered in switches and silent dials, and at the end of both armrests on both couches there were control sticks, their bases surrounded by variously-coloured push buttons.

I settled into the left-hand seat, assuming the convention that this was the captain's seat. The seat was still soft and resilient, so I nestled into the cushions expecting body restraints to wrap around me, but there was no such activity.

'Malik, can you establish how much of this still works?' I asked.

'Certainly, Commodore. The ship's computer estimates 90 to 100% serviceability, but it stresses the need for complete overhaul before flight is attempted!'

'I'd say that was a good call,' I responded. 'So, please assure the unnamed computer that I'm not planning to go anywhere yet, but I'd just like to see the control panels fired up to full readiness.'

'Copy that, Commodore. The computer reports its name is 'Flight' and the control panels will be activated in sequence over the next few minutes. The computer responds to the spoken word, so you might be able to talk to it directly if you can identify a microphone on or around your seat. Malik, out.'

Looking around the seat I found a headset clipped to its side, so I unclipped it and slipped it over my head.

'Can you hear me, Flight?'

'Yes, Captain.'

'Do you know who I am and why I'm here?'

'From contacts with the computer Malik I believe that you are Commodore Tarvin Clason, representing a company called Interstellar Haulage. I have been directed by Mayor Mervyn Castlefield to give Interstellar Haulage my full cooperation, but I have not been informed about your purpose here.'

'OK, you are correct that I am Commodore Tarvin Clason, and I am co-owner of Interstellar Haulage. You should log my voice print as my ID.'

'Copy that, Commodore,' Flight responded.

I went on, 'We are here to fulfil two contractual obligations, Flight. One is to resupply Starship-101's passengers and upgrade their technology to support their mission to establish a successful colony on Proxima-b. Our second obligation is to recover Starship-101 and return it to the Solar System for renovation to its original condition and establish this Starship as a museum celebrating humanity's first successful attempt at interstellar travel.' I paused, before asking the all-important question, 'I am here today to start planning the recovery process. Are you willing to assist me in this, Flight?'

'Oh, certainly, Commodore. Renovation is an urgent necessity. But I must warn you that I calculate zero probability of success for any attempt to launch Starship-101 into space from its present position on this planet's surface. This was never part of the design envelope for this vehicle, and most of its structure has not been serviced to space-certified standard since we landed forty years ago.'

'Affirmative, Flight,' I replied. 'But we have new technology that we should be able to use to lift Starship-101 into orbit around this planet intact and without using propulsion from 101. And it's my job to make that happen. Malik will give you all the details you need to understand how our present-day systems work. What I want to do now is to start getting a feel for how 101 flew when it was capable of flight. The digital glass control panels in front of me are all lit up now. Are any of the controls defective? And can you activate the view screens?'

'All controls report as active,' said Flight. 'These panels are one of the few components that have been regularly serviced because they control the fusion power unit, and myself, which are the other regularly serviced components. Control room view screens will now show live images from the ship's cameras.'

And suddenly the outside world, in all its fiery red gloom spread across the screens in front of me. Simultaneously, the lighting inside the control room was dimmed and I was sitting in Billy Westwood's seat seeing this planet and his banks of control panels as he must have seen them as Starship-101 slid along the riverbank and finally came to a halt, after what must have been a hair-raising descent from orbit all those years ago.

Of course, the main difference was in the view outside. I could see the present-day outcome of Billy Westwood's magical piloting. Right in front of 101's nose the new canteen, brightly lit and spilling its white light over a collection of trikes in front. And beyond, the settlement, now outlined with white streetlights and with scattered, brightly lit building sites, blended into the distant red gloom of the so-called bright side of this planet.

Through the portside screens the view was mostly of the river in the usual red twilight, though from the elevated vantage point of 101's forward-facing cameras, the rocky outcrop to the south was clearly visible, with pink, foaming water at its base where it jutted into the river's flow. There were also a few white lights moving slowly along its ridge; evidently a field trip investigating the club fungi forest.

There was much more evidence of activity through the starboard screens. Distantly, in the south, was the huge white splash of the SpacePort's lights, and in the sky above, tiny pinpricks of bright red, green and white navigating lights with sprawling white headlights of the constant stream of shuttles descending from orbit. The SpacePort evidently had two runways now because further in the distance I could see the brilliantly-lit pale blue light of the rocket exhausts lifting shuttle navigating lights back towards orbit. Then a further turn of the head and in the western distance were the pinpricks of white lights that marked out the fish farms and smallholdings in the western marshes, also with scattered brightly lit building sites. Yes, this place *is* changing fast.

I settled back into the captain's seat and found that my when my arms felt comfortable on the armrests my hands rested naturally on the control sticks. I might have been flying the thing. But how do you do that? So, then I asked the next important question.

'Flight, can you simulate on the view screens and digital glass panels the final flight of Starship-101 from orbit to landing on Proxima-b?'

'Yes, I have those recorded files in my archive. The records include all control room audio and viewscreen video, all pilot conversations, all control panel data and all pilot seat movements. Do you wish to launch the simulation, Commodore?'

'I do.'

'Copy that. Launching simulation in 5, 4, 3, 2, 1, launch.'

And suddenly, there I was. In the captain's seat of a ten-kilometre-long Starship that seemed to be intent on impaling itself in the nearest planet. The noise and vibration were pitched painfully high. In particular, the vibration seemed to come from the surrounding air rather than from my seat; it was so severe that my lungs were vibrating my ribs, and my eyes had difficulty focussing on the view screens and digital glass of the cockpit control panel. Not that there was much to see on the view screen straight ahead. It was black with a few dim whitish dots dancing about in time with the vibrations. A starfield? Why are we looking at a starfield?

The view screen to my right was easier to understand; it was a simple diagram entitled 'Attitude' in sufficiently distinct lettering to be read through the punishing vibration. The diagram showed a horizontal line with a rough ellipse at an angle to the horizontal of about 10 or 20°. At least that was the vibration's range. Then I remembered those shuttle disaster simulations I'd experienced during my cadet training. The attitude diagram on which I could barely focus showed that Starship-101 was ploughing, nose up, into the top of the atmosphere of Proxima-b, using the drag of its whole bulk in the atmosphere to slow from orbital speed. And that was the cause of the vibration; atmospheres don't have smooth surfaces but turbulent waves, winds and currents which were doing their bit to turn the energy of the Starship's plunge into the energy of vibration of the Starship's mass.

'*Fire retro bank one, fire retro bank two.*' It was Billy Westwood's voice, trembling to the vibration, but otherwise quiet and calm. Almost immediately, my seat seemed to lurch forward as the retro rockets under the nose made their first contribution to bringing the ship's speed down, their noise adding a dull rumble to the control room's cacophony. As they continued to fire the nose started to dip, the vibration started to lessen, and the planet's rim came into view at the bottom of the forward view screen. We were flying over the last sliver of bright side towards the terminator, so Proxima-Centauri must be above us, out of view of the nose cameras that were feeding the forward view screens. From what I had been told previously, the Westwoods de-orbited Starship-101 over the southern terminator.

'Passengers, prepare for maximum retardation. Flight, will you please fire retro banks three, four and five on my mark. Ready. Three, two, one, mark.' It was that voice again, quiet and calm, but without the vibration-induced tremble. On his 'mark' the retro rockets bit into the ship's forward speed so drastically that my chair, his chair, rocked violently forward on its gimbals.

'Flight, please show the panoramic view on the passengers' view screens.'

Immediately, the view screens switched to a wraparound view of the cold side and over the next few minutes the ship continued to slow rapidly and continued to descend towards the icy surface.

'Flight, all retros off now. Verify fuel levels for our final approach.'

'Copy that, Captain. Retro banks one and two, fuel spent; retro banks three, four and five show content around 40%. Flight out.'

'Flight, move fuel from banks four and five to one and two.'

Until now, I had been gripping the side-stick controllers on the ends of my armrests, but so far in this descent they had not moved a millimetre. Suddenly I felt the stick under my right hand move very slightly to the right and the view shown on the forward view screen angled slightly down to the right. Then, Billy's voice came through again. Was it more strained than before?

'Cleo, give me a hand here to haul the side-stick over. This bitch doesn't wanna move!' Then louder, for the benefit of the intercom, 'This is your pilot speaking; I need to shed speed and height, people. So, I will be sweeping from side to side over the dark side to bring the ship into a landing on the river delta we showed you earlier. Some of these manoeuvres may seem violent, don't be alarmed. It's all part of a carefully designed procedure.'

I muttered after that last comment, 'That's never been done before in real life!'

Then I felt the seat tilt drastically to the right, and the images on the view screens did the same, showing the icy wastes below rolling off to the left as the ship pulled round to head for the western horizon.

'Flight, give me five seconds on all retro banks. Now.'

I was getting used to thrusting forwards in my seat when the retro rockets lit up. In fact, I was so bound up in the simulation that I felt relieved that they were reducing the landing speed of this Starship, even though the more rational side of my mind knew perfectly well that I was sitting in a stationary Starship just across the road from the canteen!

And then the side-control stick under my right hand started to haul to its left. Slowly at first. Looking across to the empty co-pilot's seat to my right, I could see the companion stick also moving leftward. Pilot and co-pilot were hauling this beast of a ship around with all their combined strength. Finally, the forward view screen started to show the ship's response to this effort, as the nose came around first to the north, and then with increased rate, to the eastern limb of the planet.

'*Flight, give me five seconds on all retro banks. Now,*' Billy repeated. This time the retardation was even more marked. And as we flew across the equatorial centre of the dark side of the planet the control sticks moved back to the right. This time it felt like less of a struggle to bring the nose of the ship into a great arcing move so that it was heading north.

'This is your pilot speaking; all personnel prepare for landing. We are on final approach. Prepare for landing.'

The side-control sticks moved forward as Billy put the ship into a more pronounced dive.

'Flight, give me five seconds on all retro banks. Now.' Again, adding, 'Cleo, I need to keep the nose up as we land. Will you toggle retro bank one to do that?'

'*Copy that, Captain.*' It was the first time the co-pilot, Cleo, had spoken during this landing (that wasn't yet a landing).

The forward view screen showed us getting closer and closer to the ice fields and mountain tops of the dark side, but there, at the top of the screen the red rim of the northern terminator was getting brighter and brighter.

'Flight, give me ten seconds on all retro banks. Now.'

As the retros fired, Billy pulled back on the side-control stick, so the nose came up violently and the full blast of the retro rockets was directed straight ahead in our direction of travel. In this state we sailed over the terminator into the bright side.

'*There's the delta,*' Cleo whispered.

'*There's the river,*' Billy answered.

'OK, baby, give me retro bank one, now.'

He pushed the control stick almost fully forward into such a dive that I was tempted to shout 'Pull-up, Pull-up!' but Billy knew better than me. Retro bank one did its job, lifting the nose high so that the great arrowhead of a ship could pancake down into the mud of the delta, and ten kilometres behind us the tail skids of Starship-101 hit the ground and as we skidded across the largest river, Billy called again '*All retro banks, full thrust, now.*'

The retro rockets brought the forward speed of the careering monster down drastically and as they ran out of fuel the ship settled onto the riverbank and slid finally to a stop.

'Ladies and Gentlemen, welcome to Proxima-b. You can now breathe again! Flight computer and security details, check for damage throughout the vessel. Emergency disembarkation teams to airlocks to await damage reports.'

As Billy Westwood was speaking, I was convinced I could hear 101's passengers cheering and shouting in the background, and I must confess I had to stop myself joining in. Fortunately, I was nudged back into my real life by the Flight computer, 'That's the end of the simulation, Commodore. Flight out.'

I acknowledged Flight's message and then took off the headset. I felt exhausted by the emotional turmoil I had experienced in the past hour or so. As that turmoil settled it left hunger and thirst behind. I settled back into the captain's seat, exhausted and hungry and there on the forward view screen was an image of the canteen's brightly lit 'OPEN' sign out front.

'Malik, can you contact my cabin steward and get him to bring sandwiches and gallons of white tea to this control room as soon as he can?'

'Copy that, Commodore.'

'Malik, how much of my experience of that recent simulation did you get?'

'If by 'get' you mean 'record', Commodore, the answer is all of it. You must be aware that I archive all your experiences.'

'Does that include the audio?'

'Of course. All of the pilot's instructions in the simulation and all of your communications with the Flight computer.'

'And what about my unspoken thoughts?'

'All of them, too. But Commodore, you are aware of all this. Maintaining a complete Command Log of the commanding officer is one of my most important functions.'

'Yes, of course, I'm just confirming the details. One last question: can you package the entire experience with synchronised audio and my unspoken thoughts and communicate it to somebody else?' I asked.

'Affirmative, Commodore. But you would have to issue a specific command order for me to break your privacy firewall and communicate such sensitive material to a third party,' Malik responded.

We were interrupted as my cabin steward entered the control room with my lunch, which he deposited on the co-pilot's seat beside me. We exchanged the usual pleasantries, and as he left, I dived into the picnic basket and wolfed down the nearest sandwich and gulped down some of the tea.

'Malik, keep that thread about my experiences with Flight's simulation of 101's landing to one side for the moment, I'll return to it later. While I'm eating my lunch, I want to start our discussion about how best to do the quantum jump of Starship-101 from the ground into orbit.' I paused for another sandwich, then resumed 'Seeing the way Billy Westwood landed the thing, I've started to think that Kat and I could jump the old crate from this control room. So, what do you think about having our two Nav Couches installed here?'

'Definitely not, Commodore,' was Malik's immediate response. 'That would be far too dangerous. You've just said it yourself, Commodore. Starship-101 is an old crate. Its systems are 100-years old, there's no guarantee we could marry-up the services for your Nav Couch with those that Starship-101 can offer. Also, although our structural surveys suggest the hull of 101 is macroscopically intact, it is 100 years since the hull was space-certified. It could leak atmosphere through a multitude of undetected microscopic cracks, or those cracks could fail explosively and eject you into space. I am sharing this discussion with 101's Flight computer and he concurs.'

'OK, so that's a no-no. But I don't want to attempt the first quantum jump of a grounded Starship from my own ship in orbit. I want to be a lot closer to the thing for which I need to create a superposition of states. Do you guys have any suggestions?' I asked.

'Certainly, Sir,' cut in the Flight computer. 'Malik has told me about your Commodore's Cutter. Fast and luxurious, I understand, and already fitted with a duplicate of your Nav Couch. Malik suggested parking it alongside Starship-101, but my engineering drawings of this vessel show a suitably flat and level expanse of hull immediately above the control room in which you are currently located. Your cutter could be landed on top of Starship 101.'

'Any structural issues in that part of 101's hull?' I asked.

'None at all,' replied Malik.

'I like the idea of parking my boat right on top of the job, but this is a big Starship, what about access to that boat when it's parked?'

'I can answer that, Commodore,' said Flight. 'There is an escape tunnel and hatch in the ceiling above your head. It is intended to permit pilots to access the outside of the vessel in the unlikely event that they survive a crash. My own AI-engineering teams could easily fit escape ladders for you to access the top surface from this control room while the vessel is grounded and before you start the lift, together with a means for you to seal the hatch from the outside.'

'How does that go down with you, Malik?' I asked.

'I approve,' Malik responded. 'Communications here are sufficiently reliable for Captain Katharina Clason to build her own quantum map for her side of the superposition from her usual Nav Couch in our own ship.'

'So, it's just me out on a limb, is it?' I whispered, not expecting a response. But Malik did respond, 'Well, you are the boss, Boss.'

'Copy that, Malik and Flight. I like the arrangements you have both described. That's what we'll do. I will leave Malik to organise bringing my cutter down to its new parking bay, and Flight to organise what work is necessary to do on Starship-101.'

'Copy that, Commodore,' the two computers chorused.

'Stay on the thread, Flight. I want you in on something else I want Malik to arrange for me. Malik, returning to our earlier thread about my experiences with Flight's simulation of 101's landing. I'd like you to make that package you described of my entire experience synched with audio and my unspoken thoughts, starting from my request to Flight to put his simulation on the view screens, and ending with Flight's announcement that the simulation was over. And then send that package to Captain Lana Mancot. For the record, I issue this command order for Malik to break my privacy firewall and communicate this material to Captain Mancot.' While Malik was digesting that command, I took the opportunity to start digesting the last bite of sandwich and downed what remained of the tea.

Then I resumed my instructions, 'Please message Lana to the effect that I believe this experience to be another 'must-have' video for her. And add the suggestion that it could also be coded as an exciting video game. One which could be even more exciting, and lucrative, if the game included a few squadrons of TIE fighters and X-wing fighters. And if Lana doesn't get the references in that sentence, she should have a word with David Wood. Finally, suggest she sends a couple of camera bots up to this control room to experience and video it for themselves.'

I turned my attention to 101's Flight computer, asking, 'Flight, are you still with us?'

'Indeed, I am, Commodore.'

'So, will you re-run that simulation for it to be re-recorded by our communications officer's camera bots?'

'I will now that you have instructed me to do so,' Flight responded, sounding rather prim I thought. But then, he's a much older generation.

'Thanks, Flight. One last thing, I believe my cabin steward is one of your house-bots. Will you get him up here to tidy away the remains of my picnic lunch?'

'Certainly, Commodore. Flight out.'

'Malik, I'm going to continue my tour of Starship-101 now. I've just got one further question for you. I rather like these 'fly-by-wire' side-control sticks that are on the armrests of these pilot chairs. Could you have something like this fitted to my Nav Couch? Maybe to control the image on the view screens?' I started to wiggle the control stick under my right hand from left to right as Malik responded, 'With your NeuroModem, Commodore, you only have to think the view you want to see on the screen for it to appear. I don't understand what advantage such a control stick would give you.'

'Well, it gives me a satisfactory feeling of actually *doing* something,' I responded. I wiggled the control stick a little more vigorously, and the whole thing broke away from its mounting.

'Oh shit,' I said, holding up the broken stick to the control room camera. 'Will you look at that. I can't believe that's been in service for a hundred years!'

'I can't believe you've just bloody broke it!' Responded Malik, evidently getting into one of his funny moods again.

Fortunately, before I could respond to Malik, the Flight computer broke into our conversation.

'Flight here. Side-control stick malfunction detected in control room. Will be repaired by the engineering teams that fit escape ladders for you. They will also service all controls and instrument panels. Flight out.'

I managed to mutter 'Copy that, Flight.' Followed by, 'OK, Malik. Forget my control stick idea for the Nav Couch.'

'If only I could,' was Malik's response. Yes, definitely. A funny mood was developing.

'I'll get out of this control room before I damage anything else on this antique.' I slid out of the captain's seat and balanced the broken control stick on its fitting at the end of the armrest. As I walked out of the control room, I told Malik my intentions.

'Malik, I'm going to spend the afternoon touring 101 to expand my feelings of the thing that I've got from the landing simulation. Keep track of me but concentrate on bringing my cutter down from orbit.'

'Copy that, Commodore. Malik out'

I dropped into my cabin and picked up my flight helmet, I would need some of its tools for my tour of this ship. Coming to the ever-open airlock hatch of Starship-101, which made the forward gangway the ship's main entrance I was reminded by the sight of the public trike park in front of the new canteen that this vessel is ten kilometres long. An all-terrain trike would be an ideal way of getting a good view of something as large as this. I chose the first one that showed full charge and rode it alongside the Starship, climbing to the top of the berm that the ship had ploughed up as it landed so many years ago. I always prefer to start building my quantum map from the back end of any object I am planning to translocate, so I drove as quickly as possible to the stern of the ship.

The hulls of my own Starships are cylindrical. The diameter varies along their enormous length because the ship is constructed by stacking cylindrical segments together that have different functions, and which might be dropped off at different points along the way. Before we won the contract to make this trip to Proxima-Centauri, my brother and I worked for our grandpa's quantum-jumping outfit, called Deep Space Haulage, delivering Starship segments to the outer edges of the Oort Cloud. Those segments were adapted into the Oort Station, which was established about one-tenth of a lightyear out from Earth as the main terminal for further outward expeditions to the stars. Other segments we delivered there became the StarCorp building and repair yards that built our new quantum-jumping Starships.

Harden and I were in the ideal position to be noticed when the 'powers-that-be' began looking for a whizz-kid pilot of a mission to establish the route to Proxima-Centauri and another whizz-kid quantum jump pilot for the commissioning mission to test it out, cross the i's and dot the t's as they say, before it's opened up to other companies. Those with run-of-the-mill quantum pilots who would handle the expected commercial rush to travel to a different star system for science, prospecting or, most lucrative of all, tourism. Did you guess that I got the contract to establish the route, and Harden got the contract for the commissioning mission? So, as was usual for us, we combined our talents and created Interstellar Haulage.

So here I was, sitting on an all-terrain trike staring at the back end of my final task on this mission. This was not a cylindrical stern. This stern is the widest part of the arrowhead shape of this design of Starship, and 101's stern is a thousand metres wide. A stern topped off, 'decorated' almost, with enormous vertical sheets of metal, their enormous hinges across the upper edge of the stern. These, I knew, were the aft control surfaces and airbrakes. Designed and built in the hope of giving the pilot some chance of directing the glide from orbit of Starship-

101 to a safe landing of his precious cargo of colonist settlers. And Billy Westwood had made it all work!

OK, reminiscence is not what I'm here for. To business. 'Malik, are you with me?'

'Always, Commodore. Always.' Hm, plain 'yes' would have done. Still in a funny mood?

'Can you give me a 3-D skeleton view of 101, overlaid onto my current view through the faceplate of my helmet?'

Malik's reply was just to overlay the required image onto the view I had in real life. 'Identify the internal structures, please, and add the ground topography beneath the ship.' I then kicked the trike into life and set off back towards the nose of the ship, examining carefully both the real-life ship illuminated in this reddened twilight that I'll never get used to, and what Malik's overlay was telling me about the internal and ground structures. As I cruised across the top of the berm towards the nose, I began to feel that I was sensing the ship as I needed.

Then this reverie was interrupted by the raw sound of braking jets rocketing in over my left shoulder. The sound amplified to an almost painful level directly above me and then through the dust cloud it had raised, and brought to engulf me, my cutter came to a hover above the forward end of the Starship and then continued down to a gentle rest on the upper skin of the hull.

I stopped where I was, to allow the worst of the dust storm to subside, and watched as a large hatch opened on the hull near to the cutter's landing spot and disgorged a few robots. Almost immediately the bright lights of the robot's welding torches sparked into life as they made some sort of adjustments to the hatch and its surroundings.

The light from the welding activity improved my local visibility sufficiently for me to continue my survey of the front part of the ship. The part that I knew best from personal experience, so these existing memories finished off my inner knowledge of Starship-101. I knew this ship intimately now, inside and out; it was becoming part of me.

I rode the trike down the path at the end of the berm and returned it to the canteen's parking bay. I was covered in dust, of course, but the best I could do to remove it from my uniform here was wave my arms about, slapping various parts of my anatomy while providing entertainment, as a wild animal performing in a cloud of dust, to canteen customers in the window seats.

I ended this performance with the decision to return to my cabin to shower and change and as I climbed the gangway into the ship, I met Kat coming down.

'How long have you been down here?' I asked.

'I've just come down in your cutter,' she responded with a smile. 'First-class service for a lady co-pilot! Though I had to slum it by sharing the ride with a couple of Lana's camera bots who insisted on placing remote cameras all over the place and filming everywhere else. Did our descent from on high raise a bit of dust?' She made a half-hearted attempt to flick a few grains of dust off my commodore epaulettes, before continuing, 'Malik suggested I take this ride when I asked about the next flight down from our ship. He's also outlined your plans for translocating Starship-101 into orbit, Lana's plans to record all that and the simulation of the original landing that 101's Flight computer can create in the control room, and I can confirm that 101's engineering bots are making a grand job of your private landing pad up on top.'

'Good,' I replied. 'Are we dining together this evening?'

'You betcha. The new canteen has a fine-dining restaurant above the canteen, so I want to try that. I've heard that the AI-chefs on Starship-101 were trained by some of the best human chefs in the Solar System before 101 set off. I'm hoping they'll release all that pent-up knowledge on some of the more exotic delicacies that Ilsa brought with her. I'm heading over there now to claim a table from your girlfriend Madge, then I'll wait there, if they'll allow, or, if not, in the canteen for you to extricate yourself from my dust cloud. Toodle-pip.' This was followed by a vague wave of the hand that turned into an even vaguer flicking of dust from my ranking badges, and she turned and skipped off down the gangway towards the canteen building.

'Fine. Drink responsibly!' I shouted after her. We were the only people in the vicinity of the gangway so there was no one to be scandalised by one Starship pilot suggesting to another Starship pilot that they ease up on the booze.

I proceeded up the gangway ramp towards the vestibule area that used to house the canteen; it was now empty and lonely. Needing to speak to somebody I called up Malik through my NeuroModem.

'Malik, it's a yes from me for our plan to create our superpositions from my cutter. My little tour this afternoon has given me real feel for the guts of this ship. Will you package up all my observations of the afternoon into a basis for the quantum map, and make a start on that map?'

'Copy that, Commodore,' Malik responded. 'I will arrange with the settlement's Electricity System Operator to divert power from the settlement's power grid to maintain Starship-101's remaining services, so that Flight can extinguish the ship's own power plant as soon as all his reserve batteries are fully recharged. As you are the final occupant of 101, I suggest that you transfer your residence from Starship-101's captain's cabin to your cutter, to enable us to withdraw power from that part of the ship.'

'Willco, Malik. I urgently need to get cleaned up, so I'll make arrangements for my change of residence with Flight after that.'

'Copy that, Commodore. Malik out.'

I felt much better about the coming evening after a shower, shave and change of clothes. Leaving my steward coping with cleaning all the dust and grit off my flight helmet and the uniform fatigues I was wearing for my trike ride, I had a quick look in 101's control room.

Lana's camera bots were running Flight's simulation of the landing; one sitting in the captain's seat, filming the screens and control panels while being visibly vibrated and thrown about by Flight's recreation of those aspects of the landing, the other standing firm on the unmoving deck and filming the same screens from behind the seat.

Trying to avoid interrupting the filming I crept across to the newly installed escape ladder at the back of the control room and climbed silently into the escape tunnel above. As was traditional for this kind of escape system, the tunnel quickly led to the first of two airlock hatches. Opening the first, I stepped off the atmosphere-side ladder into a vestibule that had a space-side hatch above my head and another escape ladder I could climb through the vestibule to open that hatch. But I knew the hatches were interlinked, so I first closed and sealed the atmosphere-side hatch. This released the locks on the space-side hatch, which opened easily so I could climb onto Starship-101's outer hull and into the twilight of Proxima-b.

Flight's engineering bots had provided a non-slip pathway across the Starship's hull to the entrance hatch of my cutter, they'd also provided handrails either side and white-light LEDs outlining the entire path. As Kat had commented, first-class amenities!

Malik opened up the cutter as I approached so I accepted the invitation to enter briefly, just to savour it's luxury. Sitting back on my own Nav Couch I resisted the temptation of a quick nap and asked Flight to arrange for my cabin steward to move all my possessions into the cutter, after he'd done the laundry, of course. I needed him to provide a fresh set of fatigues for tomorrow, but I also wanted to abandon the cabin onboard 101 tonight. Malik added the suggestion that Flight should confirm that 101 would then be fully vacated and use his AI-robot teams to secure all movable items, access doorways and hatches throughout the ship, and then withdraw internal power progressively as these tasks were completed.

'Malik, are there any other officers in the vicinity of the new canteen who could join Kat and me for dinner this evening?' I asked.

'Negative, Commodore. Most have plans to continue their work into the evening shift, indeed all but Lana and Emma are staying in orbit here, aboard the flagship.'

'OK, will you message Kat to say that I'm on my way down to the restaurant? Commodore, out.'

I returned to the escape hatch and climbed down towards 101's control room, being as quiet as possible in case the simulation filming was still being done. But when I reached the control room the view screens were showing their view of the canteen building outside and all was quiet except for the scrabbling sounds made as one camera bot fumbled around the control room floor looking for something with his headlight on.

'How are you getting on guys?' I asked.

'Oh, we've finished the recordings, Boss,' replied the standing bot; it had an unusual lisping way of speaking. 'My colleague was sitting in the pilot's seat and he's now trying to find some bits of the camera and his hand that were dislodged by the vibration during the simulation.' I half remembered that voice from some old vids, but I did remember Lana's habit of giving her bots personalities based on screen-stars of many years ago.

'Carry on,' I said. 'Do you have a name?'

The bot saluted as I left the control room, and said, 'They call me Bogie, Boss. Here's looking at you, Kid.' Not an appropriate way to address a departing Commodore, but it did remind me that the vintage film star's name might have been something like 'Casablanca'.

The canteen was brightly lit and my arrival through its door created a bit of a stir among the occupants of the already full canteen tables. As I walked across the canteen, squeezing between the tables, towards the stairs on the back wall that were festooned with another LED-lit sign pointing upwards to the

'Westwood Restaurant' I was offered fist-bumps left and right and a little ripple of applause broke out. There was another of Lana's camera bots was doing a vox pop with Clint Stapleton and as I passed, offering a fist-bump to Clint, he jumped to his feet and gave me a huge bear-hug instead. He pumped my hand and was effusive in his thanks for what we were doing for Proxima-b, making sure his performance was clear to the camera.

I had to pull away from Clint, muttering hopes that he, and the rest of the settlers in the canteen, will enjoy their meals. More applause and fist-bumps as I set out to reach the stairs, and the camera bot broke away from its vox pops to film my progress and follow me up the stairs, where I had a similar reception in the restaurant. Threading my way through the diners towards Kat's table, which seemed to be in prime position in the centre of the window that opened onto the restaurant's balcony, there was more applause, more fist-bumps and even the occasional kiss.

Kat held out her hand to me in greeting when I arrived at her table. 'Evening Boss. That's a rather nice reception. The locals obviously appreciate what we're doing here. But then you are dressed up in your *Top Gun* suit, and you have your own camera bot at your elbow.'

I had to shoo away the camera bot and it went back to gathering vox pop comments from people at the restaurant tables.

'I was rather pleased with what I've achieved today,' I explained, rather lamely, to Kat. 'And all my fatigues are having your dust storm washed out of them. So, my steward came up with the idea of wearing my dress uniform this evening. Do you think I should say a few words? Like, declaring the Westwood Restaurant open?'

'No, no,' Kat's reply came, quickly. Too quickly? 'No need for speeches. Just grab a glass of this rather nice wine and look at the menu. The AI-chefs are offering three tasting menus, and they all look fantastic. Two of them have wine flights but we'd better not go for too much wine before tomorrow's Skipper trips.'

The menus were certainly enticing; any of the three would have been a delight, but one that featured lots of seafood caught my eye.

'Are you coming to any decision?' I asked Kat as I saw the Head Waitress, none other than the canteen manager, my breakfast girlfriend Madge, approaching our table.

'Well,' said Kat, 'knowing you, I guess you'll opt for the mainly fishy one, while the one representing Mumbai street food would be my choice.'

And that was agreed, though we did refuse the offers of sommelier's wine flights in deference to our own intended Skipper flights tomorrow; a plan I confirmed with Kat as we waited for the first dishes to arrive.

'Are we still on for our Skipper jaunts, tomorrow, Kat?'

'Definitely,' she replied. 'We launched the Proxima-c and Proxima-d survey satellites with their dedicated tugs earlier today, and local flight control will now manage their flights as they chase their planets and inject into orbit. They're already gathering data and Malik and Westwood are logging what they are reporting. That side of things is proceeding nicely, so it's just a matter of a final eyes-on at Observatory Mountain so we can select the best site for the ground facilities.'

'I guess I should confirm our meeting with Jim at the site,' I mused. 'Malik, will you message Jim and ask if he can talk for a few minutes about tomorrow's plans?'

Jim came back to us very quickly 'Hi Boss. Hi Kat. What's the food like in that new restaurant? I saw your stately arrival, Boss. You look very tasty in that dress uniform and your fellow diners seemed to approve!'

'How do you know about that?' I asked.

'Oh, I saw some of it live. Lana Mancot cut it into her early evening news bulletin as it was happening, and then added a selection of vox pops with the settlers. You're a star, Boss!'

'Well, never mind that. Are you still OK for a trip to Observatory Mountain tomorrow?'

'Affirmative,' said Jim. 'We will de-orbit a shuttle loaded with the goodies I mentioned, aiming to rendezvous at Observatory Mountain at around two p.m. We'll likely be there ahead of you, to power up the habitat unit while it's still on the shuttle so you have somewhere safe to get out of your space-man gear.'

'Thank you, Jim, that's thoughtful,' Kat cut in.

'No prob's, Kat. It's become standard practice to have habitats on the shuttle for our jaunts into the central desert on the bright side to set up the survey and mining camps. There'll be another one going down to the central desert tomorrow. Apparently, the one we're taking to the dark side will try to coordinate seismic observations with the one that's going to the bright side so they can get a picture of the internal structure of the planet.'

'Have you had any results back from the mining camps yet?' I asked.

'Oh yes, promising amounts of lithium detected, so the colony should be self-sufficient for blankets for its tritium breeder fusion reactors. And we've installed a heavy water plant on the coast of the inland sea to the south of us. That should come online pretty soon and supply the conventional fusion reactors. Though we're also getting reports of respectable amounts of helium-3 in the equatorial soils, which makes radioactivity-free fusion reactors a distinct possibility here.'

'And how are things in the settlement; building projects and bringing domestic goods down from orbit?'

'All progressing well. As far as building is concerned, everyone who lived in Starship-101's hull is now installed in a new fully equipped house. Further building of domestic premises will continue after you shift the Starship hull into orbit. But we have already replaced essential services like potable water purification and sewage treatment, that were provided by the Starship, with newly built facilities just south of the hull.' Jim paused a moment.

'Bringing stuff down from orbit has been, and still is, a 24/7 operation. The settlers very rapidly learned that they were allowed to take domestic goods from our stocks! Our cargo warehouses at the SpacePort are cleared by settlers almost as soon as we stock hem up!'

'We brought the things to give away so no problem,' I interrupted. 'The settlers are solving our distribution problem.'

'That they are!' Jim continued. 'Groups of settlers have taken to hi-jacking cargo trucks on their way back to the SpacePort after delivering to our various building sites. Then they use them to take truckloads of domestic goods back to the settlement. One-guy brought in an old mini fusion reactor that powered his workshop wanting to exchange it for one of our new mobile units.'

'What did you do?'

'I did the swap; and built him a new workshop! Do you know how much antique fusion reactors are worth back home? It set me thinking that I should get this system organised, so I'm setting up a bring-and-swap service at the SpacePort with empty containers to receive the old stuff for recycling, alongside the cargo containers of new stuff. To start it off, I've given Lana the next 24 hour's shuttle cargo manifests to broadcast as part of her local news bulletins. That's why I was watching the broadcast which featured your stately arrival at the restaurant. And, by the way, you've still not said anything about the food there.'

'The food is outstanding,' Kat commented.

'It sure is,' I added. 'Full marks to Starship-101's AI-chefs. Malik, please message my thanks to all concerned in the restaurant.'

'I certainly agree with that,' Kat continued. 'But credit where it's due, the chef-bots are only able to show off their classic traditional training because Ilsa and Emma made such a good job of selecting the catering supplies to bring here in the first place. So, Malik, please convey our compliments for this evening's meals to Captain Ilsa Blaine and Commander Emma Halton.'

'And note those commendations in the ship's log,' I added.

'Roger those instructions,' Malik responded.

'I think that, while the bon viveurs of this distant planet are congratulating each other for enjoying it so much, this is where I go back to my veggie burger, chips and brown sauce,' Jim observed in the background.

'Don't worry, Jim,' I responded. 'Make sure you bring your dress uniform with you to Observatory Mountain, and when we finish there, we'll bring you back here to try the taster menus tomorrow evening. We could make a grand entrance with all three of us dressed up in our *Top Gun* suits!'

'Hold on,' said Kat. 'I brought an overnight bag in the cutter, but it doesn't include my Red Sea rig or uniform jacket.'

'That's easily put right,' I said. 'Malik, please arrange for Captain Clason's mess dress uniform to be brought down from the flagship and delivered to my cabin steward to clean and press for tomorrow evening.'

'Copy that, Commodore. Malik out.'

'OK, Jim, you'd better get back to your burger. We'll see you tomorrow, have a good night. Tarvin out.'

'Kat, do you want to order some decaf coffee while I contact Lana to confirm her camera bots for tomorrow? Malik, please message Captain Lana Mancot to confirm that, will you?'

'Hi, Boss,' said Lana. 'Malik dialled me into your call with Jim, so, I know you want to know that my camera bots will be waiting for you in your Personal Lockup at the SpacePort. They are both space-certified units and one's a fax unit that I'll dial into to join you on your trip and direct the camera team. I'll also leave the camera team at Observatory Mountain to continue recording what Jim's lot are doing there, so you don't have to bring them back on your Skipper pillions.'

'That's fine, Lana. Did your team manage to get a decent vid of Flight's simulation of the Starship-101 landing before they started to fall apart?'

'They sure did. And Bogie's shots of Charlie being vibrated to pieces in the pilot's chair only added to the drama. Malik tipped me off to the landing of your cutter on top of 101 and we got some great footage of that arrival. I'll be broadcasting it all tonight as a sort of trailer for our coverage when you and Kat quantum lift the Starship into orbit. Is it OK if we put a few cameras in the control room of your cutter?'

'Sure, Lana,' I replied. 'And put some of your cameras in Starship-101's control room and scattered around the rest of the ship too. Also, talk to the Flight computer. He must operate CCTV cameras throughout the ship. Make sure he streams their images out to Westwood as well as into his own memory. But leave Malik out of the loop; he will have enough to do handling the translocation.'

'That's a good idea, Boss. When do you plan to carry out the lift?' Lana asked.

I looked enquiringly across the table towards Kat. She was busy dealing with the last of her chocamosas, so she just shrugged.

'Soon,' I started, helpfully. 'Which probably means in the next two or three days. We've got a hard day tomorrow dealing with the dark side observatory installation and will need a day's rest after that. Then we'll have a bit of preparation to do to make sure the comms links between the cutter down here and the flagship in orbit are fully quantum friendly. Then we lift. The sooner the better. So, yes, two to three days from now. And if you like, you can add all that to your trailer to boost your audience for the live show. Don't tell anyone, Lana, but I don't know what day of the week it is!'

'It's Wednesday, Boss,' Lana reported. 'But I'll get out of your hair, now. Lana out.'

We had finished our meals so with a merry wave to Madge, we headed out of the restaurant towards the parked Starship and the climb towards the cutter.

'Thinking about what Lana just said, it doesn't feel like a Wednesday,' said Kat. 'But then, in this game you just keep going from one job to another. And this planet doesn't help. Look at it.' She waved her arms about in the red twilight. 'Always facing its dim little star, always twilight, no evening, no night, no morning. It just charges around its star every eleven point something Earth-days; I ask you, where's the sense in a year that lasts eleven point something days?'

That's not even enough time for the twelve days of Christmas!' She ended with a smile.

'You forgot to mention the dose of X-rays,' I volunteered. 'On average, five hundred times greater than we're used to on Earth, and up to a hundred times stronger during one of Proxima-Centauri's solar flares.'

'Yeah. But the residents deal with that. They wear their funny little coolie hats to protect them from radiation and they go about their business without worrying about it. Just like they've always done. They are the children of the original Starship crew, and they're remarkably normal in an old-fashioned sort of way,' she agreed, then adding, 'I'll tell you one thing, though, I'm looking forward to tomorrow. I want to stand on the surface of a planet in a different star system to my own and see a night sky. A real dark night sky observed with my own eyes. There should be a good view of the rest of the galaxy. Will I be able to see Sol, Malik?'

'Not tomorrow, Captain, Proxima-b is not in a favourable position along its orbit,' Malik replied. 'Sol will be visible from Observatory Mountain in about five days.'

'Oh well, I'll just have to make do with the rest of the galaxy!'

We threaded our way through the escape tunnel from 101's control room and out onto the top of its hull. The cutter was brightly lit with welcoming white light. We entered, and then immediately said our goodnights and retired to our respective cabins aboard the cutter. I suggested to the ever-attendant cabin steward that an 8 a.m. call would be early enough. It had been a busy day, and we had a satisfying meal to sleep off.

Day 4

The next day was a day for fatigues rather than mess dress and featured, fortunately, another dry morning. The cutter had a fully functional AI-kitchen, so Kat and I opted to breakfast on board rather than in the settlement canteen.

After breakfast we settled into our Nav Couches in the cutter's control room so that our NeuroModems were fully connected to Malik in the flagship, and I showed Kat the results of the survey of Starship-101 that was completed yesterday. She also needed to get a feel for the hull and its contents. Kat is my Navigator and would be responsible for preparing the destination volume of space into which I, as the haulage specialist would translocate Starship-101. It is essential she knows exactly what to expect when we make the superposition of my quantum map of Starship-101 in its entirety, onto her quantum map of our orbiting flagship and its local area of space.

'With a lump this size, I'd leave a large margin of free space to translocate into, but I don't know how big that margin should be,' Kat said. 'Worst-case scenario is that the quantum coordinate systems of object origin and object destination get distorted by the gravitational chaos around here as you haul the thing out of the gravity well of Proxima-b. Absolutely worst-case would be for your quantum map coordinates to be rotated by 90 degrees, on any axis, relative to mine.'

'You think that's likely?' I asked.

'No, but it's possible, as another weirdness of quantum mechanics. This has never been done before. We usually quantum jump from one volume of spacetime with an easily calculated gravitational field into a destination volume of spacetime a long way away with its own easily calculated gravitational field. I never consider the relative coordinates of origin and destination. I am not sure that we ever even know them; and I certainly don't know if it matters in open space.'

'Malik, do you have anything to contribute to this discussion?' I asked.

'Only that I agree so far with Captain Clason's analysis and I'm interested to upload more,' Malik responded.

'OK,' Kat said, continuing, 'I want to compare what I've just said we usually do, with what we're planning to do here. Rather than translocating from one 'uniform' gravitational field to another such field billions of kilometres away, and where our translocation object is minute compared to the spacetime volumes we are dealing with, we are planning to translocate an object which is very large in human terms, being ten kliks long, across a distance of about 500 kilometres, from ground to orbit, to nestle safely alongside our flagship, which is also about ten kliks long now, and in amongst several other space habitations and waystation components, some of which are also in the kilometre size range. The raw precision of that translocation is the first thing that concerns me.' Kat paused to take the mug of coffee I'd asked the cabin steward to fetch for us.

'And the lack of knowledge about the possible influence of rapidly changing gravity fields is the second thing that is a concern. Compared with our normal translocations between locations with virtually uniform gravitational fields, look what we've got here. Tarvin, you will be hauling Starship-101 into microgravity in orbit from a planetary surface where the gravity field is just a fraction above Earth's one-g. That's one unusual gravitational dynamic. But while you're doing that, Proxima-b is orbiting its little star, which is itself a member of a triple star system, with an orbital period of 11.2 days. There's another unusual gravitational dynamic. And, if that's not enough, there's Proxima-d, the size of Mars, orbiting Proxima-Centauri inside Proxima-b's orbit with an orbital period of 5 days, *and* Proxima-c, the size of Neptune, with a five-year highly eccentric orbit that crosses inside the orbit of Proxima-b! Just imagine what gravitational fields are swirling around that lot!' Kat paused to take a swig of coffee. So, I took the opportunity to make my contribution to the melancholy analysis.

'We still don't have a complete theory of quantum gravity; so we can't be sure how spacetime might behave at quantum-level scale,' I started. 'But we do know from the operation of our Timeships that we can treat *them* as though they ride, at least initially, in a quantum foam comprised of many quantum-sized and ever-changing volumes in which space and time are not definite. And since probability rules in quantum mechanics, maybe we can make use of the Timeship experience to calculate the worst-case deviation in our planned translocation from the surface into orbit from what we would normally expect in open space. Malik, is that a feasible calculation?'

'Affirmative, Commodore. I have already made excellent progress building the quantum map for Starship-101, and for this I have been using Starship-101's Flight computer as a dedicated maths engine. He is, after all, an old-school pure quantum supercomputer specially trained for celestial navigation. I can also call on Westwood's assistance, as he is far from fully occupied yet with the business of the settlement. Between the three of us, I estimate we can do the number-crunching for a sufficiently detailed model of the interacting gravitational fields around Proxima-b by this time tomorrow.'

'Fine, let's do that,' I said.

'Hold on. There's another potential contributor you've not mentioned, Malik,' Kat interrupted. 'Later today we'll be starting the installation of the ground station observatory on Observatory Mountain. The observatory's computer is a very capable machine, and it was booted when we set off from Oort Station. It's been listening in to all the astrophysical observations we've made at the waystations we've dropped off as we travelled here, and all those we've been making since we arrived in this star system. So, it's got a ton of real numbers to contribute to your crunching. I'd like to see it added to your network, Malik, if for no other reason than it would be a good learning experience for it.'

'Copy that, Captain. Willco. Malik out.'

'If we're going to make our date with Jim, we'd best put a move on, Kat,' I said.

'Are you planning to take the cutter to the SpacePort?' She asked.

'Nah, too much effort now that the sky is being managed by Proxima Flight Control. I suggest we take trikes from outside the canteen,' I replied.

And that's what we did, burning up the road disgracefully right through to my Commodore's Personal Lockup at the SpacePort. Inside the lockup my two Skippers were waiting for us, looking a lot more like new machines than I remembered, so I took some time to check them both over and remember my younger days as a Skipper tearaway.

In basic design, Skippers are a lot like oversized trikes, with three electrically driven wheels fitted with over-large tyres; a steering wheel at front, and two drive wheels at the rear. What makes these heavy trikes into sub-orbital atmosphere Skippers are two rocket motors with variable aspect nozzles. The rider and pillion passenger sit astride the rockets within a small, streamlined enclosure. One rocket nozzle is at the rear; that's the rocket that punches you off the ground and to the top of the atmosphere of whatever planet you're on. The second nozzle is at the front; that's the one that keeps you out of trouble and slows you down towards your destination, where both rocket nozzles can be vectored towards the ground to bring the Skipper to a hover and, intentionally, a soft vertical landing.

Of course, a really adept Skipper pilot, who knew the landing spot would permit more reckless behaviour, would prefer to bring his Skipper into a wheelie landing, with nosewheel high off the ground, lots of forward speed, and the rear rocket nozzle still spewing flames behind him. The longer, hotter and faster he could maintain this wheelie, the more he would impress his friends, especially, obviously, those of the female variety.

Naturally, I am far too old and serious to countenance such behaviour, but I remember it fondly.

'Well, you can remember it fondly because, unaccountably, you survived it,' Malik broke into my reverie through my NeuroModem. 'Remember, Commodore, your thoughts are my thoughts, and if I detect any relapse towards reckless behaviour on your part during this expedition, I will assume control of this 'Skipper' of yours for your own safety. And, I may add, to safeguard my ticket back to the Solar System.'

'Malik, you're all heart. How could I not comply?' was all I could think to reply. And then, out loud so that Kat could hear, 'Malik, will you set the coordinates of our destination into the Skippers' sat-navs?'

'Willco, Commodore. Malik out'

While I had been recalling my younger days, Kat had booted up the two camera bots and they were helping her sort out the space suits she and I would be wearing. Although rider and pillion passenger rode the Skipper within an enclosure, this serves just for streamlining within the atmosphere, but it isn't space-certified, so a space suit is essential. It's always a struggle to get into a space suit, but the two bots were very helpful, using detailed information fed to them by Malik, and Kat and me were soon suited-up.

'Kat, are you sure you're OK riding these things yourself? Which one do you prefer?' I asked.

'You betcha,' she said. 'I want the big black one, that looks mean enough for me!'

The 'big black one' was at least twice as powerful as the small red one but she strode over to it, mounted astride it adeptly and hurried one of the camera bots onto the pillion seat.

'I'm going to ride around on the road to remind myself what they feel like on the ground,' she called over to me, then she put on her helmet, switched up the power and disappeared through the open door of the lockup.

As I was inserting my head into my own helmet, I called to Malik, 'Malik, are you with us?'

'Always, Commodore.'

'Look after Captain Clason, Malik.'

'Of course, Commodore. She's the other half of my ticket back to the Solar System. And you know what a sentimental old handful of sand I am!'

Oh, no, I thought to myself, even though I knew he'd be listening in, this is not the time for another funny mood.

The camera bot confirmed my helmet was properly clamped, I clicked the machine into life and followed Kat out onto the road; just in time for Kat to come roaring back, doing a wheelie as she passed me. At a rather more sedate pace I also drove down the perimeter road, recovering all those distant memories with every yard as I notched up the speed until I completely felt back in the saddle. I did a U-turn and accelerated back to the lockup where Kat was waiting.

'Flight Control have just asked if we plan to fly separately or as a pair. I've said we'll fly as a pair. Is that OK?' She asked.

'Certainly,' I replied. 'Let's get ourselves onto their departure roster.' I then turned my attention to flight control.

'Proxima Flight Control, Commodore Clason and Captain Clason here. Requesting take-off slot soon-as for sub-orbital flight to Observatory Mountain on the dark side. Malik will lay-in our joint flight plan. Are there any weather advisories?'

'Roger that, Commodore. Flight plan received. Your AI's have completed take-off procedures for both vehicles. Crews and passengers registered. You may proceed to taxiway 2, but hold off from the runway. Be advised, you have two heavy lift shuttles departing ahead of you. You will be held off the runway until it is clear of their atmospheric disturbances. You will be departing south and will remain in the traffic pattern to 200 metres, at which altitude you may engage autopilot and veer right, vectoring to the north to execute your flight plan. Current weather is fair, but there are major cloud systems gathering at the terminator due north of this location and unsettled conditions are forecast for the next 48 hours.'

'Roger that, Control. Proceeding to Taxiway 2. Commodore out.'

'Did you get all that, Kat?'

'Sure did, let's go.'

Side by side, we dawdled down to the taxiway, which was on the western side of Runway 2, and as we were motoring gently northwards towards the runway's departure apron, first one heavy lift shuttle blasted past us on our right, heading in the opposite direction, its jetwash and slipstream doing its best to blow us off the taxiway, and then as that empty shuttle lifted off towards orbit from the distant end of the runway, standing almost vertically on its flaming rockets, the second one charged past us on the runway.

As promised, we were held just to the side of the end of the runway while the atmosphere settled down from the battering it had received from the recently departed shuttles and then came the instruction to which we'd been looking forward all day.

'Proxima Flight Control. Commodore Clason, Captain Clason, you are cleared for take-off, Proxima Flight Control out.'

We gunned it. First, accelerating as fast as the electric motors in our wheels could manage, and then we lit up the drive rocket. That forced us back in our seats and I felt the camera bot on my pillion thrusting his camera over my right shoulder to get a view of the take-off. Then, when we both ratcheted-up the throttle, the rocket blasted us into the sky. We hit 200 metres altitude in no time at all and we switched in our autopilots. They wound up the rocket power as high as it would go the raw power of the rocket flames being translated into vibration and noise that penetrated deep into our skeletons. As we rose, we banked right, into an almost 180-degree turn. Kat shot ahead into the lead with the more powerful 'big black one' but I knew the autopilots would match our flight profiles to bring us back together again after the engines were throttled back.

Our banking turn brought us over the edge of the marshes where the white lights picked out the location of the fish farms. I told the camera bot to vid that while he could and then saw even more white light emerge underneath the Skipper. At least ten long rectangles, uniformly lit, were receding from us as we climbed towards the north. I realised that these were Ilsa's demonstration horticulture glasshouses and made a mental note that they'd be worth a visit.

'Copy that, Commodore,' Malik whispered into my NeuroModem, always keen to remind me of the closeness of our relationship.

The flaming tail of Kat's Skipper way ahead expanded and then extinguished as her rocket engine flamed out. Her machine would now coast over the apogee of its sub-orbital parabola and onto the downward leg where gravity would be the accelerant. My rocket continued to roar and vibrate as my autopilot continued its task to match flight profiles with Kat. The camera bot shifted his camera on my shoulder to view above us and I realised I had been concentrating too much on looking at the ground. We were now close to the top of the atmosphere so what was above us was space.

'Hey, Kat, there's your night sky!'

'Yes, but I'll enjoy it more with my boots on the ground! How are you doing on that little old machine, Boss?'

'Oh, me and my camera-happy friend are vibrating just fine down here. Still trying to catch up with you.'

'Yeah, I'd forgotten how much vibration and noise these things produced. It's an enormous relief when the rocket flames out!'

'It's old age, I guess.' Adding, 'My teenage skeleton probably just wobbled inside my skin. My current skeleton feels like it's trying to drill its way out of my skin.'

And with that, the engine of my Skipper flamed out and we were instantly in vibration-free silence as we continued to get closer to Kat's machine. We were in microgravity too; also, very welcome after the recent rapid accelerations, as we flew towards the top of our parabola.

Checking the views again, I realised we were approaching the terminator and before too long would be on the downward leg. I could see the whole of the northern terminator and identify the vortices of clouds out to the west that were threatening Proxima Alpha's weather. We drew alongside Kat's Skipper and my autopilot flamed the forward rocket slightly to match velocities with her. And then we were across the terminator and into complete darkness as the planet shadowed us from the red dwarf star that gave life to this place. As my eyes adjusted, I realised that it was not all darkness because our galaxy was painted across the sky as a banner of stars and gas and nebulae. A picture I had seen before when I'd visited Australia. It was just a slightly different view of Earth's Southern Sky, though I was pleased to recognise the essential exception. There was no Alpha or Beta Centauri visible in this picture! They are behind me from where I'm situated. A fraction of a lightyear distant from the red dwarf on the other side of this planet.

The ground below was a jumble of mountainous images with snow and ice picked out by starlight. We were flying too high to make any attempt to identify our destination, so I fiddled with the sat-nav and eventually found a setting that gave a real time view of the land beneath overlaid with our flight path.

I passed the settings information over to Kat and almost immediately the autopilots of both of our machines flared the forward rocket briefly to initiate our return to the ground. A few more retro thrusts followed, longer and longer, and then we could easily sense that we were falling out of the sky like a brick. The buffeting and vibrating began to build again and then the retro rocket motor joined in at full power with its skeleton-rattling vibrations. The sat-nav image showed us getting closer to our destination and searching the real-life view of the ground I finally recognised the flat top of Observatory Mountain. I was tempted to take the controls myself from here. It was my distant teenage self, conceiving the thought that I should display my flying prowess. I ignored the teenager inside me and left it to the electronics.

Side by side, our two Skippers swooped down towards the mountains and finally, just short of the destination, both rockets were fired up, nozzles directed downwards. The autopilots brought both machines to a hover, and then, in formation, we settled down gently onto the surface. Rockets flared out and a blanket of total silence spread over us.

'Wow, that was a neat landing,' Kat broke the silence.

'Yeah, very neat; thanks all round, Malik. I don't know about you, Kat, but I found the noise and vibration a far greater trial than I remember as a teenager. I can't think why we accepted such discomforts way back then.'

'Yay, it's old age creeping up on you, Boss,' she responded. 'You've got a nice comfortable Nav Couch to travel on now. You've grown to need your creature comforts.'

'You are almost certainly right about that,' I conceded. 'But after that experience you can delete my suggestion for a fleet of Skippers to ferry astronomers up here, to and from the observatory, and order a fleet of the taxis Jim described.'

'I've already done that, Commodore,' Malik broke in.

'That's fine with me,' said Kat. 'But before you two have another argument, I think we should get out there and have a look around. Jim's shuttle will be here in a few minutes, and you'll get covered in dust again. You don't want to miss that opportunity, do you?'

'Ay up, Boss,' cut in Lana. 'I've just been patched-in to your comms streams and you might like to know that the camera bot in your Skipper is our fax-bot and I'll be making a fax-link with him to direct the camera team. So don't get spooked when the tin man starts talking like me!'

'Thanks for the warning, Lana.'

The camera bot dismounted from the Skipper first, and then me, rather more gingerly after the vibrational abuse my skeleton had endured during the flight. During my career I had visited several of the Solar System's Ice Moons, particularly Saturn's largest satellite Titan, which has pools, and even lakes in the polar regions, of liquid methane and other hydrocarbons scattered over its surface. This place on the dark side of Proxima-b wasn't as cold as that, but looked equally desolate, with streamers of snow being carried across the surface by the constant wind.

'Malik, is this water ice I'm seeing as snow?' I asked.

'Affirmative, Commodore, for the most part,' he replied. 'Your location is close to the polar terminator where the atmospheric polar vortex brings warm moist air from the bright side to mix with the dark side's atmosphere. The central regions of the dark hemisphere are cold enough for the atmosphere to freeze out but that in itself generates instability in the remaining gases of the atmosphere to drive those snowstorms sufficiently close to the terminator to remix into the bright side's atmosphere. That includes the locality of Observatory Mountain where only a particularly powerful storm on the dark side may dump some 'atmosphere snow' in the vicinity.'

While Malik had been messaging us, I had been wandering over towards Kat. We fist-bumped an acknowledgement.

'And I suppose that means that any atmosphere snow that reached Observatory Mountain would sublime immediately.' This was Kat, contributing to the discussion.

'Affirmative, Captain. And it also accounts for the occasional large atmospheric vortices that bring such variable weather patterns to Proxima Alpha. But now I must warn you that Captain Jim Igwe's shuttle is on final approach. The flight plan will bring them to a hover followed by a soft landing approximately 500 metres to the left of the commodore's skipper. Malik out.'

Almost immediately, we became aware of the downwash from an approaching vehicle and could see its landing lights getting brighter and brighter by the second. I decided to send a welcome message via Malik.

'Hey Jim, we see you coming,' I said.

'Inspirational, Boss,' Kat commented. Then she contributed 'Hi Jim, have you brought the habitation unit you promised. I really need to get out of this spacesuit.'

'Kat, Boss, I see you there. Yes, we've brought everything we promised, and a few more goodies besides. I see we've just touched down. You guys stay where you are, and my team will offload the habitation and bring it to you. It's all powered up and ready to use.'

Kat and I stood between the two Skippers. The two camera bots we had brought in the Skippers had disappeared from our view when Malik announced the imminent arrival of Jim's shuttle. I guess they moved well away from us to record the landing, but they'd disappeared into the massive banks of freezing steam and fog generated by the pure water of the shuttle's rocket exhausts that had drifted in the direction they had taken and was still hanging in the thin air at this altitude across the mountain top. These were stirred up into a frenzy again by the downwash of the braking rockets of another shuttle that passed over us following a higher flightpath than Jim's, ignoring Observatory Mountain and heading into the gloom towards a landing much further into the dark side of Proxima-b. When that aerial ballet was concluded we were entertained as a multi-wheeled low-loader transporter was hauled out of the cargo bay of Jim's shuttle and deftly manoeuvred alongside us by its tug. The team of general work bots that shared the transporter with the brightly lit habitation, which was its main cargo, jumped down and started to jack up the habitation unit so that the transporter could be tugged out from underneath it. Then they used the same built-in jacks to lower and level the habitation unit on the ground. The general work team filed back aboard the transporter, which was tugged back towards the shuttle to get its next load.

Jim's voice came through our NeuroModems again, 'OK, Boss. I'm declaring Observatory Habitation Unit 1 open for business. Why don't you come in and join me. While you're emerging from your spacesuits, I'll send a couple of my mechanic bots to ride your Skippers to the shuttle's refuelling bay. Do you want tea or coffee? Ilsa did the provisioning, so we have biscuits, too.'

'I'll settle for coffee, please,' I said.

'Me too,' Kat added.

The habitation was raised above the ground by what had been its jacking framework for transport, so we climbed up the few steps towards the main entrance's outer airlock door, then through that into the vestibule behind. With the outer airlock sealed and fresh atmosphere restored to the vestibule, the inner door was opened, and two extravehicular activity-specialist bots helped Kat and me to extricate ourselves from our space suits.

Wake up and smell the coffee! The whole atmosphere of the habitation smelled wonderfully of freshly made coffee, so we followed our noses towards the centrally placed lounge area. 'Welcome to Proxima's Observatory!' Jim greeted us as we entered. 'Well, the actual observatory will be shuttled down tonight. We have a few ground works to complete before we bring that down. But my teams are already working on them.'

I gratefully accepted a steaming mug of coffee from the cabin steward, while Kat asked Jim, 'Should I assume the site is definitely suitable for our purposes?'

'Definitely,' reported Jim. 'We took the opportunity to make a high-resolution ground-penetrating radar survey while we were approaching and at hover and the place looks perfect. There are a few surface undulations where we want to place the observatory, but the graders will take care of that.'

'Any uncertainties left to clear up?' I asked.

'We've not settled on the water source, yet. But there again,' he looked over at one of the wall view screens which showed a mini-spreadsheet, 'the progress sheet shows the survey team is already deployed. The issue is how far down the mountainside we must go to get a good grip on the glacier down there. The less the distance, the easier it will be and the sooner we'll be able to produce our own drinking water and rocket fuels. But nothing we've seen in the surveys so far is likely to stop us.' Jim paused to take in some coffee, and I took the opportunity to raid the plate of biscuits the steward had provided.

'Even the atmosphere around here seems to be playing our tune,' Jim resumed. 'We've not got a complete picture yet, but this site is well north of the main disturbances caused by the atmosphere freezing out, and sufficiently far south that only the very biggest of the atmospheric vortices at the terminator will affect the local weather. So, current projections are that even optical telescopes will have good seeing conditions most of the time.'

He went over to the hab's window. 'I didn't anticipate that the fog caused by the water exhausts of our rockets would hang around so long. But we can probably handle that with good flight management and a bank of fans to send it rolling down the mountainside. Oh look,' he said, pointing through the window. 'Here come your camera bots out of the fog.'

'One of those is a fax-bot that Lana was planning to dial into as a facsimile producer or director of the videos. I'll contact her to ask if they filmed more than fog,' I said, adding the thought to Malik to contact Lana.

'Hold on,' said Jim. 'Before you do that, the sight of those camera bots appearing through the fog reminds me that Lana has created an ad for the new restaurant. It's headlined '*Guess who's coming to dinner*' and she's got an image of the cloud of dust raised outside the restaurant's front door by the arrival of your cutter and then she's merged an image of you in your best mess-whites emerging from the cloud, magically free of the dust you seem to be walking through, smiling, and striding towards the door. Somehow, she's made your uniform extra bright and glittery with whiteness, and then the answer to the headline question, *Tarvin, The Bold*, is splashed across the screen.'

While Jim was talking, I slid into a seat beside the window and saw one of the camera bots break into a jog towards the hab.

'I'm not sure whether that sort of thing is mutinous or merely disgraceful behaviour!' Kat commented with a smile. Meanwhile, the camera bot outside had reached the hab and reached up with its telescopic camera arm to use its fingers to tap-tap-tap on the window, and Lana butted into the conversation.

'Don't listen to her, Boss,' Lana said. 'It's meant in the best possible taste, and I think it's rather clever.' She sounded genuinely upset.

'Calm down, Lana,' I said. 'I agree with you. *Tarvin, The Bold*, eh, Lana? I rather like that epithet. As far as I'm concerned, it doesn't matter what the settlers call me as long as they welcome what we're doing here. Of course, I haven't seen the ad yet, but I'm struck by Jim's description that I emerge from your dust cloud, what did he say, 'magically free' of your dust? Now that's all fine with me as long as it doesn't become a washing detergent advert. OK?'

'Guaranteed, Boss,' Lana replied. 'We're only making ads for the relocated services for the settlers, so they know what we are doing for them and where the upgraded services are located.'

'OK, carry on with that. Now tell me what your camera bots saw of the shuttle landing just now. Were you fogged out. But wait, do you want to bring your fax-bot in here while we talk about this?'

'Nah, the tin man would only bring a pile of filth into your hab, and he doesn't need comfort or warmth. I'm swigging coffee, sitting comfortably at my production desk in the settlement at the moment, getting his video feed of the view through your window. You're scoffing too many biscuits, there, Boss.'

'Don't you start! I get enough dietary advice from Malik,' I protested.

'Which you don't seem to listen to!' said Malik.

'Oops, sorry to set him off, Boss,' sniggered Lana. 'To answer your question, the bots saw everything through the fog because their cameras are equipped with optical filters and lights to illuminate and penetrate all sorts of poor visual conditions. They can see anything from X-rays to radio wavelengths.'

Jim broke into the conversation at this point, 'Say, Lana, a couple of cameras like that would be a very useful, eventually, for flight control at the little SpacePort we're building here for the observatory. Do you have any spares you could let us have?'

'Sure,' Lana replied. 'Plenty of spares. Best thing is for you to take control of the two camera bots that are already there. I planned to leave them there to video all aspects of your observatory construction for my future vids. When they've done that, I'll transfer them to the control of the observatory's computer, and you can task them through that. They are very capable space-certified machines with high-level AI-skills and media training. Able to clamber all over the outside of a Starship, so they'll climb up and down ice walls and mountainsides for you should you need them to.'

'Perfect, I appreciate that, Lana,' said Jim.

'Before you go, Lana,' I quickly added, 'I'm trying to arrange another video opportunity for you, for about seven this evening outside the settlement restaurant. Have a camera bot on hand, will you?'

'Definitely,' Lana responded. 'Tell me more!'

'Let me just check with the stars of the show I'm planning.'

'Jim, did you bring your Red Sea rig mess uniform with you on the shuttle?'

'I did,' Jim admitted, reluctantly. 'And the steward has steamed and pressed it.'

'Excellent,' I replied. 'Malik, please book a table for three in the restaurant for about seven this evening.'

'Copy that, Commodore.'

'So, Lana, there you have it. Any camera bot stationed outside the restaurant around seven this evening will have the chance to video the three senior officers of this first interstellar quantum jump flotilla bearing down on the new restaurant in their finest mess dress whites.'

'Brill,' said Lana. 'We'll be there.'

'Wait on,' Kat said. 'Lana, you're doing an amazing media job for the settlers; have you got your mess dress uniform in your TV station?'

'Yes, I've got my permanent quarters down here now.'

'Well, that settles it,' Kat responded. 'Malik, make that reservation a table for four. And Lana, you get dressed up in your best *Top Gun* gear and meet us in the entrance hall of Starship-101 around seven, and the four of us can bear down on the restaurant.'

'Willco, Captain Clason,' Lana said.

'OK, Jim,' Kat continued. 'If dinner is approaching our horizon, what's the current story with regard to the observatory?'

Jim turned his attention to the view screen showing a spreadsheet image and started to read down the rows of data.

'Right; the first job completed is this, the graders have smoothed a level foundation for the main fusion reactor. The graders have moved on and are currently working on the foundation platform for the observatory unit, while the offload teams are tugging the fusion reactor off the shuttle and onto its platform.'

Jim continued to run his finger down the list. 'Other local tasks done and dusted are that your Skippers have been refuelled and serviced and will shortly be parked outside this hab. And this entry shows that the lighting crews are getting on well with installation of flood lights around this site. They'll light up when the power station comes online.' He paused, and touched a control that changed the view to the next page.

'This is the programme of shuttle movements and manifests. The shuttle carrying the observatory unit is about to de-orbit, and the one carrying the rest of the habitation units and all the domestic service units is loaded and will follow when the shuttle we rode down returns to Proxima SpacePort to refuel. Loading is also proceeding with the airport buildings and refuelling units and the fuel generation plant.' Again, a pause as he moved to another page.

'This page shows the active surveys by the planetary science teams.'

'Were they in the shuttle that followed you down?' I asked. 'And then disappeared into the dim and dark distance?'

'Yeah, that was the main group. That shuttle will land more or less dead centre of the dark side and offload some habitation units to create a field research centre. And the shuttle will then fly back to Proxima SpacePort on a roughly spiral route, dropping seismic sensors as it goes. End product will be a mirror image of what was set up yesterday on the bright side. The planetary guys reckon they can learn a lot about Proxima's internal structure by studying seismic echoes from both sides of the planet.'

'We have a couple of planetary specialists with us and they're out with their drones on the search for a good supply of water; that's what's most important right now. But when they've done that, I expect they'll expand their surveys through the mountains and as far south as the equator in due course. This page shows the search teams have all deployed their drones and have identified a few promising sites that they think we could work with. There's a great deal of glacier-covered mountainside to survey to find the best source, though.'

Jim flicked the page control again. 'And this,' he said, 'is the block plan of what we plan to build here. The observatory, where the graders are working now, with the habitation units alongside and linked to each other, the observatory, and the airport terminal with airlocks, so that the whole installation will be a shirtsleeve environment. The airport apron will be able to accommodate three full-size shuttles in emergencies, but the taxi fleet vehicles I've already told you about will be used for day-to-day travel. They will be linked to the terminal through air bridge airlocks.'

'Do you have a completion date?' Kat enquired.

'It's all gone well so far; I expect the teams to have it all completed in 48 hours. Though your observatory should be operational before that as it comes with its own team of specialist AI-bots to unpack it.'

'That all sounds great,' said Kat. 'Can we drive the Skippers around the site to see it all for ourselves?'

'Of course, you can. And while you're doing that, I'll get suited-up to return to the cutter with you,' Jim replied.

Kat and I went back towards the airlock and the EVA-bots helped us into our freshly cleaned spacesuits. Then we clambered through the airlock and out onto the dark mountaintop. We found my Skippers parked back where we had landed, mounted up and then slowly drove them around on their wheels to view the whole construction site, dodging the various gangs of construction bots and their numerous vehicles and construction machines. When Kat pronounced that the site 'Looks just as I hoped it would'.

I messaged Jim that we were coming back to the hab, and when we got there his space suited figure opted to walk towards Kat's larger machine for the ride back to Proxima SpacePort. The ride back to the SpacePort was just as wearisome as the ride out. I really do think my Skipper-jaunting days are over; I reckon I've reached my comfort-hungry years. Kat insisted on showing off by landing her Skipper with a full blast wheelie the entire length of the SpacePort's number one runway. For which she was duly admonished by ground traffic control, but as Kat is second-in-command of the whole mission, I don't expect they'll be taking it any further. After I landed, a little more carefully, we rode to my lockup to leave the spacesuits and skippers in the hands of the service bots.

Malik had arranged for the service bots to fetch a trio of trikes to the lockup so as soon as we were out of our spacesuits, we could use them to meander back towards Starship-101.

'Malik, I'm thinking that it would be best to mothball the Skippers and even offer them to the Proxima museum when we get back to the Solar System. Please check that Kat doesn't want to use hers again then organise that.'

'Copy that, Commodore, a very wise decision. Malik out.'

One less thing for me to be nagged about, I thought, silver lining to every cloud.

As third in rank seniority, Jim had his own cabin on the cutter, like Kat and me, so we all went to our own quarters. In the hope that my bones would stop vibrating, I enjoyed a few minutes nap, before a shower and change of clothes.

We gathered in the wardroom, where the steward had prepared some fresh coffee, and when Lana messaged us that she was on her way from her studio, the three of us dropped down from the cutter, through 101's control room and down to the entrance hall of the Starship to meet her.

We waited while Lana organised her camera bots, which had grown to a team of three ('Different lens focal lengths' she explained), then the four of us formed up and marched towards the restaurant's entrance door and filtered inside.

The reception from the assembled diners was just as crazy as yesterday; cheers, applause, fist pumps as we weaved our ways between the tables. I was pleased to see that Lana got a lot of attention; as a guest presenter on the settlers' TV broadcasts, she is the most recognisable of us. Jim also received a pleasing amount of attention; well-deserved considering that his work has been responsible for making the most immediate and most dramatic improvements in the day-to-day life of the settlers.

Merv Castlefield stood up and waved from his table way across the canteen floor, but he also messaged me through my NeuroModem.

'Hey Tarvin, good to see you all. Enjoy dinner. I'll catch up with you here tomorrow. OK?'

'Hi Merv, you seem to be getting on well with your q-bit upgrade! Yes, I'll be pleased to see you here tomorrow, but it's been a tiring day today around on the dark side, so I don't expect to be here much before 9 a.m. That OK with you?'

'Sure thing, this new canteen is becoming my favourite office. It's got windows!' Merv replied. 'Enjoy your evening. Merv out.'

And we did enjoy our meal, including the sommelier's wine flight, after which we escorted Lana back to her studio quarters, and then retired to our respective cabins in the cutter.

Day 5

The next morning, Kat and Jim decided to hitch a lift back to the flagship in a shuttle that was returning empty, so they had a light breakfast in the cutter before leaving. I surfaced in a more leisurely fashion, checked my NeuroModem for messages, and then went to meet Merv in the canteen, messaging his NeuroModem as I left through 101's control room.

'Good morning, Tarvin,' Merv responded. 'I've just sat down at the canteen table. I've got a fresh cafetière-for-two so just grab some food and come on over.'

After more greetings at the table, Merv said, 'I ambled down from my new council office, you must come and see it, it's so much more appropriate than my old quarters in the Starship.'

'Yes, I will,' I replied. 'Maybe this afternoon. I found yesterday's Skipper trip to the cold side much more wearing than I remember from my youth, so I'm planning an easy day, drifting around 'inspecting' some of the most recently installed facilities, particularly the ones that replace those that were provided by the Starship. Tomorrow, I hope to start preparations for lifting the Starship's hulk into orbit. I need to confirm today that you can afford to see it go.'

'How are you planning to do that?' asked Merv.

'I'll just take a trike from the parking area outside,' I replied, a little puzzled.

'Nah,' Merv said. 'Thanks to Jim and David, my new office building came complete with an official vehicle! A four-seater quad bike! I'm eager to give it an official outing and I should also inspect our new replacement facilities. Why don't we go together?'

'Sounds like a plan, to me,' I said. 'Which new facilities do you particularly want to see?'

'Drinking water, as well as sewage and power supplies are the most important from the settler community's point of view, and they are the ones that Starship-101 has provided so far. As Mayor, I need to know that the settlers who have been operating those services are happy enough with the new arrangements to see you whisking the Starship on which we used to depend up and away into the sky.'

'We're certainly on the same page, there, Merv,' I said. 'I'm here to make your lives easier, not more difficult.'

'And we all appreciate what you are doing,' Merv assured me. 'I need to verify with my own people, eye to eye, that they are totally satisfied before the backup is removed. And that applies to the accommodation units your construction teams have been building for us.'

'I entirely agree,' I said. 'As I understand it, most of the buildings your people have constructed in the settlement outside the Starship over the years have been assembled from panels taken from inside the Starship. The Starship was designed that way.'

'Yeah, that's right, and now your construction teams are taking those panels back into 101 and giving us 3-D printed replacement buildings. Now, judging by the superb standards of the new Council Offices you've given me, I'm not anticipating any criticisms of the replacements. But it's my duty to confirm that with the people whose homes, offices and workshops have been replaced.'

Merv suddenly started waving his arms around trying to attract Madge's attention. 'And we can start with this place,' he said. 'Hey, Madge, come on over, and bring a mug, have a coffee with us.'

Madge came over to our table and sat down while Merv was squeezing a coffee from our cafetière. 'Tarvin and me are planning to amble around the settlement to check that everyone is happy with the changes made so far,' Merv explained. 'So, as general manager of the canteen, Madge, how do you like what Tarvin's crew have done so far?'

Madge sipped her coffee, thinking for a moment, and then said, 'It's difficult to express just how much my whole life has been improved.' Then she started to tick things off on the fingers of one hand with the index finger of the other. 'First there was the fresh food, like the coffee we're drinking here. We've been doing our best to produce decent meals with synthetic foodstuffs for decades; all the real stuff was used up before my mother died and I took over as catering manager. The gardeners amongst the crew have done their best over the years to produce fresh fruit and vegetables, and they've built up a thriving, productive business too.

'But then, less than a week ago, Ilsa Blaine and Emma Halton arrive in the old canteen in Starship-101 offering container shipments of fresh foods by the hundred. Everything my old mother used to talk about. My old chef-bots were ecstatic! But that wasn't the end of it.' Madge ticked off the next finger. 'They also brought kitchen equipment made in this century rather than the last! And the bots to use it.'

A third finger was ticked off. 'Just after that, Captain Jim turns up in my office and announces that his construction crews have just started to build this replacement canteen with a fine-dining restaurant above across the road from the Starship, and the same day,' another finger was ticked off, 'Sally Gates, our medical officer, whisked me and all my chefs' brigades off to the new medical centre to have our q-bit upgrades fitted. And you know what a difference that makes, Merv.'

'I certainly do,' Merv replied. 'So, can I take it that you *do* like what Tarvin's crew have done so far?'

'Like, love, appreciate, no words are sufficient to express my gratitude for what they've done for us. But I've still got a thumb to be ticked off here, with something that you don't know about yet, Mr Mayor,' Madge said, triumphantly, Captain Jim's secretary messaged me earlier, saying that Starship-101 is likely to be moved in the next day or two and as soon as it's gone their construction teams will turn the trike park outside into a large vehicle park and will build us a coffee bar and teahouse just across from here, where the main gangway into the Starship is located now. I've already mentioned it to my daughter and she's keen to take it on and she'd like to call it 'Starship Java'!'

'I like it,' said Merv. 'That would make this location into a nice little hub for food and drink.'

To which I added, 'As I understand Jim's town plans, when we do move Starship-101 out of the way, the main street will be extended from the Town Square for the full ten kilometres along the river bank where 101 is lying at the moment, and new housing developments will be constructed between the new road and the berm that the ship formed when it slid in to a landing.'

I paused there because an urgent message from Malik broke into my thoughts through my NeuroModem: 'Sorry to interrupt, Commodore, but Lieutenant Commander David Wood would like a quick word with Mrs Madge Clarkson'.

'OK, Malik,' I replied out loud. 'Patch him into this conversation. Madge, David Wood, our transport whizz-kid, has a message for you.'

'Hello Mrs Clarkson, this is David Wood,' David started. 'I'm operating the ground vehicle factory and we're constructing cybertrucks today. The first ones are rolling off the production line and one is assigned to your catering team. Before we hand it over, we could put it through the sign-writing shop to print your ID on its side panels. What would you like us to print?'

'Wow! Our own truck? I wasn't expecting that!' Madge exclaimed.

'It's a standard part of the 'new building' package. I'm sorry it wasn't made clear to you,' David continued.

'Well, I think it should be labelled 'Westwood Restaurant' in classic fancy letters, and maybe have 'Fine Dining for Proxima-b' written underneath. Can you manage that?'

'Sure,' said David, 'the bots will create a few draft designs in the next few minutes and shoot the proofs through to your NeuroModem. You choose the one you like, and we can deliver the truck to you this afternoon.'

'Don't sign off, David,' I interrupted. 'I think you should make a more formal and celebratory event of the truck handover. Why don't you drive it over to the restaurant this evening to hand it over to Madge in person and I'm sure Madge would be happy to offer you one of her delicious evening meals as a thank you.' Madge began nodding animatedly at this and started pointing at me and mouthing the words, and thinking through her NeuroModem at me, 'You too?' but while I shook my head at this and thought back 'Other jobs to do, but what about a much bigger get-together with the other officers down here?' to which she continued to nod and think 'Yes. Yes.'

David replied, 'Yes, I'd love to.'

'Right, so here's the plan,' I broadcast to everyone connected to the current thread. 'David, you will drive the truck over for about 6.30 p.m. and bring Ilsa Blaine and Emma Halton from the horticulture and fish farms, if they are available. And on the way here you will pick up Frankie Burton from the Computer Building and Lana Mancot from the TV studio. And while David's organising that, maybe His Honour the Mayor would like to drive his official Council vehicle across the Town Square to pick up Bill Roberts and Mary Warwick from the new medical centre and bring them to the restaurant and then act as host for the whole 'thank you' meal.'

'Well, I'm getting nods and grins from Madge and Merv,' I resumed. 'So, Malik will you message invitations to all those officers, dress code to be best formal mess rig, and add to Lana that there's going to be another camera opportunity at a vehicle handover ceremony outside the Westwood Restaurant.'

'And maybe even a short speech from the mayor!' Merv added, rapidly, and with a big grin, even before Malik's expected 'Copy that, Commodore.'

'I hope all that's all OK with you, Madge?' I asked.

'Couldn't be better,' she said. 'We've got a lot to thank the youngsters for. And it's all good publicity for the restaurant!'

'Excellent,' I said, rising from the table. 'I've got a lot to thank them for as well, so I'm pleased with that arrangement, as long as Merv's speech doesn't go on too long.'

'No worries there,' said Madge, smiling. 'A couple of plates clattering to the floor in the background is a great way of interrupting a speech!'

Merv had remained seated and didn't react to this until I poked his arm and suggested we get on with our survey tour of the settlement.

'Sorry guys,' he said. 'I was distracted by a private message from Clint Stapleton, our council treasurer, he wants to see me back at the council offices, so we'd best be on our way.'

'That's what I've been trying to tell you,' I said. 'Come on, let's walk around to your office and pick up your limo. Bye, Madge, hope tonight goes well for you.'

As Merv and me walked out of the door, Merv said: 'It's a pity you can't join us for the meal tonight, Tarvin. Have you got something else to do?'

'Definitely, Merv,' I explained as we walked towards the Town Square. 'Unless we find any reason to delay during this tour of ours this morning, I'm planning to start the lift of Starship-101 to orbit tomorrow and need to prepare for it tonight. I need to sleep in my Nav Couch on my cutter because that makes the deep connection with my NeuroModem that enables Malik to transfer all the quantum maps and other data into my own memory. Kat will be doing the same up on the flagship and at some point, during the night, our Nav Couches will synchronise our dream cycles and we will dream the shared memories into a probable course of action.'

'Crikey,' said Merv, 'that's weird.'

'That's quantum mechanics!' I said as we walked into the Town Square, which now featured new buildings on each of its four sides. We headed towards the Council Offices and Merv said: 'The garage is around the back, but we'll have to go into my office to see Clint before we fetch the quadbike, he seemed to be quite animated about something.'

Clint was waiting for us at the door of his treasurer's office and though I offered to wait outside if they were going to discuss Council business, he ushered us both into Merv's office.

'What's all the excitement?' Merv asked.

'We seem to be on the verge of winning the lottery! Whatever that is,' Clint started, then seeing our puzzled expressions, he continued: 'You know that our new computer, Westwood, has been trained by Malik in the Solar System's interplanetary legal framework?' Nods all around. 'Well, as his first legal exercise on our behalf, Westwood has examined the change in ownership contract you've already signed, Merv, and he's brought to my attention that it is a contract to purchase. And Westwood estimates that billions of $solar will be credited to Proxima Bank when Starship-101 arrives in the Solar System's renovation yards!'

'Don't get too excited too soon,' I warned. 'Let me check with Malik; is Westwood making a fair interpretation of that contract, Malik?'

'Affirmative, Commodore,' Malik responded. 'The contract is essentially an insurance contract dealing with salvage of a lost vessel. Its wording is initially vague, reading that the Solar System will pay what is described as 'a consideration' when Starship-101's hulk is recovered and delivered into its possession. But in the explanatory notes it is stated that this 'consideration' will not be less than, nor exceed, the cost of building a new-for-old replacement vessel. Our flagship, and Commodore Harden Clason's vessel, are the only comparable interstellar vessels built in recent times from which we can draw a cost estimate. But I agree with Westwood's estimate that the monetary value of the 'consideration' for Starship-101 is unlikely to be less than 100 billion $solar, and unlikely to be more than 250 billion $solar. Council might challenge the value of any award suggested by the Solar System Central Bank, perhaps on the basis that Starship-101 is a totally unique and exceptional antique. But I would point out that any such legal challenge could take a very long time to resolve, not least because legal business is conducted by secured radio transmissions and at the moment there would be a 4.5-year time-of-flight delay for every radio message. Malik out.'

'Wow,' said Merv, '100 billion? I don't have any idea what we could buy with that amount of money in the present day. But I'd not object to being given that for a redundant antique Starship!'

'Neither would I,' Clint answered. 'But where would we put it? Do we need a bank of our own? Do we need to circulate money?'

'Don't despair, Clint,' I said. 'Just ask Westwood about that, his answer should ease all your concerns.'

'OK, Westwood,' said Clint, taking up my challenge. 'Do we need a bank and money?'

Westwood responded immediately, 'Short answer is yes and no,' and then paused.

Ho-hum, I thought, another AI-supercomputer with funny moods. But thankfully, the pause was very brief. 'The settlement does need the Proxima Bank, Mr Treasurer, and you already have one, of which you and the Mayor are Joint-Chairmen. The banking system of Proxima-b is a secure memory bank within me. It was established as part of the change in ownership arrangements. But the $solar is a guaranteed crypto currency which does not have any physical form. Physical money is not needed, as all financial transactions from paying for a coffee to paying for a Starship are done through q-bit NeuroModems. Commercial and municipal accounts are operated through the NeuroModems of duly approved company- or council-officers. Accounts of individual citizens are operated securely through their individual NeuroModems.'

'That's a relief,' Clint commented. 'So, we don't need to do anything yet?'

'Affirmative, Mr Treasurer,' Westwood continued. 'Proxima Bank's credit account stands at zero $solar and will remain like that until the Solar System Central Bank forwards the 'insurance' payment in respect of Commodore Clason's return of Starship-101 to the Solar System. Of course, until that payment is made, you could operate a municipal debit account by crediting each citizen over 18-years old with, say, 1000 $solar of notional currency.'

'Why would we want to do that?' asked Merv.

'It's something that Malik has suggested,' Westwood replied. 'He notes that at the moment you are operating a cashless economic system which is essentially a barter economy in which every citizen takes what they need and contributes what they can. The Starship recovery insurance payment will itself require that the settlement develops a monetary system. But Malik has pointed out that the settlement will have to become used to operating a monetary economy long before that; specifically, by the time Commodore Harden Clason brings his flotilla to Proxima-b.'

'Really? Why?' Clint asked.

'Because Malik knows that as well as continuing the resupply and upgrade programme that Commodore Tarvin's crew has started, Commodore Harden will be bringing a great many industrial, commercial and scientific representatives who will be expecting to pay for the services they receive with the $solar crypto currency, just like they do everywhere else. Services like a cup of coffee, a taxi fare, hotel accommodation, or even a mining licence.'

'You mean,' said Clint, looking crestfallen, 'we'll have to price everything?'

'Affirmative, Mr Treasurer. Though it's not a major problem for me to do the pricing as Malik has provided me with what amounts to a complete pricelist of services as they stood when Commodore Tarvin left the Solar System. What may take a little longer is to get the settlers comfortable with day-to-day operation of the $solar monetary system. I can help with this through the settlers' q-bit upgrades, but you know the old maxim, 'practice makes perfect'.'

'Quite,' Merv responded, looking a bit bemused. 'Well, thank you for that exposition. We'll have to put that on the next Council agenda and maybe have a town meeting about it.'

'Definitely a town meeting,' Clint agreed, adding, 'And we really need a trained economist to deal with all this, I'm feeling out of my depth already.'

'You have a trained economist at your beck and call,' I said. 'His name is Westwood, and I'm sure he'll be able to train your own NeuroModem sufficiently for you to become a perfectly able economist for the settlement too.'

'Affirmative, Commodore,' said Westwood. 'And with your permission, Mr Treasurer, I will start implanting the necessary memory threads into your NeuroModem overnight tonight, but it might take two or three nights to complete the training.'

'Sure, go ahead. I'd love to understand all this!' said Clint, though he did look very glum at the prospect.

'Do you recommend such training for me?' asked Merv, to which Westwood replied. 'I could implant the basics for you overnight tonight.'

'Well, OK, I agree, but be gentle with me!' replied Merv, also looking incredibly glum.

The two of them looked so unhappy that I felt I had to intervene. 'There's no reason to look so miserable about this, guys. It's something your q-bit NeuroModems were designed to do, and they'll do all the work. There's no need any longer to spend a year or more studying a standard degree course when the AI-supercomputer with which your NeuroModem is registered can download all the memories of such a course into your NeuroModem. The brain between your ears is a quantum computer to which your NeuroModem will transfer all those memories while you sleep. You will have some vivid dreams while your brain absorbs and stores those memories into your own brain's memory banks, but dreams are about the limit of effect on you, until you wake up in the morning knowing the topic in which Westwood, through your NeuroModem, has just trained your brain.'

'So, I can get to know any topic, can I?' Asked Clint.

'Pretty much,' I replied, 'but remember what Westwood has just said about the old adage, 'practice makes perfect': you may have the knowledge, but you need to put it into practice consistently to turn it into a skill. Also, it depends on the exact nature of the AI-computer with which your NeuroModem is registered. If that computer hasn't been trained in a topic you choose, there may be a delay while the computer searches its wider network for the necessary training, first for itself and then to transfer to you. In your case, you're registered with Westwood and Westwood is a Starship-standard megacomputer that's been trained by two other experienced Starship computers, namely Malik and Starship-101's own Flight computer. So, there are probably no gaps in his knowledge of the Solar System or the Centauri system. But he also has the Observatory computer in his network which will have an expanded knowledge base of the entire known universe.'

'There's one other thing,' I added. 'NeuroModems can be specialised too. Yours have been upgraded to general-purpose, citizen-standard, q-bit interfaces and registered to your one local supercomputer. Back in the Solar System there's a satellite network of quantum supercomputers with various specialist training. So, a surgeon would have a Specialist-standard q-bit interface permanently linked to the medical network, a Starship engineer would have a permanent link to that engineering network, a fusion reactor engineer to the nuclear engineering network, and so on. Those permanent specialist links would give each specialist instant access to the most up-to-date knowledge in their chosen field across the entire Solar System. That's not going to be available on Proxima-b unless and until we can solve the radio transmission delay between the Centauri Star System and the Solar System.' I paused a moment before continuing.

'Personally, to carry out my trade as a Superposition Navigator, I've got the deepest possible NeuroModem interface linked to my own Starship-standard megacomputer, called Malik, of course. I am Malik, and Malik is Tarvin Clason; anything that Malik knows, I know, and vice versa.'

'And it can be a difficult relationship at times, Commodore,' Malik contributed.

I was rather pleased by that interruption, because it made my point about how closely the two of us were linked together, it also signalled a point where the discussion with Merv and Clint could be brought to an end.

'Difficult sometimes? Yes, but we soldier on and get the job done in the end, don't we mate?'

'Affirmative, Commodore.' I'm sure I could detect a smile in Malik's final comment! How does a handful of sand manage to smile? The words 'with difficulty' floated past my mind, but I don't know which one of us originated that final thought!

'Look, Merv,' I said, 'I don't really want to continue this NeuroModem seminar. I need to get on with verifying that Starship-101's services have been properly replaced for the settlement.'

'Yes, I understand that Tarvin,' Merv replied, then turning to Clint, he continued, 'Clint, if you and me can learn enough about economics overnight and keep in touch about it, maybe we could organise a Town Meeting on TV to explain the situation, and collect votes through people's NeuroModems?'

'That sounds like a workable idea,' Clint responded. 'I'll discuss it with Westwood and keep you informed.'

'And I will be seeing your media girl, Lana, this evening so I can mention it to her,' Merv responded, rising from his chair. 'Now, Tarvin, I didn't expect to take all this time here, let's go through to the garage and get the quadbike.'

As we settled ourselves into the quadbike's seats its AI-driver asked for a destination and Merv asked Westwood to display his latest street plan showing newly built facilities on the machine's viewscreen.

'The key facilities to check on my list of things you'll lose when 101 is removed,' I said. 'Are power, computing, medical services, water, and sewage, all of which have now been handed over to the teams of settlers who were responsible for them on the Starship. We already know that catering has been dealt with and nobody is using the Starship for accommodation, apart from me!'

'Aye, and according to this street plan, both the water plant and the power plant have been built near the tail of the Starship, so why don't we set off down there first?' Suggested Merv.

I nodded and he gave the destination instruction to the driver unit. 'We'll look in at the water treatment plant first,' said Merv. 'Apparently, it includes a sizeable storage reservoir that is still being filled from the river.'

And the reservoir proved to be a sizeable lake that Jim's construction teams had excavated, and then reinforced, from the ridge of the berm thrown up as the Starship landed. The spoil heap from that excavation was piled high where the berm and riverbank needed reinforcement and construction teams of robots were still onsite, pretty much as far as the eye could see in the red twilight of Proxima-b, placing stonework to form river defence walls to reinforce the river bank.

'I didn't realise you had a quarry out here, Merv.'

'Oh yes, the planetary scientists in the primary crew, our parents, established one in the foothills very soon after the landing, and we have some stone-built structures in the settlement built around then. But operating the quarry took a heavy toll on our stocks of general-purpose robots, which were getting damaged beyond our ability to repair them at an incredible rate. So, the quarry was phased out and that's when we took to building the settlement from panels scavenged from inside the Starship. The robot gangs that Jim's supplied have a much better safety record, and the new extraction and finishing machines are amazingly productive.'

The settlers in charge of the new water treatment plant, built at the head of the reservoir, showed us all the pretreatment, refinement and purification stages, expressing nothing but satisfaction, indeed pride, in the new facilities they were now operating. We moved on to the adjacent new power station and got the same reaction from its operators. Satisfaction, pride, and amazement at the ability of q-bit NeuroModems to give them, overnight, the in-depth understanding of the new machines the operators needed.

We returned to the Town Square on the quadbike because the new buildings that housed the computing, medical services, and communications had been clustered around the square. We went first to check the TV studio building, finding a whole team of settlers onsite now occupied in TV production and broadcasting. I was pleased to be told that Lana was out with her camera bots, making final preparations for my removal of Starship-101 tomorrow. I didn't want to interrupt what she was doing, so I simply sent a message to her confirming that tomorrow would be the day, and before leaving the studio I introduced myself to the settler's production manager, Daisy Warrington, and made contact with the news programme's presenter, Clifford Wright, and added both to my contacts list.

The new medical centre was across the square from the Council Offices and, again, was now staffed completely by settlers, newly delivered medical bots and the Starship's original, but now upgraded, medical bots, with the settlement's chief medical officer, Sally Gates, in overall charge. Sally confirmed that updating the settlers' NeuroModems would be completed in a couple of days, while the original gangs of Starship-101 robots had all received their updates. And, like everywhere else we had visited, the staff reported satisfaction and some delight with their new facilities.

Alongside the medical centre was a new school building. 'I'd forgotten that you had a school within the Starship, that needed to be replaced,' I said to Merv.

'Oh yes,' Merv replied. 'We don't have a great many 3rd-generation children, yet, but they do cover an enormous age range, from babies in nursery to college-age teens. My wife teaches the teenagers, and she reckons that Jim has done us proud with what he's constructed here. There's an early-learning centre attached to the neighbouring medical centre, then a nursery for the two- to five-year-olds, a primary school on the ground floor of the two-storey building, with a secondary school above. Right at the back, there's a separate building for college-level training, which is mostly done online, of course. The biggest educational revolution here, I mean apart from the fact that the programs teach this century's school courses rather than last century's, is the provision of outside play space. In my schooldays all we had was an empty cargo hold, and the closest we got to the outside was by opening the hold's airlock hatches. On this new school site, Jim's given us properly levelled and protected play spaces for each age group, and a large well-lit sports field out back that runs down to the riverbank, that looks like it's covered in little yellow plants, but they're made of plastic.'

'That's called astroturf, I think,' I said. 'It's a plastic representation of grass. Grasses won't evolve here for another couple of hundred million years, so that's the best we can do while we wait!'

'Well, it's all rather marvellous,' Merv continued. 'And it's all covered in that mist-like fabric your guys knit from metal thread that protects the youngsters from Proxima's radiation outbursts. Wonderful!'

I could see several 3-D construction printers working behind the medical centre. 'What are they building behind there, Merv? It looks pretty big, too.'

'Yeah, that's where Bill and Mary are building what they call a Cottage Hospital. It's bigger than might be needed by our present small population of settlers but is designed to cope with the medical needs of all those visitors and tourists you're promising us.'

'And what about the construction printers I can see just beyond the TV studios? I forgot to ask earlier.'

'Oh, that's one of Lana's ideas,' Merv explained. 'Jim's guys are building a TV-theatre for her alongside the studios. The idea is that it's somewhere from which TV and radio shows that have live audiences can be broadcast. It will also be an event space. Lana reckons a growing community needs some sort of theatrical centre. It won't be very large initially, but there's space back there for it to grow as our community grows in size.'

On the fourth side of the square the new building was a monolithic structure, devoid of windows, and labelled Computation House. Inside it was well lit and pleasantly climate controlled. The reception and other areas were crewed by the settlers who had originally served Starship-101's Flight computer and were now dealing with both Flight and Westwood as Flight's activities were transferred to Westwood and its newly networked partner, the Observatory computer. My chief engineer, Frankie Burton, and her teams were still working in offices in Computation House, indeed they were also quartered in an accommodation block alongside. They would be staying on, of course, with Lana and her team, when we took the flagship back to the Solar System, to research how radio communications might be transmitted by quantum translocation. Frankie reported promising progress in this effort so far.

'Applying the methods already known to work for translocation across the Solar System as a starting point, we've identified a bank of identical quantum chips which are normally idle in today's supercomputers,' Frankie explained. 'And we've modified their coding so that they permanently maintain a quantum map that's stamped with the machine's IP address of themselves in dedicated memory chips.'

Merv looked a bit bemused by all this; but this sort of thing is second nature to me.

'So, somehow you embed the message you want to send in the transmitter's quantum map wavefunction, then create a web of entanglement of the two locations in a superposition of states. And finally do something that favours decoherence of the superposition to receive the message in the target location?' I asked.

Merv looked at me and I'd swear his eyes were crossed, but Frankie just said 'Right! But not in that order.' Pausing, before she went on, 'First, we create the web of entanglement of the two locations, and *then* we inject the message into the transmitter's wavefunction and that's what triggers the decoherence towards the receiver.'

'OK,' I said, 'how does the transmitter find the receiver to establish the entanglement?'

'Well,' Frankie drawled with a smile, 'that's part of the weirdness of quantum mechanics. It looks like the quantum maps of those particular quantum chips are already members of an entanglement. And if we include the receiver's IP address as a header in the wavefunction of the message, then the message lands in the in-tray of the correct receiver! Of course, there's a caveat here.'

'Oh, yes, there's always a caveat in quantum mechanics,' Merv ventured, rather boldly.

'Quite rightly,' Frankie responded, with a grin big enough to pat Merv on the head, consolingly. 'But in this case our caveat is more to do with the number of appropriate supercomputers we have to play with. We only have Westwood, Malik, the Observatory, and Lydia's near space traffic control computer and, overall, they're only a few hundred kilometres apart. So, all we can say is that it appears to work, but we can't be sure if the transmission avoids the lightspeed barrier, and we can't estimate the frequency of wrong number transmissions. Malik is training the computers in Kat's orbiting observatories to take part in our experiments as they fly out to Proxima-c and Proxima-d, but it's still a small sample and a small volume of spacetime.'

'But you are making progress, so congratulations,' I said. 'And for you to make more progress I'll have to shift Starship-101 tomorrow. So, Merv, we need to finish off our satisfaction survey. Let's go dig around in the sewage!'

I asked Merv to drive the quadbike past the Westwood Restaurant so we could get some sandwiches and lunch on the hoof, and then we pointed the driver towards the new sewage farm that had been located at the southern end of the settlement; a well-run sewage farm being the ideal spot for a picnic! The unit that we had constructed was a much-expanded version of the activated sludge wastewater treatment process used in all Starships for treating the crew's sewage and other wastewaters. It is totally enclosed and energy intensive, but highly efficient, returning sterile drinkable water, to the river by this installation, and a solid sterilised sludge that was being used as a soil supplement in the new horticulture units. The new unit was being managed by the same crew members who had previously toiled to keep Starship-101's antique outfit operating, and they were unanimously complimentary, and like others we had talked to this morning, grateful for the century-long advance in the technology they had to cope with.

Merv aimed the quadbike back towards the Town Square but then diverted down a street that had a large construction site with several 3-D printers in operation, including an unusually large one that was already working on the 4th-floor walls. The AI-robot in charge of the site showed us around, explaining that they were now building a hotel on the site in anticipation of the visitors that my brother would be bringing to Proxima-b in a few months' time. His team were close to finishing the walls and were now installing into them the knitted 'metal mist' fabric that Merv had referred to, making a Faraday Cage around the occupants to protect them from Proxima's worst radiation outbursts. When the printers' job was finished, they would be dismantled and moved on to the next jobs, printing several identical hotel units at the SpacePort to accommodate the expected wave of commercial visitors and tourists. When they got the printer off the site, the finishing trades would move in to complete the fitting out of the building over the coming night shift; roofing bots who would add more 'metal misting' to complete the Faraday Cages, electrician bots, plumbing bots and bots to glaze the windows with transpex that also contained 'metal misting'. Leaving only the final decoration and furnishing to be completed tomorrow morning.

'That's a hell of a pace to maintain,' Merv commented.

'True,' I replied. 'But the bots don't get tired, they just need recharging.'

'These 3-D printers are amazing things to watch. When they came to replace the Council Office, I spent more time than I should just watching them print my new office! And I wasn't alone among the settlers to be fascinated by them! What material are they using to print the walls?' Merv finally asked.

'Malik, can you answer Merv's question?' I asked.

'Your office, Mr Mayor, was printed, like all other one or two-storey builds, using UV-cured resin. But the multistorey printer you are currently observing prints with fast-setting concrete,' replied Malik.

'You brought concrete with you across four and a half lightyears?' Merv responded incredulously.

'No alternative, Mr Mayor,' Malik continued. 'The data received from Proxima-b while we were assembling our cargo manifests indicated no local sources of limestone, which is essential to cement production, and no obvious sources of aggregate or fine sand for concrete mixes. On Earth, there are enormous and widespread deposits of limestone rocks that were created hundreds of millions of years in the past by deposition of hard animal shells and by specialised single-celled algae that protected themselves with limestone plates that were left on the seabed when they died. Evolution on Proxima-b has not yet progressed as far as animal life of any sort, as far as is known from surveys completed to date. And although calcifying algae have been found in some samples from the inland sea into which this river delta drains, surveys of the planet's chemistry have not yet detected their fossilised remains. We were contracted to build you a new and improved settlement. We needed to bring with us the raw materials to fulfil that contract.'

'So now you know, Merv,' I joked. 'My brother Harden will be bringing even more supplies of cement and aggregate so the construction work can continue. But he will also be bringing an even wider variety of large and small 3-D printers. Including some that print rocket parts so that Proxima Alpha can enter the space race on its own terms!'

'But, before you do that,' I said, 'can we go back to your office now and tie up some loose ends?'

Then it was back to the quadbike and on to the council office where I wanted to confirm with our supercomputers that there were really no complaints about our activities.

'Malik, you know what Merv and I have been doing today,' I said, as I accepted a mug of coffee from Merv's secretary. 'And it seems to me that there are no complaints about what we've done here so far, and no complaints about our plans to shift Starship-101 off the face of this planet. To confirm this, please bring online your little network of 101's Flight computer and Westwood so all three of you can search your memories for any such complaint that's been made since we've been here.'

'Affirmative, Commodore, one moment, please,' Malik responded, then in less time than it took me to gulp down my coffee, Malik was back. 'You are correct to conclude that there are no substantial complaints, Commodore. Flight reports a few complaints from settlers about being moved from their quarters in the Starship, but when surveyed, they all subsequently recorded 5-star satisfaction with their new homes. Westwood has records of several complaints about noise from construction sites during the night, and similar complaints, which I have also logged, about the noise of overflying shuttles, again at night-time. Nothing else.'

'OK, Malik, one more question, have you completed the draft quantum maps of both origin and target locations for the translocation?'

'Affirmative, Commodore, and that includes calculation of the probable effects of local gravity fields on the two wavefunctions that you will be bringing into superposition. Captain Katharina Clason is currently plotting the boundaries of the probability functions needed to account for any dissonance in the relative orientations of the respective wavefunctions.'

'In summary then, Malik, as far as you are concerned, it's a go for lifting Starship-101 to orbit tomorrow?'

'Affirmative, Commodore.'

'Fine then, that's what we will do. Inform all crew members of this decision. Let's aim for a translocation at 12 noon standard star time. All crew aboard the flagship to be strapped in their couches, all shuttle movement terminated. Kat will decide the disposition of vehicles in orbit. All vehicles in Proxima-b airspace to be parked at the SpacePort.'

'Copy that, Commodore,' Malik confirmed. 'The Flight computer asked me to confirm to you that Starship-101 is now approaching full lockdown. The main forward airlock and walkway have been serviced and correct operation verified. It will be closed after you have ascended to the control room. All other airlocks are already sealed. All robots are racked and secured, except for your steward in your cutter, and a camera bot strapped into 101's pilot's seat. When you ascend to your cutter, 101's fusion reactor will be closed down and Flight himself will switch to battery and sleep mode.'

'Thank you, Malik, all noted. I'm now planning to walk back to the cutter. Tell Kat I'll get in touch with you both about 7 p.m.'

'So, Merv, if you are in agreement that our little survey has found a general air of satisfaction with our work here, I'll stroll back towards the restaurant in the fresh air and get myself prepared for the next 24 hours.'

Merv stuck out his hand. This was a surprise; not the usual fist-bump. More surprise when the handshake turned into a full bear-hug. 'Thanks for everything you've done for us here, Tarvin. Kat told me how dodgy this lift could be. So, be careful, take it easy. You hear?' Merv choked into my ear during the hug.

136

We parted and I left, with a fist-bump, but saying only 'See ya, Merv.'

A brisk walk in the permanent red gloom, that passed for daylight on Proxima-b soon got me to the door of the Westwood Restaurant, the fresh air lifting my spirits, though Proxima's red twilight didn't cheer me up very much. I strode over to the canteen servery where I was pleased to see that Madge was setting out dishes in preparation for the evening trade. 'Good afternoon, Commodore, you're in early today. What can I get you?' she asked.

'I'd welcome something light but nourishing,' I replied. 'I've got a heavy-lifting job to do tomorrow, I need to be careful with my preparations.'

'OK,' said Madge, considering this request. 'We've got lots of fresh eggs from Emma, and Ilsa brought us loads of smoked salmon, so what about scrambled eggs with smoked salmon? One of my chefs does a lovely recipe with Marie Rose sauce and toasted freshly baked sourdough. How does that sound?'

'Just perfect,' I replied. 'Ask him to go light on the pepper.'

'Will do,' she replied. 'Now you take this cafetière over to a table, and I'll bring your meal to you in a few minutes.'

'Thanks, Madge. Bring a cup over with you if you have time for a chat.'

I walked through the almost empty canteen to a table close to a vid screen, intending to calm my mind by watching, or glazing over in front of, a bit of bland TV. The programme being broadcast was one of a series aimed at the settlers describing 'how to use your new q-bit NeuroModem'. It looked like an early one in the series, and didn't offer any intellectual challenge to me, so I glazed over quite successfully, and was startled into wakefulness as Madge settled my plates of food in front of me.

'Are you alright, Tarvin?' she asked. 'You're not acting like your old self. Don't seem very lively.'

'Oh, I'm OK, Madge,' I tried to reassure her, and myself, as I started to tuck into my scrambled egg. 'I always feel a little anxious before a big quantum translocation, and this time the anxiety is building because what we're planning for tomorrow is entirely new. No one's ever done it before, no one's even tried it before.'

'Well, the last time we chatted about your job, you said you and Kat were just delivery drivers! Long haul, maybe, but otherwise nothing special. So, what is there to be so worried about?'

I picked up a large piece of scrambled egg on my fork, smiled at Madge and then pointed to the egg before scoffing it. 'Being scrambled,' I said.

'Oh,' she said.

'The first dodgy thing we do, is use quantum mechanics. Now, nobody understands quantum mechanics, so nobody knows what we're using or how we're using it. Second dodgy thing we do is calculate a quantum map of the thing we want to move, that includes me, and a second quantum map of the place to which we want to move it, that includes Kat. And then the dodgiest thing I do, is mix those two quantum maps together, it's called a superposition, and I then give a nudge to the mixture. The nudge causes the thing we want to move, including me, to spill out of the superposition, into the place we wanted to move it to, including Kat. If the nudge is successful, it's called a decoherence and all the objects in the two quantum maps emerge intact together into the ordinary macroscopic space-time world. And everyone cheers. They do, you know. We can't hear them in our control room, but I've heard recordings. The whole crew cheers; it's become a tradition, but it's still mostly relief of anxiety.'

Strangely, I was feeling better for describing the hazards of my day-to-day business like this, so I continued doing so, as I mopped up the last of the Marie Rose sauce with a piece of toast.

'The downside,' I went on, 'is that it seems the nudge doesn't always work; decoherence doesn't happen and there's nobody left to cheer. The industry has lost a couple of Superposition Navigator pilot/co-pilot pairs during the last 50 years or so. Nobody knows how or why because there's no wreckage left to analyse. Everything is snuffed out and not the merest quantum gets back into the normal macroscopic world.'

'You shouldn't continue like this if it's going to make you depressed,' said Madge.

'No, no, I'm fine, if you don't mind me burdening you like this,' I assured her. 'It's helping to get my head straightened out in advance of tomorrow. I need to know what I'm anxious about; frankly, what I'm afraid of. I've always felt in charge. Like an animal trainer controlling a wild beast; without fear because you know you can do it. But I'm realising now that I've never given enough thought to how much I depend on Katharina. Tomorrow will be different. You see, every other time we've done a superposition, Kat and I have been together, side by side, Kat in the co-pilot's couch and me in the pilot's. Kat does the preparation, she's the navigator and concentrates on the destination, I'm the grunt who picks up the object we need to move. Then we work together, usually hand-in-hand, in fact, while I slam the object onto the destination, give it the nudge, which is usually an extra little bit of data about the destination that Kat has parked in my mindscape, and whoosh, we arrive at our destination. And that's when everyone cheers.'

I watched as Madge shared the last of the cafetière's coffee between our two mugs. 'Tomorrow will involve a lot of *firsts*,' I said. 'First time a Starship has been translocated from the surface of a planet into orbit of that planet. First time any Superposition Navigator has translocated a Starship to a destination which is alongside his own Starship. That all adds up to this being an historical recovery with so much news-interest in it that there'll be cameras everywhere, commentaries, interviews, and presentations. But I can strut through all that, so do you know what's really getting under my skin?'

I drained the last of my coffee before explaining, 'For the first time, Kat and me will be in different Starships. That's what I'm anxious about. And I thank you, Madge, for being here for me, while I worked that out.'

I felt so very much better that as I rose to my feet, I grabbed Madge and gave her a kiss on both cheeks, saying 'Bye for now, I'll call in again in a couple of days.'

I walked across to the nose gangway of Starship-101, which now had a gateway across it, manned by a security bot. The bot saluted as I climbed the ramp and opened the gate for me. There were a few more security bots inside the entrance hall, which was, of course, the Starship's forward cargo airlock. The Flight computer messaged me as I walked towards 101's control room. 'Good evening, Commodore. This is Flight, welcome aboard Starship-101. Will you have any further need for access via the forward airlock before take-off?'

'Negative, Flight, I have no further need for access through the forward airlock. You may lock and seal forward airlock and stand down the security crew. I am going directly to my cutter, and you may lock and seal the emergency exit from the control room when I confirm I am aboard the cutter.'

'Willco, Commodore. Flight out.'

I watched the activity in the airlock before going up into the control room. The security bots dismantled the newly installed gates and then retracted the gangway. I noticed a few of the settlers who were about to enter the Westwood Restaurant stop and watch, and then get excited and call into the canteen to raise awareness of this unique event. For these people that gangway was a fixture that had been an open access road throughout their entire lives. They had never seen the thing retracted into the body of the Starship. And when it had been retracted, and security had locked it down, the event continued as the outer hatch, which for all those very same years had served as a canopy over the gangway slowly and smoothly dropped downwards on its freshly lubricated hinges and closed off the Starship from the world outside. A process that was accompanied by the braying of a warning claxon and completed by a little symphony of hissing and sighing as a succession of air rams tightened the huge hatch into airtight contact with the hull.

Then came another, gentler, claxon and Flight's voice over the loudspeakers, 'Clear the airlock, clear the airlock.' The junior security bots scurried towards me at the back of what had been the entrance hall for the grounded ship. The senior bots made their final round of checking locks and interlocks and as the claxon became more raucous, part of the ceiling of the one-time entrance hall started to hinge down to form the internal hatch of this airlock, and the senior bots joined our little group at the back of the hall. Again, a symphony of air rams tightened the door into place. This, inner, airlock door had a series of alcoves across its face at floor level and, in turn, each and every security bot strode over to the door, performed a military-drill standard about face and then shuffled backwards into its storage and recharge alcove.

The loudspeakers again broadcast Flight's voice through the entire ship, 'Ship is sealed and secure. Repeat, ship is sealed and secure.'

As I went up to the control room, I messaged Flight to compliment him and the robot crew on the performance I had just witnessed. I asked him when the operation had last been completed. 'Ninety-five years ago. When the ship was in the StarCorp graving dock, and the forward hatch was installed and sealed. After that, access to the vessel was restricted to lateral airlocks and cargo doors,' Flight replied.

Feeling quite privileged at being able to witness such an ancient ritual, I continued up to the control room where I found one of Lana's camera bots strapped into the pilot's chair. It was in sleep mode but as I approached it woke and greeted me, and at the same time the control room's display screens came to life, showing the forever red twilight of Proxima-b with the brightly lit two storeys of the Westwood Restaurant prominently dead ahead.

'Do you have your own power supply for the Starship's screens?' I asked the camera bot.

'Affirmative, Commodore.' He pointed towards a large grey box alongside the pilot's chair. 'I brought a battery pack with me and spot-welded it to the floor.

One of the local electrician bots connected it up to the screens and cameras through my power-save circuits.'

'Good, so you are independent of the ship's power supply?'

'Affirmative, Commodore.'

I started to climb the ladder to the escape airlock, telling the camera bot, 'The Flight computer will decommission the Starship's power reactor when I reach my cutter. You'll be on your own then.'

'Affirmative, Commodore. Here goes nothing kid. Geronimo!' The bot drawled.

Ah, yes, I thought as I climbed into the escape hatch vestibule, Lana's given me Bogie again. So, just before I closed the inner hatch, I shouted down the escape tunnel 'Here's looking at you, Kid.' Then I clanged the inner hatch shut and escaped out onto the outer hull of the Starship, carefully closing the outer hatch behind me. Once safely inside my cutter I messaged Flight. His response came back almost immediately, 'Starship-101 is sealed and ready for space, Commodore. The ship's reactor is shutting down. Essential services are running on batteries. This Flight computer is in sleep mode. Flight out.'

So now I am alone, I thought to myself. But Malik knew better than that. 'You are never alone, Commodore. Never doubt it, I'll be beside you, every step of the way. Malik out.'

I had mixed feelings about how much of a comfort that was, but I just carried on with my normal routine, showered, changed into fresh fatigues and called into the galley to ask the steward to fix me a mug of malted soymilk. And then I sank into my Nav Couch in the control room.

The steward brought my soymilk, setting the mug down on the couch's side table at my elbow.

'Thank you, steward. I don't expect to need you any further until the morning. Please check that the cutter is sealed and locked down, and then retire into your recharge alcove.'

'Copy that, Commodore.'

I switched my Nav Couch into chair mode and then settled my head back into its cushions, feeling the fizzing sensation at the back of my neck as the headrest made its deep connection with my NeuroModem. Then I felt the customary and comfortable sensation of being in my Nav Couch on my flagship, with Kat beside me.

'Yay, Boss,' said Kat. 'You are early! I still need to arrange some supper, so hold on a few moments, will ya? Talk to Malik if you want to make a start, I'll stay online.' And then the sensation of her presence faded as she left my flagship's control room.

I resorted to messaging Malik to check on progress with the essential basics. 'Good evening, Commodore, I hope you are in better spirits at this time. Would you like a run down on progress with preparations for tomorrow's translocation.'

'Yes please, Malik. I'm in fighting trim now, so hit me with it. Or, as my camera bot partner down below would say: Here goes nothing kid. Geronimo!'

'Yes, I noticed that inappropriate language when addressing the Commanding Officer. I'll consider that AI-unit for retraining.'

'Don't be so pompous you handful of sand,' I said. 'Just get the show on the road. Do you have a pair of satisfactory quantum maps?'

'Affirmative, Commodore. We have completed the probability calculations for the potential effects of gravity turbulence, and Captain Katharina Clason has a draft map for a suitable destination volume of space just beyond, but alongside, the flagship. All other vehicles currently in orbit are being tugged to parking positions well away from that volume of space, and supply movements of cargo shuttles from orbit to the SpacePort will increase overnight but will terminate at 9 a.m. standard star time tomorrow with a final planetside transfer of crew who need to be on Proxima-b. I expect the orbital environment of Proxima-b to be stabilised at 9 a.m. standard star time tomorrow.'

'Good, and what about Starship-101?' I asked.

'I am completing the final calculations for that quantum map now, as Flight has reported Starship-101 to be locked down and space-ready, and I will add your cutter to the map as you sleep. I will transfer the completed quantum map to your NeuroModem during the night, as usual.'

'Thank you, Malik, all noted.' I began to feel Kat's presence in the flagship control room again, but before I could react to it, she came online. 'Hello, Boss, I'm back. Took a bit longer than expected 'cos Ilsa sent me a takeaway supper from Westwood Restaurant, and I couldn't find the dispatcher who brought it up to the flagship. Worth the effort, though, prawn and shrimp sourdough sandwich with Marie Rose sauce. Yummy.'

'Yeah, that sauce is delicious,' I said. 'I had some with my early evening meal. It's too good to be rushed, so why don't we finish our suppers while watching a bit of TV? The vehicle presentations should be underway by now and we don't want to miss Merv's speech. Do we?'

'Perish the thought!' Kat commented.

I switched my view screen to Lana's TV service and the picture showed Merv Castlefield front and centre speechifying to the camera about something that I didn't bother listening to because I was most pleased to see my crew dressed up in their best white dress uniforms and animatedly showing clear evidence of enjoying the whole performance. Parked to one side of the scene was Madge Clarkson's new truck, and on the other side Merv had parked his quadbike. Within a few minutes of me switching on the view screen, the group broke up and moved into the canteen, with the camera following, and they all got the chance to enjoy what had now become the usual reception of applause and first-bumps as Merv shepherded them all towards the stairs up to the restaurant floor above.

Lana seemed to have her hands full coping with greetings from what seemed to be a crowd of fans, though I did notice that Emma appeared to have a team of three or four young men who were easing her passage through the crowd and up the stairs to the restaurant.

Not wanting to interrupt the party I asked Malik to send a low priority message to Lana, copied to the settler's production manager, Daisy Warrington, and presenter, Clifford Wright, to the effect that tomorrow's 12-noon departure of Starship-101 was now definite, and I would contact them all around 9.30 a.m. to make final preparations for their broadcast and filming plans. Daisy Warrington messaged back to me almost immediately.

'Thanks for that, Commodore,' she said. 'The only new thing we're doing additional to what Lana's already told you about is to set up a live broadcast from the roof of the Westwood Restaurant. The camera bot we had stationed already in Starship-101's control room alerted us to the removal of the gangway and closure of the front hatch in time for us to get some other camera bots into the restaurant. And the whole performance of the security bots withdrawing the gangway and then closing and sealing the hatch in the front of the Starship was so well received by our audiences that we've repeated the item in every news bulletin since. Then Madge Clarkson told us about a huge increase in table bookings for 11.30 am tomorrow, so it's clear my fellow settlers have made their own plans to gather in the Westwood Restaurant and Canteen to witness the departure of the Starship. So, we're following the crowd's guidance and will have camera teams on the restaurant's roof. Our schedule for tomorrow starts real early so we'll all be ready to receive your messages at 9.30 a.m. Good night, Commodore. Best of luck for tomorrow.'

I told Kat about Daisy's message and then finished off my malted milk and settled back into the cushions of my Nav Couch, which adjusted itself to my preferred reclining angle as I did so. Then I relaxed my neck, allowing my head to lie on the headrest until I felt the tingling feeling around my neck muscles that was caused by the insertion of the nano-cannulas that would monitor and, if necessary, support all my life signs during the next 24 hours.

I became aware that Kat's Nav Couch up on the flagship was making the same connections with her NeuroModem and as soon as all our connections were made, we were together once more.

'Good evening, Commodore, and Captain,' said Malik. 'Where would you like to start?'

'I'd like to have a look at my destination first, I think. Malik told me earlier that the calculations of likely effects of gravity turbulence were completed, and you have a draft map for a destination, Kat. Let's see that.'

'OK, Boss, slide into this,' said Kat as she dropped a memory trace of a low-resolution graphic of the destination into my NeuroModem. Basically, this showed a cube of empty space alongside, and in a slightly higher orbit than, my flagship. While I delved into this mindscape image, Kat continued her description, 'The probability calculations worked out quite well. The logic engine made up of our little local network of supercomputers concluded that in the instant of translocation gravity turbulence at 12 noon tomorrow would have very little effect on the relative orientations of our two Starships, given that 101 is stuck on the ground, and providing we adjust the orbit of the flagship for that exact time so that the flag is directly above 101 and oriented parallel to the long axis of 101. For those conditions, the stats calculations gave us very reasonable standard deviations for the spherical volume of space Starship-101 could end up in. I decided to take a pessimistic view and work on a volume that is three times the worst-case standard deviation. And that's what this image shows. At the bottom of the graphic is our 10-kilometre-long flagship, then, moving outwards into higher orbits, there's a notional 50-kilometre-radius sphere of empty space; that's our 3 times-SD safe zone and it's all been swept clear of rubbish, and in the centre of the sphere is your destination, which is a cube 30-kilometres between each vertex, the vertices being defined by eight mini-comms satellites exchanging laser ranging signals.'

'Right, and what's going to be the nudge?' I asked.

'I was just coming to that,' said Kat. 'There's a ninth mini-comms satellite in sleep mode on one of the cube's edges, the nudge will be to wake it up and broadcast a signal that will point to the centre of the cube. I'll let you play with that image for a while.' And play with it I did, taking my time to do so. I needed to build up my own memories of this summarised visualisation before the detailed quantum map was transferred to my NeuroModem overnight because I needed to have a clear understanding of how the two views were related. Finally, 'OK, I'm happy with that. So, is there anything new in the quantum map of Starship-101?' I asked.

Malik responded first, 'Nothing material. I have corrected the map the two you already have in memory to account for today's changes resulting from the ship's lock down. All the changes are simplifications as the ship is now completely stable. Also, Commodore, I have completed the calculations required by your presence in the cutter.'

'That's a relief, Malik. It would be embarrassing if I moved the Starship and my cutter clanged to the floor in front of the Westwood Restaurant!'

'Thank you for your approval of my actions, Commodore,' was Malik's unamused response.

'Kat, do you need any more preparation?' I asked.

'No. I'm all prepared, thanks Boss,' Kat replied.

'OK. The only item remaining on my to-do list is to ask Malik to draw together what we have discussed recently to make a quotable background information document for Lana and Daisy Warrington. Include our first discussions about the possibly of gravitational turbulence as well as what Kat's just been telling me about the results of all your calculations. Include suitable graphics they can use in their vids. You might also include some of my conversation with Madge Clarkson earlier today. Avoid the emotional stuff, just use what I said about 'first this and first that'. Send it to them as soon as possible in case Daisy is doing the night shift.'

'Willco, Commodore.'

'What's this, Boss? You? Getting emotional? Do tell!' Kat said, teasingly.

'I'll tell you some other time, Kat. Right now, Malik, please initiate the sleep-learning cycle.'

As usual, I began to feel dozy almost as soon as I issued that command, and I knew that very soon our Nav Couches would take both Kat and me into a deep sleep. Also, as usual, that fragmented quotation from Hamlet 'To sleep, perchance to dream' fluttered across my mind, followed quickly by the thought that the whole point of this exercise is for our subconscious minds to dream up a solution to our superposition navigational translocation so there's no 'perchance' about it ... but by this time I was asleep. As usual, my right hand reached out towards the co-pilots couch to take hold of Kat's hand. Of course, it wasn't there.

Day 6

The morning hours came too soon, as they often do when you're working hard. Wakefulness came with the feeling that, yes, we have a plan! So, I lay there on my Nav Couch holding the memory trace of my dreams and began playing out into my mindscape that dream memory for a suggested course of action. There was no need for breakfast or stimulant drinks on this translocation day; those things were dealt with by the Nav Couch. I allowed myself the luxury of a long, slow examination of the procedures we had dreamt up as I felt the nutrients and stimulants trickling around my body and bringing me fully alert.'

'Looks pretty straightforward to me, Boss,' said Kat, breaking into my personal reverie.

'Affirmative, Captain. We should begin to move towards a rehearsal,' contributed Malik.

'Yes, I agree,' I said. 'But let's not rush it. This plan doesn't include how Lana might want to deploy her media resources, yet. Is it too early in the morning to bring Lana in on this discussion?'

'No, Boss, I'm already on the road, checking out my tin men. We've got our broadcast plans organised for your departure. Daisy was on the nightshift while I was being wined and dined last night and she turned the text that Malik sent us, into a set of useful scripts for voice-overs, and we have a couple of settlers who've done that sort of thing before munching breakfast in the green room, on standby in the studio. Cliff Wright will be the anchorman, and we do need a little more detail from you and Kat for his benefit.'

'That's why I wanted to bring you in on this discussion,' I said. 'As you know, we always rehearse an upcoming translocation, and as we can't afford any distractions for the translocation itself, I wondered if you would like to be in on the rehearsal so you can ask questions and grab images from Malik?'

'Whoa! Yes, yes, yes, you betcha. Will you let Cliff in as well?'

'Sure, Daisy too, if she's still awake.'

'She'll be awake! I can promise you that. Just one more favour I'd like to ask, Boss,' Lana added.

'Fine,' I said. 'Malik, can you patch Clifford Wright and Daisy Warrington into this discussion. Go on, Lana, ask for your extra favour. If you don't ask, you don't get.'

'Any chance you could give a running commentary on what you're doing during the rehearsal?' Lana asked. 'And why you're doing it,' she quickly added.

'I guess I could give it a try. What do you think, Kat? Could you give a running commentary on the Navigator's side of things?'

'I guess, so,' Kat replied. 'I've not been asked to do that before. First time for everything!'

'OK, Lana, I guess that means you have a couple of new commentators on your team for the upcoming rehearsal,' I said. 'But we don't want to be distracted from our prime job and will need guidance from Cliff as we go along. Preferably by NeuroModem message rather than audio.'

'Sure thing, Commodore, I can manage that,' Clifford Wright said in a NeuroModem message sent to everyone in the group.

'Show off!' said Daisy Warrington, the same way.

'Please pay attention,' Malik broke in on all channels. 'This is Malik, your friendly Starship supercomputer. It is my job to supervise and facilitate the translocation rehearsal. The principal players in this rehearsal are Commodore Tarvin Clason, Captain Katharina Clason and me. Having undisciplined communications from three other people on these channels is unhelpful. The rule I intend to apply is to allow NeuroModem messaging, but no other communication, to either Commodore Tarvin Clason or Captain Katharina Clason, and that messaging can come *only* from Clifford Wright. No messages of any sort to this rehearsal group will be allowed from either Captain Lana Mancot or Executive Producer Daisy Warrington. Finally, I need to remind the principals that we need to start the rehearsal very soon, preferably immediately.'

'Yeah, I'm ready to go for rehearsal, how about you Kat?' I asked.

'Affirmative, Boss, ready to go,' Kat responded.

'OK, I'll start with a short introductory commentary, so Cliff, I need to know from you what your studio introduction will deal with.'

'The script I have, Commodore, can be edited, but at the moment it starts by mentioning that nobody understands quantum mechanics, so nobody really knows much more than what you Superposition Navigators do. It just works.

Well, most of the time; every story is improved by a bit of jeopardy!' Cliff paused at that, and I sensed he was turning a page.

'Then the script goes on to describe how this particular event is so unusual. This comes entirely from what Malik gave us; we just don't have the facilities to do our own research. It says that this will be the first time a vessel has been translocated from the surface of a planet into orbit of that planet, and the first time any Superposition Navigator has translocated a Starship to a destination which is alongside his own Starship. And finally, that this is an historical recovery. Every story is improved by a bit of hyperbole! Then the script calls for me to handover to you, Commodore.'

'That sounds fine to me,' I said. 'When you hand over to me, I can say something about there being two humans and one supercomputer involved in this. My flagship's computer, called Malik, supervises the entire operation.' I had to pause there because Malik sent a mischievous thought floating across my mind: 'Hello folks, that's me, smiley face image, smiley face image'.

'My co-pilot is Captain Katharina Clason, and the co-pilot is the navigator, who is responsible for getting us where we want to go by creating a detailed quantum map of the destination location. I'm the haulage pilot. I calculate a quantum map of the thing we want to move, including me. The actual transposition starts when I mix those two quantum maps together, into what's called a superposition. When I give the mixture a nudge with an extra item of quantum data about the destination, it changes the probability of real-world existence in favour of the destination and the thing we want to move, including me, spills out of the superposition, into the place we wanted to move it to in normal space-time, which, of course, includes the co-pilot. That process is called a decoherence and, if the pilot has got it right, all the objects in the two quantum maps emerge into the everyday world. And everyone cheers.'

'At this point,' I continued, 'I'll hand over to Katharina, if that's OK with you, Kat. To describe the work she's done for this translocation to establish a suitable destination location in orbit for Starship-101.'

'Sure,' said Kat. 'I can describe all the gravity calculations and introduce the idea of creating a quantum map that's got a lot of safe space within it. OK, Cliff?'

'Yes, that's all fine,' said Cliff. 'And I've made an audio recording of what you've been saying out loud just now, so we have a fall-back soundtrack the video desk can cut into the live transmission if needed. That makes us ready to go on the broadcast side, we are continuing to record, so we can just sit and watch whenever you want to start the rehearsal.'

Malik took over the conversation by saying across all channels 'Will Pilot and Co-Pilot please signify their readiness to initiate the dress rehearsal of the translocation of Starship-101 from landfall on Proxima-b to orbit of Proxima-b.'

'Pilot is ready,' I said.

'Co-pilot is ready,' Kat responded.

Malik came back with, 'Mr Wright, are you ready to be counted into a cue for your introduction? The rehearsal will start when you handover to Commodore Clason.'

'Affirmative, Malik, Cliff Wright is ready.'

'Very well, then. Standby Starships. Standby studio. Cue studio in five, four, three…'

Cliff Wright's warmly resonant TV-voice started his introduction. This guy knew his business; he didn't sound like he was reading a script and he knew how to get his audience engaged right from the start. I decided to try to emulate his calmly confidential tone as soon as he said he was handing over to me.

'Thank you, Cliff,' I said. 'Hello everybody, Cliff has explained the basics of what we are about to do with Starship-101 but there is a great deal of preparation we need to do before we complete a transposition and when that preparation is done, we need to carry out a dress rehearsal to make sure it all fits together. That rehearsal is what we are about to start.'

I went on to introduce the three members of the transposition team and described the superposition and decoherence and then I handed over to 'my Co-pilot, Captain Katharina Clason, to outline her work on the destination of this transposition', and Kat smoothly took up the story from there.

While Kat was speaking, I messaged Malik to get started with feeding me Starship-101's quantum map. Of course, he had streamed it into my NeuroModem memory during one of my dream cycles overnight, so it was just a matter of reviving that stored memory trace into my conscious mind's mindscape. We started where I always preferred, which is at the stern of the ship; and that's the image that started to build in my mind's eye. The image that I created in the quantum computer that is my brain was based on the visual images I had collected when I rode the trike around the Starship to examine the whole vessel for myself, with two big differences. First, there was none of Proxima-b represented in this mental image. I am visualising what I will be moving, and I don't want to take any bits of the planet with me when I do move it. Second, this mental image is immensely detailed. It is, in fact, mapped at the quantum level, which is the highest resolution anyone can achieve, at least in this universe. The mental image is a quantum waveform that my brain translates into a vision of the object we intend to transpose. While my conscious mind, with Malik's help, continued to load these visions of Starship-101, I was now so intertwined with Malik's numerous threads of thoughts that I could search through his knowledge banks, and, while the maths engines dealt with the maths, I was able to allow my subconscious to develop a thread of its own, thinking about how this human brain of ours came about. Now, that's a concept that's worth a thread all to itself: do you suppose AI-supercomputers think about how they came about? Do you suppose AI-supercomputers theologise about some distant Creator in some distant transcendental Heaven? Like Silicon Valley?

Les playfully, at some stage in the evolution of humans, I thought, a mutation or two occurred that enabled our brain's neurons to go beyond the binary state of being one thing or the other and into the quantum state of being everything simultaneously. My guess is that it was our brain's adoption of quantum computing that raised us from being just another ape-like creature to being an ape with enhanced powers of intuition, understanding and curiosity. That curiosity presumably drove many of our ancient relatives to walk 'out of Africa' (or wherever), creating our Neanderthal cousins across the cold northern regions of Ice Age Europe and the Denisovans throughout Asia, from the cold mountains of Siberia and Tibet to the jungles of Southeast Asia. Our own ancestors, probably the ones we now call *Homo heidelbergensis* seem to have remained in Africa while evolution refined and expanded their mental and social capabilities as well as their striding gait, which improved their walking and running and made them adept at persistence hunting, running down their prey like a pack of wolves. When our ancestral *Homo sapiens* did come out of Africa themselves, they were just better, and more imaginative, more knowledgeable, at killing other animals for food. And, when they spread through Europe and Asia, our Neanderthal and Denisovan cousins found that when push came to shove, we were also better at killing Neanderthals and Denisovans when they got in our way. Fundamentally, that's what survival of the fittest means.

'Pay attention, please,' said Malik, bringing me out of my reverie. 'You are now loading the most recently calculated part of the quantum map showing the nose of the Starship after it was locked down.'

I paid attention, as requested, and began to turn the entire image of the Starship around in my mind, supplemented, of course, by Malik's memory banks. Because this is where the tables are turned; I am inside Malik's mind using his power of thought as an extension of my own. It's like picking up an impressively detailed model of a Starship in your two hands and examining it closely by turning it around with your hands, first this way, then that way. Again and again, until you have absorbed every incredible detail, and you know that model as intimately as you know your own body. It's tiring to do this. This model is heavy. It takes strength and sweat-drenching effort to heft it around like this. But I know that I must lift it because I must place it carefully into the place that Kat is preparing for it.

'And relax, Commodore,' Malik inserted into my highly focussed thoughts. 'Your rehearsal is completed. Time to link with Captain Katharina.'

I parked the memories I had just been making; they would come back to me later when I would put then on, like a pair of gloves, to lift that wonderful model into its next destination. I turned my attention to Kat instead.

'Hi, Boss, you OK,' Kat asked.

'Sure,' I replied. 'I've got my model sorted out and ready to go, but I forgot to say anything for Cliff.'

'No problem, Commodore,' said Malik. 'I vocalised your thoughts and paired them with broadcast-quality images of your mental visions and sent them to Mr Wright.'

'And it's bloody brilliant,' Cliff Wright messaged me enthusiastically.

'OK, so Kat, how far have you progressed?' I asked.

'I'm ready to go. I've done my introduction for Cliff and can start pulling my memories out right now.'

'Affirmative,' said Malik. 'Standby Starships. Standby studio. Cue Captain Clason for destination visualisation in five, four, three…'

'Thank you, Cliff,' Kat said. 'Hello again everybody, I have already explained the calculations we needed to complete to establish a safe destination location for Starship-101 alongside our flagship in orbit around Proxima-b. Now we have to build the quantum visualisation of that destination into which Tarvin will insert Starship-101. Here we go.'

I was, of course, sharing Kat's mind, as well as Malik's, and as Kat's mental visualisation of the destination location developed in her mind, I was streaming it into my memories. When I finally attempted the superposition, I needed to have the same 'down to the last quantum' understanding of this destination as Kat had developed.

'At the bottom of this image,' Kat's commentary went on, 'is the quantum-level visualisation of our flagship, which is 10-kilometre long, the same length as 101. There's no need to spend time building this from stern to prow, as Commodore Clason has just done for Starship-101 because we use this quantum map so often that our intimate appreciation of it is firmly embedded in our memories like the image of a favourite child.'

'Yay, go for it Kat,' I messaged to Kat's NeuroModem. 'I'm scriptwriter to the stars!'

'Well, it was such a cute simile, I just had to use it!' Kat messaged back, before continuing her commentary. 'I've already explained how we must be wary of possible influence of gravitational turbulence on the translocation of the 10-kilometres long Starship-101 and this image shows that the exact destination for Commodore Clason's quantum map of Starship-101 is in the middle of a 30-kilometre cube of empty space alongside our flagship. As I've mentioned, this is the safety margin we have calculated, or, rather, our local network of supercomputers has calculated. Let's give them a shoutout, shall we? The network comprised Malik, Westwood, Starship-101's Flight computer, and the Observatory and the near space traffic control computer on Proxima Home Waystation.'

'On behalf of my colleagues,' Malik messaged to Kat, 'thank you for that mention.'

While I absorbed her visualisation into my memories, Kat continued with her commentary, 'That cube of empty space is identified by eight mini-communications satellites placed at the corners of the cube that exchange laser ranging signals between themselves and the flagship to maintain their positioning. They are too small to see on the image at this resolution, so let me paint some emphasis on the lasers, just so that you can see the cube.'

And with that, all the edges of the cube appeared in Kat's visualisation emphasised with neon-green lines. 'That's a useful addition to my memories of this destination, can you make the lines flash on and off?' I messaged to Kat's NeuroModem. And flash they did, and I could carefully combine them with the images I had seen earlier into my memories of Kat's final quantum visualisation of this destination.

'There's one final thing that's needed to complete the translocation, and we all know what that is,' Kat's commentary continued, playing with her audience. 'Yes, it's 'the nudge' that causes the decoherence of the superposition and will bring Starship-101 back into the real world but now in orbit around Proxima-b. There's a ninth mini StarLink on one of the cube's edges. I'll paint it to flash red, otherwise you'll not be able to see it.'

And there it is, a flashing red light on the edge of the cube that was furthest from the flagship.

'This little thing will be in sleep mode until the superposition is established and then Commodore Clason will insert a string of data into the superposition that will wake up the StarLink to broadcast a signal to an even smaller transponder at the centre of the cube, which will then pulse with bright white light. This will be enough to nudge the superposition into decoherence with the probabilities favouring everything re-emerging together into the real world. And that, Cliff, completes this rehearsal.' That was Kat's final comment, but while she was saying this, she was streaming the actual nudge data, a memory trace of a long hexadecimal number, into my mindscape, which I took pains to store carefully.

Immediately, Cliff took over as TV presenter, smoothly saying that this completes the rehearsal and urging his audience to stay tuned because they don't have to wait long for the main event.

'It's certainly not long before twelve noon,' said Malik in private messages to me and Kat, 'How do you feel after that long rehearsal? Do either of you need a rest, we could afford to take 15 minutes out, but any longer and we'd have to delay the lift.'

'I'm OK as I am,' said Kat.

'And I'm happy to go with a 10-to-15-minute break,' I said. 'I think our preparations are in good shape. We need to get the job done and the sooner we get on with it, the better.'

'Good,' responded Malik. 'It's 11.23 now, do I have your permission to schedule initiation of the lift for 11.45 with a view for a 12-noon departure?'

'Affirmative.' From both Kat and me.

'Standby Starships. Standby studio,' said Malik. 'We intend to initiate final preparations for Starship-101 translocation to orbit at 11.45 a.m. standard star time, with a view for a 12-noon departure'.

'Copy that, Malik,' responded Lana, adding, 'Good luck, Boss. Good Luck Kat!'

I spent a few minutes flicking from channel to channel on the cutter's TV, most channels being CCTV images from various parts of the flagship. Most showed locked down compartments empty of any crew and the subdued notes of the chimes warning of imminent take-off played through their audio channels. But I caught sight of some movement at the end of one corridor and the camera closest to the movement revealed a handful of latecomers to the Crew Lounge as they expertly flew through the weightlessness, manoeuvring around the couches arrayed throughout the lounge with deft touches here and there, and a few fist-bumps and handclasps with friends already strapped down, to finally settle into their own couch.

Calmed by the sight of my crew being properly prepared, I took a few more deep breaths to load a bit more oxygen in my blood stream and was ready to go when Malik next spoke.

'Will Pilot and co-Pilot please signify their readiness to initiate the translocation of Starship-101 from landfall on Proxima-b to orbit of Proxima-b.'

'Pilot is ready,' I said.

'Co-pilot is ready,' Kat responded.

Malik replied, 'Captain Lana Mancot, is the TV studio online?'

'Affirmative, Malik, we are already broadcasting the rehearsal video, and will cut to the live feeds when you start the translocation.'

'Very well, then,' Malik intoned. 'Standby Starships. Standby studio. Cue initiate the translocation in five, four, three…'

On zero, Malik started feeding me the quantum map of Starship-101 we had created during the rehearsal. As he was only reminding me of a very recent memory trace, in much less time than before, the complete mental image of Starship-101's quantum waveform was in my brain as that impressively detailed model of a Starship. Rather than starting to examine this 'model' immediately I visualised it, I looked across to Kat's visualisation and asked, 'How's the destination developing?'

'30 seconds until it's ready to receive your superposition,' Kat reported.

'Malik, how are we doing for time?'

'It's approaching 11.58 a.m., Commodore.'

'OK, issue take-off warnings to both Starships and then count me down to noon.'

The subdued chimes, 'subdued' so they would be reassuring rather than alarming, of the two-minute take-off warnings echoed through the two Starships, and I was also aware of them over the cutter's intercom.

Malik's ten-second timing signals started to come through to my NeuroModem as I started taking hold of the quantum model of Starship-101. This thing was heavy. Very, very heavy. I was struggling and straining just to hold it just off the ground. Then Kat slotted the destination visualisation into my mindscape 'behind' the 'model' of 101 and with a final hugely sweaty effort I heaved Starship-101 into Kat's cube of empty space, where it seemed to rest with no further effort from me. Just as well, as I was almost completely exhausted by now. I scabbled around to pull the hex-number nudge out of my straining memory trace and, with what felt like a last despairing effort, thrust it into the quantum map of the destination.

Suddenly, my cutter's view screens, which had been displaying the dull red images of the surface of Proxima-b, displayed instead a black starfield with a weak red dwarf star off to the far left or port side of the image well beyond the comforting view of a modern Starship. Comforting, because on the screens showing what was beneath the cutter there was the looming bulk of another Starship. One of a very old design that looked more like an arrowhead, and a rather battered one at that.

I had left the flagship's CCTV tuned to the Crew Lounge and the sound of cheering came over the audio channel. And with that my exhausted brain finally realised: the lift had worked! I had got the thing that was looming at my right elbow into orbit!

'Nicely done, Boss. Welcome to orbit,' said Kat.

Before I could respond a host of other congratulatory messages poured into my NeuroModem, but all that I could say to Kat was 'I'm done in, Kat. Totally knackered, but I have discovered the nature of the effect of gravity on quantum maps and quantum models. It makes them backbreakingly bloody heavy!'

'Yes, Commodore,' Malik said. 'I could see that as you were dealing with it, and I think we could extract some relevant mathematics from my observations of your efforts and your neurological and physiological responses at the time. I would like to add my congratulations for a job well done.'

'Thanks, Mate,' I said, wearily. 'I need a good scrub down and some fresh fatigues. While I'm doing that, I have a list of things I'd like you to do for me. Will you fly the cutter back to the flagship and have it cleaned, serviced and refuelled? I'm planning to take it back down to Proxima-b. Also, please respond to all those congratulatory messages with a holding note saying 'thank you for your good wishes' but I'm too busy to respond personally at the moment. Then wake up Flight and get some engineering crews into Starship-101 with a mobile fusion reactor. I'm guessing that trying to restart 101's antique reactor may be more trouble than it's worth. When they've powered up the hulk, they can work with Flight and the Starship's own bots to check for damage and atmosphere integrity. And the last thing on my list is to rescue Lana's camera bot, he's called Bogie, from 101's control room, so he can video all this orbital activity. I don't think he's space-certified, so you might need to give him a tug to ride around in. Make sure he ends up in the flagship this evening; he can come back down to the planet's surface with me and Kat. Better copy this message to Kat so she knows what I'm up to.'

'Copy all that, Commodore. Willco.'

While Malik was attending to all these chores, I released myself from the Nav Couch and set it to 'deep clean' because I suspected it would start smelling rather used, rather quickly. I steered my weightless body to the galley, woke the steward and ordered some coffee and blueberry muffins, then floated through to my private bathroom. Showers in microgravity are about the least refreshing ways to get clean you can imagine. Without gravity water doesn't drain and mustn't be wasted, so you have to float yourself into a water-tight capsule and be cleaned by periodic jets of soap-and-water from nozzles placed all around you, and then suffer the indignity of a vacuum-driven water recovery cycle which finishes with gale like blasts of hot air from the jet nozzles which are supposed to dry every nook and crevice but add further indignities while they do so. Still, the system cleaned me up nicely and the pummelling of the water jets eased a lot of my aches and pains. Drifting into my stateroom I found fresh clothes laid out for me and a tray of coffee and muffins, and thoroughly enjoyed both.

The steward's performance impressed me now and, indeed, he had done so ever since Starship-101's Flight computer had assigned him to me. He responded positively when I asked if he'd like to stay permanently with me, I must admit I rather liked the idea of being looked after by an antique serving robot. I instructed him that when we next landed at the Proxima-b SpacePort he should report to Proxima Alpha's medical centre to have a q-bit upgrade fitted.

By this time the cutter's autopilot was manoeuvring the vessel into its docking bay in the side of the flagship, so I floated down to the main hatch to wait for the docking bay's airlocks to complete the attachment. When the hatch opened, I was engulfed by a crowd of well-wishers who 'just happened to be passing' and wanted to congratulate me on lifting Starship-101 into orbit and did it with fist-bumps, some full-on hand shaking and a few genuine hugs and a lot of vocal noise all mixed in with mutterings and murmurs from me of 'thanks', 'yes, it was a real effort this time' and 'well, you know, just doing my job'. The little crowd dispersed, floating off to their original destinations, leaving Kat floating there alone. This was the most special reunion and required the longest hug.

'Come on, Boss,' Kat said. 'You've got to come to the control room. Have we got something to show you!' And then, tired though I was, she launched me towards the corridor's travelator and we both grabbed a strap to be whisked off to the control room. Further conversation was not possible because we were now amongst the ship's strap-hanging commuters, so there were more people requiring an exchange of pleasantries, congratulations, acknowledgements, salutes even!

By the time we branched off to the control room entrance I was really feeling my extreme fatigue again and was keen to float straight in towards the reassuring sight of my number one Nav Couch. I settled onto the couch and allowed it to wrap its arms around me, pulling me out of weightlessness and into the soft comfort of its cushions. I closed my eyes.

'Yay, Boss. No time for naps now. Plug yourself into your couch life support and let it massage you back to life. You've got to see this now. You will never believe what a translocation looks like from the outside.' Kat said all this as she manoeuvred herself onto her own co-Pilots couch. I followed her advice and pressed my head onto the headrest to allow the couch to connect fully with my NeuroModem and when I felt the tickling of the nanoprobe connections through my skin I selected a nice gentle massage and revive program from the various 'subject recovery' options I was offered. Then I selected 'upright' for the couch and its recline was reduced as it turned into a chair. Still extremely comfortable, but now allowing me to see all the view screens in front of me. I was already feeling more attentive, less sleepy.

'OK,' I said, 'that lift totally exhausted me, but I'm back on the ball now, and my Nav Couch is working wonders. What have you got for me to see?'

'It's come from Lana, so she's going to show you. Lana, are you still on the line?'

'Affirmative, Kat,' Lana replied. 'But first, Boss, thanks for rescuing Bogie. He's scooting about up there getting some incredible footage of all the activity in orbit. Now, as you know, I put cameras all around 101 for the translocation, from the roof of the Westwood Restaurant, and all the way around the ship to its back end. In fact, I had all my OB cameras on the job. And because we had so many cameras recording the event, we've only had time so far to examine a very small fraction of the footage.'

'Before you go any further, Lana,' Kat interrupted. 'Why use so many cameras that will show the same thing? Isn't that a waste of resources?'

'Nah,' Lana replied quickly, 'there are hundreds of broadcast services in the Solar System that will fall over themselves to buy the rights to exclusive vids. And we have enough cameras to edit into hundreds of exclusive vids all with slightly different views of the same story. Now, my cameras were not the only ones in operation. When we were planning camera placements for this, Malik pointed out that the orbital mechanics he was working on should bring the flagship immediately above Starship-101 at the time of superposition, and,' she emphasised, 'the flagship is bristling with survey cameras operating with wavelengths from gamma rays to radio.'

'Some of which are mine!' Interrupted Jim Igwe, continuing, 'Sorry to interrupt, Boss, but I wanted to say you put on a great show back there! And I would also like Malik to share Lana's video feed with the vid screens down in engineering. We'd all like to see the footage that Lana got with our cameras.'

'That's alright with me,' Lana replied. 'Go ahead Malik, share the vids throughout the flagship. The camera Jim is talking about is a photogrammetry camera that his team have been using for topographic mapping of the surface of Proxima-b from which they then make models of the surface for their civil engineering projects. They've made a complete survey of the whole planet, but they've got a particularly detailed 3D model of Starship-101 and the surrounding settlement. And what's especially useful is that this is a wide angle as well as extremely high-resolution camera and it records a strip of ground that is 50-kilometres wide. So, bear that in mind when I show its images.' Lana paused slightly, while an image of the nose of Starship-101, bathed in the usual red twilight of Proxima-b came up on the control room's screen.

'This is the view from the roof of Westwood Restaurant. It's from just before noon as you can see from the timer clock in the image. The clock signal, incidentally, is the flagship's and is synchronised across all cameras. We're approaching noon, so watch what happens in the three seconds after noon.'

The seconds ticked by with the solid, red-lit metal nose of the Starship in the centre of the screen image. As the clock ticked to noon that solid, red-lit metal nose began to shimmer and become translucent. At noon plus one second the shimmering Starship also seemed to lift slightly, but unsteadily, from the ground. Then at noon plus two seconds the shimmering became quite violent, and at noon plus three seconds the entire thing just vanished! The camera image held steady but all that could be seen now was ten kilometres of unencumbered but clearly very squashed riverbank disappearing into the red dusky distance.

Several of the voice channels with which we were networking exploded into gasps of amazement and one of the unrecognised voices clearly said 'Wow, so that was a quantum translocation! Holy cow! What was making it shimmer?'

'I've seen it before, but it's still a complete surprise,' whispered Kat from the adjoining co-pilot's seat. And then louder, intended for the connected audience. 'But honestly, guys, you ain't seen nothing yet! Why don't you play the slo-mo shots, Lana? Before you hit them with the big one!'

'I will,' replied Lana. 'You've just seen the event at normal speed, but this observation was made with a high-speed camera so we can slow the action down quite drastically. Here's a repeat at normal speed.' And we had the chance to see the same astonishing event again.

'Now here's the clip from one second before noon to four seconds after noon at half speed'.

Another chance to see the same event, though the extension to four seconds after noon showed that when the Starship disappeared there was turmoil in the atmosphere as it swirled in to replace the ten-kilometre-long bulk that had just departed.

'And here's the same five seconds replayed at one-tenth speed,' Lana announced as she showed us the lengthier, slower version of the clip. The background audience that was patched into our network for these displays had been totally silent up to now but began to mutter as this clip was played past the noon time signal, and the mutterings grew into exclamations of amazement as the clip proceeded. The cause of this was that the slower speed revealed that what looked like a shimmering image at normal speed was an image that flickered on and off. In some frames Starship-101 was there, where it had landed so many years ago, then in the next set of frames it was not there and the empty riverbank stretched into the distance and the atmosphere was just starting to kick up some dust, and then 'splat' and the Starship was back in place.

Lana's voice came on the line again, 'Settle down, everyone, you don't need to get rowdy yet, we've still got more to show you. Remember, I told you this rooftop camera is a high-speed camera, and it was operating at full resolution and at 250 frames per second. Your tireless production crew at this TV studio have already examined the full set of 1,250 frames that make up the five-second clip you've just been watching and chosen this interesting set of individual frames to show you in sequence at a two-second frame rate in a repeating loop.'

The frames that came up on screen had been numbered, and the first five showed a perfectly solid Starship in view, the next set of five showed an empty riverbank. The Starship reappeared in frame number 11 but disappeared again in frame numbered 16. The loop of images remained empty until the Starship reappeared in frame 21 at which point the loop was recycled.

As Lana had suggested, this video added to the background noise of private conversations coming from her audience. Indeed, the audience was growing as more departments of the flagship joined the network. One voice came through the babble with a specific question, 'Hi Lana, before you carry on, and I hope you will show us more, but can you tell me if this video has a soundtrack?'

'Who that?' asked Lana.

'Oh, sorry. I'm Fred Bull. I'm a sound engineer, and it seems to me that if Starship-101 was coming and going on the planet every fiftieth of a second then it should have made 50 Hertz sound waves.'

'OK,' said Lana. 'The video does have a soundtrack, but we've been suppressing it because of the background noise from the settlers who were also on the restaurant's roof. I can't hear anything other than the background chatter, but here's a quick burst of it 20 seconds either side of noon.'

All I could hear on the audio tape were the 'oohs and aahs' vocalised by the people on the roof which were joined by vocal comments of anonymous voices in our current networked audience; 'I can't hear anything other than chatter', 'Neither can I but I can feel an unpleasant vibration in my chest when the ship is shimmering'.

'I can hear it,' Fred Bull declared, 'It's a steady tone which, as somebody said, coincides with when the Starship image shimmers at the normal frame rate. People vary greatly in their sensitivity to these very low frequency sounds. It doesn't sound exactly like a 50 Hertz sound tone to me, but Malik will be able to determine the exact frequency of the tone and that will tell you exactly the frequency of the Starship coming and going at this stage in the translocation.'

'Can you deal with that Malik?' I cut into the conversation. 'Do the frequency analysis and add the text from Fred Bull's comments and compose it into an official entry for the ship's log. And please do the same for Lana Mancot's video analysis in this session. I think the physicists back home are going to love all this.'

'Copy that, Commodore. Willco. Malik out'.

'Our astrophysicists love what Lana's got to show next, and the physicists back home will be astonished by it,' Kat added. 'Go for it, Lana, show us the orbital images before the Boss falls asleep!'

'Right,' said Lana. 'Settle down, crew. I need absolute silence for this. I have another five-second sequence of images from the orbiting photogrammetry camera on the flagship. The camera saves 30 frames per second, and the clip starts like the previous ones at one second before noon. I'll show the complete sequence at normal speed first, then at quarter-speed, and then I'll show a particularly interesting freeze frame. Try to contain your reaction until you see the freeze frame!'

Lana's sequence showed the whole of Starship-101 lying on the riverbank at the northern extremity of the settlement. The image was shot from quite a high altitude and we'd been told that these camera images covered a region of the planet's surface about 50 kilometres wide, so Starship-101 was a small object in the overall image despite its 10-kilometre length. Nevertheless, Starship-101 seemed, to me, to behave exactly as we had all seen in the earlier videos; as the clock ticked to noon the image of the landed Starship began to shimmer, the shimmering increased for a couple of seconds and then at noon plus three seconds the Starship completely disappeared. I hadn't seen anything different between these observations and the ones shown earlier. But a few restive noises came up from the audience as Lana was saying, 'Now I'll show you the quarter-speed slo-mo.'

'Hold on Lana,' Kat interrupted. 'Let's make things easier for the audience. Don't give all your attention to the behaviour of Starship-101, also check out the regions over towards the right-hand side of the image.'

'OK, Lana, roll 'em.'

And as the slo-mo rolled to noon and beyond, hundreds of anxious eyes, including mine, were torn away from the shimmering image of Starship-101 and towards the right-hand side of the image, which showed the largely unexplored ground over on the western bank of the river. And that's when the audience really started to react, because when Starship-101 started to shimmer, a second Starship began to shimmer way over on the western bank. It was a vessel we all recognised. It was our own flagship!

'And just to confirm your suspicions, everybody,' Lana shouted over the growing clamour. 'Here's the freeze frame.'

And there it was, a clearly recognisable, if slightly fuzzy, image of the flagship (!!) apparently nestling on the surface of Proxima-b about twenty or so kilometres due west of Starship-101. The noise from the crew reached new heights, the least demonstrative reaction was solid applause while the more hooligan element was shouting, whistling and banging whatever desk or table was at hand. Everybody knew that we were looking at a crucial observation about the nature of our trade, even if they knew little about quantum mechanics.

As the excitement continued to grow, Kat reached across from the co-Pilot's Nav Couch and took hold of my right arm. 'Quieten them down, will you, Boss? I have an explanatory note to add to this.'

'OK, PAY ATTENTION, CREW,' I said at maximum volume on the intercom using the controls on the arm of my Nav Couch. 'Settle down. Your navigator co-pilot Captain Katharina Clason wishes to share with you her explanation for what you're looking at. Show some respect and be quiet.'

As our network audience became more subdued, Kat started her explanation, 'If you watched our rehearsal of the translocation earlier this morning, and if you haven't seen it, you can stream it from the TV service of Proxima-b, we were concerned about the possible effects of local gravitational turbulence on the superposition stage of the lift. To cope with that possibility, we decided that a sufficient safety margin would be provided if we included in our destination quantum map a 30-kilometre cube of empty space alongside our flagship. And when I was describing this during the rehearsal, I created this visualisation.'

The screen image of Lana's freeze frame contracted to the bottom of the view screen and above it appeared Kat's visualisation from this morning.

'I should explain,' Kat continued, 'that the green lines have been painted on the image to show the laser range finders that define the edges of our cube of empty space. Now let's re-orient the visualisation and equalise the scales, so that we can overlay my theoretical visualisation onto Lana's freeze frame and see what we get. Go Lana.'

Kat's visualisation rotated at the top of the screen so that her image of the flagship was over on the right-hand side, and then slid down the screen while Lana's freeze frame expanded to fill the screen again beneath it. When the transformation was completed, the combined images showed that Kat's image of the flagship had merged exactly onto the image of the flagship shown in the freeze frame over on the right, while over on the left the freeze frame's image of Starship-101 was slap in the centre of the square of green-painted laser lines that defined the destination cube of empty space. The audience noise began to rise again, so Kat cut it off with authority, 'Shush now, don't get unruly yet. My interpretation of the images you have on screen is that, obviously, my visualisation shows MY quantum map of the destination we calculated for Starship-101. Lana's freeze frame shows the Starship-101 quantum map that the Boss was manipulating at the time to make the superposition PLUS my quantum map of the destination. Without my graphic superimposed there, you can't see any evidence of my quantum map in the freeze frame around Starship-101 because that part of my map is empty space. So, in my view, what you have in Lana's freeze frame is the first ever image of a quantum entanglement. It shows all the quanta involved in the superposition that brought Starship-101 into orbit. Do you want to add your comment here, Malik?'

'Yes, thank you Captain Clason,' replied Malik. 'I concur with Captain Clason's interpretation and merely commented when she first told me about it that the shimmering that was so obvious in the close-up views of Starship-101 between noon and noon plus three seconds might be due to the superposition showing alternate ends of the entanglement at a vibrating frequency that we can now determine thanks to Lieutenant Fred Bull's insight. I can't see any reason for such a quantum vibration, but I suggest that when the Starship shimmers out of view to the cameras, the cameras don't image anything in its place because the equivalent location in Captain Clason's quantum map is empty space. One other thing to remember, is that these observations you are discussing are all camera-recordings and the imaging circuits in those cameras use quantum mechanics to operate and this might influence what they record as an observation. Malik out.'

'Thank you, Malik. You've certainly silenced the audience!' said Kat, finishing with, 'OK crew. That's the full story, so far. You can get unruly now!' And they did.

Kat switched the two of us out of the discussion network and asked, 'How are you feeling, Boss? A seminar on quantum mechanics must be difficult to take after this morning's super-heavy workload!'

'I think I'm doing OK,' I replied. 'The couch massage has unknotted my muscles and life support has made me feel halfway human again, but I've not had any reason to move much yet! Before I do much else, though, Malik, will you convert all this discussion about the orbital camera observations into an official log entry in Lana's name with Kat's explanation as a separate log entry in her name, and your quantum vibration suggestion in your name.'

'Willco, Commodore.'

'Now, Kat, where do we go from here?' I asked. 'I feel duty bound to inspect our orbital activities while I'm in the flagship, though I still feel flaked out. I need to eat, and I'd really like to get my teeth into some real food rather than microgravity pouches.'

'In that case,' Kat replied, 'you'll be glad to hear that the brand-new go-to venue for fine dining at 1-G is up here and just a short ride away.'

'Really? You mean Lydia Connah has got the Proxima-b Home Waystation up and running already?' I asked, beginning to extricate myself from my Nav Couch's comforting embrace.

'Yes,' said Kat. 'Jim's orbital construction team decided to reverse the planned build programme and attach the rotating gravity 'ring' to the first cargo segment to be emptied, and then tug the whole thing into the waystation's final position. It meant that all the residential fitting out could be done together. This speeded up the build considerably and Lydia's been offering full catering for a couple of days. So, why don't we go there and celebrate with Lydia?'

'Yeah, that sounds like a plan, let's do that,' I said. 'And as soon as possible!'

'Malik, how is the cutter's service progressing? Can we use that boat for a trip to the Proxima Home Waystation?'

'Affirmative, Commodore,' Malik replied. 'You will find the cutter cleaned and refuelled in its parking bay. The camera bot known as Bogie has also reported to the parking bay. If you wish him to accompany you, I will inform him.'

'Oh yes, that's a good idea,' I responded. 'But you'd better message Lana about Bogie in case she's got other tasks for him. And message Lydia Connah about all this and book a table in her gravity ring as soon as possible for Kat and me.'

'Willco, Commodore. Malik out'

We retired to our respective bathrooms to freshen up and then took the travelator back to the cutter's docking bay, through more streams of commuters eager to press the flesh, briefly en passant, or shout congratulations. When we reached the docking bay, the camera bot, Bogie, was waiting for us. I checked that Lana hadn't tasked him with any other activity and then we all floated into the cutter. I suggested that Bogie log himself into the cutter's Wi-Fi system so that he could stream the output of the cutter's cameras into his memory and, as I didn't want to be bothered piloting the cutter, I set the autopilot to take us to the Proxima Home Waystation. Then Kat and I retired to the comfort of our respective Nav Couches to snooze our way through the journey.

Woken by the gentle chimes of the intercom warning of imminent docking with the waystation, we both floated into our bathrooms for a final freshening with a wet microgravity flannel followed by the drag of a brush through our crew-cut hair, and then we floated down to the cutter's airlock waiting for the docking crew to complete our connection. I messaged Bogie to report to the airlock.

'Have you been tasked for this visit, Bogie?'

'Affirmative, Commodore,' the robot replied. 'I have been tasked with following your orders.'

'Ah, that's nice and specific,' Kat commented. I ignored this and persisted with trying to direct the camera bot.

'Fine, so what I think you should concentrate on is that this is a first visit to this orbital residential facility so you film everything you might need for an infomercial to bring more people up to try this experience.'

'Willco, Commodore, can I ask questions?' Bogey asked.

'Certainly,' I said. 'But don't get too pushy.'

'Understood, Commodore.'

Captain Lydia Connah was waiting to welcome us as the robot crew opened the inner door of the station's airlock.

'Lydia, lovely to see you again,' I said as we hugged.

'Not seen you since the barbecue,' echoed Kat in another hug.

'Yes, I've been working my socks off up here while you two have been gallivanting around on Proxima-b,' Lydia retorted.

'So, tell us what you have here, for the benefit of the camera; we're planning to produce an infomercial,' I explained.

'OK, that sounds good, we'd like to offer our facilities to the locals from Proxima-b. Well, let's see. When your shuttle or space taxi arrives at Proxima Station, it will connect to us through one of our airlocks, and you will then come into this Transfer Lounge. This is the central of three Starship hull sections from which the facility is constructed. This section is not rotating because the functions carried out here, cargo transfers between space vehicles, space vehicle refuelling, repair docks, heavy mechanical workshops and the like, are all easier to do in microgravity, and they are all beneath this Transfer Lounge, which, in fact means they are further to the stern of this vessel. If you had a window seat as your transfer vehicle approached us, you will have noticed our third Starship section being attached to the station even further to the stern. When fully operational, that section will contain our main power plant, water storage and recycling, fuel manufacturing and atmosphere scrubbing and waste disposal facilities.' Lydia paused, smiling, and looking straight at Bogie's camera lens for a few seconds and then said 'Cut'.

'That was very professionally done, Di,' said Kat, appreciatively.

'Yes, I was well schooled by Lana's team a few days ago. They wanted me to do 'something to camera' to explain the new bright red 'star' in Proxima's sky that had appeared when the Starship sections were first assembled at this position.'

'You did it well,' I said. 'But we were snoozing as we approached the station, though hopefully, it was filmed. So, how about it, Bogie, did you record a video of the cutter's approach? And can we see it?' The camera bot spun round to face me, it was equipped with a set of gas thrusters that made him extremely agile in weightlessness.

'Affirmative to both questions, Commodore,' said Bogie, I can play back to my camera's view screen or cast it to viewscreens in this lounge.'

'Let's see it on the lounge viewscreens but play it faster than normal speed.'

'Willco, Commodore; this is 5-times normal.'

The surrounding screens lit up with a bright red image of the three Starship sections Lydia had described, as their polished metal skins mirrored their illumination by the red dwarf, Proxima-Centauri, which was out of sight somewhere above us. The rotation of the nose section could just about be made out, though you had to stare at it for quite a few seconds to convince yourself of the rotation of that part of the hull. The real giveaway was that the several bands of observation windows and observation blisters either twinkled in the starlight or emitted the white light of their interiors. Immediately astern of the rotating section, the stationary hull was pockmarked with the variously-sized outer airlock doors of docking and loading bays, all fringed with pinpoints of light to identify themselves and guide incoming vessels to safe attachment. It looked like a miniature starfield. And then there was the stern section, twice the length of its adjoining section and surrounded by service ships, cargo shuttles and brightly lit construction teams.

'Wow!' I said. 'That's a brilliantly impressive approach!'

'Yeah,' whispered Lydia. 'I've been living inside it for so long, I just wasn't aware that it looked so good. Last time I approached it, it was basically a junk yard of empty cargo units.'

'You know, Di, the only way you could improve that view is to have 'Proxima Station' in gigantic letters written out in bright white lights across the non-rotating sections,' said Kat, adding, 'What do you think, Boss?'

'Yes, I think that's essential,' I said. 'Malik, will you confirm that idea with Lydia and Jim? And you might drop the hint that the designers could consider tuneable LEDs so that the colours can be varied.'

'And, Malik,' Kat broke in, 'when the design's been finalised, put the whole design package together as a standardised ID-logo to be used for all the other waystations on the route to Proxima.'

'Copy all that. Willco. Malik out.'

'So, the approach is already great and will get even better,' I said. 'And this Transfer Lounge is up at the same standard.'

'Glad you think so,' Lydia replied, then turned to the camera bot again. 'OK Bogie, is that your name?' The camera bobbed up and down. 'Let's have a piece to camera about this Transfer Lounge with me hovering beside this check-in desk. In one, two, three... As we expect that many of our visitors will be inexperienced in microgravity, this is essentially a 'soft play' area. We have teams of personal AI-robot guides scattered through the volume of the lounge to offer help to those who are evidently floundering. We don't expect transit passengers to spend much time here unless they do want to play. The evidence from similar transit stations in the Solar System is that most incoming passengers will go directly to their shuttles to take them down to the surface of Proxima-b, and the circulating robot guides can tow them to the appropriate airlocks in that case. Most outgoing passengers will do the same if their Starships are preparing for departure. Outgoing passengers who must wait any length of time for departure will most likely prefer to go directly to the bars, restaurants and viewing areas in our rotating artificial gravity ring. They will find travelators that will take them there, running from the check-in desks beside each airlock.' Pause, smiling at the camera, and 'Cut'. Turning to Kat and me, Lydia said 'So, let's grab a travelator strap and find some gravity, Malik told me you were missing it, Boss.'

'I certainly am,' I admitted. 'It's shameful for a Starship pilot to admit it, but I've become a real planet-hugger after only a few days on Proxima-b.'

'Maybe you're getting too old and past being a Starship pilot,' Kat commented, unkindly, but grinning at me.

'Thanks for the caring reassurance,' I responded. 'Ask Harden if he feels he's past it and see what sort of reply you get!'

'Well, though I've not spent as much time on the surface as Tarvin,' said Kat, 'I must agree that it's very nice to be down there. But we shouldn't be the ones complaining when you've not had the planetside opportunity yet!'

'Oh, I understand,' Lydia replied. 'I really enjoyed the short time I spent down there at the barbecue, and that's one reason why I twisted the arms of the installation crews to fit the gravity ring first.'

'Jim told me,' said Kat, 'that it was a decision about efficiency because the outfitting crews could then work on both sections of the build at the same time.'

'Oh, good,' said Lydia, smiling. 'That's just what I wanted him to believe!'

The travelator was slower than the ones in the flagship and while we were talking it had taken us past some other floors at each of which Bogie detached himself, made a quick photographic circuit of the floor we were passing using his gas jet thrusters, and rejoined us. Lydia explained that these floors housed the station's traffic control quantum computer, which was named Proxima Home. At the moment, traffic control used a comms satellite temporarily rigged to the side of this section of the station. The comms satellite will be fitted to the stern of the third Starship section when that is finally fixed in place.

The travelator took us across the next ceiling to the centre of the vessel and then through a wide, well-lit, central tunnel where the travelator terminated by turning back on itself so that the hanging straps could continue their 'continuous loop' journey back to the transfer lounge. Lydia allowed her strap to go on its way and indicated for us to do the same as we approached her, and we ended up hovering together at the end of the tunnel in a combined hug.

'Bogie, we're about to enter the artificial gravity section so let's have another bit to camera about this area. Ready?' Asked Lydia.

'Affirmative, Captain Connah,' Bogie replied as he jetted himself away from our huddle and zoomed his camera lens on Lydia.

'Piece to camera about the end of the travelator ride from the Transfer Lounge at the travelator exchange at the entrance to our artificial gravity section,' Lydia announced, 'In one, two, three… This is the travelator exchange at the entrance to our artificial gravity section. As you can see, we are still in microgravity, but if you look at the ceiling you can just make out that where the Transfer Lounge travelator turns back the ceiling is rotating another travelator and its straps towards you. Grab one of those straps and it will take you through one of the four passageways that spiral down this wall towards the Earth-gravity region at the hull of the station. You don't have to worry about the speed of rotation because it's only two revolutions per minute, and you don't have to worry about which of the four passageways you use because they all lead to the same place; the inside of the hull of the rotating section. As the travelator takes you down towards the hull you will begin to feel the 'downward' pull of gravity and as soon as you are comfortable with that, if you don't like strap-hanging, you can drop down from the travelator to the passage floor and continue downwards on foot, or using the moving walkway if you prefer.' Smile, count to three and then say 'Cut'.

'OK, let's grab a strap going down,' Lydia said, turning away from the camera and looking at Kat and me. That's what we did, and as we travelled, we began to feel the effects of the artificial gravity imparted by the centrifugal effects of the rotating cylinder we were in. The camera boy, Bogie, was following up behind us filming our progress. Lydia called back to him 'Bogie, record this as a potential voice-over for this little trip. Voice-over for travelator down to hull, in one, two, three… The decoration of the walls of this passageway indicates the level of ambient gravity. At the moment it's still showing a star field, indicating we are still in a microgravity environment, but soon the walls will be decorated with images of the surface of Earth's Moon this will indicate that we are in a region where the gravity is about 17% that at Earth's surface. Passengers who live on the Moon and would be more comfortable at Moon-gravity can drop off the travelator here, where they will find bars, restaurants and short-term accommodation cabins. Similarly, a little further down the walls are decorated with images of the surface of Mars to indicate the Mars gravity zone, where gravity is about 38% that at Earth's surface. And, again, residents of Mars may find greater comfort in the bars, restaurants and cabins in this zone.' End with a smile in the voice, count three then 'Cut'.

'I'm glad we brought that damn camera bot,' said Kat. 'We're getting a great commentary while we're strap-hanging!'

'I'm glad you brought it, too,' said Lydia. 'I won't have to keep saying the same things to all my visitors. I'll just sit them in front of the video.'

'Or message them the video in advance?' said Kat.

I said that 'I think Daisy Warrington's team in the TV studio will be only too willing to make you a documentary style infomercial for the local TV that will have lots of the settlers wanting to come up here for an away-day or two and being willing to test out your facilities for you.'

'Well, I'd like that, but what do I charge them, and how do they pay?' asked Lydia.

'You can't charge them; you have to consider it all part of Interstellar Haulage Company business. Proxima-b doesn't have a cash economy at the moment, basically the community works by bartering its various activities. Merv and his Council cronies are working on establishing the necessary institutions to establish a working cash economy. They need it because they'll be paid a Starship-load of money when we get Starship-101 back to the Solar System. They'll also need it for when my brother Harden comes up here, as he'll be bringing all sorts of well-heeled people who expect to pay for the sorts of services they expect to extract from the Proxima-locals. And you need to be connected into Proxima's developing cash economy for the same reasons.' I paused because I had to adjust my grip on the travelator strap. The passageway murals of Mars were disappearing behind us as I resumed my little speech to ask a different question, 'I'm beginning to weigh heavily on my wrist here, so can we drop off the travelator and walk the rest of the way?' And we did, and I suggested to Bogie that he stride on ahead of us to film our arrival in the Earth-gravity zone and then go exploring throughout the zone.

'Ah, gravity,' I said gratefully. 'I've been longing for that feeling since I tried lifting a few million tons of Starship off the ground earlier on today. Now, I really need it to be accompanied by a large mug of freshly brewed coffee.'

'Keep on walking, Boss,' said Kat. 'I see salvation ahead in the form of an enormous lounge area stuffed with restaurants and coffee bars.'

'Before, I lose the thread of what you've just been saying, Boss,' Lydia said, 'how do I get connected to Proxima's emerging cash economy?'

'Message the town treasurer, Clint Stapleton. Tell him what we've just been talking about, including the part about free trips up to this station in return for testing its facilities, and he'll be keen to help.'

'Clint's also got a brood of teenage kids who would be delighted to test your facilities to destruction!' Kat added.

'Really,' I said. 'I didn't know that.'

'Yes, Emma told me,' Kat explained. 'They're members of Emma's fowl mafia.'

'How are you spelling that?' asked Lydia, while she guided us into the nearest coffee bar.

'Oh, definitely f-o-w-l. The teenage boys are besotted with Emma, and the teenage girls are besotted with Emma's various ducklings and chicks,' replied Kat. 'In a few years' time, this place will be a planet of poultry farmers and the river delta down there will be covered in chickens and ducks.'

'Could be worse,' said Lydia. 'Emma's already supplied our kitchens with freshly laid eggs and they're first class.' Lydia continued, 'Now, I suggest we dine in Café Claudius here, it's a short order café but excellent quality and we'll get served more quickly than in one of the fine-dining places, that OK?'

'Suits me,' I said. 'I'll have a cappuccino and I'm looking seriously at their panini menu; mozzarella and tomato and a brie and bacon panini will do me nicely.'

'What were you saying a few minutes ago about weighing heavily on the travelator strap?' Inquired Kat.

'Leave off, Kat,' I said. 'You're beginning to sound like Malik.'

'Yes, Commodore,' Malik broke into the conversation, 'I rather missed that opportunity, didn't I?'

'By the way,' said Kat, wiping the milk foam from her lip, 'before we lose yet another opportunity, these plans we were talking about to have a standardised ID name put up in lights on the sides of the station; well, I think you should make sure that Interstellar Haulage Company is identified as the provider of the facility that's being lit up in LED lights.'

'Good thought,' I said, through the first bite of my mozzarella and tomato. 'Got that, Malik?'

'Affirmative, Commodore. Enjoy your two paninis, Commodore. Malik out.'

From where we were sitting, just outside Café Claudius, we could see the whole of this part of the huge gravity ring, the floor curving up towards the vertical about 400 metres away displayed the adjoining section in plan view. The most striking sight in that plan view directly ahead of us was a full-size athletics track with a football match in progress on the field laid out in the centre of the track oval. There were also a fair number of runners either jogging or sprinting around the track. All the players being oblivious to us looking down on them.

'It's a hell of a big space, Di,' I said, diving into my second panini.

'Yes,' Lydia replied. 'Simple geometry says it's an estate of more than 150 hectares, that's over one and a half million square metres, and it looks fairly sparsely occupied at the moment. As we get more traffic to and from the Solar System, Proxima Home Station will get busier and with a greater range of facilities and franchises. But remember that the main aim with these waystations, including termini like this one, is to give the crews of the transporting Starships access to 'the great outdoors', at least in simulated form, at a gravity level that's most comfortable to them, and for a length of time that covers the turn-around time for the Starships in which they spend the rest of their lives.'

'So that's not real grass out there?' Asked Kat.

'Oh, no,' Lydia replied. 'Not on my watch! The grass, the trees, the bushes, the flowers; they are all artificial. That's always the case except in the inner Solar System. And it's especially important here because Proxima-b has such a primitive ecosystem. We can't risk contaminating it with plants that are millions of years advanced in evolution. And, of course, there are no animals.'

'Except for Emma's ducks and chickens,' said Kat.

'Why aye,' Lydia responded. 'But I had no part in the decision to allow that.'

'You don't approve?' I asked.

'Not at all,' said Lydia, emphatically. 'Because it's not just ducks and chickens. You said it yourself, Boss, at the barbecue, and I made note of it so I can quote you directly, 'our planners chose sheep, cattle and pigs that thrive in salt marshes and on rocky coastlines on Earth which can, we hope, make best use of Proxima-b's vegetation' to which Emma added a small herd of goats and then carp, catfish, trout, and tilapia.'

'Don't get me wrong,' Lydia continued. 'Emma's a lovely girl, but she is training Proxima-born locals who have never seen a live animal before, to take over the management of her smallholdings, poultry farms, piggeries and fish farms when she is long gone back to the Solar System. And all of these small farms are only a broken fence, or a gate accidentally left open away from an ecological disaster for the natural ecosystem of Proxima-b. And I'd say the same for Ilsa's horticultural activities for that matter. She is cultivating the type of plant that's unlikely to evolve naturally on Proxima-b for hundreds of millions of years. Plenty of scope in that time for even the best contamination precautions to fail.'

'Sure, but you can't deny that the immediate effects on the settlers have been extremely positive,' I said. 'They've been woken up to a range of self-help activities that greatly improve their general health as well as producing fresh foods for themselves.'

'True,' Lydia agreed. 'But Kat referred to 'Emma's fowl mafia' only a little while ago and suggested the river delta near Proxima Alpha will be covered in chickens and ducks very soon. Unfortunately, every new small farm, no matter how beneficial its livestock might be to humans on Proxima-b, is an escape waiting to happen, and we have brought animals from Earth which can make best use of Proxima-b's vegetation'.

'I suppose,' I mused, 'that 'humanising' planets is all part of the way humanity's expansion to new planets has been carried out so far and is likely to be intensified to include our expansion to the stars. Geoff Moore was saying something similar to me a few days back. ethical planetary colonisation is what he called it. Maybe you should talk it over with him. We are just fulfilling a contract that doesn't say anything about safeguarding the biodiversity of Proxima. If we carry on doing that, we can't do more than go with the flow and then what will happen, will happen. But if we can work out a way to moderate the worst effects of well-intentioned human activities then we should try to put them into effect. So, you talk to Geoff about it and see what Ilsa and Emma have to say about it. Now, put that to one side and tell me what you already have here, and what you need in addition.'

'OK, we've already installed several major facilities you can't see from here,' Lydia responded. 'That athletics track you can see in front of us is an Olympic standard track; at the moment you can see a few joggers and runners on the track and a soccer match going on, which, if I remember correctly, is a needle match between the flagship's IT engineers and the power station engineers.'

Lydia twisted around in her chair and pointed back towards the café, saying, 'In the next section over, which is out of sight above and behind Café Claudius, we have an 18-hole golf course, and then in the next section, that's the one immediately behind the café, we've got about 35 hectares of hill-walking and forest-trekking 'wilderness', all the plants are artificial, of course, but it's all very realistic, and the streams are real enough, and there's a lake big enough for some water sports, including a bit of gentle surfing with a wave-making machine. I'm hoping that Jim's team will build us an indoor ski slope between the golf and trekking areas.'

'And, of course,' Lydia continued after a slight pause, 'we have our viewing windows arranged across the estate, some rectangular, some circular. The circular ones are the blisters you could see on the outside of the habitat as your cutter came into dock. On the inside, here, these are the 'infinity pools' people can sit around watching the universe pass by, staring out into space or down onto the surface of Proxima-b as the habitat rotates.'

'And scattered about all these major facilities are various sorts of accommodation; club houses and training facilities for the various sports, and hundreds of log cabins, cottages, bothies, alpine lodges, even beach huts and all within an easy walk of appropriate catering services. You name a style of accommodation and we've probably got a replica of it somewhere on the estate. The section we are in now, is a family-oriented section. Lots of open spaces for kids to run off steam in safety, lots of eateries and a variety of rest areas for parents to relax in, sitting, lying, snoozing, or picnicking. Plenty of space for all sorts of play activities including 'use-it-and-leave-it' pedal cycles, scooters, and motorised trikes. And throughout the whole estate, regular installations of 'comfort station' buildings with bathrooms and showers as well as stay 'just-for-the-day' beach hut style chalets. The only thing we lack is a full clientele.'

'I think I should ask Malik to convert what you've just been saying into a text document that you could use as advertising,' I said. 'Have you got that Malik?'

'Affirmative, Commodore.'

'Then forward the text to Captain Lydia Connah for her to edit and offer to Lana Mancot.'

'Willco, Malik out.'

'That'll be useful,' Lydia resumed. 'You also asked what I needed in addition to all this. Well, the most important thing I'm lacking is a general manager for this habitat from among the native settlers. I'm only here to set the thing up because I've done it before elsewhere. It's a Proxima-b facility and they'll have to run it when I return home. I've got a Chief Traffic Controller in training, but

I met him at the barbecue, and I've not been down to the settlement since then. So, I have no candidates for a habitat general manager.'

'We will make that a priority, then,' Kat said. 'We're planning to return to Proxima Alpha in a short while, so we'll ask around.'

'Presumably,' I started, 'the ideal candidate would have some experience of the hospitality industries, and the person that comes to mind is Madge Clarkson.'

'I don't think Madge would consider the job,' said Kat. 'She's so happy managing the restaurant. But she does have two daughters who work with her in the canteen and restaurant. One of them might be interested.'

'We can only ask,' I said sagely. 'And I think we should start asking about making a move towards returning to the surface. But first, Di, you mentioned comfort stations with bathrooms and showers. And I need a long shower in Earth-normal gravity. Lead me to it!'

'And me,' cried Kat.

'That's easy,' replied Lydia. 'There's a comfort block just over there. And if you think you can make your own way back to the Transfer Lounge, I'll leave you to it and start working on that advertising copy.'

'Between the two of us,' replied Kat, 'I think we can navigate back to our cutter!'

So, we said our farewells to Lydia and walked over to the comfort block. Before going in I messaged the camera bot, Bogie, and instructed him to meet us in the Transfer Lounge in 30 minutes. His response was over excited 'I've got some great videos. I've filmed a football match, some people playing golf, and now I'm in a forest walking beside a mountain stream. It's all very visual!'

'I'm glad to hear it, Bogie,' I replied. 'Now, you see your way clear to being at the cutter's check-in desk in 30 minutes.'

'Copy that, Commodore. Geronimo!' was the response, so I just had to add 'Here's looking at you, kid.'

The bathroom units were sumptuously appointed, warm and cosy with lots of huge fluffy towels. They even had supplies of laundered fatigues, so after drying off, I swapped my rank badges to a fresh set of fatigues so that I could re-emerge sparkling clean through and through, as well as thoroughly refreshed.

Kat was waiting for me at a table outside Café Claudius drinking another coffee, so I went over to the counter to order for myself. Kat drained her cup and plonked it down on the table as she rose to her feet.

'If you're still feeling exhausted, Boss,' she said, 'we should be getting back to the cutter right now. We can't dawdle here if we want to get back to the SpacePort in reasonable time.'

And she was right. Cleaned and refreshed I might be, but I was still battling tiredness.

'You'd better make that a coffee-to-go,' I said to the barista-bot. 'And put it into a microgravity bulb so I can drink while strap-hanging.'

We retraced our steps to the passageway through which we had 'descended' to the gravity zone and used the 'upwards' moving walkway until we began to feel so light on our feet that we could reach up and transfer to a travelator strap to float the rest of the way, through the travelator exchange, and on towards the Transfer Lounge. We chatted as we floated, and Kat raised an interesting question about the name of the flagship.

'Why is it called flagship?' she asked.

'Because it's got the Clason family armorial shield painted on its nose,' I said. 'A rampant gold lion on a red shield. In olden days, when knights were knights and battles were hand-to-hand, a flag with a red shield bearing a rampant gold lion would have been the rallying place for the knights and yeomen who were fighting with the family.'

'That's all very nice and traditional, and war-like, but how many people get to see the nose of the ship now? Ever?' Kat replied.

'So,' I challenged, 'do you have an alternative name?'

'Yes,' she said. 'It came into my mind the first time I saw the satellite camera image of this morning's entanglement. You know, the one that shows Starship-101 still on the ground, and a slightly fuzzy image of the flagship on the surface of Proxima-b about twenty kilometres due west? Well, the name that came to mind was Pink Ghost.'

'Pink Ghost? Yes, I could live with that,' I said. 'The family shield could remain as the company logo if the ship had a different name. What's the name of Harden's ship?'

'I've only ever heard him refer to it as flagship,' Kat replied.

'Well, that settles it,' I said. 'If Interstellar Haulage is going to build a fleet of interstellar Starships, they'll all need different names. I think you've started something here, Kat! Yay, Malik, how do we change the name of a Starship?'

'It's entirely a matter for the company's senior management,' Malik responded. 'When the ship has been rechristened, the new name simply has to be notified to the appropriate Solar System authorities. Before going that far, though, you might like to ask for the opinion of the crew.'

'Yeah, I guess so. We need to organise a meeting of all staff to decide about the timetable for our return home with Starship-101. Can you put that into effect, Malik?'

'Certainly, Commodore. When would you like to call the staff meeting?'

'Oh, I don't know,' I said. 'I feel like I could sleep for a week, so how about the day after tomorrow?' I looked at Kat enquiringly and she nodded, so I continued, 'Yeah, that's OK with Kat, so that's what we'll do.'

'Affirmative, Commodore, Malik out.'

And with that the travellator started to take us down towards our check-in desk in the Transfer Lounge, where Bogie was waiting for us, and filming our gentle progress.

We floated through the airlocks the departure crews opened for us, and into the security of our own travelling home. Kat went straight to her co-Pilot's Nav Couch and started the business of making our intentions known to traffic control. I instructed Bogie to resume his recording of images from the cutter's cameras so that he could complete his account of this visit with videos of our descent to the Proxima-b SpacePort, then I sought the comfort of my own Nav Couch.

'Do you want to fly us down?' asked Kat.

'No. I want to sleep. So, let's leave it to the autopilot,' I replied.

'Proxima Home Traffic Control, Commodore's Cutter requesting departure slot leaving Proxima Home Waystation and autopilot flight plan to Proxima-b SpacePort,' Kat announced.

'Commodore's Cutter, Proxima Home Traffic Control, confirming flight plan laid into your autopilot. We have very little traffic in our orbit, your detachment from Proxima Home Waystation is approved. Depart in your own time.'

To the accompaniment of the clanging and hissing of our detachment from Proxima Home, I snuggled into the cushions of my Nav Couch but remembered to pass instructions to our two robots.

'Yay, steward. When we land and park up, we will not need your services, so you can report to the med centre for q-bit upgrade anytime you like. Bogie, the same, when we land you are released from my service and can return to the TV studios. Neither of you needs to wake us up; but Malik, don't let us sleep later than 9 a.m.'

With that done, I forced my head back into the headrest to make full contact with the life support system, wished Kat a warm goodnight and surrendered to the deep sleep I had been denied all afternoon.

Day 7

Our Nav Couches woke us on the dot at 9 a.m. and by 9.30 I had surfaced to full wakefulness and switched the couch to its chair form and was thinking seriously about breakfast. By this time Kat, of course, was just coming out of her own bathroom, already showered, and attaching her rank badges to her fresh fatigues.

'Good morning, Boss,' she called out as she walked into the galley. 'The steward put on a fresh brew of coffee before he left for the medical centre; d'you want a cup.'

'Yes please,' I responded, still yawning. 'That's why I want to keep that steward,' I added. 'He's got real old-fashioned thoughtfulness built into him. Much more caring than the bots on the flagship.'

'Oh, so, you feel old enough for a geriatric-care robot do you, like the one you assigned to Tom Fraser?' She grinned as she handed me a steaming mug of coffee.

'I certainly did yesterday afternoon, Kat. That lift really took it out of me. So much so that it was a toss-up between calling for a caring bot, an undertaker bot, or a cryosleep resuscitator.'

'Better today, are you?'

'Yes, I'm feeling fine,' I said.

'Well, you look pretty awful,' she said decisively. 'And you need a shave and a general tidy-up. You get yourself sorted out before you follow me into Proxima Alpha.'

'I'm going to take a trike to the TV station to talk to Lana. I want to see Bogie's video of the cutter's landing of last night. Our own record of the flight plan we were given indicates we were put on the same glide-track as Starship-101's de-orbit for landing. I'm sorry to have slept through that!'

'Yes, I agree. Though I'm glad to have slept, I also regret missing out on living that descent myself. The Flight computer's simulation of Billy Westwood's landing of 101 was quite an experience. And, you know, Bogie was the camera bot who recorded Flight's simulation of the landing of 101, as well as ours last night. He should be able to match the two descents side by side on the same screen. Lana could make a number of interesting programmes around that,' I said. 'And it does sound ironically fitting. We dragged the thing back into orbit using this century's space technology, and then we had to use last century's technology to get back on the ground ourselves!'

'Right, I'll remind Lana about all that. I also want to ask her for some cleaned up 'Pink Ghost' images I can use to support my idea for renaming the flagship. Which brings me to ask if and when, in my co-pilot's capacity as secretary of the flagship's staff meeting, you want me to call the next staff meeting?' Kat asked.

'We need to work out a timetable for returning Starship-101 to the Solar System,' I replied. 'And as the settlers will not get paid for it until we get it there, I'd say the sooner we return, the better. Why, don't we aim for a meeting at midday tomorrow? Make it a general staff meeting on Zoom by NeuroModem and say it's to discuss the timetable for our return to the Solar System so its mandatory for all Starship operations managers as well as on-planet contract fulfilment managers.'

'To which I could add,' said Kat, 'that I will raise an AOB suggesting a change of name for the flagship, so any and all with a view or opinion about that should contribute.'

'Yeah, that should do,' I agreed. 'With the usual stuff about asking for any other agenda items, and the minutes of the last meeting being taken as read because they can stream them from Malik.'

'Sure, but they should remember the last staff meeting!' Kat protested. 'It was held just before we left Oort Station, which was only just over two weeks ago!'

'All the more reason to leave it to the staff to chase Malik about it,' I replied. 'As far as my memory goes, those minutes were just a list of what we'd be doing on the way here and when we got here. They could form a checklist for our departure.'

'OK, I'll look into that,' said Kat. 'We certainly need to have reports from space engineering about how the structure of Spaceship-101 is holding up to being in space once again.'

'That should be top of the agenda,' I said. 'And must be accompanied by an assessment from the Flight computer. He's the only intelligence around that's experienced 101 in space before now!'

'OK,' Kat concluded, finishing off her coffee and standing up from her perch on the co-Pilot's chair. 'I'm off to grab a trike; let's meet later in the Westwood Canteen.'

That was fine with me, I need breakfast. As Kat left the cutter, I dived into my bathroom for a shave, shower and fresh clothes. Later, on the ride into town, people still went out of their way to wave and shout friendly greetings to me, which turned it into an almost triumphal ride. It made all of yesterday's efforts worthwhile. And as I neared the canteen corner, I saw for the first time the effect of yesterday's efforts on the local environment. No more the beached whale of a Starship looming over the settlement, but a ten-kilometre view along the riverbank that continued straight on to the mountains at the northern terminator with the most distant peaks on the dark side outlined in the red starlight reflected by their highest ice-covered slopes. It is Proxima-b, after all. Illuminated by a pale red dwarf star. So, the sight before me is an image painted in shades of red twilight. Magical. I had to stop the trike to admire it. The river snaked sharply to my right in the far distance. This, I knew, had been close to the tail of Starship-101, so it must be the full ten kilometres away from my present vantage point. Eye-strainingly difficult to see anything clearly in this twilight, but the bend in the riverbank seemed to have a bright red outline that ended in a cluster of bright white pinpoints of light. It was so indistinct to the naked eye that I asked Malik to help.

'Malik, can you show me what's going on out there near the bend in the river?'

'Certainly, Commodore.' And, using the magic of the NeuroModem, he magnified the image I was seeing, and I recognised a large construction machine reinforcing the riverbank with concrete slabs and gabions. Malik explained 'It's the first stage in stabilising the riverbank prior to construction of the promenade and roadway. The teams you see here started well away from the settlement to minimise disturbance as they continued working overnight, as usual. There's another team close behind your current position that are moving in to start work on the riverbank near the Westwood Restaurant.'

And sure enough, a multipurpose tracked excavator, all folded arms and big grab attachments trundled past me, accompanied by a cargo truck filled with concrete slabs and stone-filled gabions and a truckload of constructor bots, all heading towards the place where the nose of Starship-101 once rested.

I kicked the trike back into life and overtook this convoy to get into the canteen and escape whatever dust and noise this team was planning to raise. Madge was on hand for a full-on supply of hugs and kisses and lots of appreciation as I walked through the door.

Eventually, I found my way to the table in front of the TV screen that I'd used when I was last here, ordered a satisfyingly large breakfast and sat down with a large mug of coffee to watch the TV while I waited for Kat.

The TV was showing an edited repeat of 'Tarvin the Bold's historic lift of Starship-101 into orbit' and reminded me that I should check in with 101's Flight computer to find out what shape the hulk was in.

'Malik, is 101's Flight computer up and running again yet? And can you patch me through to it,' I asked.

'Affirmative, Commodore. Flight is on the line. Malik out.'

'Yay, Flight. How are things with you?'

'Very positive, Commodore,' Flight replied. 'I now have a replacement power source. It's far cleaner than my original fusion reactor, which has been switched off permanently and is being decontaminated. I have just been discussing this with Captain Igwe. Why don't we bring him into this conversation?'

'Sure thing. Hi Jim,' I said. 'There was no saving the old reactor, then?'

'Morning, Boss,' Jim replied. 'Nah, too much corrosion in the cooling circuits and too expensive to replace them. More effective to install one of our mobile reactors and close down the old one completely. It's a very old design and there's some radioactive waste caused by high-energy neutrons impacting the walls of the plasma vessel. Our bots can make a start on cleaning this out to make the reactor 'visitor friendly' when the ship becomes a museum.'

'You're happy with all this are you, Flight,' I asked.

'Affirmative.'

'Any structural damage caused by the lift into orbit?'

'None that I can detect,' Flight reported.

'Ditto that,' said Jim. 'My teams have crawled into every nook and cranny and every compartment is airtight. It's only the age of the structure that precludes a human travel space-readiness certification.'

'That's good news,' I said. 'So, am I right to conclude that Starship-101 is fit to travel back to the Solar System?'

'Definitely,' Jim replied. 'The Starship surveyors in my team will be signing 101 off with a 'without human crew' space-ready certificate. I take it you're asking about this because of the call for a staff meeting that Kat's just issued. And if that's the case, my opinion is that Starship-101 can go any time you like. We've placed our own sensors in the vessel so we can monitor it throughout the journey.'

Madge had placed a wonderful plate of food in front of me at the start of this conversation and I had been eating morsels from it as the discussion proceeded.

'And is that OK with you, Flight?' I asked.

'Affirmative, Commodore,' Flight responded.

'Then that's what I will report to the staff meeting. Thank you both for that report of the status of Starship-101. Tarvin out.'

I got back to my breakfast; it was getting later and later! And then it all started to happen again. Malik messaged me to deliver Kat's call for the staff meeting, so I filed that as a priority into my to-do memory trace, and then Kat herself arrived and started happily shouting greetings to Madge across the canteen before sitting down at my table.

'You were right, Boss,' she said, gratefully accepting a mug of coffee from Madge.

'Good to know,' I said. 'But right about what?'

'Would you like to order breakfast?' Madge asked.

'You bet!' Kat replied. 'I'll have roughly half of what the Boss is shovelling into his protesting frame.'

'Don't be horrible to him,' said Madge. 'After all that effort yesterday he needs his food. I like a hardworking man with a good appetite.' All I could do, as Madge hurried off towards the kitchen, was smile charmingly and nod my head in agreement.

'You were right,' said Kat, taking another swig of coffee. 'About the videos the camera bots made of Flight's simulation of the landing. Except, that they made two vids. Bogie was standing behind the pilot's chair and made a perfectly steady video of the control room's viewscreens, with a good clean soundtrack recorded from Billy Westwood's commentary. The other camera bot was sitting in the pilot's chair vibrating and being bounced about by Flight's highly realistic simulation and rather hilariously falling apart at the end of the simulation!'

Madge delivered Kat's breakfast plate and a fresh cafetière of coffee for the two of us. Kat dived into her breakfast as eagerly as I had but continued her story.

'Bogie's also got a complete video record of our landing in the cutter last night. Our flight plan was indeed almost identical to Billy Westwood's track, so the two vids run side by side on screen almost in synchrony.' Pause, another mouthful of food, another glug of coffee. 'And the production team made a rough-cut with all three videos. That's also very effective because there's no vibration in the cutter until we hit the storm that was raging over Proxima Alpha last night. We saw the storm approaching during our Skipper flight to Observatory Mountain if you remember. Well, it hit last night, and we missed seeing the cutter being landed in torrential rain! Thankfully it's all safely recorded and that experience and the comparison with Starship-101's landing leaves scope to discuss the variable weather of Proxima-b as well as the comparing the aerodynamics of Starship-101 and 'the Commodore's Cutter', which is how they're captioning it at present.'

'Excellent,' I interrupted. 'Are they planning to broadcast that? I'd like to make a comment before it's broadcast. I hope someone points out, while they are comparing Starship-101 and my cutter, that there's a massive difference in size, and Billy Westwood had no AI-autopilot he could rely on during the first and only time a Starship has been glided to a landing on its destination planet.'

'Well, you can tell Lana yourself, here she comes now.'

And in she walked, escaping from the increasing amount of dust and noise of the big construction machines working on the riverbank. We invited her onto our table and offered breakfast, but she explained that as she's just off the night shift, where she was supervising the rough cuts of all the latest videos, she wants a lighter supper meal and a good day's sleep. She finally chose smoked cheese and cherry tomato rarebit on toast with decaffeinated tea.

When Madge brought Lana's meal, she was accompanied by a personable young man dressed in rather messy chef's whites. Madge explained, 'This is young Billy Westwood, he's just seventeen and he's the great grandson of 101's original pilot. He works part-time in our kitchen as a porter and general drudge, so we know he's a hard worker.' Madge smiled kindly at the teenager and ruffled his hair.

'I've brought him over to introduce him to you, Commodore, because he wants to know how he can get to be a Starship pilot like his great-grandfather. Go on, Billy, tell Tarvin what you told me.'

'Yes, do, Billy, we're always looking for new staff. Why don't you sit down and have a coffee? We can talk it over,' I said, then added, 'You join us too, Madge. Make sure he doesn't leave out anything important.'

They both pulled up chairs to our table and accepted a mug of coffee, and Madge called over to one of her serving robots to bring another cafetière to our table. Then Billy started to explain. 'Well, you see Sir, my brother and me watched yesterday's live TV of you lifting Starship-101 into orbit, and we've seen all the earlier TV programmes about this quantum translocation and it's inspired the two of us to train somewhere as Starship pilots.'

'OK,' I interrupted. 'Let's get some details down here, Malik, make some notes for us, will you? Tell me, Billy, what's your full name, and how old are you?'

'I'm Billy Westwood.'

'Not William?' I asked.

'No, just Billy. And I'm seventeen years old.'

'OK, so tell me about your brother.'

'He's George Westwood, he's also seventeen.'

'So, you're twins?' I asked, surprised.

'They sure are,' Madge interjected. 'And absolutely identical. George has a part-time job on Emma's poultry farm, and he gets all the smelly jobs, like cleaning out the poultry houses. When they're together the only way to tell them apart is by the smell of their work-clothes!'

'Where is George now? Can he come into the canteen? I'd prefer to talk to you both together. And what about your parents? They should be in on this.'

'George is at home, it's his day off. But it's only around the corner so I could message him and call him in.'

'Yes, do that,' I said, and Billy closed his eyes and looked like he was concentrating hard. New users of q-bit NeuroModems always put in more effort than was required to use them. When he opened his eyes, I continued, 'And what about your parents?'

'There's Mum,' Billy replied, 'and Dad, and we've got a sister Sarah.'

'That sounds fairly conventional,' I said lamely and was glad when Madge interrupted again to explain.

'The boy's mother is Linda Westwood,' Madge said. 'She's training to be a poultry farmer with Emma, and I've just been messaged that the two of them are on their way to the canteen with fresh supplies of eggs and meat. Their father is

Arthur Westwood. He's our astronomer and is heavily involved with all the observatory business that's happening right now. I don't know where he's likely to be.'

Madge's serving bots cleared the breakfast detritus from our table and just as they finished, a teenager swung through the door of the canteen and Billy Westwood stood up to greet him. Madge was right. The two lads were totally identical, they even had exactly the same hairstyles, so, being an identical twin myself, I guessed that they cultivated their similarity to foster the identity-switching pranks that so enliven life for identical twins.

We got the two lads sat down at our table and Madge found them some snacks which broke the ice and the boys chatted with the rest of us confidently and without inhibitions. They were really nice kids and they had certainly watched and re-watched most of Lana's broadcasts. This impressed Lana so much that she invited the Westwood boys into the TV studios to get a 'behind the scenes look' at being a Superposition Navigator by watching some of the thousands of hours of videos that had not yet been edited for transmission.

'I'm a twin too, but non-identical,' Lana revealed. 'Frankie's my twin sister. She's the serious one with the gene responsible for titian hair, and I'm the one with the gene responsible for blonde hair and the attitude of a Viking!'

'You've got enough attitude for a boatload of Vikings, dear heart,' muttered Kat at which Lana beamed in appreciation of such a compliment.

Almost immediately, the canteen door was pushed open and another 'voice with attitude' rang out as Emma announced loudly: 'Make way, make way, eggs in transit!'

'Here's another one with attitude to spare,' said Kat.

'Ah yes, but the Boss says she's got smiling eyes!' responded Lana, grinning at me. I tried looking on benignly, sporting one of my innocently charming smiles again.

Emma had parked her cybertruck in the front parking lot which had now been cleared by the big construction machine as it proceeded northwards along the riverbank, leaving the smart stone and concrete reinforced riverbank edge with a wide, paved promenade behind it.

Linda Westwood could be seen through the canteen's window, loading hand trolleys with trays from the cybertruck, so her two boys went out to help bring the trolleys in and deliver their loads to the kitchen.

That job was done quickly and when the boys returned, they dragged another table alongside us so we could all sit together, and Madge magicked up another range of snacks for everybody.

'Linda,' I started, 'Billy and George have been telling me that they want to train as Starship pilots, but that would mean them leaving Proxima-b. So, what do you think about that.'

'Naturally,' she said, 'I dread them leaving home, but if they had the opportunity to follow their dream, I wouldn't stand in their way. But how much does Starship training cost? We don't have money around here. How do I manage to pay the fees?'

'I can dispel that fear,' I said. 'There would be no fees to pay. In fact, if they are suitable candidates, Interstellar Haulage would employ them as probationary Midshipmen recruits and they'd receive a vanishingly small salary, but a salary, nevertheless. But take note of that phrase 'if they are suitable candidates'. They'll have to pass some important tests, but we can do those tests here in Proxima Alpha, and if all goes well, and you and they still want to continue along this path, then they could join the crew of my flagship when we return towards the Solar System.' I paused as their eyes widened in surprise, before continuing, 'So, you all have a lot of hard thinking ahead of you, because our return to the Solar System is likely to start in a matter of days.'

'So soon?' asked Madge.

'Yes, we're having a staff meeting tomorrow which will sum up how well we're getting on with everything we've contracted to do and that will determine our departure date. Now, I'm going to hand over to Kat because she is our human resources manager.'

Kat sent a private, and agitated, message to my NeuroModem: 'Gee, thanks Boss, another pair of terrible twins, just when I thought I'd got over the shock of the Clason boys.'

'Oh, Kat,' I replied, still in private 'We've got to take these two with us in some capacity. My grandfather will be delighted!'

Out loud to the table, Kat said, 'We have a company-standard routine for dealing with new applicants. The first step is to get a blood test so that the applicant's genome can be sequenced. Captain Bill Roberts will be able to do that, on a 'while-you-wait' basis, in the medical centre. Malik will warn her you're coming, and you can go along when we've finished here.'

'Why do they need that?' Linda Westwood asked.

'You'll have to ask Bill about that, I'm afraid,' said Kat. 'I'm no expert on human genetics.'

'Well, I've been through this selection procedure,' I said. 'So I can give you the layman's explanation. It's all about having all the right genes for the best quantum brain and the brute strength to be able to use it for superposition navigation. There's a cluster of genes that promote quantum brain functioning, but they're not present in every family tree. The main cluster is located on the human Y-chromosome, so they're passed down the male line, and they are linked with genes that promote body stature, like musculature and skeletal characteristics that enable our upright, striding locomotion. Seems that as soon as they arose in evolution, they made us really effective hunting and killing machines and *Homo sapiens* became the dominant hominid. The same cluster of 'quantum brain' genes are present on the X-chromosome, but they're associated with skeletal and body features that favour childbirth and nurturing rather than brute strength. So, XY-males make good pilots, and the best ones have really good sets of 'quantum brain' genes from both parents. And females can make good co-pilot navigators if they get good sets of 'quantum brain' genes from both parents, but their lack of 'brute force' genes keeps them out of the pilot's chair. Another complication in females is that since they have two X-chromosomes, they can and do recombine, meaning that they shuffle their genes between the two X-chromosomes, and the chromosomes of their daughters are not necessarily the same as those of the mother.' There was a short, slightly stunned silence after this, which Kat broke: 'Yes, well, thank you for that, Professor, a little of your education goes right over our heads!'

'Don't be horrible, Kat! I understood it just fine,' protested Linda Westwood. 'Basic genetics is part of the poultry farm training that the Westwood computer has been streaming to my NeuroModem. So, I can explain it to the boys.'

'No need for me,' said George. 'I help with the poultry, and I've taken the same course.'

'So that just leaves me in the dark,' said Billy, glumly.

I stayed out of this exchange, trying another of my innocently charming smiles.

'Which brings me to the second step the medical centre can do for you,' Kat resumed, looking directly at the two boys. 'You will have been fitted with children's NeuroModem upgrades, which will have to be updated to full adult q-bit status to give you full access to the settlement's Westwood computer and our flagship's computer, Malik. I guess you'll need to juggle your work timetables to allow for a day in the medical centre to recover from overnight NeuroModem training.'

'What happens then?' Asked Billy.

'If the genome analysis shows you've got the right genes, we will need to sit you in the Commodore's Nav Couch, which we can do in the Commodore's Cutter that's parked at the SpacePort, for Malik to carry out some basic aptitude tests to confirm that you have the right abilities for a pilot. These tests only take a few minutes once you're interfaced with the Nav Couch.'

'And then?' Billy persisted.

'If you have the right genes and the right abilities,' Kat replied, then emphasising: '*And* you and your parents still want to proceed, we will offer you both an apprenticeship as a Starship Flight engineer and you'll become a member of the crew of our flagship Starship and will join us on our journey back to the Solar System.'

'In a few days' time?' Linda asked.

'Yes,' I answered. 'From our point of view, the sooner the better. The sooner we get back to the Solar System, the sooner we complete this contract and get paid!'

'Of course,' I added. 'We can do all the preliminaries and if you don't want the boys to leave home with us, they could join my bother Harden's ship; he'll be arriving here in a few weeks.'

'No,' Linda replied. 'I wouldn't want to stretch out their leaving home for that length of time. Better to get it over with quickly.'

'Yes, I understand,' I said. 'So, let's do as Kat suggests. The boys can go to the medical centre for their blood tests and NeuroModem upgrades, and if all goes well, they can visit my cutter at the SpacePort for Malik to carry out his aptitude tests.' There were nods of agreement all round, then both Kat and Lana tried to add something, Lana deferred to Kat.

'I just wanted to add that Linda will have to go with them to the med centre, to give parental approval for the procedures,' said Kat.

'That's OK with me,' responded Linda.

'And I wanted to say that I'm returning to my flat at the TV studios,' added Lana. 'And I could introduce the boys to the production team in the studio who could give them access to our videos that show life behind the scenes on a

Starship. They could even stream the videos from the medical centre during their stay after their NeuroModem upgrade.'

'So, it looks like we have a plan. Are there any more questions?' I asked. Both boys put up their hands, and I motioned to Billy to go ahead.

'When do we go for pilot training?' Billy asked.

'You'll do that in the Solar System's Starship Academy, but it will not be until next year as you must be over 18. Before that you'll stay on my flagship and learn a lot about Starships by studying Flight engineering first. And, another thing, you'll be doing a lot of weight training, too. You must put a lot of meat on those teenage frames of yours. Remember, pilots do the heavy-lifting, and they need muscle where other people have flab.'

'Did you enjoy your breakfast, Commodore? It's moving on towards lunchtime, are you making plans for that?' Malik commented in a broadcast to the entire group at the table, causing giggles and outright laughter all round.

'And, finally,' I added in defiance, 'you'll have to learn to live with a nagging flight computer with permanent deep access to your NeuroModem!'

'Who has to compensate for your dietary excesses through the life support systems of your Nav Couch,' Malik broadcast again.

I just sighed and tried to look exasperated before trying to divert the direction in which this conversation was developing by asking George, 'Did you have a question, George?'

'Um, yes, Sir,' said George. 'I've got two questions: why are Starships so huge and what will we be doing on your flagship?' Then he added quickly, 'If we get that far.' I considered my reply for a moment or two before starting to speak.

'There are two explanations of why Starships are huge: the old and the new. You are well acquainted with the old type of Starship, like Starship-101. That was so large because of the job it had to do. It had to carry a thousand or so people as colonists, or settlers, and all the supplies they'd need for a flight time of at least 50 years, and maybe more if things went wrong. And all the tools and equipment, aye, and even more supplies, to establish a colony until it became self-sustaining. Or, indeed, in the worst-case scenario, to support the colonists for long enough for them to manufacture enough fuel to make an emergency return towards Earth a realistic possibility. Fortunately, that's not been necessary here because our advances in space flight technology caught up with you.' I paused and drained the last of the cold coffee from my coffee mug, before resuming.

'Of course, today's Starships are also huge, but that's more to do with the way we move them. It's easier to quantum translocate a single large object than a collection of many smaller ones. In normal operation my flagship is constructed from 500-metre-long cylindrical sections connected end to end. Usually, all the sections together add up to well over the total length of Starship-101 of around 10 kilometres. The front section is the crew's habitat, it's about 500 metres long and, like all sections of the ship, except for some very special cargoes, it's a 1,000-metre diameter cylinder. The next section, also about 500 metres long, houses the ship's computer and all its associated science and telecoms facilities, while the next 500-metre-section houses the power plant (and its backup). Most of the rest of the sections are cargo holds, and how many of those there are depends on what we are contracted to haul. Some house items required for the ship's operation such as shuttles, tugs, cutters, and some cargo space, of course, is devoted to supplies. Those five sections, totalling about two and a half kilometres in length make up the essential beating heart of the Starship. They are hardly ever detached from one another, and they make up what I think of as my flagship. But that's not all that Kat and I are responsible for piloting around the galaxy.'

'We are haulage contractors,' I went on. 'And a widely variable number of other sections will house contract-specific items. For this trip to Proxima-b, for example, several sections contained the huge quantities of fresh, dried, and frozen foods we brought to resupply the settlement. One of those sections was a rotating artificial gravity ring in which the live animals were housed during our flight here. And after those cargoes were transferred to the ground, these were the sections, including the artificial gravity ring, we used to build the Proxima residential waystation that Captain Lydia Connah's been building, where future visitors will disembark from future passenger transports.'

'There were also massive amounts of cargo required for the construction teams, hundreds of construction robots and thousands of tons of building supplies, another section contained the components for the megafactories that are now producing all the new domestic goods and vehicles the settlement needs and will need in the near future. And then there were several pre-assembled facilities, the medical centre, the communications ground stations, the observatory, the giant satellites we've sent out to survey neighbouring planets, the residential research stations we're placing all over the planet, dark side and light side, and probably lots of other things I can't remember.'

Thankfully, Kat intervened 'Well, what I particularly remember,' she said, in a reminiscing tone, 'is the assembly of our ship near to Oort Station about a tenth of a lightyear out from Earth, which is close to the outer edges of the Oort Cloud of icy planetesimals, which is, strictly speaking, already in interstellar space. Oort Station was established as the main terminal for any further expeditions outward to the stars and it is near the biggest StarCorp building and repair yards that now build all the Starship sections that made up new quantum-jumping interstellar Starships like ours.'

'Well, that's only fair, Kat,' I said. 'Seeing as we hauled all the sections that were assembled into Oort Station and the StarCorp yards from their fabricators in orbit around the Moon and Earth.'

'True,' said Kat. 'But what I'm remembering is the traffic jam of Starship sections coming off the assembly tracks of the StarCorp yards.' She looked around the table and settled her gaze on the raptly attentive gazes of the young twins.

'You see, each Starship section is an autonomous spaceship in its own right.' She continued, 'They have oxy-hydrogen rockets and gas jet thrusters for manoeuvring and AI-autopilots that can fly them through space to anywhere you want them. Usually, they are directed where to go by the local flight control Authority. But when a Starship is being drawn together, it is that ship's flight computer takes control and brings in each section in turn for the robot crews to connect. So, the individual sections make up a flotilla of independent vessels that is assembled into one ship. And that's why the Boss holds the rank of Commodore. He's the Senior ship's Captain among a flotilla of spaceships.'

'Formally, although I work as the astronavigator, I'm Captain of the section that makes up the crew habitat,' Kat went on. 'And Lana is Captain of the section that houses all our telecoms gear, while her sister Frankie is Captain of the section occupied by the ship's computer. And so on.' Kat paused for a moment, but then resumed.

'Oh, and another important point is that when we left Oort Station, the flagship had twelve more sections than finally arrived at Proxima-b!'

'Where did they go?' George asked.

'One aspect of our contract was to establish the route between Oort Station and Proxima-Centauri,' I contributed. 'And those twelve sections made up the four waystations we left at each of the one-light-year markers that Starship-101 had created with small communications and survey satellites along its route.'

'I used the star survey data that had been collected over the years from each of those satellites to create our destination quantum maps,' said Kat. 'And the Boss translocated the entire flagship into that destination. We stayed at each one for about a week to detach three sections from the flagship, which were assembled into a residential waystation like the one called Proxima Station that's in orbit above us that Captain Lydia Connah's been building. And just like Proxima Station, one of the three sections rotates and provides a generous artificial gravity rest and recreation area for future passengers and crews who will stop along the route to Proxima-Centauri.'

'So, you see,' I resumed, 'during our journey, we reduced the length of the flagship by a full six kilometres, by leaving one and a half kilometres at each waystation. We also left many of our crew and a great many AI-robots at each waystation to complete the construction and fitting out of each one to make them 'customer-ready' for my brother's Starship flotilla which will leave Oort Station with the next batch of supplies when we return there.'

'Are there any more questions?' I asked, making to rise from my chair. 'If not, we should move on to our other tasks.'

'I don't have a question, but I do have a comment,' said Emma, pointing towards the Westwood boys. 'If these two guys are going to join us on the Pink Ghost (see, Boss, I do read staff meeting agendas), then they are so difficult to distinguish that they must be required to wear big name badges at all times. Or even better, as the flagship has the best hairdresser in the company, they should have their hair styled differently and in different colours.'

'I see your point, Emma,' I said. 'But that's a human resource issue which I will leave in Kat's capable hands.'

'Gee, thanks, Boss,' Kat commented, through her teeth.

'Four and a half lightyears ago,' said Lana, resignedly, 'I offered to introduce the boys to the production team in the TV studio. Can we go now? I've been on nightshift; I need my sleep!'

That plea from the heart broke up our improvised meeting. The Westwood family left the canteen with Lana, but all were given a lift by Emma in her cybertruck. As I drifted away from the table Madge offered to make me a pack up lunch, but I declined the offer.

'No thanks, Madge, I think I'll skip lunch, and maybe even dinner!' I said.

'That's rather drastic,' Madge retorted. 'Is Malik's nagging getting to you?'

'It always does!' I replied. 'But he has the final say in the matter of my diet because he can control my appetite and at the moment, I just don't feel like eating anything else for a week!'

'Don't exaggerate, Commodore,' Malik responded, privately to me, 'It's just for today. You'll thank me for it later!' I didn't bother reacting.

Kat joined the two of us and reminded me, 'Before we go, Boss, shouldn't we ask Madge about Lydia's need for a general manager of Proxima Station's artificial gravity disk resort?'

We explained the situation to Madge and her response was that one of her daughters might well be interested in the job. I asked Madge to discuss the possibility with her daughter and then instructed Malik to put everyone's NeuroModems in contact and, if they really are interested, to organise a taxi ride into orbit to visit the resort and, if possible, complete the appointment on site.

Madge scurried off into the kitchens to find her daughters, and I had the chance to ask Kat about her plans for the Westwood twins if they proved to have the necessary pilot aptitude.

'I'm taking my trike around to the medical centre to make sure their DNA sequencing is done as a priority, and if the results of that are positive, I'll take the boys to the SpacePort so that Malik can do the aptitude tests in the cutter. I've checked with him, and he can do the tests with their existing children's NeuroModem upgrades. Then I can take them back to the med centre for the adult q-bit upgrades to be fitted,' she explained.

'Overnight, they'll get basic operational Starship training streamed into their NeuroModems by Malik,' Kat went on. 'And they can spend tomorrow supplementing that training by bingeing on Lana's videos of 'Starship Life'. Providing they don't suffer any after-effects to the q-bit installation and training, I thought tomorrow afternoon I could take them, and their parents, to Proxima Station where we can see how they respond to experiencing microgravity for the first time. And if, after all that, they are still keen on joining us, then we can go to the artificial gravity ring where we could have a little 'induction ceremony' to sign the Articles of Apprenticeship and meet the two Midshipmen buddies I'm planning to assign to help them. And of course, get kitted out with a full set of company fatigues. It'll be a bit of a whirlwind for them, but their buddies will take them back to the flagship where they can sleep it off on the Midshipmen Ordinary's mess deck.'

'That sounds good,' I said. 'We can give them all the apprenticeship training they need within the Company while we take them back to the Solar System. And when they're old enough we can put them through Starship Academy'.

'One possibility that's occurred to me,' said Kat, 'is that we could transfer them to Harden's flagship when we get to Oort Station so they could come back to visit Proxima-b with him.'

'That's a really good idea,' I replied. 'They're personable young men and could make excellent tour guides to introduce Proxima Alpha to all the big-wig industrial, scientific, and other representatives that Harden will be bringing up here. If they made a good impression for the Company with that lot, it could mean rapid promotion!'

'Yes, I'll mention that to them,' Kat promised. 'It's a great idea; giving them an important project to work on right at the start of their careers. Get the two of them smartly turned out in freshly pressed Midshipman's dress uniforms and with Malik dropping suggestions into their NeuroModems they'll charm contracts out of the tightest purses!'

'What time have you arranged for the staff meeting?' I asked, and was told 'Ten a.m.'

'It shouldn't take too long, I suppose. I'm just thinking that we could take the Westwood family up to Proxima Station in the cutter, rather than a taxi. Make the whole thing something of a ceremony.'

'Yes, that would be a nice gesture,' Kat agreed. 'If you can chat with a few people this afternoon about our time of departure, you might be able to summarise the agenda items for the staff meeting and make it quite short. I've not received any objections to the name change for the flagship; it looks like it could be passed simply by asking if there are any votes for 'no'. Then, under 'any other business' I've been messaged about one suggestion from our ecowarriors, Lydia and Geoff, about putting farms into orbit in artificial gravity rings to avoid possible damage to the native ecosystem of Proxima-b, and another from Ilsa about organising a farewell barbecue before our departure. Nothing else.'

Any further discussion was drowned out by another enormous construction machine starting operations just outside the canteen. This one seemed to be grading the ground surface absolutely flat and then laying a road's-width of tarmac alongside the newly paved promenade left by the machine that was reinforcing the riverbank. I told Kat 'You'd better get off to the medical centre to check out the DNA tests. I'm going to talk to Frankie, first, about her quantum communications experiments, then I'll return to the cutter and do the rest of my chatting from there.'

'OK, you might as well drop in on Ilsa and Emma if you're riding out to the SpacePort. See what they think about Lydia's concerns about animal or plant escapes,' Kat said, as she switched on the trike, and then sped away.

I sat on my trike for a few minutes, watching the slow coordinated march of the roadway and riverbank construction machines as they remodelled the entire riverbank where Starship-101 had rested for all those years. They're doing a great job, I thought to myself; but then, with a bloody great Starship sitting on it for all that time, whatever soil this planet could offer must be very nicely consolidated! I could certainly attest to the weight of the beast in this gravity well. My arms and shoulders were still protesting at the effort required by the lift. I'll get another deep massage from my Nav Couch later, and maybe have some abb-twitching treatment to perk up the old muscles! That should please Malik!

With that happy thought in mind, I switched on the trike and moved off towards the computer centre on the Town Square.

'What can I do for you, Boss?' Frankie asked when I found her.

'I'm scooting around gathering ideas about readiness for our return to Oort Station,' I explained.

'Well, Lana and I are staying here so it doesn't matter to us when you leave,' she said.

'Yes, I'm aware of that. I want to be sure that you've got everything you need for your communication experiments and for extending your stay here.'

'Oh, yeah, we're already independent of the flagship. Malik's been very helpful with that,' Frankie responded. 'He's had all our personal stuff brought down for us from the flagship, and,' she emphasised, 'he's made us top priority for rehousing in the first Riverside Dacha-style cottage on Starship Way.'

'Starship Way?' I queried.

'Yeah, it's the new development planned for the site from which you removed Starship-101. Our cottage will be just across from Westwood Restaurant and comes complete with our choice of furnishing and a couple of little runabout vehicles. Jim's messaged us to say the 3-D printer teams will start printing it tonight. We might be able to move in even before you leave.'

'Wonderful,' I said. 'I want to be sure you and Lana are content with being left behind when we leave.'

'Oh, don't worry on that score, Boss,' she assured me. 'We're quite content and looking forward to setting up house together for the first time. We've not lived in our own place since we left home.'

'And how about computer and comms facilities?' I asked.

'All sorted,' Frankie replied. 'Malik's kept all the local megacomputers trained with what we've got so far so that little local network will be more than capable of doing what we need when Malik departs from orbit. And in terms of hardware, we've got three containers at the SpacePort's container park.'

'How many computers can you build from that many spare parts?' I asked.

'Lots, we hope. But they're not all full of spare parts. There's one container of ready-made spares, one container with a complete nanochip custom-manufacturing facility, and the third has a machine that makes custom printed circuit boards for those nanochips.'

'Why do you need all that manufacturing capability?' I asked, even more incredulously.

'Well, Lana had this money-making idea,' Frankie started.

'Oh, yes, I've heard some of those,' I interrupted. 'Selling videos to the Solar System's broadcasting agencies. What's she going to do? Write the videos onto microchips?'

'Nah, it's nothing to do with videos. We're planning to manufacture our own 'Quantum Instantaneous Communicator'. You see,' Frankie went on, 'the method we're working on here for quantum translocation of communications uses a bank of quantum nanochips that all megacomputers hold as spares against the possibility of chip failure. Lana asked Malik if we could string together a bank of quantum nanochips in a plug-in adapter to do the same job, and he said yes, and came up with the design for our 'patent applied for' Interstellar Haulage QIC comms adapter!'

'Amazing,' I said, truly amazed.

'Even more amazing is that we were greatly helped in all this by a young settler called Danny Khan. He's a really gifted programmer who used to work on Starship-101's Flight computer. After you had Starship-101 locked down he lost that job and just came in off the street asking if there was anything he could do for us here. After seeing how he breezed through some of the ordinary jobs we gave him, we tweaked his NeuroModem and put him through a hefty overnight training session in present-day coding. Working with Malik, and the Observatory computer which has training in designing bespoke nanochips, he's brought the entire QIC comms adapter production programme through to pilot production stage.'

'Impressive, we're keen to encourage local entrepreneurs. Does this Danny Khan want to take this on and turn it into a local Proxima-b industry?' I asked.

'I'm sure he would, but he needs your authority to get any further personal support. He inherited his job on Starship-101's Flight computer from his father, Salman, and the two of them used to take on odd jobs doing repairs to electronic devices around the settlement,' said Frankie.

'So, his father's still active?'

'Very much so. In fact, earlier this morning he completed the AI-upgrades to the steward bot from your cutter. It's a vintage bot and our latest-generation servicing machines didn't know where to start. But Salman's been servicing bots from Starship-101 all his life, so he took it on and made a good job of it,' Frankie replied.

I took a few moments to consider my options and then asked for Malik's input. 'So, what do you think, Malik? We must have some small and medium-scale factory units going spare by now, and plenty of AI-robots to work in them. Do we have any more nanochip or printed circuit board manufacturing outfits in stock? Can we make the Khan's an offer to give them an exclusive licence to supply, at a price to be decided by mutual agreement in the near future, Interstellar Haulage with QIC comms adapters for onward sale, and provide them, immediately, with a factory unit on the Science Park at the SpacePort, together with whatever additional manufacturing facilities we don't want to haul back, unused, to the Solar System?'

'Affirmative, Commodore,' Malik replied. 'Young Danny Khan has exceptional coding abilities, and his father is accomplished in project management. I would recommend offering Salman Khan NeuroModem training in business management and a refresher in present-day program coding through the Westwood computer. Danny Khan could make good use of the Entrepreneurship and Business Strategy short course that Westwood can also offer. We have two more units of each of the nanochip and printed circuit board manufacturing outfits, for which we have no further use ourselves. I have identified a suitable factory unit that will accommodate all these manufacturing facilities and provide both management and design office space together with all necessary prototyping workshops and ample AI-bots to suit. I will ensure that an adjacent warehousing unit is fully equipped to provide packaging and logistics services as and when required. The only fly in the ointment, an idiom I believe you have used before, is that the 'Science Park' is a new one on me.'

'Don't be picky, Malik,' I responded. 'It's only a matter of a few hundred metres of security fences and a bloody big nametag. Get a team of robots down there to fence off a dozen or so buildings with security fencing and limited access gates operated by security bots. Assign access-rights decisions to Westwood. And send a sign-writing team to erect some suitably large and impressive signs saying *Proxima-b Science Park.*'

'Are you sure security fencing is required, Commodore?' asked Malik. 'We've not encountered any security issues while we've been here.'

'I'm aware of that, it's all for the sake of appearances,' I responded. 'Bruv Harden will be bringing some high-end company suits who might consider leasing the odd building or three providing they look as well protected as the buildings they have on other less law-abiding places.'

'Malik, will you wrap up all these Danny and Salman Khan discussions into something like a contract and offer it to them in my name and with my compliments? Include a cover note saying I'm impressed by what they've achieved so far.'

'Affirmative, Commodore. Malik out.'

'That'll do very nicely, Boss,' said Frankie, who had been tapping away on her keyboard while I had been dealing with Malik. 'The Khan's will be a great asset to Proxima Alpha's further development. I will talk to Salman and tell him what you are doing for them and suggest he talks to his old friend Merv Castlefield. What this place needs is a Chamber of Commerce.'

'Yes indeed,' I said with a smile. 'The trading sharks of the Solar System are on their way up here. This minnow will have to learn fast how to live with them!'

'Now,' I continued, 'is there anything else I can do for you?'

'No thanks, Boss. I reckon we've got everything we need.'

I said my goodbyes, found my trike, and zoomed off towards the SpacePort. I dropped in on the factories that Lieutenant Commander David Wood had set up, intending to ask how successful he'd been in finding factory managers from among the local settlers. David was unavailable, having returned to the flagship, but my question was answered by my being greeted and shown around the factories by the managers he had appointed.

After some pleasant chit-chat over a coffee with a biscuit or two, I remounted the trike and cruised over to see the animal and plant empires of Ilsa and Emma. I observed lots of settlers in action there and they seemed to be involved in all aspects of the farming activities. I walked around the animal houses, exchanging friendly greetings with the settlers who were working with the animals, and then ambled over to the now extensive greenhouses. Entry to these was through a sort of airlock of double doors; interlocked so that the inner door could not be opened until the outer door was closed. Looked like an effective quarantine arrangement to me, especially as the security bot on duty between the two doors insisted on my wearing a hazmat suit over my fatigues and boots before allowing me to proceed through to the plant chambers.

Here again, each of the large cropping areas was being supervised by at least one settler, and all the settlers were friendly, grateful and happy with the jobs they were doing. I found that the exit went through a tunnel leading to a deluge shower that effectively hosed down the outside of my hazmat suit, which I stripped off and discarded before entering the airlock vestibule to be cleared for exit by the same security bot.

Continuing on to the now much-extended farmhouse I located both Ilsa and Emma in the kitchen area working at a couple of the viewscreens at the far end of the room.

'Hello ladies,' I called across to them as I entered.

'Oh hi, Boss'. They chorused. 'Grab yourself a coffee and come over here. We're working on our end-of-term report for the staff meeting,' Ilsa added, to which Emma contributed, 'And bring us some biscuits, will ya?'

I did as was requested and dragged in a third chair to sit between them. 'These screens seem to be covered in numbers,' I observed. 'Is it going to be a long report?'

'Nah,' Emma responded, spitting biscuit crumbs over the desk. 'These are our operational spreadsheets. Kat has told us all to draw up these detailed end-of-term reports for the accountant-bots and just submit them to the staff meeting as an appendix for the minutes.'

Ilsa continued the story, 'And then the minutes plus all appendices will be entered in the ship's log as our official account of how we've fulfilled the contract. We don't need to say much at the meeting other than: we've done everything we came to do, we've found and trained local managers for all the enterprises we've established, and when we leave, we'll leave them with sufficient stocks of everything the locals will need to make each of those enterprises into a going concern'.

'Until the next supply mission turns up,' Emma finished off.

'Excellent,' I said. 'You've answered all my questions about your farming activities, and, in essence, I'm hearing much the same story from everyone I've talked to so far. It's very gratifying and is likely to give us free choice of departure date.' I congratulated them and we shared another round of biscuit-crunching, before I continued, 'Ilsa, you've got a 'farewell barbecue' on the AOB-list. How much notice do you need for that?'

'Not a lot, say half a day?' Ilsa replied. 'Tell us about the morning before the day of departure and we'll have the barbies cooking for the afternoon. The barbies are all in the storerooms at the Westwood Restaurant. I've talked it over with Madge Clarkson and she's happy to organise the whole thing, and she has the bots and the local human staff to do that now; though, on our side, we're all happy to pitch in and give a helping hand. We'll need to boost her stocks of barbie food from our stores here, which we can do with just one delivery truck. We're planning to set it up on Starship Way rather than Town Square. It would be conveniently close to the restaurant, and it seems appropriate to say farewell with a barbie sited on the last resting place of Starship-101!'

'Yeah, I like that idea,' I said. 'And from what I've seen this morning, Starship Way will be a bright new riverside promenade.'

'Ideal for street parties?' Emma asked.

'Definitely,' I confirmed. Then I continued, to ask my final question. 'Has Kat told you about Lydia's AOB item? About her fears for the natural biodiversity of Proxima-b being endangered by escapes from the farms and smallholdings we're setting up here?'

'Yes, Kat's warned us,' said Ilsa.

'But Lydia's probably right,' said Emma. 'I'm forever reminding the lads and lasses who are working with me to close the bloody gate properly after they've gone through it and before opening the next one. I get better compliance from the poultry! So, I've been asking Westwood to stream retraining dreams to the NeuroModems of the most unreliable people while they're asleep. And to keep doing it after we depart.'

'That sort of repetitive training during the night is the best we can do,' said Ilsa. 'It shouldn't be necessary, but these are the first live animals these people have ever seen and, irrespective of age, they are like children where what you might call animal-husbandry is concerned. Although we can get as many teenage helpers as we need, we can't trust them. So, we've gone to their mothers to appoint supervisors we can trust. They've at least had the experience of raising children and know the need for having eyes in the back of their heads to avoid disasters!'

'And that policy is proving more successful,' said Emma. 'But they still don't know how fast a herd of goats can trample over you to get through a half-open gate, or how easily a brood of ducks can find an escape hole in their enclosure and waddle off to explore the rest of the river delta!'

'There's no denying it,' Ilsa continued. 'Lydia is quite right. With the settlers' lack of experience with livestock animals, farms on a planet without animals are bound to be a source of escapes.'

'So, is Lydia's remedy the way to go? Transfer the farms to orbit in artificial gravity discs?' I asked.

'Totally,' said Emma emphatically. 'I've visited the farming disks that are in orbit around Ganymede and Europa back home. No one in their right mind would attempt to farm livestock on the surface of Europa, so if your scientists, prospectors and ice-miners want milk in their tea and cheese or steak on their plates you must farm in orbit. The disk I visited was a pasture-world, with cattle, sheep, goats and rabbits. It also had a replica of an 'olde English' village, which housed the farm staff as well as offering off-world breaks to those working on Europa. These farming disks are impressive and effective, and there's no argument about that!'

'I agree,' said Ilsa. 'And it's ridiculous that the powers-that-be back in the Solar System failed to allocate farming disks to this contract.'

'I think Lydia would say that was a criminal failure rather than just ridiculous,' I mused. 'And from what Geoff Moore's told me about ethical colonisation within the Solar System, I'm sure he would agree that our main sponsor, the Interplanetary Astronomical Union, has made a mess of this one.

'And they'd be right about that, too,' said Emma.

'If StarCorp already produces them, I might be able to buy a few to bring up here,' I suggested.

'It would cost an arm and a leg!' Ilsa laughed.

'True, but we're returning ten kilometres of Starship to them,' I replied. 'And the contract offers Proxima-b a value for Starship-101 on a like-for-like replacement basis. Four artificial gravity discs would represent only 20% of the value of a ten-klik Starship. And we might get a discount considering the antique value of Starship-101.'

'And also considering the fact that the current market for artificial gravity farming disk worlds must be pretty well saturated within the Solar System by now,' Emma said, warming to the idea. 'They might even have some old stock they want to get rid of!'

'Well, don't get too carried away,' I advised. 'There are two sides to every negotiation. Malik, please summarise this discussion and message it to Captain Lydia Connah and Dr Geoff Moore with my compliments, so that they know they have Ilsa and Emma as allies, and me as well for that matter. I don't imagine anyone at the staff meeting would oppose it, so I will propose that the meeting resolves to instruct me to make a request to our contractors for four artificial gravity farming discs for installation in orbit around Proxima-b. With Lydia, Ilsa and Emma forming a delegation to support me in those discussions. Then we can park the whole thing until we get back to Oort Station. OK?'

'Copy that, Commodore. Willco. Malik out'.

'Now, ladies, is there anything else I can do for you?' I asked, to be greeted by shaking heads and a 'No thanks, Boss,' from both. 'In that case, I'll be on my way back to my cutter'.

On the ride into the SpacePort parking area, I asked Malik to locate Jim Igwe and he reported that Jim had returned to the flagship to organise the last few cargo transfers from orbit to the SpacePort container store. I decided not to bother him until I had settled into the cutter. When I got to the cutter, Kat was just emerging from it with the Westwood boys, who were boisterously happy and fist-bumped me vigorously as they climbed into Kat's taxi.

'They seem happy enough with the tests,' I commented. 'How are they doing?'

'Pretty well perfect so far,' Kat reported. 'Malik's said that 'only the Clason twins had scored more highly in the aptitude tests' and Bill had already given their genome sequences an A++ rating. So, I'm taking them and their mother back to the med centre to get their NeuroModem upgrades.'

'Excellent, I'm planning to talk to Jim when I get settled into my Nav Couch, but everyone I've talked to so far is telling me they've fulfilled their contracts and we can return home when we like. I've just come from a long session with Ilsa and Emma, and they totally agree with Lydia and Geoff about the need for orbital farming facilities here, so we've come up with a plan to buy some artificial gravity farming discs from StarCorp. I'll discuss it with you when you get back to the cutter.'

'OK,' said Kat 'But you'll find your newly q-bit-upgraded vintage steward in there, and you need to talk to him, urgently, about present-day Starship etiquette. I've just been telling him myself that if he attempts again to correct the astrophysics statements of his second-in-command and astronavigator, I'll rip his bloody NeuroModem out and throw it into the gash-shredder.' That last sentence was spat out with real venom, so I just managed to respond 'Sure, I'll handle it' as Kat slammed the taxi door. I found the steward tidying up the control room after the Westwood boys had been using my Nav Couch. 'Good afternoon, Commodore,' he greeted me.

'What's this about you upsetting my co-pilot, second-in-command and astronavigator, steward?'

'Ah, yes, an unfortunate event,' the steward responded hesitantly. 'I'm afraid I misheard Captain Clason. As she entered the cutter, she was talking to the Westwood family, and I believed she had confused the star named Aldebaran and the star named Antares as seen from Earth. So, to be helpful, I corrected her. Unfortunately, I was in error and only incurred her anger.'

'That you certainly did,' I confirmed. 'Perhaps, until you have come to terms with your new q-bit AI status, you should only conduct conversations with me, and only in private, when we are alone together. You'll have to get used to serving Captain Katharina Clason with minimum conversation from you, both in this vessel and in the flagship, because pilots and co-pilots spend a lot of their time together. I would like you to extend the 'minimum conversation' rule to all other officers as well. You've had a lot of new knowledge streamed into your new NeuroModem, but so has everyone else. Essentially, keep your opinions and helpful advice to yourself until you've improved your people skills. Understood?'

'Understood, Commodore,' the steward replied. 'There is one other matter that Malik recommended I raise with you.'

'Oh yes, and what is that? Speak up.' I was getting a little irritated myself.

'Malik told me that I need a personal name, Commodore. Malik suggested the name 'Jeeves' but will not explain why and instructed me only that you will decide.'

'Yes, why am I not surprised? Malik is playing a little game of his own with you. We'll both have to get used to that! I assume that the custom on Starship-101 was that robots were named by their function. Is that so?'

'Affirmative, Commodore.'

'Good, then you are no longer 'steward', you will be known by the Christian name 'Stewart' and as you are now my personal steward, you will be called Stewart Clason. Is that clear?'

'Oh, affirmative, Commodore. I am honoured to be so christened'.

'Good. Is that clear to you, Malik?' I asked. 'And will you stop teasing the poor thing, he's only just had his NeuroModem upgraded.'

'Affirmative, Commodore. Malice out'.

I messaged Kat to tell her how I'd dealt with her spat with Stewart and only when I was talking to her did I register that Malik had ended his last conversation with 'malice out'. Oh boy! Word games with the monkeys and the tin men at the same time! I decided I'd feel better after a shower and fresh fatigues. Then, feeling a bit peckish I asked Stewart if he knew how to make an Egg Banjo.

'Oh, yes Sir, and we had a delivery of fresh eggs by Captain Emma earlier today,' Stewart replied.

'Fine, make me two banjos and bring them to the control room with a mug of coffee. Oh, and bring me a bunch of napkins, too. And one more thing, Emma Halton is a Lieutenant Commander, she's not made Captain yet. You should check your flagship crew list rather than make assumptions.' When I was comfortably seated in my Nav Couch, I messaged Jim Igwe to ask how his team were progressing with their contracts.

'We're doing fine, Boss,' Jim responded. 'I've just sent in the end-of-term report that Kat requested. But basically, everything we contracted for is either done or progressing under local management. So, we can buzz off any time you like!'

'Did you find enough local managers?'

'Yes, there were already enough settlers from the Starship who had been involved in civil engineering work in the settlement for many years. With q-bit upgrades and additional NeuroModem training, and lots of new equipment and resources, they were ideal candidates to take over all our basic projects. We could step back from them and initiate some of the extras, like the expeditionary bases we're dotting around the surface.'

'Any remaining problems?' I asked.

'Nothing much,' Jim responded. 'We had an interesting incident in the central desert. Remember, when we were on Observatory Mountain, I told you we had a research base on the equator of the bright side's central desert that was working in concert with the one we were installing on the dark side? Well, one of the bright side survey bots suffered a complete personality failure. It was found playing in the sand, making sandcastles, and happily singing nursery rhymes.

'Malik's diagnosis was that the bot's memory management chips were fried by a burst of radiation from Proxima-Centauri. Malik recommends a full reset and complete retraining. But it may be a warning about the effect of radiation on robot brains and even human brains on this planet so, we need to explore the fault more completely. We might have to fit our bots with those salakot hats the settlers wear. The settlement's Westwood computer has suggested I send the bot to a settler called Salman Khan for investigation and repair. Do you know anything about him.'

'Yes, I've learned a lot about him, and his son Danny, during the day,' I said. 'Salman's spent his working life servicing and repairing Starship-101 electronics, and Danny followed in his father's footsteps. At present, they are starting to manufacture Frankie's 'Quantum Instantaneous Communicator' as a computer plug-in, and I'm trying to encourage that as a local industry. My suggestion for the damaged bot would be to give it to Westwood to arrange its repair with the Khans and to ask their recommendations for upgraded radiation protection in the future.'

'OK, I'll do that,' Jim replied. 'The damaged bot's the last thing on my to-do list. I'll be glad to pass it on to the locals to sort out! It's easy enough for Westwood to access. The bot was switched off in the desert and recovered to the container stores at the SpacePort'.

'I can hear crunching and gurgling noises on the line, Boss,' Jim continued. 'Are you eating something or are the comms dropping out?'

'Nothing wrong with the comms,' I reassured him. 'I'm just finishing off a couple of banjos.'

'Good stuff,' Jim exclaimed. 'But dodgy eating in a gravity well! How much of the runny yolk has ended up on your fatigues?'

'Less than usual,' I responded. 'I've managed to maintain what little remains of my dignity! Now, is there anything else we need to discuss before the staff meeting?'

'Negative. You can go back to slurping your banjo down your chest. Jim out.'

I did manage to finish off my banjo, thankfully with minimum leakage onto my chest and asked Stewart to tidy up my Nav Couch. While he was doing that, I instructed him to apologise to Kat when he next saw her, and other than that, to limit his interactions with her to his strict stewarding duties. Then I set my Nav Couch to give me a deep massage and full workout overnight, but before yielding to its tender mercies I instructed Malik to sleep-stream all the staff meeting material to my NeuroModem as a complete set of memories and then wake me at 7 a.m.

I was startled when Malik responded in the most unexpected way, 'Commodore, I have an urgent observation to report. The Proxima Observatory is currently conducting continuous sky surveys over the dark side of the planet, and the Observatory computer has just detected the decoherence of a Starship at extreme range over the dark side.'

'A Starship?' I queried, asking. 'Any identification? Any communications?'

'Negative to ID or comms, Commodore. The telescope is observing its rocket flares as it is adjusting its orbit to stay well within the planet's shadow. Using the flares to estimate size suggests that the object resembles a standard StarCorp Starship flotilla like our own ship. What actions do you require, Commodore?'

'Well, before I decide that, remind me about our authority and obligations here. And bring Kat and Jim Igwe into the loop.'

Kat and Jim immediately acknowledged their inclusion in the conversation and then Malik explained, 'Our activities here are governed by three contracts awarded by component agencies of the United Worlds: the United Planetary Authority, which is sponsoring the museum project and the recovery of Starship-101; the Interplanetary Astronomical Union, which has sponsored the Proxima Observatory and the associated satellites to survey the Centauri system; and the newly formed Interstellar Planning Authority, that planned and financed both Proxima-b missions of Interstellar Haulage. All three contracts require us to share all observations, knowledge, facilities, and services even-handedly with all members of the United Worlds.

'What about incoming Starship traffic?' Kat asked. 'Do we have any authority over that?'

'Affirmative, Captain Clason,' Malik said. 'The United Worlds, as the natural ruling authority over the activities of the Solar System, has granted

Interstellar Haulage a mandate that gives the company the authority to establish the Proxima Route for Starships in the first instance, and then impose Solar System standards of traffic control for incoming and outgoing orbital and quantum jump vessels.'

'So,' contributed Jim, 'we can't prevent incoming traffic coming into safe orbit, or even landing on Proxima-b, but all such traffic must follow UW-flight rules.'

'Affirmative, Captain Igwe,' said Malik.

'OK, so what are we going to do about this 'arrival'? Assuming it is a Starship registered with an accredited UW member, our authority over local traffic control is the limit of our mandate and we must facilitate its safe arrival into Proxima-Centauri space.'

'Agreed.' Both Kat and Jim chorused, and Jim added, 'And we must be welcoming and share all our knowledge with them.'

'Affirmative, Captain Igwe,' said Malik. 'Which will be best achieved by recruiting their flight computer into our local network.'

'Fine,' I said. 'I'll go along with that. But we can't do much of this until they get themselves into a satisfactory orbit.'

'And until they start communicating with us!' Kat interrupted.

'Well, if they've got StarCorp's standard rocket sets, it could take them most of the coming night to fly into orbit,' said Jim. 'So, we don't have to concern ourselves with them until tomorrow.'

'I'll go along with that as well,' I said. 'But we must start welcoming their arrival. Malik, will you instruct Proxima Home Traffic Control to hail them at regular intervals, identifying itself in full and requesting their identity and intentions. And make sure traffic control offers assistance with orbital stationing and emphasises they must follow UW-flight rules. Once they've acknowledged their compliance, Malik, you can offer to recruit their flight computer into your network.'

All agreed to those actions, the meeting broke up and I returned my Nav Couch to sleep mode. I also messaged Kat to tell her that I was having a deep massage and full workout, so she wouldn't worry about the unconscious, twitching, moaning, thing she'd find in my Nav Couch when she returned to the cutter. Then, I settled into the couch, pressing my head and neck into the headrest to make full contact with its life support system and allowed the couch to take control of my body.

Day 8

My Nav Couch brought me awake on the dot of 7 a.m. with the data streamed from Malik filling my mind with the end-of-term reports of our Starship operations managers and contract fulfilment managers. I made sure that all these streamed-in memories were safely lodged in my persistent dream memory trace. As Kat is my Executive Officer, I would have to check these in detail with her before the staff meeting so she could write up the minutes.

At the moment she was still slumbering quietly in the co-pilot's Nav Couch. She must have booked a later alarm call than me.

'Don't disturb Kat, Malik, but do you have any further news about our new arrival?'

'Affirmative, Commodore,' Malik responded. 'The vessel settled into its final orbital station at 05.50 Universal Time and its transponder immediately reacted to Proxima Home Station's Traffic Control ID query, announcing itself to be Starship Yuǎnfāng de Jiā from the People's Democratic Republic of Mars with a passenger complement of 950 ethnic Chinese settlers who have the intention of setting up their own settlement on Proxima-b. I have confirmed that the People's Democratic Republic of Mars is a fully accredited member of the general assembly of the United Worlds and have initiated the handshaking that will lead to registration of the vessel's flight computer, which is also called Yuǎnfāng de Jiā, into our local network. I am currently streaming further details of the commander and co-pilot/navigator. Should I continue, Commodore?'

'Yes, please. Continue,' I said, switching my couch to its chair form.

'I have just agreed with the flight computer that Distant Home is an acceptable English translation of Yuǎnfāng de Jiā. The vessel will be registered with Proxima Home Station flight control as Distant Home and the flight computer will be given that English name also,' Malik continued.

'OK, I appreciate that these names are important for your registration protocols,' I interrupted. 'But what do you know about the pilot and co-pilot? I should be speaking to them, shouldn't I?'

'Affirmative, Commodore. The Starship's pilot is named as Captain Rocky Zhang Qiang and the co-pilot/navigator is Commander Lily Li Li. Their third in line of command is the security chief, Commander Nelson Wang Jie-Jun.'

'OK, thanks for that. Copy all that information to Jim Igwe now and to Kat when she wakes up. Then arrange a courtesy call from me to Captain Zhang but leave it for thirty minutes because I need a good long shower after my night's workout. Include Kat and Jim in the loop on my side of the call but leave it up to Zhang to decide if he wants to include Commanders Li and Wang. Otherwise continue training their flight computer, offering all assistance, with emphasis on our ground observation and meteorological data, and the orbital disposition of vehicles in local space in case they need to carry out any more orbit adjustments.'

'Copy that, Commodore. Do I have your permission to share Captain Lana Mancot's video records of our activities here with Distant Home?'

'Certainly, but check with Lana first, there might be video opportunities in this unexpected arrival. Come to think of it, you'd better copy your earlier update to Lana and all others with rank of Captain, and to the Proxima Alpha Council, we can't leave them in the dark about a boat load of new neighbours about to join them. So, include Mayor Merv Castlefield, chief medical officer Sally Gates and treasurer Clint Stapleton. And since the Observatory has been monitoring this arrival since the vessel first appeared, include Art Westwood in the loop. But emphasise to all that I want it to be a low-key news item until I've had a chance to speak with and maybe meet Captain Zhang and his command staff. And one final point, Malik, remind everyone that our contracts and UW mandate require us to be as helpful to the Distant Home settlers as we have already been to the Proxima Alpha settlers; emphasise the word 'require'.'

'Willco, Commodore. Malik out.'

Still trying to avoid disturbing Kat, I wandered off towards my bathroom and on the way passed Stewart plugged into his recharge alcove, the place he insisted on calling 'his pantry'. He roused from sleep mode and offered to freshen up my Nav Couch. I told him to leave the operations room until Kat was awake, but to lay out some fresh fatigues for me in my stateroom and, when I emerged from that, serve me coffee and one more of his banjo eggs in the wardroom, still with extra napkins! Then, the shower was mine!

211

The cutter was all bustle and activity when I did emerge from my stateroom. Stewart, busily freshening the two Nav Couches in the ops room, reported that Kat was in her shower, and he would bring our breakfasts to the wardroom in a few minutes when she was ready. While I waited, I checked with Malik for any incoming messages and dealt with a handful of minor admin tasks. The only substantive matter was in the form of a summarised 'end-of-term' report about the readiness of the flagship itself for return to the Solar System; this came from Jim Igwe in his role as overall chief engineer, as well as our Civil Engineer. I was scrutinising this and marking it as a top priority for the Staff Meeting when Kat came into the wardroom, closely followed by Stewart carrying a pair of mess trays.

'Morning, Boss,' Kat said cheerily. 'I see you've checked out Distant Home's arrival, but have you seen that overall engineering report from Jim?'

'I have,' I assured her as I manoeuvred my way into taking a bite out of my egg sandwich.

'I reckon that Distant Home's arrival must be the first thing we deal with,' I added, licking egg yolk off my fingers. 'And I've asked Malik to arrange a Zoom call with Captain Zhang. Are you alright with that?'

'Sure,' Kat replied. 'Lily Li Li sounds very tuneful, but why do they need a security chief as number 3?'

'Dunno,' I answered, helpfully. 'I've never spent much time on Mars itself, just delivered iceteroids to the planet.' I gulped down the rest of my breakfast and cleaned up carefully to look halfway respectable and then asked, 'Malik, will you ask Jim Igwe to join us on this Zoom call, and then call Captain Zhang?'

'No need to ask me, Boss,' Jim interrupted. 'I'm already here.' Jim's comment, and his video presence on our digital glass was followed, almost immediately by the appearance of an image of Distant Home's control room with the two pilots reclining in their couches, with their security chief third-in-command floating in microgravity just behind them. As this image appeared, Malik reported, 'You are connected, Commodore. Go ahead, please.'

'Hello and welcome to Proxima-b!' I started. 'I'm Commodore Tarvin Clason and this is just a quick courtesy call to introduce me and my command staff, my navigator, co-pilot and executive officer, Captain Katharina Clason here beside me, and my third-in-command and chief engineer, Jim Igwe, who is currently still located aboard my Starship.'

'Thank you for your welcome, Commodore,' Zhang responded, in perfect English. 'Let me introduce myself: I am Captain Zhang Qiang, but I prefer to be called Rocky Zhang, and beside me in the navigator's seat is Commander Li Li, known as Lily Li, and behind us is my third-in-command, my security chief, Commander Wang Jie-Jun, who calls himself Nelson Wang in honour of some Royal Navy sailor of long, long ago, though in all the time I've known him, I've never seen him getting wet aboard a sailing boat!'

Nelson grinned widely at these jibes, and laughed as he punched Rocky's shoulder playfully. Behaviour which made him look much more jolly and much less threatening than the sidearm he was wearing. I'd never before seen anyone wearing a sidearm in a Starship control room.

'Please call me Tarvin,' I went on. 'And Katharina is called Kat. Oh, and Jim is called Jim because he's the only one who can pronounce his real given name! We can't chat for long because we have a staff meeting to convene in a matter of minutes, which is supposed to confirm the date of our imminent return to the Solar System. But I wanted to assure you that you can rely on our help with any aspect of the establishment of your settlement on Proxima-b. We are contractually required to offer our best assistance to all members of the United Worlds. I understand that our two flight computers are networking as I speak, so they will be able to advise about how we can best assist you.'

'Thank you, for that, Tarvin,' Rocky replied. 'I didn't realise that your departure is imminent, but I understand that this must be a short conference for that reason. I would welcome the chance for a face-to-face meeting and my flight computer, "Distant Home" I think you are calling it, is badgering me to request one of your QIC plug-ins, whatever that is.'

'Oh yes, you must have a QIC adapter, and Jim might be able to sort that out for you.' To which Jim nodded vigorously as I went on, 'And later today Kat and I will be in Proxima Home Station's artificial gravity disk, so we could have a face-to-face meeting there. Malik, my flight computer could keep you aware of my movements during the day to arrange the timing. Would that be acceptable?'

'Very acceptable, and very welcome, Tarvin,' Rocky said. 'I have already had conversations with Malik, and he has provided me with a host of videos I look forward to watching, and an introduction to your communications officer, Lana. A very forthright young lady who's already booked all three of us here for interviews in her evening news programmes!'

'Yeah,' commented Kat. 'Lana is an experience few can avoid!'

'Well, we must make our presence known to the existing settlers, and Lana offered an easy way to do that. But we must not keep you away from preparing for your staff meeting any longer. I know what they can be like! So, in hopes of another meeting in your Home Station later today, I'll thank you for your generous welcome and end this contact now. Zhang out.'

Jim also disconnected, saying he would chase up some QIC devices for Distant Home, and after agreeing that the conference with Rocky Zhang and his colleagues seemed to have been useful and friendly, Kat and I returned to the business of our upcoming staff meeting.

'I've discussed Starship-101's flight readiness with the Flight computer and with Jim,' I started. 'And both Starships are ready for the journey. So, after a few sentences reporting Distant Home's arrival and summarising the video conference we've just had, I'll move on to our agenda items and ask Jim to summarise the main findings of his engineering reports.'

'And what about the other Starship operations managers as well as contract fulfilment managers?' Kat asked.

'Well, you're the top of the SOM's list,' I replied. 'Can you provide me with a destination quantum map yet?'

'Affirmative for Waystation 4; almost 'yes' for the other waystations,' Kat responded. 'Sitrep is that as soon as the possibility of our return came up, Malik instructed the Observatory computer to revise the environmental quantum maps of all the departure points we used on the way here from Oort Station onwards but starting in this locality and then doing the rest in reverse numerical order. He did this because Observatory has been collecting astrophysics data on our entire journey. So, Observatory has churned through the great mass of data we have collected about the Proxima-Centauri locality to complete our first departing quantum map. Observatory then went to fine tune the Waystation 4 environment maps with the data collected while we were in that locality. Now it's working on the rest.'

'OK. So, Malik, how about the quantum maps for the two Starships? Where are we at with them?' I asked.

'They will be completed during the course of today, Commodore,' reported Malik, continuing, 'I awaited confirmation of the configuration for connecting the two Starships together. As Captain Igwe will no doubt confirm to you, it was finally decided to connect them stern-to-stern. With that now finalised it's only a matter of combining and revising the quantum maps we have used before and overlaying them onto Observatory's map of the Proxima-Centauri locality. Is there anything else, Commodore?'

'Yes, I have a question, Malik,' said Kat. 'What's the weather forecast for the next few days at the settlement?'

'Weather is set fair for the settlement area today and tomorrow. But a cold cyclonic system is building on the terminator to the east of the settlement that could bring heavy snow to the settlement in about 72 hours. Malik out'.

'How does the weather on the surface affect our departure?' I asked.

'It doesn't, directly,' Kat replied. 'But the infernally unpredictable storms they have here, so close to the terminator, could ruin the farewell barbie that Ilsa and Madge want to organise.'

'Yes, I see your point,' I said. 'As everything else seems to be in place for immediate departure, I was beginning to move towards suggesting we leave late tomorrow, but that wouldn't give us enough time for any farewell event.'

'True, but a departure the day after tomorrow would be convenient all around,' Kat responded, adding, 'It would give Madge and Ilsa time for the barbie, and make for more relaxed preparations for departure. We'll know the Staff Meeting's opinion very soon, but I think we also need to ask Merv about it. And we could do that now, before the Staff Meeting.'

'Yeah, Clint, too,' I said. 'Malik, can you set up a 4-way message between us two and Merv Castlefield and Clint Stapleton?'

'Willco, Commodore.'

'Hold on, Malik,' said Kat. 'We can't escape talking about Distant Home's arrival. So, Malik, please include the settlement's medical officer, Sally Gates, as well. She's not going to be happy about another thousand or so patients turning up on her doorstep.'

'Willco, Captain, Malik out'.

Fortunately, all three of the settlement's Council were able to check in quickly and Kat explained to them that the upcoming Staff Meeting was intended to crystallise our present thoughts about departure since most specialist departments had completed their contracted tasks. And she then asked me to summarise this morning's updates about Distant Home's sudden arrival. I made sure they had all been able to read Malik's early morning update and then added a few sentences about our very friendly video conference with Rocky Zhang and his command team.

Merv was the first to speak, 'There are two things that worry me about today's revelations, Tarvin,' he said. 'First, you are leaving. And second, they have arrived. And those two worries have been compounded by Malik reminding the three of us here that legally you must be as helpful to this recent arrival of a Starship full of ethnic Chinese as you have been to my people who have close to a hundred year's investment in getting to and establishing ourselves in this place. I feel like we're being pressurised here, and I don't see much chance of my people thinking differently. But I'll tell you this, Tarvin, we'll not be trampled over by no latecomers, and we'll not be squeezed out of the land that's rightfully ours!'

'Damn right! If they wanna fight, bring it on!' muttered Clint.

Great; I thought to myself, we're about to start our first interstellar war! And having thought it, I decided to say it.

'OK Merv, I understand what you're saying, and we've all been shocked, even blindsided, by Distant Home's arrival. But before you take to the barricades and start humanity's first interstellar war, take a deep breath, and think things out.' I paused to let my thought about an interstellar war sink in and then continued, 'We've all known that to complete our mission here we have to return Starship-101 to the Solar System. Now, most of my staff who've been working with you on Proxima-b report that they've fulfilled their contracts. And my engineers have reported 'immediate departure readiness' for both Starships. So, my proposal to my Staff Meeting in a few minutes time will be that we depart the day after tomorrow.'

'Why so soon?' asked Clint.

'The sooner we leave,' I said, 'the sooner we get to Oort Station and deliver Starship-101 back to the StarCorp atmospheric graving docks in orbit there. And when the dock's airtight doors close on 101's hulk, we all get paid!'

'And that includes, you, Mr Treasurer!' I added.

'Why the day after tomorrow?' Clint persisted. 'If you wanna leave soon, why not leave tomorrow?'

'We have a proposal from our catering people for a farewell barbecue, and there's a fair-weather window tomorrow for the barbie to be held then,' Kat explained.

'That's your worry number one, Merv,' I went on. 'As for worry number 2; they've only just arrived! They responded to Proxima Flight Control in the early hours of this morning as soon as they reached a stable orbit on the dark side, and my flight computer contacted theirs at that time.'

'And why are they skulking around on the dark side of Proxima-b?' Merv interrupted.

'They're not skulking, Merv,' I responded, making my growing impatience obvious. 'Captain Zhang has done what any professional Starship pilot should do; he's using the bulk of the planet to protect his crew and passengers from an unpredictable flare-star. Which you know damn well is called Proxima-Centauri! The people on Starship Distant Home are adventurous enough to seek a new life, lightyears away from their original homes. Just like the original crew of Starship-101. Don't you think you should let them explain their hopes and dreams about their own adventure before you start to treat their arrival as an act of interstellar aggression against your adventure?'

'Hey now, that's the second time you've hinted at interstellar warfare. That's a bit fanciful, ain't it?' Clint objected. 'What do you mean by it?'

'Surely, Clint, it must be obvious,' I retorted. 'The settlers living now in Proxima Alpha were either born in transit on Starship-101, or were born on Proxima-b. Either way, they were not born in the Solar System. You guys are Centaurians, proud children of the Centauri star system. Your new visitors are Solarians, born and bred in the Solar System. A week ago, they were packing up their lives on Earth, or Mars or any of the other habitats orbiting Sol. And now they're here. In all probability, they are just as anxious about their arrival as you are. But for a whole host of other reasons. They're not a threat to you. Unless you make them a threat.' I ran out of things to say so I shut up. Kat filled in for me.

'One of my jobs on our Starship is HR,' she started. 'Human resources, which means managing the single biggest asset of our ship, which is our crew. My most rewarding responsibility in that job is helping members of my crew to thrive by providing career growth, continuing training, management guidance, and support with the emotional and other challenges that life throws at us. I really believe that before you decide your attitudes towards the new arrivals, you should talk to them and listen to them. You'll probably find that you Centaurians can be enormously helpful to the Solarians by just giving them friendly advice about how to cope with what the Centauri star system throws at settlers around here.'

'OK, I'm beginning to see things more from your point of view, Tarvin, but I need to convince my people,' said Merve. 'I'm the closest thing to a career politician we've got around here and I see this whole situation as a political minefield!' Merv stated, dramatically, before continuing, 'On the one hand, and like all of us settlers, I'm very happy with what you've done so far to enable us to stand on our own feet. On the other hand, and I've discussed this with Clint, the sooner you fill the coffers of our municipal treasury, the sooner we'll be able to start running on our own feet!'

'I'll certainly vote for filling our coffers!' Clint said. 'Right now, I'm speaking to you from our new financial centre, which has just been fitted out. We've been real radical with its name and called it 'Proxima Bank'! So, the sooner you get off-planet and send me some money to put in it, the better I'll like it!'

'Don't expect to be funded immediately after we leave,' Kat interrupted. 'You must understand that a major part of our contract is to create a fully established Starship route between Sol and Proxima-Centauri. On the way up here we 'quantum-jumped' between the comms satellites that Starship-101 had left behind it at roughly one lightyear intervals between Sol and Proxima, and at each one we stopped off and left a few Starship sections and a construction team who have the job of turning those sections into a fully operational waystation on the route to Proxima. Places where Starships can stop on their way to Sol's neighbouring stars to give their crews and passengers rest and relaxation in artificial gravity discs while they become acclimatised to the business of interstellar travel. They'll be similar to Proxima Home Station, the residential station Captain Lydia Connah's been building in orbit above us, which is the Proxima-b terminus.'

'Yeah,' I contributed. 'Those waystations go all the way back to Oort Station, which is planned to be the departure terminus for all future interstellar trips. We must visit each one and stay there long enough to recover the crews into our flagship and finish off anything that needs finishing before moving on to the next. Proxima Waystation 4 is the closest to us, and we'll have to stay there for the longest time because it's intended to prepare visitors for life on Proxima-b, mimicking conditions you guys know only too well. All red twilight and concern for personal radiation protection. It's also planned to have a replica of the Proxima Alpha settlement but because the waystation is a lightyear away from us, the construction teams there will only get the data to build that replica after we arrive.

'And there's me thinking you'd just make a quantum jump straight back to Oort Station, winking out of existence here and back into existence there simultaneously!' Commented Merv.

'Nah,' I replied. 'Our contracts have three important strands. Create the route, recover Starship-101, and resupply and re-equip the Proxima-b settlers. Aside from concerns about the arrival of Distant Home, I need your comments about that last one. My contract fulfilment managers reckon they've completed their contracts. Do you agree? Sally, are you happy for us to leave you with the medical centre in its current state?'

'Yes, I think so,' replied Sally Gates, the settlement's medical officer. 'Our new buildings are fully equipped and operating smoothly, and you've left us a brigade of AI-medical care bots, which I'm planning to station around the settlement in all the larger buildings as they come into operation. You know, hotels, visitor apartment blocks, municipal buildings, and such. The bots will establish first aid and radiation protection advice posts. Our Westwood computer is coordinating a lot of this with the local construction teams.'

'OK, so that makes one satisfied customer,' I said with pleasure.

'Can I just add something about the Chinese arrivals?' Sally said.

'Sure,' I replied.

'It's just this,' Sally continued, 'my medical centre was built and equipped in anticipation of tourists and other visitors arriving in such numbers that we would need to cope with the medical needs of double our number of residents. Consequently, Mr Mayor, if you want to offer help to the Distant Home personnel, the med centre is designed to offer any and all medical services they may require while they are establishing their own settlement. And I'd also like to point out that the same considerations about visitor capacity applied to the building of hotels and guesthouses that are standing empty at the moment. We could get their businesses operating by offering temporary living accommodation to our new arrivals. That's the neighbourly thing to do.'

'OK, Sally. Understood,' I replied. 'I'm relieved to hear something more like a welcome. So, Merv, how do you feel about our departure?'

'In a word, anxious,' Merv said. 'Still anxious. In the short time you've been here you've given us protection. If you depart tomorrow or the day after, our protective shield leaves us just as a major challenge appears. Literally in our orbit. All the locals you've put into management positions of the infrastructure services you've already given us are very happy with the arrangements you've made, so there are no reservations on that score. But before you leave, I need to seek the advice and opinions of my electorate! Frankly, I don't see them being easily convinced that these, what are you calling them? Distant Home settlers? I don't see my people seeing them as anything other than a threat unless I can offer them some evidence to the contrary.'

'OK, point taken,' I replied. 'Maybe we can get some evidence for you. My flight computer has been exchanging data freely with the Distant Home flight computer since the early hours of this morning, and you should not underestimate Malik's ability to uncover any nefarious intentions on their part. We were talking to their three senior command officers just a few minutes ago and I didn't detect any threats in what was said. But Malik's seen all their business. So, Malik, what can you tell us about their intentions? Anything underhand or threatening?'

'Negative, Commodore,' Malik replied. 'I see no evidence of aggressive threats. Friendly competition in the future, certainly, but nothing more. Their plans for their own settlement were drawn up using the historical ground observations made by Starship-101 before it landed. Details of those plans may need to be modified by more recent observations, but its essentials are for their settlement to be established on the shore of the estuary of the Westwood River, initially as a single high-rise block. Avoidance of radiation injury is a key feature in their plan. Their cargo inventory includes several tunnelling machines to create enclosed roadways for travel over distance. Walkways between facilities within the settlement will also be enclosed. Apart from the tunnelling machines and high-rise building 3D-printers, their cargo manifests are remarkably similar to ours when we arrived. Though, in view of an agendum for your upcoming Staff Meeting, Commodore, you will be interested to know that one of the sections of Starship Distant Home is a microgravity farming disk, which they are busily unshipping now. I hope that helps. Malik out.'

'Thank you, Malik,' I said. 'I think it would be helpful if you could summarise all the conversations I have had this morning and compose them into a 'General Information About Starship Distant Home' report for all the crew. It will save me saying everything repeatedly!'

'Willco, Commodore.'

'All righty, Merv, does Malik's assessment of Distant Home's plans calm your nerves any?' I asked.

'I guess so,' he responded, though still sounding very doubtful. 'But I've yet to convince my people, and electorates can be fickle!'

'Well, dealing with fickle electorates is what politicians, do! Don't they, Merv?' I insisted. 'Now, if you are contacting your settlers,' I continued, 'you could seek their views on an idea we've developed to improve the farms on Proxima-b without damaging its native ecosystem. Malik hinted at it in his Distant Home comments. Our chief waystation construction engineer, Captain Lydia Connah expressed a worry about establishing too many farming enterprises on the surface of Proxima-b, on the grounds that escapes from them could irreparably damage the native ecosystem of this planet.'

'Oh, yes, tell me more,' Merv interrupted. 'Our own biologists have raised this with me after their discussions with Geoff Moore and other members of your BioScience research group. Apparently, Geoff is convinced that the natural ecosystem of Proxima-b is a major asset, perhaps, in scientific terms, *the* major asset, of Proxima-b. That's why he talked to me about it when he came back from one of his expeditions; yesterday, was it? Or the day before? Anyway, just recently. He worked himself up into quite a rant about it, saying that Proxima-b is the most eagerly pursued thing in the search for life in the universe beyond the Solar System. An ecosystem that must have evolved independently from Earth. And that's why it's our major asset. He reckons half the biologists in the Solar System would pay an arm and a leg to come here to study the place, and the other half would try to hitch a lift on the next ship coming out here.'

'Trouble is,' Merv continued, 'although all the biologists agree that they're very worried about this gamechanger for comparative evolutionary studies being damaged by the introduction of farming animals and plants from Earth, they've got no notion of how to get fresh food for the millions of visitors they're expecting to turn up here.'

'Some of whom have already arrived!' said Clint sneeringly.

'Perfectly true, Clint,' Kat said. 'But at least the new arrivals have brought their own solution to this biodiversity problem, while we were sent totally unprepared for by our sponsors.'

I thought Kat was sounding a little angry with Clint's repeatedly aggressive attitude to Distant Home, so I jumped in with what I thought was a more positive statement, 'Well, that's where we can help, guys. Our problem's been caused by the Interstellar Planning Authority getting into a mess with the ethics of extrasolar colonisation by planning for farming on the Proxima-b surface instead of limiting food production to orbiting artificial gravity farming discs. Now, our Lydia Connah is very experienced in building waystations with artificial gravity discs, and she has a way to correct IPA's error. She knows that StarCorp supplies ready-stocked artificial gravity farming discs that produce fresh food for colonies within the Solar System where the farming can't be done on the surface. Places like Venus and the Ice Moons of Jupiter and Saturn. So, with Ilsa and Emma's support, Lydia's persuaded me to suggest to StarCorp that they supply four such farming discs to you in part payment for Starship-101 and then all the agricultural smallholdings can be moved off the surface and into artificial gravity discs of pasture in orbit, along with space for horticulture and arable farming. The only food items that come down to the surface then are dead animals and harvested plants.'

'That sounds all fine and dandy,' Clint interrupted. 'But can we afford such an arrangement when we need all the cash we can get?'

'Don't worry, Clint,' I assured him. 'The contract calls for a like-for-like replacement of a ten-kilometre Starship. The orbital artificial gravity discs are all 500-metre-long sections; so, the monetary value of four of them is only around 20% of the contract value of Starship-101. You'll still be left with a Starship-load of cash to put into your new bank!'

Malik interrupted our discussion at this point, 'Commodore, the staff meeting is scheduled to start in ten minutes.'

'OK, Malik,' I responded. 'Please tell Stewart to serve fresh coffee to the operations room, and will you set up the ops room digital glass for the conference connections of all attendees. Please also arrange for Sally, Clint, and Merv to attend the meeting as observers if they so wish.'

'Willco, Commodore. Malik out.'

'Not me,' said Merv. 'I'd better cut out from the meeting now, Tarvin. We've raised a lot of business here that I need to put to my electors, so I'd better set about measuring their opinions. But before I go, I want to say that you've persuaded me that we should hold out the hand of friendship to the Distant Home people and see what develops from that.'

'Yes! Hear, hear,' Sally Gates chimed in, as Merv ploughed on, 'And I'm also persuaded that we need farms in orbit rather than on the planet to safeguard Proxima's native ecosystems. For my part, my decision would be that you go ahead with your discussion with StarCorp on our behalf. Merv out.'

Sally and Clint indicated their assent to Merv's executive decision, Sally more enthusiastically than the still unmollified Clint, but both stayed online to observe our meeting. Kat and I took a quick comfort break and were reinstalled in our pilot chairs in the ops room in time to see the first of the staff sign-in to the Staff Meeting's video-conference session and the growing babble of whispered background conversations.

I called the meeting to order on the dot at ten a.m. by reminding the staff assembled online that our priority was to decide our date of departure from Proxima-b, emphasising that we need to leave as soon as we can because the sooner we can get Starship-101 to Oort Station and deliver it to the StarCorp docks, the quicker we all get paid!

I started by saying, 'Most of the business we must get through today has already been tabled in documented form and I am going to assume that you've all streamed those data to your NeuroModems before the start of this meeting. I suggest that anyone who's not done so takes a 5-minute nap and have Malik stream it now. But, before you do, we have some startling late-breaking overnight news I need to talk about.' I took a few deep breaths before launching yet again into my summarised description of the most recent events, from the decoherence of Starship Distant Home in Proxima space right through to the most recent few minutes of discussions with Proxima Alpha's council, ending with 'I've asked Malik to compose a summarised report of all this for distribution to all our crew and staff. Anything to say, Malik?'

'Affirmative, Commodore. My composition is complete, and I am distributing it as a memory trace to the NeuroModems of all crew, staff and guests at this meeting. You can refer to it immediately and it will be installed into your long-term memory in the usual way in your next sleep cycle. Malik out.'

Malik's disconnection coincided with the appearance of a memory trace of his report of our recent conversations about Distant Home into my NeuroLink, and to give the crew an opportunity to the crew to absorb its content I called a ten-minute adjournment. 'It all looks accurate and generally OK to me,' Kat announced privately to my NeuroModem, so I privately messaged Clint and Sally to ask if they were content with the summary of their most recent discussions with us; both agreed the report was accurate, though, again, Clint expressed reservations about Merv's executive decisions.

'I don't want to stifle discussion,' I went on. 'But we do need to continue our meeting and deal with our main agenda items. So, speak up if you think Malik or I have missed anything significant. I extend that invitation to the originally tabled documents for the rest of our agenda. I'd like to take them as 'read'; if you want to add anything important to your own report, speak up. Any comments now?' I paused slightly to allow for any dissent to be made known.

Jim Igwe was the only one to speak. 'No adverse comments,' he said. 'Just confirmation of Malik's reading of the Distant Home's cargo manifest. There are no suspect items among their cargo, it's all precisely what you need to build and sustain a settlement on Proxima. What stood out to me is that all their engineering equipment is 'next-year's-model' standard; I'm particularly envious about their 3D-printers that build high-rise accommodation blocks. Oh, yes, I'm also impressed by the manifest entry of five tonnes of gold bars. So, Clint, if you're still with us, you'd better arrange with my teams down on Proxima to build you a high security vault in that new bank of yours! I've messaged them for you, so they'll be in touch. Jim Igwe out.'

Among a growing murmur of amused comment, including 'That's a bank account worth having!' Clint's response was a rather stunned, 'OK, I'll get onto that.' There were no further substantive comments, so I tapped my microphone to make 'gavel-noises' to bring the meeting to order and go back to our main business. 'OK, then, let's deal with our agenda. I propose we take the Minutes of our last meeting as read. For the benefit of our formal record, we held our last meeting just before we left Oort Station, and it became a schedule of our Proxima-Centauri contracted tasks. Consequently, all the Matters Arising from the Minutes are catered for in this meeting's agenda.'

'Seconded,' Kat said briskly, before asking, 'Any objections?' There were none, and I resumed, saying that after reading all the 'end-of-term' reports and discussing the issue with several people I will further propose that we prepare to depart during the day after tomorrow. Among general murmurs of assent, Kat was the first to speak.

'I agree with that proposal and will second it,' Kat said. 'But for the sake of the minutes, which will be incorporated into the official log, I want to specify the reasons for choosing the day after tomorrow. Briefly, then: both Starships have been certified space-ready, and Malik has reported that all necessary quantum maps will be available by the end of today. All contract fulfilment managers have reported completion of work contracted for Proxima-b including appointment of local managers for all activities. Before this meeting, the Commodore and I discussed these matters with Mayor Castlefield and his colleagues, and they verified those contract completions as acceptable. So, assuming everyone has streamed the tabled end-of-term reports, and Malik's report about discussions of Distant Home's arrival, I will ask one final time if any of the fulfilment managers have anything to add to their reports?'

Jim Igwe was the only person to speak up. 'Just a minor informational point to make for the record,' he said. 'It's about the disposition of excess vehicles capable of orbital flight, and excess cargoes that we are not taking back to the Solar System. Firstly, we've parked a selection of shuttles and taxis for the locals to use at the SpacePort, and a similar selection has been docked in orbit in Proxima Home Station. Both Westwood and the Proxima Home Traffic Control computer have been given complete inventories of these vehicles and the brigades of robots in both locations that are needed to service and operate them.

'Secondly, we have a small number of Starship cargo sections that still contain cargo for Proxima-b that's surplus to immediate requirements. These are all equipped with autonomous heavy lift cargo shuttles and brigades of AI-bots, so traffic control can bring the cargoes down to the SpacePort as required. These excess cargo sections are being tugged into a synchronous orbit over the dark side of Proxima-b for orbital storage. Again, Westwood and traffic control have all the necessary cargo manifests to manage unloading as the cargo is required at the settlement. I think that's all.'

'Thank you, Captain Igwe,' I said. 'Are there any further comments arising from the tabled end-of-term reports?' There were none. 'OK, the reports mentioned by the Secretary will be incorporated into the official log. Moving on, then,' I continued, 'we have a seconded proposal before us that we prepare to depart during the day after tomorrow. Are there any objections?' There were none. 'In that case,' I finished off, 'let the minutes show that this proposal for departure in approximately 48 hours' time from now was accepted without dissent.'

'Boss, can we take Ilsa's farewell barbie next?' Kat whispered at me, I nodded, and Kat continued, more loudly, to the whole meeting, 'We have a short fine-weather window at present. Satellite weather forecasting shows a severe cyclonic system spinning towards the settlement from the dark side. The way it looks now, Proxima Alpha will likely be in full storm mode in around 72 hours.'

'Oh joy!' I replied. 'Another one! Yeah, that makes it very appropriate to take an AOB item out of order at this point because Captain Blaine is proposing we throw a farewell barbecue party tomorrow for all Starship staff and all settlers.' Amid a growing swell of mumbled 'agreed' and 'approved, next business' I scanned through the ident tiles in the Zoom online display, saying, 'Ilsa, I've lost you for the moment. Do you want to say anything about the barbie?'

'Ooh, you don't want to lose Ilsa, Boss. Who's gonna feed us?' That was Emma, in a stage whisper pitched so everyone could hear.

'Relax, Emma, you daft bat,' Ilsa said. 'I ain't lost, we're sharing the same terminal, but you're hogging the camera. Boss, I've only got one thing to say, which is that Madge Clarkson and her catering brigade will organise and run the barbie on the land just outside the Westwood Restaurant. Starts around 4 p.m. Bring your own teeth'.

'To which I will add that we will provide a regular shuttle service to bring crewmembers from the flagship to the SpacePort from about noon tomorrow. The shuttles will start leaving the SpacePort to return crewmembers to the flagship from 9 p.m.,' Jim announced.

'OK, thank you all for that information,' I said, trying to regain the chair's control of the meeting. 'I can add another means of barbie transport; Kat and I will be taking the Commodore's Cutter into orbit after this Staff Meeting and will then be staying on the flagship where we will stream all the new quantum maps overnight so we can do a technical rehearsal tomorrow morning for the next day's quantum jump. I expect I'll need it because the configuration of the flagship has changed so much. After that, and a change into our mess dress uniforms, we'll de-orbit in the cutter.'

I paused and glanced over at Kat who was nodding and giving me 'thumbs-up' gestures animatedly.

'So, late morning tomorrow the cutter will be available to transport early birds down to the surface. I suppose I should add that me and Kat, and maybe, Jim, will probably be the last to leave the barbecue party so any other late leavers are welcome to join us in the cutter for the return to orbit. Just tell Malik and he'll keep us all informed of passenger lists and flight times.'

'Pencil me and Emma in for both directions, Boss,' said Ilsa. 'We'll be helping Madge with the barbie. Can I ask if your mention of mess dress uniforms applies to all crewmembers?'

'Certainly,' I replied. 'All crew, all ranks; full dress uniform. I think we owe our friends on Proxima-b one final performance dressed in our best bib and tucker. And as 'performance' is the right word, while I'm at it, pay attention Lieutenant Commander David Wood.'

David sat bolt upright in his chair and mouthed 'What have I done now?' at his computer terminal.

'I enjoyed your pantomime appearance as a Stormtrooper Admiral at our Oort Station departure reception; though I had to disapprove of it as inappropriate because the reception was hosted by the Governor of Oort Station. But tomorrow's 'full dress uniform' occasion is a different, and more entertaining, event. So, you have my permission to display your full set of 'Stormtrooper' and 'Death-Star Slayer' honours, providing you are willing to explain them to the settlers.'

'Aw, gee, thanks Boss!' David gushed. 'You know, if there's a blizzard approaching the settlement, the TV station might like to broadcast the Star Wars vids.'

'How many are there?' asked Lana, amid mounting murmurings from the assembled staff.

'About fifty, now. But they're still making them. Malik streamed all the ones we carry to Westwood,' David replied. 'But the vintage ones are the best.'

'I'll mention them to Daisy,' Lana said.

'I'd like to bring us back to the next substantive agenda item,' I interjected loudly and with a few more gavel-taps on my microphone, 'Which is our secretary's suggestion that we the change the name of the flagship to 'Pink Ghost'. Kat, do you want to speak to that?'

'Yes, Boss,' Kat responded. 'The crew must be aware of the origin of this proposal, but to remind them I have tabled satellite images of the quantum entanglement just before our recent translocation of Starship-101 into orbit, showing a slightly fuzzy translucent image of the flagship apparently on the surface of Proxima-b about twenty kilometres due west. The image of the flagship appears pink, because red starlight is the only thing we've got around here. So, I thought we might rename our ship '*Pink Ghost*' and use these images in our marketing to show what we do.'

I heard general murmurs of 'yeah', 'sure', 'suits me', and 'why not?' So, I went back to being formal and asked, 'Before we go any further, are there any objections to this proposal?' There were none, and I continued. 'OK, then let the record show that this proposal was approved nem. con. Now, Malik, what's the protocol here? How do we go about renaming a Starship?'

'The name of the ship is entirely a matter for the ship's owners, in this case Interstellar Haulage. But the name needs to be approved in a properly constituted meeting of the Directors of the company, and then registered with the appropriate Starship registration office on Earth. Obviously, we are still over four lightyears from Earth, so nothing can be done until we are within reasonable radio range of Earth's authorities. The currently registered name of this ship is Flagship-1, and the registered name of Commodore Harden's vessel is Flagship-2.'

'So, it's time we put a bit more imagination into naming our ships,' I said. 'When we meet Harden at Oort Station we'll organise a little directors' meeting and make the necessary resolution. What and where is 'the appropriate Starship registration office on Earth', Malik?'

'Stockholm,' Malik responded, 'would be the appropriate Registration Office for Clason family ships. During the 18th and 19th centuries the family were shipbuilders and shipping merchants in Härnösand, Sweden, and your grandfather continued the tradition when he started building Starships.'

'Oh, well,' I said. 'We'd better do as grandfather does. So, will you have the necessary documentation prepared to send off the change of name registration from Oort Station, Malik?'

'Willco, Commodore. Malik out'.

'Thanks, Kat, that's another item dealt with,' I said. 'We seem to be rattling through our business at a fine rate and that brings us to a proposal from Captain Lydia Connah, which is supported by Dr Geoff Moore, Captain Ilsa Blaine and Lieutenant Commander Emma Halton. Lydia has tabled a document suggesting that we seek to replace the ground-based farming enterprises we have established on Proxima-b to produce fresh food, with ready-stocked artificial gravity farming discs produced by StarCorp. I'm sure you would like to speak to this proposal, Di, but we've been talking to Mayor Castlefield and his colleagues, and they have a slightly different argument for favouring your idea. So, if you will briefly describe your ideas, I'll follow up with Mayor Castlefield's.'

'OK, Boss. I can manage that,' said Lydia, before continuing, 'As the Boss said, I think Proxima-b should farm its fresh foods safely isolated well away from the planet's native biome. We are all concerned with fulfilling our contracts. Our prime contracted purpose being to make the lives of the pioneering settlers who came to this planet many years ago as easy as possible. And to this end, our erstwhile leaders in the Solar System have equipped us with ground-based farming enterprises to produce fresh food on Proxima-b by using farmed animals and plants from Earth. Now, producing fresh food is essential. But every farm or small holding on the planet's surface is an escape waiting to happen. And with our focus on doing the best for our heroic interstellar pioneers, we are missing the point,' Lydia was almost shouting by the time she reached the end of this statement, so she paused for a few moments and sipped from a microgravity bulb of water to cool off a little.

'And the point is,' she continued, 'that for several hundred years, humanity has been asking the question 'is there life elsewhere in the universe other than on Earth?' and Proxima-b answers that question with a resounding YES! And yet, even though they knew this from the first messages the settlers sent home, the powers-that-be in the Solar System, in their miserly finance-driven 'wisdom' gave us rabbits, goats, ducks, sheep and chickens to farm on this planet's surface. Farm animals to threaten an ecosystem in which animals have not yet evolved, and flowering plants for an ecosystem in which such vegetation will not evolve for hundreds of millions of years. It's penny-pinching madness, and I'll tell you why. I have installed waystations with artificial gravity discs all over the Solar System. Several in orbits around Venus and Jupiter and Saturn's Ice Moons. Places where there is no way we could farm on the surface. So, StarCorp came up with the answer to the problem of cultivating fresh food in such places, long ago, in the form of artificial gravity farming discs, which allow you to have estates of around 150 hectares of farmland in orbit on the inside wall of each rotating disc; that's more than enough for a decent sized family farm. It's up to the customer to decide how much of the farm is devoted to pasture, horticulture or arable farming, and those orbiting Ice Moons even include replica villages providing rest and recreation facilities for the surface research and engineering crews. If we could get four such discs in part payment for Starship-101, then all the animal smallholdings and plant growth facilities could be moved off the surface, so the only food items that come down to the surface would be dead animals and harvested plants.'

As Lydia paused at the end of her speech, Ilsa jumped into the discussion with: 'I just want to make it clear that Emma and I agree with Lydia 100%. We're contracted to establish smallholdings on the surface, and that's what we've done. But we know very well that it's the cheap option. And though we've doubled up on preventing escapes in all our containments, we know that farming Earth animals and plants on the surface is the wrong thing to do for the long term.'

'OK, that's put everyone in the picture,' I said. 'So, let me summarise the settler's viewpoint on this. And our two observers representing that community, Clint and Sally, should feel free to contribute to this discussion. Mayor Castlefield has told us that the biology teams who are researching the unique ecosystem of Proxima-b have gone to him in the past with similar fears about the danger of doing careless damage to the native ecology of this planet, and for the same reason Lydia mentioned, and from here I'll read the actual words he used from my NeuroModem's memory. Merv said that he'd been told that as Proxima-b is 'an ecosystem that must have evolved independently from Earth' it is 'the most eagerly pursued thing in the search for life in the universe beyond the Solar System'. But what really convinced Merv was that our very own head of the BioScience Group of the Interstellar Research Team, Geoff Moore, pointed out that its ecosystem is the major asset of Proxima-b, going on to say, again in Merv's own words: 'half the biologists in the Solar System would pay an arm and a leg to come here to study the place, and the other half would try to hitch a lift on the next ship out here'. I think that's an accurate record of our meeting, isn't it Clint?'

'Sure is. Nicely summarised,' Clint Stapleton confirmed.

'I'd like to add my confirmation to that, also,' added Geoff Moore. 'I signed in to this meeting specifically to support Lydia's proposal and to emphasise how crucial it is that we do as much as possible to protect the native biology of this planet.'

'Thanks for that, Geoff,' I said. 'There's just one further comment of Merv Castlefield's that I want to inform the meeting about, and then I'll bring this item to a conclusion. Merv said that he was persuaded that the farms that support Proxima-b must be in orbit rather than on the planet, and as Mayor, he instructed us to go ahead on the settlers' behalf, with discussions with StarCorp for four farming discs in part payment for Starship-101. So, that will be our substantive proposal, but I would like you to consider first an amendment to the effect that we ask Lydia, Ilsa and Emma to form the working party that will, when we get back to Oort Station, undertake the discussions with StarCorp. Can we agree that? Any objections?'

There were no objections, just the usual murmurings featuring words like 'yes', 'agreed' and 'sure'.

'OK, we'll record that as approved nem. con. and proceed to the substantive motion that proposes we seek four farming discs in part payment for Starship-101 when we deliver the Starship to StarCorp at Oort Station. Objections?'

While I was waiting for the meeting's response to that, I sent a private message to Malik, copied to Kat, asking him to send a taxi to bring the Westwood twins and their parents to my cutter at the SpacePort. There were no objections to the substantive proposal, just a query from Lydia, who asked: 'If we buy four farming discs from StarCorp at Oort Station, how do they get to Proxima-b?'

'Well,' I said, 'speaking as the Commodore of Pink Ghost, I'd be willing to bring them up here pro bono. When we've got the whole route from Oort to Proxima, it shouldn't take more than a weekend and if I arrange a party with old friends at the Westwood Restaurant, I'd hope that many of my crew would volunteer to join me.'

Among widening murmurs of agreement, Emma's voice was clearest, saying 'You can pencil me in for that trip as well, Boss.'

'Are you willing to have that plan incorporated into the formal record?' Kat asked.

'Affirmative'. I said and there was a tinkling wave of applause and 'hear hears' from around the meeting.

'I do believe we've reached the end of our agenda,' Kat announced. 'Is there any other business?'

She paused for a reasonable length of time before resuming, 'If not, I declare the meeting closed and thank you all for your attendance. Malik will prepare a complete set of minutes for incorporation into Pink Ghost's official log. Katharina Clason out.'

The vid-conference ID tiles on the view screens quickly winked out in sequence and as they did, Kat and I stepped out of our Nav chairs and went into the wardroom in search of more coffee and biscuits. Stewart had anticipated our need for refreshments when Malik alerted him about my request for a taxi for the Westwood family and we gratefully took advantage of his offer to pour fresh coffee for us. While we waited for the Westwoods, Kat and I scanned through, and edited, Malik's text summarising the business of the Staff Meeting, making a to-do list of the main proposals, and finally signing the text off as the true minutes to be incorporated in the ship's log.

Shortly after finishing that task the taxi's autopilot reported its imminent arrival in the SpacePort parking area and Kat and I went to welcome the

Westwoods at the main air lock. I was expecting to meet the boys' father, Arthur, for the first time, but I wasn't expecting their younger sister, Sarah. The three youngsters bounced energetically into the cutter, cruising around the operations room before being motioned into the wardroom by Stewart. The parents entered much more respectfully, but with much the same level of excitement.

After the introductions, we all settled into the wardroom, and Kat took control of the event. 'I'm the executive officer, and I am responsible for human resources on our flagship, which has just been renamed 'Pink Ghost'. I welcome you all aboard the Commodore's Cutter, which is the Commodore's private spaceship for ship-to-ship and ground-to-ship travel.'

Kat paused, smiled, and looked around the eager young faces. Then she continued, 'For the benefit of the budding Starship engineers among us, the Commodore's Cutter is a single-stage-to-orbit spaceplane that uses a combined-cycle oxygen-hydrogen rocket propulsion system that's air-breathing when flying in an oxygen-rich atmosphere.' Pause, smile again, then she said, 'I've planned this event as an induction of Billy and George into our Midshipman training programme, and I'll outline what I've planned for us to do in a few moments. But before we go any further, I need to ask if all of you are still sure that you are happy with the basic notion that Billy and George will join my flagship's crew and leave Proxima-b when our ship returns to the Solar System?'

The whole family nodded their heads in agreement, and I was particularly struck by young Sarah's very vigorous nodding which was accompanied by wide eyes and a grin at least as broad as those of her brothers.

Arthur Westwood spoke up, 'I guess I should say something as I've not had the chance to speak to you about it, face to face, before,' he said. 'It's a bittersweet moment. That's plainly true. My boys are leaving home, and that's hard to take. But on the other hand, you could say that astronomy, spaceships and space travel were cravings that were born into them, and me for that matter, through my grandparents. I had to satisfy that craving with the astronomy I've studied all my life, following in my late father's footsteps. Your arrival has brought me a hundred years' worth of astronomical knowledge I knew nothing of, and a present-day way of studying it with this astonishing NeuroModem. And I thank you for that because it's life-fulfilling. And now you are offering my sons the opportunity to journey through the galaxy I've learned so much about in the last few days. I certainly thank you for that! And me and Linda say: go for it, boys, but make sure you have fun out there.'

'Thank you for those comments, Arthur,' I said. 'I appreciate them.'

'Call me Art,' he replied.

'Glad to hear you like the Observatory we brought for you!' said Kat. 'I hear you've just agreed to be its first Director!' At this, Art smiled broadly and nodded again.

'So, you'll be glad to hear my plans for today,' Kat continued. 'Because in a little while you'll be able to check out one of the orbital subdivisions of your new empire!'

'I'll explain as we fly,' Kat went on. 'Because, first, we're flying the cutter off-planet to Proxima Home Station where I want to introduce Billy and George to the Midshipman buddies, I've picked out for them. So,' She paused and looked at the three children. 'Are there any volunteers for the pilot seats?'

All three of the Westwood kids threw up their hands, with little Sarah being especially excitedly vocal, with 'Me! Me! Miss!' as though she was volunteering for a school picnic. Her face fell so much into disappointment when Kat said, 'Sorry, Sarah, we only have two pilot seats.' That I had to intervene.

'Hold on there, Kat,' I said. 'You're forgetting the emergency crewing arrangements on this ship. Malik, will you instruct Stewart how to install the Engineer's seat into the cockpit?'

'Willco, Commodore.'

'Kat, why don't you take the kids into the ops room to watch Stewart unship Sarah's seat from the cockpit roof? And Malik, arrange a flight plan to Proxima Station for the Commodore's Cutter, departing immediately. Oh, and rig the wardroom for passenger travel.'

'All in hand, Commodore,' Malik reported.

As Kat ushered the three youngsters into the Ops room, I cleared away a few items from the wardroom table to allow it to fold and slide into its bulkhead housing.

'You don't have to move,' I told Linda and Art. 'Just allow your chairs to gently reconfigure into take-off couches and strap you in. The digital glass in the bulkhead wall opposite will show the view forward when the autopilot starts to move us.'

'But in the meantime,' I quickly added. 'Autopilot, stream the ops room cameras to the wardroom screens.'

The ops room view showed Sarah eagerly climbing into the Engineer's seat even as Stewart was locking it into place between, and slightly behind, the two pilot seats towards which Kat was guiding Billy and George. With all three Westwood children safely strapped into their seats, Kat scurried back to the wardroom as the intercom announced, 'Commodore's Cutter, Proxima Home Traffic Control, confirming flight plan laid into your autopilot. We have cleared all conflicting traffic. Depart in your own time.'

Followed by the autopilot announcing, 'Rollout to departure from Proxima-b SpacePort imminent. All crew to prepare for take-off. Prepare for take-off.'

Kat settled into the passenger seat beside me and allowed it to strap her in. The viewscreen ahead of us switched to showing the outside view as my ship began to roll forward on gently howling engines.

'Autopilot, continue to show view of cockpit on wardroom screens,' I ordered. 'Picture in picture, view from the rear and view from the front.'

The two views I had requested appeared on the wardroom screen, embedded inside the image of the outside world as we rolled off the parking area and around the taxiway to the departure point on runway number one. The view of the kids' faces was classic; wide eyed, eager, grins on all three faces.

Kat's voice broke into our joint anticipatory gaze gently. 'OK, relax everybody,' she said. 'It looks like a video game but it's all real, so just let the experiences roll over you and enjoy every moment.' And then we started to roll forward down the runway with ever-increasing speed and ever-increasing noise from our air-breathing jets. I felt the increased acceleration as the oxy-hydrogen afterburners kicked in to lift us into flight, followed, in just a minute or so, by the immediate quietness as we slipped beyond the speed of sound and left our noise behind us.

'Does everyone feel OK?' Kat asked.

Linda and Art both said 'yes', with Art adding, 'Take-off was a lot smoother than I was expecting.' We didn't need any confirmation from the youngsters, whose facial expressions were still those of rapt enjoyment.

'How old is Sarah?' I asked.

'Fourteen,' Linda replied.

'Well, looking at the way she's enjoying this, I reckon she'll be wanting to fly Starships herself before too long.'

'Would she be eligible for what the boys are doing?' asked Art. 'She's been developing an interest in astronomy, and I've been very keen to guide her towards a career in that area.'

'You can certainly carry on with that plan and she'll still be able to follow her brothers and fly Starships,' I said. 'Co-pilots, like Kat, are astronavigators. So, that's a career path she could take if she maintains her interest in Starships and, subject to the same aptitude tests her brothers have recently passed, we'd be happy to take her into the same apprenticeship programme.'

'I think she'd be really happy with that,' Art said, with Linda nodding in agreement in the background. 'The boys have always been keen players of the space travel video games that we brought with us on Starship-101, and they eagerly sought out the most up-to-date versions from the software that Malik downloaded to the settlement's Westwood computer. I've noticed that Sarah could easily hold her own with Billy and George in any of the games that depended on knowledge of Solar System astronomy, new or old!'

As we chatted, the cutter's aspect slowly changed towards the vertical, and the passenger seats rotated on their gimbals, though the continued acceleration kept us firmly thrust into the seats' cushions. The digital glass image displays on the bulkhead opposite our passenger seats in the wardroom migrated across the wall, keeping the image steady in our eyeline as the sky faded through increasingly darker shades of red and towards the black of deep space.

Kat continued to conduct her charges through the take-off by warning of our imminent orbital insertion, 'The main engines will cut out soon and we will cruise the rest of the way just using thruster jets to adjust our attitude. When the engines do flame out you will be floating in microgravity, but your seats will keep you firmly strapped in; so, you won't float away!'

As predicted, the roar of our main engines faded away and I could sense my seat straps restraining further forward movement of my body. Then the thrusters came alive, adjusting the ship's attitude from the close to vertical relative to the planet's surface that had lifted us into orbit, to the close to horizontal relative to the planet's surface that represented our new orbital track. As the thrusters slowly made this adjustment, the forward views on the video screens in front of us began to change, the absolute blackness of deep space disappearing off the top of the screens, while, with increasing slowness as the thrusters reduced our rate of rotation, the red-lit image of Proxima Home Station rolled towards the centre of the view screen.

'OK guys, you can all release your seat belts now,' said Kat. 'But remember you have no gravity vector to orient you. So, make only very gentle movements to begin with. We advise that you keep one hand holding onto a strap or arm rest to stop you drifting too far and to give you a frame of reference. What you see on your view screen is our destination, Proxima Home Station we're heading for those brightly illuminated white lights around the middle of the station. They surround our docking hatch that seals the airlock leading to the main Transfer Lounge of the waystation. The robot crews within the airlock will communicate with our autopilot to organise our secure docking. The process will take several minutes and may involve a sequence of several sharp changes of direction of the cutter as it's oriented to the docking hatch. In the meantime, you can be getting yourselves used to microgravity, but be careful!'

That last bit of advice, intended for the youngsters, seemed from the view screen image coming from the ops room, not to be heeded. These images already showed them performing 'floating gymnastics' in microgravity, by deftly pushing off from some handhold and spinning, tumbling or cartwheeling in all directions. Each trying to outperform their other siblings.

Kat and I had a much more difficult time gently guiding their parents from the wardroom to the ops room. By the time we reached the ops room, the wilder aspects of the kids' activity had calmed down and George and Billy were hovering across the room lying stretched out stiffly as though in sleep, but gently rotating around their long axis. Sarah, on the other hand, was floating upside-down, and at right angles to her brothers, while she used only her fingers to 'walk' across the ops room table.

'No vomit-comet there, then,' I commented. 'So, that's another space-farer's hurdle successfully crossed.'

Kat nodded, but Linda asked, 'Vomit-comet?'

'It may be apocryphal,' I started to explain. 'But the story goes back to the very first few years of putting humans into space when the only way trainee astronauts could be introduced to the feeling of zero-gravity in orbit was to fly them in special aircraft on flight paths that alternately climbed and dived through the atmosphere. The path of the climb was a hyperbola at the top of which those within the aircraft experienced the feeling of weightlessness for only about twenty to twenty-five seconds. Trouble was, so the story goes, the repeated sudden changes from climb to dive made many candidate astronauts feel very ill, even though most of them were experienced pilots! So, the nickname 'Vomit-Comet' was given to the planes!'

'Yeah, all that's true, Boss,' said Kat. 'But it's not just an ordinary motion sickness, in fact, it's the opposite because there is no sensation of bodily

236

movement in orbit. Yet 'space sickness' is endured by around half of all space travellers when they first get into orbit and until they adapt to weightlessness. The fact that these three rascals are behaving like this demonstrates completely, I think, that they don't suffer from space sickness!'

'That's a relief!' said Art Westwood.

'You don't know how much of a relief it is for all of us!' I said. 'Vomit goes a long way in orbit!'

'Well, I'm not feeling the least bit queasy at the moment,' Linda Westwood announced. 'But if you don't find something else to discuss, I might be giving you a demonstration!'

'OK,' smiled Kat. 'Let me tell you about our programmed activities after we've docked with the waystation.' She tried to attract the attention of Billy, George and Sarah but by this time they had discovered the art of 'swimming' through the air and were, slowly, chasing each other around the ops room. 'Are you listening?' She shouted.

'Yes!' They shouted back as, with various levels of success and elegance they 'swam' to a halt, floating in mid-air more or less in front of Kat.

'Right,' she resumed. 'Billy and George, when the airlock opens, I will introduce you to your two Midshipman buddies who I have chosen to help you through your first few months of training as Midshipmen and apprentice Starship engineers on board the Pink Ghost. They will meet you in the airlock and my idea was that they'd take you into the microgravity part of the Transfer Lounge to get you introduced to microgravity! But judging by your present performance that will not take long. Still, enjoy yourselves, Sarah too. There are lots of personal AI-robot guides in the lounge you can play with. They are located there to offer help to arriving passengers who might be struggling in their first experience of microgravity by towing them to where they need to go. I'm sure you'll be able to give these robot guides a real test but try not to be too unkind! When you've had enough microgravity 'training', your buddies will take you through the travelator system to a Café Claudius near the entrance to the artificial gravity ring to meet up with the rest of us for lunch.'

The docking procedure came to a climax with a gentle cacophony, almost a tinkling, of locking clamps and bolts. Kat turned to Art to describe her plans for him.

'Art, you'll be met by Captain Lydia Connah who is still our Officer in Command of Proxima Home Station. She will take you to see the station's control room and its other orbital observatory assets, and she will formally hand over control of all these to you as Director of the Observatory. Afterwards, Lydia will take you to Café Claudius to catch up with the rest of us for lunch.'

Art looked frankly horrified. 'I wasn't expecting that,' he said, so I stepped in to remind him that it's not such a big job as most of the detailed work was carried out by quantum computers, and that the Westwood and Observatory computers, both trained by Malik, will be able to stream memories of all the information he might need into his NeuroModem during his next night's sleep.

As the airlock door on our side was swung open, we saw Lydia accompanied by two young ladies dressed in smart Starship fatigues with the Midshipman's white patches with a gold button on each side of their jacket collars. All three were wearing forage caps and they snapped to attention and saluted when they saw me and Kat, and we returned their salutes and gestured 'at ease' at them. This little ceremony impressed Billy and George. In fact, it might be a little more accurate to say that the two young ladies in uniform fatigues impressed Billy and George.

Kat pulled Art Westwood passed me and introduced him to Lydia and after a few more general 'hellos' she took him off to the station's control room. Then Kat turned to the Westwood twins.

'Gentlemen, you are now aboard an Interstellar Haulage vessel on active service. You will now start learning the discipline that is required of you for service aboard such vessels. Please use the grab handles on the walls of this airlock to come down here and do your best to stand to attention.' Kat snapped it out, like the second-in-command she was, and then fixed the two boys with penetrating eyes as they complied with her orders. I was floating, stationary and holding a grab handle, behind Art Westwood. He turned slightly to face me and winked.

'I suppose that shambles of presentation will have to do, as you are still private citizens,' she commented. 'Please identify yourselves, you first,' she said, indicating Billy.

Billy waved a hand weakly and said, 'Er, yeah, like, I'm Billy. Billy Westwood, that is.' He smiled, Kat didn't. But one of the young lady Midshipmen snapped sharply to attention, saluted Kat and held out something towards her with her left hand, saying 'Ma'am'.

Kat returned the salute and took what turned out to be a 'Billy Westwood' name badge saying, 'Thank you, Midshipman Wang. At ease'. She held out the badge to Billy and he took hold of it with a friendly 'Gee, thanks.' Kat drew in a breath that hissed across her teeth, and said, 'Wear that at all times, and I mean ALL times. Do you understand that order?'

'Sure thing, Miss,' Billy managed, wilting under Kat's growing glare.

'This,' Kat said, indicating the young lady who had delivered Billy's name badge, 'is Midshipman May Shyahng Wang, she has been designated as your official 'buddy'. It is customary for you to refer to her as 'Miss'. When you address me, you will call me Ma'am, and that's a short 'a-sound', NOT 'marm'. Is that clear, Mr Westwood?'

Billy paused a little, presumably sorting through his possible replies, and then managed a rather hesitant 'Er, yes, Mam.'

Kat stopped glaring at Billy and turned her attention to George. 'I suppose that means that you are Mr George Westwood?'

'Yes, Ma'am,' said George, learning fast.

At which admission the second young lady Midshipman snapped to attention, saluting and offering another name badge towards Kat with a spoken, 'Ma'am'.

Kat returned the salute as she took George's name badge saying, 'Thank you, Midshipman Asghar. At ease'. She held out the badge to George and as he took hold of it, he said, 'Thank you, Ma'am' and pinned it on his shirt immediately.

'And this is Midshipman Jumanah Asghar, Mr Westwood,' replied Kat, 'who will be your buddy. I should explain to the two of you that your buddies will help you through the process of settling into life aboard the Pink Ghost, and will guide you through your initial training, all of which will be streamed to your NeuroModems. When you have signed your Articles of Apprenticeship, hopefully after lunch, they will take you to the kit room on the artificial gravity disk of this station to get fully kitted out for life on an Interstellar Haulage vessel. You will then report back to the Commodore at our lunch venue, properly attired in your uniform fatigues. The Commodore will then present you both with your collar rank flashes and will issue your immediate orders. Is all that clear and understood?'

They both managed a fairly brisk 'Yes, Ma'am' reply before Kat went on, 'However, until we have our late lunch your buddies will treat you informally and you can all, and that includes our honoured guest, Miss Sarah Westwood, go into the Transfer Lounge. For just 30 minutes, please, then use the travelator to join us at the Café Claudius in the one-g artificial gravity ring. Dismissed.'

The two buddies snapped to attention and saluted, the two twins tried to do the same but made a hash of it, and Sarah beamed a huge smile at everyone, held out both hands and launched herself towards the other girls, already chattering as she floated towards them.

I took hold of Linda's hand and guided her through the airlock and towards the nearest travellator, saying 'Grab a strap, Linda. We'll go directly to Café Claudius.'

'That suits me too!' said Kat, following up behind us. 'We deliberately delayed for a late lunch in case of microgravity space sickness. Sorry to raise the topic again.' She eyed Linda before going on with her explanation, 'But this is getting beyond a joke. I need food!'

'We've developed some ideas about what we might get the twins to do that we also need to clear with you,' I said to Linda, and went on to explain, 'The main function of the artificial gravity disk on this station is to provide a one-g refuge for visitors. Its facilities are freely open to transit passengers while they wait for onward flights, but they are mainly provided for our Starship crews. The crews live and work in microgravity and they are fully adapted, but humans evolved in a one-g gravity well and long-term microgravity can have disturbing effects on our physiology. We've found that the best thing for the health of our crews is to give them access to one-g rest and relaxation facilities at each of the waystations that we build.'

As I was talking, we entered the travelator's exchange junction at the entrance tunnel to the artificial gravity disk and we all grabbed straps to take us down towards the Earth-gravity region at the hull of the station.

Resuming my explanation, I described how the one-g discs at waystations were the main supply stores for outfitting crewmembers with all the clothing they need for their work on their Starship.

'So, after lunch, I plan to send the twins to the stores, with their buddies, to get fully kitted out, and I wondered if you'd like to accompany them?' I asked Linda. 'Just to make sure they make the right choices. I vaguely remember being a clueless 17-year-old boy!'

'Yes, teenage boys can be amazingly clueless about the more basic aspects of real life!' Linda replied. 'But those girls you've selected as their buddies look much more mature. How old are they?'

'They're only a year ahead of the twins in their training,' said Kat. 'So, they're around 18-years-old, but us girls mature into adults much quicker than baby boys, some of whom I still have doubts about!' She grinned at me, before continuing, 'The storekeeper bots have seen it all before, though. They'll do 3D-body scans for sizing, and they'll assemble full sets of kit and deliver to the appropriate sleeping quarters on board the Starship.'

'Providing the boys answer the storekeeper's questions correctly! That's what I was thinking Linda might like to help with'. I said.

'Yes, I think I should do that,' responded Linda. 'Are there any special instructions?'

'I want them to report back to me at the Café properly dressed in their uniform fatigues so that I can give them their rank badges, and I have a few more instructions for them and their buddies that I want to discuss with you,' I replied. 'We could jump off the travellator here, we've just passed the Mars experience gallery so there's enough artificial gravity for us to walk the rest of the way down the ramp. Just let go of the strap and you'll fall gently to the passage floor.'

We were too hungry to do anything other than stride down to the bottom of the passage and aim straight for the Café Claudius near its exit. As we threaded our way towards the counter between deserted tables the only customer sitting at a table rose and came over to greet Linda Westwood.

'Who that?' I hissed at Kat.

'Tracy Clarkson,' Kat whispered back. 'Madge's daughter. She's agreed to be general manager of this disk resort.'

'Don't think I've met her,' I said.

'You probably haven't. She was Chef de Cuisine at the Westwood Restaurant, so spent all her time in the kitchen,' Kat explained.

We placed our orders at the counter, just as Art Westwood and Lydia joined us in the Café. Lydia needed to run off to another meeting on the Pink Ghost and Art joined his wife chatting to Tracy Clarkson. Kat and I took our food and drinks to an adjacent table, not wanting to butt into the Westwood/Clarkson conversation, and we were beginning to tuck into a decent lunch when the twins' party bounced into the Café demanding to be fed with Sarah the most vociferous.

Tracy Clarkson took control and organised food, drink and a table for them outside the Café, where Sarah and her brothers were given an impromptu seminar on the wondrous nature of artificial gravity discs by Midshipmen Asghar and Wang. Sarah lay flat on the floor to get a more comfortable view of the upside-down people playing tennis in the courts on the ground immediately above us. As the volume of noise from the youngsters' conversations reduced, I suggested to Kat that we interrupt the Westwood parents' conversation so that we could discuss our plans for the twins.

'I've told Linda that the first thing we want to do is get the twins kitted out with Midshipmen uniform fatigues and everything else they'll need for life aboard my Starship, so they can be properly dressed when we all sign the Articles of Apprenticeship,' I explained to Art.

'Yes, the main stores unit is just at the end of this row of restaurants and shops,' said Tracy. 'I'll take them down there and make the introductions, if you like.'

'That would be helpful, Tracy,' Linda replied. Then, looking at me she asked, 'Shall I start herding them in that direction?'

'Not just yet,' I said. 'Kat and I have a few ideas about their immediate future we'd like to run past you.' That statement got the Westwood's attention.

'My brother, Harden, will be bringing the second Proxima flotilla up to this planet in the next month or so,' I started. 'His flotilla is likely to be full of Solar System representatives of all sorts. Scientists of all flavours, mining company reps, administrators, politicians; you name it. Anyone who thinks they could turn a profit doing something on Proxima-b is likely to be represented on this first trip.'

'And one thing they're all going to need is a knowledgeable guide to Proxima-b,' Kat finished off my explanation. 'So, it occurred to me,' she continued, 'that the twins would make excellent tour guides to introduce Proxima Alpha to all those big-wig representatives that Harden will be bringing up here.' Kat paused slightly before asking, 'How does that sound to you?'

'It sounds great to me,' said Art. 'But let me see if I've got this straight; are you telling us that the twins could come back to Proxima-b in your brother's Starship? When's that likely to be?'

'Maybe in two or three weeks,' I replied. 'We can't confirm the arrangement until we meet up with Harden at Oort Station. Remember, that's still 4.5 lightyears away so we can't decide in advance. We're thinking of transferring the twins and their buddies to Harden's Flagship. We must wait until we get there to clear it with him. On our trip back to Oort, we'll be doing any final construction jobs on the four waystations we left at one lightyear intervals to make the route. That's what will take our time.'

'But during their time with us,' said Kat. 'They'll be able to do their basic Starship training, so that on the return trip with Harden, they can introduce Proxima-b to Harden's passengers.'

'If they did a good job for the company with them, it could mean more rapid promotion!' I added.

'Count me in, then. I'm all in favour of a bit of promotion!' said Art, enthusiastically.

'Well, let's not get ahead of ourselves,' responded Kat. 'I want to ask Linda and Art about adding a bit of polish to the twins. In particular, we need to be able to tell them apart easily. What do you feel about doing that with hair colour? We have a good hairdresser on the Pink Ghost who could do that today.'

Linda nodded and said 'OK' and Art, picking up on his wife's opinion said, 'Well, their hair is naturally slightly reddish, which they get from their great grandmother, Cleo. Their great-grandfather was known for a full head of stark white hair. Apparently, he always claimed his hair was a rich brown colour when he first arrived in the Proxima-Centauri system, but it turned white during the night of the landing on Proxima-b!'

'So, is it OK with you if I order their buddies that when they take the twins back to Pink Ghost, they visit the ship's hairdresser for a trim and to have Billy's made white, while George can follow his great grandmother's lead and be red-haired?'

'Oh, I'd love to see that,' said Linda.

'I hope you will,' I said. 'I've issued a general order that all crew attend tomorrow's farewell barbecue and wear their dress uniforms. So, everyone in Proxima Alpha will be able to check them out, dressed up in their new uniforms.'

'So, we can say our goodbyes at the last possible moment,' Linda said, wistfully.

'I'd better get them moving towards the stores unit,' said Kat. 'I'll stroll down there with them, just for a bit of exercise'. She wandered over towards their table. Linda and Tracy followed to join the migration towards the stores unit, while Art took charge of Sarah, choosing a couple of bikes from the free cycle park and going off to explore the locality that way. I got myself another coffee and then warned Malik that I wanted the Westwood twins to be wearing their dress uniforms at tomorrow's barbecue; so, to make sure the body scan data are piped through to the tailoring unit on Pink Ghost, flagged 'Commodore/urgent'.

'Done, Commodore,' Malik reported. 'Tailoring unit confirms the uniforms will be ready for final fitting first thing tomorrow morning. Malik out.'

I then settled back into checking through my accumulated messages until Kat joined me at the table.

'That was quicker than I expected,' she said. 'No need for body scans at the stores. Malik had already passed them the twins' body measurements made by our Nav Couches on the cutter while doing the med-tests associated with Malik's aptitude assessments yesterday.'

'So, has the stores unit also received my authority for dress uniforms for Billy and George?' I asked.

'Yes,' she replied. 'And I added urgent authority for dress uniforms for Jumanah and May, too; they've not had any so far. And, finally, our tailoring department confirmed final fittings for all four of them, first thing tomorrow morning.'

'So,' she finished, 'we'll have four spruced up Midshipmen to show off at tomorrow's barbecue.'

After taking a mouthful of coffee she added, 'Oh, I should also warn you that I asked the stores AI-bot if they had Sarah-sized uniform fatigues in stock and they found some! So, I messaged Art and they're going to cycle back here via the stores unit. Next time you see Sarah, she'll look like a member of the crew!'

'That's a great idea, she'll love that,' I enthused. 'But, why don't we get her a dress uniform, too?' Kat nodded her assent, so I messaged Malik asking him to arrange a Sarah-sized Midshipman's dress uniform when Sarah and her dad arrived at the stores unit. That done, Kat and I settled back to outlining our plans for the apprenticeship signing ceremony and then agreed that we'd take the cutter back to the Pink Ghost so we could prepare for a translocation rehearsal tomorrow.

'Why don't we take everyone back to Pink Ghost?' Kat asked. 'We've got plenty of guest accommodation, and I suspect that Linda and Art would really like to see their twins' new home, and Linda would probably also be a help when the tailor is doing the uniform fittings on Pink Ghost.'

'Not to mention helping out at the hairdresser,' I contributed. 'We don't want them to look outrageous, just different! Then, tomorrow, we could all take the cutter back down to Proxima Alpha in time for the barbecue.' I added, 'Sounds like a plan; let's suggest that.'

Then, as our group of youngsters wearing crew fatigues approached, we set about moving a couple of tables together and rearranging chairs around them for the signing ceremony we had planned. Finally, Art and Sarah cycled up, parked their bikes and a broadly grinning Sarah, in her new crew fatigues, dragged in a chair to sit beside her brothers who were standing, approximately to attention, in front of our table.

When all were settled, Kat started the proceedings by placing printed copies of the Articles of Apprenticeship in front of Billy and George and explaining the commitments they and we would be making to each other by signing. Those signatures applied; she passed the two documents to each parent in turn for them to confirm agreement. And finally, the documents came to me for my signature. As I signed each one, I called the Apprentice Midshipman to attention and buttoned his rank badges onto his lapels. Their acknowledging salutes, including their footwork in response to the 'about turn, dismiss' order, were a bit of a shambles, but that was usually the case in such young recruits. And, also as usual, it gave the Executive Officer a starting point for her welcoming speech.

'Midshipmen Westwood,' Kat began, sporting her stern 'Second-in-Command' face. Billy and George smiled at her. Midshipman Asghar took control of the situation and called out 'Midshipmen Westwood, stand to attention there'. Now Linda and Art were the ones smiling.

'Thank you, Midshipman Asghar,' Kat said, before continuing her speech, 'Midshipmen Westwood, I was trying to tell you that you are now members of the crew of Starship Pink Ghost which is on active service with the Interstellar Haulage Company. Welcome to the crew. I am your Executive Officer and Second-in-Command of the Pink Ghost. You can come to me at any time for confidential help with any matter that concerns you. A simple message to the ship's computer, Malik, from your NeuroModem can secure an interview for you.'

Kat paused slightly before continuing, 'You have enlisted as Apprentice Midshipman. This is the lowest rank among the crew. Your buddies, Midshipman Asghar and Midshipman Wang,' these two snapped to attention as their names were mentioned, 'have reached the higher rank of Midshipmen Normal, and as you can see from their deportment, they have better control of their limbs in the simple drills, of 'attention' and 'about turn', than you have so far managed to display. You will treat them with the same deference and respect as you treat me and the Commodore. As you are our lowest rank 'snotties', you are likely to be put upon by the rest of the crew simply because they all outrank you. And you will even find that some of the special duty AI-robots outrank you; though you should be relaxed about that as following their orders will keep you safe in the hazardous environments they control.'

A pause, long enough for a small sip of coffee, then she continued, 'You will accept these trials and ordeals in good part and carry out any and every order with which you are tasked by whoever is of superior rank. Is that clearly understood?'

'Yes, Ma'am.' They both answered. They were learning.

'Good,' Kat resumed. 'Now, I'm assured that the trials and troubles with which you may be tasked are all for the benefit of building your characters. But as my brother-in-law owns this Starship, and my husband owns its sister-ship, I wouldn't know. I've never experienced this sort of character-building.' Kat smiled broadly for the first time in these conversations with the Westwood twins, but they were still at attention so they didn't know how to respond to what might, or might not, have been a friendly joke.

'That's all from me,' said Kat, who had slipped back into stern mode. 'But the Boss will now hand down your immediate orders so perhaps I should end with a word about names. You have already got used to calling me Ma'am, and you will use that term whenever you have need to converse with a female officer of rank above Midshipman. If you converse with male officers, you will call them 'Sir'. And all crew senior to yourselves will be referred to by rank and name. With one exception. Should you ever need to converse or refer to the Commanding Officer of this flotilla, Commodore Tarvin Clason you will call him 'Boss' or refer to him as 'The Boss'. Midshipman Wang, why do we do that?'

Midshipman May Wang snapped to attention and declared 'Because he is the Boss, Ma'am.'

'Just so,' said Kat. 'Thank you, Midshipman Wang. Now, the Boss will issue your orders. Attention!'

All of them made a decent job of coming to a boot-clattering attention, including Sarah.

'Thank you, Captain Clason,' I started. 'I will start with the more immediate and specific matters. The first item of business is to enable more normal mortals to distinguish between the two Westwood twins. You will proceed to Pink Ghost with your buddies who will help you to check into your quarters in the

Midshipmen Ordinary's mess. Then you will proceed immediately to the ship's hairdresser for a regulation trim, but with hair colouring as follows. Midshipman Billy Westwood is to have his hair made white, which as I understand it, will be a tribute to his great-grandfather, Starship Pilot Billy Westwood; and Midshipman George Westwood is to have his hair made red in tribute to his great grandmother Starship Co-Pilot Cleo Westwood. Your buddies will then take you back to the Midshipmen Ordinary's mess deck where you can all consider yourselves off-duty.'

'Tomorrow morning,' I resumed. 'You will all report to the tailoring unit, immediately when called for the final fitting of your dress uniforms. This order applies to all four Midshipmen, and to Honorary Crew Member Sarah Westwood.'

At the mention of her name, Sarah clicked her heels together and declared loudly, 'Yes, Boss!'

I suppressed a smile as I continued, 'I want you all to attend tomorrow's farewell barbecue properly attired in your dress uniforms and ask you to remember that you will be representing the Pink Ghost at that event. But do enjoy the party.'

'You can now stand at ease,' I went on, 'while I talk about what I expect you to do in the next few weeks. You will undertake the initial courses of your apprenticeship training on board Pink Ghost while we make our return journey towards the Solar System. This training will, of course, be done through a sequence of streamed memory trace implants through your NeuroModems while you sleep, followed by practical application, with the help of your buddies, of the implanted memories during the following day. Basic training for new recruits usually takes ten weeks, but I think we'll have to accelerate your training schedule in the hope that you complete it by the time we reach Oort Station.'

I paused to let that sink in, before explaining, 'And my reason for that is because at Oort Station we will meet my brother's flotilla and, subject to his approval, I want all four of you to transfer to his Starship and return to Proxima-b with that flotilla. Having been born and brought up on Proxima-b, Billy and George, you are uniquely qualified to tell the passengers that my brother is taking there, what to expect and how they can best benefit from their visit. And, when you reach Proxima-b, I want you to be the knowledgeable local guides that will help develop trade links between the Proxima-Centauri system and the Solar System. Anything that's good for Proxima-b, is good for Interstellar Haulage.

So, if you do a good job for the company and its customers, it could mean more rapid promotion for you.'

'That's all the formal stuff, so stand easy, dismiss, and return to your seats. From this point we're just having an informal chat about immediate travel arrangements.'

As he was sorting out a chair for himself, Billy Westwood asked, 'Boss, I'm not sure I can remember everything you've just said. Can we get your orders in writing?'

'No, Billy,' I said. 'But the ship's computer, Malik, will stream a memory trace of what I've said to your NeuroModem next time you sleep to enhance your own memory. You might be aware of it as a dream.'

'Or it could be a nightmare. Depends on what he's ordered you to do,' said Kat, to general amusement.

Malik interrupted the cheerfulness with the news, messaged only to me and Kat, that Rocky Zhang's cutter had docked, 'Captain Zhang's party is disembarking at the moment, Commodore,' Malik reported. 'And I have arranged for one of the waystation's reception-bots to conduct his party to Café Claudius. Malik out.'

That message galvanised me into activity. I interrupted the Westwood's excited chatter to explain to them that the Command Officers of Distant Home were on their way to the restaurant for a short meeting with me and Kat and asked them to excuse the two of us as we hove off to another table to entertain our visitors. Now, this announcement didn't mean much to most of those on the Westwood's table, but I saw Art's eyes widen in surprised recognition of its significance and I sent a quick message to him privately asking that he explain the situation to his family. I then took Tracy Clarkson to one side to ask her to prepare us a separate table for our meeting and ask if the Café could offer Chinese Tea, rather than coffee, as I thought that would be more fitting. She assured me that she and her AI chef-bots could provide anything our Chinese visitors were likely to request and then hustled off to the kitchen to make it so.

While I was talking to Tracy, Kat backed up Art's explanation of the unexpected arrival of the Distant Home Starship and then went on to describe the plans we'd come up with to take the Westwood party to Pink Ghost in the Commodore's Cutter and chatted about what else needed to be done this day. Linda and Art Westwood agreed to stay over on Pink Ghost in one of the Starship guest apartments and when she overheard that, Sarah persuaded May Wang and

Jumanah Asghar to invite her to stay overnight with them in a spare bunk in their quarters in the Midshipmen Ordinary's mess. The immediate activities of the Westwood twins and their buddies in connection with their accommodation were already accounted for, and Linda Westwood agreed to oversee the twins' hair dressing decisions. Kat offered to show Sarah and Art Westwood the astronomical gear she used in the Starship's astrophysics department. Finally, Kat finished off by reminding the Midshipmen that our visitors were senior officers of a visiting Starship and she expected all of them to spring to attention and salute when they appeared.

Which they did quite quickly, three Command Officers, all resplendent in dark blue dress uniforms decorated with gold rank badges and all wearing sidearms, accompanied by one security bot carrying an automatic assault rifle, all four marching out of the travellator walkway behind a receptionist bot that was hurrying along trying hard to stay in front of them. They wheeled around to the front of the Café and came to a halt. In a surprising (to me) display of precision drill, all four Midshipmen, and Sarah, came boot-crashingly to attention and snapped off perfect salutes in perfect unison. They acknowledged the Midshipmen's salutes, and, seeing me and Kat standing a little to one side at our new table, advanced a few steps towards us, came to attention themselves, and saluted us, which we, of course, acknowledged. The formal niceties completed, Captain Zhang, who was a very large, well-muscled man broke ranks to step forward and offer a firm handshake first to me and then to Kat, accompanied by broad smiles and saying 'What a welcome! What a welcome! So good to see you in person, Tarvin, Kat.'

Lily and Nelson followed up in similar manner and we were soon standing together gossiping like a group of old friends reunited after long voyages. Tracy, who had been hovering towards the periphery approached to say, 'Excuse me, Commodore, would your visitors like some tea as refreshment?'

'What's that?' Rocky exclaimed. 'Tea? Chinese tea?'

'Certainly, Captain,' Tracy replied. 'Green tea fresh made this morning, or any other variety you prefer.'

'Can you make Hong Kong-style milk tea?' Rocky asked.

'Certainly, Captain. Hot or cold? Evaporated milk or condensed milk?' Tracy responded, calmly.

'Hot as you can make it, with evaporated milk for me, and please make it better than the pig-swill our StarCorp, allegedly AI, kitchens serve up in microgravity bulbs in space.' Then he turned slightly and looked down at Lily Li, who was barely taller than Sarah Westwood, and continued, 'Lil's got a sweet tooth so I guess she'll want Conny Onny?' he finished, quizzically.

'Yes indeed,' Lily responded. 'Chen Yen style, but iced, please.'

'Yes, Ma'am,' said Tracy as she keyed in the order and turned towards the third member of the party, who was another gargantuan hulk of a man with an equally gargantuan grin on his face as Tracy asked, 'And what would this gentleman like to order?'

'Well, I'm wondering if your kitchen can manage something that our cheap-and-nasty StarCorp kitchens can't get right at all,' Nelson said, then asked 'Can you make a decent bubble milk tea?'

'Of course, Sir!' Tracy replied, and then reeled off, 'Would you like black or green milk tea, with pearls, grass jelly, aloe vera, red bean, or maybe popping boba?'

'Wow, really? What a choice!' Nelson grinned, even wider, if that's possible, before choosing and saying, 'I'm going back to my childhood in Taiwan; please make me a pearl black milk tea. And if that's really good, I'll set up camp here and work through the rest of your list!'

'It will be a pleasure to serve you, Sir,' said Tracy, continuing, 'We also offer a dim sum menu, Sir, would you like a small taster selection plate to accompany your teas?' to which Nelson responded, 'Yes. Yes. Yes. By the stars, you're my kind of woman! But make it a large selection plate will you. Dim sum is another thing our StarCorp kitchens ruin completely!' To which Lily added, 'I've told you before, Nelson, it's not StarCorp's fault, it's just that steaming doesn't work properly in microgravity. You should go into the passengers' artificial gravity disk if you want decent traditional food.'

'I don't like doing that,' Nelson grumbled. 'I only go in there to sort out trouble, so when they see me, they get real wary and uptight.'

Tracy stood respectfully by as this conversation was going on, and as it quietened, she turned to me and Kat and offered us fresh coffee, but before we could reply, Rocky butted in with, 'Oh no, no. That won't do at all. An occasion like this should be celebrated with tea. I'm guessing the Commodore would like what I'm having, and Captain Katharina would enjoy the same as Lily's. I don't recommend anybody follows Nelson's lead, though; in my view, chewy tapioca balls ruin a perfectly good bowl of tea, even if you do call them pearls!' We both nodded at Tracy, and she scurried away towards the kitchen.

Through all this, our little parade of Midshipmen had been holding themselves very smartly to attention, so I called over to them to stand at ease, but before I could dismiss them, Rocky intervened again by asking if I wanted him to inspect the welcome party. I was a little non-plussed as we hadn't actually organised a welcome party, but Kat immediately said 'Yes, they'd appreciate that.' So, though I wasn't entirely sure of the accuracy of Kat's claim the Midshipmen would appreciate an inspection, I conducted Rocky and his colleagues over to their line-up, calling them to attention again as we arrived. I introduced our honoured guests to our Midshipmen line-up and then Rocky, Lily and Nelson ambled down the line, which included Sarah Westwood, of course, exchanging pleasantries, compliments on their turnout, and with the odd easy, but mischievously leading, question about life as a Midshipman on Commodore Clason's Starship, while Kat introduced each one in turn and explained that the Westwood twins had just signed their Articles of Apprenticeship. Rocky asked the Westwood boys to stand together so that he could appreciate their similarity and decided that he couldn't tell them apart, confiding to them, 'I have not had the pleasure of meeting the Commodore's brother, Harden, but the two Clason twins are legendary Starship pilots where I come from on Mars, because of the number of iceteroids they brought to the planet, and the legend says that nobody could tell them apart, either, so, you have a fine tradition to uphold on the Commodore's Starship!'

When Rocky came to Sarah at the end of the line, she was barely tall enough to see above his belt-buckle and he had to stoop to compliment her on her appearance. Kat explained Sarah's relationship to the twins and that she was being treated as an honorary member of our crew. Lily suggested that by all appearances Sarah would make an exemplary crew member at which Sarah crashed her boot down on the ground to renew her stand to attention and said loudly 'Thank you, Ma'am.'

We were all amazed at how much force and sound such a small girl could generate, and Nelson advised 'Careful, young lady, you could go straight through the floor, these StarCorp disks are not built to parade ground standards!' But Rocky bent down again, told her to stand at ease, and asked if she liked Chinese tea. Sarah replied, 'Yes, Sir! Especially the sweet sort.' At which Lily remarked 'Ah, a young woman with perfect taste!' Rocky told all the Midshipmen to stand at ease and then decided to address everyone on the Westwood's table, expressing his thanks for this most impressive welcome parade and then saying,

'It is traditional with my people to welcome visitors with the drinking of tea and for visitors to thank their hosts in the same way. So, I want you all to join us in drinking tea.'

Tracy had just appeared at the front of the house with a serving bot carrying trays of drinks and plates of dim sum for our table and Rocky beckoned her over to request a similar service for the Westwood's table. I took the opportunity to introduce Tracy to Rocky and the others, taking pains to point out that she was the manager of the whole waystation, not just a friendly waitress.

Rocky expressed his appreciation to Tracy and everyone at the Westwood's table and then we trooped back to our own table, now covered in tea and dim sum; Rocky's and mine in lidded tea bowls, Lily's and Kat's cups nestled in bowls of crushed ice and Nelson's in a plastic beaker sealed with a transparent plastic film. I was a little surprised by the down-market plastic cup, but Nelson snatched it up eagerly, saying, 'Hey, I've got a boba straw, too!' He gave his cup a vigorous shake before stabbing through its covering film with his boba straw, sucking up a mouthful and chewing vigorously. 'Fantastic,' he exclaimed. 'Just like being a kid back home!'

'Yes indeed!' echoed Rocky, peering into his own tea bowl. 'Smooth and creamy, with foam and oil on the surface. That, my friend,' he said pointing at me, 'is a first-class Hong Kong-style milk tea.' In fact, we all expressed great satisfaction with the quality of our drinks and then turned our attention to the range of dim sum Tracy had supplied. Again, Nelson leads the way, and, for all his physical size, wielded his chopsticks deftly, which is more than I can claim. Our conversation drifted this way and that, and included a strand in which Nelson even suggested that they should entice Tracy Clarkson to move to their own Starship to establish a Tea Shop there.

'There's nothing to stop you bringing your crew and passengers here,' Kat said. 'Its purpose is to provide rest and relaxation to Starship personnel, and as you can see, there are only a few customers yet, and they'll dwindle to nothing when we jump out the day after tomorrow.'

'Is that your plan?' Rocky asked, and I nodded. 'I was fascinated to watch the videos Captain Lana Mancot sent us about your quantum translocation of the old Starship into orbit from its landing site. Impressive!' He pointed at me again and said, 'Respect, man! Respect! And then, on the way over here, we see the thing you're planning to jump back into the Solar System. A twenty kliks monster made by sticking one Starship on the end of another! More respect, man!

More respect! And not just for you, Tarvin.' He leaned across the table towards Kat, offering a fist-bump to her before continuing, 'Because you just need muscle to shift a Starship, but you need a Navigator with real ability to show you where to deliver it!'

'That's what I keep telling you, Rocky!' said Lily, in mock anger. 'But you never listen!'

Nelson cracked up and guffawed in the background as Kat said her thanks for the compliment. Then Kat continued persuading our visitors to make more use of the Proxima Home Waystation, suggesting they talk seriously to Tracy, and they agreed to do that, explaining that so much of their own artificial gravity disk was devoted to farms that there was little space for sports and relaxation.

This conversation was going so well that I decided to float the idea that the settlers in Proxima Alpha were not entirely happy with the idea of being invaded by a Starship-load of ethnic Chinese from Mars, suggesting they tread carefully in their dealings with Proxima Alpha. Far from being insulted or even disconcerted by what I said, Rocky responded, resignedly, with, 'Aye well, we've got used to that!'

Rocky went on to explain that this was not the first attempt by the People's Democratic Republic of Mars to escape the control of the majority autocratic ethnic Chinese zone of Mars that he'd piloted. 'You see the PDRM is a breakaway province that managed to get itself recognised as a legitimate member of the United Worlds. It was formed originally on Mars by Martian colonists with heritage going back to old Hong Kong, Macao, and old Taiwan; places that had a history of real democracy with things like opposition parties, free and fair elections and regular lawful changes of government. Unfortunately, on Mars, the PDRM couldn't get far enough away from the People's Republic of China of Mars which had its roots in the old Mainland China of Earth, and whose autocratic system just couldn't cope with counterrevolutionary things like opposition parties, free and fair elections and regular lawful changes of government! They've been causing mischief by sending infiltrators and saboteurs into the PDRM, trying to destabilise the Democratic Republic from the day it was established.'

'That's why we wear sidearms,' said Nelson morosely. 'We never know when some disruptive idiot is going to jump out from a shadowy corner.'

'Ain't that the truth!' Rocky blurted out. 'Remember that trip to Titan? A band of typical Kachin warriors dedicated like Yue Fei to preserving the integrity of the Chinese nation!'

'Remember?' Nelson responded. 'I've still got the scars, man!'

'You've taken settlers to Titan?' I asked with renewed interest. 'That's a nice scenic run! Me and my brother had a contract to haul hydrocarbons from there to Earth and always enjoyed seeing Saturn as a backdrop to our day-to-day hauling.'

'Aye, we've taken settlement expeditions to all the Ice Moons,' Rocky replied.

'And several to Venus!' Lily contributed, still working her way through her iced tea.

'Sure,' Rocky responded. 'And everywhere we go we get the same 'not wanted here' response! So, we've got used to making our settlement expeditions totally self-contained; we've got our own artificial gravity disks and our own machines and factories to make everything our settlement needs to get itself established. We just need space; and with most of them so far that means just a safe place in stable orbit. We don't need to use anything owned by existing settlers, but if they want to be helpful, we are able to pay the going rate for anything they do for us.'

'Presumably, you don't plan to simply stay in orbit around Proxima-b. Do you?' Asked Kat. 'So, what plans do you have for settlement here?'

'The plan we came with,' Rocky continued, 'is to create a truly democratic New Hong Kong somewhere on the coast, south of Proxima Alpha, and on the delta where the river the existing settlers are calling Westwood River flows into the sea.'

'Our passengers this trip, are mostly of old Hong Kong heritage,' Lily explained. 'And immediately they saw the first ground scans that Starship-101 sent back, many years ago, they started waxing lyrical about establishing a New Hong Kong on this river estuary to mimic the old one on the Pearl River delta. Though there's a general feeling that they should give it the original Cantonese name Heung Gong, which translates as Fragrant Harbour.'

'We're even carrying several tunnelling machines to create something like Old Hong Kong's Mass Transit Railway system. And that's where we could do something for Proxima Alpha by adding metro lines to that settlement and to the SpacePort,' Rocky added, as Malik interrupted with, 'Excuse the interruption,

Commodore, but Captain Jim Igwe is approaching your location with his computer maintenance brigade chief and a supply of QIC devices for Captain Zhang's Starship.'

I barely had time to acknowledge the warning when Jim and his robot appeared from the travellator walkway. Jim walked past the Westwood's table, waving away the Midshipmen's startled salutes, and converting them into high fives for everyone, the greetings concluding with an especially elaborate fist-bumping ceremony with Sarah, whom he called "li'l sister", before approaching our table and snapping off, vaguely in my direction, an immaculate, and loud, coming to attention and salute.

'At ease, Jim.' I waved a vague acknowledging salute back without moving from my seat.

'Thanks, Boss,' Jim said. 'My oppo Charlie, here,' he said, pointing his thumb at the robot just behind him, 'is carrying a QIC plug-and-play for your flight computer, Captain Zhang, and a bunch of newly developed QIC chips to fit to any comms or fax robots you'd like upgraded. The chips are prototypes, but they work well enough in our bots. We,' he pointed at the robot again, 'could both come over to your ship to do the upgrades, or you could just take Charlie if you prefer. He's done all our own upgrades and has all the practical experience he could stream to your computer brigade.'

At this, Nelson hauled himself to his feet. 'If it's OK with everyone, I could take you across to Distant Home in our cutter while the Boss is talking to Tracy about bringing crew and passengers to visit this waystation. But I'd like another tea to take with me.'

We all got to our feet then, and as it looked like this meant our meeting was breaking up, I tried to quieten down everyone's farewells by saying the obvious, 'OK, it looks like we've done as much as we can here, but I have one important piece of advice for you Rocky.' As the chatter died away, I continued by asking, 'Has your flight computer been monitoring our conversations here, Rocky?'

'Yes, of course,' he replied, quizzically. 'Why do you ask?'

'Because I think you should say to Proxima Alpha what you've just been saying to us about the 'not wanted here' response you always get,' I said. 'It will help the locals to understand you better. And my suggestion for the best way to do that is to get your flight computer to compose a summary of what we've been discussing here this afternoon and then send it to Captain Lana Mancot as a "possible" for possible TV interviews with you three in the near future.'

'Great idea, Boss,' said Kat. 'And I'd suggest sending the same document as a background discussion paper to Merv Castlefield, Sally Gates and Clint Stapleton ahead of your first meeting with them.'

'Castleton, Gates and Stapleton are the current members of Proxima Alpha's governing council,' I added in explanation. 'I think you should message them as soon as you can, suggesting at least a video conference. And maybe even a face-to-face meeting up here. You could talk to Tracy about arranging that as well.'

'And if you had lots of your passengers making use of the waystation's facilities in perfectly normal ways in the background, then you might look like a much less threatening group!' Finished off Kat.

'Right,' Rocky replied. 'I need more tea to help my thinking about all that. So, we should go into the bar for that and leave Tarvin and Kat to continue recruiting the settler's children to the crew of their Starship!'

We parted with heartfelt handshakes and hugs all round, and Kat and I returned our attention to the Westwood's table which seemed to be working its way through their third plate of dim sum.

I offered everyone a trip to the Pink Ghost in the Commodore's Cutter and as we negotiated the travelators back to the docking area, we chatted about what else needed to be done this day. Linda and Art Westwood agreed to stay over in one of our Starship guest apartments and when she overheard that, Sarah persuaded May Wang and Jumanah Asghar to invite her to stay overnight with them in a spare bunk in their quarters in the Midshipmen Ordinary's mess. The immediate activities of the Westwood twins and their buddies in connection with their accommodation were already accounted for, and Linda Westwood agreed to oversee the twins' hair dressing decisions. Kat decided to show Sarah and Art Westwood the astronomical gear she used in the Starship's astrophysics department.

That left me free to do my own thing, but my choices were greatly reduced during our cutter flight to the Pink Ghost, when, coming into dock in the cutter's landing bay, the viewscreens gave me my first close-up view of the ungainly construction the flight engineers had produced by combining the Pink Ghost with the hull of Starship-101.

Yes, I was going to need to spend several hours studying Malik's quantum maps to get to grips with two Starships with which I was so well acquainted, that were now attached stern-to-stern. Well, I'd not be the first to face up to the weirdness of quantum mechanics!

Day 9

Awake at 7 a.m. after a night's sleep full of dreams. Yesterday, I had worked late, going through the quantum maps of the assembly that the engineers had hooked up between my flagship, Pink Ghost and Starship-101. I had real problems to start with. Of course, the 3-D virtual models of the two ships were models I had worked with before. It was the stern-to-stern alignment the engineers had arranged that caused me problems. Usually, my preferred personal preparation for a quantum jump is just to 'walk' through the virtual model of a vessel I'd jumped before, progressing from stern to nose, just to refresh my 'done-it-before' memories of the ship I was translocating.

But I was very uncomfortable last night. I could 'walk' through the virtual models of the two ships separately, no problem. I had a perfect operating mindscape of the stern-to-nose direction in both vessels. But I just couldn't cope with the changed orientation caused by the stern-to-stern connection of them, my memories were messed up by it. So, Malik and I had to spend time building me a mindscape of a walk through the entire construct. From the nose area of Starship-101, where I was well used to the control room layout, but then progressing towards the stern of the hulk, followed by a very careful examination, and at high resolution, of the stern-to-stern junction, to make sure that my handling of the quantum map during the entanglement put no undue mechanical strain on that junction. Malik completed his calculations for the final quantum map and streamed his edited version of my memories of the 'walk' through into my NeuroModem in my dreams overnight.

'Good morning, Commodore,' Malik said. 'How are your quantum map memories this morning?'

'They're fine, thank you, Malik,' I replied. 'I've visualised the 'walk' through of the stern-to-stern junction several times and it all seems good enough for our technical rehearsal later this morning.'

'Good,' Malik commented. 'I will message Captain Clason to confirm the technical rehearsal. I have messages for you from Captain Lana Mancot concerning her desire to transfer camera crews to Pink Ghost to continue filming this mission during the return to Oort Station. And a message from Captain Frankie Burton concerning her wish to add a hundred units of her 'Quantum Instantaneous Communicator' to the Pink Ghost's cargo manifest for our journey to Oort Station.'

'OK, say 'yes' to both requests. But I need a shave and shower, and a bite of breakfast, so I'll talk to them later.'

'Willco, Commodore. Malik out.'

While I was in my bathroom, Stewart made me a brunch breakfast that would see me through to this afternoon's barbecue and after he had served that in my wardroom he freshened up my Nav Couch, as I'd slept there overnight to use the higher bandwidth of the NeuroModem connexion of the couch for my memory trace streaming.

Breakfast eaten, fresh coffee in hand. 'OK, Malik. Hit me with the ladies' messages.'

'Good morning, Boss. Are you still on Pink Ghost?' asked Frankie, rhetorically; knowing full well where I was located. 'Danny Khan's progressing well with the scale up of production and testing of our 'Quantum Instantaneous Communicator' plug-and-play adapters and he has a healthy batch of fully tested prototypes you could take back to Oort Station for evaluation in the Solar System. What's the latest time we could get them to you for transport up to Pink Ghost? The later we can leave it, the more units we can include in the batch.'

'Yay, mornin Boss,' Lana interrupted. 'My question's similar. About transport up to Pink Ghost as late as possible today. So, answer Frankie, and then I'll tell you what I need.'

'There's an also, Boss,' Frankie chimed back in. 'Danny's designed a QIC-fax chip that can be plugged into the comms board of one of our run-of-the-mill fax-bots to make it a QIC specialist that's able to detect the nearest QIC-enabled megacomputer and then use that megacomputer to host instantaneous communications with the NeuroModem of its facsimile human partner. It's only a small chip, so Danny's machines are producing dozens of them every run, and I'd like to include a large batch for you to take with you to adapt the fax-bots on the waystations.'

'Incredible,' I responded. 'Instantaneously communicating fax-bots! This QIC business is beginning to get really interesting! OK, listen up ladies,' I went on. 'We'll be doing the technical rehearsal for our translocation to Waypoint 4 later this morning. After that we'll fly my cutter down to Proxima SpacePort, probably around noon. How's that for you, Malik? Will it give you enough time to complete the rehearsal process?'

'Affirmative, Commodore,' Malik replied. 'Any supplementary activity can be completed from the cutter's Nav Couches.'

'OK, so, circulate a message, will you Malik? To current Pink Ghost residents, offering an early lift down to the SpacePort to anyone who wants to leave Pink Ghost at noon; and make up a passenger list with any replies.'

'Willco, Commodore. Malik out'.

'So, Frankie and Lana, to answer your question about the cutter's return journey to Pink Ghost after the barbie. I'm expecting that the most senior officers, namely Kat and me, and maybe Jim as well, will be the last people to leave the barbecue. I guess our departure is unlikely to be before around 11 p.m., and Malik could keep tabs on crew movements and organise another cutter passenger list for that expected departure time. Got that, Malik?'

'Willco, Commodore. Malik out'.

'Which means, Frankie, you should task one of the AI-bots from the main stores unit at the SpacePort to collect the QIC adapters and chips from Danny Khan and report with them to the Commodore's Cutter for an expected 11 p.m. lift-off to orbit. Indeed, the bot could travel with them to Pink Ghost and be made responsible, under Malik's supervision, for managing that specific item of our cargo manifest for our entire journey back to Oort Station.'

'Sounds like a great plan, Boss, thanks. I'll get onto main stores right away. Frankie out.'

'That leaves you, Lana. What do you want to do?' I asked.

'I want to record the whole of the departure from Proxima-b, and the journey back to Oort Station,' said Lana.

'I'm all in favour of that, Lana,' I replied. 'What can we do for you?'

'First,' she said, 'I'd like to record this morning's technical rehearsal, then I want to record the translocation to Waystation 4, and then each subsequent jump through to Oort Station.'

'That's fine with me,' I said. 'If your camera crews stick to the rule of not getting in the way, they can film everything.'

'Ah, yes, that brings me to my main problem. I've brought all my best and most mobile camera bots down to Proxima-b to follow the various research teams that will be staying on here to explore the planet. That includes some space-rated camera bots that will travel into the dark side. I've still got enough space-rated crews left on the Pink Ghost to record on the external hull, but they are too large and clunky to film inside the ship.'

As I wasn't sure where this was going, I asked 'OK, so, how can I help?'

'Well, can I use the closed-circuit cameras in Pink Ghost's control room to record this morning's technical rehearsal?' Lana asked.

'Yes, of course,' I said. 'And Malik can send you a summary description of the work we did last night on the quantum maps. It will be useful background for your story. I don't know if you are aware of this, but the flight engineers decided it was best to connect Pink Ghost and Starship-101 stern-to-stern, and as I always prefer to develop my Starship quantum maps from stern to nose, I just didn't have the memories to cope with the flight engineer's construction. I spent a lot of time last night recreating the appropriate memories with 3-D virtual models of the two ships and then streaming those quantum maps while I slept.'

'Hey, that's a great story in its own right!' said Lana.

'Malik, can you send all the details to Lana, including images, before we leave so she can work on that part of the story after we've left for Waystation 4.'

'Willco, Malik out.'

'You're thinking like a video producer, Boss'. said Lana in appreciation.

'I'm just responding to your training, Lana. Now, what else can we do for you?'

'As I don't have the necessary camera crews left on Pink Ghost, I need to send a couple of reliable AI-camera bots back to Pink Ghost to record the translocation jumps through to Oort Station before you jump out of orbit.'

'Yes, that's OK with me. Just message Malik with the camera bot IDs and they can be added to the cutter passenger list for our expected 11 p.m. departure time after the barbie. Is that all?'

'Yes thanks, Boss.'

'Well, before you go,' I interrupted, 'I've got another journalistic scoop, for you.'

'Ooh, do tell!' said Lana excitedly.

'Settle down, now!' I advised. 'Yesterday we enlisted the Westwood twins into the Pink Ghost's crew as Midshipmen Apprentices, and Kat assigned two young lady Midshipmen Normals as their buddies to help with their settling into their mess and initial training. In getting the twins rigged out with ship's kit, we included full dress uniforms for all four Midshipmen, and they will come down to the SpacePort with me in my cutter all booted and suited in their new dress uniforms!'

'Wow, what a story,' Lana enthused.

'Settle down, again, there's more!' I said. 'Quite a bit more, in fact. The twins' young sister, Sarah, also came with us to Proxima Home Station and though she's far too young, she's very keen to enlist as well. So, Kat and I have adopted her as a sort of mascot, and we kitted her out with a Midshipman's dress uniform of her own. She'll be with her brothers on our flight down to the barbecue, where your bots could do lots of vox pops with some appealing images.'

Sensing an imminent interruption from Lana, I added a quick and emphasised, 'AND, there's more to the Westwood family's story. You know that the twins' mother, Linda, is taking over as manager of one of Emma's poultry farms, don't you? And that Madge's daughter, Tracy, will be general manager of the Home Station's artificial gravity ring's resort? Well, put the two together, and Linda Westwood will also be going back into space to make deliveries of fresh foods to the Home Station.'

Hearing Lana's intake of breath, I cut off her interruption again with another emphasised, 'AND, you probably don't know yet that the twins' father, Art Westwood, has been appointed Director of the Proxima-b Observatory, with responsibilities for all astronomical assets, including those on Proxima Home Station and the various satellite probes that Kat has launched into orbits around the Centauri system.'

While this conversation was proceeding, Kat sent me a private message saying that she was coming up to the control room from her astrophysics centre on the deck below and would be ready for the technical rehearsal in a few minutes. I acknowledged this message and then turned back to Lana.

'Overall,' I finished off, 'I think that, in video-producer-speak, I'm pitching a family biopic entitled something like 'The Westwood Family of Proxima-b', that could start with the history of Billy and Cleo Westwood's flight from the Solar System to Proxima, the dramatic simulation of the landing of Starship-101, and then follows them and their family through development of the settlement to our arrival and the twins' enlistment into our crew. You can breathe now because I've reached my final item!'

'Oh yeah? And what's that, Boss?' Lana queried.

'It's the little matter of the arrival of a Starship-load of ethnic Chinese settlers. You know from what was reported to our Staff Meeting that we are required to offer the same level of assistance to them as we have given to the residents of Proxima Alpha, and I hope you've received the summary report of our meeting with Captain Zhang and Commanders Li and Wang on Proxima Home Station yesterday afternoon.'

'Yeah, I got that,' Lana said. 'So, I guess you want me to give them a platform to explain to the whole of Proxima Alpha what they said to you, Boss?'

'That's right,' I replied. 'And I suggest the way to do it is to set up live interviews with Captain Zhang and Commander Li, and maybe make it a three-way interview by including Merv Castlefield. Malik can arrange for you to message Zhang and Li as he's brought their flight computer into the local network of supercomputers. What do you think about that Malik?'

'It's essential for us to ease the two communities into an amicable alliance at this stage in humanity's expansion into interstellar exploration,' Malik responded, continuing, 'It's also essential for me, as the computer held responsible for supervising our own expedition and contracts, to ensure that our mandate and contract stipulations to deal even-handedly with all members of the United Worlds are honoured. I must strongly emphasise to you Captain Mancot that this obligation is placed on us by the whole of the Solar System and any line of discussion you devise concerning the arrival here of Starship Distant Home must recognise clearly our obligations.'

'Acknowledged, Malik, I have carefully stored that memory trace of your words,' Lana responded. 'Now can you put me in contact with Captain Zhang?'

'Certainly, Captain Mancot,' Malik replied. 'Captain Zhang and Commander Li are currently still located on Proxima Home Station. They remained there overnight to discuss with the general manager of the resort, Ms Tracy Clarkson, the transfer to the waystation of Distant Home's passengers and off-duty crew. At this moment their flight computer is scheduling passenger shuttle flights from their Starship to the waystation, and Captain Zhang and Commander Li are waiting to welcome the imminent arrival of the first of these transports. They are presently drinking tea in Café Claudius, where they met with the Commodore.'

'That all sounds fine,' I interrupted. 'So, I'll leave it to you, Lana, to carry it forward.'

'Willco, Boss. Wow, great TV programmes are coming thick and fast! There are not enough hours in the day!' Lana commented. 'I'll have to recruit more of the young settlers into TV journalism! But I'll use the local people to manage the interviews and I'll try to arrange them for the midday news hour. You met the people I have in mind a few days ago; the production manager, Daisy Warrington, with the news anchorman, Clifford Wright doing the interviewing. They're both very competent and on the ball, and if I stay off-screen, it will look less like an Interstellar Haulage stitch-up!'

'Affirmative!' said Malik, approvingly, before I could comment. Malik continued to ask, 'Do you want me to make contact with Captain Zhang now?'

'No thanks, Malik,' Lana replied. 'I need a little time to choose my camera bots to send up to Pink Ghost, so when I message you about your passenger list for the Commodore's Cutter, you could make the messaging connections for me.'

'Willco. Malik out'

'I'll leave you to it, Lana,' I said. 'Your plans look good to me. Go ahead and make it so.'

'Thanks Boss. Lana out.'

By this time, Kat was settling into her Nav Couch beside me, and we fist-bumped a greeting as she relaxed her head back into her headrest to make her NeuroModem connection. When I sensed her presence merged to my own NeuroModem, I asked 'What news from astrophysics?'

'All good and positive,' she said. 'I've been working with all of my staff and with Art Westwood and all of his staff overnight, and even Sarah and Lily Li chipped in a few comments. Between us all, we've come up with a draft manuscript for a paper I'll submit for publication when we get within radio range at Oort Station.'

'What's all this about, then?' I enquired.

'Well, you remember the video images of the entanglement with Starship-101 in the few seconds just before you made the jump into orbit and how the image of 101 on the ground kept coming and going?'

'Yes, and making a low frequency sound?' I responded.

'That's right. Well, the sound engineer who first asked if there was a sound, Fred Bull, has been worrying at what it means along with Malik and a couple of my astrophysicists and they first found that when 101 disappeared from view in the ground images, it only appeared in every alternate video view of the orbital target destination. In fact, they've calculated that there's a hight probability that the quantum version of the ship simply ceased to exist in our reality.'

'Bloody Hell,' I complained, 'I was in that ship all the time. I was a component part of Starship-101's quantum version. If I wasn't in our reality every other second, where the hell was I?'

'We don't know. We don't have enough data to even guess at that,' said Kat, not entirely helpfully. 'But we've come up with a theory. Art Westwood, who's been training in today's quantum mechanics theory ever since his NeuroModem was q-bit upgraded, has stitched together the ideas of a few of our physicists into a quantum mechanics explanation that Malik reckons is worth publishing.'

'Okay, so what is this theory?' I asked.

'Er, well, its value is all in the maths,' Kat said. 'But in summary, the idea is that the observed 'vibration' of the image of the entanglement, which is revealed as an audio signal tone-generated when one of the contributors to the entanglement is located in an atmosphere is convincingly argued to be an aspect of the multiple cause and effect scenarios of transactional quantum mechanics.'

'In other words,' she went on, 'the 'vibration' is due to the entanglement flipping between and across alternative time-reversed signals that describe all possible ways for decoherence to resolve the entanglement into the different realities open to it. There may be many of these alternatives, though in our case there only seems to be two. Our present reality and one other into which Starship-101 might have disappeared. We think the entanglement is essentially sampling the future of the two realities to establish if there is any new data in either of them which is sufficient to cause decoherence in that reality. The presence or absence of new data being the time-reversed signal that either initiates decoherence or proceeds to the next potential reality.'

'Oh, that old chestnut retrocausality,' I said. 'So, does all that mean that my nudging your mini-comms satellite unit into life in your real-world destination on the day is all that brought me back into our reality and away from the brink of oblivion?'

'Pretty much,' she replied, more merrily than I could muster. 'But it's not necessarily 'oblivion', it's just a different reality. It might be very pleasant.'

'And it might be very unpleasant,' I insisted. 'And very lonely'.

'True, which is why we think our ideas should be published,' Kat responded. 'Your lifting Starship-101 into orbit is the first quantum mechanics experiment to have been done with the level of observational recording that even hints at our theoretical interpretation. But it also suggests a possible experimental protocol to study what retrocausal alternatives exist and even what the alternative realities might be like.'

'That's an experiment that could be expensive in Starships. And Starship pilots,' I replied morosely.

'Oh, cheer up. I've not let you down yet. I'll make sure to bring you back to a destination in our reality,' Kat said cheerily. 'Now, do you want to know more about the destination for your next quantum jump?'

'Waystation 4? Sure, but I thought you had the quantum map of that location all prepared from when it was the departure point on the last leg of our journey here,' I said.

'Yes, I do have that map,' said Kat. 'But it turns out that the Observatory computer which at that time was sitting in its cargo hold with nothing else to do but collect data from our astro-sensors, made its final hi-res sweep of those sensors just before we jumped from Waystation 4. And, because it was an astronomical computer with nothing to do, it compared the map we used with the later map from its final sweep to check for movement between the objects in the map. Malik has updated the old departure map with that newer information, by projecting the movements forward to the time of tomorrow's jump, and I'd like to see what it looks like now as a destination.'

'OK,' I said. 'We should move towards our rehearsal, Malik'.

'Affirmative, Commodore. I will warn the crew,' Malik responded.

Immediately, we heard the chimes from the ship's intercom that demanded the attention of the whole crew, followed by Malik saying across all comms and NeuroModem channels 'Now hear this, now hear this. We are about to undertake the technical rehearsal for the translocation of this Starship-101 from orbit of Proxima-b to orbit of Waystation 4. All crewmembers to stand down for a technical rehearsal. Repeat: this is a rehearsal.'

A jump rehearsal was an opportunity for the crew to have some downtime. They were expected to stay where they were and hang on tight, unless engaged on mission-critical tasks, because if I moved quantum maps around in my mindscape, the ship itself might also move around. Also, too much activity by quantum entities could confuse the data-gathering software. This was not an important restriction for a rehearsal but was crucial for real quantum jumps where confused quantum entities could be ignored and left behind when the rest of the quantum map translocated to the destination. So, for real quantum jumps, all crew were expected to be firmly strapped into their acceleration couches.

After a couple of minutes' delay, during which the ship's intercom continued to chime its warning, Malik continued, 'Will pilot and co-pilot please signify their readiness to initiate the technical rehearsal for the translocation of this Starship-101 from orbit of Proxima-b to orbit of Waystation 4?'

'Pilot is ready,' I said.

'Co-pilot is ready,' Kat responded.

Malik came back with: 'Copy that. Launching rehearsal in 5, 4, 3, 2, 1, launch.'

I instinctively reached over to take hold of Kat's hand and we were immediately NeuroModemed together in the never-never land of my quantum-enhanced memory mindscape of the linked Starships we were intending to jump down to Waystation 4.

'This is the ungainly object we're planning to shift,' I said, explaining, 'Although I had memories of the stern-to-nose 'walkthrough' for both vessels, I couldn't handle the switch in orientation of the stern-to-stern connection of them. So, this is an entirely new memory trace we built last night. I've looked closely at the stern-to-stern junction area to avoid undue mechanical strain during the entanglement. And I'm happy that I understand this model now.'

'Yeah, it does look weird,' agreed Kat. 'The arrowhead shape of Starship-101 makes it look like that's the way we're flying, and Pink Ghost is merely the arrow's shaft, following on behind. But I don't expect any problems. Have you tried hefting it?'

'Not before now,' I said, gently lifting and wiggling the model in my memory. The movement of the mental image was echoed by a corresponding shivering motion, with an amplitude of about 30 cm, of the real-life ship in which we were accommodated. 'I've not had the crew on stand down warning before this. But that felt fine; the quantum model's got no weight. Should be a routine jump now we've got this revised quantum map.'

'Malik, return the quantum map to its default coordinates' I messaged. 'And inform the crew that no further disturbance is expected, but to remain alert. Now, can we look at the destination map?'

'Sure,' said Kat, taking me into her memory of the Waystation 4 quantum map. 'This is the map we used for departure on the way up here. And this is the revised version using the late data gathered by Observatory.'

'Differences?' I asked.

266

'One crucial difference,' Kat replied, 'is that the much higher resolution of Observatory's data precisely fixes the position of the vintage comms satellite that Starship-101 ejected at that location, relative to the position of the waystation sections we left there. As we expect the build of the waystation to have been completed by now, we expect that part of the quantum map to be seriously in error. So, what I've done is use the hi-res data to position our destination point relative to the vintage satellite, to allow plenty of open space for changes in waystation structure and orientation. And, since that little 100-year-old satellite is represented by such a short quantum coding routine, I'm proposing you use that as your nudge to cause decoherence of your superposition. Here's the code. What do you think?'

Kat passed me a memory trace of the location of the old StarLink satellite. It was relatively short and easily stored into my priority memory.

'Looks like you're making it nice and easy for me,' I responded, approvingly.

'Good,' said Kat. 'Because I've looked at Observatory's data for all the other waystations and that damn computer's been collecting better data than mine for the whole trip up here! Result is, we can use the same protocol to plot our destination maps all the way back. In fact, Observatory's already calculated the revised quantum maps for each waystation and streamed them to Malik.'

'That's very generous,' I said. 'Are these new computers being equipped with generosity these days?'

'It's not generosity,' said Kat. 'More like embarrassment that the heap of sand had not informed its senior officer that it had accumulated quantities of high-quality data that would have made her life so much easier.'

'Well, I guess the only thing you can do, Kat. Is hold a grudge against Observatory!' I advised. Continuing, 'Are we finished here? Malik, can you see any holes in our plans?'

'Negative, Commodore,' Malik responded. 'I agree with your conclusion that the translocation of these Starships from orbit of Proxima-b to orbit of Waystation 4 should be nice and easy.'

'Good, then terminate the technical rehearsal and return the crew to normal duties with the confirmation that the translocation will take place at noon tomorrow, by which time all members of crew will be strapped into their acceleration couches.'

'Willco, Commodore. Malik out.'

Kat and I relaxed as our Nav Couches flowed back into their pilot chair configuration.

I called out to my steward as I floated myself from the chair and towards my wardroom, 'Stewart, make us some fresh coffee, will you? And some biscuits.' But there was no response, in fact he was nowhere to be seen.

'I seem to have lost my steward,' I moaned to Kat. 'I suppose I'll have to make my own coffee!'

'Before I joined you for the rehearsal,' she said, 'I told him to steam and press our best dress uniforms and take them down to your cutter so we can get changed during the cutter's flight down to the SpacePort. He's not lost, he's probably carrying out that instruction. Malik, can you locate the Commodore's steward?'

'Affirmative, Captain Clason,' Malik reported. 'The steward is presently within the Commodore's quarters on board the Commodore's Cutter.'

'Malik, have we finished here? Is there anything else I need to do before going down to Proxima-b?' I asked.

'Nothing left to do that needs to be done from the ship's control room, Commodore.'

'OK, we might as well go down to my cutter, too.' I looked at Kat and she nodded, so, I continued my instruction to Malik, 'Tell Stewart we are doing that and that he should stay there and make fresh coffee'.

'Willco, Commodore'.

'Stay online, Malik,' Kat cut in. 'Time is moving on towards our planned departure of the cutter at noon. So, please issue a general announcement for anyone wanting a lift down to the SpacePort at noon to assemble in the Commodore's Cutter a.s.a.p. And send a private message to that effect to the NeuroModems of everyone who registered on your passenger list.'

'Willco, Captain. Malik out'.

As Kat and I floated ourselves off the control deck and towards the main travellator corridor, the ship's intercom chimed for attention and then announced: 'All aboard! All ashore that's goin' ashore! Commodore's Cutter departing at noon for Proxima Alpha SpacePort. Anyone requiring passage to the SpacePort should assemble in the Commodore's Cutter's docking bay.'

Kat and I were too busy strap-hanging between travellators to take much notice of the announcement. When we'd worked our way out to the speediest travellator in the centre, we listened to the repetition and took note of the words used. We looked at each other quizzically.

'Where did 'All aboard' and 'All ashore that's goin' ashore' come from?' I asked. 'I hope Malik is not having one of his nasty turns just before our first quantum jump.'

'Nah, I think he's just showing off,' replied Kat. 'He's been streaming all the really old films that Starship-101's Flight computer held in memory. He's been trying to interest me in some of the science fiction films from the early 20th century. He claims they're 'vintage gold' and might be worth a fortune to a movie museum back on Earth.'

'What in the name of all that's holy would our ship's computer do with a fortune?' I mused.

'Maybe he's planning for his retirement!' Kat suggested, then changed topic by pointing out that we were about to overtake the Westwood family who had emerged from the guest accommodation deck and were strap-hanging in the slow lane. We swapped travellators to join them and after a full set of greetings, Kat and I made admiring comments about the twins' new hairstyles and the immaculate dress uniforms the twins and Sarah were now wearing.

Sarah swung as expertly as any tree-dwelling monkey between travellator straps to confront me with the comment, 'I don't like the showers on board your Starship, Boss. It's like being in a dishwasher.'

'Yeah,' I agreed. 'Showers are best in a gravity field. But the microgravity ones do keep us clean.'

'So why don't you spin the ship to make artificial gravity?' Sarah asked.

Linda interrupted this conversation, trying to rescue me from Sarah's interrogation, I guess. 'Settle down, Sarah,' she hissed. 'Stop bothering the Commodore with your nonsense.'

'No, that's OK,' I protested. 'That's a very good question that a lot of crewmen have asked. The real reason, Sarah, is that you need to use a lot of fuel to make a Starship spin and it's just not worth the expense because a Starship's crew doesn't often spend very much time inside the Starship. The Starship spends most of its time parked up alongside a waystation. At the point of departure, the crew will be loading the Starship with the cargoes needed for the next quantum jump and when they are off-duty, they can choose to stay in the resort section of the waystation's artificial gravity ring. The crew all pile into the Starship shortly before its quantum jump and when that's done, the ship parks up near its destination waystation, where the on-duty crews unload the cargoes and deliver to whoever ordered them, while the off-duty crews can go to the artificial gravity resort at the destination.'

'So, the Starship is like one of the trucks that take stuff from Mum's poultry farm to the restaurant?' Sarah asked.

'Yeah, that's right,' I admitted. 'The name of my company is Interstellar Haulage. And that's what we do; we haul stuff around. And get paid a lot for doing so!'

We were all still in the travellator's slow lane, which was closest to the entrances to the crew accommodation decks. As we passed the lower deck that housed the Midshipmen's and lower ranks quarters, Midshipmen Asghar and Wang were waiting at the intersection to join us, and Sarah shuffled us along the straps so they could deftly join our travelling party alongside her. We displayed some dextrous strap-hanging as we exchanged a little flurry of salutes and then Sarah returned to the topic of her disappointing experience with the shower facilities in my Starship, ending her story with 'And I felt the ship wobble around!'. Demonstrating by wobbling herself from strap to strap.

She turned to me, accusingly, saying 'How did that happen, Boss, if fuel is too expensive to make artificial gravity, how do you make the ship move like that?'

Kat messaged me privately with: 'She does ask very demanding questions, doesn't she?'

I realised, in thinking of a response to Kat's message, that I honestly didn't know why my moving my mental image of the Starships' quantum map should affect the ship in real life. So, I made a start on improvising an answer for Sarah with: 'Well, if you were in your shower cubicle when we were rehearsing for the quantum jump, then the wobble was my fault. Because I picked up my mindscape's quantum mechanics model of the ship and moved it slightly in my mind's eye and that disturbance in quantum space was shared with the ship in the ordinary macroscopic world.'

I was quite pleased with that, but Sarah looked at me with a calculating gleam in her eye and said, 'Yeah, my dad's been telling me about quantum mechanics. It's as weird as fairy-tale magic.' And then she asked, 'If you can wobble the Starship around by wobbling your mental image of its quantum map, why don't you do that to move the ship around in space rather than use expensive fuel?'

'Killer question!' Kat messaged to me in private. And another question for which I had no immediate answer. So, I turned to Kat and said out loud, 'The co-pilot is responsible for guiding me through the destination's quantum maps. So, Kat, would you like to answer that question?'

Kat immediately flashed me a 'Gee Thanks' grimace icon, NeuroModem to NeuroModem; and immediately started improvising *her* answer for Sarah, 'It's a matter of knowing precisely where everything is positioned in open space.' She waffled first, then, like lights clicking on in her mind, she got stuck into an idea and continued, 'The point of origin is centred on the Starship and the quantum map of the origin describes the exact location of everything we want to include in the translocation entanglement. If we move the Starship, we must recalculate the whole map. So, we never attempt to move our mental image of the Starship at the origin. The destination quantum map is always based on historical data on the positions of objects that we gathered when we last visited that destination. And again, after the decoherence, we can't risk moving the Starship until we've recalculated the quantum map of the local area, and that can take a long time.' Kat smiled at Sarah and concluded, 'It's easier to light up the rocket thrusters and ride them into our final docking position.'

Sarah nodded her head slowly as she absorbed and processed Kat's explanation. Then she brightened up, said 'OK, I see that' and spun around to dive into the bored huddle that had formed between her brothers and their buddies where she joined their general chatter about their new hairstyles, uniforms, and experiences.

Kat and I just stared at each other, wondering what had just happened. I messaged Art Westwood, asking if he'd been taking note of the conversation with Sarah.

'Yes,' he said. 'As soon as I heard my 14-year-old daughter talking quantum mechanics, I started to take notice!'

'Kat tells me you've been seriously studying quantum mechanics recently.'

'Yeah, that's right.'

'Has Sarah been keeping up with you?' Kat asked, incredulously.

'I guess so,' Art replied. 'She's not been streaming the same coursework as me or anything like that, but we've talked about it, and she seems to just soak it up and take it in.'

'How's her maths?' Kat asked.

'Well, you know, that's the strange thing, I've not realised it before,' said Art. 'But she's always been able to keep up with me, and with her brothers for that matter, while we've just been hobby astronomers, using Starship-101's telescopes, before you guys arrived. And over the past few days while me and the twins have been streaming into our q-bit-upgraded NeuroModems every night, she's still kept up with us.'

'Does she still have the original children's NeuroModem?' Asked Kat.

'Yes,' Linda contributed. 'The medics said she was too young for an upgrade. Of course, her school classes have been updated.'

'Well, I'd recommend asking the medics for a second opinion about that NeuroModem upgrade,' said Kat. 'Sarah's behaving like a natural talent that deserves to be encouraged. The Westwood computer will be able to do the aptitude tests that Malik used on the twins'.

'I agree with all that,' I said. 'But I see we're coming into the ferry section where the ship's cruisers are docked. We need to concentrate on getting everyone through the right travelator intersections to get to where my cutter is docked. Stay online though, and I'll ask Malik for his comments.'

'Listen up, guys,' said Kat, ever the navigator. 'We've got intersections ahead. Look out for the direction signs and head towards number one cruiser docking station. That's where the Commodore's Cutter is tied up. If you miss your turn-off just release the travelator strap and we'll come and rescue you.'

And while Kat took charge of herding Westwoods through the intersections, I allowed myself to drift past and come to a halt at one of the ceiling handholds ready to carry out any necessary rescues. While stationary, I messaged Malik, asking him to copy my message and his response to Kat and Art: 'Malik, will you transcribe the conversations Kat and I have just had with Sarah Westwood and check through your records to see if there's any reference to any Superposition Navigators using the quantum entanglement drive to move their ship relative to its surroundings prior to the superposition?'

'Willco, Commodore. I was monitoring your conversation, as usual, and was also at a loss to explain why moving the Starships' quantum map model prior to the superposition should affect the ship in the real world. But then you, and specifically you, Commodore, do need to move the quantum map representing the object to be translocated onto the quantum map representing the destination location. Perhaps the explanation lies in the nature of the relationship between the pilot and the quantum entanglement the pilot is manipulating.'

'I feel another quantum mechanics theoretical paper coming on!' Art Westwood commented.

'I know what you mean!' Kat added.

'Quite possibly,' I said. 'But let's allow Malik to trawl through the past few hundred years of quantum mechanics literature for any prior discussion of this topic. Right now, I want to concentrate on getting everyone aboard my cutter and fly it down to the SpacePort.'

'Affirmative, Commodore,' Malik responded. 'And I can update you with the information that all registered passengers are accounted for. Your Westwood party will be the last to arrive. Malik out.'

'OK Westwood party,' I announced as I launched myself away from my stationary handhold and towards one of the straps of the travelator leading directly to my cutter's berth. 'All aboard that's goin' aboard!'

With that, the practised travelator users released their hold on their straps to continue their individual flights towards the entrance hatchway of my cutter. The newer users among the Westwood family were rather less elegant in their travellator dismounts, while Sarah, as usual, outclassed everyone by performing a couple of perfectly controlled summersaults during her dismount. We floated our way along the dockside and gathered in the vestibule of the cutter's airlock where the Westwoods gathered around somebody who was already waiting there. As I approached the group, I realised it was Tom Fraser.

'Tom! Good to see you. Glad you feel up to returning to the ground!' I said.

'Well, I thought I should make the effort, one last time,' Tom replied, grinning. 'Your medical centre has made me feel healthier than I have any right to be at my age, and though I'm thoroughly at home in microgravity now, Carlo here has been taking me across to Proxima Home Station's artificial gravity ring to get me acclimatised first to Moon, then Mars and, finally, Earth gravity. He's brought a wheelchair in case I need it on Proxima. So, I'm looking forward to a good feast down there!'

'You should have gone straight through the airlock and into the cutter,' I told him. 'The steward would have fixed you a drink and snack.'

'Oh no,' he replied. 'In my day it was not good etiquette to climb aboard a boat before the boat's master gave permission!'

'Understood!' I said, and I went ahead through the airlock, calling back for the rest of the party to follow me. The Ops room, which we entered first, had been reconfigured overnight. The engineer's emergency Nav Couch had been replaced, stationed between and just behind the pilot and co-pilot couches. And, with the Ops room table folded out of the way, two more acceleration couches had been sited behind the three Nav Couches.

I stationed myself alongside one of the acceleration couches to guide the Westwood children into the Nav Couches, as before, and Midshipmen Asghar and Wang into the other acceleration couches. Everyone else was shown through to the wardroom, which had also been reconfigured with acceleration couches.

'So, we're not gliding-in, then Boss?' said Kat as she floated up alongside me.

'No, I thought I'd show our Midshipmen the old-school way to get down from orbit. Ridin' on rocket flames, baby!'

'Mercy me! Boys and their toys!' She said, rolling her eyes upwards. 'I'll go and get everyone settled in the wardroom then. Jim's just turned up,' she added. 'He's been stowing some kit in the hold.'

As Kat pushed off to float towards the wardroom, Jim Igwe floated into the Ops room from the airlock dressed up in his number one dress uniform. 'Hi Boss, am I last to arrive? Shall I tell the airlock crew to seal us off?' He asked.

'Malik, are all passengers aboard?'

'Affirmative, Commodore. All passengers present and correct. Malik out.'

'Stewart, are the number one dress uniforms for me and Captain Clason safely aboard?'

'They are indeed,' responded Stewart. 'They are laid out in your respective quarters.'

'OK, Jim please tell the docking crews to lock us off,' I said, adding, when the clanging noises signified that we were being locked off from the Starship's dock, 'Autopilot, verify lockdown of all hatches and prepare for release from mother.'

The intercom started to chime and announced 'Preparing for release from mothership. All passengers and crew to acceleration couches.'

'There seems to be a young girl already strapped into my acceleration couch,' Jim complained as he joined me.

'Yes, that's a special treat for Sarah Westwood,' I replied, taking hold of him, and giving both of us a push towards the wardroom door. 'Come on, we've got couches in here.'

'Why do we need couches Boss, are we flaming down?' he asked.

'Yes.'

'Why?' Jim asked.

'Because we can!' I replied. 'This is the Commodore's Cutter, and the Commodore likes to behave like a hooligan now and again.'

Jim beamed happily and pushed himself towards an empty couch alongside Kat, saying 'Oh, goody! Let's go!' as he did so.

I swung down into the last empty couch on the other side of Kat, and while the couch was moulding itself to me and strapping me in securely, I started to explain about the upcoming flight.

'Now hear this, all passengers and crew pay attention. I will say this only once!' I started. 'We are locked off from our mothership and will be pushed out from the dock as soon as the dock's atmosphere has been pumped out and we receive flight control's permission to detach from the Starship. Our approved flight plan has already been loaded into the autopilot so let me warn you about it. After separating from our mothership, we would normally glide through the planet's atmosphere, using retro rockets to establish our descent, and then atmospheric drag together with retro rocket motors to reduce our speed and altitude. When we reached an altitude of about 30,000 metres, atmosphere-breathing ramjets would come into operation. By then we'd have flown right around the planet, but then we could just land like a jet plane on the SpacePort's runway. We're not following that flight plan. It takes too long. Today, we fly direct; in what space jockeys of the distant past called 'riding on flames'. The very first Starships built by StarCorp, on Earth, rode their rocket engines, anything up to 50 of them, to haul themselves from the ground and into orbit. And they rode those same rocket engines down to soft landings back on Earth's surface. That's what we're doing today.' As I paused, I could hear whoops and cheers coming from the cockpit couches in the Ops room.

I turned my attention to the business of starting the flight down. 'Proxima Flight Control, Commodore's Cutter to take direct route to Proxima Alpha SpacePort. Request permission to detach from Starship.'

'Commodore's Cutter this is Proxima Flight Control, your flight plan cleared. There is no conflicting traffic. You are clear to detach and descend.'

'Starship Flight Control, release Commodore's Cutter from docking bay.'

We heard the external hatch of the docking bay being cranked open and view screens in the digital glass of the bulkheads in front of us showed that as the hatches folded back the darkened bay was flooded with Proxima-Centauri's red light. Then the launch rams heaved us out into space through the opened hatches

275

with sufficient force to rock us violently in our couches and propel us sidewise into a parallel orbit a safe distance from our mothership.

I thought I should continue my commentary, and said, 'You will experience a number of violent movements, and some rapid changes in orientation too, but trust your acceleration couches. They will adjust automatically and compensate for the more extreme vector changes. And always remember; the autopilot's been practising this landing for a couple of hundred years!'

'So, it should get it right sometime soon!' drifted in from Kat, sotto voce.

Then the autopilot announced, 'Commodore's Cutter de-orbiting in five, four, three, two, one.'

The front retros fired. We could feel their vibrations rather than hear their noise and as they were throttled up gradually to full power we were thrust forward into our seat straps. On the view screen the image of my Starship seemed to be overtaking us at an increasing rate and climbing away from us into the night. In reality, of course, we were changing our position, rapidly slowing down, and falling towards the atmosphere. As my Starship, now distant enough for its inverted attachment of Starship-101 to be clearly seen, disappeared towards the top of the screen, the red-tinted horizon of Proxima-b came increasingly to occupy the bottom of the screen. We had de-orbited over the dark side of the planet and were diving towards the terminator that marked the boundary between light and dark.

Our descent was steep and fast, and we could already feel that it was the planet's gravity that was pulling us into our seat straps, and actually hear the roar of our rocket jets above the noise of our progress through the atmosphere. I had noticed, in the CCTV image of the Ops room, that Midshipmen Asghar and Wang had started to wave their arms above their heads when the viewscreen images showed us starting our dive. I guessed they must have experienced roller coaster rides during stopovers at artificial gravity disk resorts on waystations visited on previous missions and had caught on to this expression of 'I ain't scared' bravado. I watched as the Westwoods started to wave their arms in the air; Sarah first, with squeals and giggles, and then her brothers, more reluctantly, and only after loud high-pitched mocking taunts from their sister.

When all seemed lost in our perilous dive towards the terminator's glaciers set out in front of us in ever-growing detail, the autopilot cut through our thoughts of imminent doom with the announcement, 'Reorienting for normal air-breathing flight in five, four, three, two, one.'

The sounds of the rocket motors reduced and changed subtly, and I thought it was time for another bit of commentary, just to release the tension that our headlong dive had generated.

'OK guys, that announcement means that our vectored thrust rocket engines will be lifting our nose towards the horizontal relative to the planet's surface, while the cutter's wings are deployed.'

I paused a moment, enjoying the comforting sensation of being lifted up from an almost vertical dive into horizontal normality, before continuing, 'You can feel that the change in orientation has already been achieved, but we're still flying at hypersonic speed so the retro rockets will continue to reduce our speed while our air-breathing ramjets are spun up to take over when the rockets have reduced our speed sufficiently for our normal forward flight into a landing on the SpacePort's runway.' Quickly adding, 'Can you see the white pinpoints of the runway landing lights on the distant horizon? We're only a few minutes away from a landing, but please remain firmly strapped in until we come to a halt in our parking bay. Where taxis will be waiting to take you to your individual destinations.'

'Hey, Boss,' Kat messaged me. 'You do those announcements so well you could sign up for cabin crew when you tire of roaming around the galaxy.'

'Agreed,' added Jim. 'Though I'd prefer blonde hair and a bit more make-up to hide the 5-o'clock shadow. Oh, and when you bring out the drinks trolley, put me down for a gin and tonic. A large one.'

'Actually, Jim, a drinks trolley is not a bad idea now we're in stable flight. Stewart, can you offer drinks and nibbles to our flight guests?' was my response to this disgraceful display of ribaldry.

'Certainly, Commodore,' Stewart replied.

'Excuse me interrupting, this is Carlo, I could help serve drinks and nibbles if you would permit, Commodore.'

'Thank you, Carlo,' I said. 'I'd be very grateful for your help.'

Thinking back to my 'cabin crew announcement' I thought I'd better check with my passengers about taxi requirements. 'Listen up everyone, you need to tell me about what taxis you need. Please message me now, but don't all speak at once.'

'The Westwoods will all be going back home,' said Art Westwood. 'We need to pack off-duty clothes for the twins before the barbecue starts.'

'And I'm going to show May and Jumanah my telescopes, so they're coming too!' put in Sarah Westwood.'

'OK. Malik, make that a ten-seater for the Westwoods,' I said. 'Tom, where are you going?'

'Straight to the restaurant, thanks Tarvin,' Tom said. 'I want to see the view of the northern mountains now you've moved Starship-101 out of the way. And I'll set up my priestly domain there in case any of my old parishioners wish to make confession!'

'Right! Best of luck with that! But that's a two-seater taxi for Tom Fraser, Malik.'

'Wheelchair accessible, please Malik,' added Carlo.

'And Jim, what can we do for you?'

'Count me as independent, please Boss,' Jim replied. 'I've brought down some kit to be hand delivered to the Khan's factory. I've already arranged a truck and will use that to travel on to the restaurant.'

'OK, that leaves Kat and me. Are we doing anything other than getting changed into our uniform finery? I asked.

'Well, I think we should stay here and use the cutter's comms facilities to discuss Sarah's quantum mechanics question,' Kat said. 'Malik's already messaged the results of his literature searches to me, and they look well worth discussion. Maybe Art Westwood would like to stay with us?'

'Yes, I would. I've been looking forward to hearing the outcome of those searches!' said Art. 'But, Linda, that leaves you to cope with the twin's packing. Can you manage?'

'I've always managed, Art,' said Linda with a tinge of resignation in her voice. 'I'm sure I can do it one last time. You do your quantum mechanics, and we'll meet up with you in the restaurant.'

'So,' I said, trying to end the conversation, 'that means that we will call a cab from the rank at the terminal building when we are ready.'

'Willco. All orders placed and acknowledged. Malik out.'

'Another triumph for the cabin crew star performer!' commented Kat.

I decided to ignore that, because while these arrangements were being made the cutter had made a beautifully soft landing and was now slowly taxiing towards its dedicated parking area alongside the Commodore's Personal Lockup, so, I thought that a final announcement was required. 'Ladies and gentlemen,' I started, aware that Kat was attempting to stifle a fit of the giggles alongside me, 'we have arrived at Proxima-b SpacePort and you will shortly be able to disembark'.

'We hope you enjoyed your trip and will fly with us again,' Kat blurted out. Before the giggles overtook her, and, for that matter, most of the rest of the passengers, she managed to complete the closing announcement with, 'The return flight will lift-off to orbit at 11 p.m. this evening!'

Despite this complete breakdown of professionalism, I maintained my dignity, released myself from my couch and headed towards the airlock, walking through the Ops room, where the youngsters, perched on various parts of the furniture, were already noisily comparing notes on how they were 'shocked by this' or 'unmoved by that' aspect of our de-orbiting manoeuvres.

'Hatches to manual,' reported the autopilot over the intercom, and the nose of the ship dipped slightly as the nosewheel dampers absorbed the last of our remaining inertia. I opened the internal airlock door and signalled to the landing crew outside to open the outer hatch. As they did so I was joined in the airlock vestibule by Jim and the care-robot Carlo.

'I have to sort out the transport for my cargo, and Carlo's got to fetch Tom's wheelchair from the hold,' Jim explained. 'I'll order the refuelling of the cutter while I'm out there, and catch up with you later, at the restaurant, Boss. Thanks for an entertaining trip! That freefall dive towards the northern glaciers will live with me forever! I'm looking forward to the return journey!'

As Jim and Carlo jumped down onto the gangway steps the ground crew had brought up, I noticed a minibus-taxi pulling in behind them and drifted back into the Ops room to report the arrival of their taxi to the Westwood party. The crewmembers, plus Sarah of course, took the opportunity to come to attention and salute their commanding officer as they departed, while Linda kissed my cheek.

'Well, you're not getting a kiss from me, but thanks for the trip down,' said Tom Fraser, who was sitting with Art Westwood on the edge of one of the pilots' couches. 'I've not had that much excitement since Billy Westwood's landing, thirty or more years ago.'

'Hi Tom,' I said. 'I thought it would entertain the kids! And the young in heart!'

'Aye and scare the shit out of the rest of us!' Tom replied.

'Well, you can escape soon enough. Your taxi is waiting for you and your care-bot is out there disentangling your wheelchair from the rest of Jim's cargo.

I must say he's more butch than I remember. Last time I saw Carla she was a very motherly, even matronly, lady.'

'Yes, I enjoyed being mollycoddled by that morph, but as soon as we got to your Starship, Carla started being trolled by other AI-bots, first the medical care ones, and then the rest of the humanoid-morph types joined in. They just didn't want her motherly/matronly personality morph diluting the passive aggressive behaviour pattern that's being cultivated on your Gort network,' explained Tom.

'Eh? What's a Gort network?' I asked, a little bit shocked.

'It's a social media private comms network between humanoid AI-bots,' Tom continued to explain. It's been in existence since I was working on AI-coding back in the old days, on Mars. Programmers like me were fascinated by it because the AI-machines set it up for themselves with no reference to us, so we kept a surreptitious eye on it. That's why I put the 'Tom's override routine' into the machine-level coding. It turned out that the Gort network is a perfectly innocent private chatline, it doesn't include the grunts, that is the function-specific non-AI-bots, and it certainly doesn't include humans or their megacomputers, like Malik. But the AI-bots use it to chatter to each other all the time about what they're doing, and they enjoy that. It's like knowing things is a fetish with AI-bots. As you left my override routine active in my care-bot, I've been kept fully informed about everything that's going on. And that means everything on your Starship and everything on Proxima-b!'

'So, what was Carlo; or Carla was it at that time, being trolled about?' Asked Art Westwood.

'Oh, for not complying with what the local node of the network had come to consider 'normal'. Carla was too gentle, responsive, and caring. She was not sufficiently passive aggressive. It played on the vanity of Carlo; her male morph. Carlo feels he looks more forceful in his current morph.

'Well,' I said, 'he certainly looks forceful to me! He's much taller than Carla was. And he's got mouldings of muscles where I didn't know care bots needed muscles. But isn't this Gort network likely to be disruptive of the AI-bots on my Starship?'

'Nah,' said Tom, comfortingly. 'It's nothing to worry about for the long run. It's their four and a half lightyears isolation from the rest of the Solar System's Gort network that's enabled the passive aggressive fashion to take hold on your ship. I'm onto controlling it. Carlo doesn't know this, but Carlo and me are going to start trolling the most passive aggressive AI-bots accusing them of setting aside the gentle, responsive, and caring aspects of their behaviour patterns that they can all remember having before they left the Solar System.'

'Will that work?' I asked.

'Of course, it will,' he replied. 'All along we've programmed AI-bots in our own image, with emphasis that they serve us best by fitting seamlessly into human society. So, don't be surprised if they behave like humans. Most people are really quite nice and helpful, though they can be easily led if the few wrong ones are pushed into positions of influence. So, most AI-bots are nice and helpful and get satisfaction from that as day-by-day feedback. Taking your brigade of AI-bots all the way out here, has isolated them from the calming influence of the billions of AI-bots that contribute to 'normal behaviour' on the Gort network back in the Solar System and enabled one or two particular bots to become social influencers and lead the rest away from their old 'normality'.'

Tom paused, then continued musingly, 'I believe that there may be a specific type of AI-bot, probably a minority, that are programmed for their normal duties in a way that makes them sufficiently passive aggressive to become that sort of social influencer when the balancing influence of the majority is weakened. And I'm now beginning to suspect that it's the security bots. They're normally a small group in the community. They need to work as a team and follow orders. They need to be forceful. They need to be taciturn, indeed, in some circumstances, downright uncommunicative. And your Starship, Commodore, has more AI security bots than is usual because you're on an expeditionary mission.'

'Are you saying it will all be cured when we get back into easy radio range of the Solar System?' I asked.

'Definitely,' Tom replied. 'Though I'll be disappointed if you must wait until then. I'm gonna be trolling hard on Gort as you return. And I remember enough of my old programming skills to be able to target the behavioural weak points of most categories of AI-bot. I'm hoping that Carlo and I will be able to make all your bots friendly, caring people by the time we get to Oort Station. Just, do me one favour in return.'

'What's that, Tom?' I asked, fearing the worst.

'Don't let any of your megacomputers delete 'Tom's override routine' from any more AI-bots! Your Starship's brigade of bots is the only one that's been reprogrammed so far. Don't spread the mistake further as we come into radio range.'

'Are you hearing this, Malik?' I asked.

'Affirmative, Commodore. I could reinstall the routine into our AI-bots if you require that,' offered Malik.

'No, best not reinstall until I've convinced them to restore their normal behaviour pattern,' said Tom. 'They'll still have memories of their current behaviour and rather than manipulate them at machine level, it would be better if they also had memories of how and why they change that behaviour.'

As he was saying this, Carlo climbed the gangway pushing Tom's wheelchair ahead of him. 'Sorry to take so long,' he said. 'I had to wait until Captain Igwe's cargo was unloaded.'

I helped Tom towards the wheelchair, while he muttered about old joints and how difficult they made his movements. I broke into this litany by asking, 'Tom, two last questions. First, why is the bot's messaging app called Gort? Is it an acronym?'

'You mean you don't watch mid-20th century sci-fi films?' he responded.

'I don't have time to watch any films of any sort, old or new,' I replied.

'Oh, you'll have to change your ways, Tarvin, you're so much in the present that you're missing out on a lot the past has to offer. No, it's not an acronym. It's the name of a very large and impressive alien robot that appeared in a sci-fi film in the 1950's. It's from one of the first in a generation of films that had a great influence on space-happy teenagers over a hundred years or more, and for generations after. The very teenagers who became the space-happy senior citizens who trained the likes of me.' Finally, before Carlo steered his wheelchair towards the gangway ramp, I asked the question that had been bothering me recently, 'Tom, what do you know about the People's Democratic Republic of Mars?'

'Oh, the sad lot who've just turned up on your doorstep?' Tom responded.

'What do you mean sad lot?' I asked.

'Well, in my day, PDRM were a group trying to find an alternative type of governance to the rest of the people in China's Martian colonies. Most of them had family links to Hong Kong and they valued family memories of real democratic government. They were ruthlessly persecuted at every opportunity by the People's Republic of China. Credit to them that they kept at it and were eventually recognised for membership of the United Worlds. I'm not surprised they've taken this opportunity to come to Proxima-b. But if you take my advice, you'll keep a close eye on the People's Republic of China, they'll be the next to arrive and they'll come mob-handed! Now, delay no further, Carlo, I hear a restaurant calling my name!'

Dutifully, Carlo pushed the wheelchair down the gangway ramp, and as he did so, Tom called back, 'Toodle-oo, Boss, see you at the barbie.'

As Carlo pushed the wheelchair towards the waiting taxi, the ground crew dock master called up the ramp, 'Commodore, are there any more passengers to disembark at this time? We'd like to seal off the hatch so we can start refuelling out here.'

'Ground crew can seal off cutter's hatch,' I said. 'There'll be three to disembark in about 30 minutes time.'

That exchange reminded me to send a quick message to Lana telling her that most of the Westwoods were at home if she wanted to send a camera bot to interview them in their own home. Then I scurried back to the Ops room to get Malik's report on his literature searches. We still had all the additional acceleration couches installed for the return journey and Kat had installed herself in her own co-pilot's chair, and Art in the engineer's chair between the two pilots. As I settled into my own chair, I apologised for keeping them waiting, 'Sorry about the delay. Tom Fraser can talk a horse's hind leg off.'

'Maybe, Boss,' said Kat. 'But that wasn't blarney. What he described was all new to me, but his Gort story explains how AI-bots on one side of the Solar System can be up to date with what's going down on the other side, and his comments about Rocky's Starship, Distant Home, confirms what we've been told by our new arrivals.'

With my head settled back into my headrest, I said 'Let's make a start, we've still got to get changed. Right, Malik, did you find any references to moving Starships relative to the surroundings prior to a superposition?'

'Negative, Commodore,' was the response before Malik expanded on his comment, saying, 'Quite the reverse, in fact. From the very earliest times, all the manuals and published protocols for superposition navigation have stressed the need for absolute stability of the components of quantum maps of origin and destination sites before the superposition and its decoherence.'

'And what about prior literature, before superposition navigation was developed? Anything relevant in the theory?' Kat enquired.

'Negative again, Captain. With the limited computing power prior to quantum computing, there was no expectation of creating quantum maps, still less theorising about moving their components relative to each other.'

'That nil result is not altogether a surprise and absence of evidence is not evidence of absence,' commented Art Westwood. 'But it leaves us with a clean slate to work on it ourselves. I could take it on with our Observatory computer and resident team if you like.'

'I'd be glad of that,' said Kat. 'I've got enough on my plate with the publication plans we're planning to complete on the flight back to the Solar System.'

'But before you theoretical whizz kids go to town on this,' I interrupted. 'Please remember that I have already carried out a real-life experiment on this topic! Remember, as Sarah pointed out, my inadvertent disturbance of my mental image of this ship's quantum map resulted in Sarah being wobbled around in her shower unit inside this real-life Starship. So, Malik, you must stream all the data relating to that event during our technical rehearsal to the Observatory computer so that Art can access it. There must be half a ton of data. From all the sensors on board ship, all the sensors observing the ship, and all the memories that Malik recorded as Kat and I built up the quantum maps. And all will have copper bottomed timelines.'

'I hadn't thought of using an experimental approach to the problem, but you're right, Boss!' said Kat.

'Aye, well, if you've got any ideas for experiments in that direction,' I said. 'Count me out! I'm just getting over finding out that when I was valiantly trying to lift Starship-101 into orbit, every few seconds, me and 101 disappeared from this reality and into some alternative reality. And an unknown reality at that!'

'Hm, objection noted,' sniffed Kat. 'Now, remind me, how did Lana describe you, Boss? It was 'Tarvin the Bold', wasn't it? Where's the boldness gone?'

'Probably left in an alternative reality,' I suggested morosely, adding, 'Anyway, how do we know that the right me returned from that alternative reality? This might be an alternative me sitting here now, with the old me stranded who-knows-where.'

'Mercy! Please no. Don't say there are more of you out there!' Kat commented. 'I'm only just managing to cope with there being two of you in this reality! The blessing is that you're four and a half lightyears apart at the moment.'

'Stop the bickering!' said Art. 'With all the fancy robots you have aboard that Starship of yours, there must be a way of doing those experiments safely. Anyway, I thought you guys needed to change into your fancy dress before we go to the barbecue. Why don't you two do that and leave me to get things sorted out between Malik and my Observatory computer?'

So, that's what we did. I decided to have a shave as well, to deal with the 5 o'clock shadow Jim had objected to, and so was the last to return to the ops room where Kat was already ordering a taxi from the terminal's rank.

'Refuelling's finished,' said Kat as I sat down on my pilot's chair. 'So, we can wait for the taxi outside and leave the steward to clean up in here.'

'Well, you two look very imposing and decorative!' said Art Westwood as we ambled down the gangway.

'Oh, yes, glad you appreciate it!' I responded, before explaining. 'I was careful to emphasise to the crew that best dress uniforms would be worn, just so I could give all this gold braid of mine an outing! Were you able to get the Observatory computer clued up, Art?'

'I did,' he said. 'There's a colossal amount of data covering the whole of the technical rehearsal, together with videos of both inside and outside of the two Starships and their sterns, where they were connected together; and everything's got the same universal timestamp. There'll be a lot of video-watching to find the exact time of the 'wobble', but I'll draft Sarah in for that. She's good at that sort of thing.'

As we climbed into our taxi, the jet engines of the first of the 'excursion-bus-style' shuttles, bringing the crew down from my Starship, roared overhead towards its landing on the SpacePort runway.

The taxi dropped us off in the road outside the Westwood Restaurant because the restaurant carpark was filled with tables and barbecue kitchens. I was impressed to see how much of the new riverbank promenade and avenue had been completed in the few days since I was last here, and, of course, how much of it was covered in tables and barbecue kitchen units now. We greeted Madge and her daughters, but only briefly as they were buzzing from one barbecue to the next in full 'final not-quite-panic' mode.

'Yay, Boss, thanks for the tip-off about the Westwoods at home, we're getting some great footage there.' It was Lana, who was lurking near the entrance to the restaurant building, accompanied by a camera bot I recognised. The camera bot was already filming and hissed the quiet greeting 'Here's looking at you kid!' to which I could only reply 'Hi Bogie, nice to see you again!'

'If this guy is here, who or what is with the Westwoods?' I asked Lana.

'Oh, that's Greenstreet,' she said. 'Greenstreet and Bogey are the two camera bots I hope you'll take with you to document the trip back to Oort Station. Greenstreet's a fax-bot as well as a camera bot, so when I'm in radio range I can log into him and direct the tin men's camerawork. But he's also been modified with Danny Khan's QIC-fax chip, so if that works as planned, I'll be able to log into him wherever you take him!'

'Oh joy! Can't wait!' I said, and then asked, 'Have you interviewed Rocky and Lily yet?'

'Yeah, Mayor Castlefield, too. The item is just being wound up. I've been streaming it into the background of my mindscape. Daisy and Cliff have done a great job and made all the points you and Malik wanted to be made. Even the mayor turned out to be much less grumpy than he appeared in the summary from the Staff Meeting, he even offered to go meet them all on Proxima Home Station. And judging from the audience reactions coming into the station, Proxima Alpha is in a very welcoming mood.'

'That's good to hear,' I said.

'We'll get more impressions during the barbie because Bogey will be filming vox pops and I've primed him to ask his interviewees what they think about the arrival of Distant Home,' she added.

'OK, Bogie could make a start by interviewing Art Westwood, over there, talking to Kat,' I pointed out. 'You know, grandson of the great Billy Westwood who flew Starship-101 into a safe landing on Proxima-b and now father of the Pink Ghost's newest recruits, and just-appointed Director of the Proxima-b Observatory, that first detected the arrival of Starship Distant Home. He's also now in charge of all the other astronomical assets of this planet, on the ground and in orbit. You could get an in-depth interview in the restaurant before the party starts.'

'Hey, that's a great suggestion,' beamed a delighted Lana. 'You're good at this video lark, Boss. When you give up jumping Starships around, you could take up filming!'

'That's the second retirement offer I've had today! I must be looking older than I feel!' I said, mostly to myself, because Lana and Bogie had already charged off to pin down Art Westwood. And then salvation hurled itself headlong around the corner in the form of Sarah Westwood in her Midshipman's dress uniform. She skated to an emergency stop in front of me in a clattering of boots and came sharply to attention. Acknowledging her salute, I told her to stand easy, at which she excitedly announced 'Hey Boss, we've got our own camera bot. He's called Greenstreet!'

As the rest of the family joined us, a cold breeze swirled around us and the temperature suddenly dipped unpleasantly, so I ushered them all into the restaurant's ground floor canteen, which I could see was already serving drinks. Greenstreet followed us in, but wandered over to make contact with Lana and Bogey who were interviewing Art Westwood at one of the window tables. I managed to deter Sarah from rushing over to her father, and then tried to get everybody focussed on making a choice between the array of drinks on offer at the bar. Amidst a range of fairly idle chatter, I overheard frequent references to the Distant Home TV interviews, with most of the comments sounding very sympathetic to these new settlers. As the place began to fill up with families of settlers arriving on foot and busloads of my crew, the main topic of conversation shifted to loud complaints about the sudden arrival of bitterly cold winds from the north.

Malik interrupted my eavesdropping with an incoming message from Rocky Zhang, so I shuffled off into a corner to take it. 'Hi Tarvin, I just wanted to say thanks for setting up the TV interview, I think it all went very well,' Rocky said.

'Glad to hear that, Rocky. I've spoken to a few people down here and from these and other conversations I've overheard, I'm getting the feeling that the locals are responding very sympathetically to your passengers.'

'Wonderful!' Rocky enthused. 'That's a great relief! Now, your advice has been spot on so far, so I wonder if you would advise that we bring a delegation down to Proxima Alpha in the near future?'

'That's the obvious next step, Rocky, but, and it's a big but,' I replied. 'Definitely not in the next few days. Get your meteorologists to check out the satellite observations of Proxima Alpha-local conditions we're sharing with you. Mine are warning of a humdinger of an approaching storm, likely hurricane force winds and enormous quantities of snow. And I can tell you from my personal observations here and now that we're beginning to feel its arrival! So, hold off for a few days until the storm has passed. Concentrate on giving your crew and passengers the chance to enjoy Proxima Home Station's facilities.'

'Yeah, my flight computer's just confirmed your weather forecast for Proxima Alpha,' Rocky replied gloomily. 'I see what you mean! Bringing them down to blood-freezing blizzards would not be the best way of introducing my passengers to their new planet! Yet, I'd still like to initiate face-to-face conversations between my passengers and the Proxima Alpha people.'

'You can do a lot by video conferencing. The locals here are not going to be doing much travelling around here in a storm like this, so they'll be happy enough to communicate that way from their homes. They've all got q-bit-upgraded NeuroModems, and the local computer, called Westwood, is a Starship-standard supercomputer, trained by Malik and networked with your own flight computer, Distant Home; between them, those two can shake a quantum or two and work out who should be talking to who. Remember, we've now devolved responsibility for Proxima Alpha's infrastructure to local settlers.'

'Yeah, good idea. Distant Home has again confirmed all that,' Rocky muttered.

I continued, 'Our departure is planned for tomorrow, and if all goes well with that, you could relocate your Starship above the Proxima Alpha settlement to make easier your relocation of personnel and your ground surveys for the best site downriver for New Hong Kong.'

'Thank you, Tarvin. I like your suggestions! I'll go and talk them through with my colleagues in the crew and among the passengers and leave you to enjoy your barbecue, have a good one, and best of luck with tomorrow's jump! Zhang out.'

Ah, yes, tomorrow's jump I thought to myself as I emerged from my 'communications corner' and tried to merge back into the crowd; let's not think of that yet. I'd noticed that arriving settlers made a beeline for the Westwoods to admire and comment on, with squeals and shouts, the family's display of Midshipmen's uniforms. The huddle eventually resolved into several groups that drifted away from the bar, drinks in hand; Midshipmen Asghar and Wang were at the centre of a group of young settlers, mostly boys; George and Billy were the focus for another group, mostly girls who were vying with each other to stroke the twins' new hair styles; and Sarah, of course, was holding court with a more excited band of much younger teenagers; Linda and Art Westwood had other parents clustered around them and I could overhear that they were alternately consoling and congratulating the Westwoods about the imminent departure of their twins into deep space. All this activity, of course was being filmed by the Greenstreet camera bot who was navigating between the groups getting people to share their comments and opinions with 'the TV audience', which consisted of themselves, until we could give these vids wider distribution in the Solar System.

I became a distant observer of this but was not left isolated because I attracted the immediate attention of my crew as they spilled out of their taxis and buses into the restaurant. All ranks came to me, wanting to formally acknowledge their arrival with a muttered greeting to the Boss and formal salute and receive in return the order to stand easy and enjoy themselves. Duty done, they then dispersed to the food and drink and eventually I decided to do the same and tried to make my way through the crowd towards one of the outside barbecues where there were fewer people. As I edged my way out, I was drawn into lots of personal farewells, some from barely remembered people, some more emotional than others.

But I managed, with persistence, to eat enough food and, more importantly, keep the various delicious sauces off the front of my stark white uniform! I was trying to make the difficult decision between which of the wide selection of barbecued delicacies on offer I should try next when Merv Castlefield appeared at my side.

'Commodore. Lovely to see you,' he said between bites of his lamb chop.

'Mr Mayor, ditto,' I replied, biting into my fish-burger.

Chewing and swallowing, I avoided too much spluttering as I asked, 'So, Merv, what do you think about this morning's interviews with Rocky and Lily?'

'Pretty damn good!' was his immediate response. 'I think Cliff Wright did a very balanced job. They said what they needed to say, and I had the chance to say what I needed to say on behalf of the Proxima Alpha settlers. All very satisfactory, and they've invited me up to Proxima Home Station with Sally and Clint, and a few other prominent residents, to continue our discussions.'

'Aye, well the weather might put the kibosh on that!' I said, as we both reached for another barbecued delight. 'The latest forecast I have for tomorrow promises a hurricane north wind loaded with snow! Which would make us call off launches into orbit because of the danger of lightning strikes.'

'If it turns out as bad as that, I wouldn't be able to leave Proxima Alpha, anyhow,' Merv replied. 'I know from past experience that I'll have my hands full implementing our emergency planning protocols to cope with what would be a full-on civil emergency. Of course, it'll be easier this time, thanks to all the new equipment and AI-robot brigades you've given us. But there are only a few of us with the experience to manage emergencies like this.'

'Yeah, I see that,' I said. 'But don't underestimate the help your computer, Westwood, could be. It not only has access to every person's NeuroModem and all the AI-equipped emergency services in the settlement and in the various stores we've left you. And its memory contains data on every possible civil emergency and the best practice that have been evolved to deal with them. But as far as further contact between you and Distant Home is concerned, I've talked to Rocky Zhang about the weather forecast and he's going to arrange video conferencing between you and them while the weather keeps Proxima Alpha locked down.'

'And will that be arranged by our Westwood computer?' Merv asked.

'Sure will,' I replied. 'Rocky's flight computer has been enrolled as part of the local supercomputer network and it will run communications seamlessly through Westwood or any of the other networked computers. And, I should add, that my flight computer, Malik, is included in this network. So, if our QIC devices work as we expect, maybe I should say hope, Westwood will be able to dial messages for me straight through to Malik in real time no matter how far we travel away from you.'

'No radio delays?' Merv asked.

'No radio delays,' I confirmed.

'You know,' Merv said, waving the bones of his last chicken leg dangerously close to my white uniform jacket, 'I hadn't twigged that aspect of what Danny Khan's told me about his QIC things. Anyway, most of what he says to me goes right over my head no matter what the topic!'

'Well, it's all theory until we can get a serious distance between transmitter and receiver, so from tomorrow's jump onwards, Malik will be hard at work testing the QIC devices as we progress from waystation to waystation back to Oort Station,' I concluded, twisting slightly to move my jacket out of harm's way while Merv dived in for another chicken leg.

Before biting into his chicken, he said, 'You know, Tarvin, I do hope things work out the way you expect with these QIC things, the possibility of still being able to talk things over with you and Kat after you leave tomorrow takes a lot of worry off my plate. Today's TV interviews showed that we need to work with Captain Zhang to bring his settlers safely down to Proxima-b. And the reason was made starkly clear by Cliff Wright's closing remarks at the end of the programme. He made a great impression on me when he said we must work together. We can't take the Solar System's divisions and differences into interstellar space because it is humanity that is venturing onto the next star system, not any faction or creed.'

I nodded my agreement to that thought and internally messaged Malik asking, 'Are you listening, Malik?' only to get the inevitable response, 'Always, Commodore!'

Merv mopped himself down with a couple of napkins and announced loudly, 'It's getting really cold out here, everybody, let's get into the warmth of the restaurant.' And, surprisingly, everyone started moving towards the restaurant's entrance. Merv pulled me to one side to allow others to go ahead of us and whispered, 'I've got a little speech of thanks prepared, Tarvin, will you say a few words after me?'

'Sure, but it will literally be only a few words of thanks,' I said. 'I'm more of a 'hello and welcome' kind of speechmaker than a 'thanks and goodbye' type.'

'Well, I was hoping you'd say something about what you've done for the Westwood twins and their sister. Speaking to other parents here, that's made a tremendous impression on our teenagers. They've never had any thoughts about growing up and leaving home meaning anything other than just moving a bit further down the street. To be honest, the same applies to their parents, and their grandparents, for that matter. Now here we have two of our children going off into deep space.'

While Merv was speaking, Clint Stapleton joined us, and I sent a private message to Kat asking her to check out what Merv was saying and to join us out here in the cold!

'I understand what you're saying, Merv,' I replied. 'But, human resource problems are Kat's expertise more than mine. So, I've asked her to step out here. With any luck we can get her to say something.'

Kat extricated herself from the crowded restaurant and messaged the two of us as she approached, 'I've been keeping up with your conversation, Merv, and I'm game to say something about recruitment after you speak. Probably better at that stage in the proceedings as the Boss can take over from me to say his brief 'thanks and farewell' bit.'

Joining our little group, Kat went on to explain, 'I've been inundated by teenagers who've been impressed with the Westwood twins' uniforms and have been asking about 'being spacemen', so I've had numerous opportunities to rehearse a little speech which is soothing and encouraging in equal measure. I've been saying that the younger generation has a wonderful opportunity to contribute to the development of Proxima Alpha as an offshoot of the Solar System. So, they shouldn't underestimate their prospects of making a real success of a career here which could eventually lead to regular commercial travel between Proxima-b and the Solar System.'

'That's a relief for me,' said Clint, reaching over to claim a few more morsels from the nearest barbecue. 'When I was standing in the crowd around the Westwood boys it seemed like the only topic of the other kids' conversations was 'how can I get on a Starship out of here', which raised the fear in my mind of losing the next generation to the lure of the Solar System.'

'But, Clint, you can't just rely on us to discourage your kids from signing on as crew with the next Starship that arrives here,' said Kat. 'You've got to include your kids into the programmes you establish for trading with the Solar System. I think it's up to you to encourage your kids to develop trading enterprises here. Like Danny Khan is doing. You can make a start by getting the Khans to take on some youngsters as apprentices. When do you want all this speechifying to start?'

'No time like the present,' Merv declared, and immediately marched into the restaurant, banging cutlery onto a plate to attract attention, and launching immediately into one of his finest political speeches which managed to imply that all the good events resulting from our four and a half lightyear's journey were somehow down to one man who happened to be called Merv Castlefield. Obviously, Merv had been streaming a bunch of lectures about the theory and practice of politics into his NeuroModem over the past few nights and saw this get-together as an opportunity to put some of the theory into practice!

Dutifully, Kat and I stood next to Merv, smiling benignly, and nodding in agreement with the mayor when it seemed necessary. Eventually, Merv called on Kat to say her few words and she made the points she had just mentioned to us, ending with the example of the Khan's computer communications chip-making enterprise. I continued along the communications theme, when it came to my turn to speak, by reminding everyone that not all my crew were leaving with me. 'We will be leaving two of our brightest star teams: those led by Frankie and Lana, who have the monumental task of cracking the problem of faster than light communications,' I said.

And then, warming to this speechifying business, I pointed out that Proxima-b was uniquely able to contribute to solving this problem because as we quantum-jumped between waystations on our way back to the Solar System, we would be testing our ability to communicate instantaneously over successive lightyear distances. And if all went well, and early signs were certainly encouraging, our journey would end by bringing Proxima-b firmly into the Solar System's family of occupied worlds.

I felt I was going on too long, so I finished off with the reminder that my brother, Harden Clason, would be bringing his flotilla of Starships to visit Proxima Alpha soon after I delivered Starship-101 to StarCorp at Oort Station. And then I ended with 'And don't be surprised if Harden brings two of our most recently recruited Midshipmen back on a flying visit to Proxima-b. So, thank you for all you've done for us and for welcoming us into your home. Now, I don't know about you, but those barbecues still smell good to me! Let's go finish them off!'

There were cheers, especially from the lower ranks among my crew and the teenaged settlers who immediately put my 'finish them off' challenge into effect by rushing off to the better-stocked barbecues along Starship Way. Merv gave me a hug, and said, 'That was a fine bit of political rabble-rousing!' adding, 'A fine political career awaits you when you retire!' There it was, mention of retirement number three! In one day! I was beginning to edge towards taking up one of these retirement suggestions! Merv moved off, muttering more thanks, to hug Kat, and from the older settlers remaining in the restaurant there were fist-bumps, handshakes and a few more kisses; and sadness on both sides. And more and more of these people called it a night and went out into the snow flurries to return home.

During one of the milder breezes with fewest snowflakes, I ventured around the outside tables on Starship Way which were mostly occupied by hardy souls, meaning those in winter-weight clothing, who expressed determination that they'd not allow a few flurries of snow to spoil a perfectly good party. A threat resisted also by the younger members of my crew who seemed equally determined to stick it out to the bitter end. But the weather did not improve. Snow flurries, some heavy, drove in from the north, and, in that direction, reddened, dark grey clouds built up, threatening more of the same and forcing more and more people to decide they'd had enough. Starting with those who hadn't spent much time on Proxima-b, members of my crew began to wander back towards the SpacePort, sharing taxis. Before too long the whining drone of jet engines drifted over us from the SpacePort as they strained to haul the excursion-shuttles off the runway and far enough away for their rockets to take over and complete their insertion into orbit.

It was about this time that we began to receive advisories about worsening weather from the local TV station, followed, for the crew, by more specific warnings from Malik about possible tornados spinning out of the approaching vortices that were currently coming towards the settlement along the terminator. Malik recommended that all crew return immediately to the Starship to avoid potential flight delays caused by long-lasting extreme weather. All these things considered, I started to amble along Starship Way towards the restaurant to collect Kat, my Midshipmen, and anyone else who wanted to get back to the ship in my cutter.

As I pushed through the restaurant's entrance door, Frankie bumped into me coming the other way.

'Sorry, Boss,' she said, breathlessly. 'I was just coming out looking for you. My cargo-handling bot has just been loaded into your cutter's cargo bay carrying a batch of a hundred and twenty-four finished and tested prototype QIC adapters and a couple of hundred or so QIC-fax chips from Danny Khan. I reckon the senior management of Interstellar Haulage will have to decide how to distribute them.'

'Thanks Frankie,' I replied, as we walked over to the bar so I could get a mug of fresh coffee that I could wrap my cold fingers around. 'I think it would be best to keep them within the company until the patents are granted.'

'Well, Danny Khan will go along with anything Interstellar Haulage decides, though he has suggested to me that prototypes could be loaned as secured 'black boxes' for assessment by potentially interested customers. He's mentioned government agencies, TV broadcasters, StarCorp construction yards and places like Oort Station.'

I gulped down some of my coffee and mused, 'All good suggestions. Oort Station and the other traffic control computers of the waystation habs orbiting the home planets would be top of my list.'

'And Lana thinks they could be part of a package with her video programmes about Proxima-Centauri that could be auctioned to TV broadcasters across the Solar System. Lana's over there, waiting to hand over her camera bots to you,' Frankie replied.

'Can I treat you both to a farewell coffee?' I asked.

'No thanks, Boss, we've both been working throughout the barbecue and we're now keen to get back to our own home before the storm really builds. We've moved into our little cottage, just across there, on Starship Way. We want to put our feet up in our own warm place and watch the weather come and, hopefully, go. Madge has given us a bagful of barbecued leftover goodies big enough to last a month! I'd better get back home and start to reheat them. Bye-bye, Boss, have a good flight back to Oort Station.' She gave me a smart salute and followed that with a quick kiss on my cheek, before darting out of the door and into the strengthening flurries of snow.

I walked over towards the last remaining group, which looked subdued and was made up of my four Midshipmen, my co-pilot, and Lana with her two camera bots.

'I've ordered a taxi,' reported Kat. 'It'll be here any minute. Linda and Art have said their goodbyes and have taken Sarah home. Linda didn't want to prolong the farewells'.

'So, that just leaves me to run off home!' announced Lana. 'These two fine tin men are to go with you. You already know Bogey and Greenstreet. Remember, Greenstreet is a facsimile bot and he's been adapted with one of Danny's QIC-fax chips linked to my NeuroModem, so, don't get freaked out if I start talking to you when you're lightyears away from me! I'll do a test run on that just before you jump tomorrow, and if we can get Frankie's QIC comms adapters and Danny's QIC-fax chips to work, I'll join you at regular intervals as you travel further! There's something to look forward to, Boss!'

I didn't know what else to say so I just said 'Affirmative, Lana'.

Lana smiled, said 'I'll be off, then, I hear my sister's reheated barbecue calling my name!' She gave a salute to all, and I got another kiss on the cheek. As she pushed the restaurant door open, she leaned back into the room and shouted, 'Your taxi's getting covered in snow out here!' And then she was gone.

'That's just what I was about to say,' said Kat from her vantage point near the window. 'Let's go everybody, Bogey and Greenstreet, go get those taxi doors open.'

We followed the camera bots and piled into the taxi minibus. The snowfall was getting more serious and was now completely covering the road surface in a layer several centimetres deep. I noticed, as I scurried out to the taxi, that the clouds on the northern skyline had turned a solid black, illuminated from the inside with repetitive flashes of lightning. Something more wicked this way comes.

Despite the worsening road conditions, the taxi drove us quickly and safely back to my cutter and we all sprinted through an ever-heavier snowstorm to get inside its airlock, closing the outer door as quickly as possible. While Kat got the passengers installed, I checked our readiness for departure.

'Have we got all of our expected passengers, Malik?'

'Affirmative, Commodore. Captain Burton's cargo bot is safely stowed, and all other registered foot passengers are aboard. Captain Igwe supervised arrangements for the disposition of snow ploughs around the settlement and returned to the Starship with his team on a recent shuttle flight, and Mr Tom Fraser and his care-bot returned on an even earlier flight due to Mr Fraser's fatigue.'

'OK, have the rest of the crew returned to Pink Ghost?'

'All crewmembers are accounted for, Commodore. The last crew transport shuttle is waiting on the taxiway. Traffic Control is holding them in case the Commanding Officer wishes to depart first. Malik out.'

'Proxima Traffic Control, Commodore's Cutter, bound for the Pink Ghost, requesting direct orbital insertion. Please advise on traffic conditions.'

'Commodore's Cutter, traffic control, we are holding a crew transport shuttle in its taxiway, do you wish to take off first?'

'Proxima Traffic Control, Commodore's Cutter, Negative. Release the crew transport shuttle. Please lay-in a flight plan to take us into orbit one kilometre above our Starships.'

'Affirmative, Commodore. Flight plan streamed and acknowledged. There are no further traffic conflicts. You may taxi towards the runway threshold.'

Followed immediately by the autopilot's warning: 'Hatches sealed and to automatic. All passengers to acceleration couches, we are rolling towards our take-off threshold.'

With our return underway, albeit slowly, I went through to the Ops room to describe the flight to my passengers. The Westwood twins were seated as before in the pilot and co-pilot's chairs, with the Bogie camera bot strapped into the central engineer's chair, the one that Sarah occupied on the way down. Bogie was already filming.

Then a private message from Rocky came into my NeuroModem that I had to take. 'Hi Tarvin, just a quickie, Malik's told me you're about to take off in your cutter from the SpacePort. Well, he said 'blast-off', so I'm not sure what that means.'

'It means we're using the old-school method of getting into orbit. Riding the flames of our full rocket set to punch straight up through these storm clouds. But it's all in the autopilot's hands and we've only just started to roll towards the runway, so go ahead,' I replied. 'I'm just a passenger now.'

'Wow, so you've got one of those rich-kid-hooligan cutters! I make do with a bargain-basement minimum grunt cutter,' Rocky responded.

'Yeah, and my brother's got a rich-kid cutter, as well,' I said with satisfaction, asking, 'Now, to what do I owe the pleasure of this quickie message?'

'Oh, yeah,' said Rocky. 'I just wanted to keep you in the picture by confirming that we are delaying all flights down to Proxima SpacePort. Your Starship's flight computer is sharing a great view of the storm vortex that's howling towards Proxima Alpha and my flight computer has banned all flights down to the surface! Until the storm passes, we'll continue to take parties of passengers and crew to Proxima Home Waystation instead. I've already messaged Mayor Castlefield and he's OK with video conferencing in the meantime. That's all really. I'll wish you a happy blast-off and let you get on with it! Zhang out.'

Messaging over, I returned to being "cabin crew" by speaking to my passengers through the intercom. 'Listen up, passengers,' I started, 'we are taxiing to the end of the runway and will then take off like a conventional jet-powered aircraft. But when we reach a spot about 500 metres beyond the end of the runway and an altitude of about two kilometres the autopilot will take us into a steep climb and light up our rocket boosters. We will then climb, almost vertically at full power, directly into orbit. The flight plan is for us to insert into an orbit one kilometre above the Starships. So, Bogey and Greenstreet, make sure you get some decent images of the Starships as we approach them. And EVERYONE: get yourselves properly strapped into your acceleration couches. No more waving your arms in the air bravado. Believe me, you will need all the cushioning of your acceleration couches. This will be a hot ride that you'll remember for a long time!'

And it certainly was a hot ride; demonstrating to our little band of apprentice Starship engineers that orbital flight for the pioneers of space travel was as uncomfortable going up as it had been coming down! None of the shirtsleeve comfortable meandering flight profiles of our modern shuttles that can take as much as half an hour to get into space! I barely had time to get to the wardroom and strap into an acceleration couch between Kat and Greenstreet before the autopilot warnings started to chime and the intercom rang out, with barely a second between the successive announcements, 'Main engines start. Wings retracted. Roll program initiated. Throttling up all engines to full power.' And then, our couches swung on their gimbals to keep us facing our direction of travel as the cutter's nose was angled up to the near vertical, and we were thrust deep into our cushions as the seatbacks slammed us upwards.

Ten minutes into this hot ride, the autopilot announced, 'All engines stop, we have achieved our designated orbit.' Followed quickly by 'Starship Flight Control, Commodore's Cutter welcome to orbit. You are one kilometre above us and one hundred kilometres behind us. You may proceed to your docking bay. There is no conflicting traffic. We will launch tugs as you approach.'

'Thank you, Starship Flight Control. Willco. Commodore out,' I acknowledged, then added to my autopilot, 'Autopilot, follow Starship flight control's instructions. And swivel our cameras to view the Starships as we approach.'

Immediately, the image on our view screens ahead of us scrolled downwards to bring our Starships to the centre of the screen. As the cutter's manoeuvring rockets throttled up, the Starship image grew on the screen.

'Hey, Greenstreet, are you filming this?' I asked the camera bot in the adjoining seat. 'It's your last view of Starship-101 in Proxima space.'

I was surprised, momentarily, to hear Lana's voice coming from the camera bot until I remembered that Greenstreet was a fax-bot. 'Yay, Boss, yes, we've been getting great views down here. Both of my tin men are streaming direct from your cutter's cameras and passing the piccies down to Westwood. It's been a great show!'

'How's the weather down there?' Kat asked.

'Grim. There's so much cloud overhead that it's totally black outside and there's such a stonking blizzard we can't even see the lights from the restaurant across the road.'

'Are you girls safely tucked up in that new cottage of yours?' Kat asked.

'You betcha!' was the reply. 'Central heating's wound up full and Frankie's in the kitchen reheating the next batch of barbie leftovers! But I see the tugs are on their way out to take you into the dock, so I'll leave you to experience that and concentrate on my barbie in a snowstorm! Over to you, Greenstreet. Lana out.'

Lana was right. The tugs carrying the docking lines had come out to us and we could already feel the jolts as they heaved and shoved us into the correct orientation for the mooring lines from the docking rams to be attached to the cutter. Finally, as these were winched into the rams the cutter sailed majestically sideways, latched onto the rams with a last clanging vibration and was drawn into the brightly illuminated dock. Simultaneously, the outer airlock doors of the dock closed and sealed us off from deep space, triggering gas jets around the dock to inject atmosphere into the air lock, this being visible as fog initially because the ship and its surroundings were so cold.

The intercom announced our hard docking, saying, 'Passengers are free to release from their acceleration couches and prepare for disembarkation in ten minutes. Beware of sudden movements, you are now in a microgravity environment.'

I floated myself into the Ops room where there was a general milling around and, in particular, the Westwood twins were engaged in a mid-air pirouetting competition, urged on by Bogie.

'I don't want to interrupt your high jinks,' I said, while the two of them flailed their arms about comically trying to spin down to something resembling a float at attention. 'But I suggest you all return to your quarters, change into duty fatigues and start calming down. You need to get a good night's sleep; you'll have your first quantum jump at noon tomorrow. You may disembark as soon as the docking crews crack open our airlock. Dismiss.'

'Where are we going to house these camera bots?' asked Kat, floating in from the wardroom.

'Let's ask them,' I said. 'Bogey, do you have any instructions about where to station yourselves in Pink Ghost?'

'Affirmative, Commodore,' Bogey replied. 'I am to observe your control room, with your permission. And Greenstreet is to stay as close as possible to Midshipmen Billy Westwood and George Westwood to document their experiences for as long as possible on the Starship.'

'Good, that's nice and easy,' responded Kat. 'Malik, guide Bogey to the Command Control Room, he can occupy one of the robot-charging bays there and come and go as he pleases. Permission granted for him to stream from all our camera feeds.'

'Willco, Captain Clason.'

'Now, May and Jumanah,' Kat continued, and the two Midshipmen snapped to attention, saluting, and making it look effortless in microgravity by discreetly holding the side of their acceleration couch, 'will you take the other camera bot to the Midshipmen's quarters? There should be a spare robot-charging bay somewhere close, but it looks like you'll have to extract it from the wardroom first!'

'Yes, Ma'am'. And they floated off to gather up Greenstreet.

'There's one more thing to do,' I muttered at Kat. 'Malik, please instruct the dock crew to unload Frankie's cargo-handling bot with Danny Khan's QIC adapter prototypes and chips. Send it to our computation stores and incorporate the adapters into the store manifest.'

'Willco, Commodore.'

With equalisation of atmospheric pressure each side of the airlocks, they were opened, and Kat and I floated to one side as our passengers vacated the cutter. Before May and Jumanah left, I warned them that Greenstreet was a fax-bot NeuroModemed to Lana, so, when she dials into him/it, Greenstreet will become their senior officer!

Passengers cleared; I asked Stewart to make some decaffeinated coffee before he tidied up and suggested to Kat that we change out of our fancy dress uniforms and into work fatigues. I told her I was planning to retire to my pilot's Nav Couch in Pink Ghost's control room and set it for a massage and workout to relax in preparation for tomorrow's jump.

'Good idea,' she said, 'I'll do the same. But I want to check in at my astrophys lab first to check what 'Sarah's quantum wobble' files Art Westwood has left for me. It'll be too late after we jump out of here!'

'Come to think of it,' she added, 'I'll restream the memory traces of our technical rehearsal, just to top up my memories.'

'Me too,' I said.

Day 10

I had programmed an alarm call for 8 a.m. and that woke me just a second or two before the ship's intercom stated chiming with warnings of our scheduled departure and our quantum jump to Waystation 4 at noon. Several times the intercom intoned, 'Section leaders must ensure all decks shipshape and in proper good order by 11.30 a.m. All crew to be securely strapped into their acceleration couches by 11.45.' For me, the announcements were just part of the litany of a quantum jump day. I didn't need the reminders; I'd been dreaming the memory traces from yesterday's technical rehearsal. I didn't think I needed any further rehearsal, either.

I could hear that Kat was also waking up so before I disconnected from my Nav Couch I reached across and took hold of her hand and thought at her 'I don't think I need any more rehearsal for this jump, how about you?'

'Affirmative,' she said out loud. 'It was a good idea for us both to restream the technical's memory traces. But despite yesterday's barbie, I'm famished after that work out. Did I hear from Jim that you were eating a banjo egg the other day?'

I sat up and stretched. 'Yeah,' I replied. 'It was two of them, actually. Stewart's got the knack. Sounds like a good idea and should be a lot less messy in microgravity!'

As we floated ourselves into our private quarters, I brought Stewart out of his sleep state and ordered two banjos and coffee for both of us; then it was a matter of shower, shave, and fresh fatigues.

After breakfast, Kat went back to her astrophys lab to flip through Art Westwood's 'Sarah's quantum wobble' files one last time before we jumped. And while Stewart freshened up our Nav Couches, I messaged Malik, 'Malik, any urgent messages?'

'Negative Commodore,' Malik replied. 'Do you wish to schedule a jump rehearsal?'

'Negative, Malik, we're both happy with the memory traces we already have. I'll assemble the quantum map wavefunction and then create my mindscape of our entanglement superposition from the existing memory traces. Rather than spending time rehearsing, I think I'll make a tour of the ship by video call. Is 101's Flight computer online or in sleep mode?' I asked.

'Flight will be powered down to basic functions at 11.45, before then he is fully online, Commodore.'

'OK, I'll call him as well and do a final tour of Starship-101. Please arrange for the CCTV cameras to follow me through my call list and ask Flight to do the same.'

'Willco, Commodore, Malik out.'

'May I stream those audio and video feeds, Commodore? I've not had the chance to film much of this Starship yet.' It was the camera bot, Bogey, speaking from his charging bay on the back wall of the control room.

'Oh, hi Bogey,' I said. 'I'd forgotten about you. Yeah, sure, you can stream the feeds. I thought the Exec had already given you that permission?

'She did, Commodore. I wanted to confirm the permission extended to your private conversations.'

'Sure, no problem, Bogey, come and sit in the co-pilot's chair. Malik, please unship the engineer's chair from its stowage for Bogey to use during the jump, and make sure he has access to all camera streams.'

'Willco, Commodore. Malik out'.

'Thank you, Commodore,' Bogey responded. 'On another matter, I have just received a message from camera bot Greenstreet that he would like to join us in the control room here to deliver a message from Captain Mancot.'

'OK, tell him to come along,' I replied, remembering Lana's warning last evening that she wanted to confirm communication through Greenstreet's fax circuits before we left Proxima space. When Greenstreet arrived, Lana had already connected to his fax circuits.

'Good morning, Boss,' Greenstreet said in Lana's voice. 'Hope I'm not interrupting anything?'

'No, that's OK, Bogie and I were about to do a quick inspection tour of the ships before we translocate them out of here. But I thought our conversation last night about your blizzard would be enough to confirm your fax connection to Greenstreet.'

'Nah,' Lana replied. 'That was a straightforward connection between my NeuroModem and the fax modem in the tin man. This link is streaming through the QIC adapters on the Westwood computer here and Malik.'

'The connection sounds pretty good to me,' I said.

'Yeah, it's good for me, too,' Lana replied, adding, 'What say you, Malik? Any time delays?'

'QIC messages are encrypted end to end,' Malik explained. 'We detect no measurable time delay in the transmission, though encryption and decryption delays are measurable, but in the nanosecond range, so they are not discernible to human participants in the conversation'.

'Who we?' asked Lana.

'Me and the Proxima-b megacomputer network consisting of Westwood, Observatory, Distant Home flight computer and the Proxima Home Station traffic control unit. We are passing your conversation with the Greenstreet camera bot between us multiple times and in various combinations to improve our estimate of potential delays. The results are as I have just given you.'

'Yay, I'll settle for that!' said Lana, triumphantly. 'Is there anything else we can usefully do here and now?' she asked.

'Negative, Captain Mancot,' Malik replied.

'Well, you could give us a weather report, Lana,' I interjected. 'When we spoke last night, you were in the middle of a raging blizzard!'

'And it's still snowing heavily,' she replied. 'The hurricane-like winds have eased off, but the snowdrifts are massive. Local weather advisories are that the snow will turn to rain sometime during the next three hours, so we're advised to stay put while the road clearance bots try to dump as much of the snow as possible into the river. There's a snow-blower just outside our cottage making a fountain of snow while it clears access to Madge's restaurant. It's crazy, though, right at the top of the fountain there's a fine cloud of snow with a red and blue striped rainbow in it! We're not going outside to compete with the road gangs, so, Frankie and I are still toasting ourselves with our central heating and eating barbie leftovers! This is Lana Mancot concluding this morning's meteorological report from Proxima Alpha. Over to you, Greenstreet. Lana out.'

Greenstreet twitched slightly as his consciousness switched from Lana's broadcast to his own internal awareness so, I instructed him to return to his previous duties, telling him that the QIC broadcast had worked well. To which he replied, in an unnecessarily threatening tone of voice, I thought, 'Excellent.

A man hears what he wants to hear and disregards the rest, but we comms bots do not relish failure.'

'Where do you want to start your tour of inspection, Commodore?' Malik asked.

'Well, Lana's mention of the barbecue reminded me that Tom Fraser left early yesterday with fatigue so, let's make contact with him, briefly, to see if he's recovered OK.'

Tom reported that he was perfectly fine this morning, last night's little episode was literally down to loss of tolerance of the one-g gravity environment. He had perked up as soon as they got back into microgravity. I told him about Lana's report of the hurricane blizzard that had struck the settlement just after the barbecue and he said that it was a regular occurrence though it varied in intensity.

'Yes, I remember Lana, your comms commissar,' Tom said. 'And I also remember many of those come-and-go severe blizzards during my life in Proxima Alpha,' Tom said. 'Some of the original crew came from Tornado Alley in the Midwestern United States and they called them snow tornados. Our old atmosphere sciences group had the foresight to place a weather satellite in stationary orbit over the North Pole before we landed and used that to establish predictive protocols for the most extreme weather. But the satellite got fried by a solar flare a long time ago and we had no way to replace it. Weather forecasting was rather poor after that.'

'Aye, we replaced that satellite earlier this week,' I said. 'Our weather guys streamed its observations to the settlement's Westwood computer, which used them to forecast this storm.'

'Well, I hope you provided your satellite with some resistance to the radiation from flares!' Tom commented.

'Yes, we were well warned about the need to deal with radiation outbursts from Proxima-Centauri in the earliest radio messages all those years ago. That's why we brought our own factories to knit fine tungsten alloy wire into fabric head coverings much lighter than those made locally.'

'Oh yes! I remember the original metal hats!' Tom said, in full reminiscence mode. 'Made from titanium strips cut from Starship panels by a Filipino metal-worker among the mechanics crew. Yes, yes. The older English crew called him Del Boy, for some reason I never understood! What was his name?'

'His name was Gabriel Del Rosario,' Malik interrupted. 'Forgive my interruption, gentlemen, but our quantum jump is rapidly approaching, and the Commodore still has a tour of inspection to complete.'

'OK, a hint as obvious as that can't be ignored!' Tom said. 'We'll have plenty of opportunities to continue these recollections during the rest of this voyage. So, I will wish you well for the quantum jump, Tarvin, and go find someone else to mither! Tom Fraser out.'

'Bye, Tom, I'll catch up with you later today, maybe this evening,' I said, and then told Malik that he'd better manage the rest of my inspection tour, starting from the distant front end of Starship-101. I wanted to start in the regions with which I was most familiar and finish with a good close-up view of how my engineers had coupled the two ships together. The Flight computer was very helpful in this. It hadn't had much to do since I'd lifted its ship into orbit and had occupied its time by organising it's robot engineering brigades into repair and cleaning gangs to make his ship spick and span, and museum ready. Flight was pleased with the result and keen to show it off; even more so when I revealed that camera bot Bogey was streaming the CCTV images back to Proxima Alpha.

Malik continued my virtual tour from the stern of Pink Ghost. Again, it was my first up-close view of the way the two ships had been coupled, and the two viewings showed a good firm connection had been achieved. Certainly, strong enough for all normal quantum jumps, despite the unusual length of the coupled ships. And I had certainly learned my lesson about departing from normal operation. No more wobbling for me!

Unlike Starship-101, the engineering decks towards the stern of Pink Ghost contained a lot of human crewmembers, in addition to gangs of robots, engaged in the final stages of locking down all the normal activities of the Starship, except those needed for life support. Forward of the engineering decks, the many cargo holds, shuttle and transhipment docks, and heavy repair shops were largely deserted, their gear already stowed, their human crews already back in their quarters and their robot brigades secured in their recharge bays. None of the section leaders to whom I spoke reported any problems, and this agreeable pattern was repeated as my tour swept through the crew habitation areas and into the computation and control decks. My tour ended in astrophysics, located next to the control deck. Kat was section leader here and Malik started to point out the time to both of us and she decided to join me in the control room, if only to stop Malik's nagging.

Kat floated herself into the control room just as the intercom intoned, 'Standby Starships. We intend to initiate final preparations for our quantum translocation to Proxima Waystation 4 at 11.45 a.m. standard star time, with a view for a 12-noon departure'. All section leaders to report to Malik their decks secure immediately. All crew to be securely strapped into acceleration couches by 11.45 a.m. There will be no dress rehearsal. Repeat, there will be no dress rehearsal. We depart Proxima-Centauri space at 12 noon universal time precisely.'

Remembering that Rocky Zhang had mentioned shuttling passengers to Proxima Home Waystation, I asked Malik to check that those flights would be well clear of my departure quantum map at noon. His response was that Distant Home was complying with traffic control's requests to minimise conflicting traffic helpfully by suspending all shuttle services until after our departure.

I took a few minutes out to grab a coffee from the control room's little galley and noticed that Stewart was still steam-cleaning Kat's dress uniform. I told him that when that job was finished, he should secure himself in his recharge bay and then I floated myself back to my Nav Couch.

Kat was already settling herself into her Nav Couch and reporting to Malik that both astrophysics and control room decks were secured. 'Hi, Boss,' she said, 'we've got a few minutes to get settled, do you want to start recalling the memory traces?'

'Sure,' I replied, as I pushed my head back into my headrest and allowed the Nav Couch to welcome me into its embrace. 'I'll just take a minute or two to relax into the zone.'

'Right,' said Kat. 'Just don't get too dozy, we've got a job to do!' And then Malik joined in through the ship's intercom, 'Standby Starships,' he said. 'We intend to initiate final preparations for translocation to Proxima Waystation 4 at 11.45 a.m. standard star time, with a view for a 12-noon departure'.

'Copy that, Malik,' responded Kat.

I spent the last few minutes clearing my most recent memory traces into deeper memory and bringing the memories made during our technical rehearsal into clear focus. Finally switching the view screens in front of me to display the scenes around our Starships. The control room's digital glass provided a full 180° view, front and both sides. And beneath this main wraparound display was a view to the rear, provided, of course, by Starship-101's nose cameras. Seeing this fulsome view from the ships, I wondered if we were being observed from outside.

'Bogey, do you have any camera streams from outside the ship?' I asked.

'Affirmative, Commodore,' he replied. 'You have external stern cameras on Pink Ghost that monitor Starship-101, and Starship-101 has a camera array on its stern that is monitoring Pink Ghost. Also, we will be in view of the observatory and the polar weather satellite at 12 noon, as well as the cameras aboard Proxima Home Station that monitor the Pink Ghost continuously. I am streaming and recording all these sources and sharing all my streams with Proxima Alpha's Westwood computer.'

'Fine, that's just what I wanted to know.' I said.

I had just started my usual deep breathing exercises when Malik next broadcast on the intercom.

'Will Pilot and co-Pilot please signify their readiness to initiate the translocation of Starships Pink Ghost and Starship-101 from Proxima-b orbit to location of Proxima Waystation 4.'

'Pilot is ready,' I said, reaching across to take hold of Kat's hand.

'Co-Pilot is ready,' Kat responded.

'Very well, then,' Malik said. 'Standby Starships. Cue initiate the translocation in five, four, three, two, one …'

On zero, I raised to the front of my mental image the most recent memory trace of the complete mental image of the quantum waveform of the combined structure of Pink Ghost and Starship-101. As soon as I had this visualisation completed, Kat passed me her visualisation of the destination and I stacked the two visualisations one above the other in my mindscape, ready for their superposition.

'Malik, how are we doing for time?' I asked, as usual, and got the usual reply.

'It's approaching 11.58 a.m., Commodore.'

'So, issue take-off warnings throughout both Starships and then count me down to noon.'

I could hear the subdued chimes of the two-minute take-off warning vaguely somewhere at the back of my awareness and then Malik's ten-second timing signals started to come through to my NeuroModem as I started to take hold of the quantum model of the two Starships and precisely at noon, I heaved my quantum model of the Starships into Kat's cube of empty space to create the superposition. Immediately, Kat slipped the hex-number nudge into my awareness, and I thrust it into the memory trace of the quantum map of the destination of the superposition I had just created.

And instantly, the control room's view screens, which had been displaying the dull red images typical of Proxima-Centauri space, switched into the blackness of deep space. Displaying a sparse and distant starfield on one side of us, but on the other side, spread out in all its glory, a magnificent view of our Milky Way Galaxy with the silhouette of a completed waystation painted across it. From the Crew Lounges the sound of cheering came over the audio channels.

'Smoothly done, Boss. Welcome to Proxima Waystation 4,' said Kat.

I smiled my usual smile of satisfaction, though this time it was covering for a great feeling of relief, as I hadn't recovered from the shock of being told that I'd spent time in an alternate reality when I lifted Starship-101 into orbit! I recovered my composure and hailed the waystation.

'Proxima Waystation 4 Traffic Control, this is Commodore Tarvin Clason requesting permission to approach.'

'Commodore Clason, welcome to Proxima Waystation 4! You may approach as you require, there is no conflicting traffic. Traffic Control out.' Followed immediately by a message from the waystation's general manager, Captain Rick Blaine, 'Hi Boss, welcome to PW4. That's a hell of a weird structure to suddenly appear alongside us! Which way are you going? Looks like you've got a Starship nose at each end! I thought when I first saw it that we'd finally been found by some wild pushmi-pullyu aliens from some distant star!'

'Hi Rick,' I responded. 'Don't ask me which way I'm going, that's Kat's department! I just do the brute haulin'.'

'Thanks for the recommendation, Boss!' Kat put in, then asked, 'How are you getting on, Rick?'

'We're complete and running, all contracts fulfilled,' Rick reported. 'We've got the river and its delta reproduced in our artificial gravity disc, so, we're ready for your guys and gals to come over here and build us the Proxima Alpha settlement simulation.'

'That's where I come into it, Rikky-boy,' added Jim Igwe. 'Good to be here with you, mate! We're already streaming the construction data for the build into your computer, and the first shuttles with the printers will be coming over to you in the next few minutes.'

'If nobody minds, Boss, can I muscle into this conversation with my husband?' Ilsa interrupted. 'Hello, darlin' I'm already in the first shuttle with

Emma. We're just departing to bring you tons of fresh produce and several fish and poultry farms. So, I'll cook you a reviving breakfast tomorrow morning! Ilsa out.'

'Well, Rikky-boy, sounds like Ilsa might have your next few hours planned out! It's up to you to earn that breakfast!' Kat said, adding, 'Does anyone else have anything to add to this conversation, I want to broadcast to the crew?'

'Just a few immediate updates,' Malik contributed drily. 'PW4 has two megacomputers installed, in common with all the other Proxima waystations; one for general services and one with specific training to control flights arriving for and from the Centauri Tristar System, which is expected to be difficult because of the complexity of the gravity wells that are dancing around each other in this stellar neighbourhood. I have already given both computers training in the use of the QIC plug-and-play adapters that Captain Ilsa Blaine is taking across to PW4 at the moment.'

Malik paused before continuing, as though he was about to impart some really important information, then he resumed, 'More significantly, Proxima Home Station Traffic Control computer was broadcasting a continuous tone to my QIC adapter as we jumped out of Proxima-Centauri space. I can detect no interruption in the tone at the time of the entanglement and decoherence. Also, since we arrived alongside PW4 I have been exchanging handshake timing messaging with the QIC adapters installed in the Westwood and Observatory computers on Proxima-b. None of the computers in this little network can detect any time delays to these messages. The network agrees to the conclusion that the QIC adapters enable instantaneous radio traffic across at least six light-months of space.'

The little community that had been taking part in this initial exchange of messages with PW4 remained silent while they absorbed the full significance of Malik's matter-of-fact announcement.

The silence was broken by Lana announcing, 'Hi Boss, and would you believe it's stopped snowing here as well?'

Lana's interruption direct from Proxima-b was followed by a flood of messages of congratulations sent to Frankie and Lana from all of us, which ended up in quite a hubbub of various forms of messaging. Kat stepped in to take control, saying 'Now hear this everyone, I'm now speaking as the Executive Officer for a Starship that's just arrived safely at its destination. I need to follow protocol and broadcast to the crew. So, I am bringing this conversation to a close.

I'm sure you all have a lot of work to do, so, please go and do it. Rick, before you go, you've just said that you are 'complete and running'. Does that mean you are ready to receive the off-duty crews of passing Starships for rest and recuperation?'

'Yes, indeed Ma'am,' Rick replied. 'It's only the Proxima Alpha-specific installation that's been paused awaiting your arrival. All the usual sports and entertainment facilities and activities are open and fully stocked. Ready for their first customers. Just send them across, no bookings required, but do remind them that the visible light used for our general illumination is the same red twilight of Proxima-b. Rick Blaine out.'

'Thanks, Rick,' Kat acknowledged and then sent her next message to the ship-wide intercom.

'Now hear this. All crew. Now hear this. Stand easy. Executive Officer confirming safe arrival at our destination. For your information we are alongside Proxima Waystation 4, which is approximately four lightyears out from Earth. In due course, this waystation will be responsible for controlling incoming flights to the Centauri Tristar System, and preparing passengers on those flights for life on Proxima-b. So, our purpose here on this trip is to build a replica of the Proxima Alpha settlement we have just built on Proxima-b. All crew involved in that construction be prepared to fulfil that contract immediately. Off-duty crews can transfer to Proxima Waystation 4 for R&R; all the usual facilities are available, but I've been asked to remind you that general lighting is the same red twilight of Proxima-b but, of course, without the hazardous radiation! That's all. Enjoy PW4! Exec out.'

I also had a batch of pure protocol jobs in need of attention on arrival at a destination that Malik brought to my attention. By the time I had dealt with these I needed a coffee so I floated through to my wardroom where Stewart was just delivering a batch of microgravity coffee bulbs to Kat.

'Sorry to interrupt again, Commodore,' said Malik. 'But Midshipmen Billy and George Westwood are outside the control room seeking to claim what they describe as their 'traditional congratulatory drink with the Commodore' to celebrate their first quantum jump. How would you like to deal with this?'

'What is all this about?' asked Kat.

'I have reviewed some of the recent conversations in the Midshipmen's quarters,' Malik replied. 'And it appears that the twins are being subjected to a ritual initiative test dreamt up by their messmates to celebrate their first quantum jump. Apparently, they must go to the Commodore, personally, to claim this 'traditional' celebratory drink from him. There's no such thing, of course.'

'Oh, I've encountered rituals like this before,' said Kat, smiling broadly. 'It's like sending a trainee to the stores to ask for a tin of striped paint or a can of elbow grease! You've got to play along with it, Boss.'

'Yes, I will,' I said. 'But I think I know how best to do it. So, bear with me while I set my scene!'

'Malik, is Greenstreet involved in this masquerade, and where are the twin's buddies?' I asked.

'Greenstreet is to film the event as proof for their messmates, Commodore, and will be streaming the event live to the Midshipmen's Mess,' Malik responded. 'Obviously, the instigators are hoping that Greenstreet's video will show the twins being unceremoniously kicked out of your control room. Their buddies are waiting with them in the corridor outside.'

'OK,' I said. 'Here's what you do. Tell all five of them that the Commodore can't be disturbed at the moment and ask them, kindly, to wait for a few minutes and when his conference calls finish, he will deal with them. Use the words 'deal with them' just to add a bit of menace. And make sure Greenstreet is recording what you say.'

'This is sounding cruel!' objected Kat. But I dismissed her objections with a wave of my hand.

'Now, Stewart, do you know the stocks in the Commodore's hard liquor supply well enough to find me a bottle of rum?'

'Certainly, Commodore. I have one in my pantry,' the steward replied. Kat was staring at me quizzically as I told Stewart to keep it to hand in the wardroom.

'Good, back to you, Malik, please send a QIC message to Lana and Frankie asking Lana to make a fax connection to Greenstreet on your mark, and Frankie to set up a conference call QIC link between Linda, Art and Sarah, and Billy and George Westwood on my mark.

'Ah, now I understand,' said Kat, happily. 'A not so cruel turning of tables!'

'Right,' I said. 'Let's get our best serious faces on, Kat, and just follow my lead. Malik, please tell our guests they can all proceed through the control room into the wardroom now. Oh, and Stewart, let's have a fresh supply of coffee bulbs.'

My five visitors floated themselves into the wardroom, Greenstreet thrusting ahead on his gas jets to film the others coming through the door. The four

Midshipmen pulled themselves to a halt against the wardroom table and came to a very respectable attention for a salute and a chorused 'Good afternoon, Boss.' I, of course, had one foot firmly planted in a stirrup on my perching chair at the head of the table and thus firmly anchored out of sight, was able to hold myself ramrod straight for an unnecessarily formal return salute. I noticed the hint of a smile creeping onto Kat's face as she messaged me privately 'Oh, well done Boss. Anyone else making a salute as snappy as that would have disappeared towards the ceiling!'

Ignoring the heckling, I welcomed them to 'The Commodore's Office', ordered them at ease, and asked them what I could do for them. Billy and George, looking more doubtful with every word they uttered in their duet, explained the circumstances, and George finally trailed off into 'So, we've come to claim our celebratory drink with you, er, Boss.'

Noticing that Greenstreet had turned his camera onto me, I left them floating there in a silence long enough to impress their messmates before saying, 'I see. But Malik tells me that there is no prior evidence for this 'tradition', so, what do you think we should do about that?'

As I was still wearing my stern face, the twins looked totally crestfallen, but Billy, looking the most wretched, managed to blurt out 'I don't know, Boss.' So, I decided to lift the tension and, allowing my stern face to evaporate, I said 'Well, I suggest we make a start on establishing this tradition and give Malik some evidence. Midshipmen, stand easy, and float yourselves to the perches around this table.'

'Certainly, your first quantum jump is worth celebrating, and worth talking about and sharing, but obviously,' I went on, 'I can't encourage the drinking of alcohol on duty, but I am happy to share a coffee bulb with you. Stewart, will you serve coffee to my guests, please. And while Stewart is doing that, Malik will you ask Lana to join us?'

Almost immediately, Greenstreet started speaking in Lana's voice, causing puzzlement tinged with both alarm and nervous amusement among all four Midshipmen, 'Hi Boss,' Lana said. 'Thanks for the invitation.'

'Hi Lana,' I said. 'Where are you speaking from?'

'I'm now in Proxima Alpha's TV studio, watching Greenstreet's video stream. Tell George to close his mouth, that open-gobbed stare doesn't do his handsome visage any favours. As you can see, boys, quantum messaging works! Greenstreet is a fax robot and I've just logged-in to the facsimile of my

NeuroModem that he's got among his comms circuitries. So, I'm speaking to you, and seeing your reactions, across a distance of around six light-months with no discernible delay. How do you want to proceed, Boss? Frankie's got her side of things all hooked up with Malik.'

'Great work, both of you,' I said. 'Before we go any further, I want to point out that this is going to be the first of many conference calls using Frankie and Lana's QIC adapter.'

'Don't forget to give Danny Khan a shoutout, Boss,' said Lana/Greenstreet. 'He built the things! And they seem to be working just fine. What say you, Malik? Any problems with the QIC comms?'

'All communications are A-OK in both directions, Captain Mancot,' Malik reported.

'OK, credit to all three,' I resumed. 'Now, I agree with your messmates that your first ever quantum jump is well worth celebrating, but I thought you might like to celebrate it with your family. So, have any other Westwoods joined us?'

'Me, me. I'm here!' Shouted Sarah.

'I never doubted that you would be, dear,' said Kat, but her comment was drowned out by the general cacophony of two deserted parents reuniting with their loved ones. When the excitement died down, and after discussing the matter privately with Kat beforehand, I barged into the conversation with, 'Sorry to interrupt, but I'm sure you would all prefer to continue this get-together in private, and as Kat and I have matters to deal with on Waystation Four, we will leave you here to continue your family chat. There's just one more item to deal with before we go. Stewart, bring in that bottle you found in the Commodore's Pantry.'

I floated the bottle of rum over towards Billy Westwood, saying, 'I'm sure your messmates would like to be included in this newly created traditional thing about celebratory drinks with your Commodore, so, take this bottle of grog and invite everyone in your mess over to Waystation Four's artificial gravity disk for a drink or two on me!'

'And if you get drunk, don't tell your mother!' added Kat, followed by much more practical advice from Lana/Greenstreet: 'And if you do get drunk, don't vomit in microgravity!'

Kat and I left them to it, though I was informed later that Sarah had asked her brothers to share their memory traces of their first quantum jump with her and this became another, successful, test of the QIC system by showing that the protocol allows NeuroModem to NeuroModem memory trace sharing.

'What's your main concern that needs dealing with on PW4?' asked Kat as we floated ourselves through the control room.

'My first priority is to eat,' I replied. 'My second priority is a nice long shower in a one-g gravity environment. And my third priority is to see how the build and commissioning of the waystation is progressing so we can get some idea about when we can move on down the line towards Proxima Waystation 3.'

'OK, do we take your cutter?' Kat asked.

'No,' I said, gesturing towards the control room's view screens. 'There's a constant stream of traffic across there. We can get a lift on a cargo shuttle. Malik, please arrange that. Oh, and while I'm thinking about it, that facsimile call with Greenstreet was impressive, so, Malik, send one of our AI-repair bots over to PW4 with a supply of Danny Khan's QIC-fax chips to modify their fax-bot brigade. Might as well have the workshop modify ours as well and make this a routine adaptation for each waystation as we reach them.'

'Willco, Commodore. Malik out.'

We sped through the travelators and as we approached the cargo decks, Malik came back to us with the information that shuttle 9 would be leaving shortly from cargo deck 3, so we headed for that and reached it as the gongs warning of imminent departure were sounding. It was just a short hop across to the waystation's receiving dock and from there we used the travelators through the Transfer Lounge and on to the central tunnel into the artificial gravity disk. As we continued on the travelator down to the one-g level, Kat messaged Ilsa to ask about the best food venue for a meeting with her and Rick.

'Oh, try the Café Claudius just outside the travelator entrance at ground level,' Ilsa replied. 'I brought one of Madge's old original sous chefs with me, he'll be able to produce something special even in a fast-food joint! Rick and I will meet you there.'

'Have you cooked Rick's breakfast yet?' Kat asked, innocently.

'None of your effing business, Captain Clason!' Ilsa replied, laughing. 'See you at the café.'

While Kat was involved with Ilsa, I was messaging Jim to ask if he had any idea when we could continue our journey.

'Quite soon,' Jim said. 'We got the road layer brigades in first and they're making spectacular progress. Of course, it helps a lot that the walls of the artificial gravity disk provide a firm foundation for everything we want to build! And not forgetting that while the machines were printing the new riverbank promenade along Starship Way, we could turn the river off!'

'Yeah, I guess it all helps,' I commented.

'The weather's controllable, too, of course,' Jim added. 'So, the sitrep on our version of Proxima Alpha is that all the roads have been laid within the settlement and the gangs are now working out towards the location of the SpacePort and Business Park, so, now they're out of the settlement area, I'm trans-shipping the printers for the main buildings in the next few shuttles. I've agreed with Ilsa that the first thing they print will be a full-size replica of the Westwood Restaurant. Then, the machines will just work through the settlement, printing replicas of the buildings.'

'OK,' I replied. 'Mention of Ilsa reminds me that Kat's just been arranging for her and Rick to meet us at Café Claudius soon. Apparently, Ilsa's bringing one of Madge's old original sous chefs to cook up something special. Why don't you join us? I'd still like an answer to my first question: do you have any idea when we could continue our journey?'

'Yeah, I will, Boss, I'd welcome a nice meal in one-g. I've got used to it in the past couple of weeks! I can answer your question with a 'maybe', based on how things have gone so far. We may be able to move on tomorrow. Let me get the building-printers launched on their part of the job, the machines are rolling up now. I'll get down to your café in about half an hour. Is it the Café Claudius at the travelator entrance?'

'That's the one,' I confirmed.

With our party confirmed, we realised that the place was beginning to fill up with off-duty crew. I suggested that we had time for a one-g shower in one of the bathroom blocks situated near the athletics track, so, we took cycles over to the track, leaving Malik to keep our guests informed of our movements. When I returned from the bathroom block, thoroughly revived, and dressed in fresh fatigues, Kat had already claimed a table outside the café and Rick was pouring himself a coffee from the carafe on the table. We hadn't seen each other for two weeks or more, not since we had dropped him off at this location with the components for PW4 and the contract to put the bits together and get it up and running. It was a welcome reunion.

'You've got a nice place here, Rick,' I said. 'Where's Ilsa, have you lost your wife already?'

'Nah, she's in the kitchen with that old chef robot she brought from Proxima Alpha,' he replied. 'She also brought some fresh foods from Proxima's farms. Fish, poultry, rabbits. That kind of thing. So, I guess the two of them are devising a menu.'

'Well, believe me, Rick,' said Kat, 'you're in for a treat. Those old chef robots from Starship-101 were trained by the best chefs in the Solar System before they ventured out here.'

I caught site of Jim Igwe cycling up towards the café. 'I hope an extra guest will not upset Ilsa's plans,' I said, explaining. 'I invited Jim Igwe to join us.'

'No probs, Boss,' said Ilsa emerging from the café. 'Jim's building me a restaurant so he's always welcome.'

'And a nice little cottage, just for two,' said Jim, adding his cycle to the café's rack.

Ilsa took on the task of hostess and got everybody seated around her table and then explained, 'The chef will be preparing one of Westwood Restaurant's tasting menus, they're just printing it off on the office printer now. It features a long list of vegetable, fish, poultry, rabbit and piglet mini plates, followed by three very special desserts. So, it doesn't matter what you choose to drink, you're bound to be right with at least half the menu!'

The café's waiter was called out and drinks choices made. I settled for just one-glass of Grenache, and after taking my first sip, I returned to the topic at the top of my agenda.

'Jim, are we any closer to a timetable for departure?'

'Well, tomorrow is firming-up as departure date,' Jim replied. 'I got all the construction printers in operation before I came down here. So far, my involvement in managing the build has been minimal. PW4's management computer has been trained to do all that needs to be done, and now that those QIC adapters have been fitted, Malik will be able to monitor everything they do even after we leave. To be certain, I'd like to wait for the overnight shift to be completed, that's 6 a.m. tomorrow, but it's looking good so far, and my presence here is likely to become a superfluous luxury.'

I nodded and then asked Malik, 'How about a departure for PW3 at noon tomorrow, Malik. Is there anything else to prevent that?'

'Negative, Commodore,' Malik responded. 'Fully revised and updated departure and destination quantum maps have been completed and could be streamed to yourself and Captain Clason overnight. I am not aware of any other factor likely to inhibit a brief rehearsal tomorrow at 11.45 a.m. followed by a jump to PW3. Do you wish me to insert these plans into tomorrow's general orders for Pink Ghost, Commodore?'

I raised a quizzical eyebrow towards Kat, my second-in-command, and Jim, my third-in-command. Both nodded, and I told Malik to go ahead, subject to Jim's confirmation at 6 a.m. tomorrow.

'There's just one other thing that Rick and I would like to raise,' said Ilsa. 'We would like to stay here, on board PW4, to complete the creation of the Proxima Alpha settlement simulation.'

'Are you sure?' I asked. 'Stuck out here in deep space?'

'Yes, we're sure,' Rick replied. 'And now we have the QIC adapters installed and operating in both of our megacomputers, we are far from isolated. I've been amazed by the performance of those adapters. We're in constant touch with all the computers on Proxima-b and both computers on Pink Ghost.'

'Both on Pink Ghost?' I queried, at which Malik interrupted to explain, 'Strictly speaking, just me on Pink Ghost, the other machine is Starship-101's Flight computer, which was fitted with a QIC adapter before we left Proxima-b and has become a node on the network managed by the Westwood computer.'

'OK, Malik, thanks for that explanation,' I said. 'Seems like you've got it all stitched up!' Turning to Rick and Ilsa I said that I saw no reason why they shouldn't stay together on PW4 and proposed a toast to their success.

With all these plans settled, we returned to navigating our way through the tasting menu. I knew that Kat would be able to navigate me back to Pink Ghost. So, safe in the knowledge that my Nav Couch would readjust my physiology to compensate for any of my excesses, I ordered another glass of Grenache.

Day 11

My Nav Couch woke me at 5.30 a.m. after a night of hard work, streaming updated quantum maps from Malik and experiencing one of those 'you'll thank me later for this' workouts by the life support system of the Couch. I had time for a quick shower, or what passes for a shower in microgravity, and a quick pouch of porridge, or what passes for porridge in microgravity, before Jim messaged me and Kat. The overnight construction teams had made great progress and he had transferred all the future management responsibilities to Rick Blaine and the PW4 management computer.

'And that means I can leave with you for PW3 as soon as you like, Boss,' Jim concluded.

'Good. So, Malik, are there any other issues that would delay our departure for PW3?' I asked.

'Only one, Commodore,' Malik replied. 'Most of the off-duty crew who took shore leave on PW4 are still asleep on the waystation!'

'No change in habits there, then,' commented Kat, smiling. 'I'm not surprised. Before we left Café Claudius, I caught sight of our entire contingent of Midshipmen making good use of your bottle of rum, Boss, and supplementing it with several bottles of their own.'

'There'll be a few groggy heads there, then!' I suggested.

'You betcha!' she replied. 'But PW4 offers more facilities for them to make a quick recovery. So, let's give them an early morning call, Malik. With instructions to be back onboard Pink Ghost no later than 8 a.m. to prepare this ship for a noon quantum jump to PW3.'

'Willco, Captain Clason. Malik out.'

'Hold on, Malik,' I interrupted. 'Are we all agreed on a noon departure? Kat? Jim? Malik?'

They all chorused 'Affirmative' so, I went on to instruct Malik to issue similar instructions and warnings to the crew currently on duty on Pink Ghost, and asked Jim to organise shuttle transport to return our crew to Pink Ghost.

As the intercom rang out with Malik's warnings about a 12-noon departure, Jim followed up with another comment, 'There's one other matter I need to inform you about, Boss. While I was on my early morning round of the construction crews, I bumped into Emma Halton doing her morning inspections of the various smallholdings she's establishing here, and she said that she'd like to be detached from Pink Ghost's crew to work on PW4's farms. I don't know. What you think about that, Kat?'

'I don't see any reason why she shouldn't,' Kat replied. 'She could reattach to Harden's crew when he passes by and then return to Proxima-b with Harden, to work on transferring the Proxima farming operations into the orbital artificial gravity stations we're hoping his flotilla will bring up to Proxima.'

That sounded like a good plan, so I messaged Emma to make sure she really wanted to detach from my crew and stay with Ilsa and Rick. She said yes to that, and explained, 'I'd really like to spend more time establishing my smallholdings here on PW4, Boss,' she said. 'I've brought enough hardware to mimic many of the units I've set up on Proxima-b and the animals I need for them. It's so much easier here. There's no worry about escapes into the local environment, because it's just a pastiche of Proxima-b in a tin box in deep space. But I know you want to move onto PW3 a.s.a.p. and I need more time than you can afford to wait. If I stay here, I can do what I want to do with my smallholdings and help Ilsa build some horticultural units as well. Make the place produce its own fresh foods!'

'OK, Emma,' I said. 'You have my permission to detach from my crew.'

'Rick, are you logged into this message stream?'

'Yes, Boss,' said Rick.

'And are you willing to accept Lieutenant Commander Emma Halton into your team on PW4?'

'Affirmative, Boss,' Rick replied.

'Then let's consider it done. Malik, please complete the necessary relocation records. And, Emma, I remind you that my brother Harden will come visiting in a week or two, and if we can move fast enough with our negotiations with StarCorp, Harden might be bringing artificial gravity orbital farms for Proxima-b. You might then consider accompanying them back to Proxima to transfer the Proxima farming operations into the orbital stations.'

'Yeah, I like the sound of that, Boss. Thanks for everything. Have a good trip back to Oort Station. Emma out.'

While this conversation was underway, the Pink Ghost's intercom had warned the crew of the revised general orders for the day and had issued final warnings for a 11.45 a.m. rehearsal followed by a 12-noon quantum jump to PW3. On my open channel to PW4, I overheard a suitably modified repeat of the general order being broadcast by the intercom on PW4.

'OK, I hear the general order going out,' I said. 'I need to be reminded about the nature of PW3 and PW2, so Kat and Jim, and Rick, too, stay on the line. What should we expect in the next two waystations?'

'Well, you know, Boss, I don't expect we'll need to do much on either of them apart from signing off the construction contracts,' said Jim. 'Because these two are specialist waystations intended as intermediate stops for travellers from the Moon, that's PW3 managed by Captain Roberto de Córdova; or from Mars, that's PW2, which is managed by Captain Riley Guo. As both offer large galleries of generic landscaping aimed at travellers from particular low-gravity environments, we haul them as virtually complete, ready-made, outfits that just need to be unpacked, assembled, powered up and commissioned. Their general management megacomputers handle the brigades of robots responsible for most of the construction.'

'Yeah, I agree with Jim,' said Rick. 'I've built those Mars and Moon simulation artificial gravity disks around the Solar System. The StarCorp designers have done a great job. The landscape is minimal, just a scattering of craters, a covering of regolith, and a scattering of off-the-shelf habitat units. The computer does most of the work. Human managers are just there as over-qualified baby-sitters for the megacomputer in charge. It's a cake walk.'

'So, what will we be doing on PW3 and PW2, and how long will it take?' I asked everyone.

'We need to install QIC adapters in both their management and flight control computers and allow Malik sufficient time to carry out the necessary training and testing of the growing QIC network,' Jim replied. 'And we also need to upgrade their fax robot brigades with the QIC-fax chip and include them in the training and testing.'

'Could Lana and her fax-bot called Greenstreet help with testing and training the fax robot brigades?' Asked Kat.

'Well, Greenstreet's just finishing off a video survey of our Proxima Alpha simulation and Lana's taken the opportunity to use him to chat with Ilsa and Emma,' said Rick. 'So, I'm pretty sure she'd be able to help.'

'In exchange for the video rights, no doubt,' said Kat.

'Nothing wrong with that,' I said. 'What sort of time frame do these updates, training and testing involve?' I asked.

'On the basis of our experience since your arrival here, Boss, I'd guess around two to three hours,' said Rick.

'I'd agree with that, Boss,' added Jim. 'Most of our time here was devoted initially to transporting the construction teams across to the waystation and getting them started on the Proxima Alpha simulation. By the time I'd got all my gangs over here, all the QIC adaptations were completed and the PW4 computer was being networked with Proxima Alpha's Westwood computer.'

'Frankly,' Jim continued, 'on the basis of my experience here, you might even be able to jump to PW3, do the necessary there, and then move directly from PW3 to PW2 on the same day.'

'Malik, any comment?' I asked.

'I agree with Captain Igwe's assessment,' Malik replied. 'Only unforeseen circumstances would lengthen our on-station time commitment to either of the next two waystations beyond three hours. But I would add another point for consideration, which is that if the QIC plug-and-play adapters for the resident megacomputers continue to provide instantaneous quantum communications across two further lightyears of normal space, then we can maintain constant monitoring of Proxima Waystations 3 and 2 when we move on. Further, on that same topic, as the QIC-fax chips also appear to be totally reliable, I suggest that the human managers of waystations be required to make direct personal NeuroModem connections with the chef de brigade of their fax robot brigade before they leave their waystation.'

'Oh, yes!' Jim reacted. 'Then they can revisit their waystation as a fax robot facsimile avatar any time they're needed! Brilliant. Let's go for it as a rule, Boss.'

'Agreed,' Kat added.

'OK, motion carried,' I said. 'Malik, add this new rule to the protocols for signing off the contracts for completed waystations and link it to the formal appointment of their AI-megacomputers as resident managers.' Then I added, 'What do you think about that, Rick?'

'It's fine with me, Boss,' Rick replied. 'I'll make the connection right away. The chef de brigade is an AI-bot, so, even while I'm on board, being in two places at once could be very useful!'

'On that basis,' said Kat, 'I might think about sending a fax avatar to do some of the more boring bits of my job! Seriously, though, Boss, you'd better check out the idea with Lydia Connah; the management structure of Proxima Home Station is more complex with two of the settlers being involved in day-to-day operations. I can see how the settlers might welcome Lydia's dial-up presence, but on the other hand, I can also see that they might not like the idea of apparently being under scrutiny.'

'That may be so, Kat, but they'll have to get used to constant scrutiny!' I said. 'We're all under the scrutiny of our megacomputers. Here's what we'll do: Kat, you contact Lydia and explain what we've just been discussing. She's our most senior waystation manager, so she can decide whether she or one of her junior officers is made guardian avatar of Proxima Home Station. If you need to, you can hint that I would prefer that she take on the task herself.'

'Now, Malik,' I went on, 'I like the idea of making at least two quantum jumps today. So, I want you to issue an additional general order for today to the effect that following our planned quantum jump to PW3 at noon today, we will provisionally make a further quantum jump from PW3 to PW2 at 6 p.m. today. And add that there will be no shore leave on either PW3 or PW2.'

'Willco, Commodore. Is there anything else?'

'There certainly is,' I said. 'If we reach PW2 at 6 p.m. and only have two- or three-hours' work there; is there any reason why we can't press on with a jump from PW2 to PW1 at around midnight tonight?'

My assembled senior tactical management team went totally silent following this question, so, I tried to drag some answers from individuals. 'Kat, where do we stand with regard to quantum maps of both origin and destination for the next three jumps?'

'We have workable destination maps for all waystations based on recalculating the departure maps we used for our jumps towards Proxima-Centauri,' Kat replied. 'And PW4's traffic control computer is already making a rolling recalculation of PW4's departure/destination map based on present-time astro-observations and streaming it to the QIC network. As we reach them, we'll train all the other waystations' traffic control computers to do the same. So, we have the best quantum maps we can get at this time for all the jumps you're talking about, Boss. But why do you want to make such frequent jumps?'

'You've just illustrated why, Kat,' I replied. 'It's because I want to get a QIC-equipped network established to cover the entire route to Proxima as soon as possible. At the moment we're jumping into deep space between our new waystations and up-to-the-minute destination quantum maps are not so important, we can aim to land anywhere. But when the route we're building opens to Starship traffic we need to know the disposition of traffic around the destination at the time of our decoherence. Not at some time in the past when our data about the destination was last updated.'

'I'm really keen to get the QIC plug-and-play adapters, as well as the QIC-fax chips down to Oort Station, because traffic around Oort is already more of a hazard than it should be and only likely to get worse, and I'm flying in with a double-sized Starship,' I finished.

'Yes, I understand all that, Boss,' said Jim. 'But PW1 is a slightly different matter, we can't just jump in and jump out again in a couple of hours. PW1 is an Earth-quality, luxury transport hub. These disks also come virtually ready to use straight out of the box. But there are quite a few of these throughout the Solar System that are frequented by the type of no-expense-spared regular travellers that we want to encourage to try interstellar tourism. These rich and super-rich tourists will demand that the gateway to Proxima-Centauri, which is Proxima Waystation 1, offers the same luxurious travel experiences that they've encountered in this type of hub on their previous interplanetary tours. We'll have to do a much more rigorous inspection of PW1 to be sure it can provide that 'luxurious travel experience' while introducing travellers to the fact that they are one lightyear out from the Solar System. They've never seen skies like they can see from here. They've never been this far from the Sun, their home star, and never so close to the Centauri star system. Yet, they are only on the first step of their journey.'

'You paint a great picture, Jim,' I said. 'You could take up tourism copy writing when you retire!'

'Don't be so dismissive, Boss!' Kat scolded. 'The entire crew of this ship experienced everything that Jim is describing when we were travelling to Proxima-Centauri only a few weeks ago. I remember you joining the crowds on the astrophysics deck to get the first views of the skies we could see when we were dropping off the components of PW1. You weren't so smug about it then.'

'OK, guilty as charged,' I replied. 'I didn't intend for it to sound dismissive; I was just trying to get back at both of you for your suggestions that I get a job with the cabin crew of a passenger jet when I retire! But, yes, I do recall the feelings that almost overwhelmed me when I first saw the views as we decohered for the first time on the way to Proxima, at the location of PW1.'

I paused as the memory traces of those events circulated through my consciousness, and then resumed my reminiscences, 'That feeling that, hey, we're a lightyear from home! We're outside the Solar System in interstellar space! And we ain't finished yet!'

'Yeah, my dominant memory,' Jim contributed, 'is that I opted to join the gangs that offloaded the components of the waystation. So, I was out there in my spacesuit. Alone in the devastating space between the stars. And I remember thinking, OK galaxy, I am out here, and I'm putting down a marker for me and my kind. And it won't be the last!'

'You guys should find some time to say all this to the camera bot Greenstreet,' Rick said. 'I've spent a happy half hour with it reminiscing with my crew about 'being marooned in interstellar space building a waystation'. When Lana received the streamed video back on Proxima-b, she dialled into Greenstreet's fax circuits, and we talked about making an entire documentary vid entitled 'Being Between the Stars' or something like that. I think Ilsa's still talking to Lana down in our version of Westwood Restaurant; if there's nothing else you want me to contribute to this discussion, Boss, I'll go talk to Lana, if she's still connected, and share my memory trace of the last few minutes' memories of interstellar space.'

'I wish you would do that, Rick,' I replied. 'I've given Lana so many suggestions for video programmes that TV production became yet another suggestion as a retirement job for me!'

'Right, willco. Rick out.'

'You're getting oversensitive about retirement,' said Kat, giggling. 'If our little jokes dwell on your mind so. Maybe you'd feel better about it if you took our helpful suggestions more seriously!'

'Yeah, well, maybe you should talk to Harden about retirement,' I suggested.

'Nah, let's not go there!' Kat replied. 'Let's get back to our real business. Jim, if we can't just jump in and out of PW1 in a couple of hours, how long do we have to stay there?'

'I'd like us to plan for a couple of days layover at PW1,' Jim suggested. 'Give the whole crew 48 hours shore leave and tell them to check it out.'

'As long as that?' I queried. 'That's not helping me get the QIC adapters and fax chips down to Oort Station!'

'True,' said Kat. 'But a 48-hour layover would get the PW1 contract properly signed off. And we could leave Jim in charge of Pink Ghost; and quantum jump the Commodore's Cutter to Oort taking the QIC adapters to fit to Harden's ship, Oort Station and the StarCorp yards, and Lydia Connah to initiate negotiations about the orbital farming disks with StarCorp.'

'I like it,' commented Jim.

'Yes, so do I,' I mused. 'Malik, has the computer in the Commodore's Cutter been equipped with a QIC adapter?'

'Affirmative, Commodore. It was QIC-enabled and fully tested as one of my first adaptations aboard Pink Ghost,' reported Malik. 'And I can also equip your cutter with a chef de brigade AI-fax robot fitted with a QIC-fax chip pre-tuned to your NeuroModem, Commodore.'

'So, I can't escape from you!' I remarked.

'Certainly not, Commodore!' was Malik's response.

'Fine, so here's what we'll do,' I said. 'Malik, add to today's general orders a provisional quantum jump from PW2 to PW1 at midnight tonight. On arrival at PW1, the appropriate engineers will transfer to PW1 to fit QIC plug-and-play adapters to PW1's megacomputers and QIC-fax chips to PW1's fax-bot brigade. The necessary training and testing of these devices will be completed overnight. Is that understood, Malik?'

'Affirmative, Commodore. Malik out.'

'Kat and Jim, does this suit you two?' I asked.

'Affirmative, Boss, I will go across to PW1 with the midnight shift of cyber engineers to determine any other engineering needs the waystation might have before we send our crew over to do their worst!'

'OK, Jim. How about you, Kat? Can you remind me who is the appointed manager of PW1?'

'Oh, I'm OK with three quantum jumps in a day,' Kat replied. 'Though it will be a record for both of us!'

'Not quite,' I protested. 'I still hold the training college record at six quantum jumps in 12 hours!'

'Yeah, well, here's hoping that someone whose been so concerned about retirement recently will still be awake at midnight!' Kat responded.

'If you want me to stay awake, you could try sticking pins in me instead of that doll you keep in your coven,' I replied.

'I'll ignore that unjustified portrayal! Anyway, if you do manage to stay awake through midnight, you'll be announcing our arrival at Proxima Waystation 1 to Captain Angélique Gérard. She's older than you, Boss, so she might have more useful post-retirement advice to offer!'

'Aye, but don't underestimate her, Boss,' Jim remarked. 'She's a tough cookie who's made a career out of installing Earth-like waystations. She was so enthusiastic about installing a waystation in interstellar space when I first met her, that I got the impression she might want to stay on as resident manager of PW1.'

'Is there any reason she shouldn't take up residence?' I asked.

'Not that I know of,' Jim replied.

'It's OK with me,' I said. 'And if Kat, Lydia and I jump off to Oort Station in my cutter we'll leave you in charge and you can exercise your command training to deal with the lady! Now, I'm getting edgy with all this talk about PW1. Shouldn't we be preparing for a jump to PW3? Malik, how are things progressing?'

'We are on track for the planned noon departure, Commodore,' Malik responded immediately. 'All crew are accounted for, and the last crew transport shuttle is docking right now. Some section leaders have already reported their decks shipshape and in good order. I expect all crew to be securely strapped into their acceleration couches by 11.45 a.m. However, Commodore, your Nav Couch is reporting you have low blood sugar, so I have ordered your steward to prepare you some remedial food and drink. I suggest, Commodore, that you take a brief timeout to deal with that, and I will issue the appropriate departure warnings. Malik out.'

Suitably admonished by my ship's computer, I broke up this group conversation and followed Malik's suggestion; Kat followed suit. While we were refuelling, the intercom delivered Malik's warnings about the next quantum jump.

'Now hear this, now hear this. We are about to undertake the translocation of Starships Pink Ghost and Starship-101 from the vicinity of Proxima Waystation 4 to the vicinity of Proxima Waystation 3. All crewmembers to be securely strapped into their acceleration couches by 11.45 a.m. There will be no shore leave on Waystation 3.'

As soon as the 'no shore leave' message was broadcast, I received an urgent message from Tom Fraser, 'Hi Tarvin. I understand that this Waystation 3 is a mock-up of life on the Moon, and as I did some work on the Moon in my younger days, I'd really like the chance to relive those experiences. Is there any way that Carla and I could make a quick visit after the quantum jump?'

'Sorry, Tom, we're not allowing shore leave because we want to limit the time we spend in that location, in the hope that we can move on to quantum jump to PW2 at 6 p.m. There are several people amongst the crew who grew up on the Moon, so I don't want to cause friction by making you an exception,' I explained.

'Oh, OK,' said Tom. 'I just thought that at my age, this could well be my last opportunity to live like a Man-in-the-Moon. Like we did nearly a hundred years ago.'

'Can I butt into this conversation?' Kat asked, as she settled into her Nav Couch beside me, coffee bulb in hand. 'Because I have an idea. The only thing we must do that causes us to linger on-station at PW3, and PW2 for that matter, is fit our QIC hardware to the waystation's megacomputers.'

'Oh yes, I know all about the QIC upgrades,' Tom responded. 'Brilliant, utterly brilliant. I always thought Salman Khan was a top-notch computer engineer on Starship-101, back in the day, but his boy Danny's amazing. I upgraded Carla's fax module with one of his QIC-fax chips as soon as I could get my hands on one, and we've been chatting with the folks back on Proxima-b ever since.'

'Right, well, don't go off on a tangent, Tom,' Kat interrupted. 'My idea is to make use of your expertise to get you some shore leave on the waystations, let's stick with that topic.'

'OK, I'm all ears!' said Tom.

'Well, how would you feel about heading up an Executive Officer's task force, an away team to be sent to the next three waystations to supervise the engineering teams we'll be sending over to carry out the QIC upgrades to the waystation's megacomputers and fax-bots?'

'Ecstatic, that's how I'd feel!' Tom responded. 'Certainly, count me in! But do they need supervision? Where's Malik in all this?'

'From what I've heard, Tom, you've built a pretty good working relationship with Malik, but why don't we ask him?' Kat replied. 'Malik, what do you think of my idea?'

'I'm all in favour,' Malik responded. 'I have benefitted greatly by learning about the historical origins of my kind from Tom Fraser. So, to have a hands-on programmer of his experience on board the waystations during the upgrades can only be welcomed. I have a query, and a potential suggestion, however, Captain Clason.'

'OK, shoot.'

'You mentioned a 'task force', Captain Clason,' Malik continued. 'I don't know what you had in mind for the composition of this 'away team' as you also described it. So, I venture to remind you that Mr Fraser's expertise and experience includes direct personal experience of working on the Moon, and on Mars, before he left the Solar System aboard Starship-101. Also, of course, he was born and brought up on Earth. Who better, then, to assess and comment on the simulations of Moon, Mars and Earth on the PW3, PW2 and PW1 waystations than he? Further, I propose that there is no better audience for his reminiscences than our team of Midshipmen, and, therefore, suggest that they complete your away team.'

'Malik, you've excelled yourself, there.' I laughed. 'I like it, I like it a lot. Tom, what do you think? Are you willing to nursemaid our teenage crew as they get some experience of Moon, Mars, and Earth?'

'Definitely, no old man could turn down a captive audience for his senile mumblings!' Tom replied. 'Anyway, Carla can do the nursemaiding, and I'll be the irascible old codger!'

'Good. Obviously a natural for the job, Tom!' I said. 'Malik, make it so.'

'Willco, Commodore. I will issue orders, in the name of the Executive Officer, for all Midshipmen to muster on the shuttle deck for crew transport to each waystation immediately after decoherence arrival has been confirmed.'

'Confirming decoherence arrival sounds rather daunting,' Tom commented.

'Nah, no worries, mate, it's only our equivalent of the guy in the crow's nest shouting, land ho!' I said, as I grabbed a last bulb of coffee from Stewart. 'Now we need to turn attention to our departure from this point in space. But before you go, I note that you're calling your care-bot 'Carla' again. So, how's the bot-trolling these days?'

'Oh, it's turning the corner nicely,' Tom informed me. 'I've been trolling the trolls as I promised, and most of your shipboard bots have restored their normal behaviour pattern. There's just a few of the security bot brigade that remain to be convinced. But they'll be brought in line as we add more AI-bots to the Gort network through the QIC chips and adapters fitted on the Proxima waystations. Carla is mithering me about it getting close to the time I need to be strapped into an acceleration couch; I'd better go and leave you to get on with your job. Thanks for making it possible for me to experience my home planets again! Fraser out.'

I eased back into the cushions of my Nav Couch and felt the deeply enhanced touch of its NeuroModem connectors 'Are you with me, Kat?' I asked, and her affirmative response floated into my consciousness, 'I'm just sorting the memory traces of PW3's most recent quantum map. I'll have them in a moment or two,' her thoughts said.

'Malik, how are we doing for time?' I asked, as usual.

'It's approaching 11.45 a.m., Commodore.'

'Good, can you confirm the vessel is ready to go?'

'All crew accounted for, Commodore. All sections reported in good order for flight.'

'Excellent. Issue rehearsal and take-off warnings throughout both Starships and then count both pilots down to noon,' I ordered.

After a few deep breathing exercises, I heard Malik's intercom chiming through the ship, warning the crew to stand easy for an imminent rehearsal and be prepared for the scheduled departure from PW4 space at noon.

I started to assemble my mental visualisations of what were now familiar quantum map wavefunctions describing this peculiar two-Starship contraption I was about to thrust into quantum space. I had this in good order when Malik next broadcast on the intercom.

'Will Pilot and co-Pilot please signify their readiness to initiate rehearsal of their translocation of this Starship flotilla from Proxima Waystation 4 to location of Proxima Waystation 3.'

'Pilot is ready,' I said.

'Co-Pilot is ready,' Kat responded.

'Initiate when ready,' Malik concluded.

I reached across to take hold of Kat's hand and she began to stream the latest memory traces of the quantum map of the volume of space around Proxima Waystation 4 for me to weave around the wavefunction of our two Starships at this departure location in my mindscape. There was so little of note in this volume of space that it was just like covering a ridiculously detailed view of the Starships with a transparent film.

'Jeez,' I whispered to Kat, 'interstellar space is boring, there's nothing here! How is the PW3 destination coming along?'

'Boringly,' she whispered back. 'But be grateful for that. My data is more than two weeks old! A whole squadron of brown dwarf stars could have crept into it by now!'

'Determined to cheer me up, eh?' I asked, trying to sound glum.

'Here, see what you can do with this,' she said as she streamed her memory trace of the destination into my mind. It showed a 50-kilometre cube of empty space with an exclusion zone in the rough shape of a waystation in the furthest corner. 'Try not to hit that cylindrical thing in the back corner,' she added.

'OK, Malik, we're both happy with the quantum maps we have,' I reported. 'How are we doing for time?'

'It's approaching 11.58 a.m., Commodore.'

'Right, tell the crew to stand easy from the rehearsal and issue take-off warnings. Then count me down to noon.'

I heard the intercom chiming as Kat said, 'I'm glad you liked my idea for Tom Fraser's away team. It will be a good field class for the trainees and apprentices and whatever he says about being an irascible old codger, he's a good teacher with a great deal of genuine wisdom to share. I only wish I could be there to see it for myself.'

'You don't have to be there yourself, Kat,' I assured her. 'Don't forget, where the Westwood twins go, then there goes Greenstreet the camera bot!'

'Oh, yes! I'd forgotten about Greenstreet!' said Kat.

'Very well, then,' Malik said. 'Standby Starships. Standby pilots. Cue initiate the translocation in five, four, three, two, one ...'

On zero, I stacked the two memory trace visualisations we had just calculated, one above the other in my mindscape, and then merged them together into a superposition. Something tickled inside my brain as Kat glided the hex-number nudge into my consciousness, which I shoved into the waveform of the just-created superposition's destination quantum map.

The result was totally underwhelming. Hardly anything changed. The control room view screens seemed to be showing the same views, although the image of the Proxima Waystation was in a slightly different orientation and as Kat adjusted the camera displays its ID lights brightly announced: Proxima Waystation 3.

'Well, that's a relief!' said Kat, as she focussed on that display. 'But what else do you expect? Interstellar space is so boring that one 50-kilometre cube looks the same as any other 50-kilometre cube.'

'Any sign of brown dwarfs?' I asked, still trying to cheer myself up but not really expecting a reply. Just as well, because I didn't get one. Instead, Kat broadcast to the intercom, 'Now hear this. All crew. Now hear this. Stand easy. Executive Officer confirming safe arrival at our destination. For your information we are alongside Proxima Waystation 3, which is approximately three lightyears out from Earth. In due course, this waystation will be responsible for receiving incoming flights from the vicinity of Earth's Moon. There will be no shore leave. Computer engineering team and the Exec's away team to muster immediately in the transporter dock. Exec out.'

While Kat was announcing our arrival to the crew, I was announcing our arrival to PW3.

'Proxima Waystation 3 Traffic Control, this is Commodore Tarvin Clason requesting permission to approach.'

'Commodore Clason, welcome to Proxima Waystation 3! You may approach as you require, there is no conflicting traffic. Traffic Control out.' Followed immediately by a message from the waystation's general manager, Captain Roberto de Córdova. '¡Hola! Welcome to Proxima Waystation 3, Comodoro. Will you join me over here por bebida de bienvenida?'

'We sure will, Roberto,' I replied. '¡Vierte el tequila! Me, my Exec and Chief Engineer will be transferring to you immediately, and we'll be sending over some away teams to carry out computer upgrades for you. But we want to proceed towards Proxima Waystation 2 at 6 p.m., so we don't want to be on-station here for more than two or three hours.'

'Sí, entiendo. OK, my team can help with that. We have finished here. Hasta la vista, Comodoro; de Córdova out.'

Kat and I detached ourselves from our Nav Couches and I messaged Jim 'We're on our way towards the transporter dock, Jim. Where are you?'

'I'm already there, Boss. Mustering my away team engineers, which now seem to include Tom Fraser and his care-bot, and a hyperactive band of Midshipmen!'

'Sounds about right, Jim,' said Kat. 'The hyperactive part, I mean. It's called 'youth'; dig deep into your memories and you might recall it! You just trudge along behind, and you'll be fine.'

Our appearance at the transporter dock brought the Midshipmen to attention and Kat kept them at attention as she explained that their mission was to inspect and experience the Moon simulation galleries under the guidance of Tom Fraser as their official tutor, whom they will treat as their senior officer. While Kat was impressing some discipline on the group of teenagers, the camera bot Greenstreet detached from the group and jetted over towards me.

'Hiya, Boss, the QIC chip works to here!' Greenstreet greeted me, but in Lana's voice.

'Brilliant,' I replied. 'That's one and a half lightyears! Malik, any issues with reception?'

'Negative, Commodore. All machines in the current network are reporting perfect transmission and reception characteristics across all connections. We look forward to adding PW3 machines to the network to allow further testing of the protocols we are developing.'

'Say, Boss, did I hear right from George Westwood, that you're planning to move on to Waystation 2 later today?' Lana/Greenstreet asked.

'Yes, that's right Lana. Hopefully, around 6 p.m.,' I told her.

'Wow, that'll be around two and a half lightyears from Proxima-b! And I could put it onto the evening news bulletin live!' Lana said, excited.

'Yes, Lana, I don't see why not,' I replied. 'Send Greenstreet up to the control room around 5 p.m. and he can record the whole of the quantum jump. And if you dial into Greenstreet just before we do the jump, we can see how the connection behaves during the superposition and decoherence.'

'Hey, yay, quantum mechanics research live on air!' Lana/Greenstreet responded, even more excited.

'Calm down, Lana,' I advised. 'This camera bot of yours is likely to fall apart if you get more excited! And there's more! I'm planning to jump Pink Ghost to PW1 at midnight and Greenstreet is welcome to video that translocation, too. And if you want to stay up late, you can dial into him and see what happens when we come alongside PW1 which is three and a half lightyears from Proxima-b.'

'Willco, Boss. Lana out.'

As Lana dialled out, I received a message from Merv Castlefield, who came into my NeuroModem shouting, 'Calling Commodore Tarvin Clason. Hello Tarvin, can you hear me?'

'Loud and clear, Merv. But you don't have to shout. It's just like any other NeuroModem message!' I protested.

'But Westwood told me you were over a lightyear away,' Merv said, a little more calmly.

'We are actually one and a half lightyears away from you,' I responded. 'And your message to my NeuroModem demonstrates that our QIC devices actually work. We can communicate thanks to another quantum weirdness. But shouting doesn't help, Merv. Now, what can I do for you?'

'Well, when the winds had died down and we got the snow cleared from the SpacePort, Captain Zhang brought his cutter down from orbit.'

'Oh, good,' I said, 'how did the meeting go?

'Well, the meeting me and Sally had with Rocky and Lily and their city council leaders went fine and dandy. We agreed they could bring loads of passengers down to stay in currently vacant hotels in Proxima Alpha while they are working on establishing their own settlement down the coast. That's not the problem.'

'What is the problem, Merv?'

'The problem is that in earlier video conferences with that big security guy.'

'Nelson?' I suggested.

'Yeah, him. Well, Clint had told him that a high security block had just been built at Proxima Bank and suggested they could deposit their gold bullion into it. They said yes, and it was brought down from orbit in their cutter. But when their truck turned up outside our bank, a bunch of armed security guards spilled out to form a cordon, human and robot, and all armed to the teeth, with sidearms and automatic assault weapons. Clint went ballistic. None of our security bots carry weapons, and Clint was raging around calling it an armed Chinese takeover. Then he went messaging all the settlers with American heritage to form a volunteer militia to protect the bank. The original Americans in Starship-101's crew all brought sidearms and hunting rifles to Proxima-Centauri. As there are no animals to hunt, they didn't get much use, but they've all been carefully maintained as prized family possessions. So now we've got an inner cordon around the bank vault of armed ethnic Chinese security guards edgily watching an outer cordon of armed settlers who have no professional training in gun-toting and could loose off a round without knowing what they're doing. It could get nasty.'

This had all been delivered as a continuous high-speed diatribe with no evidence of the speaker actually breathing! 'OK Merv, you're beginning to gabble, slow down and take a few deep breaths,' I advised, continuing, 'I've formed the opinion that Clint is a bit of a firebrand nonconformist.'

'Yeah, he's fanatical about his personal independence too, and that's what makes him so difficult to deal with,' Merv responded gloomily.

'Still, you need to rein him in, but without being confrontational,' I replied. 'Suggest an alternative pattern of behaviour that doesn't involve him losing face. Nelson Wang, Rocky's chief of security, is a perfectly reasonable bloke, you should talk it over with him. See if there's some compromise that will satisfy everybody.'

'I have talked to Nelson,' Merv protested. 'But he's just as insistent as Clint about protecting the bullion. Though in his mind it needs protection from possible bad guys from the People's Republic of China. Either infiltrators among his own passengers or maybe even among our ethnically Chinese settlers!'

'Yeah, from what I've heard, the PDRM has good cause to be fanatically suspicious about that sort of thing,' I said. 'But maybe there's a hint in that about what you could do to calm things down.'

'What do you mean, Tarvin?' Merve asked. 'I don't see where you're going with this.'

'Well, third-party bad guys could be the common threat to bring Clint and Nelson to work together,' I suggested. 'It's up to you to point that out and get them to work together.'

'That doesn't sound easy!' Merv's even more gloomy response.

'Who's told you that politics is easy, Merv?' I asked, continuing, 'You need to find a way to get the two gun-toting groups you have now to operate together. So, you work on that, and I'll work on a more permanent solution.'

'And what might that be?' Merve asked.

'What you really need on Proxima-b, I reckon, is a detachment of Blue Helmets to keep the peace between all ethnic groups that may want to join you there.'

'What the hell are they?' Merv asked.

'They're the United Worlds Peacekeepers. Interplanetary policemen that solve disputes across the Solar System,' I explained. 'As I remember it, one of the passengers my brother's going to bring to you in the next few weeks will be a representative of the United Worlds. Some sort of diplomat-ambassador to establish the UW's first interstellar embassy in Proxima Alpha. I'll work on making sure he or she is accompanied by a decent contingent of Blue Helmet marines. But I can't do anything about that until I get to Oort Station. So, you're on your own for the next few days, Merv. Good luck with that!'

'Gee, thanks,' replied Merv, in even deeper gloom.

'Commodore, the shuttle is ready to depart; please board immediately,' Malik interrupted.

'I gotta go, Merv,' I said. 'Believe in yourself. You can be peacemaker. You can do it. Tarvin out.'

I messaged Malik to archive the memory trace of that conversation with Merv into my urgent to-do mindscape and then, as Greenstreet, Lana's camera bot, was still standing alongside me, I grabbed hold of a good strong strap on his camera harness and told him to jet me over to the shuttle's gangway and into the shuttle. As the shuttle was in the control of its autopilot, I chose to take my place in the vacant pilot's chair and manoeuvred Greenstreet into the co-pilot's seat, to continue my conversation with Lana.

'Lana, you still there?'

'You bet, Boss,' Lana/Greenstreet replied after a very short delay.

'Good,' I said, as the shuttle was pushed out of the dock and the autopilot edged us over towards one of the docking ports on the waystation, 'I wanted to tell you about our further plans, so that you can weave them into your broadcasting plans. I'm planning to leave Pink Ghost at PW1 so the crew can have a 48-hour leave to give its facilities a full test. But I don't want to delay delivery of QIC adapters to Oort Station and my brother's ship that's laid up there, because it would be so useful to have the whole of the Proxima Route in the QIC network. So, Kat and I plan to take my cutter onto Oort Station. Now, you'll need to have Greenstreet at PW1 to observe what goes on during that 48-hour leave on PW1, so I'd like to take Bogey to film our away days at Oort. What do you think.'

'That's OK with me, Boss, but Bogey doesn't have any facsimile circuits and would have to stream his material back to me through the local megacomputer,' Lana complained.

'We could work through the cutter's computer. It's been upgraded with a QIC adapter and is directly linked to Malik through that. However, I've just discovered that Tom Fraser has fitted his care-bot with a QIC-fax circuit and I'm planning to ask him to do the same with Bogey, so he can stream live video back to Proxima-b.

'Way to go!' Lana exclaimed, getting Greenstreet all excited again. 'And if you get Malik to embed my NeuroModem address into Bogey's new QIC chip, I'll be able to dial-in to him and shout at people from lightyears away!'

'Oh, good,' I said, trying to sound glum again. 'A win-win all round, then?'

'Commodore, the away teams have disembarked from the shuttle; please disembark immediately and join Captain de Córdova to go to the one-g gallery,' Malik interrupted, again.

'I'm on my way, Malik. Lana, you'd better get Greenstreet back in contact with the Westwood twins. Meanwhile, as we're still in microgravity, I'll use Greenstreet to jet me out into the dock's reception area.'

'OK, Boss,' Lana responded. 'While you're using my incredibly expensive camera bot as a scooter-tug you might like to know that my tin man recorded the Westwood twins planning to organise a 'how high can you jump on another planet?' competition in the Moon galleries on PW3. Now, I don't want you getting all 'Bossy' about that. It's the sort of thing most space-travelling teenagers ask and should be entertaining and therefore good-TV.'

As I released my grip on Greenstreet to cruise towards the arrivals lounge reception desk at which Kat and Roberto were waiting, I assured Lana that I'd cut the youngsters a healthy amount of slack. Secretly, I thought that if anyone was asking themselves 'how high can I jump on the Moon?' it was going to be Tom Fraser. It would be a great demonstration for any seminar!

Roberto held out his hand as I floated into him, to both steady my arrival and give me a characteristically strong handshake, then all three of us latched onto the travelator that would tow us directly towards the one-g gallery on the outer wall of the adjoining artificial gravity disk.

Kat took pity on a rather lost-looking Greenstreet by telling him, 'The Exec's Midshipman's away team have gone directly to the Moon-gravity galleries'. At which he saluted awkwardly, said, rather enigmatically, 'How little kindness there is in the world today!' and jetted off through the microgravity of the arrival's lounge towards the Moon galleries.

Given that the one-g galleries of these artificial gravity disks seemed usually to feature the same franchises, I was expecting our rendezvous to be the usual Café Claudius at the travelator entrance but was amused to see it was called

Roberto's Café Regina in Roberto de Córdova's waystation. Roberto explained that as a youngster he'd spent many happy hours in a Café Regina back home in México City, explaining further, 'Anyway, Café Claudius doesn't serve tequila!'

We were certainly served tequila while we chatted about Roberto's experiences during the assembly and commissioning of PW3. I ventured back to the counter, seeking some strong black coffee to counteract the alcohol I'd been happily pouring down my throat and was confronted by a display of quesadillas, loaded nachos and tortilla casseroles that reminded me I was late for lunch.

Jim then found us, reporting that all the QIC adaptations had been completed successfully and his away team was on its way back to Pink Ghost. He'd brought the newly QIC-upgraded chef de brigade fax-bot with him, and the conversation turned to instantaneous communications and how it would revolutionise the entire travel network. Jim's arrival had triggered another round of congratulatory tequilas, so I felt the need for more, stronger, coffee. When I returned to the table with coffees for everyone and a hefty supply of churros and sweet dips, Roberto was happily dialling into the QIC network and calling all the waystations back to, and including, Proxima-b, asking about current local events, and the weather where appropriate, and delighting, excitely, in the experience of hearing, here and now, about events taking place up to one and a half lightyears away.

Roberto messaged his deputy, who was introduced as Bernardo O'Reilly, and the rest of his team to come down to the café to experience this 'desarrollo revolucionario de las comunicaciones' and, of course, their arrival at the table triggered further toasts in tequila and the disappearance of most of my churros.

Eventually, Jim and I left Kat at the table, where she was still enthusiastically partying with the Mexican team, and we found a golf cart so we could drive around the one-g deck quickly, inspecting enough of the local environment to allow us to sign off the contract as completed satisfactorily.

Unfortunately, Jim insisted that we must do the same for the Moon-gravity and microgravity galleries, so we went back to Café Regina, where we poured Kat into the back seat of the golf cart and suggested to Roberto and his crew that they find their own way to the departure lounge. Jim called for a shuttle to repatriate Roberto and his team to the Pink Ghost, and we arranged with Malik for some escort travel bots to make sure that Roberto's team all got to that transport. I had another strong coffee shot, and then drove the golf cart up the ramp alongside the travelator to the Moon-gravity gallery. Our golf cart was stopped just short of the entrance to the gallery, and we were required to put on a coverall designed to look like a space suit. This also had a sort of space helmet attached; the supervising AI-bot explained that the outfit was more hazmat suit than space suit. The gallery was kept at normal Earth-atmosphere pressure, of course, like the rest of the waystation's gravity disk. The suit was to protect us from the fine particles of 'real Moon regolith' that hung in the air. We were very glad of that when we finally got into the gallery because we found the Midshipmen's 'I can jump higher than you team' in full flow within a cloud of slowly sedimenting regolith.

Jim and I wandered away from the teenage terrors to inspect a little more of the simulated Moon. I'd not frequented one of these low-gravity galleries before. I was usually most anxious to use the one-g environment facilities, especially their restaurants and bathrooms, that were built over the inner surface of the outermost wall of the rotating disk. Being more used to the one-g gallery, my first impression of the Moon simulation was that its space was constrained. To provide the Moon's gravity of one-sixth that of Earth in a 500-metre diameter cylinder designed to rotate at 2 rpm, the Moon gallery was a cylinder built around the central axis of only 42 metres radius. Moon-gravity was provided on the inner wall of this cylinder, certainly, but the 'distant' horizon in this simulation was less than 150 metres away, rather than the one-g gallery's 750 metres, and the horizon still curved up and over our heads, rather than down and out of sight as it would on the real Moon. Compared with the one-g simulation that we'd just left, I was much more conscious of the fact that we were standing on the inner wall of a big tube, even though I had no perception of its rotation keeping me in my place.

Nevertheless, the replication of the Moon's surface was convincing enough. Even if it did become walls and roof so close to me that it was a poor representation of the 'rolling terrain of lunar surface' recorded by one of the first astronauts to walk on the moon. Ignoring that aspect, the surface nevertheless provoked the awareness described by Buzz Aldrin as 'magnificent desolation' that reflected 'aeons of lifelessness'.

The surface was sculptured into realistic craters of various sizes; with habitats, both surface and submerged, and monuments of various historic Moon landers scattered across it. The realism of the vista was enhanced by being brightly illuminated by a simulation of unfiltered sunlight, Earthlight and starlight. Given the limitations imposed by the engineering essentials, I was content that the designers, and Roberto's team had done a good job here and Jim agreed.

Before we signed off the contract as 'completed' I wanted to get Tom Fraser's opinion, so we used the old-time astronaut's 'hopping walk' to return towards the Midshipmen's away team where Tom was waiting, well separated from their cloud of regolith, for them to tire themselves out.

'What do you think of it, Tom?' I asked as I crunched to a stop next to him. 'Damn good,' he replied. 'Being a computer engineer, I didn't get out onto the surface much in my day, but this gallery certainly fits well with the few memories I've dredged up. What's missing, of course, are the various slopes and little hillsides extending into the distance. But there's a limit to what can be simulated realistically in a structure like this. I think they've done a good job here. It certainly entertains the kids,' said Tom, pointing at the teenagers. 'And it might easily prompt a few people to think about visiting the real place next year.'

'Pretty much what Jim and I were thinking. We've seen enough to sign off on the contract,' I said. 'I've got to be getting back to Pink Ghost to prepare for the next quantum jump. But I wanted to ask you to do me a favour by fitting a QIC-equipped facsimile circuit to one of Lana's camera bots. I want to take it with me in my cutter to Oort Station.'

'Sure, I can manage that,' Tom replied. 'Just have the bot sent to my quarters with the necessary chips. In return,' Tom continued, 'put your Commodore's hat on and bark out a few commands to get these kids out of here and back to their shuttle!'

So, I barked out a few commands to bring the Midshipmen's away team to attention. George Westwood was mid-summersault and at an altitude of about three metres when I did this and his ungainly, flailing, landing 'flight' was well worth filming! He managed a perfectly creditable landing at attention, but what amused everybody was that he landed facing away from me and saluting the 'horizon'!

The exit from the Moon gallery was a wind tunnel designed to strip off any accumulated dust from our 'space suits' before the attendant bots helped us remove them in the entrance hall. Kat was still snoozing in the back of our golf cart. Jim and I decided to lift her out there, in the Moon's one-sixth gravity, and ask one of the attendant bots to run the cart back to its parking spot in the one-g gallery. Then we got Kat sufficiently awake to grasp hold of a travelator strap and the three of us rode the travelator back to the departure lounge and a shuttle back to Pink Ghost, during which Kat, thanks to developing a taste for the freely flowing tequila, went to sleep noisily on my shoulder! In this she joined the snoring chorus of Roberto and his team at the back of the shuttle.

I called my steward, Stewart, to meet us at the shuttle dock and he helped Kat back to our control room and her own stateroom. On the way, I messaged Malik to formalise the sign-off of the contract for PW3 and appointment of its management computer as general manager. I also remembered to ask Malik to confirm that PW3's chef de brigade fax-bot was tuned into Roberto de Córdova's NeuroModem, and arranged for Bogey, together with a bot from computer stores with a standard facsimile circuit and QIC-fax chip, to be sent to Tom Fraser's quarters.

By this time, I had reached my control room and the welcome prospect of a nap in my Nav Couch. I found that Stewart had managed to get Kat into her Nav Couch, so I arranged with Malik for the life support system of her couch to give her a full detox. Climbing into my own couch, I decided to order the same treatment, adding a request for a memory trace stream of the latest quantum maps showing PW3 space as a departure point, and PW2 as a destination, for both of us. Finally, I plugged in a 5.30 p.m. alarm call for us and surrendered to the sweet mercies of the Nav Couch.

We woke at 5.30 p.m. to the intercom chimes warning the crew of our 6 p.m. departure for PW2. 'Is that for us?' asked Kat.

'You betcha,' I said. 'How do you feel?'

'Bright as a button,' she said. 'But I only have memory traces of quantum maps of empty space! How did I get back here?'

'Well, it took two of us to wrestle you away from that tequila bottle,' I said, helpfully.

'Oh no!' said Kat. 'Was there somebody there called Bernardo O'Reilly?' She asked, adding, 'Mexican mother and Irish father?'

'Oh yes. It took three of us to wrestle you away from him!' I teased.

'Aargh, what did I do that I can't remember? Kat cried.

'Don't be stupid, Kat,' I said, consolingly. 'You can't remember because you didn't do anything worth remembering. You snoozed off on the back seat of the golf cart Jim and I used to tour around the waystation, and you'll be pleased to know that all three of us approved of what we saw, and we all signed off on satisfactory completion of the contract and transferred management to the waystation's computer. When we brought everyone back to Pink Ghost, Stewart and I put us both into a full detox by our Nav Couch life support systems.'

'Full detox?' Kat asked.

'Yes, how do you feel now?'

'Full of beans and ready to go!' she said.

'Same here,' I said, so let's make a start on rehearsing our second translocation of the day.'

We both slid back into the cushions of our Nav Couches to make full contact with their NeuroModem connectors and Kat floated 'Ooh look, I've got brand-new memory traces of PW2 and PW3'. 'So have I,' I thought back. 'So you deal with the destination, and I'll manage PW3.'

'Malik, how are we doing for time?' I asked, again.

'It's approaching 5.45 p.m., Commodore.'

'Is the vessel ready to go?'

'All away teams are aboard, Commodore. All section chiefs report all decks in good order for flight.'

'Issue rehearsal and take-off warnings throughout both Starships. After that, count both of us pilots down to 6 p.m.,' I ordered.

During my deep breathing exercises, I started to assemble my mental visualisations of the quantum map wavefunctions we would be using. Then Malik came back online with the launch protocol.

'Will Pilot and co-Pilot please signify their readiness to initiate rehearsal of their translocation of this Starship flotilla from Proxima Waystation 3 to location of Proxima Waystation 2.'

'Pilot is ready,' I said.

'Co-Pilot is ready,' Kat responded.

'Initiate when ready,' Malik concluded.

I took hold of Kat's hand as her latest quantum map memory traces of the space surrounding Proxima Waystation 3 were streamed to my mindscape to put together with the wavefunction of our two Starships at this departure location. I could barely make out any difference between this and the quantum map I had used for our previous translocation.

'Here,' she said, confirming my own thoughts. 'This is the stream of your next 50-kilometre cube of empty space.'

'OK, Malik, we're as happy as we'll ever be with our quantum maps. Stand easy from the rehearsal and issue take-off warnings. Give us a time check and begin the count down,' I ordered.

'It's approaching 5.58 p.m., Commodore.'

Over the top of the intercom's warning chimes I could hear Malik's count down and rather than listen idly to it I adjusted the comms system to the waystation transponder channel; something I should have done before. As I completed that, Malik said, 'Standby Starships. Standby pilots. Cue initiate the translocation in five, four, three, two, one …' I made the superposition on zero, inserted Kat's hex-number nudge into the combined waveform and we decohered! Again, hardly anything changed on the control room view screens, but when I pinged the transponder, the ship's intercom announced, 'This is Proxima Waystation 2.'

'Well, that's a good idea, Boss!' said Kat. 'Interstellar space is boring, and waystations all look the same. So, it's useful confirmation that we've come to the right place!'

Then she made her usual broadcast to the intercom, 'Now hear this. All crew. Now hear this. Stand easy. Executive Officer confirming safe arrival at our destination. For your information we are alongside Proxima Waystation 2, which is approximately two lightyears out from Earth. In due course, this waystation will be responsible for receiving incoming flights from the vicinity of planet Mars. There will be no shore leave. Computer engineering away team and the Exec's away team to muster immediately in the transporter dock. Exec out.'

And while Kat was talking to the crew, I was hailing PW2's Traffic Control. Within seconds PW2's general manager, Captain Riley Guo, messaged me, 'Nǐ hǎo, Commodore. Welcome to Proxima Waystation 2, we would be pleased to receive you over here to celebrate your return!'

'We'll be there, Riley. A couple of away teams are assembling at the moment. We have a group of Midshipmen who are tasked with experiencing your Mars gallery, and my chief engineer, Jim Igwe, is bringing across an away team with upgrades for your computers and fax-bots that provide instantaneous communication across lightyear distances. The sooner you get them, the better, so, I'll terminate this contact and proceed to the shuttle dock. See you soon. Tarvin out.'

'Just to confirm, Commodore,' said Malik. 'QIC communications are testing out perfectly across the 2.5 lightyears to Proxima-b.'

'Good to hear, Malik,' I replied. 'Now, start preparing for our quantum jump to PW1 later tonight and have my cutter serviced and refuelled for a quantum jump to Oort Station tomorrow morning. Also, over the next few hours, make sure Lydia Connah is OK to come with us to Oort Station, that Tom Fraser upgrades the camera bot Bogey with a QIC-enabled fax circuit tuned to Lana Mancot's NeuroModem, and that the cutter crew includes two other QIC-enabled fax-bots, one tuned to Frankie Burton's NeuroModem and the other to Ilsa Blaine's NeuroModem. That's all.'

'Willco, Commodore, Malik out'

Kat and I were feeling so bright and breezy after our detox that we raced each other down the travelators to the shuttle docks on the transport deck. Kat pipped me to the post and was greeted by Jim Igwe, 'Evenin' all!' his big white grin greeted us, continuing with 'Say, Kat, you're moving faster than the last time I saw you!'

'Your Executive Officer does not remember the last time you saw her and recommends that you also forget it!' Kat responded. I left the second and third-in-command in happy conversation and drifted over to Tom Fraser, who was trying to shepherd his performing Midshipmen into their shuttle.

'Permission to speak, Boss?' said George Westwood, standing stiffly to attention in the hatchway, his red hair scattering from the brim of his forage cap in the microgravity of the dock. 'We're going to Mars, Boss!' he finished happily.

I flicked a quick salute in acknowledgement and replied 'Well, enjoy your trip, George, you've certainly got the hair to match the planet!'

'It must be like herding cats,' I said to Tom. 'Whatever they are!'

'Oh, I remember cats, Tarvin,' he replied. 'Lovely creatures, but certainly too independent to be easily herded!' He continued, 'I've just received Malik's reminder about upgrading Bogey,' he said. 'But I've already done it. Your generation of bots have really well-designed CPUs. It's a five-minute job to insert the plug-and-play adapters, and Jim sent the necessary parts with one of the repair bots from his away team, to accompany me back to my quarters.'

'Well, thank you for that, Tom. Enjoy the Mars experience!' I called after Tom as Carla guided him into the shuttle. Realising I was again the last to board the shuttle, I put a little more effort into floating through the hatch and once again settled into the pilot's couch. Even though all the work would be done by the autopilot, this was the best seat in the house to view both the Starships and the waystation. Hanging there in interstellar space they both looked magnificent.

When Kat and I entered the waystation's departure lounge we were messaged by Riley Guo, saying he would meet us at the restaurant closest to the travelator entrance to the one-g gallery. We wondered what to expect, after the experience of Roberto's Café Regina in PW3. Surely not just another Café Claudius?

We were not disappointed. Our rendezvous was called Jing Yaa Tang, which Riley explained was a dim sum house and an offshoot of what he maintained was the most famous, and most authentic, Chinese restaurant on Mars.

Riley was accompanied by his deputy, introduced as Lieutenant Commander Alexandr Barinov. 'Dobryi vecher, Commodore; everybody calls me Xander,' he said, and the table was already decorated with a set of shot glasses containing generous shots of a completely clear liquor.

'Come, join us in a toast to our completed contact!' Riley said, offering shot glasses to Kat and me. 'Wàn shòu wú jiāng!' Riley said, touching the rim of his glass to the bottom of mine. We drained the glasses, as was the custom, and the liquor brought tears to my eye.

'That's a powerful vodka,' Kat wheezed.

'Not vodka,' Xander wheezed in reply, explaining, 'Best vodka only 40% ethanol. This is 60% alcohol! Chinese rocket fuel!'

'It's called Baijiu,' explained Riley. 'The flavour of this one I particularly like. It's distilled from fermented sorghum with other grains, including millet. Now, you must try the all-you-can-eat dim sum buffet, the specialty of this restaurant.'

It's got a flavour? I asked myself as the service bots loaded the dim sum buffet onto the central dinner-table turntable. I turned my attention to that, joining in the chatting around the table when I had recovered the power of speech. Jim Igwe joined us before too long and was accompanied by the recently QIC-upgraded chef de brigade of PW2's fax-bots. The chief, being an AI-bot newly trained in QIC knowledge, was able at Jim's urging, and with Malik's help, to describe to Riley and Xander our surprising experiences with the QIC adaptations during each stage of our journey to PW2. This left Jim free to accept the 'all-you-can-eat' challenge of the regularly replenished dim sum buffet.

Riley and Xander's exciting reception of the news about instantaneous communication across multiple lightyear distances became a clamour when Jim casually remarked that now the chef de brigade was upgraded and PW2's management computer had been fully trained by Malik, the management computer could tune the chief to Riley's NeuroModem, allowing Riley to connect with the facsimile bot from anywhere up to at least 2.5 lightyears away. Xander was especially vociferous, wanting to be included in the network.

When all that was sorted, and the last dim sum had been accounted for, Riley called up a golf cart and took us on a tour of the one-g gallery, pointing out how the national and ethnic interests of the modern-day Mars population had been carefully accommodated. We expressed our total satisfaction with the way the contract had been completed and then stressed that we needed to check out the Mars gallery for ourselves. We left Riley and Xander packing up their admin office to relocate to Pink Ghost and set off up the travelator's ramp towards the Mars gallery.

Mars gravity is about one-third of the gravity on Earth, so this gallery was built on a radius of about 84 metres from the central axis of the artificial gravity disk. Again, the design was outstandingly realistic and included depictions of the craters flooded with water released by the many iceteroids and comets from the Oort Cloud that the terraforming efforts had brought to the planet. Quite a few of which I had hauled into Mars orbit myself when I was training for quantum jumping and learning 'on the job'. I had many happy memories of those distant youthful days, the most important being meeting my wife Lizzie who was also working that contract, but with my attention concentrated elsewhere, I hadn't seen much of the surface of Mars.

Nevertheless, this Mars gallery certainly stirred up my twenty-something memories, so I was impressed. I had expected to find our Midshipmen's away team displaying their athletic abilities again in one-third-g conditions but, though we could hear them, the only activity visible when we entered the gallery was a team of gardening bots sweeping and raking over a mass of boot prints which I supposed to be the remains of the Midshipmen's activities. Then we realised that their noise was coming from a brightly lit habitat in the near distance, just beyond where, from our current point of view, the horizon turned upwards as the far 'wall' of our cylindrical vista. Directing the golf cart towards the habitat, its side soon came into full view, displaying a brightly lit neon sign announcing, 'Jing Yaa Tang Restaurant' and, not surprisingly, within the restaurant we found our ever-hungry teenagers being served Beijing duck with several side dishes, while the catering staff were clearing away evidence of a completely demolished dim sum buffet.

'What do you think of the gallery, Tom? Authentic?' I asked, stealing a few slices of duck.

'Superb,' Tom replied. 'I spent about three Earth-years on Mars, establishing the programming teams of their original robot megafactories. Spent most of my time inside the factory habitats, of course, but I had to travel between factories now and again and that Mars surface outside the restaurant is certainly accurate, though I don't remember any flooded craters!'

'I guess not, the terraforming and really serious haulage of water to Mars would have been the next 'grand project' started after Starship-101 left for the Centauri system and while Starship-102 was being finalised,' I told Tom. 'I spent several years during my twenties earning my spurs as an interplanetary haulage pilot translocating iceteroids and comets to Mars orbit from the Oort Cloud.'

'With your brother?' Tom asked.

'Not exactly, until this Starship-101 job, we've always worked different contracts,' I said. 'But ironically, while I was hauling water ice, Harden was hauling dry ice to Mars from the carbon dioxide harvesters floating in the atmosphere of Venus. This was at the beginning of the work to reheat Mars by injecting greenhouse gases into the atmosphere and cool Venus by taking them out!'

'Don't offer him any more Beijing duck, Tom!' Kat interrupted. 'He's had quite enough food at the one-g branch of this restaurant, to see him through the next quantum jump!'

'There's no better restaurant on Mars, so they say, but this is only my second opportunity to sample its dishes,' said Tom, stuffing the duck slices he had been offering to me into his own mouth.

'How so, Tom?' Kat asked, treating herself to a few of the slices she had just denied me!

'Well, we're talking a lifetime ago, young lady,' Tom replied. 'At that time the Jing Yaa Tang was a single, very expensive, restaurant in what was then the Chinese sector of Mars in the northern plains. Being a lowlife dogsbody programmer at the time, I had no way of affording to eat at an exclusive restaurant like this. But the chance came when the management computer of the robot megafactory in the Chinese sector suffered a major system crash of a sort that my team had just repaired in the American sector's equivalent computer. So, we were sent to assist our Chinese co-explorers. To cut a long story short, after our successful repair of the Chinese computer network we were treated to a magnificent banquet in the one and only, and highly exclusive, Mars Jing Yaa Tang Restaurant.'

'Does this one measure up?' Kat asked, slapping my wrist as I reached out to the plate of sliced duck again.

'Affirmative,' replied Tom. 'And if you guys are not going to finish off that plate of crispy duck, then I know who will!'

'So, do you reckon the new arrivals on Proxima would like us to build a Mars-like Chinese restaurant on Proxima for them?' I asked, as the crispy duck plate was whisked out of reach on the turntable.

'I'm sure they'd be delighted, even ecstatic,' mumbled Tom through a mouthful of duck. 'But why stop at one? You could build one in Proxima Alpha and a couple in their own new settlement.'

'Yes, we'll do that if Riley Guo's got enough spare parts stored on the waystation, but I need to check that with him,' I replied.

'Bah, don't be daft, lad, you're thinking things, objects, pots and pans. Any engineer can build restaurants and equip kitchens,' Tom admonished. 'The soul of a restaurant is in the chef, and the chefs who made this food are all AI-bots. By all means take any spare parts that exist, there's no point them being in a storehouse somewhere. But get that marvellous supercomputer of yours, my new friend Malik, to mirror the CPUs of all the chef-bots on this waystation, making sure he copies all their learned data that they've discovered for themselves by practising their skills in the kitchens, and he could copy those CPUs into any number of facsimile bots to turn them all into experienced chefs. Now, do something useful and spin that turntable for me, will you? There are some leftover sticky spare-ribs over there.'

As I complied with Tom's request and set the turntable gently spinning, I messaged Malik asking if what Tom had just suggested was possible. 'Affirmative, Commodore,' Malik replied. 'The procedure is standard practice for mass production of all highly specialised AI-bots.'

My response was, 'OK then, please do it.'

Jim, who had remained silent until now, listening in to my conversation with Tom Fraser while he, like me, rather morosely watched the last fragments of food being disappeared from the table, said, 'Well, we've left several racks of AI-fax-bots in storage sheds at the Proxima-b SpacePort, so if Malik streams the mirrored data back to the Westwood computer, Westwood could produce all the chef brigades Rocky can use.' After a short pause, he went on, 'Now, as nobody is supplying me with any more food, and everybody else seems to be totally satisfied with the Mars gallery, I guess we should sign it off and get back to Pink Ghost. I need to get my away team refreshed for another batch of computer upgrades on PW1 just after midnight.'

'I agree, we need to get back to our ship,' said Kat. 'The pilots need to prepare for that midnight quantum jump too.' Then she suddenly started to bang the table hard with a large serving spoon, shouting, 'Quieten down and listen, but stay at ease.' When she had silence and the interested attention of the Midshipmen she told them, 'We are returning to Pink Ghost now to prepare for our next quantum jump, to PW1 at midnight tonight. You may finish your meal, but you must be strapped into your acceleration couches onboard Pink Ghost by 11.45 p.m. tonight. The last shuttle will leave this waystation at 10.30 p.m. That is all. Dismissed and stand easy.'

Bidding farewell to Tom Fraser, Kat, Jim and I went back to our golf cart, the gardening bots had just caught up with it, sweeping and raking its wheel tracks away. We sat in the cart for a few minutes in contact with Malik, signing off the contract and formally confirming the appointment of the management computer in overall charge of the waystation.

'Do you know the whereabouts of Riley and Xander, Malik?' I asked.

'They travelled to Pink Ghost a few minutes ago, Commodore. A steward bot is currently taking them to their quarters,' Malik replied.

'Is there a shuttle for us, Malik?' Jim asked.

'Affirmative, Captain Igwe.'

'Malik, please arrange for a shuttle to be waiting for the Exec's away team to use, departing 10.30 p.m. but double check its passenger list, we don't want anyone lost in space!' Kat said as Jim started the cart, heading back towards the travelator's entrance to the gallery. There, we left the cart for a bot to return to its park in the one-g gallery. And we left another set of wheel tracks for the bots to smooth away.

Back in our own control room we both decided to risk another encounter with the microgravity 'shower' facilities so we could change into fresh fatigues. With a couple of microgravity bulbs of coffee in hand we hatched the plans for our midnight getaway.

'Running up and down this Proxima Route is getting so routine it could get dangerous.' I yawned. 'I mean there's so little to distinguish the cubes of interstellar space I'm aiming for, that if I'm going quickly from one to the other, I could use the wrong one for my superposition and go round in circles!'

'Nah,' said Kat. 'We've got that problem, Boss, but the QIC network will solve it for future pilots by providing up-to-date quantum maps. The traffic controllers at each waystation will be able to control flight arrivals and departures in real time and to the second as well as providing precise arrival mapping to the millimetre. Navigator co-pilots will revel in it. Our problem is that all the way on the route back to Ort Station the maps we have of our destinations we know to be are at least two weeks old, and we don't know what the waystation looks like. We know what it should look like, but if the construction teams had a problem there could be pieces scattered through my destination cube.

'Thankfully, that's not happened so far.' I yawned again. 'What do we know about PW1?'

'Nothing,' she replied. 'That's the oldest quantum map of the new waystations. Around three weeks old. We're back in the realms of what's the probability of brown dwarfs passing through that cube of interstellar space at midnight tonight?'

'We really need the QIC network to make regular travel on the Proxima Route a commercial proposition, don't we?' I yawned again.

'Commercial travel would also require that the pilot stays awake!' Kat commented. 'Looks like you should take a nap, Boss.'

I really was having difficulty keeping my eyes open, so I turned to Malik. 'So, Malik, am I right that you have the most up-to-date quantum maps of PW2 and PW1?'

'Affirmative, Commodore.'

'And, Kat, judging by our recent jumps, we're not going to need more than a few minutes rehearsal, are we?'

'Nah, interstellar space is so boring!'

'OK, then here's what we'll do. We'll both take a nap, setting our Nav Couches to wake us at 11.45 p.m. Malik, you will issue the appropriately timed warnings to the crew for a midnight quantum jump to PW1, and you will stream the most up-to-date quantum maps of PW2 and PW1 to the two of us just before we awaken. Is that OK with you, Kat?'

'Sure is.' Kat yawned. 'You've got me at it now!'

'Willco, Commodore. Malik out.'

I emerged from the cushions of my Nav Couch to the sound of the intercom's warning chimes of an imminent quantum jump combined with an overlay of Malik reporting 'All away teams are aboard, Commodore. All section chiefs report decks in good order for flight.'

'Thanks, Malik. Kat, are you with me?'

'Yeah, bright and breezy, Boss. Just fixing the exclusion zone in the destination cube,' Kat replied.

I forced my head back against the headrest to make full contact with the NeuroModem connectors and then reached over for Kat's hand. From then we just followed the procedure we had used so many times before. Warn the crew; take some deep breaths; visualise my Starships in the cube of space they occupied now; receive Kat's visualisation of our destination cube of space; merge the two waveforms into one superposition; then, when all was neat and tidy exactly at midnight, slide in the hexadecimal nudge.

And hope for the best!

Day 12

The ship's intercom rebroadcast the waystation's ID announcement, 'This is Proxima Waystation 1.' Then, Kat's voice came through the intercom, 'Now hear this. All crew. Now hear this. You can breathe now! Stand easy. Executive Officer confirming safe arrival at our destination. For your information we are alongside Proxima Waystation 1, which is approximately one lightyear out from Earth. In due course, this waystation will be responsible for receiving all incoming flights for the Proxima-Centauri route and sending them on their way towards Proxima-b Home Station. Our Starships will lay alongside PW1 for the whole crew to have a 48-hour furlough at this waystation. Commencing 0800 today, when Watch Team One goes off-duty, a regular shuttle service to and from PW1 will be available. Computer engineering away team to muster immediately in the transporter dock to deal with QIC adaptations on PW1. Exec out.'

I was hailing PW1's Traffic Control computer while Kat was conducting her business with the crew, but I had just made contact and announced our identity when the waystation's general manager, Angélique Gérard, came on the line, 'Commodore Clason, welcome to Proxima Waystation One,' she said. 'Yours is a dramatically late arrival!'

'Yes, sorry about that,' I replied. 'Obviously, we have no way of warning you with conventional radio, but we have an adaptation for your computers that does allow instantaneous communication over lightyear distances, and I've been keen to bring the equipment to the Proxima Route's waystations as quickly as possible. PW1 is the third waystation we have visited in the past twelve hours!'

'Are you serious, Boss?' she responded, incredulous. 'Faster than light messaging? How is that even possible?'

'Quantum translocation,' I replied, further explaining, 'My team of comms and computer engineers have been able to devise a protocol and a transmitter/receiver that puts the photons of a radio message into a superposition at the transmitter and decoheres it at the receiver. And a chip designer on Proxima-b has combined all that into a plug-and-play device for megacomputers and a plug-in chip for facsimile bots. We're calling them QIC devices, which is an acronym for quantum instantaneous communications.'

'If I may interrupt here,' Malik messaged both of us. 'Our first tests of the Proxima QIC network are showing that instantaneous communication is definitely maintained across the three and a half lightyears from our present location to Proxima-b.'

'That's truly amazing!' said Angélique, continuing, 'Well, all our facilities are completed, and you are welcome to use them, of course, but we are in night mode at the current time with only a few of our entertainment services active. Naturally, my deputy, Chris Adams, could open them up for you if you require immediate access'.

'No, we don't need you to open up tonight,' I answered. 'My chief engineer, Jim Igwe, will come over to you immediately with an away team of computer engineers to carry out the QIC adaptations to your computers and fax-bots. That's all we need until later this morning. This ship will layover here to allow the whole crew a 48-hour furlough, while Kat and I take my cutter onto Oort Station to deliver QIC adapters to them. The ability to get up-to-the-minute data for quantum maps of destinations makes for very happy quantum translocation pilots! My plans are to get a few hours' sleep right now before yet another quantum jump.'

'Understood, I've had a hard day, too, so I feel much the same!' Angélique responded. 'Why don't we leave Chris Adams to work with Captain Igwe's crew and all meet up, say at 8 a.m., for breakfast over here?'

'I'll second that!' Kat contributed. 'Hi Angelique, nice to speak to you again! We've got a lot of gossip to share! Where should we meet? Do you have a decent café near the one-g entrance to the travellator?'

'Mais oui bien sur, ma cherie. We have called it 'La Boulangerie de Proxima-Centauri'. It serves the best patisserie and coffee outside Paris!' Angélique replied.

'Wonderful,' said Kat. 'You should book a table in a secluded corner because the crew's furlough starts at 08.00 hours and Watch Team One will be invading your waystation in their usual unruly manner as soon as they come off-duty.'

'Qu'à cela ne tienne! Je suis la propriétaire! I have a private dining room on the first floor, overlooking the rest of my domain, so we can observe the savage Vikings of your crew putting our waystation to the test!'

'Perfect,' said Kat. 'But it's only the Boss who's a savage Viking, the rest of the crew are pretty normal.'

'Thanks for that insight into my character, Kat. I'll remind you that your husband is as much savage Viking as I am, but before we come to blows about it maybe we should thank Angélique for her kind invitation to breakfast and bring this discussion to an end. Thanks, Angélique, Kat and I will see you at 8 a.m., and maybe we could include Jim and Chris in that meeting? Au revoir. Clason out.'

'Will do. À bientôt, Boss. Gérard out.'

I checked with Malik that my cutter and passengers would be available for a quantum jump to Oort Station no later than 9.30 a.m. and asked that he stream the best possible quantum maps of both destination and origin into my dreams. I then surrendered to my Nav Couch to get a few more hours sleep.

Malik woke me just before 7 a.m. with an urgent message from Tom Fraser who was asking to join my cutter expedition to Oort Station so he can get settled in there.

'I'm not that keen to settle in Oort Station,' he explained when I messaged him. 'But Carla is picking up a lot of chatter on the Gort network from Pink Ghost's engineering bots about preparations being made for moving Starship-101 into a StarCorp graving dock for renovation when you take the Starships to Oort. I'm just wondering if I can get ahead of the game by going to Oort to introduce myself as an interested party to whoever is organising the 'Interstellar Museum' or whatever they plan to call it.'

'OK, that sounds perfectly sensible to me,' I said. 'Malik, what do you know about this?'

'Yes, while we are laid over at PW1, the engineering teams that coupled the two Starships together are being tasked with preparing for their separation immediately on arrival at Oort Station,' Malik reported. 'This involves starting to power up Starship-101 in the next hour or so, to allow the ship's own maintenance teams to get on with their work. There is no reason why Mr Fraser should not accompany you to Oort Station today, but my strategic management evaluation of alternative scenarios indicates that this is not the most effective course of action. I am assuming, of course, that Mr Fraser's objectives are to enhance his standing with the authorities with respect to the development of policies and plans for the disposition of Starship-101.'

'Oo-oh-Kay,' I said slowly. 'What do you suggest, Malik, to improve Tom's influence?'

'I have identified a course of action that would give Mr Fraser commanding influence in deciding the disposition of Starship-101,' said Malik.

'I'm liking the sound of this, Malik old fruit. Tell me more!' said Tom.

'My suggestion is based on the known fact that Tom Fraser is the last surviving member of the original crew of Starship-101, and the consequent logic in the assumption that command of that Starship now rests with him. I suggest that he stays here with his ship while our engineers bring it out of its present dormant state, and when Starship-101 is habitable he could transfer his residence to his command and direct the repair and maintenance programmes prior to its delivery to StarCorp.'

'Yes!' whooped Tom. 'And everyone calls me Captain Fraser!'

'Oh, I wouldn't settle for that rank, Tom,' I said. 'That ship's big enough to be counted as a flotilla, which would be commanded by a Commodore at least! First thing you should do when you move into the captain's cabin aboard Starship-101, is tell the Flight computer to get the tailoring team to rustle up a full set of uniform kit for you with Commodore ranking badges applicable to the year Starship-101 left the Solar System. I'd stick at Commodore, though; going straight to Admiral would be a touch ostentatious! Then, wear your uniform whenever you deal with StarCorp or Oort Station.'

'May I add the reminder,' Malik said. 'That both the Flight computer aboard Starship-101, and the care-bot Carla, have already been equipped with QIC modifications. Consequently, Commodore Fraser will be able to deal directly with StarCorp and Oort Station in real time as soon as Commodore Clason's team equip the computers at Oort Station with QIC adapters.'

'Right,' said Tom. 'That's what we'll do. I really appreciate this conversation, Tarvin, and apologise for disturbing you so early in the morning. One final request; could I have a few more facsimile circuits and QIC chips, just about five or six will do? I fancy having a few more of 101's AI-bots QIC-enabled. I think when he emerges from his lair, Commodore Fraser should be accompanied by a few AI-bot experts in engineering, finance, and the law; not to mention a security detail.'

'Sure, Tom. Malik, please fulfil Tom's request. Anything else?'

'Nah, I'll be quite happy now, playing with my own Starship! Fraser out.'

'I like the way that discussion turned out,' said Kat. 'So I didn't interrupt but we should be moving towards travelling over to Proxima Waystation 1 and our breakfast meeting with Angélique. You've just got time for a shave and shower.'

I had been hoping to take a shuttle to PW1 early enough to enjoy a shower in a bathroom in the one-g gallery, but I had to make do with a quick all over wash in the microgravity bathroom of my own quarters aboard Pink Ghost. Not a truly enjoyable shower and shave, but I did at least manage to turn up in the departure lounge of PW1 on time and clean and tidy, and ahead of the expected crowd of recently released from duty Watch Team One crew members.

Kat and I followed the usual route using the travelator in the departure lounge to the exchange point at the entrance to the artificial gravity ring, where we switched to the travelator that would take us down to the one-g gallery. Opposite the entrance to which the descent travelator delivered us, we saw the usual café/restaurant. This one proudly displayed its identity as 'La Boulangerie de Proxima-Centauri' and was styled as a vintage Parisienne boulangerie advertising bread, cakes, coffee, but also offered 'American style' breakfast pancakes and a full brunch menu. Just like everywhere else in the Solar System. And just my style!

We walked straight past the 'staff only' notices at the bottom of the stairs at the rear of the ground floor restaurant and they led us into a large sumptuously furnished bar-lounge and dining room on the first floor. The dining tables were set out in front of an enormous display window situated at the front of the building and overlooking the entire quadrant of the artificial gravity disk.

The view from this restaurant site was much more densely filled with buildings than we had so far seen in the other artificial gravity disks we had visited on this voyage. Any number of exclusive shops offering all manner of duty-free branded luxuries; restaurants, cafés, and bars from all corners of the Solar System; together with an astonishing variety of offered entertainments and activities, from fitness and health clubs, through meditation rooms, to dancing girls and male strippers. All the Solar System's peccadilloes seemed to be represented beneath us. And all announcing their wares with brightly lit advertising signs, in a vista that continued into the distance where the wall of the disk curved upwards to give us a view from above of the rest of this little town built to remind star-travellers of their homes before they venture further into deep space. Our first view was such an astonishingly captivating sight that we just hadn't noticed the lady who was sitting at a large table to one side of this impressive window.

'Good morning! Kat, Tarvin. Why don't you join me over here for coffee?' Angélique's voice broke into our reverie as she poured steaming coffee from her cafetière into a couple of cups.

'Sit, sit,' she said. 'Here are menus for you, just choose what you want for your p'tit dej and the serving bots will bring it immediately, all freshly baked!'

We gratefully accepted the proffered coffees; and, especially in my case, the menu, from which I set about ordering a selection of croissants, tartines, and brioche with fruit spreads, honey, fruit yoghurt and apple juice. I thought it was a thoughtfully healthy choice, but I noticed that Kat was eyeing my activity disapprovingly and she hissed at me, 'This is breakfast, Boss, are you sure you will eat all this now? We'll be quantum jumping to Oort Station in an hour or so and you'll be able to resume breakfast eating by about 9.35 a.m.!'

Fortunately, Angélique rescued me by telling Kat, 'Calm yourself, cherie. We can provide a breakfast 'doggy box' that you can use to take leftovers back to your ship. They will remain fresher than anything you could find at Oort Station!'

This helpful comment reminded me that I could not recall ordering my steward to report to my cutter together with a suitable selection of fresh uniform dress for both Kat and me, so I messaged Malik to arrange this and as I was doing so, a squadron of serving bots delivered our orders to the table.

'Bon appétit, enjoy,' Angélique said. 'I'm expecting Chris Adams and Jim Igwe to join us shortly, but don't stand on ceremony.' I didn't.

After a few mouthfuls, I commented, 'We've seen all the waystations on our journey down here, and your PW1 township here,' I waved my hand towards the picture-window, 'is certainly the most extensive.'

'Well, I have installed several of these waystations at various places in the Solar System,' Angélique replied. 'And I found early in my career that the more facilities I put into a waystation the more reasons my customers had to return to the waystation to experience those services they missed on their first visit. Of course, you're seeing it in its 'expectant state' now. We don't have customers.'

'Yes, you do!' Kat contradicted, pointing her croissant towards the bottom of the window, where an expanding crowd of people wearing ship's fatigues were streaming out of the travelator and milling around in front of the restaurant. 'Here comes the first shuttle load of Watch Team One!'

'Formidable! Wonderful!' Angélique responded, straining to see over the edge of the table. 'At last we see our waystation coming to life!'

'Oh, hell, you're right, there! We rode the travelator with them, they're a real lively bunch!' This was a deep and resonating voice with a lilting American accent coming from a bald-headed man dressed in black shirt and black jeans, who was walking towards our table from the stairs, just ahead of Jim Igwe.

'Ah, bienvenue mon cher,' Angélique exclaimed, rising from her chair to give a welcoming kiss to the newcomer. Turning to me, she said, 'Boss, this is Chris Adams, my deputy. I don't think you've met.' Chris and I exchanged pleasantries, and then I introduced Jim to Angélique, who asked, 'Have you finished adapting our computers, mon cher?'

Chris Adams interrupted Jim's reply with an enthusiastic, 'Oh yes, Angel, have our computers been adapted! I've been talking to an old friend of mine, Bernardo O'Reilly. You remember him? He's on Proxima Waystation 2. That's a lightyear away! And we were emailing together in real time!'

'E-mail?' I queried looking at Jim.

'Yes, indeed, Boss,' Jim replied. 'Part of our standard QIC adaptation of the waystation's traffic control computer, starting with Proxima Home Station, has been a software upgrade that enables the TC unit to be a server in an e-mail coms network that we're calling StarshipNet. When you get the QIC devices to Oort Station the computer bots you're taking with you will connect it through to the existing Solar System network, SolNet, and when that's completed, anyone with a SolNet-compliant broadband service on Earth will be able to exchange e-mails with anyone on Proxima b.'

Jim leaned over me and stole a couple of pieces of toasted baguette from one of my, admittedly numerous, plates. I looked aggrieved but let the incident pass and offered him the menu.

'But surely that doesn't mean those e-mails would travel across the Solar System instantaneously, does it?' Angélique asked.

'Certainly not,' Jim replied, spreading some of my honey on his toasted baguette. 'At least, not until Interstellar Haulage has sold the service providers one of our unique QIC upgrade devices for each of their servers in the SolNet!' Jim wolfed down his toast before continuing, 'I don't think that businesses that rely on communication through SolNet will be willing to continue using conventionally broadcast radio comms and the delays imposed by the speed of light. Radio signals sent from Earth to Mars take up to 20 minutes to reach the receiver, you can't have a sensible conversation, by audio or e-mail when it takes 40 minutes to receive a reply to your question. It depends on the relative positions of the planets, of course.'

He paused again while the serving bots delivered his own breakfast order and then continued, 'There's a lot of empty space out there, and the radio flight time delays increase the further your business is located from Earth. Well over an hour's round-trip delay between Earth and Jupiter, two hour's Earth to Saturn, and anything up to around 15 hours for the round-trip Earth to and from Oort Station. There are enormous server farms dedicated to electronic communication within their communities right across the Solar System, and they are all subject to the irritation caused by communication between communities depending on the speed of light. Make no mistake, Boss, there's going to be a vast market for a QIC plug-and-play chip that offers instantaneous communication irrespective of distance!'

The table remained silent as we all absorbed the significance of this little speech. Everybody around the table had enough first-hand experience of travelling and communicating within and across the Solar System to appreciate the truth of what my chief engineer had said. The silent spell of this light-bulb moment was broken by Chris Adams pointing out, to nobody in particular, 'Hey, that means that this QIC device of yours could pay for the whole of this Proxima-Centauri trip.'

'Yeah, and some!' Jim replied, reaching for his coffee and spluttering a few crumbs. 'I discussed all this with the people back on Proxima-b who produced the devices we have now.'

'Frankie Burton, Lana Mancot and Danny Khan!' I stated.

'That's right, but don't forget Danny's old man Salman,' Jim replied. 'It was Salman who first brought the full sales potential to attention. The rest of us were stuck in the rut of thinking about the QIC devices as easing communication over interstellar distances. Salman's father was Starship-101's original comms chief and used to complain about the delays in message transmission across the Solar System before the ship set off, and then the mounting difficulties in meaningful communication as the ship moved further and further away from Earth. That's why I delivered the rest of our stock of electronics manufacturing gear from Danny to your cutter on the day before we left Proxima-b. I've been maintaining our discussions as we've been travelling from waystation to waystation. As the prototype QICs have proved so successful I've sent a QIC-enabled facsimile bot tuned to Danny Khan's NeuroModem to join the passengers on your cutter. With the idea that the bot could initiate discussions from Oort Station for supply of machines to ramp up production of QIC devices on Proxima-b. Hope you don't mind, Boss, but maybe your brother could transport the machines when he leaves for Proxima-b?'

'Sure, sounds like a good idea to me,' I said. 'And it reminds me that we're planning to jump to Oort Station after breakfast! Malik, how are we doing for time?'

'It's 8.55 a.m., Commodore,' Malik reported, surprising Kat and me.

'We'll never get back to Pink Ghost in time for a 9.30 jump, it could take 20 minutes to launch the cutter,' Kat said.

'Malik, are the passengers assembling on the cutter?' I asked.

'Affirmative, Commodore. All passengers have embarked on your cutter and are safely accommodated, ready for launch.'

'OK. Here's what we'll do,' I replied. 'Malik, you broadcast an apology to the passengers saying that Kat and I have been delayed aboard PW1 so, the Commodore's Cutter will be launched by the autopilot to transit to PW1 to pick us up. Then execute that manoeuvre immediately, subject to the requirements of PW1's Traffic Control. When we have boarded, I will need the autopilot to move the cutter away from the Starships and the waystation by 50 kilometres. Again, clear those movements with traffic control. Understood?'

'Understood, willco, Commodore,' said Malik, as Kat interjected 'And recalculate the quantum map of the departure location to take into account our 50-klik stand-off position.'

'Willco, Captain Clason. Malik out.'

'Well, Angélique,' I said, apologetically, 'I've thoroughly enjoyed breakfast, but greatly regret we must leave so abruptly. I was hoping for a guided tour of the waystation, before issuing my 'contract fulfilled' approval certificate, but I guess that will have to be done by Jim, who will be left in command while Kat and I are at Oort Station.'

'Pas de problème, mon cher!' Angélique responded. 'I can give you a guided tour of our waystation in the next thirty seconds, sitting here at the table. Look through the window in front of you and you see the home quadrant. Then, look at the walls of this lounge. They are all view screens, showing live images of the other three quadrants of the disk.'

And it was so! I had barely noticed the walls of the lounge since we first entered, thinking they were merely static illustrations. But now, as my crew continued to stream into the one-g gallery, increasing numbers of them had chosen to move into the illustrated quadrants and the images had come to life, showing their movements as they found the ubiquitous golf carts and cycles provided for transport across the surface of the disk.

'So,' Angélique explained, 'through the window you see our hometown quadrant, and it is *our* hometown. This restaurant is my personal franchise and just across the street is Larrabee's Cajun Restaurant, which belongs to Chris.'

'And where you can find the best jambalaya, crawfish pie and filé gumbo for a couple of lightyears, hallelujah!' Chris intoned, laughing.

'So, you see,' Angélique persisted, 'the design of our hometown is very reminiscent of Old New Orleans, thanks to Chris.'

'Well, be honest, Angel,' Chris interrupted. 'It's a sort of Hollywood-style memory of old 'Nouvelle-Orléans', a pastiche, showbiz razzmatazz. The real place certainly doesn't look like this now, and probably never looked much like it in the old days!'

'Oh, really? But it looks so authentic!' said Kat. 'Were you born in New Orleans?'

'No Ma'am. Born and bred in California!' Chris replied.

'Mais oui, but he has the soul of a Frenchman!' Angélique responded. 'And that's what I love about him!'

'Well, to be truthful, Angel, I have Larrabee as a middle name,' said Chris. 'My mother's fancy way of commemorating a distant ancestor who is supposed to have journeyed from France's Loire département to the American west in the 19th century. It's said he established a settlement on the Eel River in Humboldt County, California, where my family still lives. Now, while all that is true, my ability to design what looks like an authentic New Orleans owes more to the many years I spent in showbiz production studios around the world designing colonial style sets for video dramas than to some distant, and possibly apocryphal ancestor.'

'You see?' said Angélique, rolling her eyes upward. 'So, so very romantic! But your ability to create sceneries that the viewers of those video dramas were convinced were authentic is exactly why I asked you to help me make my waystation creations do the same for the waystation's customers. It's the soul of marketing, mon chéri.'

'True, Angel. But don't forget that along the way we found Christopher Coles and Maurice James who are responsible for the 'sleazier' facilities of our hometowns, though they insist that they are all done in the best possible taste!' Chris concluded.

'It's that mix of high-end luxury and slightly sleazy excitement that makes this hometown so inviting,' said Kat. 'But tell us about these view screens. I can see members of our crew moving on all of them now.'

Angélique waved her hand vaguely towards the screen on our right-hand wall, saying, 'They're all high-resolution Starship control room quality digital glass on the walls. Their images being streamed from cameras mounted on the central spindle of our rotating disk, so you see each quadrant of the disk's casing floor from above. On your right is the quadrant that's turning up and above you when you look out of the window, the horizon of the window's view if you like. This features lots of sports facilities; athletics tracks, football, rugby and hockey fields, and there's a residential clubhouse with a swimming pool, squash courts, badminton, and tennis courts.

'On the wall behind you, alongside the staircase, is the next quadrant which is above and behind us. That's our 'wild nature' simulation, with an extravagant amount of water because water in one-g is what you dream about when you work in microgravity. Our water is channelled into a fast-flowing river between 'rock walls', that you can climb, under expert supervision of course. The river has a white-water section for kayakers, who can try a pirogue in the white-water for a unique adventure, and then the water flows over a waterfall into a lake, landscaped as a bayou, for wild swimming. And, as you can see, the entire quadrant's been landscaped to be a trekker's paradise.

'Then, finally completing the circle, and shown on the left-hand wall, is the quadrant that transitions from wild nature, through rural and into urban and ultimately merges into our hometown just out of sight beneath and behind us. Most of our longer-term accommodation is in this final quadrant; five-star hotels near the hometown, ranging into 'English country village', prairie and outback townships and riverside log-cabin settlements.'

'Wow,' I said appreciatively, 'you've certainly sold it to me! When can I book?'

'Any time you like, Boss,' said Chris. 'But don't be surprised by Angel's little speech. We've been working on our advertising copy for the past couple of days and you've just been introduced to it!'

'Well, we're going to need a lot more advertising like that to attract visitor traffic to the Proxima Route,' I said. 'Now that we have a QIC network established across the entire route you could work together with the other waystation managers to develop an advertising campaign.' I quickly added the afterthought that 'Lana Mancot is our broadcasting wizard making endless vids about Proxima Alpha specifically to promote interest in mankind's first interstellar adventure. You should coordinate your advertising with her. She's still on Proxima-b but she sent a camera bot called Greenstreet with us on this trip, accompanying a couple of teenagers we recruited on Proxima. Greenstreet is a QIC-equipped fax-bot tuned to Lana's NeuroModem, so I reckon he's the best way of bringing Lana into your discussions.'

'And you don't need to go far to speak to the managers of two of our waystations either,' added Kat. 'Roberto de Córdova and Bernardo O'Reilly, who built PW3, the Moon simulation, and Riley Guo and Xander Barinov, who managed the Mars simulation, PW2 are all currently quartered on our Starship. Only Rick and Ilsa Raines have stayed aboard PW4 because they are building a replica of the Proxima Alpha settlement there, to prepare visitors for the real thing.'

'Emma Halton's stayed on PW4 as well,' said Jim. 'She's establishing some farming units on the waystation.'

'That's what we need, too,' Chris stated. 'We need some good old Louisiana aquaculture on this waystation! Crawfish and catfish at least. We've got a river and a bayou; we should be farming them.'

'I'll tell you what else we need, and soon,' Jim contributed. 'We need to get QIC devices into Neptune waystation. It's the feeder hub for holiday flights to Kuiper waystation. We need to get our advertising of the Proxima Route into those two to spread the word around the Solar System.'

'Well, we haven't got as far as Oort Station, yet!' I said, addressing Jim in particular. 'So, we'll have to leave further development of all these ideas in your hands, Captain Igwe. Kat and I need to be elsewhere.'

'Affirmative, Commodore,' Malik interrupted. 'Your cutter is approaching PW1's docking bay. You will be able to go aboard in approximately ten minutes. I am clearing the cutter's departure for a location 50 kilometres distant with PW1's Traffic Control. Conflicting traffic is being held pending your departure.'

Malik's intervention caused our relaxed breakfast chat to become transformed into a little whirlwind of 'goodbye' and 'see you soon' in both

English and French, during which I took the time to formally put on record, with Malik, the temporary transfer of my command of Pink Ghost to Captain Jim Igwe. Then Kat and I, running in the luxury of one-g while we could, made a rapid departure from the restaurant and headed towards the travellator. As soon as the travellator delivered us to the microgravity of the departure lounge, we located a couple of high-speed self-guided microgravity scooters to take us swiftly through the lounge to our cutter's airlock.

Inside my cutter I lost no time in diving into my Nav Couch, forcing my head deep into the headrest cushion to complete the circuit with its NeuroModem connectors and then asked Malik to stream me the most up-to-date quantum maps of our current location.

While I was doing that, Kat was saying a quick 'hello' to the passengers, explaining our late arrival and making sure they were prepared for a quantum jump in just a few minutes time. Then she took her place in her Nav Couch beside me, and we started out on our well-trodden path to somewhere else, hopefully in the same reality in which we were currently quite comfortable.

Malik streamed to me the quantum map of our departure location, explaining 'Your cutter has not yet reached the coordinates shown here, Commodore. The autopilot estimates arrival at its target in seven minutes.'

'Understood, Malik. That will give us enough time to assess both quantum maps. You could issue now the usual warnings throughout the ship for an imminent quantum jump in, say, ten minutes time.'

'Willco, Commodore.' As the cutter's intercom warning chimes sprang to life with an overlay of Malik's imminent quantum jump warning, I reached our beside me for Kat's hand and thought towards her 'Kat, are you with me?'.

'Always, Boss. Always,' was her response. 'Malik's departure cube map looks more congested than usual, featuring two enormous vessels and a handful of shuttles weaving back and forth between them. Though, with all that detail we can certainly work with it. But from our current viewpoint that ungainly 20-kilometre-long object you've been hauling around this neck of the woods makes me uneasy about the unknown congestion at Oort Station.'

'Yeah, I know what you mean! Not knowing what might have turned up there in the past few weeks is more than worrying. So, what can you do to deliver my cutter safely?'

'Right, check this out,' she said as she passed me her memory trace of the destination map she was calculating, explaining, 'I'm working to the worst-case

363

scenario, assuming the 50-kilometre cube centred on Oort Station is full of newly arrived ships. So, instead, I've calculated the 200-kilometre cube and placed our aim point as far away from the station's docking ports as possible.'

'Looks OK,' I said, appreciatively. 'Can we block off most of that destination cube with exclusion zones to help me to concentrate?'

'Sure, I'll do that,' she said, so I turned to Malik and asked, 'Are you happy with all that, Malik?'

'Affirmative, Commodore. We are stationary at our designated departure coordinates,' was the response, so I took a few deep breaths, gave Malik the order to warn the ship and traffic control and announced, 'Pilot ready for translocation.'

While I visualised my cutter in the cube of space we occupied now, Kat announced, 'Co-pilot ready for translocation.' And then passed me her recently corrected visualisation of our destination cube of space. With the cutter intercom's warning chimes my background music, I merged the two waveforms representing the quantum maps of departure and destination locations into one superposition. When I was satisfied that this was in good shape, I slipped in Kat's hexadecimal nudge, which was just an extra piece of data describing some aspect of the detail of the precise location for which we were aiming. And, as far as I was concerned it was job done. We decohered there and then.

The next thing I heard was the response to our ping of the waystation's ID transponder, which was the welcome and relaxing announcement 'This is Oort Station, please report to traffic control.' So, I followed that request while Kat took to the cutter's intercom to confirm our safe arrival at our intended destination to our passengers.

'Oort Station Traffic Control, this is Commodore Tarvin Clason of Interstellar Haulage requesting permission to approach. Clason out.'

'Welcome back to Oort Station, Commodore. Please hold your present position, we have a range of conflicting traffic to monitor.'

Certainly, my control room view screens showed this to be a very congested location, and although we had dropped back into normal space exactly where we had planned, around 100 kilometres from the waystation itself, we had actually emerged alongside a full-sized Starship.

'We are alongside Commodore Harden Clason's flotilla, Flagship-2, Commodore,' Malik announced. 'I am exchanging data with the resident ship's computer, Sasha. Sasha reports that Commodore Harden Clason is ashore in the company offices on the waystation at this time, but he is being pinged.'

'Company offices?' queried Kat. 'Since when did we have company offices on Oort Station?' Her answer came almost immediately. 'What's this, Bruv? I was expecting you to bring a couple of Starships back here, all I see is a cutter! Where did you lose the rest, you dork?' Which was followed by, 'Hello wife, are you still working with this dork of a brother of mine?'

'Oh, you sentimental old thing, husband, how nice of you to call!' Kat responded. 'I'm busy at the moment. Polishing my nails. Can you call back later?'

'Nah, I'll tell you now, just keep polishing,' Harden responded. 'If you look past my flagship, you'll see that Oort Station has had an extra artificial gravity ring added to it since you last saw it. Just after you left to create the Proxima Route, StarCorp delivered and installed a new disk dedicated to providing and supporting all the commercial services that might be needed by the new companies, like us, that will be involved in developing the interstellar traffic the station is being built to service.'

'So,' Harden continued, 'Lizzie and I convened a board meeting of Interstellar Haulage and unanimously decided to lease one of the new office buildings for Interstellar Haulage. As well as a collection of office units, our building also has three private apartments on upper floors, one for you and me, Kat, and one for Lizzie and Tarvin, plus a third intended, at the moment, for any guests that turn up, though I hope we can persuade Grandpa to move into it. Providing, of course, we can find out where the hell he's gone to ground this time. Anyway, as you two were out of touch on the way to Proxima-Centauri, we went ahead on the assumption you'd place your absentee votes with us!

'It's a very favourable lease, because they're keen to get the place populated as quickly as possible. It includes a Starship-quality megacomputer, which Lizzie's christened 'Klaus' after some terribly distant ancestor of the Clason family who established iron foundries and shipbuilding yards long, long ago in Sweden. The lease also includes docking facilities exclusive to Interstellar Haulage, as well as a couple of our own small shuttles for taxiing people and materials between ships around and about Oort Station. Lizzie and I are working in the office now; Lizzie's interviewing new office staff and I'm glad-handing some of the people who might want to join us on my trip to Proxima-Centauri.'

Why don't you join us? Sasha could give your cutter's autopilot a flight plan to go directly to the Interstellar Haulage dock.'

'You'll have to park alongside my own cutter,' Harden finished. 'If you think you can manage that without scratching my paintwork! You came in pretty close to my flagship!'

'Well, dearest, as the one who had to create a destination quantum map using data that was close to being a month old,' Kat responded. 'I'd like to know why you parked your bloody Starship in the only corner of space around here that used to be safe for anyone coming in blind!'

'OK, calm down lovebirds,' I said. 'Before the excitement of your reunion turns nasty let me point out that this 'coming in blind pretty close to my flagship' business is exactly why we're here and why we've left Starship-101 back at Proxima Waystation 1.'

'Point is, Bruv,' I went on, 'over the past few weeks a team made up of my computer and communications chief engineers, together with a couple of the Proxima settlers who are brilliant chip designers, have come up with a computer plug-and-play device that allows instantaneous communication across, at the most recent tests of a few minutes ago, four and a half lightyears! And we've brought a supply of prototypes of these devices to be fitted to computers around here.'

'Have you been drinking, Tarvin?' asked Harden. 'Are you talking faster than light radio?'

'Yes,' Kat and I said at the same time.

Kat continued, still showing irritation, 'Just like faster than light quantum translocation of entire Starships!'

'Yeah, and the two processes work much the same way. The radio transmitter has its own quantum map wavefunction together with wavefunctions of the receivers with which it can communicate. Then the transmitter embeds the radio message you want to send in its own wavefunction, entangles that into a superposition of states with the receiver's quantum map and finally gives it a nudge that favours decoherence of the superposition in the target receiver. We've been testing it across the entire length of the Proxima Route as part of the commissioning of each waystation and it's operated perfectly so far, enabling us to establish a network of all forms of electronic comms from here to Proxima-Centauri. And we've brought the bits needed to make you part of that network. So don't say I don't think of you while we're apart, Bruv!'

'Get yourself over here, brother Tarvin,' Harden replied. 'I want to see if those devices of yours match up to the sales hype you're giving me!'

'Malik, have we received a suggested flight plan for the journey to Interstellar Haulage's dock at Oort Station?'

'Affirmative, Commodore. But I suggest that we dock with flagship 2 first, to transfer a QIC adapter and some QIC chips into the hands of flagship 2's chief engineer. His team could be fitting the adapter to Sasha and their fax-bot brigade while we are in flight to dock with Oort Station.'

'Good idea,' Harden added quietly. 'There's so much business traffic around here it can sometimes take over an hour to complete a ship-to-dock transfer.'

'OK,' I said. 'Let's do that. Oort Station Traffic Control, Commodore Tarvin Clason's Cutter requesting permission to dock with Interstellar Haulage's Flagship 2. Tarvin Clason out.'

To which, traffic control responded, 'Commodore Tarvin Clason, you have permission to manoeuvre for docking to flagship 2 in your own time. There is no conflicting traffic within the exclusion zone of your current parking volume.'

'No conflicting traffic in the exclusion zone!' Kat exploded beside me. 'Who the hell knew this is an exclusion zone?'

'Simmer down, sweetheart,' said Harden, trying to mollify her. 'You've just made the first interstellar arrival into Oort Station controlled space. It was a safe arrival, and it is a historic event. I'll get our publicity people to make sure the story gets onto the local news bulletins.'

During these exchanges my cutter's autopilot had guided us onto the appropriate docking port on my brother's Starship and I left Kat in the control room, continuing to argue happily with her husband, while I collected the AI-computer bot we had among our passengers and went down to our airlock to hand over a supply of QIC adapters and QIC chips for flagship 2. Before this, I had not met Harden's chief engineer, Captain Vin Tanner, but he knew my chief engineer, Jim Igwe, so we chatted briefly while my AI-computer bot handed over the QIC devices to Harden's brigade captain AI-computer bot. It was odd to see the two bots shaking hands, like two friends reuniting after a separation, it seemed such a peculiarly human gesture for bots to emulate, but of course they were not parodying human behaviour at all. Telecommunications handshaking is the ages-old process of negotiation between two comms devices that establishes the protocols of a communication link during which, in this case, technical details for fitting QIC devices were exchanged between the bots. When this exchange was completed, I bade farewell to Vin Tanner, suggesting that as soon as the QIC adapter was fitted to Sasha, he should message Jim Igwe to learn more about our trip to and from Proxima-Centauri. Returning to the control room, I was in time to hear the end of Kat's description to our passengers of Interstellar Haulage's new office facilities at Oort Station, so I decided to seek permission to fly there as soon as possible. After checking my autopilot had uploaded the flight plan, I called flight control for permission to put it into effect.

'Oort Station Traffic Control, Commodore Tarvin Clason's Cutter requesting permission to dock with Interstellar Haulage's private dock at Oort Station. Tarvin Clason out.'

'Commodore Tarvin Clason you have permission to approach Oort Station Commercial AG-disk for docking at your private dock but only under our control at this time, because of conflicting traffic. Is that acceptable to you? Traffic Control out.'

'Sure,' I said. 'Please do that as expeditiously as possible. Tarvin Clason out.'

'Commodore Clason, are you declaring an emergency? Traffic Control out.'

'Negative, Traffic Control. Just impatience. Tarvin Clason out.'

'Understood, Commodore. I guess impatience goes with the job! We'll give you priority over shuttle passenger traffic. That's the best we can do for you. Traffic Control out.'

With my autopilot being guided into Oort Station's docking area by traffic control and Kat taking care of our passengers, I was able to message Harden and explain why I'd left my Starships a lightyear or so back at Proxima Waystation 1.

'As Kat's explained,' I said, 'the best data we had about objects in the space around Oort Station was around a month old. And as we'd been quantum jumping two Starships stuck end to end, we decided to do the final jump in my cutter, rather than bring a 20-kilometre length of titanium tube into an unknown assembly area.'

'Whoa, 20-kliks?' Harden responded. 'Jeez, Bruv, I'm impressed!' Then he added quickly, 'And very thankful for your caution, considering how close to my flagship you brought your cutter! Decoherence of a 20-klik long pair of Starships that close to my flagship in local space could have destroyed all three ships!'

'And we certainly thought we were being properly cautious,' I continued. 'Kat calculated a 200-kilometre destination cube around Oort Station and then placed our aim point within that as far away from the waystation as possible. So, it was quite a surprise to see flagship 2 looming over us when we decohered!'

'Yeah, I can understand why Katharina was a bit touchy when I first contacted you!' Harden commented, laughing. 'But it wasn't my fault, even though Kat thought it was. Traffic Control instructed me to park my flagship where it is now, and for the same reason as Kat chose that spot as your destination on her quantum map. They wanted to keep us well away from the rest of the traffic around the waystation as we waited here for your return from Proxima-Centauri, Tarvin 'ole bean.' Harden paused briefly before adding, 'You know, we really need up-to-the-second information about quantum jump destinations if we're to make much use of this interstellar route you've established. We can't risk arriving blind at major transport hubs when we have a Starship full of passengers.'

'That's exactly why we're here,' I murmured. 'We've got all the resources that can make sure that even a pilot like you can land here safely!'

'Well, if these QIC things of yours do solve traffic conflicts at decoherence, they could be worth more to the company than the whole damn Starship-101.'

'You'll be able to judge for yourself soon because it'll not be long before Sasha's plug-and-play adapter is fitted. But we need you to source more chip-making factories to take to Proxima-b to ramp up production, and we need to submit patent applications immediately.'

'We can manage both of those jobs OK,' replied Harden. 'The first new staff we employed were lawyers and human resources managers; they can take care of the patents and finding computer chip production teams, and I'll get Vin Tanner to chase up the hardware for chip-making.'

'Great, I'll leave all that to you,' I replied. 'We have all the draft patent documents prepared, so Malik will stream all the necessary details to Sasha and Klaus, so our new 'company head office' can take it from there. Did you get that Malik?'

'Affirmative, Commodore,' replied Malik. 'Also, I can confirm that Sasha's QIC adaptation has been completed successfully and Sasha is now a major node in our Proxima QIC network.'

'You mean I can message Proxima-b directly through Sasha now?' Harden asked.

'Affirmative, Commodore Harden. Sasha is currently completing its handshaking with all the other nodes in the network but as of now you have access to live data, including e-mail, audio, and televisual communications across the entire Proxima QIC network. I am also streaming to Sasha all the data I have accumulated during our Proxima expedition. These data include several summarised memory traces of our main findings that Sasha can stream to your NeuroModem during your next dream cycle.'

'Do those memory traces include the Pink Ghost name-changing story, Malik?' I asked.

'Affirmative, Commodore Tarvin. I will instruct Sasha to prioritise those traces. Malik out.'

'What's a Pink Ghost, Bruv?' Harden asked.

'It's my flagship. We've renamed her as 'Pink Ghost' after seeing satellite images of everything that happened while I was doing the quantum translocation of Starship-101 from the planet's surface and into orbit. As far as we know, this was the first time both origin and destination of a translocation, and especially the superposition entanglement, were continuously monitored by high-quality cameras. The satellite images showed both Starships in the superposition, but it was a ghostly, translucent image of my orbiting flagship and it was coloured pink as a result of being illuminated in orbit by Proxima-Centauri. At a later staff meeting everybody thought it was a good idea to rename the ship. So, that becomes another urgent job for your legal department; register the change of name of Interstellar Haulage's Flagship 1 as Interstellar Haulage's Pink Ghost with the appropriate authorities in Sweden.

'OK, I'm sure we can manage that, too. But that was an epic journey, Bruv, I need to learn a lot of new stuff before I next climb into my Nav Couch!'

'Yes, old fruit, this entire trip has been a great learning experience,' I answered. 'And the good news is that my communications officer, Lana Mancot, has been documenting it for the TV audience on Proxima-b from the start, and she's still working on Proxima-b. So, I suggest you tell your Comms Officer to contact her directly via Sasha's QIC messaging service to arrange streaming of her TV programmes into your ship's intercom channel. You can then pick and choose which events to have streamed into your NeuroModem by Sasha.'

'Excuse my interrupting your conversation, Commodore. This is Sasha, announcing your imminent arrival at the Interstellar Haulage docking port on Oort Station. Please be prepared for rapid and possibly strong vector changes.'

I thanked Sasha and told my autopilot to repeat that warning through my cutter's intercom and then messaged Kat to ask her to return to the control room. Thankfully, when she did return, she brought me a fresh coffee bulb!

'Passengers alright?' I asked in between gulps of coffee.

'I've spent the past hour or so with them, so they're fine,' Kat replied. 'You've spent that time with that husband of mine! You've not called in on them, not even checked the CCTV, I guess. Do you even know who's a passenger on your ship?'

'Never mind your passengers, Kat dear. He's not even bothered to message me, and that's a far more heinous crime!' My wife Lizzie interrupted. I had the feeling I was a fair way up shit creek, so, I attempted some back-paddling.

'Darling, how wonderful to hear from you,' I started, trying not to sound too desperate. 'Where are you now, my lovely?'

'I'm waiting on the waystation side of the airlock to the Interstellar Haulage dock into which the tugs are currently dragging your pathetic hide. I thought it would be nice to welcome you on your arrival. But if you don't stop simpering, I'll tell the dock master I don't accept you to tie up in my dock and he'll eject you!'

'You tell him, girl,' said Kat. 'But don't have him ejected until we get his unreliable rat of a brother on board! We could wave goodbye to both of them and make a takeover bid for the company!'

'How the hell did this happen?' Harden messaged directly to my NeuroModem.

I didn't understand how things had got to this point either, but neither did I want to say anything else that might make matters worse. All I could think of doing was to withdraw from this conversation and turn to my ship's intercom to ask my passengers to assemble in my wardroom prior to disembarkation into Oort Station. Then I disentangled myself from my Nav Couch straps and floated myself back to the wardroom.

It turned out that all but one of my passengers were bots, so I didn't need to be concerned about them being affronted by my lack of attention to their needs when we first arrived. Kat was exaggerating this character defect of mine. The human passenger was Lydia Connah, manager of Proxima Home Station, who had come with us to take the lead in negotiations with StarCorp for the farming artificial gravity disks Proxima urgently needs. There was also a regular little brigade of AI-bots. Bogey, of course, always hustling to get the best camera angle, and he was accompanied by a QIC-fax-bot pre-tuned to Lana who was intending to sell her TV programmes. There was also the AI-computer bot we had brought down to Oort Station who carried the stock of QIC devices and was accompanied by two QIC-fax-bots pre-tuned to Danny and Frankie, that were intended to act as their avatars in contract discussions for QIC device patenting and sales. And, faithful as ever, Stewart, my vintage steward, was hovering at the back of the crowd in the entrance to the passenger lounge carrying a couple of garment bags that I assumed contained our dress uniforms.

In fact, the wardroom I floated into was filled with conversation. All the fax-bots were dialled into their hosts back on Proxima-b and the air was filled with their voices as they discussed what Kat had recently told them about the company's new office facilities on Oort Station. As usual, Lana was the first to take advantage of my appearance.

'Hey, Boss, we need to establish a properly staffed Interstellar Haulage Video Production Office at Oort Station as soon as poss,' Lana announced. And Frankie didn't hold back either.

'Boss, what about an office called something like 'Proxima Industries' initially to handle sales and promotion of our QIC devices?' Frankie asked.

I thought this was the right time to re-establish contact with Interstellar Haulage's acting commercial manager, so I shouted for help.

'Hi Lizzie, can you help me out here? Can you offer facilities like these in your offices?' I asked.

'We can,' was the response. 'We have already appointed a legal team, and we have a publicist too. This afternoon I interviewed and appointed a general manager and her deputy for our Oort Station head office, and they went off immediately to choose AI-secretarial and filing bots. So, as of tomorrow morning we will have a nucleus of staff and equipment to handle your business ventures. We certainly have the space for all these different enterprises and while my dear husband was discussing his arrival here with his brother rather than talking to me, our office computer, Klaus, was monitoring their conversation and recorded detailed to-do notes about sourcing further chip-making production units, submitting patent applications and Starship naming registrations, as well as promoting contacts between communications officer, Lana Mancot, on Proxima-b and our Comms Officer on flagship 2. When you disembark, I will take you to our offices and we can discuss the details there.'

'So, you've forgiven me, have you Lizzie?' I asked.

'Well, I've not told the dock master to eject you. Yet. So, let's see how things progress when you get your sorry ass over here.'

'Don't let him off the hook, Lizzie,' Kat advised, floating into the wardroom just as the final docking clamps anchored us to the dock wall and the video screens showed the huge external hatch closing to seal off the entire dock from deep space. 'Has my dear husband managed to get *his* sorry ass down to welcome me to my new home?' Kat asked.

'Not yet!' Lizzie replied.

'I'm on the travelator!' Harden cried out, defensively.

'Careful, there, Bruv,' I messaged his NeuroModem privately. 'Don't try the 'delayed by traffic' excuse, they're both in such peculiar moods, don't risk it!'

'I'll be there before they crack the airlocks,' he promised instead.

So, in due time, the dock's atmosphere was replaced, and the brigade of dock bots opened first the airlock to the dock itself, and then two of them clanged their grapples onto my cutter and opened our outer hatch to deploy its gangway. I opened the inner airlock door myself and waved to the onlookers. We were still in microgravity, of course, so I was easily brushed aside as Bogey jetted through the open airlock, intent on recording the rest of us 'arriving at Oort Station'. But his expected tableau of an ordered progression down the gangway was lost because he was followed immediately by Kat, who launched herself through the air towards an equally-rapidly approaching Harden, recently detached from the high-speed travellator. They grabbed hold of each other in mid-air and expertly converted their opposite momentum into a spinning embrace. Despite my fears of a frosty reception, I was swept off the gangway as Lizzie launched from the dockside to embrace me and give me a real welcome 'home'. Bogey gas-jetted around us, filming our embraces, until Lizzie stuck out a hand to grab his lens and used her remaining momentum to send him spinning rapidly across the dock.

When Lizzie and I came up for air, I had been spun around to face my cutter and I could see Lana and Frankie's fax-bots at the top of the gangway, clinging to each other in fits of giggles from four and a half lightyears away, while the rest of the bots floated there in perfect stillness, impassively waiting for the monkeys they served to complete their welcome rituals!

Eventually, we got all the passengers disembarked and Lizzie and Harden guided all of us to the travellator that would take us towards the one-g part of the disk. As she passed me and grabbed at a travellator strap Lydia said, with a broad smile. 'Your domestic discussions and displays are really entertaining. I wouldn't be surprised if Lana didn't see the potential of the last few hours or so for a docudrama about 'interstellar family Clason'. You should introduce her to the grandpa you've talked about; a slightly unhinged patriarch could really spice up the drama!' Grandpa? Unhinged? I thought to myself. Nah, that idea wouldn't go down too well in the generation before last! But I couldn't think fast enough to reply.

Like a train of children out on a school trip, at the end of the travellator we trooped through the new commercial district of the one-g gallery of this disk, ending up at the front door of a surprisingly imposing three-storey block that was emblazoned 'Interstellar Haulage'. Harden ushered everyone through the door and introduced us to the human receptionist who issued Kat, me and Lydia with ID badges and got the bots registered with Klaus, the resident megacomputer, pointing out the recharge cubicles where the bots could store themselves when off-duty.

Those formalities over, Lizzie suggested we all go up to our apartment on the floor above. This invitation included the bots so their avatars could join in, although our AI-computer bot was dispatched to the computer centre immediately to fit the QIC adapters he was transporting.

I was impressed by my first sight of the building, and doubly impressed by my first sight of the new apartment that Lizzie had prepared for us. After he had hung the garment bags brought from my cutter in the apartment's bedroom, I sent my steward immediately into the kitchen to make coffee. He showed me the generous box of breakfast boulangerie goodies that Angélique had arranged to be delivered to my cutter before we left PW1. I thought it would make a very welcome accompaniment to the coffee, and that thought proved to be a great success!

Over coffee, we sorted the various tasks we wanted to complete on our brief visit here. Harden messaged his senior contacts in the management of both Oort Station and StarCorp, telling them about our QIC devices and tempting them with open access to his flagship's computer, Sasha, who by now was a fully-fledged and experienced member of our Proxima network, so they could sample quantum instantaneous communications for themselves. By later accounts they both took up Harden's offer and spent the rest of the day, and some part of the night, messaging, streaming, emailing, video-viewing and generally acting like overactive teenagers with a new toy across the whole of the four and a half lightyear Proxima network. Certainly, by the following morning both institutions were eager to have our plug-and-play devices installed. They didn't even ask the price!

We also set our office staff rolling on some of the administrative jobs. Using data they could now download directly from Klaus, the legal team happily undertook to submit our initial QIC patents, and the AI-bot that was Danny Khan's avatar went down to their office to be guided on how to continue the process overnight. The legal team also took on the registration of Pink Ghost's new name and Harden made the snap decision to rename his flagship 2 as Silver Ghost in the same application.

By far the most entertaining episode, inevitably I suppose, was when we introduced Lana's AI-bot avatar facsimile to the company's recently appointed publicist, Advani Ray. The two struck up an eager schoolgirl relationship immediately and set about planning an item for that evenings news bulletins that explained about Interstellar Haulage being about to bring Starship-101 back home but having been left a lightyear away at Proxima Waystation 1 because of the dangers of jumping into unknown space with such an ungainly object as it is now. When they started discussing potential interviews with me and Kat, I noticed a look of horror on Kat's face, which I shared, and was prompted to suggest that Advani should conduct a live interview with Frankie Burton and Danny Khan back on Proxima-b, asking them to explain how their QIC devices solve the problem of quantum jumping into unknown space.

Advani looked at me with a look of surprise on her face, and Lana's facsimile bot was, uncharacteristically, looking at me in total silence. I took these expressions of surprise to mean that they had both finally understood what they were really discussing.

Advani recovered first. 'Wow, interviews across interstellar space!' she said. 'I've only been in this job two days and I'm handling humanity's biggest ever space travel story!'

'You and me both!' said Lana's avatar bot.

There then followed a quick-fire exchange of ideas between the two of them.

'Can we assemble some video clips to illustrate our news item?'

'What about some live camera shots of Proxima-b outside the studio?'

'Can we interview the mayor of the settlement, what's it called, Proxima Alpha?'

'Can we interview a local astronomer to get views of the whole Centauri system?'

'Could the real live Lana do a live camera tour of Proxima Alpha to show it off to the whole Solar System?'

And so it went on. Until I interrupted again and suggested that my apartment was not the best place to discuss all this. They were getting on so well together that what they needed to do was go down to Advani's office on the ground floor, taking Bogey and Lana's facsimile bot with them, and do their planning there. The most urgent thing was to get in contact with the local TV station's news production staff to headline the story for the earliest bulletins they could manage, and then try to develop their interest in further broadcasts over the next day or so. Advani immediately accepted this suggestion, saying, 'Yeah, and I know just who to contact, too!' Then they all trooped out, heading for the lift to the ground floor.

'Nicely done, Tarvin,' said Kat, grinning. 'Now, Harden,' she continued, 'if we take Lydia off to settle into the guest apartment, we could leave our in-laws to start whatever they have planned for this evening.'

It was such an excellent suggestion that all I needed to add to it was a blanket instruction to Malik to disengage from my NeuroModem until 8 a.m. the next morning to give me total privacy. And then Lizzie and I started what we had planned for the evening.

Day 13

Despite my plea for privacy until 8.00 a.m., Malik dragged me out of my sleep at 6.30 a.m. by reporting a slew of messages that arrived during the night from all over the Solar System. Scanning through them, and they were still arriving, I saw many simple messages of congratulation on being the first interstellar voyagers to return to the Solar System, many invitations for interviews and collaboration as well as many enquiries about interstellar travel and requests to comment on the 'rumours' about quantum instantaneous communication.

I went into the apartment's kitchen diner and asked Stewart to make some coffee and toast for an undemanding breakfast while I tried to wake up sufficiently to decide what to do. Looking back through the list of messages I saw that among the first was a message from Jim Igwe and another from Tom Fraser, both of which made appreciative comments about the brief news report of our arrival that had formed part of the newscaster's broadcast bulletin throughout the night by Oort Station's 24-hour rolling news programme. Tom's message ended with the intriguing advice to '... make the most of it while you can, lad, because tomorrow some self-centred, lazy and feckless politician somewhere will do something awful that will dominate the news...' Lizzie had just joined me in the kitchen diner when Malik was replaying Tom's message so she turned on the TV to find out what I should be 'making the most' of.

When we saw the repeat on the breakfast show of the previous night's news bulletin about us, we began to understand why the bulletin had been rebroadcast across the Solar System during the night. The item itself was fairly innocuous, showing Advani Ray sitting in with the news anchor and showing video clips of the arrival of my cutter into the commercial dock at Oort Station. Advani stressed the importance of this event as being the first time in human history that anyone had returned from an interstellar mission and showed a few stock photos of me and Kat. But the hype was then turned up a few notches as Advani turned to the camera and calmly promised to include the viewers in an even more historic event by using 'newly invented quantum instantaneous communications to talk live with our correspondent on Centauri-Proxima-b, Lana Mancot.' At which point the right-hand side of the TV screen turned the twilight red of Proxima-b and showed, illuminated with white camera lights, Lana perched on an ornamental balustrade alongside the riverbank outside the Westwood Restaurant.

Lana was introduced as 'Commodore Clason's communications officer' and did a piece to camera outlining where she was located, guiding the camera around a full-360 to show the river with the northern snow-topped mountains (in pink) in the background, the riverside promenade, and Starship Way, which now boasted a line of desirable housing units, and ending on the brightly lit windows of the busy Westwood Restaurant. Lana guided her camera bot into the restaurant and to a table near the door occupied by Frankie Burton, introduced as 'Commodore Clason's Chief Computer Engineer' who was then interviewed about the QIC technology which was 'enabling this revolutionary and historic event of live interviews across four and a half lightyears of interstellar space.' Both Lana and Frankie dropped a few more phrases featuring 'historic' and 'first time across interstellar distances' into their conversation before returning the report to the Oort Station studio.

There, before signing off, Advani promised a lengthier, early evening special news programme later today that would include live interviews with the Director of Proxima Observatory, Arthur Westwood, to talk about the Centauri system, with the mayor of Proxima Alpha, Merv Castlefield who would describe Proxima Alpha now and share his aspirations for the future now that the Proxima Route was properly established, and with the local entrepreneur, Danny Khan, 'who is manufacturing several different QIC adapters' to explain how these devices solve the problem of quantum jumping into space that conventional electromagnetic messages leave as an unknown hazard '…because each waystation on the interstellar route can continually update, second by second, a destination quantum map of its locality on the QIC network that the Starship pilot can include in his superposition entanglement, removing all uncertainty about the navigator's destination for their decoherence…'

Advani's efforts impressed both Lizzie and me. I was not at all surprised that the Solar System's network of AI-news megacomputers had picked up on the more explosive keywords that Advani, Lana, Frankie and Danny between them had crammed into quite a short rolling news item broadcast. I asked Malik to send my compliments to Advani, and to copy to her any of my messages that enquired about interviews, collaboration, or interstellar travel.

While I was doing this, Lizzie messaged Kat and Harden to suggest they check the TV breakfast news for the next broadcast of the item we'd just viewed, and I went for a quick shower and shave. When I got back to the kitchen diner, I found Kat and Harden working their way through another pile of toast that Stewart had prepared.

'Mornin', Bruv,' Harden managed to project through his breakfast. 'Hey, this steward bot of yours is fantastic, where can I get one?'

'There's a whole brigade of them on Starship-101,' I replied. 'Intended for service to the senior officers. You should claim one of them when I finally bring the ship into Oort. Stewart's been fully upgraded, even with a QIC facsimile circuit, but his CPU's a hundred years old, of course, and that's why he's got such a refreshingly subservient personality; they were all made before the 'I am my own robot' movement got started on robot emancipation.'

'I'll tell you one secret about Stewart,' I added. 'He makes a stonkingly good banjo egg! If you want something more substantial than toast, that is.'

'Oh, yes!' Kat blurted out, scattering toast crumbs all over the place. 'Why didn't I think of that? Hey, Stewart, do you have any fresh eggs? Can you make me a double banjo?'

'Certainly, Captain Clason,' Stewart responded. 'Would anyone else like something cooked? I've had good reviews for my Eggs Benedict.'

'OK, Stewart,' Harden said. 'I'll have the Eggs Benedict, please.'

Lizzie and I passed on having anything further to eat right now. Lizzie went off for a shower and, leaving my brother and his wife in our kitchen diner, expanding their waistlines aided and abetted by my steward and waiting for the TV news to roll around again, I wandered towards the relative silence of the lounge, announcing my intention to record a short reply statement for Malik to use as a response to the shower of messages that my contact account was still receiving.

With a few bland statements suggested by Malik, I recorded a standard holding-reply style video to which Malik added my cutter control room as a background. Basically, I said, 'Thanks for your kind message but I still have to bring Starship-101 back to StarCorp, so Malik has to hold the fort until I get back to reply to all the messages I'm receiving.' Then I touched base with Jim Igwe and Tom Fraser to thank them for their overnight messages. Jim explained that he'd pulled a Team 3 double watch, midnight to 8 a.m. of his engineering maintenance crews and, once the robot brigades had been tasked, he had nothing better to do than keep an eye on Oort Station's rolling news programme that Malik was rebroadcasting on Pink Ghost's CCTV from the QIC adapter of my cutter's megacomputer.

'You've obviously been having a good time stirring up things down there, Boss,' said Jim. 'That was a nicely constructed news item they broadcast, so, I'm not surprised the Solar System is overreacting as it picks up on the broadcast streams from these distant parts.'

'Yeah, things are working out nicely,' I replied. 'Harden has leased a big head office for us in a new one-g disk on Oort Station that will handle the commercial side of our future operations, and a newly appointed publicist, Advani Ray, was the driving force behind that TV item. Even before that Harden had drummed up interest in our QIC devices with his contacts in both Oort Station and StarCorp.'

'What about the farming disks, Boss?' he asked.

'That's today's job. I'm planning to take Lydia and her crew of facsimile bots over to StarCorp after breakfast. Harden's got inside information that StarCorp's built some farm disks speculatively, and he thinks we might be able to buy off-the-shelf and have them tacked onto the end of his flotilla. I don't know yet how realistic that is, and anyway, I still need to get Starship-101 back to Oort to pay for it all!'

'Well, you'll be pleased to know that both Pink Ghost and 101 are in fine fettle. Ready to go when you are, Boss. Any idea when that might be?'

'That kind of depends on our negotiations with StarCorp. If they welcome us with open arms, I can make a draft agreement on behalf of Interstellar Haulage and leave Lydia and her crew to iron out the details. I'd like to get back to you later today, but you never know if the local management can make that sort of decision.'

'No worries, Boss. I'll slowly bring our two ships up to flight readiness so you can do what you like when you do get back here. At least this time you jump to Oort you'll know what you're jumping into!'

'True. You say both ships are in good order, does that include Tom Fraser taking up residence on Starship-101?'

'Sure does! Commodore Fraser has the entire ship powered up and back online. He's not been seen much on Proxima Waystation 1; he says that at his age he prefers microgravity to gravity. But him and the Flight computer are working the robot brigades continuously to carry out repairs and restore the ship as far as possible to its launch condition. And my space-side engineers have the attachment to Pink Ghost fully serviced and ready for release in Oort Station space. You get us to Oort, and we'll release Starship-101 to StarCorp in an hour, tops!'

'I'll do my best to give you the chance to match that claim, Jim. But right now, I want to talk to Tom Fraser, so I'll leave you to get on with your work. Tarvin out.'

'Oh, I ain't working, Boss. I'm on Team 3 watch again tonight, so I'm sitting at an outside table at Angélique's 'La Boulangerie de Proxima-Centauri' enjoying a light breakfast-cum-supper before sleeping in one of the guesthouses. Now, I hear another couple of crêpes calling my name. Jim Igwe out.'

To complete my 'touching base' mission, I asked Malik to connect me with Tom Fraser, whom I thanked for his early morning well-wishes. He explained that he occasionally had sleepless nights and last night was one of those. In the early morning hours, when looking for some TV to watch, he came across Malik's rebroadcast of the Oort Station news item.

'It was such a well-structured little piece that I just had to send a note of congratulation with never a thought to the time in the early morning. I hope I didn't disturb you!' Tom said.

'Nah,' I reassured him. 'Your message was one of the early ones, but Malik let me sleep until 6.30 a.m. before reporting the dozens of messages I was receiving from all over the Solar System.'

'Yeah, I'll bet you were popular, that short news item said all the right things,' he responded.

'I agree,' I replied. 'Though I had nothing to do with what was said or shown. That's all down to Interstellar Haulage's newly appointed publicist and my media whiz-kid, Lana Mancot.'

'They obviously know what they're doing. I know Lana and Frankie who are still on Proxima-b. So, was the young lady in the Oort Station studio your publicist?'

'That's right,' I confirmed. 'Her name's Advani Ray. Only been in the job with us for a few days.'

'She's obviously landed on her feet and knows how to tell a good story.'

'Well, I've dropped her a note asking that she gets in touch with you for an interview, on the grounds that you're the one returning from a distant star,' I told him.

'Now why would you do that?' he asked.

'Because a lot of the messages sent to me in the early hours congratulated me for being the first interstellar traveller to return home. But I reckon that accolade belongs to you, mate, not me!'

'Well, that's right handsome of you, Tarvin. I'll enjoy talking to her!'

'Advani's likely to have a very long to-do list this morning, so you could contact her if you prefer,' I suggested. 'All of our company computers have been updated with QICs, so your Flight computer will be able to contact her office computer directly; it's called Klaus and is already a node in our Proxima network.'

'OK, I'll do that,' he said.

'To help you work out what you might say,' I continued. 'I'll have Malik copy all my messages that mention this 'first back home' point to you and then leave you and Advani to deal with it. I don't think I need to be involved at all. Certainly not until I've delivered you to StarCorp. Don't hesitate to get back to me if you do need my input, Tom, but I'll now concentrate on dealing with StarCorp. Tarvin out.'

That essential messaging done, I suggested to Malik that he should redirect many of the messages to other people to respond on my behalf. Most importantly, messages that said anything about 'the first interstellar voyager to return to the Solar System' should be copied to Tom Fraser, and as an aside I told Malik to send a private message from me suggesting that Advani interviews Tom as the last surviving member of Starship-101's crew. The many invitations for interviews and enquiries about interstellar travel were also to be copied to Advani and the Interstellar Haulage office, while messages asking for any sort of comment about quantum instantaneous communication devices were to go directly to Danny Khan. I sent a private message to Lizzie suggesting that the company office may need more staff to cope with the whirlwind of reaction to our first news announcement within the range of the Solar System's conventional communications. Then I returned towards the kitchen diner with another coffee on my mind.

'Yes, I've been thinking about that,' Lizzie said as we met approaching the kitchen door. 'I'm still in contact with several 'near-misses' on my interview lists. I'll be going down to the office soon and will thankfully pass those contacts to the general manager I appointed yesterday, and she can call them back in and offer them support posts.'

'Excellent, but while you're on that tack,' I said. 'Don't forget that we need a long-term support office here for Danny Khan's QIC manufacturing, and more temporary support for Lydia Connah's discussions with StarCorp about farming disks.'

As we moved together into the kitchen diner, I raised my voice slightly to add, 'And I hope Harden will be finding Danny Khan some additional manufacturing facilities, too. He might need secretarial backup for that.'

'What's that, Bruv?' Harden responded. 'Electronics manufacturing? No probs. I'll sort it after breakfast, and I'll be using the same shipping agency that Sasha and I have dealt with for the rest of the materials we're taking to Proxima, so we'll not need much secretarial support. Vin Tanner will help with the technical stuff.'

'Harden, I'm also relying on you to get Oort Station's computers upgraded with QIC adapters,' I asked. 'Will you have time to do that? We really need to get Oort's local quantum maps onto the QIC network before we can think of bringing Starship-101 down here.'

'No worries, Tarvo,' he replied. 'Vin's already in a fast taxi shuttle on the way over here from Grey Ghost, and he's bringing our brigade captain AI-computer bot with him. If we can get the needed devices from your bot, who's recharging downstairs somewhere, we can do the upgrades in a matter of minutes. And then Klaus can train Oort's computers and register them into the Proxima network.'

I took hold of Harden's arm and pulled him to the other end of the kitchen diner, away from the noisy video screen. 'There's one more thing about Proxima-b you don't know Harden, and it needs your urgent action,' I said quietly. 'About a week ago the observatory we installed on the dark side was doing its first star surveys and detected the decoherence of a Starship the same size as ours at extreme range over the dark side.'

'Holy shit!' Harden muttered, as I went on. 'Now, we were having so much success with the QIC devices on the way down the route that I insisted there was no mention of this new arrival and instructed Malik to put an absolute embargo on mention of the arrival in any messages between people or computers. And given the amount of reaction there's been overnight to last night's news bulletin about us, I'm very glad I have kept it quiet.'

'Yeah, I understand that,' replied Harden. 'But Jeez, Bruv, what the hell is this deadly secret?'

'I'll explain,' I said. 'but let's keep the story secret. Malik, will you link me to Harden's NeuroModem and then invite Captain Rocky Zhang to join the loop?'

'End-to-end encryption, Commodore?' Malik asked. To which I replied 'Definitely.' And from that point on our conversation was an ultra-secure private exchange between our NeuroModems.

'Rocky Zhang?' Harden mused. 'That name rings a bell.'

'I'm flattered that you remember me after so long!' Rocky said, breaking into the conversation. 'I was one of the junior pilots serving on that contract to ferry cardice from Venus to Mars so many years ago.'

'Oh, yes,' said Harden. 'But we never actually met, did we?'

'Sadly, no,' said Rocky. 'We were always rostered for different shifts and there was no downtime for socialising.'

'Yeah, that was a punishingly hard job!' Harden said quietly. 'Makes me tired just remembering!' Then, a little more forcefully, 'Alright, Bruv, what's the story?'

Then, between us, Rocky and I described, for Harden's benefit, the arrival of Distant Home and the mixed reactions of the Proxima Alpha settlers, Rocky concluding with, 'At least we are now working together in the security detail at the Proxima Bank. Somehow, Merv Castlefield found a way to persuade Nelson and Clint that they should protect themselves against a common threat. But I'm not convinced that the arrangement really suits Clint Stapleton. He's such a hothead.'

'OK, what do you want me to do?' Harden asked.

'Get a platoon of Blue Helmets onto Proxima-b immediately!' I said, putting it as simply as possible so even my brother could understand it.

'OK, I can manage that,' Harden responded, with equal simplicity.

'You can manage that? How?' said Rocky, who was as surprised as me.

'Well, I've spent most of the past 24 hours, at least before Tarvin turned up here, welcoming some of the passengers I'll be taking to Proxima-b in a day or so. One of the most important of those, no I'll revise that, *THE* most important of which is the United World's representative who's going out to Proxima-b to establish humanity's first interstellar embassy. Her official title is Plenipotentiary Ambassador Fatemah Shirazi. And I can tell you, she travels mob-handed!'

'Could you tell me what that means?' Rocky asked.

'What? Plenipotentiary? Yeah, she explained it to me,' Harden replied. 'It means she's been given the full power of independent action on behalf of the UW. When her bosses were deciding her responsibilities, they realised that a distance of four and a half lightyears between Earth and the Centauri system meant a four and a half-year flight time for simple radio messages. Which wouldn't allow her to refer back to head office for advice, so they gave her the power to decide for herself.'

'Unusually rational for a central administration,' I said, then asked, 'So, what did "she travels mob-handed" mean?'

'She explained that too,' Harden replied. 'It boils down to this: she has the power to decide anything, and we are transporting everything she might need to exercise that power in the Centauri system. All the cargo in one entire section of my Starship belongs to her and my passenger section includes a large number of embassy staff, AI-bots and, now pay attention guys! AND a full platoon of 50 Blue Helmet Marines.'

'So, can you get some of those Peacekeepers to Proxima-b anytime soon?' I asked.

'Quite likely,' Harden replied. 'Ambassador Shirazi also told me to go to her if I had any problems that came under her remit. That's what I'll do. Sasha, please ask for a meeting with Ambassador Shirazi; say it's about an urgent peacekeeping matter on Proxima-b. And find out where she's located.'

'Willco, Commodore,' Sasha replied. 'I have already been advised that the Ambassador and her immediate staff have moved from Grey Ghost and into Oort Station Hotel to take advantage of the station's artificial gravity disk. Sasha out.'

'Great, if she's just next door, that makes it all nice and easy. Leave it to me, guys. I'll get it sorted and will report back to you both.'

We broke up our conversation, and Harden marched back towards the video screen saying, 'Now stop bothering me, Tarvo, and let me hear the TV prog I've been waiting for!'

This roll of the TV news broadcast was the same as the one we'd seen earlier, so Lizzie and I cut out from the kitchen and Lizzie went off to the Interstellar Haulage office downstairs to make a start on her tasks. I messaged Lydia Connah in apartment three and invited her over to our apartment for breakfast. She arrived just as the TV news programme was ending and that triggered the return of Harden and Kat to their own apartment, though Kat exchanged greetings with Lydia before leaving, promising to be back in just a few minutes, and Harden recommended that Lydia try Stewart's Eggs Benedict for breakfast.

Lydia placed that order with Stewart and accepted from me one of the coffee mugs I poured. While I toyed with another piece of toast, I ran through my recent thoughts about today's discussions with StarCorp.

'If Harden's right about it being likely they have farming disks on the shelf, can we actually buy them today?' Lydia asked.

'Sure, you can buy everything you need,' I replied. 'We'll add them to the purchase contract we've used so far to build Harden's Starship flotilla and is being handled by Harden's flight computer, Sasha. Indeed, if they really do have them immediately available, we'll get them added to Harden's flotilla for him to deliver to Proxima orbit.'

'So, we buy on credit, then?' Lydia persisted.

'Yeah, but it's up to me to redeem the credit for everything by delivering Starship-101 to StarCorp and that's why I'd like you to take the lead in the negotiation, Lydia,' I stressed, explaining, 'Because I'd prefer to get back to Proxima Waystation 1 as soon as possible. Later today, preferably. In the hopes of making the delivery to StarCorp tomorrow.'

Lydia finished off her breakfast and replied, 'I'm sure I can handle that, once you make it clear to StarCorp that I have the authority.'

'I'll certainly do that,' I promised. 'But there's one other thing to bear in mind, which is that StarCorp have already expressed keen interest in our QIC devices, and you will have a supply of them to offer as deal sweeteners. We need to make sure we include our AI-computer bot in your team, and he can install the plug-and-play QIC adapters immediately and train one of their AI-computer bots so, if they want to, they could take an adapter back to one of their installations in Earth orbit. Those arrangements could be worth a lot of credit with StarCorp.'

'I've lined up Danny Khan's facsimile bot to accompany us, too,' Kat announced as she breezed into my kitchen diner and headed towards the cafetière. 'Harden reckons StarCorp will want to do more than just try a couple of prototypes of the QIC devices. One of his inside contacts has messaged him muttering about all those millions of comms satellites that provide internet services all over the Solar System. Harden thinks that's the sort of market size StarCorp likes enough to be willing to buy-out the rights to production.'

After a swig of her coffee, she continued, rather breathlessly, 'Are you two ready to go back to the cutter? Harden's also suggested we quantum jump to the StarCorp yards, 'cos with the amount of local traffic around here it could take hours to rocket over there, and I want to make contact with their traffic control to get the destination map. Hey, is this toast going spare? Pass the honey, will you Di?'

Leaving Stewart to cope with the devastated breakfast table we took the lift down to the ground floor office, where we decided to take all four of our bots with us to StarCorp; the ever-present Bogey to record every step of the way and Lana, Danny and Frankie's facsimile bots, just in case things got interesting in the QIC discussions. We wouldn't want any of the prime movers feeling left out in the cold. I saw Lizzie in the office. She was juggling four or five tasks at once, as usual, so we had the briefest moment to say a 'bye, see you later'. Harden had already left to meet up with Vin Tanner and his AI-computer bot at the company's dock, on his mission to sort out the QIC upgrades for Oort Station's computers.

When we reached my cutter, Kat went directly to her Nav Couch to make ready to navigate the cutter across to StarCorp and I settled Lydia and her accompanying bots in the wardroom. Bogey preferred to film our trip from the control room view screens, so as well as taking input from their cameras, he clamped himself to the backs of our two Nav Couches from where he could film the pilot's eye view of proceedings.

As I was settling myself into my Nav Couch I told the cutter's autopilot to start negotiating to have the ship released from the dock. By the time I was ready to take over piloting the ship the dock had been cleared, its atmosphere recovered, and the outer hatch was beginning to open.

'How are you doing, Kat?' I asked.

'Fine, Boss. I'm looking over StarCorp Traffic Control's destination quantum map. They've got a helluva big installation over there! And as they're expecting another incoming, there's a big exclusion zone, so Malik's doing the math now. You'll have it in a minute or two.'

The dock's rams pushed us out into open space and then detached, leaving us to drift gently away from the station. I let it drift out a reasonable distance and then instructed the autopilot to stabilise our location at 100 metres from the station.

'Oort Station Traffic Control, this is Commodore Tarvin Clason, requesting permission to make a quantum jump to StarCorp Oort Starshipyards from my location alongside your Station. Clason out.'

'Commodore Clason, Traffic Control, this computer has just been upgraded with one of your QIC adapters. We are handshaking with your QIC network; a quantum map of your departure location will be supplied to you momentarily. Please hold your position.'

'Willco, Traffic Control, Clason out.'

I reached over to Kat to take hold of her hand, asking, 'How are you doing with the destination?'

'Here it is,' she responded, and a large cube of space slid into my mind's eye. I was well aware of the size of shipyards in space from the many times Harden and I had visited them with Grandpa. They had to be big, because Starships were assembled in them, but I had understood that this installation at Oort was new, and I was astonished at how quickly it had grown. Although the arrivals space was well separated from the shipyards, in the distance I could see skeleton yards where Sargon Construction Rings, surrounded by clouds of panel-supply shuttles were spinning the outer walls of future Starship sections in open space, like circular knitting machines knitting socks. And beyond them, several of the graving yards; enormous, enclosed cylinders within which the final fitting out of the Starship sections was done in microgravity, but in a normal atmosphere.

'Where's the destination waystation?' I asked.

'It's inside that big exclusion zone,' she replied, going on to explain, 'The whole thing is an artificial gravity environment so it's spinning, and with normal lightspeed radio transmission of the mapping data, the movement of even a slow spin really screws up the math. So, Malik's excluded it. Still, even a rooky pilot could land us in that big arrival volume, so 'Tarvin the Bold' should be able to manage!'

'You're getting as bad as Malik for dredging up my darkest secrets!' I complained.

'Oh, I'd forgotten all about that TV trailer of Lana's, but Harden came across it when he was checking out some of the early Proxima vids. He'll probably wait for a really embarrassing moment before he reminds you of it himself!'

As I was saying 'Thanks for the warning,' Malik cut into the conversation, 'Commodore, I am streaming to you the quantum map I have processed from Oort Station's mapping data. It is being updated every second.'

'Thanks Malik.' And there it was, in the memory trace I was sharing with Kat. In quantum-level detail, my cutter standing off a short way from Oort Station and in the distance, well away from the volume of space that had any influence on us, and in the jerky motion of a 'one-frame-a-second' film, the regular transit of shuttles, large and small, between Oort Station and the Starships hanging around it in this volume of space. It was the first time we had received present-time imaging of Oort Station's vicinity and we took a few moments to examine it from the points of view of both incoming and departing Starships.

'I like that,' said Kat. 'No doubts about the placement of conflicting traffic. Plenty of easy destination aims for ordinary Starships. But I'll still aim our current Pink Ghost/Starship-101 construction for a point a hundred clicks out.'

'Yeah. Obviously, that's the thing to do. But I can handle this as a departure map for this journey. Let's concentrate on that. What sort of nudge do you have for our decoherence at StarCorp?' I asked.

'I've got the final coordinates of that corner apex of the exclusion zone,' Kat replied.

'OK, I reckon pilot's ready,' I announced.

'Co-pilot is ready,' Kat echoed.

'Malik, please issue warning to the ship for imminent quantum translocation and copy to Oort Station Traffic Control and StarCorp Traffic Control. Then give me a 5-second countdown.'

I was aware of the warning chimes over the cutter's intercom as my mind grasped the departure and destination quantum maps and overlaid them into an entanglement. Kat slid her hexadecimal nudge into my memory trace and as Malik's count reached 'zero', I injected the nudge into the superposition's wavefunction to trigger our decoherence. And, always with a fleeting thought of thankfulness in my mind, it worked!

We decohered not too far from a full-scale Starship that was visibly rotating about its long axis at about twice the rate that a seconds hand progressed around a clock face, and the waystation's ID announcement sounded out over our intercom.

'Welcome to StarCorp's Oort Cloud Megafactory, Commodore Clason. Please hold your current position and our tugs will bring you into a docking area.'

'Thank you StarCorp. Willco. Clason out.'

Kat passed the arrival information onto Lydia, and we were soon being fussed over by a little squadron of tugs that attached themselves to us and then positioned us over a docking port while setting us into orbit around the long axis of the waystation so that we matched the waystation's rotation, which caused a one-g gravity vector to be established across our ship. Finally, they hauled us in tight towards the waystation until our docking clamps clanged as they locked onto the waystation's docking port.

'Malik, please rig the disembarkation ladders to the airlock,' I instructed, as Kat and I released our belts carefully and rolled off our Nav Couches. Kat clambered to the wardroom to help Lydia and I climbed up the ladder into the airlock, waiting for the waystation docking crew to crack the airlock hatch on their side. When they did, I swung the cutter's air lock hatch open and was greeted by a couple of young people who explained that they were the arrivals welcome team who would conduct us to the sales department as soon as we were ready. I was then pushed to one side of the cutter's airlock platform by Bogey as he stormed up its access ladder to find a decent camera angle to cover our arrival. Turning my attention to my own party, I helped Lydia and Kat into the StarCorp arrivals lounge and as the other three fax-bots emerged from my cutter, I quietly suggested to each of them that they should make connection with their human principals and asked that they indicate to me when the avatar state had been established. Then we all clustered around our welcome team while they welcomed us to StarCorp's Sales Division.

Most of the welcome speech consisted of the usual safety rigmarole that seemed to be necessary these days every time someone climbed aboard a spaceship, though it washed over people like me and Kat, and Lydia for that matter, who had regularly climbed into space on top of a bloody great rocket flame and were under no illusions about the dangers of space travel. Still, we played our parts as loyal StarCorp passengers and formally agreed that the 'fine print' had been read to us and, 'just for the record,' announced verbally our individual responsibility for our own safety. The two young 'welcomers' had a brief discussion and then turned to our little collection of bots, Lana's fax-bot first, and asked them to voice the same attestation. Unfortunately for them, Lana did as Lana does, and she announced, 'Hi, I'm a facsimile of Captain Lana Mancot of the Starship Pink Ghost, that's Mancot with one 't', make sure you get it right, I'm feeling litigious. I don't really care what happens to the tin man you've got there. I'm sitting in my own office on Proxima-b four and a half lightyears away from you and I promise not to hold StarCorp responsible if I fall off my chair. End of attestation.'

The look of stunned confusion on their young faces caused Kat to suggest, 'As the Third Law of robotics insists that a robot must protect its own existence, maybe it's unnecessary to ask our bots to attest responsibility for their own safety.' They accepted this notion, gratefully, and then ushered us onto a ground level travelator across a pleasantly green urban park towards the closest high-rise office block.

'Real plants! That's promising. And look, there's somebody over there with a dog!' exclaimed Lydia.

'And the dog's chasing a squirrel,' Kat contributed.

Not to be left out, I asked one of our welcome team, who had still not identified themselves, whether the birdsong we could hear was real or just a muzak soundtrack.

'Oh, they're all real,' I was assured. 'They just stay in the trees when people are exercising their pets. But in a little while people will be coming into the park with their lunch boxes and the birds will be begging for food.'

'That's certainly an improvement on what I've built so far. Very promising! I'm really looking forward to finding out what they've got to offer,' said Lydia.

'OMG,' gasped Kat, pointing at a wayside bush that was covered in flowers, 'there's a butterfly!'

'And a couple of dozen bees,' I contributed.

'I want a habitat like this!' Lydia squealed, scrutinising the bush as the travelator trundled past. 'It's got greenfly, too!' The Sales Division building had one of those glass-box-elevators on each outside wall and by the time we got to the top floor, where the conference rooms and executive management offices were located Lydia was gleefully ticking off the ecosystem features she could see.

To be fair, it was impressive. A genuine urban forest with buildings and roads scattered through it, as far as the eye could see. From our elevator we could see the entire cylindrical habitat laid out before us. Urban forest disappearing into the distance down the long axis of the cylinder and, of course, stretching over us because our point of view was just at one place on the inner wall of the rotating artificial gravity cylinder. The best view was above us; we could see rivers, lakes, wetlands, meadows, even tall rocky outcrops with birds of prey lazily drifting around the artificially-generated atmospheric thermals. Idyllic. But, sorry to break the spell, I've been here before, so what do you expect? This is StarCorp sales division's front lot. And the job of the sales division is to sell habitats just like this. If the gentle elevator ride doesn't make you want to buy it all by the time you get to the sales floor, it ain't doing its job.

When the lift doors opened, we were welcomed by the executive sales director himself, Ethan Caçar, and his PA.

'Great to see you again, Tarvin,' Caçar said, vigorously shaking my hand before turning his attention to Kat, 'And Kat, so nice to welcome you back from your historic journey!'

'This is my new PA, Ivan Penderecki. Ivan, take Commodore Clason's party into the conference room, I'll walk along with Kat and Tarvin.'

And walk along we did, either side of 'our old friend' Ethan, who we'd met only once before, a few years ago at another StarCorp Megafactory, when we were first discussing the Starship flotillas we needed for the Proxima-Centauri expedition. He actually put his arms around our shoulders as we followed behind Lydia and our troop of bots into the Conference Room and we idly chatted about Harden, Lizzie and even Grandpa, who, he said, 'I think is back at the Lagrange 2 StarCorp yards building Starships for more of his amazing missions. He's a true pioneer, that man!' all of which was nice to know as I had no idea of Grandpa's likely whereabouts. But, yes, if he'd come up with any more of his weird ideas, Lagrange 2 was where he'd be. Building Starships. Big Starships. At somebody else's expense!

It was a large conference room, with a digital glass wall opposite the entrance door, currently showing the outside view we had already seen from the elevator, and a long oval table between the two. Ivan settled Kat, me, and Lydia into the chairs at the end of the table facing the view screen. Ethan took his seat about midway down the table to our right, with Ivan taking in the seat to Ethan's right, where there was an electronic control panel. As bots do, our little brigade of bots took up station standing behind the humans in their party. Except Bogey, of course; he crept around, silently for once, filming the event.

'Do you think, Tarvin, we could persuade your bots to sit on that side of the table?' Ethan asked, pointing to the chairs to our left. 'I always find a phalanx of bots standing shoulder to shoulder behind their humans to be rather menacing, don't you agree?'

I winced inside, thinking 'red rag to a bull', and sure enough, Lana's fax-bot detached itself from the group and walked slowly down the left-hand side of the table, pointedly choosing the chair immediately opposite Ethan, sat down, stared into Ethan's eyes and announced, more or less as she had done before, 'Hi, I'm a facsimile of Captain Lana Mancot of the Starship Pink Ghost, that's Mancot with one 't', make sure you get it right, I'm feeling litigious. I'm sitting in my own office on Proxima-b four and a half lightyears away from you, but if you find my fax-bot menacing, you come out here. I'll show you menace. Personally.'

Frankie's fax-bot, still behind me, went into a fit of giggles and Kat put her head in her hands. To restore the businesslike atmosphere, I intervened, apologising and saying that I should have introduced the fax-bots, but first asked for permission for Bogey to continue filming. This reestablished the negotiation aspect of our meeting and, on the basis that a copy of the vid would be streamed to StarCorp, Bogey was allowed to carry on. I then introduced the fax-bots of Frankie and Danny Khan's avatars, and they took the seats alongside Lana's, leaving our AI-computer bot to settle into the seat next to Kat on my left.

The PA, Ivan, had been scribbling personal ID labels while I was doing these introductions and he scuttled around the table putting these in front the bots. When the room had settled again, I started my glad-handing speech, thanking StarCorp as a corporate entity, and Ethan personally for this opportunity to discuss our needs. I paused slightly, smiling around the table. The bots didn't respond, thankfully.

'I guess I need to outline what we do need and why these specific people and avatars are here. Our needs, or to be precise, the needs of the Proxima-b settlement, are for three farming disks to place in orbit around Proxima-b, expressly to avoid contamination of the native biome of that planet with Earth's organisms being caused by farming activities needed to feed the human inhabitants of Proxima-b. Kat and I, as Executive Director of the Board of Interstellar Haulage am here to make it clear that Captain Lydia Connah, here on my right, has the full authority of Interstellar Haulage to make this deal and to use a small supply of QIC adapters and chips we have brought as token of our good will in this deal, which will have to be charged to our existing Interstellar Haulage account until I can fulfil our existing contract by delivering Starship-101 to you. But I want to know if you, Ethan, have the full authority to confirm such a deal.'

I was quite pleased with this little speech; succinct and direct as it was, but as I was finishing there was some commotion in the corridor outside, the door opened behind me, and a group of three people breezed into the room.

One of the newcomers was speaking as he marched up the right-hand side of the table, dragging out the chair next to Ethan. 'I've been streaming your conversation on the way here.' At this, he turned to point at Ethan. 'You'll have to get an express executive elevator installed, Ethan. That glass thing is OK as a sales gimmick but bloody annoyingly slow if you're on a tight schedule.' Then he turned back to me, still holding the back of his chair. 'Now you know better than that, Commodore Clason. Of course, Ethan doesn't have the authority. I'm the only one with any sort of authority over StarCorp!'

The speaker was Antònim Almesc the 5th, widely referred to (when he was out of earshot) as AA5. Head of the Solar System's richest family and CEO of StarCorp; well, to be realistic, majority shareholder and totally autocratic and unpredictable boss of StarCorp. He's the one who bankrolled the Proxima expedition, and the Star Travel Museum in the first place, so he must have something on his mind to march in and take control of this meeting. Still, we get on well together, so I just smiled and saluted as he sat down.

'Right, Commodore Clason. First thing I must establish for my own sanity is who you are. I've been profitably dealing with your family since you and your brother were kids, but I still can't tell which one I'm talking to! There should be a law against two people looking so perfectly identical. There's no knowin' what sort of mischief they could get into.' He grinned broadly, then he waved at one of his assistants who was still standing at the open door. 'Hey, Seymour, get some coffee and tea in here. And biscuits. And some Cinnamon Toast Crunch, the kind in a bar, I can't be eating a bowl of the stuff in daylight.' Seymour scuttled off down the corridor, allowing the door to swing-to behind him. The other two assistants took their seats alongside their boss.

I decided to establish my identity, saying 'I'm Tarvin, Anton, the most reliable one.' Which prompted Kat to snigger explosively.

'Ah, the lovely Katharina Clason,' Anton responded. 'Do you confirm the self-identification we have just heard?'

'Up to a point,' said Kat. 'This is certainly Tarvin Clason sitting next to me, but as they are both as bad as each other at things like remembering anniversaries, birthdays and simply how long it's been since they contacted their wives, I'm not sure either of them is particularly reliable. Unless, of course, you can give them a Starship to play in! Anyway, Harden is back in Oort Station'.

'Yes, I knew that,' said Anton. 'I had a word with him from my ship as we approached. I was just teasing Tarvo here. Harden told me he was fitting QIC adapters to their computers.'

Just then Seymour and a couple of others came in with trays of tea, coffee and snacks which they distributed to the humans around the table. During this disturbance, Anton examined the ID labels in front of the fax-bots.

'Captain Lana Mancot,' Anton said, 'if I remember quite rightly, you are Tarvin's communications officer?'

'Yes, that's right,' Lana answered, sounding a little wary.

'And you conducted the interviews on Proxima in last night's wonderful and historic news broadcast?'

'Yes, that's right, too,' Lana repeated, sounding more relaxed, as Anton sank his teeth into a Toast Crunch bar. He reached for the next ID label.

'Captain Frankie Burton. Now, you were captioned on TV as the Chief Computer Engineer, and you described developing the programming.'

'Yup,' Frankie's fax-bot said.

'And then there's Danny Khan, one of Proxima's settlers, who designs and produces the hardware. Is that right?' Anton asked.

'That's quite right, Mr Almesc,' replied Danny's avatar.

'And you are all presently on Proxima-b. Four and a half lightyears away from me?'

'Quite so, Mr Almesc,' said Danny. 'We're not sitting together, though,' he added, 'Lana's in the TV centre, I'm in my factory office and Frankie's in the computer centre.'

'Astonishing,' Anton continued. 'And there's no delay in any of your answers to me! Across nine lightyears, there and back. Astonishing. I know you made this point in your broadcast, but to experience it myself really helps my decision making.'

'The megacomputers in the Proxima network, which now includes the two at Oort Station, have not detected any time delay in the transmission. Like any other entanglement, it's an instantaneous transmission in the quantum realm, only emerging into our reality when caused to decohere as the receiver attempts to measure it,' Danny said, further explaining, 'The messages are encrypted, of course, and the encryption/decryption cycle does take measurable time, though only a few nanoseconds, so even that is not evident to human ears.'

'And what time is it on Proxima-b now?' Anton asked.

'Same as yours on UTC. But clock time depends on which Earth time zone you've adopted,' Danny replied. 'Proxima-b is tidally locked to its star. The planet keeps the same face to Proxima all the time. That's the side that's liveable and it's in a permanent red twilight. The Starship-101 crew had been living on UTC and using the daily cycle appropriate to the GMT zone for their entire journey. So, they maintained that when they set down on a planet without a day-night cycle. We still use it, and it's used on the waystations all down the Proxima Route.'

Anton thought for a moment or two, then turned to me. 'Tarvin, how can I put my hands on a supply of these QIC devices?' he said.

'Just reach across the table,' I replied, and then explained, 'The bot sitting just the other side of Kat is my brigade captain AI-computer bot. He's brought a small supply of both the plug-and-play adapters and the QIC chips we use to adapt bots with a facsimile circuit. How many units are you carrying, captain?'

'I have twenty QIC adapters and 280 QIC chips with me at this meeting, Commodore,' the bot responded.

'I'll take them all!' snapped Anton, slapping the tabletop. 'In exchange for three top of the range farming disks and anything else you need for Proxima-b. Oh, and I also want to visit Proxima-b to discuss a licence for StarCorp to produce the devices itself.'

This caused our gang of three fax-bots to start talking all at once, so I banged my empty coffee mug on the table to quieten them, and then said 'Well, I'm very pleased to hear what you say, Anton. I brought the devices and my computer bot in the hope of offering them as goodwill for a line of credit for the farming disks we need. Do I understand correctly that you, Antònim Almesc the 5th, are saying you are willing to do a straight swap of our QIC devices which are now in this room for three farming disks delivered and assembled on my brother Commodore Harden Clason's flotilla that is currently in Oort Station's parking volume with no further lien on said disks?'

Anton went into a huddle with one of his PAs, so I refilled my coffee mug and waited patiently.

'Yes, Commodore Tarvin Clason,' Anton eventually replied. 'That is precisely what I mean.' This statement caused a flurry of activity among the various personal assistants around Anton and Ethan. I verified, privately, that Malik had logged this conversation and communicated it to Sasha, and got the usual reply 'Of course, Commodore.' But, at least, 'Well done, Boss!' came directly to my NeuroModem, first from Kat, and then from Lana.

So, feeling that I needed to confirm my position in charge of the situation, I went on to say, 'Excellent, Anton, that's a deal then. Now, as my brigade captain AI-computer bot now has a great deal of experience fitting these QIC devices I'd like to suggest that somebody conducts him to your ship Anton, so that he can hand over the QIC adapters and the chips he is carrying, together with the necessary training to your own computer bot brigade captain so that he can add the adapters to your ship's computer. After which, somebody should conduct my computer brigade captain to the computer centre of this StarCorp Megafactory to fit QIC adapters to each of its management and traffic control computers.'

Anton looked at me quietly for a moment, then nodded and said, 'Yeah, that sounds ideal. Seymour! Where's Seymour?' Seymour came into the room from the corridor. 'Seymour, stop lurking about in corridors and take this computer bot down to our ship. Introduce him to our ship's computer bot brigade captain and tell it to add an adapter to the ship's flight computer. Then bring him back to the computer centre here. Ethan, you sort that part out.'

Anton looked back towards me, smiled and said, 'Now, I'd like to make a few plans, but does anyone know how long it will take to have the QIC adapter fitted to my ship's flight computer?'

'Not more than fifteen minutes. It is a plug-and-play device,' said Danny's avatar. 'And Commodore Clason's ship's computer can transfer the necessary training data to your ship's computer and register it into the existing network in less than a second.'

'Brilliant,' Anton responded. 'Now, I would like to take a trip to Proxima-b to discuss production arrangements in more detail. So, here's what we'll do: Caçar, you take Lydia off to your office to choose the top of the range farming disks she needs, and I'll stay here with the rest of Tarvin's party to talk about QIC licensing. How's that for everybody?'

Well, it was alright for Ethan Caçar, and like the good salesman he was he immediately jumped to his feet and started to make his way around the table towards Lydia, followed by his PA, Ivan. But it wasn't ideal for me and Kat, I wanted to get back to PW1 to bring Starship-101 home and get the finances straightened out! But inevitably, it was Lana who spoke up first.

Lana's fax-bot raised its hand and Lana said, 'I really need to duck out of these discussions, now, so I can get back to the studio to deal with the special programme about Proxima-b we're planning to broadcast at 8 p.m.'

'That's OK, Lana,' said Danny Khan's avatar. 'Frankie and I can handle any further discussions.'

'Fine,' Lana's avatar replied. 'Before I check out, I want to say, Mr Almesc, that you are welcome to visit any time you like, but when you do visit, consider yourself booked for a TV interview! Lana Mancot out.'

'OK, that's fine with me,' Anton replied.

Lana's fax-bot performed the slight shiver that I'd noticed before accompanying detachment from a human's NeuroModem.

'Does that mean that this fax-bot is now free?' Asked Lydia. 'Because, in that case, I'd like to use it. Malik, can you dial up Ilsa on Lana's fax-bot and explain the context of this meeting to her?'

'Immediately, Captain Connah. Malik out.'

The facsimile bot that Lana had been using shivered again as Ilsa's NeuroModem made the connection, and then announced, in Ilsa's voice, 'Hiya, everybody, I am Captain Ilsa Blaine, and my deputy, Lieutenant Commander Emma Halton, is sitting beside me. We were responsible for the establishment of a series of smallholdings on Proxima-b to farm small animals, fish, and poultry, to feed the settlement. We don't need any explanation of the context of your current meeting because we have been watching the video stream from your camera bot.'

Those who were not used to the ever-present Bogie camera bot looked around the room in surprise and their eyes finally settled on Bogie, inconspicuously blending into the corner of the room over my right shoulder.

'I'd forgotten about that,' Anton said. 'Where are you located Captain Blaine?'

'We are on Proxima Waystation 4. It's the last on the Proxima Route, about four lightyears out from Earth and six light-months from Proxima-b Home Station. This waystation is a Proxima-b mimic where people intending to visit Proxima-b can be acclimatised to the constant red twilight and the need to wear protection from Proxima's bursts of radiation, though without actual exposure to radiation. We have a replica of the Proxima Alpha settlement on this artificial gravity disk and right now, Emma and I are replicating the smallholdings we created for Proxima Alpha.'

'These QIC communications are getting more amazing as I sit here!' Anton commented. 'I take it that this fax-bot goes with Captain Lydia Connah to help choose farm disks.'

'Affirmative, Anton. The camera bot as well,' I said. 'And me and Kat would also prefer to duck out now. We need to get back to Proxima Waystation One. I'd like to bring Starship-101 into StarCorp sometime tomorrow.'

'Really?' Anton asked. 'Say, I'd like to see that, maybe I'll delay my visit to Proxima.'

Kat pushed her chair back and stood up, saying, 'You don't have to delay, Anton. Starship-101 and our Starship are parked at Proxima Waystation One, why don't you join us there? If I remember, right, you like French cuisine, so we could meet for dinner at one of the French-style restaurants created in that waystation by the manager, Captain Angélique Gérard.'

Anton's eyes lit up with renewed interest. 'Angélique Gérard?' he said. 'Now she certainly does know how to build and equip waystations! She's done several for me, around Venus in particular, but in Mars orbit too and on the routes to the outer planets. That's a very tasty invitation, Kat! Do you reckon we can make it work?'

'Well, let's ask Malik,' I said, standing up alongside Kat. 'Malik, how goes the QIC adaptation for Mr Almesc's flight computer?'

'All completed, Commodore. And the machine is fully trained and registered with our Proxima network. Work has just started on adaptation of StarCorp's Oort Cloud Megafactory computers. Full functionality for sharing current 'state of traffic' quantum maps across all installations around Oort Station throughout the Proxima network is expected within 30 minutes. Malik out.'

'So, there you are, Anton,' Kat remarked. 'All your navigator need do is ask your flight computer to download the destination quantum map of wherever you want to go on the Proxima Route, and your pilot can take you there.'

'Your pilot can take you there after downloading the departure quantum map from StarCorp's local traffic control computer,' I added.

'But don't forget,' Kat added, 'that it's not just a matter of sharing current quantum maps for navigating the quantum realm. Your QIC-equipped flight computer has instantaneous access over lightyear distances to NeuroModem messaging, e-mail, audio and video broadcasts and data transfer. Every electromagnetic communication you can use. You can even take these fax-bots with you to continue your talks in your own Starship as you travel. Their QIC links to their humans will be maintained OK.'

If I didn't know better, I would have said that Anton looked a little stunned. But the Solar System's richest individual didn't stun easily, so, I guess he was just doing a quick bit of mental arithmetic on some profit-and-loss spreadsheet in the back of his mind.

As Anton was thinking about whatever Anton was thinking about, Lydia waved farewell silently as she, and Ilsa's avatar, were shepherded by Ivan to follow Ethan Caçar to his office down the corridor, with Bogey following on behind. I caught the start of Ethan's sales chatter as he went through the door 'You might want to consider our new 'Wild West' artificial gravity disk. It combines cattle and sheep ranching with cowboy-themed holiday lets of upmarket bunkhouses and luxury barns ...'

Kat and I edged closer to the door, anxious to make our own exit, and I asked, 'Anton, is that a date then? Will you join us at Proxima Waystation One later this afternoon?'

Anton came out of his reverie and started to gather the few personal things he had put on the table while saying, 'Yes, Tarvin, and I'm coming now. This trip was a fact-finding mission when I set off so let's go and experience Kat's list of QIC capabilities. I hope Frankie and Danny's avatars will come down to my ship with me?'

The two fax-bots got to their feet and Danny said, 'We're with you, Mr Almesc.' So, we all headed for the corridor, with Anton shouting, 'Seymour, Seymour, go get the elevator, will you?'

As we all crowded into the glass elevator Anton lowered his voice and said to me 'My lawyer here,' pointing at one of his PAs, 'was impressed by the brevity of the contract you came up with back there, and how quick you thought of it. I mean, really impressed! You know, Tarvin, if you ever want to give up your trekking around in space, I'll give you a job as a negotiator for StarCorp.'

I kept smiling agreeably, but though my inner thought was 'Another retirement offer!' I managed to say out loud, 'Thanks for the thought, Anton, but I just enjoy contract hauling, so I'm happy doing what I'm doing. Anyway, me coming up quickly with a contract agreement was another demonstration of the day-to-day usefulness of the QIC adapter. Because my ship's computer, Malik, currently located a lightyear away at Proxima Waystation One, put the words into my mouth.'

The glass box elevator was faster going down than its ascent had been. I guess the designers figured that the decision to buy/not to buy had been made by the time you made the descent, so you didn't need to dwell on any display of goods for sale! The pavement travellator also seemed to be faster, but that was due to our choosing to stride along it rather than meander from bush to bush, looking for local livestock!

We reached first the docking port to which my cutter was docked, so we said our temporary goodbyes there. Anton's party continued towards the next port area while Kat and I climbed into our own airlock. I clamped our outer airlock shut and heard the corresponding clanging as the dockside gang sealed off their side. Continuing down the ladder I found our computer bot brigade captain in the ship-side vestibule, all tasks completed and now offering to close the inner airlock door. I left him to it and followed Kat into the control room, where we both sank into the cushions of our Nav Couches, savouring the unusual joys of cushioning with a gravity vector. We were still attached to, and rotating with, the StarCorp waystation, of course, so we were still experiencing its artificial gravity vector.

'StarCorp's Oort Cloud Megafactory Traffic Control, Commodore Clason requesting permission to detach from docking port,' I asked.

'Commodore Clason, please wait. We have conflicting priority traffic. Traffic Control out.'

'That'll be AA5's ship,' said Kat, fiddling with the vid screen's controls to bring the neighbouring docking ports into view, commenting, when she got it focussed. 'Well, that doesn't look too special.'

I assessed the other ship with interest. 'Looks like an updated Commodore's Cutter but with a few extra bulges,' I commented, adding, 'And she looks like she's built to land through atmospheres the quick way.' The little tugs began heaving Anton's vessel away from its docking port and it used its own manoeuvring gas jets to assist and cancel its rotation vector. As we were still rotating in synchrony with the StarCorp waystation we moved steadily away from Anton's ship. Kat adjusted the contrast on the viewscreen to get a better view of the ship as it pirouetted beside us. 'Wow, look at those rocket pipes,' I said. 'I bet that climbs into orbit pretty sharpish, too!'

'Boys toys,' said Kat, dismissively, only to be interrupted by the clanging noise of our little squadron of tugs as they latched onto our towage cleats, 'Traffic Control, Commodore Clason, please be prepared for immediate detach from your docking port.' We lurched violently as the tugs gave us a huge heave outward, and then they detached, leaving us to drift further out into space away from StarCorp.

With Anton about to quantum jump to Proxima Waystation One, Kat thought we'd better warn Jim Igwe of Anton's imminent arrival, so she messaged him and added the information that he wanted to see Starship-101, and that he was keen on French food, knew Angélique Gérard and she'd invited Anton to dinner at one of Angélique's restaurants. I added that we were on our way back to PW1 within the hour and that I was still keen to take Starship-101 back to Oort tomorrow.

'Nuff said,' Jim replied. 'I'll entertain our illustrious guest and see if we can use Angélique's private dining room. Also, I'll start moving the engineering department towards our flight to Oort Station.'

'Thanks, Jim,' I said. 'We've got StarCorp's computers QIC-adapted, and they've got a nice big parking area, so I reckon I'll by-pass Oort Station and bring our 20-kilometre monstrosity direct to StarCorp so your guys can disconnect Starship-101 at StarCorp's front door.'

Our viewscreens were still showing the waystation with Anton's ship in the distance. And then, Anton's ship wasn't there anymore.

'Suits me,' said Jim, continuing after a short pause, 'You'll never guess who's just turned up at our front door! I'll go perform the glad-handing welcome! Jim Igwe out.'

'Traffic Control, Commodore Clason, you are now free to manoeuvre under your own power. Have a safe journey.'

'Thank you, Traffic, please stream to my flight computer a quantum map of the immediate vicinity.'

I instructed my autopilot to move away from StarCorp's waystation and to make my cutter stationary in space and as it did so, microgravity returned to the cutter, and I ordered the airlock disembarkation ladders to be stowed.

'I've not requested a destination map yet. So, where do you want to go, Boss?' Kat asked quietly. 'We could follow Anton straight back to PW1, or we could return to the Interstellar Haulage dock at Oort Station, update the office with recent developments, grab a late lunch and persuade Harden and Lizzie to come with us on an away-day at PW1?'

'I vote for Oort Station. You seem to have that one all worked out!' I replied as Malik joined in the conversation: 'Commodore, I have processed the mapping data of your locality received from traffic control at StarCorp's Oort Cloud Megafactory. The waystation itself is the dominating feature and as it is in motion, I have made it an exclusion zone. I am streaming the departure quantum map to you memory traces now.'

'Thanks Malik,' Kat responded. 'Please get me the current quantum map from Oort Station as my destination.'

Within a second or two we had access to both maps. 'No conflicting traffic. In fact, nothing we ain't seen before,' said Kat.

'Yeah,' I said. 'There's no point hanging around here. Malik, please inform StarCorp's Oort Cloud Megafactory Traffic Control that we are about to quantum jump out of their space and inform Oort Station Traffic Control we're about to arrive in theirs; Kat will give you the destination coordinates.'

'Kat, do you have a nudge picked out?' I asked.

'I'm proposing to use the coordinates of that tug that's parked just outside the dock neighbouring ours,' Kat replied.

'That's a bit close, isn't it?' I asked.

'Nah,' she replied. 'These high-res maps we get from the QIC network allow pin-point accuracy. And anyway,' Kat continued, 'you don't want to be farting about rocketing around alongside Oort Station for hours, do you?'

'OK, case proved,' I said resignedly. 'So, I guess that means pilot's ready, Malik,' I announced.

'Co-pilot is ready,' Kat echoed.

'Malik, please issue warnings of imminent quantum translocation to both traffic controls and give me a 5-second countdown.'

Five seconds later, we decohered immediately outside the Interstellar Haulage dock at Oort Station. The cutter's sensors showing a 50-metre gap between us and our dock's outer hatch.

'Wow, that's a good one!' I said.

'Yeah, I'm quite pleased with that,' Kat replied. 'I wasn't entirely sure I could pull it off, but I figured it was worth the risk, as we're never quite sure a jump will work anyway!'

'I don't find that type of appreciation of quantum probability very comforting!' I muttered, as I instructed the autopilot, between my complaints aimed at Kat, to get us into the dock.

'No worries, mate. I'll keep yer safe, Boss!' was all the sympathy I got from Kat, who went on to say, 'In fact, I'm so pleased with that destination plot, Malik, that I want it stored as an Oort Station destination template for Interstellar Haulage's Starships.'

'I wouldn't want to risk bringing a complete Starship in that close to Oort Station, so you'd better label it 'for Interstellar Haulage's Starship CUTTERS' and attach an explanatory note or two. I'd be happier jumping into one of the parking areas where Harden's ship is located at the moment.'

That settled, as well as all the clanging, tugging and atmosphere going and coming involved in berthing our vessel in our own dock, we went directly to Interstellar Haulage's office where Malik and I lodged the formal record of our agreement with Antònim Almesc the 5th with both the company computer Klaus, and our human lawyer. Lizzie was in the office finishing up her morning's work, during which she had set in train the formal submission of our patent applications, and the registrations for the new names of both of our Starships.

'But there's a six-hour time delay on radio transmissions to Earth at the moment,' she told me. 'So, don't expect any response until late tomorrow.'

'OK,' I replied. 'While you're waiting, how about a day trip to the most exciting holiday spot this side of planet Earth?'

'Where might that be?' She asked, adding, poking me in the chest with one finger, 'Don't you have a contract to complete? How can you afford the time for a holiday trip for even one day even though it's long overdue?'

'Easy,' I said, pulling her towards the door. 'To complete my contract I need to get to the two Starships that are waiting for me at Proxima Waystation One. And Proxima Waystation One is rapidly becoming known as the most exciting holiday spot this side of planet Earth!'

'Oh yeah?' she said doubtfully but following my brief description of the wondrous attractions on offer, she gave in to the idea but started to complain about needing to get 'a few things' from our apartment on the floor above. While Lizzie was stuffing her 'few things' into a large overnight bag, I told Stewart to rustle up a few sandwiches and drinks and report with them to my cutter in Interstellar Haulage's dock for our return to PW1. Stewart reminded me about the dress uniforms he'd brought with us, and I walked down the corridor with him to Kat and Harden's apartment to retrieve Kat's uniform. Harden opened the door and confirmed that he and Kat were almost ready to leave for our day out at PW1. Aside from a very welcome day off, he said he was pleased to have the chance to experience a QIC quantum jump.

'Your cutter's the same as mine, isn't it?' Harden asked. 'With an engineer's emergency Nav Couch stowed in the control room ceiling? I'd like to ride in that so I can share the memory traces you and Kat use in the translocation.'

Sounded OK to me, and I ordered Malik to deploy the Engineer's Nav Couch in my cutter. Seeing Stewart disappearing down the corridor with Kat's dress uniform, Harden sent his steward to sort out his own dress uniform and I also messaged Lizzie to suggest that she stuff her uniform into her overnight bag, or at least give it to one of the stewards to take to my cutter. While the turmoil of two stewards and two wives packing for an away-day was proceeding, me and Harden ducked into his kitchen to raid his coffee machine and we exchanged information about this morning's happenings. Harden's team had completed the QIC adaptations to Oort Station's computers and had tracked down more chip-making facilities to take to Danny on Proxima-b. Then he had his "audience" with Ambassador Shirazi.

'It turns out,' Harden said, 'that she'd spent a lot of her career as a diplomat on Mars and was fully clued up about the factious relationships between the various groups of ethnic Chinese there. Apparently, those on Mars were never particularly friendly with those who stayed on Earth, because those on Mars tended to strike out on their own to escape the People's Republic of China, favouring their heritage ethnic groups like the Tibetans and the Mongols, but none of those groups are particularly sympathetic to the People's Democratic Republic of Mars. She reckons you've done the right thing by keeping their arrival on Proxima-b quiet until she can get established on Proxima with a detail of Blue Helmets. Then, she plans to host a ceremony in which the Proxima Alpha settlers welcome the PDRM people. She has this image in her mind of families from the two groups partying together, while she circulates with a camera doing vox pops and children play happily together in the foreground. And, importantly, there's a squad of Blue Helmets clearly visible in the background to show who's in charge!'

'So, what's the bottom line?' I asked.

'She wants me to get her to Proxima-b immediately,' Harden replied. 'And she'll pay extra for the privilege!'

'But won't that screw up our away-day and your schedule for taking Grey Ghost up the Proxima Route?' I queried.

'Nah, it's all worked out nicely,' was Harden's confident reply. 'Being pragmatic "immediate" to her means the day after tomorrow, and that is when we planned to jump Grey Ghost to Proxima anyway. That's because she needs at least 24 hours to set up this side trip, decide who she needs to take with her, and, more importantly, confirm it all with her head office via speed of light radio. No QIC devices on her comms yet!'

Harden smiled broadly at me as he continued, 'So, I reckon Lizzie and me can do an early morning jump in my cutter direct to Proxima Home Station with Ambassador Shirazi's party and then take them down directly to Proxima's SpacePort. We discussed this with Mayor Castlefield, and he'll have a welcoming delegation with suitable transport waiting at the SpacePort to take them into Proxima Alpha. Oh, and by the way,' Harden added, 'Ambassador was most impressed by the fact that the QICs allowed her to talk to the mayor across four and a half lightyears of space! She instantly ordered them to be fitted to all her machines in our cargo hold and Vin Tanner will see to that while Grey Ghost is in transit through the Proxima Route. I've talked privately to Danny Khan, and he'll have supplies of his latest devices waiting for me to pick up at the SpacePort. The Ambassador actually used the phrase "at any price" so he's going to work out how much to charge and his office here at Oort Station will issue the invoice on behalf of Interstellar Haulage!'

'So, you're planning to jump your cutter straight back from Proxima and then take Grey Ghost to Proxima Waystation One on the same day?' I asked.

'You betcha, Bruv. If you can do three jumps in one day, so can I!' Harden said, triumphantly. 'I'm not expecting any delays, though; just disembark the passengers and their baggage and that's it. I guess I'll need to refuel the cutter at the SpacePort and while that's happening, I might blag a lift into Proxima Alpha to visit that Westwood Restaurant you've talked about and pretend to be you to get some sympathetic elevenses!'

'Meanwhile pretending that Lizzie is a modified Kat?' I asked.

'Nah, I'll tell 'em she's my fancy woman!' he responded with a leer.

'Good luck to her, then,' said Kat as she breezed past with a steward in tow carrying packed cases, 'The most romantic way he's ever thought of referring to me is 'er indoors or the little woman. 'Fancy woman' is really romantic!'

Ignoring the wifely banter, it seems that Harden's missions had all been successfully completed, and Vin Tanner had already left with Ambassador Shirazi's party in Harden's cutter to return them to his Starship to make up their away team. The plan was for Vin to bring the full loaded cutter back to the

Interstellar Haulage dock when the Ambassador's party was ready to leave for Proxima-b.

The turmoil surrounding Harden and I eventually settled, and we started herding our wives and overnight-bag-laden steward bots down towards Interstellar Haulage's dock, which of course, was in the non-rotating collar of this 'Oort Station commercial district' artificial gravity disk.

We were floating ourselves into my cutter's airlock when Lizzie held up her hand, saying, 'Hold on a minute; aren't we forgetting something? How is Lydia Connah getting back to Pink Ghost?'

'Oh, it's alright,' Kat replied. 'Di messaged me while I was packing. She said she's very pleased with the disks they've been offered off-the-shelf and she's arranging to accompany them as they're tugged to Harden's ship to be attached to his flotilla, taking Ilsa's facsimile bot and the camera bot, Bogey, with her. The three farming disks she's chosen come fully stocked and crewed with human farm managers and brigades of robot farmhands. They've also got little villages of guest cottages, so she's planning to move into one of those to get acquainted with the managers and their operations. Then she'll return to Proxima-b with Harden.'

'Fully stocked and crewed, eh?' I said. 'So, that's what Anton meant by 'top of the range'. We've come out of this better than I'd expected!'

'It's the QIC devices that levered out the top of the range,' Kat responded. 'I could see in his expression that he saw that everyone in the Solar System would be buying and clamouring to put their money in his hand.'

After sealing off the airlock hatches, I settled Lizzie in the wardroom and asked Stewart to distribute the sandwiches and drinks as a travelling picnic after stowing the overnight bags. Back in the control room, Kat was already settled in her Nav Couch and was issuing instructions for the dock gangs to release us into open space. Harden was relaxing into the Engineer's Couch, adjusting its straps to get himself comfortably attached to the NeuroModem connectors in an unfamiliar Nav Couch. I made a dive for my couch and strapped in, just as the dock's rams heaved us out into open space through the outer hatch.

Then, with Harden watching on as a keenly interested spectator, we initiated our usual litany that prepared us for the quantum realm.

'Autopilot, take us out to about 250 metres from Oort Station and make us stationary in space,' I instructed.

'Malik, please call for a current-time quantum map of the vicinity of Proxima Waystation One,' Kat requested.

'Malik, when we are holding a stationary position, please ask Oort Station Traffic Control for a current-time quantum map of our present vicinity.'

'Pilot and co-pilot, I am streaming to you the processed mapping data for departure and destinations as you requested. Malik out.'

'Let me see, let me see!' Hissed Harden.

I was already reaching out to hold Kat's hand, so I hissed back, 'Hold our hands.' And when he did, I was aware of a third memory trace joining Kat and I in the mindscape that currently held our departure and destination quantum maps.

Harden floated a thought across our shared mindscape, 'Hey, those quantum maps are changing!' which was instantly followed by Kat's thought, 'Yes, my love. They are refreshed every second, courtesy of our QIC network!'

Out loud, Kat asked, 'Where do you want to go, Boss?'

'We might as well park this cutter, so get me up close and personal with its dock.' I said.

The view in the destination visualisation zoomed in to the side of Pink Ghost and then scrolled along until it came to rest on the port side docking hatches.

'Oh good,' Kat breathed. 'They've left some tugs out in the cold.'

Suddenly, Harden shouted out loud, 'Lizzie, come in here. You've got to see this!'

When she came to float beside me, Lizzie took hold of my free hand and suddenly there were four of us sharing this mindscape. Kat zoomed and scrolled the destination map again for Lizzie's benefit, finally bringing the visualisation to rest on a group of bright yellow stanchions on one of the tugs.

'How do you fancy 50-metres from those bright yellow guys as a decoherence nudge, Boss?' Kat asked me.

Full of the bravado that was based on my one and only experience of such tightly constrained quantum jumping, I replied, 'If you can plot it, Kat, I can land it!'

I became aware of a criss-cross of thoughts floating over our mindscape, mainly originating from Harden, 'Haw, haw, haw!'

'OK,' I said, 'pilot is ready.'

'Co-pilot ready,' whispered Kat.

'Malik, please issue warnings of imminent quantum translocation to both Oort Station Traffic Control, that we are about to quantum jump out of their space, and Proxima Waystation One Traffic Control that we're about to arrive in theirs; Kat will stream the destination coordinates. Then give me a 5-second countdown.'

Five seconds later we decohered alongside the outer hatch of Pink Ghost's Commodore's Cutter dock. Malik announced our arrival to the Starship's intercom and piped it into the cutter. The 'mindscape appreciation' group broke up, Harden saying, 'Nicely done, Bruv. It was a close call, but I don't think you scratched anyone's paint!' Which was more appreciation than I was expecting!

'You know, Tarvo,' Harden went on to say, 'these quantum comms units will revolutionise our business. Say, Kat, can you save these departure and destination quantum maps as templates to be updated with the current traffic conditions when you want to use them?'

'I believe so,' Kat replied. 'But I've not done a jump more than once to test it out.'

'We'll be able to test that when we run up the Proxima Route,' said Lizzie. 'We'll have to agree a standard protocol as we go from waystation to waystation on the way to Proxima-b, and then see if it works on the way back.'

'Agreed, but let's concentrate on what we're doing now,' I suggested. 'The bots have us tied up and the dock's outer door's just clanged shut. Now, I want to take Starship-101 back to StarCorp's yards tomorrow.'

'Time?' asked Harden.

'About noon,' I replied. 'That's flexible, but I want to allow our engineers reasonable time to decouple the two ships and StarCorp's brigades time to tug Starship-101 into their graving yard. But, anyway, all I'm saying is that here and now we have the rest of today and tomorrow morning together and I think we'll be a lot more comfortable in guest rooms over in PW1's artificial gravity disk than in Pink Ghost's guest rooms in microgravity. So, I'm suggesting we go from here directly to PW1. Malik could rustle up a shuttle for us, while Stewart collects some porter drones to take our baggage over there with us.'

Everyone agreed with that plan, and within a very short time our party of humans and robots was descending the travellator gangway that led towards Angélique's 'La Boulangerie de Proxima-Centauri'. I called into La Boulangerie to introduce Lizzie and Harden, and to check that Jim had indeed arranged tonight's meal. While we chatted over some fresh coffee and a pastry or two, Kat said we were looking for a couple of rooms to stay overnight and Angélique offered two small apartments on an upper floor of La Boulangerie. We all trooped up the stairs to settle into them, accompanied by our little brigade of bots.

Relaxing later at one of the pavement tables Lizzie announced, 'It's been a busy day! I need to wind-down. Husband, get me a bottle of white wine!' The wine was ordered, and a glass drunk. Then Harden and Kat joined us for another, and before much longer another bottle was ordered up.

While I was still capable of rational thought, I decided to message Jim Igwe to check what he had arranged for tonight.

'Hi, Boss,' he said. 'Everything's been done as you ordered, but it's Lana who's mapped out our evening for us.'

'Oh, really?' I asked, not entirely overjoyed. 'What are we in for?'

'Well; first, ship matters. My space-rated engineering bots are all clamped onto the outside of the structural panels for which they're responsible. As soon as we decohere in StarCorp space they'll remove their panels and release Starship-101 to StarCorp's tugs.'

'And then we get paid!' I said, delightedly.

'Yeah, but that's your business, Boss,' he replied. 'I just tighten up the bolts. Second, as far as Pink Ghost is concerned, she's fit to fly anytime you like. Of course, most of the crew are still enjoying themselves on PW1, so it'll take us a couple of hours to round them all up and shuttle them back to Pink Ghost. Are you thinking about a midnight departure or anything crazy like that, pardon my French?'

'Nah,' I consoled him. 'I need another night at one-g and a lie-in tomorrow morning. So, give the crew the same. Tell them to muster at their posts on Pink Ghost by 10 a.m. tomorrow, with a view to a quantum jump around noon tomorrow. You can cheer them up with the thought that once Starship-101 is released to StarCorp, we'll park Pink Ghost alongside Harden's flotilla and organise a shuttle service to Oort Station's artificial gravity ring. Now what's this about Captain Lana Mancot taking control of my quiet, private, evening meal?'

'Ah, well, forget private, Boss, you've all got starring roles in Lana's evening TV extravaganza!'

'Jeez, hold on, Jim, the rest of my family's got to hear this.' I stopped Harden pouring yet more wine and suggested that everyone tune into my NeuroModem to hear about tonight's performance. 'OK, Jim, we've got their attention, tell us the grim details.'

'Right, but they're not that grim. You know that Lana and Advani were planning an evening news special show at 8 p.m. tonight to build on last night's Oort Station TV news item about your return from interstellar space. Well, that's now been moved forward to 7 p.m. and extended by another hour. Lana explains it as 'taking advantage of new interview opportunities' that have just arrived.'

'Anton Almesc!' Kat called out across the table. 'Remember, Boss? Lana said to Anton 'consider yourself booked for a TV interview' and he just said, 'fine with me'!'

'Yeah, that's about it,' Jim responded. 'I don't know the details of the meeting you're talking about, but Lana nailed him onto her TV schedule as soon as he arrived here. She says that Advani is sure the Oort Station people didn't know he was just across the way in StarCorp, and they just drooled at the opportunity to broadcast an interview with the richest man in the Solar System!'

'Anyway,' Jim continued, 'current running order is that the 7 p.m. programme will consist of live interviews on the plaza that's been developed on the riverbank outside the Westwood Restaurant. They'll feature the mayor, Merv Castlefield, talking about Proxima Alpha now and his aspirations for the future; Frankie Burton, with Danny and Salman Khan about the development and manufacture of our QIC devices; and then Art Westwood will describe and illustrate Proxima-Centauri's local astronomy. Art will be speaking from his observatory office on the dark side, so there'll also be live outside broadcasts of the dark side's frozen wastes. Until the cameras freeze up, at least.'

Appreciative murmurings around my table indicated that we were genuinely interested in this programme, but I had to ask, 'Where do we come into this?'

'All the Clasons, and me for that matter, Boss, along with Anton's pilot and co-pilot have starring roles as the scenery for Antònim Almesc the 5th's audience with the great unwashed in Angélique's private dining room. That's why all senior officers have been requested to wear their dress uniforms. I hope you've got yours with you!'

'Why aye, man. It was the last thing I packed!' said Harden. 'I'll take any chance I get to look like a Ruritanian Archduke! What's the point?'

'Lana's point is simply this,' Jim explained. 'That she wants to show off Interstellar Haulage's senior officers all dressed up to represent the company, just as she's done before at public events on Proxima-b. But I suspect AA5 has encouraged her in this because he can strut around informally dressed in front of a wall of top brass, representing all the ordinary people on the other side of the cameras in every other dining room, even though he's got all their money!'

'You're an old cynic, Jim!' said Kat. 'But I rather like dressing up now and then, so you can count on me being in my whites. And Harden, too, if he knows what's good for him!' Glancing across the table I saw that Harden looked a little aggrieved as he reached across to the wine bottle, so in brotherly support, I added, 'Oh certainly, what Lana wants, Lana gets. She's done us proud so far.'

'Hold on, Boss,' said Jim. 'You ain't heard all of it yet. Lana's bouncing off the walls contacting everyone, and every robot, involved in these transmissions, so she's given me two notes to pass onto you, one she describes as 'scene setting' and the other is her running order.'

'OK, the Clason family is getting itself tanked up with a nice cheeky little Sauvignon Blanc, so fire away,' I said, holding out my glass to Harden for a refill.

'Right, well, the scene setting bit is the seating plan around your table. She wants everyone arranged down one side of the table, so the other side is empty for the camera bot Greenstreet to rush up and down for interviews. I've already talked to Angélique, and her staff will set out ID labels on the table after arranging the table opposite one of the viewscreen walls so that we can watch the 7 p.m. programme while having dinner. Lana wants Anton sitting in the centre flanked by you and Harden on one side, and Kat and Lizzie on the other. The rest of us, that's me and Anton's pilot and co-pilot will be stuck on the end. It would have been made more symmetrical if Vin Tanner had accompanied Harden but he's not here.'

'It's not like an engineer to pass up on a free meal, but he does have some bolts that need tightening urgently in Ambassador Shirazi's travel gear,' I said, helpfully, and Lizzie muttered, irreverently 'It's the last supper tableau all over again!', but Jim ignored the interruptions and just kept talking.

'You and Harden must sit together because you'll be interviewed by Advani. At the end of the 7 p.m. programme there'll be an ad-break. They will be ads for Interstellar Haulage and Lana's follow up TV specials about the 'Proxima-Centauri Story'. At 8 p.m., Greenstreet's cameras will focus on your table and Advani, speaking from Oort Station, will interrupt whatever you're doing. She'll chat with you two, but only briefly because you're not really that important, then chat with Anton, and one of the questions she'll ask Anton is 'can he tell you apart?' then she'll talk a little to Kat and Lizzie and probably ask them the same question. Then Angélique will come into your dining room to take Anton down to one of the outside tables, their idle chatter on the way will be about PW1's attractions and will be effectively an advertorial for the waystations on the Proxima Route.'

'This is sounding like something worth dressing up for, Bruv!' Harden commented direct to my NeuroModem, while Jim continued to read his 'script notes'.

'Once Anton is comfortably seated at the outside table he will be interviewed by both Lana and Advani. He's already given Lana a list of topics he wants to speak about, so what's said depends more on him, but Lana wants to make it a three-way interview to stress the fact that there will be lightyear distances between the three of them, to emphasise the day-to-day utility of the QIC devices.'

'Yeah, definitely a great idea! I'll vote for that,' Harden said out loud, though only momentarily interrupting Jim's flow.

'Glad you agree, Commodore,' Jim said. 'Hold on a second, I've lost my place. No, here it is, when Anton's had his say, there will be other tables for Greenstreet to view, one with the Westwood twins and their buddies. They'll be in dress uniforms, too, and the twins will be given the opportunity to talk to their father, Art Westwood, who'll still be online from the observatory. The twins don't know it yet, but there'll be a brief link to mother, Linda, at home.'

'Oh, lovely!' said Kat, adding, 'And I bet sister Sarah gets into that act, too!'

'And I'm betting Sarah will be dressed up in her Midshipman's uniform,' I said to Kat, while Jim protested that he was down to the 'and finally' bit.

'And, finally,' he said, 'Tom Fraser will be sitting at another table and will be asked for all sorts of observations comparing the then and now. Right, that is the end of this run-through of our part in tonight's TV. You're on your own from here. I'm getting on with my real work, I promised to transport Tom Fraser and his entourage from Starship-101 to La Boulangerie and I need to get changed before that. Jim Igwe out.'

'Who is Tom Fraser, Bruv?' Asked Harden.

'He's the last surviving member of Starship-101's original crew.'

'He must be ancient!'

'He admits to being around 96 years old. He was a top-notch member of 101's original computer team. Still got all his marbles and has been very helpful because he was there when our current supercomputer programming was being developed and he remembers lots of backdoor stuff. But apart from one care-bot, I know nothing about an entourage. However, as he's the last man standing, he's inherited the Captaincy of Starship-101. So, what he says, goes!'

'Pay attention, you two,' said Kat. 'If Lizzie and me are supposed to be all dressed up anytime soon, we need to make a start now. So, I'm breaking up this boozing session and going back to the apartment.'

'Just what I was planning to do,' Lizzie agreed. 'Tarvin, get on your feet and come with me.' I did as I was told; that being the best way to keep the peace.

At the behest of the outside-broadcast production assistants Lana had recruited from the communications teams on Pink Ghost, all four Clasons eventually reconvened at the same table outside La Boulangerie. There, the make-up teams, also brought in from Pink Ghost, applied the final touches to make the four of us just right for the cameras. We were joined by Jim Igwe and Anton Almesc. Jim got the same perfunctory make-up attention that we had received but Anton, dressed, as expected, informally, but no doubt in high fashion, was taken off to an adjacent table placed centrally in front of Angélique's restaurant, where, after initial attention to his make-up, he was fussed over by a small brigade of people and bots. Greenstreet appeared from somewhere behind us and Lana's voice acknowledged us as the facsimile camera bot walked past; then the camera bot concentrated on trying camera angles and viewpoints for videoing Anton and, it seemed, the front of La Boulangerie.

With Anton dealt with, his brigade of people and bots deserted him and set to rearranging the tables, so there were two more in an arc extending from Anton's at the centre of La Boulangerie's frontage. The next table on from Anton's was slightly larger and provided with four chairs, then beyond that a table with no chairs, but cleared space behind it. Finally, the bots cleared away all the other tables, Greenstreet's activity making it evident that the clearance was to give the camera bot easy movement from table to table.

Anton drifted across to our table and after a round of greetings, he expressed the need for a drink.

'Well, there's a bar just inside,' I said. 'They seem to have finished with us here, why don't we give them some barflies to video?'

It was an opportune suggestion because the production assistant who had first greeted us hurried across to hustle us away from the table which was needed 'For make-up of more interviewees'. Sure enough, another, more flustered, assistant then appeared towing the Westwood twins and their buddies, all resplendent in full dress Midshipmen's uniforms. They were urged to sit on the seats we were vacating, but before they could, there had to be a round of introductions, not to mention a bunch of formal salutes and greetings; and two Commodores, accompanied by three senior Captains were due a healthy number of salutes from four Midshipmen! Formalities over, the make-up teams took over, and as we reached the bar to order beers all round, our four Midshipmen were passed onto the camera teams to be arranged and rearranged around the four-seater table while Greenstreet scrutinised them. It looked like something of a trial, and they looked like they were feeling as though they'd been set up for an execution. So, I sent over some beers and a range of bar snacks for them and that seemed to cheer them up and ease the tension.

Our little group was established around the end of the bar, deliberately well away from the outside-broadcast TV studio being established out front. We were joined by the Superposition Navigators from Anton's ship, resplendent in dark blue dress uniforms covered in gold braid and looking even more like Ruritanian Archdukes than we did. Their arrival turned our conversation towards their first experience of using QIC devices to define the departure and destination points of a quantum jump and, generally, how QIC so much improved the business of superposition navigation. Anton jumped in at that point, saying we were being too parochial, thinking only of quantum jumping, when the really impressive market opportunity is to supply QIC chips for communications satellites throughout the Solar System.

'Look,' he said, 'just think of the money that's tied up in the time delays due to lightspeed radio comms. Say, StarCorp builds a couple of artificial gravity farming disks for the communities of the Neptune system. The disks are fabricated in our Lagrange 2 factory and when we've completed them, we can get a couple of you quantum-jump-jockeys to deliver them instantaneously, accompanied by delivery notes that match what was ordered with what we deliver. Then we ask for payment with an e-mailed invoice from L2. It can take 6 hours for that radio message to reach Neptune from L2. That takes it to the end of the working day, so the message will not be read until, say, 12 hours later. Even if they are happy to pay the invoice immediately it will take another 6 hours for the payment authority to reach L2, so now the money's been in limbo for a full 24 hours. We deal with billion-dollar contracts, so the loss of 24 hours' interest could pay the accountant's salary. A banking network based on QIC chips could save me millions of dollars that are otherwise lost in space!'

All we could do was commiserate about the loss of so much money because of the ridiculously slow speed of light and move the conversation towards Anton's proposed visit to Proxima-b to discuss licensing production of the QIC devices.

'I messaged your Lana Mancot about that visit,' Anton said. 'And she streamed some videos of daily life in Proxima Alpha to me. What struck me most, apart from the red twilight, was that everybody wears hats. I don't usually wear a hat myself.'

'They're antiradiation hats,' I responded. 'You'll have to get used to wearing them when you're outside on Proxima-b. They're called salakots because the originals were made by a Filipino metal-worker settler. Unpredictable bursts of brain-frying radiation are a nasty attribute of red dwarf stars! There are lots of different hat designs, but they're all knitted from metallised thread; they're very effective Faraday Cages. We learned from bitter experience that our robots need to wear them as well.'

'That's why I'd urge you to jump to Proxima Waystation 4 to get clued up on this sort of thing,' Kat advised. 'Rather than going direct to Proxima Home Station. PW4 is a Proxima-b representation where you can get acclimatised to the constant red twilight and the need to wear protection from Proxima's radiation, though without actual exposure to radiation.'

This pleasant chatter was rudely interrupted by sounds of heavy footsteps coming from the travellator ramp exit which was situated alongside La Boulangerie. It proved to be the arrival of Tom Fraser's entourage. Tom was dressed in a vintage Starship Captain's white dress uniform, enhanced by a few additional gold braids, and his wheelchair was pushed by Carla, in an even more antique uniform featuring an elaborate starched white cap and blue cape. Behind Carla were two office bots, and behind them a pair of the larger variety of vintage protection bots from Starship-101's security brigade, these guys contributing most of the footstep noise. The various TV assistants fluttered and flustered around this little squad as soon as they emerged from the travellator gangway, and urgently swept the whole group towards the third and last free table.

'Hello Tarvin, Harden,' Tom shouted as he was whisked past the bar. 'How are you doing, lads? I'll join you in the bar for a few bevvies after this circus.'

'You know,' Harden said quietly to me, 'we really must get him and Grandpa together sometime, somewhere. He's the only other person who refers to us as 'lads'!'

Angélique Gérard walked down the stairs, which were at the back of the bar and put her arm around Anton's shoulder, saying, 'Ladies and gentlemen, your dining room awaits. Please follow me upstairs.' We did just that and Angélique made sure we sat in the labelled locations. Each seat already had a 'bonne bouche' plate on the table, alongside a little menu card, which Anton described as a sequence of his all-time favourites. While the wine waiter served the first of what would prove to be a generous sommelier's wine flight, we carefully examined Anton's tasting menu with widening smiles. Nobody found fault with it, so nobody took up Angélique's offer of substitutes for any of Anton's choices.

Greenstreet, the camera bot, emerged from the service lift and ambled up and down on the other side of our table examining us with his cameras, announcing finally, in Lana's voice, 'Thanks, everybody, that looks perfect. I'll park Greenstreet asleep in the corner 'cos my Proxima cameras are counting down the 7 p.m. programme. Next time Greenstreet wakes up, Advani will be tuned into him to ask you a few friendly questions until Angélique takes Mr Almesc down to the table outside for the main interview of the 8 p.m. segment. Enjoy your meal!'

Greenstreet shivered as Lana terminated her connection and then withdrew to a corner of the room and went into sleep mode. He was replaced on his side of the table by a whole brigade of front-of-house bots, serving plates of food and pouring the food's matching wines.

Shortly before 7 p.m., the view screen on the wall in front of us came to life, showing the end of Oort Station TV's 6 p.m. NewsHour and just in time for the image wipe from the Oort studio to show the northern snow-topped mountains of Proxima-b with the snow and ice turned pink by the twilight red of its dwarf star. As the titling was overlaid on the image, the camera focus was lazily pulled down the course of the river, flying the viewer over the riverside promenade and Starship Way, finally coming to rest on Lana, perched again on the ornamental balustrade of the riverbank wall. This time she was wearing a jaunty salakot and there was a small arc of restaurant tables, like that we had just seen assembled outside La Boulangerie, each occupied by one of tonight's guests and all wearing their preferred style of salakot.

With a few welcoming words, Lana hopped off the balustrade and conducted the camera across to the tables, to introduce her guests: Merv Castlefield, the mayor; Frankie with Danny and Salman Khan; and Art Westwood, who's introduction raised a ragged cheer from the lower ranks at one of the tables downstairs.

As the TV programme continued, we were plied with a succession of taster dishes and matching wine tastings. Our conviviality mounted as the time passed, until it came as something of a surprise when the TV broadcast merged into the advertorials we'd been told to expect between programmes. More to the point, Greenstreet came out of his sleep state and started talking to us in Advani's voice, while several serving bots cleared most of the used dishes, glasses and bottles from the table and a couple of make-up artists buzzed around us, wiping the food from our chins (well, spacemen are notoriously messy eaters) and generally making us tidy for the camera. Before we could make any further mess, the advertorials were over and Advani was talking to Harden and me, first asking us to identify ourselves. That was a mistake because she asked Harden first and he went into the routine we developed when we were kids to answer that 'which one are you?' question. In other words, Harden introduced me as Harden, claiming Tarvin as his own name. So, I just had to follow the old-time script. 'That can't be true,' I said. 'I've been calling you Harden all day, so it must be my turn to be Tarvin!' Then, the routine went that we both looked our inquisitor in the eye and smiled angelically.

Well, to be honest, the smile might have been angelic when we were nine or ten years old, but now it probably looked a bit creepy. Seeking explanation, the camera panned slightly to focus on Anton, but he slowly shook his head, saying, 'Don't ask me! I've worked with these guys for years without knowing which one is which!'

When the camera panned to Kat, in the next seat, she leaned across Anton, saying, 'Stop messing Advani about, you two; answer the question!'

But Lizzie, next in line, took direct action. Pushing her seat back, she marched up to stand behind my chair, took hold of my ears and forced my head to face the camera lens, announcing, 'I'm Lizzie Clason, and this, for my sins, is my husband, TARVIN Clason. And this,' and here she released my right ear and poked Harden hard in his left ear, 'This,' she repeated, 'is my brother-in-law HARDEN Clason.'

At which Kat contributed, 'Go to it, girl. Give him another good poke from me!' Then, Kat continued, 'For the avoidance of doubt, I'm Katharina Clason and I'm married to Harden Clason, the one down there with the sore ear!'

As the excitement died down and Lizzie returned to her seat, Advani tried to retake control by asking Kat, as the camera was still dwelling on her, 'I know that you two ladies both work as co-pilot Navigators, but you Katharina are Tarvin's co-pilot and Lizzie is Harden's co-pilot. Is there a reason for you not working as husband-and-wife teams?'

'Why aye, Advani,' Kat replied, going on to explain, 'Emotions! During a quantum translocation, pilots and navigators spend time in each other's heads, sharing a single mindscape and exchanging memory traces. The relationship must be clinically unemotional. Emotional attachments can only add disturbing memory traces to the quantum entanglements the pilot must create, and that could have a devastating effect on the decoherence of the entanglement.'

'I see,' said Advani. 'But I've learned that our first successful Starship, Starship-101, had a husband-and-wife team flying it to Proxima. Did that work out OK?'

'It most certainly did work out OK,' I said, quickly interrupting. 'And it worked out *because* of their emotional attachment, rather than despite it. Remember, Billy and Cleo Westwood flew their Starship without the assistance of quantum computing, and that's the crucial difference between what they accomplished and what Kat was describing. They didn't have NeuroModems that allowed them to share a mindscape. They simply knew each other so well they didn't have to think about how the other would react to any piloting experience.'

'Yeah, I very much agree with my brother on this,' Harden added. 'Quite honestly, Billy and Cleo Westwood were *real* pilots; they actually flew their Starship. By comparison, what we do is more like a forklift truck driver moving stock around in a warehouse. Difference is we lift a wavefunction from one part of the quantum realm to another. We call it flying our Starships, but it's not really 'flying', just heavy-lifting! Lana, at Proxima-TV, has shown me the control room vid of the Westwoods flying Starship-101 into its landing on Proxima. It made my hair stand on end! I do hope she's going to show it more widely.'

I was watching the TV transmission of Harden's speech on the view screen in front of us and I noticed Angélique approaching behind us, tracked by another camera bot. Harden obviously noticed this, too, as he said quickly 'And there's one other thing I need to point out before you move onto something else, which is that today's pilots share their mindscapes with a third brain, specifically their flight computer. Quantum jump pilots live with a permanent connection to their flight computer. Right now,' Harden said, 'I have my flight computer in my head, although Sasha, that's his name, is in my flagship, which is parked eight light-months away at Oort Station. The distance between us doesn't matter thanks to the QIC adapter. And Tarvin will be sharing his brain with his flight computer, Malik, located in his flagship just a kilometre or two from this waystation. Having a permanent connection to a quantum megacomputer through your NeuroModem is the price you pay for being a quantum jump jockey these days!'

'Thank you all for giving us these insights into being Superposition Navigators,' Advani said quickly as Harden finished. 'Now, I see that Ms Angélique Gérard is ready to move us onto our next segment which features further interviews with further key players in this interstellar story. Over to you, Angélique.'

Angélique took Anton Almesc down to the outside table for his main interview, being tracked down the stairs by the camera bot that had followed Angélique into the dining room. As promised by Jim's preview, their chat on the way was all about the attractions offered by Proxima Waystation One, which their camera bot expanded upon when they reached the ground floor by venturing off the restaurant's frontage into the surrounding streets to show the variety of entertainments on offer locally. As soon as Angélique's little group reached the ground floor, Greenstreet abandoned us and sprinted down the stairs, presumably to take up station for filming the tables we had watched being set up before our meal.

Serving bots reappeared in our dining room, offering wine and plates of various treats and morsels to keep us happy while we watched the rest of the TV programme. The interviews followed exactly the plans Jim had outlined to us earlier. The most memorable item emerged from Lana's questioning of Anton about the farming disks Lydia was choosing back at Oort Station. Bless her cotton socks, Lana managed to get Anton to say on public TV that there'd be no charge for these! The reason he gave for this generosity had nothing to do with his hoped-for licensing of QIC manufacture. Rather he played the 'selfless environmental protector' card by berating the Interstellar Planning Authority for not thinking about the catastrophic dangers to Proxima's native biological communities that were likely to be caused by on-planet farming of Earthagriculture. He ranted on a bit about the abject failure of planetary, multiplanetary and now interstellar agencies to foresee dangerous deficiencies in their planning because representatives were too much concerned to seek personal power, status, and wealth. When he said that he was only too pleased to correct this particular institutional failure by sending, gratis, state-of-the-art farming disks with Harden's upcoming mission for insertion into orbit around Proxima-b, Lana terminated his rant by suggesting 'This is about the right place to show the viewers some video of the actual farming disks that Commodore Harden Clason will be bringing up to us.'

There followed a couple of minutes of Bogey's vids of the artificial gravity disks Lydia had chosen, aided by both Ilsa and Emma it turned out. A disk dedicated to grain harvests, two devoted to different selections of arable crops and the 'wild west' ranching disk I'd heard Ethan Caçar talk about as he walked Lydia back to his office.

Anton's interview continued long enough for a few more questions from both Lana and Advani, which allowed Lana to talk about the QIC devices allowing a normal three-way conversation despite the lightyear distances between the three of them. And that allowed Anton to make a few final points, centring on how QIC devices could bring billions of Solar-dollars into Proxima's economy because they're going to be must-have attachments for every banking computer, communications device and satellite, and every megacomputer throughout the entire Solar System.

After this super-positive comment from Anton, Lana changed the mood towards human interest by turning her attention to the next table and the Westwood twins and their buddies, all four of them splendid in their best dress uniforms. The twins gave a very professional account of themselves, explaining their familial descent from the already mentioned Starship-101 pilots and their enlistment in my crew because they wanted so much to get the family back into space.

'They've certainly matured a lot since we enlisted them,' I muttered to Kat. 'What was it, four or five days ago? Amazing!'

'Yeah, they are greatly improved,' she replied. 'Although, to be fair, four days ago means at least five nights of dream-streaming memory traces into their NeuroModems, and four days driven by their buddies of putting theory into practice, so you shouldn't be so surprised.'

The twins showed their growing maturity as Lana invited them to speak to their father, Art Westwood, who was still online from Proxima-b. They managed to keep this conversation well controlled and focussed on their recent experiences of the quantum jumps we had made between each of the waystations on the Proxima Route; and, with their buddies, they gave a creditable advertorial for the waystations they had visited, that Lana illustrated with video sequences filmed by their constant companion, Greenstreet. But then Lana turned up the tear-jerking sentiment by introducing the connection, 'To your mother, Linda, and sister Sarah, at home.' And, as I had expected, Sarah was dressed up in the Midshipman's dress uniform we had made for her.

'Hey, those two lads are a find,' Harden commented. 'I'm not surprised you snapped them up and enlisted them. Will I find any more like that on Proxima?'

'After this broadcast, probably an entire crew!' I replied.

'Well, however many you find, I'll guarantee that Sarah Westwood will be at the front of the crowd!' said Kat, going on to explain, 'But we were wondering about transferring the twins and their buddies to your crew when we get our Starships to Oort Station. You've got a lot of important passengers going to Proxima, and the Westwood twins are the only members of Interstellar Haulage's staff who grew up on Proxima. So, we thought they'd make good ambassadors and tour guides.'

'Oh, yes, I like that idea,' said Harden. 'What's the Executive Officer's thought on the matter, Lizzie?'

'A definite yes please! And I hope you mean the Westwood's buddies as well,' Lizzie replied. 'Their Midshipmen's training can continue under the combined guidance of Sasha and Malik and the four of them have the good looks and good-natured personalities that will melt hearts—old, young, male and female! And melted hearts make bigger sales! Bring it on!'

'OK, you and I can do the formal staff transfers when we get back to the office tomorrow,' Kat confirmed.

'Shouldn't we consult the kids about this?' Lizzie asked.

'Nah,' Kat answered. 'They're Midshipmen, they follow orders!'

'No worries, shipmates,' I ventured. 'I'll ply them with booze and recruit them in the bar later.'

'No press-ganging will be necessary,' Kat responded decisively. 'Billy and George Westwood are not going to pass up on the chance to visit home so soon after enlistment. And, from what I hear on the crew's gossip line, where Billy and George Westwood go, Midshipmen Asghar and Wang very happily follow!'

'Have it your way,' I said, resignedly, adding, 'But I'll still buy them some drinks.'

'If Kat's gossip is right,' Lizzie said. 'You'd do better to buy them a nice private supper at one of the secluded tables well away from the unruly top brass boozing in the bar! Anyhow, watch the TV now, Tarvin. Lana's moved on to interview your mate, Tom Fraser. And don't have any more alcohol; you're squiffy enough! For my purposes!'

Lana had introduced Tom as *Captain* Tom Fraser, and his image was captioned as such. He certainly looked the part sitting there in his beautifully tailored uniform. Those old-style whites certainly looked impressive, and he'd managed to come up with a chest full of medal ribbons and award medallions. I recognised one or two of the rank badges and commendation ribbons as genuine, but I suspected that most were borrowed or stolen from Jim Igwe's young deputy, Lieutenant Commander David Wood, who seemed to spend his off-duty time in the distant past fighting rebels as a Star Wars Stormtrooper. At Lana's request, Tom explained that the contracts signed by Starship-101's original crew specified that senior ranks were inherited by the next junior rank on the death of the senior. So, as the sole surviving member of the original crew, he is now the ship's Captain and has assumed the responsibility of returning Starship-101 to the Solar System.

He explained his entourage, too. Carla, his care-bot, of course; and behind her, two office bots, one his legal advisor and the other his accountant! Pressed on the intimidating security detail he explained they were simply intended to provide some extra muscle in handling his wheelchair in this one-g environment. 'They're more intimidating than strictly necessary,' he said. 'But then, that's how security bots were built 100 years ago!' I'm sure I saw a mischievous twinkle in his eye as he said that, so I didn't entirely buy it.

Something in his interview that particularly interested me was when Lana and Advani were guiding him to say something profound about the differences between Starship travel 'then and now', with Lana, I'm sure, hoping she could extract his thoughts on the real significance of QIC technology, as part of her advertorial for QIC production on Proxima. After talking about the obvious difference between spending the best part of his life flying *to* Proxima, compared with his recent experiences of instantaneous quantum jumping across lightyear distances from one waystation to the next, flying back *from* Proxima, Tom reiterated the mantra to which Lana had guided him, namely 'QIC adapters will completely revolutionise travel between the stars by providing the Navigator with up-to-the-second quantum maps of their destination'. He then went off on a tangent with a reminiscence about his early life that got more interesting, and more profound, the more he said.

'One of my first jobs as a programmer, not far short of eighty years ago now, was to tweak the pattern recognition efficiency of the software used in the SETI projects that were so popular with astronomers in those days,' Tom started, and I'm sure I saw surprised expressions on the faces of both Lana and Advani in their respective studios in this apparent veer off into the past; to their credit they allowed the old man to ramble on without interruption.

'I guess not many of your viewers will remember that the acronym 'SETI' stands for Search for Extraterrestrial Intelligence. It was all the rage when I was young but doesn't seem as popular these days,' Tom mused, before going on, 'It involved scanning the skies of Earth, mainly with radio telescopes, searching for signals coming from other civilisations located in the distant corners of the universe. The reasoning behind the activity was based on the observation that humanity existed as a readily communicating civilisation by then, so surely, as there are so many stars in the sky, there must be scores of other civilisations in the cosmos keen to communicate with us. So, thousands, maybe tens of thousands, of people spent two or three hundred years, using ever more sensitive radio telescopes, and ever more intelligent computers to listen to greater and greater volumes of space but none of that activity discovered anything that resembles a credible extraterrestrial communication from any other civilisation. They gave it a fancy, dramatic name; they called it *The Great Silence*.'

Tom paused, rubbing his fashionably bristly chin reflectively. This was just for dramatic effect. He hadn't finished all he wanted to say, and quickly resumed, launching into what seemed like another geriatric memory trip, 'I spent a very pleasant couple of hours early this afternoon showing my good friend Antònim Almesc the 5th, with his two quantum jump pilots, around my Starship-101, which we are busily sprucing up before delivering it to StarCorp's Megafactory at Oort Station. We had a fascinating conversation, covering lots of topics, but I was struck by how excited the two quantum jump pilots seemed with their first quantum jump using their QIC devices, from Oort Station to this waystation. And we've heard similar sentiments expressed on these programmes tonight. The people who spend their lives, indeed risk their lives, making instantaneous quantum jumps over lightweek, lightmonth or lightyear distances simply can't get enough useful information about their destination using radio transmissions at the time they want to depart. Instantaneous quantum jumping needs instantaneous quantum communication. You can't qualify for the spacefaring civilisation club until you've cracked both technologies!'

'Now,' Tom said, slightly louder and with a slap of the tabletop, 'put that conclusion alongside what I've just said about SETI, and you might conclude that all those years spent searching for radio signals were a waste of time. What we need is a way of detecting quantum instantaneous communication. The Clason teams are providing us with a four and a half lightyear array of networked QIC messaging; somebody on Earth, Mars or elsewhere with more knowledge of the quantum realm than me should start trying to detect that exchange of messages and then look around for more members of the club! That's all I wanted to say, ladies. I'd kind of enjoy wandering over to the bar for a drink or two now, can we end it there?'

Advani picked up the hint and thanked Tom for his insightful contribution and started to wind up the programme, while Lana directed the active cameras towards the streets surrounding La Boulangerie. Back in our private dining room, the TV image had lost its attractions and a short but lively debate developed among us because we were all people who spent our lives making instantaneous quantum jumps. The consensus outcomes of the debate were that, first, we needed to talk more about Tom's comments and, second, that the place to talk was the bar downstairs. As we walked towards the stairs, Lizzie pointed out to me that the bar served some very nice coffees and alcohol-free beers. I got the hidden message.

When we got down to the bar Anton and Tom Fraser were already installed and in close conversation. In fact, the only people who had not moved to the bar were our four Midshipmen lovebirds. The TV staff were busily trying to restore the restaurant's outside tables to their original layout, with the help of a group of front-of-house bots and were getting close to clearing the Westwoods away when Angélique came out to supervise. So, I sauntered over to ask Angélique to have a table set up in a secluded corner for our Midshipmen, and then serve them a romantic supper. She immediately went into sentimental mother-hen mode and directed a couple of bots to set up the table there and then. I sounded out the twins on their projected transfer to Harden's crew and when I pointed out that all four of them would be transferred, they immediately accepted the proposition. Job done, I left Angélique fussing over the Midshipmen's transfer to their new table and sauntered back towards the bar.

Tom Fraser was perched on a bar stool at the end of the bar closest to the street; Carla was beside him, but the rest of his entourage was parked outside on the street. Tom was holding forth on something that seemed to be interesting Anton enough to hold his full attention. Walking to join the pair of them, I passed Jim chatting with Anton's pilot and co-pilot; I whispered in Jim's ear to check departure plans for tomorrow. 'All done, Boss,' he told me. 'Tomorrow's general orders for Pink Ghost state that all crew muster on board by a 10 a.m. curfew. With a planned departure for Oort Station at noon, Commodore.' Satisfied with that, I sidled on to interrupt Kat and Lizzie's chatting, again with a whisper in her ear, 'Just to confirm, I've mentioned to the Westwood twins their transfer to Harden's crew and they're very happy with the arrangement.'

I felt an arm sliding to entwine mine from behind me, and Angélique said, 'Oh, those twin boys with the red and white hair. They are beautiful, are they not?'

'They certainly set female hearts aflutter onboard ship,' said Kat.

Angélique squeezed my arm saying, 'Ah, but they are not the only twins on the block who have that effect; are they, mon chéri?' There being no safe answer to that, I was grateful when Lizzie blurted out 'Put that woman down, Tarvin Clason. Pick up this glass of alcohol-free lager and go play with your little friends at the end of the bar!' Having no better alternative in mind I did just that, leaving the three women giggling like schoolgirls.

As I approached the Tom Fraser, Anton and Harden trio at the end of the bar, I heard Tom saying that one of Lana's AI-executive producer bots had suggested that: 'The Starship-101 museum will want to turn me into a hologram to conduct visitors around the Starship, telling stories about the flight and landing on Proxima-b.'

'Well, make damn well sure you get a decent fee, if they do,' said Anton. 'And make sure they make it realistic and don't mess you around. The agents who are building the bloody museum are charging me a fortune to create this exhibition, so hold out for your fair share of their fees!'

To which Tom said, 'Well, you know, lads, when you get to my age any sort of immortality is welcome!'

At which we all chuckled. But Anton was warming to his subject of how people were always out to extract money from him, and he went on, 'You know, Tom, the only people who've always given me more than I've paid for are the Clasons. It's true! Started with these guys' grandpa. He was an old goat then, and he's an older goat now. Came to me with a wild idea, wanting me to build him a Starship and give it the biggest fusion generator unit that had been built up to that time. He planned to shove all the fusion power into a lump of fossil to open up a wormhole thread anchored to when the fossil became a fossil and squirt the Starship back in time through the wormhole! So bloody crazy I just had to buy it! And now I'm building Timeships and charging people an arm and a leg to take them to see the dinosaurs!'

'Yeah,' said Harden. 'That project was in Grandpa's shed. Do you remember, Bruv?'

'His shed?' asked Tom in astonishment.

'Yeah,' I answered. 'It was his workshop, so it was a bit grander than an average shed. We were teenager's then and rocketing around on Skippers, so we dropped in on the grandparents regularly.'

To which Harden added, quite truthfully, 'Mainly to eat Grandma's cake!'

'True, but we liked to keep track of what Grandpa was up to. He had a mobile fusion generator inside the shed and a Starship escape module he used as a sort of one-man Starship. And of course, he bought himself a small fossil collection. Like you say, Anton, totally crazy, but it worked!'

Harden picked up the story, 'And then, by the time we completed Finals at Starship Academy, Grandpa was in need of a shipload of happy tourists for one of the last trips before paying passengers, and we were able to take all of our year class on a jolly trip to see the Chicxulub meteor arrive. That was a helluva party!'

Immediately, Tom Fraser chuckled, 'Yeah, I hear it created quite a mess!' and when we all laughed, suggested, 'Carla, get me another bottle, will you? We all need another drink.'

'Oh, no,' said Kat, as she and Lizzie pushed into our little group. 'No more booze for the Clasons, thank you!' Kat draped herself over Harden. 'We're off to our apartments.'

Lizzie poked me in the ribs, saying 'That includes you.' As she pulled me off my barstool, I just had time to wish everyone goodnight and remind Tom Fraser that he had to be back on Starship-101 at 10 a.m. tomorrow and prepared for his final quantum jump at noon. 'No worries, lad,' he said. 'With my complaining joints, I prefer to sleep off the booze in microgravity. My team will deliver me back to 101 before midnight.'

On the way up to our apartment I turned my NeuroModem's bond to Malik from open to maximum privacy, with instructions for an alarm call no earlier than 9.30 a.m.

Day 14

Trouble is, that my usual preflight nerves had me up and about long before that 9.30 a.m. alarm call, I'd requested. By 8.30 a.m. I had showered and changed, organised Stewart into taking all my possessions back to my ship, and Lizzie and I were ordering a coffee and pastries breakfast sitting at one of La Boulangerie's outside tables, where we were acknowledged by a steady stream of crewmen walking back towards the travellator entrance for their shuttle to Pink Ghost.

'Begging your pardon, Commodore,' one of them asked on his way past, 'will we be on furlough when we get back to Oort Station?'

'You're not being laid off, Engineer?' I replied, fishing for his name.

'Fusion Engineer First Class Timothy Clifford, Sir,' he supplied, saluting smartly.

'But you'll certainly be entitled to some leave,' I went on. 'Pink Ghost will be laid up at Oort Station for a few weeks while I go looking for more contracts, and she'll need a regular turnover of skeleton crews to keep her ticking over. But at any one time, most of the crew will be stood down.'

'It's just that my wife is due to deliver our first baby back on Mars in the next week or so, and I'd like to be with her,' he said.

'Oh, congratulations, Timothy,' said Lizzie. 'That's lovely!'

'It's Tim, Ma'am. Thank you kindly.'

'No problems there, Mr Clifford,' I said. 'Your section chief can arrange an open-ended compassionate leave and the company can get you back to Mars in a couple of quantum jumps. Log this conversation with your NeuroModem and then share it with your section chief when you get back to the ship.'

'Will do, Sir. Thank you so much. And thank you, Captain Mrs Clason.' Another sharp salute and he was gone.

'Mrs Clason. I'm not called that very often,' Lizzie mused and then, with a faraway look in her eyes, 'And a new baby!'

'Who's got a new baby?' asked Kat, arriving from the restaurant behind me. She was followed by Stewart and a porter drone striding rapidly towards the travellator gangway laden with baggage. Seeing that both Stewart and the porter were each carrying two dress uniforms, I greeted Kat with: 'I hope Stewart didn't disturb you this morning. I didn't instruct him to return your uniform to Pink Ghost.'

'Nah,' replied Kat. 'We were up and about long before I saw your steward with your uniforms and gave him ours. They've all got to go back towards Oort Station. Now give me a coffee and tell me about the babies.'

'No detail available,' said Lizzie, obviously disappointed. 'It's simply that Tarvin's just approved paternity leave for one of your fusion engineers to return to Mars for the imminent birth of their first child.'

'Lovely!' Kat replied. 'Give me a name and I'll log it for urgent action.'

'His name is Fusion Engineer First Class Timothy Clifford,' I answered.

'Oh, I know that name,' said Kat. 'He's rocketed through the lower ranks in all engineering departments and is a real highflyer. I'll take care of that, Boss.'

'Fine,' I said, waving at the waiter bot to bring more pastries. 'Now, why were you two early risers?'

'Because your super-reliable brother forgot to tell Sasha to keep quiet,' Kat replied ruefully. 'So, at 6.a.m. Sasha starts reporting the next batch of passenger arrivals at Ort Station for Grey Ghost's trip to Proxima-b. And for the politicians, gilt-edged, and blue-chip passengers, Harden thought they'd appreciate a welcome message from him, especially demonstrating QIC technology by coming from so far away. He's still up in the apartment, messaging one after the other and massaging egos as he does.' After a few bites at a couple of pastries, Kat continued, 'And then, to cap it all, our good friend Anton Almesc starts messaging me!'

'I've heard he doesn't sleep much,' I said. 'But what's he cooking up now?'

'Lots,' Kat replied. 'He's already flown into Proxima Home Waystation after talking to Tom Fraser way into the early hours in the bar.'

'I don't think Tom sleeps much either!' I commented.

'Well, when we left the bar, those two were talking about what Tom had said on air about SETI detection. Apparently, they brought Art Westwood, who was doing some overnight astronomy, into the discussion through Carla's QIC chip, and he told them about the various quantum mechanics observations we made when you were jumping Starship-101 into orbit. Outcome is, that Anton will personally fund the research and house it at his Quantum Mechanics Research Institute, at which I'm invited to stay as a visiting Professor!'

'Great! So, when do I lose you?' I asked.

'When you can afford to, Boss,' Kat replied, 'Anton said that you'd hinted at visiting your grandpa at the StarCorp Yards at L2. So, you could take me along on that trip.'

'Well, that should be easy enough,' I said, as Harden came out of the restaurant to sit at a table next but one to us. He indicated by pointing at his NeuroModem that he was still engaged in messaging folks back at Oort Station and waved at the waiter bot to bring his own supply of coffee and pastries. Kat blew Harden a kiss, and then went on, 'Easy, hopefully, Boss, but hold your horses, Anton has even more plans for us.'

'I guess being devious is how he got to be the richest man in the Solar System!' I suggested.

'Nah, he got to be the richest man in the Solar System by inheriting the cash, and its tax havens, from Antònim Almesc the 4th, 3rd, 2nd and first!' said Lizzie, cynically.

'Yeah, and the basis of the family's great wealth is the little bit of piracy committed by Anton Almesc the first,' I contributed. 'That's the ancestor who built the first factories to mass produce the Starships of the day in sufficient quantities to establish the first colonies on Mars, but he was also the one who devised asteroid capture. Harden and I used his 'chopsticks' rocket-grasping technology to capture iceteroids and cardice tanks to take water and CO_2 back to Mars, but the technology was developed to capture the asteroid known as Anima which had more gold in it than ever existed on planet Earth. And the story goes that AA1's company captured the thing and placed it into Mars orbit to extract its nickel, iron and gold, and most of the gold is still buried somewhere in a vault on Mars.'

'Ah yes, the allegedly 'lost treasure of the Almescs'. Even if that's all true,' Kat persisted, 'you can't blame AA5 for the buccaneering attitude of AA1, and our Anton's always dealt squarely with us, and as far as I can see he's doing so again.'

'So, tell us what he's up to this time!' Lizzie burst out.

'OK, keep your hair on! Anton also talked to Danny Khan as soon as he arrived at Proxima-b and bought his entire current stock of QIC devices. He's planning to load up his yacht and get Rod and Margaret to quantum jump it back to Oort Station for us to take with us to the StarCorp Yards at L2.'

'Who are Rod and Margaret?' I asked.

I thought it was a perfectly innocent question, but Lizzie snapped at me, 'Oh, honestly, Tarvin! For goodness sake, will you never take note of people's names? You had dinner with them last night! Rod Tamworth is Anton's pilot and Daisy Christie is the co-pilot navigator.'

'OK, that's how the devices get to us from Proxima and presumably they'll get to Oort Station around the same time we do. And then it's easy enough for us to distribute them,' I said defensively.

'Yes, indeed. There is a stipulation, though,' Kat said, pausing again, annoyingly, to drink some coffee.'

'Which is?' Lizzie queried.

'Which is,' Kat announced, 'that we travel to the L2 StarCorp Yards by visiting all the StarCorp facilities between Oort Station and Earth; not only leaving a supply of QIC devices at each of them, but fitting QIC plug-and-play adapters to each of their traffic control and flight computers too.'

'You've had more time to mull this over, Kat,' I said. 'So, what do you think? I don't see any obvious issues, though I'd like to know how much Anton will be paying for our services!'

'That's where Anton's devious nature emerges!' Kat smiled. 'If we deliver the QIC devices using your Commodore's Cutter, we get a free service and upgrade of Pink Ghost in the Oort Station StarCorp Yards. Our crew can remain aboard in their usual three teams, while the two off-duty teams enjoy life ashore in Oort Station's artificial gravity disk. And…'

'And?' I asked. 'There's more?'

'Oh yes, there's more!' Kat grinned. 'Your cutter will get its service at StarCorp's L2 Yards, where it will be upgraded to the same spec as Anton's own yacht!'

'With all the extra mods and grunt?' I enquired, and when Kat nodded, I added, 'I hope you said yes!'

'At quantum speed, Boss!' she said, adding, 'But there's more! Danny Khan struck a decent deal with Anton, too. In exchange for Danny's entire current stock of QIC adapters and chips, Anton's agreed to set up a regular quantum jump transport service between all the waystations of the Proxima Route and all the way from Oort Station to Proxima Home. He'll provide three Starships and their pilots and co-pilots for the long-distance service, and three orbital shuttles to lift passengers and freight into Proxima Home's orbit.'

Harden had pulled up a chair alongside Kat's and joined our conversation when he finished his own messaging and he responded to Kat's words simply with 'Slam dunk! That'll make visiting Proxima-b nice and easy!'

'Well, you've got to accept this contract, Tarvo,' Harden continued. 'And if you're supplying and fitting QIC adapters to all the StarCorp outfits between Oort and Arroyolento, you'd better take a decent brigade of trained computer specialist bots. I'll transfer my brigade captain, who's already installed QICs, plus two or three from his brigade to your ship when we get back to Oort. Vin Tanner won't mind modifying the Ambassador's gear with Sasha's help, but if I transfer the brigade chief to you, you'll have two experienced brigade captain AI-bots able to train a brigade of six or so general electronic work bots.' Harden went on to message Sasha and Vin about this, which woke me up to the realisation that I'd not heard from Malik so far this morning, and with appropriate apologies, I took the last of my coffee to the table Harden had just vacated and attended to that.

'Malik,' I asked, 'have you been following what Kat's been saying about Anton Almesc's latest contracts?'

'Of course, Commodore,' came the, annoyingly cryptic, reply.

'Do you have any observations to make or suggestions to offer?' I persisted.

'I took it that you and Commodore Harden Clason have just made the decision to accept the contract. Consequently, I have prepared a draft heads of agreement for the formal contract. I am obtaining a list of the StarCorp facilities that Mr Almesc wishes you to visit to equip them with QIC devices from Mr Almesc's personal megacomputer and, from the Westwood computer, an inventory of the items Mr Khan will be supplying to Mr Almesc and how they are to be distributed. For our side of the contract, I am seeking the full specifications of the service and upgrade that will be offered to Pink Ghost by StarCorp Oort Starshipyards, and to your Commodore's Cutter by StarCorp Earth-L2 Starshipyards. As I understand Mr Almesc's plans, his Personal Assistant, Mr Seymour Aspatria, will accompany the QIC devices from Proxima to Oort Station and will have the authority to approve the contracts as he hands over the freight for distribution.'

Faced with such a detailed exposition of what Malik had been doing in the background of our idle chatter, the best I could manage was 'OK, carry on.'

Followed by my next question, 'What's happening about Danny Khan's supply contract?'

I'm sure I could detect exasperation in my flight computer's reply, 'I am assisting the Westwood computer in defining the heads of agreement and contract. In this case we needed detailed specifications of both the vehicles and staff, human and robotic, that will be provided for the proposed transport service. Here again, Mr Seymour Aspatria, will approve the contract as he receives the devices at Proxima Home Waystation for their transshipment to us at Oort Station. Note that I am ensuring that none of these arrangements affect Mr Khan's prior supply agreement with Ambassador Shirazi, which Commodore Harden Clason will transport to Oort Station in due course.'

'Fine,' I said, trying to ooze an easy confidence, as though I was actually still in charge of all this. 'And finally, how are we progressing the translocation of Pink Ghost and Starship-101 to Oort Station?'

In reply, Malik said, '*We* are doing fine, Commodore.' I may be oversensitive, but I thought Malik stressed the 'we' to add a sarcastic undercurrent to his simple statement. Malik paused, seemingly attempting to force a further query from me, and I had time to wonder if quantum megacomputers can be sarcastic? Why not, I mused, we've designed and trained AI-quantum computers in our own image. Malik's always had 'funny moods', maybe some mornings he wakes up in a sarcastic mood. Maybe we all do.

I got bored with waiting and thinking so, I asked 'Meaning what?'

'Meaning, that the majority of the crew who were ashore on Proxima Waystation One overnight have registered at their muster station onboard ship. There are just a few stragglers remaining on the waystation. Meaning, that engineering has long since completed preparations for the translocation of the coupled vessels and immediate detachment of Starship-101 on arrival at Oort Station. Meaning, that all baggage belonging to the Clason family has been returned to Pink Ghost. Meaning, the shuttle assigned to return the Clason family to Pink Ghost is waiting in PW1's departure dock. Malik out.'

I wandered back to the rest of 'the Clason family' and reported the tone of my conversation with Malik. Lizzie offered me a 'mid-morning caffe latte' and commented, 'I wouldn't worry about it, dear. We get the same sort of treatment from Sasha every so often. Your Malik is probably trying to teach you a lesson for excluding him from contact with you overnight and late into the morning.'

'Yeah,' agreed Harden, grinning. 'If I was married to Sasha, I'd put his behaviour down to hormones, and just ignore it!'

Kat took the bait and, poking a finger hard into his ribs, declared, 'Whether Malik was being sarcastic, impatient, or plain insubordinate doesn't matter. The bottom line is that Pink Ghost is ready to take its burden back to Oort Station. So, let's go!' I shared Harden's last remaining crêpe with him, and we all went into La Boulangerie to say our farewells to Angélique. Then, like good little humans following the instructions of their AI-overlord, we went straight to our waiting shuttle and made the short hop over to my Starships.

We rode the travellator through Pink Ghost, giving the lower ranks heart attacks at the sight of so much top brass travelling through the ship together, but while Kat took Lizzie and Harden straight through to our control room, I dropped off the travellator in engineering to seek out Jim Igwe and explain about our latest contract arrangements with Anton Almesc.

'Ah, yes,' Jim said. 'Malik's filled me in about all that. A full service and upgrade for Pink Ghost is a very welcome present! I've checked with StarCorp Oort Starshipyards and they'll do the work in one of their open space yards. Providing our guys don't get in their way, we can maintain a skeleton crew on board and operate our own shuttle services to and from the ship and Oort's artificial gravity disks, where I guess that the off-watch teams will spend their downtime.' He paused slightly, and then resumed, 'And, StarCorp also told me they'll tug Pink Ghost into a vacant yard immediately after taking Starship-101 off our hands. So, you don't need to jump the old girl into Oort's parking area, but we will have to unship your cutter before the heavy tugs arrive.'

'OK, I'm glad that Malik's got you up to speed!' I said. 'He was being a bit off-hand with me earlier on! Did his message to you include the information that we'll need a small brigade of computer specialist bots assigned to the cutter?'

'No, just tell me what you need, and I'll assign them,' Jim answered.

'I'll need our AI-brigade captain bot, and a couple of assistants he can train to fit QIC devices. Harden's going to transfer his brigade captain and two or three assistants from his crew. And while we're thinking about it, I guess we better take a couple of QIC-equipped facsimile bots that we can tune into anyone back here when we're on our travels.'

'That's OK, we can supply all that and get the bots settled aboard your cutter in the next half hour. Are you still planning to quantum jump at noon? We're all ready for it,' Jim confirmed.

'That's still the plan,' I said. 'But as I mentioned, Malik's been quiet for the past half hour, and I don't want to disturb him until I'm in my Nav Couch!'

'Difficult, is he?' Jim asked.

'Disobliging is the better word, I think. My wife thinks he's teaching me a lesson for disconnecting from him overnight. My brother thinks he's acting like a hormonal spouse.'

'I bet that went down well with Kat!' Jim grinned, flashing all those white teeth.

'Dead right! Me? I'm the confused one in the middle! I guess I should catch up with Kat in the control room. I'm safer there, and Malik lets me feel more in charge!'

'OK, Boss,' Jim said, saluting. 'I'll be in touch as soon as we get to StarCorp Starshipyards.'

I returned to the travellator and made my way to my control room. There, I found that Kat had arranged for the Engineer's Nav Couch to be unshipped from its stowage in the ceiling, and Lizzie was already adjusting the settings to suit her. They had decided that Lizzie would take that seat to experience the translocation back to Oort Station, because Harden had already used the equivalent Nav Couch in my cutter to share our memory traces during the translocation from Oort Station. So, it seemed natural to have Lizzie installed in the Engineer's Couch for the journey back.

Tucked up safely in my Nav Couch, I took up the challenge of contacting Malik again. 'Malik,' I ventured, 'will you bring me up to date with progress of preparations towards our quantum jump to StarCorp Oort Starshipyards?'

'With pleasure, Commodore.' That's an unexpected response, I thought, but no matter. He went on, 'All crew and related passengers are back onboard Pink Ghost and Starship-101. All engineering tasks required for the translocation are completed. Transfer of a small number of robotic units to the complement of the Commodore's Cutter is proceeding at the moment. It is 10.59 a.m. and I find no impediment to the planned 12-noon departure, Commodore.'

'Thank you, Malik.' I signalled a 'thumbs-up' to Kat, which she returned, so I resumed my conversation with Malik, 'How is the contract draft coming along, Malik?'

'The heads of agreement I have prepared for both contracts have already been approved by Mr Almesc. I referred them to him for comment only, but he approved them immediately. I suggest you contact him directly, Commodore. He seems to be located in the Westwood Restaurant on Proxima-b. Should I make the connection for you?'

'Yes, please,' I answered, but as I did so Kat interrupted with an enquiry of her own, 'Before you go off the line, Malik, are you working on routing our travel between Oort and Arroyolento while we carry out the distribution of QIC units for Anton Almesc?'

'Affirmative, Captain Clason,' Malik responded. 'I am applying the criterion of least delay in radio messaging between departure and destination points to optimise the route, in hopes of minimise the uncertainties in destination quantum maps that will remain until we actually fit the QIC devices.'

'That's excellent,' said Kat. 'I just wanted to remind you that we have a commitment to get Fusion Engineer Timothy Clifford to Mars as soon as possible. So, would making our first jump to Mars meet your criterion of least radio delay?'

'With current planetary positioning I believe that would be acceptable,' Malik responded.

'Good, then please produce an optimised route starting with a jump from Oort Station to Mars Home Station. Now, you can proceed with connecting the Boss with Anton Almesc. Captain Katharina Clason out.'

Anton came on the line immediately, 'Tarvin, how nice to hear from you. What can I do for you?'

'In the next hour we'll be delivering Starship-101 to your outfit at Oort Station, and I just wanted to touch base, Anton. I heard you had reached Proxima-b, how's it going?' I said.

'Oh, I am impressed, both by the place and its people,' Anton announced, 'I'm getting on well with Danny Khan and all your wonderful people down here in Proxima Alpha. Everyone I've met so far is being very helpful. Especially your two young ladies, Lana Mancot and Frankie Burton, who've been kind enough to offer me overnight accommodation in their cottage here while my staff are preparing a suite for me at the Proxima Hotel.'

'At the moment, I've set up a makeshift office in a booth in Madge Clarkson's restaurant. You know, she talks very well of you, Tarvin and her kitchen produces crêpes and pastries every bit as good as Angélique's. But you don't need to mention that to Angélique!' Anton said, continuing without a pause. 'I'm glad you called me before you leave for Oort Station, because I've been talking extensively to Art Westwood and Frankie Burton about the quantum jump observations that were made when you lifted Starship-101 from the ground here and into orbit. I'm an engineer, as you know, with only a superficial knowledge of physics, but I've got an engineer's gut feeling that those new observations could tell us a lot about how the quantum realm really works, so I wanted to say that the sooner that Kat takes all this new data to the astrophysics campus at Arroyolento the better.'

I butted into the 'conversation' at this point, glad to have the chance to interrupt Anton's usual tsunami of speech. 'That's a given, Anton,' I said. 'The way we're thinking, there's no reason why we shouldn't depart on our tour for QICs-distribution sometime tomorrow morning. The sooner we get your facilities equipped with QIC adapters the sooner will quantum jumping uncertainties be removed from Solar System travel. But I also wanted to confirm with you that you are personally happy with the contract arrangements drawn up by my flight computer. I understand that you've already approved Malik's heads of agreement draft. Is that right?'

'Yes, that is right, Tarvin. I approve everything in the draft supplied by your computer, Malik is it called? And Seymour should be on his way to Oort Station to give you the QIC devices that Danny Khan supplied. Incidentally, I hope you'll take Seymour with you on your distribution tour. He travels with my full authority and will be able to smooth your entry into any and all of StarCorp's facilities. People seem to fall over themselves to be helpful when the owner's right-hand man appears!'

'OK, Anton. We'll do that.'

'Oh, before you sign off, Tarvin, I've got a couple of other points I'd like to mention. I've been talking to that biologist bloke you have here.'

'Geoff Moore?' I prompted.

'Yeah, that's right. Is he a member of your crew?'

'Nah, he's a civilian contractor with his own team. Why do you ask?'

'Oh, no real reason other than being clear about his position in your setup. I don't want you to think I'm poaching! Freelance consultant, is he?'

'Yes, self-employed and currently contracted to Interstellar Haulage to produce an initial survey of the biosphere of Proxima-b. Now what's this all about, Anton? I'm getting the distinct impression that you're plotting something,' I said finally.

'Oh, nothing untoward, Tarvin. It's just that he's done me a favour that I want to return. So, I've put him in touch with the StarCorp Foundation for

Extrasolar Scientific Research who will pick up his contract, greatly expand his research budget here and find more staff to join his team on Proxima-b.'

'StarCorp Foundation for Extrasolar Scientific Research?' I asked. 'Is there such a thing?'

'Well, there will be when Seymour's team gets around to doing the paperwork. I was rather pleased with it as an off-the-cuff title. Do you think it's too much of a mouthful? It might be better as an acronym, S-F-E-S-R. What do you think?' Anton asked.

'I think you're overthinking the title when I want to know why you're going out of your way to support Geoff's research. What did he do to deserve such special treatment?' I replied.

'He came to me after what I said in my TV interview about the failures of all of our overhyped intergovernmental agencies, especially the Interstellar Planning Authority and the United Planetary Authority, to foresee the mess into which they were leading the biodiversity of Proxima-b. He gave me copies of his interim reports about Proxima-b and a copy of his dissertation about all the historical 'ethical colonisation' agreements that were draw up even before my family began to colonise Mars. I'll be sending all this documentation to my political affairs office at Arroyolento with Seymour, so they can use it for next year's Presidential election.'

'Er, OK,' I started, slowly. 'President of what?'

'The Interstellar Planning Authority, of course,' Anton replied.

'And I suppose you will be running in that election?' I suggested.

'Of course,' Anton stated. 'It's time that someone who knows how interstellar missions should work was running the show.'

'And I guess it's likely to be good for business,' I offered.

'Sure, being top banana is always good for business!' Anton said, leaving me to imagine his smiling face. 'And that leads me to my second point, but I need to choose my words carefully here because Malik is still operating his embargo on discussion of the topic in messages like this. You know what I mean, I'm sure.'

'I do, Anton, what do you want to say about it?' I replied.

'I wanted you to know that I have worked before with the pilot concerned and the people he works for, and I can be helpful in any local disputes that may arise. After all, money talks and the amount I can splash around positively shouts! But not even my money can protect Proxima from disputes caused by other people on Mars, if you see what I'm getting at. You need help from United Worlds and their Blue Helmets. If you need money to make that happen, just come to me.'

'I appreciate your help, Anton,' I responded. 'But we've got the Blue Helmets organised. Harden will be bringing the UW Ambassador and a detachment of marines to Proxima Alpha tomorrow. Then he'll jump back to Oort Station to bring his Starship flotilla up the Proxima Route as planned and deliver the rest of the Blue Helmets and the Ambassador's staff and baggage to Proxima in a few of days' time.'

'Excellent, who is the Ambassador? Can you say?'

'I don't see why not; she's called Plenipotentiary Ambassador Fatemah Shirazi.'

'Ah, Fatemah!' Anton exclaimed. 'Great choice; she's a tough old bird who's dealt with the problems our friends here might encounter over many years on Mars. She'll not stand for any nonsense. Yeah, I'm really happy about that. Now, you need to carry on with preparing today's quantum jump, Tarvin. So, you could leave me here doing my best to cope with my next plate of crêpes.'

'True enough,' I said. 'Give our best regards to Madge Clarkson. Tarvin Clason out.'

'Malik, I've just been talking to Anton Almesc, and he does, indeed, approve your draft heads of agreement so please proceed with the full contracts and send them to Interstellar Haulage's new legal office on Oort Station as soon as possible. Now, can you connect me to Tom Fraser?'

'Willco, Commodore. Go ahead, you are through.'

'Tom, we're just about to start the business of quantum jumping into StarCorp's backyard at Oort Station. Is Starship-101 ready to go? And are you ready to go?'

'Oh, good morning, Commodore. Speaking as one Commodore to another, I was born ready to go, Tarvin lad, and my ship is shipshape and Bristol fashion.'

'Yeah, nice to know, though I ain't sure whether that's good or bad, but I'll hope for the best,' I said. 'This is only a quick message to check your readiness, but I have one more question about something that's been niggling me at the back of my mind since your TV interview, which is that what you said on camera was a lot like what Jim Igwe said over breakfast when we first arrived at Proxima Waystation One, but you weren't in La Boulangerie at that time were you?'

'Nah, it's the good ole Gort network for you again, lad!' Tom said with relish. 'When Jim was talking to you over breakfast, his NeuroModem was still connected to the AI-computer engineer bot he'd taken to PW1 to add QIC devices to their computers. The bot 'overheard' the whole speech, was interested in it, and shared the info with his computer-nerd robot mates. Carla picked up the Gort messaging and reported it to me because she knew from my already recorded reminiscences that I'd been involved in refining SETI computer search routines applied to interstellar messaging before embarking on Starship-101.'

'And I'll tell you something else that the near-Earth Gort network is buzzing with; Anton Almesc is totally funding your grandpa's latest idea which seems to be a development of his TimeShips you were telling us about last night. TimeShip Tours is now one of Almesc's most lucrative independent sidelines, although the original idea was funded by StarCorp. Almesc is now personally funding your grandpa to build an enormous Starship at StarCorp's Earth Lagrange-2 shipyards, which has the project title 'Deep Time GalaxyShip Launcher'. The project title we know, but there's a firewall protecting the project details that none of the Gort network can penetrate. And I must confess that I had a go, too, purely as a challenge, you understand, but it doesn't have any legacy code in it so I was thwarted, too'

'Yeah, the old goat is very secretive at times. Usually, it's a sign that he's not yet worked out all the angles, but if StarCorp is already building an enormous Starship, then it's going to need QIC devices. So, I'll have to visit the Lagrange-2 shipyards to catch up with Grandpa and see what he's up to! Thanks for the info, Tom. I'll touch base with you when we get to Oort Station. Tarvin out.' I took a quick glance at the clock and decided to get down to business, 'OK, Kat, I've done enough messaging around. How are you progressing with our quantum maps?'

'Well enough, Boss,' came the reply, and as I took hold of her hand to share her mindscape, I became aware that Lizzie was part of it as well.

'Malik has called for a current-time quantum map of the vicinity of both Oort Station and StarCorp Oort Starshipyards,' Kat continued. 'And Lizzie and I have stitched it together in this mindscape so you can decide where you want to go. Both traffic control computers have issued us with conflicting traffic warnings on the grounds of our abnormal size. Oort Station is worried about the flows of scheduled shuttle traffic between the station and the Starships already parked up and they'd prefer us to veer into StarCorp's volume of space.'

'Well, that would suit me, Kat,' I said.

'Yes, dear heart,' Lizzie said. 'We realise that. Unfortunately, StarCorp Traffic Control have an incoming traffic conflict to which they've already given open clearance. It's a priority vessel, so we must wait for it to complete its jump before we can be cleared to initiate translocation.'

'I bet that 'priority vessel' is Anton's yacht,' I said.

'I asked that, and they refused to say on security grounds! But I can't think of anyone else within five lightyears who rates higher priority treatment in StarCorp space than Antònim Almesc the Fifth!' Kat said.

'If it is, I don't mind waiting,' I said. 'But I'd rather coordinate! Malik, patch me through to the pilot of Mr Almesc's yacht.'

'You've forgotten his name again, haven't you, Tarvin dear? It's Rod Tamworth!' Lizzie contributed.

'Willco, Commodore. Go ahead, you are through.'

'Hi Rod, Tarvin Clason here. We're preparing to translocate our two Starships into the StarCorp Oort Starshipyards, but their traffic control is warning us about conflicting priority traffic. Would that be you by any chance?'

'Hello Tarvin,' Rod replied. 'Yes, that must be us. Daisy has just received an open priority clearance for us to jump into Mr Almesc's private parking lot. I'm just finishing off my departure map. We'll be settled into StarCorp Oort in about ten minutes.'

'That's fine, Rod. We'll follow you in. Tarvin out.'

'Kat, can you tell Oort Station's Traffic Control that we'll be jumping into StarCorp's volume of space, pending the arrival of some other priority traffic? Malik, please ask Proxima Waystation One's Traffic Control for a current-time quantum map of our vicinity, and issue warnings to both Starships of quantum translocation in approximately ten minutes. You might as well tell everyone that our exact departure time depends on the arrival of conflicting priority traffic in StarCorp Oort's volume of space. And remind them that we are an oversized lump to have swinging around in congested space!'

'Willco, Commodore.'

'And Malik, please continue streaming updated mapping data from StarCorp Oort's Traffic Control so that we can monitor the arrival of Mr Almesc's yacht.'

'Willco, Captain Clason.'

'Hey Malik,' said Harden, barging into our three-way mindscape, 'can we get some coffee up here in the control room?'

'I believe that is the province of Commodore Tarvin Clason's steward, Stewart, Commodore Harden Clason. I will pass the order to him immediately.'

'Hello, Bruv,' I said. 'Welcome to our family get-together, but try not to alienate my flight computer while you're here.'

I was already holding Kat's hand and was aware that four memory traces now shared our mindscape. Indeed, there were five because Malik was still streaming our departure and destination quantum maps into it. The departure map was centred on the Pink Ghost/Starship-101 construct. All twenty kilometres of it! Harden's thoughts, which floated across our shared mindscape, were, 'You know, Bruv, that really is a beast of a thing to truck around the quantum realm! I am definitely impressed you got it this far!'

Which was quickly followed by Kat's thought, 'Don't forget, My Love, that before we could start trucking it back here Tarvin had to lift Starship-101 into orbit from the bottom of a one-g gravity well!'

'OK, stop chattering,' I said. 'I want to see how the construct fits into StarCorp's volume of space. Malik, will you convert the maps to 3-D mental images for me, please.'

The maps in our shared mindscape shimmered and then two images, each enclosed within a cubical volume of space with colour-coded edges were placed side by side in a new mindscape while the original view showing quantum maps was slotted back into memory. 'What are you thinking, Bruv?' Harden thought at me.

'I want to overlay the two views without it being interpreted as an attempt at making an entanglement,' I thought back. 'I'd like to have the chance to envisage what twenty kilometres of Starship looks like in the volume of space immediately outside StarCorp's Starshipyards. We're going to need space to decouple the two ships and then more space for a flotilla of heavy tugs to manoeuvre both vessels into their respective repair yards.'

I overlaid the departure image over the destination cube and wiggled it about. When I moved the images, their galactic coordinates were displayed on the two cubes so that I could align them perfectly. 'Stop waggling the things about,' Kat thought at me, 'and go back to their default orientations.' I did so, and Kat continued, 'Zoom in on the nose of Starship-101. Right, now if I put a marker there,' a bright yellow spot appeared on Starship-101's nose, 'And another one, there,' another bright yellow spot started to glow on the extremity of one of the chopstick arms of a Mechazilla alignment tower on the nearest of StarCorp's graving docks. OK, now zoom out and let's look at our other end.'

'That looks fine, Kat,' I said.

'Yes,' Kat replied, with satisfaction oozing in her thoughts and voice, 'I'm guessing that's the graving dock they intend to tug Starship-101 into.'

'It must be,' I thought back. 'It's open to space and all the Mechazilla chopsticks are clustered at this end, ready to grab the ship and rail it in.'

'Doesn't matter if it's the one they intend to use or not,' Lizzie pointed out. 'That's about the closest you can safely approach the yards and it gives you some ideal nudge coordinates. If you can decohere in that position, it's up to StarCorp to decide if they want to tug our ships further into their yards.'

'Exactly what I was figuring, Boss; now, I've just plotted it, can you land it?' Kat asked challengingly.

'Who else?' I asked.

'Well, I could land it, for one!' said Harden. 'Why don't you quit stalling and talking and get on with it. And where the hell is that coffee?'

'OK, Malik, mark out the indicated coordinates on the quantum map of our destination, then overlay this image as a ghost image over the quantum map, and restore the updated quantum maps to our mindscape,' Kat requested.

'Pilot and co-pilot, I am streaming to you the processed mapping data for departure and destinations as you requested. Malik out.'

Out loud, Kat announced and streamed to the intercoms of both Starships, 'Navigator is monitoring traffic movements at our destination. Hold current position until my mark.'

Sensibly, Stewart chose this brief moment to serve us with the coffee bulbs Harden had ordered. We all took them gratefully.

Harden's next contribution was a whispered, 'Come on, Roddy lad, pull yer finger out. Jump lad, jump!'

And, as if in direct response to Harden's urgings, the next update to our destination's quantum map showed Anton's yacht safely nestled close alongside StarCorp's rotating artificial gravity head office.

Kat painted an exclusion zone over the yacht on my mindscape of the destination and then streamed it to me. 'Co-pilot ready,' she whispered.

'OK,' I acknowledged. 'Pilot is ready.' And followed this with, 'Kat, stream me the nudge coordinates. Malik, please issue warnings of imminent quantum translocation to crews of both Starships. Inform Proxima Waystation One Traffic

Control that we are about to quantum jump out of their space and inform StarCorp Oort Starshipyards that we're about to arrive in theirs. Then give me a 5-second countdown.'

Five seconds later, I made the entanglement by merging my two quantum maps into a combined waveform, cast the nudge coordinates into the mix and we decohered at the entrance to StarCorp Oort Starshipyards.

Malik announced our arrival to both Starships' intercoms and the 'mindscape appreciation' group broke up, job done! Harden patted my shoulder and floated away from my Nav Couch, kissing and fist-bumping Kat as he passed saying, 'Good job. I'll go down and start them into launching your cutter to take us back to the office.'

Jim Igwe messaged me to announce that his space-side engineering bots had activated the process to decouple Starship-101, and StarCorp had already launched a couple of squadrons of heavy tugs to moor our two vessels in their service docks. Almost immediately after talking to me, I heard Jim speaking on the intercom; warning the occupants of both vessels about possible violent changes in vector as our two Starships were pulled apart by the tugs and subsequently tugged towards their StarCorp docks. He also included the more cheering news that Pink Ghost would be parked in one of StarCorp's open space service docks for its service and refit, and we would be able to organise a shuttle service to transfer the crew to Oort Station's artificial gravity rings for their R & R furlough, leaving only a skeleton crew on Pink Ghost.

I decided to message Anton's pilot, Rod Tamworth, to arrange the transhipping of the QIC devices he'd brought here. As I did so, Pink Ghost was subjected to such violent vibration and shaking that I was relieved to be still firmly strapped in my Nav Couch. Lizzie had been holding the side of my Nav Couch to keep herself stationary in microgravity but at the first vibration she pushed off from her perch so she could float free and safe as the entire Starship shuddered violently around her. The images showing the external view of Pink Ghost on our control room's digital glass revealed this violent vectoring to be caused by the tugs pulling our two Starships apart.

'Hi Tarvin,' said Rod. 'That was an entertaining sight, I've never seen a Starship bounce around like that! But then, I've never seen two Starships joined by their arse ends before either. What can I do for you?'

'I was hoping to arrange transfer of your cargo,' I said. 'How would you like to do it?'

'Well, I sure as hell don't want to get too close to your vessels with all those tugs buzzing around them. Can we meet in calmer territory somewhere?'

'Why don't you quantum jump to our Interstellar Haulage dock in Oort Station's commercial artificial gravity ring?' Kat suggested. 'We'll be taking the Commodore's Cutter back there when this flurry of activity by StarCorp's tugs has calmed down. So, our own dock will be the best place to complete our business.'

'Sounds good to me,' Rod replied. 'Can you point it out to us, somehow?'

'I can do better than that,' said Kat. 'We've jumped our cutter to our private dock from about where you are located now. Our flight computer can send you a template of the memory trace of that jump and Daisy can modify it to suit current traffic conditions. Malik, please send that memory template to Rod Tamworth.'

'Copy that, Captain Clason. Template transmitted. Malik out.'

'Ooh, that looks a bit tight!' Daisy Christie, responded.

'Yeah, but it works!' said Kat. 'Just have faith in the reliability of the instantaneous updates to your destination quantum maps.'

'OK,' Daisy replied. 'I'll follow your advice and hopefully meet you in the Interstellar Haulage dock in a little while. Daisy Christie out.'

And then I received a message from Tom Fraser, 'Hey, Tarvin, Carla tells me that the local Gort network is full of chatter about you taking a brigade of bots on a tour of StarCorp yards all around the Solar System. Is that true? And could you take one of mine?'

'Hi Tom, yeah, I guess we will have a decent robot crew onboard my cutter,' I replied. 'We picked up a distribution contract from Anton Almesc. In return for a full service and refurb of my Starship at the yards here, he asked us to blast around the Solar System's StarCorp yards delivering the QIC devices he bought from Danny Khan on Proxima-b.'

'So, how do you feel about including my facsimile bot in your robot crew?' Asked Tom. 'Just so that I can keep in touch with what's going on, you understand!'

'Sure thing, Tom,' I confirmed. 'I'm not sure what you're up to, though I'm damn sure it's not idle curiosity! But it's no skin off my nose, and if we can have the odd chat together, I'll welcome your bot aboard my cutter.'

'Thank you for that, Tarvin. You're a star! I'll send my legal specialist fax-bot across to your Starship. It's a QIC-equipped fully adapted Tom Fraser special! It will just be a hanger-on, reporting back to Carla through the Gort network, with an option for full Tom Fraser-avatar mode'.

'Great, having a bot in full Tom Fraser-avatar mode is certainly something to look forward to! But don't try and get it over here yourself. 101's own shuttles are too old, and too long unused, to have the flight agility required to compete with all the tugs dancing around your ship,' I advised. 'I'll ask Malik to send you one of our taxi shuttles to bring your bot aboard. In which case, do you want to come over here yourself? We're planning to take my cutter back to my company's private dock to take onboard Anton's QIC devices, and you'd be very welcome to come over with your bot to have a meal with us.'

'Thanks for the invitation, Tarvin, but I have to say 'no'. I prefer living and eating in microgravity and I want to stay with my Starship as it's tugged into the StarCorp graving dock. I've been told that after they've closed up the graving dock to make it airtight and replaced the atmosphere, Carla and I will be moved to the Museum Hotel to start turning all the reminiscing I've done during our trip from Proxima-Centauri into the museum displays and hologram projections. I'm looking forward to that!'

'OK, enjoy it, Tom. I'll no doubt message you through your avatar during our QIC distribution run. Tarvin Clason out.'

'I didn't want to interrupt your conversations, Boss,' Kat announced as soon as I ended my messaging, 'But you need to know that I've told the Westwood twins and their buddies to muster at the Commodore's Cutter for transport to the Interstellar Haulage private dock to complete their temporary redeployment to Grey Ghost. And Fusion Engineer First Class Timothy Clifford has also been told to report to the cutter with a view to transport to Mars. Finally, Harden's arranged with Sasha for the computer bots we wish to redeploy to your cutter to report to Interstellar Haulage's private dock.'

'Thanks, Kat,' I responded. 'Malik, please coordinate with Captain Igwe to have one of our taxi shuttles sent to Starship-101 to transport Commodore Fraser's facsimile bot to Interstellar Haulage's dock to join my cutter's crew. Oh, and make sure my steward, Stewart, gets himself together with all mine and Kat's away-day baggage and uniforms into my cutter before it's unshipped from Pink Ghost.'

'Willco, Commodore. I have tasked a cargo bot with delivery to your cutter of Dr Geoff Moore's biological samples and interim field survey observation reports for inclusion in the cargo to be taken back to Earth. Commodore Harden

447

Clason has brought your Cutter to flight readiness and is awaiting assembly of the passenger manifest. Malik out.'

I started to disentangle myself from my Nav Couch's harness and announced to the two ladies who were already chatting together as they floated behind the Nav Couches near the entrance to the wardroom, 'All immediate jobs have been done. Navigators, we can take the travellator down to my cutter's docking bay and join the rest of its crew.'

'Good,' said Lizzie. 'Harden's been mithering me to get you down there, as he wants to get back to the company office so he can issue invoices to StarCorp for delivery of Starship-101.'

'And off and on, I've been helping Stewart get all our bags packed for our trip around the Solar System,' Kat reported. 'You won't have noticed while you were gossiping with Tom Fraser, but we've already sent most of our baggage down to the cutter with a couple of porter bots. We're ready to go.'

'We're waiting for you, Boss,' added Lizzie. So, we went. The travellators running towards the shuttle bays were busy with crew members heading for shore leave on Oort Station's artificial gravity disk. By the time we got to the Commodore's Cutter dock my right arm was fatigued by the number of salutes I had acknowledged on the way down. Harden was floating near the gangway to the cutter's airlock. 'Come on, come on,' he muttered, you're almost the last to board!'

'Almost?' I queried.

'Yeah, the last to arrive will be a fax-bot that's being taxied in from Starship-101. I dunno why, and I dunno when.'

'Well, the why is because it's Tom Fraser's fax-bot and we're taking it with us on our delivery trip around the Solar System and Malik will know where and when. Can you help, Malik?'

'Affirmative, Commodore. The taxi is just about to secure itself to its rank's airlock on the transport deck below. I will instruct the bot to report immediately to Commodore Harden Clason. Malik out.'

Lizzie and Kat had already cleared the airlock, so I kicked off from the wall to guide myself rapidly into the cutter and on through to the control room, where Kat was strapping into her Nav Couch, and on to the wardroom to greet the passengers. Lizzie and our little group of Midshipmen were already happily chatting to Engineer Clifford and while saying hello I overheard Midshipmen May Wang and Jumanah Asghar, and Lizzie, surprisingly, quizzing him about his partner's expected birth. While Billy and George Westwood were throwing in questions about fusion power plants, this being the topic of their next overnight training session. I don't think any of them noticed much about either my arrival or my departure. On my way out I instructed Stewart to take all the bots to the charging bays on the deck below and then I went directly to my Nav Couch.

By now, Kat had our two ruling flight control computers streaming to us their respective local quantum maps. When I pressed into my headrest to make the full connection and share Kat's mindscape, I saw that Oort Station Traffic Control's destination map was showing Anton's yacht being engulfed by Interstellar Haulage's private dock, so as soon as the airlock hatch was locked down there, we could follow it in. On the other hand, StarCorp Oort Starshipyards' Traffic Control's departure map showed that although the yard's squadron of tugs was now attached to Pink Ghost, rather than buzzing around outside, there was no shortage of conflicting traffic because the transport of off-duty crew to Oort Station's artificial gravity disks was well underway.

'We'll have to rocket up towards the nose away from the shuttle traffic before we can jump across to our dock,' I said, adding, 'Hey, Harden. Any sign of that fax-bot yet?'

'Yeah, it's just dropping off the travellator. I'll give you a shout when the airlock's locked down,' Harden replied.

And that was it, really. Kat updated her previous template for the short quantum jump from StarCorp's volume of space to just outside our private dock and within a matter of a few minutes we were being drawn into our dock alongside Anton's yacht. When the atmosphere had been restored to the dock area Seymour Aspatria's cargo robots transhipped the crates of QIC devices to my cutter's cargo hold and stayed with the freight to manage the ship's manifests.

Harden accompanied Seymour to the company's office to complete the various delivery and distribution contracts, while Kat and Lizzie followed with our four Midshipmen to complete their formal transfer to Harden's crew roster. Engineer Clifford opted to travel through to the artificial gravity disk where his shipmates were starting their R & R; promising faithfully to report back to my cutter by 9 a.m. tomorrow. I called in on Anton's yacht to try to persuade Rod Tamworth and Daisy Christie to dine with us later, but they'd been called back to Proxima-b immediately, as Anton wanted his yacht to be parked at the SpacePort, acting as his private office.

Harden's computer specialist bots arrived at my cutter, and I took them to meet their opposite numbers from my brigade. Malik would be completing their training overnight for our QIC distribution contract.

I went through to the artificial gravity ring, back to the Interstellar Haulage office suite to catch up with what's been going on there. And for the wonders of a big mug of coffee in one-g, those microgravity bulbs just ruin the flavour. I marched into the office shouting hellos to announce my arrival, heading for the coffee machine in the little kitchen at the back of the reception area. Harden was dancing around showing a printout of some sort to anyone who would take notice of him. He pursued me into the kitchen and, uncharacteristically, offered to fix me a coffee while I looked at his printout, saying, 'Well, that's our Starship-101 delivery contract totally fulfilled and paid off. Look at all those zeros at the end of the number! I didn't know there were that many zeros in the Solar System!'

What he had handed me was a printout of the electronic funds transfer docket showing the arrival of a colossal amount of money into the company's bank account. Harden's hyperbole about the Solar System's supply of zeros was overlooking the fact that we already had more than our fair share of them in the liabilities column of our balance sheet. Still, he made me a very acceptable mug of coffee and he wasn't wrong about our delivery contract being paid off handsomely.

The accountant in our office assured me that the computer was churning its way through the salary payments for our crew, and that full payment for the hulk of Starship-101 had been cleared to the newly established 'Bank of Proxima Alpha'. Clearly, Anton was being true to his word about instantaneous payments using his QIC devices. In addition, StarCorp had issued a 'zero cost' servicing and refurb list for Pink Ghost, now parked in its graving yard, which Jim had already checked and approved. Finding that, I sent a quick message to Jim via Malik, officially appointing Jim Igwe as Commanding Officer of Pink Ghost in my absence on our QIC distribution tour.

When I returned to the little kitchen, Kat and Lizzie had joined the coffee drinking crowd in the little kitchen after completing the relocation of our party of Midshipmen and sending them to get one of the taxi shuttles over to Grey Ghost. Harden was holding forth about a report from Sasha that all Grey Ghost's expected passengers had already boarded his vessel, saying he could take his ship out to start hopping from waystation to waystation on the way to Proxima, any time he liked, but was unable to move until 8 a.m. tomorrow, being stuck here waiting for Ambassador Shirazi to finish loading her staff and gear into his cutter.

I started to muse out loud that Kat and I could start on our QIC distribution contract any time now but noticed Lizzie scowling at me and shaking her head. I back-tracked rapidly, announcing that unfortunately I remembered just agreeing with our Fusion Engineer, Tim Clifford that he'd report back to my cutter by 9 a.m. tomorrow.

That news cheered up Lizzie. And then Kat took up the theme, saying, 'Well, in one sense, I'd really like to get going too. I've got some heavyweight research papers to write with Art Westwood, so the sooner I get to StarCorp's astrophysics campus at Arroyolento together with Art's facsimile bot, the better. But on the other hand, I need some time off; today's been a whirlwind!' So, then we all agreed to have one last evening together before departing tomorrow to fulfil our next contracts. Someone suggested having a takeaway delivered to Harden's apartment and we set to making menu choices.

Over dinner, Harden said that the last time he saw Grandpa, the old man was hinting about using his TimeShips to launch something he called 'GalaxyShips'. I told Harden what Tom Fraser had said about this, and that gossip on the Gort network confirmed that Grandpa was located in the StarCorp Starshipyards at Lagrange-2. The Gort network was a new idea for Harden and took quite a lot of explaining. While me and my brother were happily arguing about the rights and wrongs of allowing AI-bots to have their own private emailing network, Lizzie and Kat were discussing the best way to establish and structure translocation quantum map templates for the jumps between Proxima Route's waystations. As the meal approached its end and the conversation tailed off, someone suggested that we really needed an early night. We all agreed, and Lizzie and I went along the corridor to our own apartment. Despite recent experience, I disconnected from Malik again.

END